Dorothea Ruggles-Brise, John Glen, David Erskine Baker

The Companion to the Play-House

Vol. 1

Dorothea Ruggles-Brise, John Glen, David Erskine Baker

The Companion to the Play-House
Vol. 1

ISBN/EAN: 9783337375904

Printed in Europe, USA, Canada, Australia, Japan

Cover: Foto ©Andreas Hilbeck / pixelio.de

More available books at **www.hansebooks.com**

THE COMPANION TO THE PLAY-HOUSE:

OR,

An Historical Account of all the Dramatic Writers (and their Works) that have appeared in *Great Britain* and *Ireland*,

FROM THE

Commencement of our Theatrical Exhibitions, down to the Present Year 1764.

Composed in the Form of a Dictionary,

For the more readily turning to any particular Author, or Performance.

VOL II.

CONTAINING

The Lives and Productions of every Dramatic Writer for the *English* or *Irish* Theatres, including not only all those Memoirs that have been formerly written, but also a great Number of new Lives and curious Anecdotes never before communicated to the Public.—Also the Lives of our most celebrated Actors, who were likewise Authors of any Theatrical Composition, from Shakespear and Johnson, down to the present Times.

LONDON:

Printed for T. Becket and P. A. Dehondt, in the *Strand* ; C. Henderson, at the *Royal Exchange* ; and T. Davies, in *Ruffel-Street, Covent-Garden.*

MDCCLXIV.

THE
PLAY-HOUSE
DICTIONARY.

R. Gent. — Thefe Initials we find prefixed to a Dramatic Piece, entitled,

The *Valiant Welchman*, Tragi-Com.

None of the Writers give any Account of this Author, nor even hint at his real Name, yet I cannot help venturing one Conjecture in Regard to him, which is, that I think it not improbable to be Mr. *Robert Armin*, Author of a Comedy called the Hiftory of the *Two Maids of* Moore Clacke. —There being fome Refemblance in the Manner and Stile of the two Titles, and the Difference of only fix Years in their Dates, the laft-nam'd Piece having been publifhed in the Year 1609, and this before us in 1615.

ADAMS, *George*, M. A.—— This is, I believe, a living Author, but has made only one Attempt in the dramatic Way, and that probably not even intended

for the Stage, but only publifhed for the more undifturb'd Perufal of the Clofet. It is called,

The *Life and Death of* SoPHOCLES. Hift. Play.

ADDISON, *Jofeph*, Efq;—This very great Ornament to the Age he lived in, his own Country in particular, and to the Caufe of polite Literature in general, was Son of the Rev. Dr. *Launcelot Addifon*, who afterwards became Dean of *Litchfield* and *Coventry*, but at the Time of this Son's Birth was Rector of *Milefton*, near *Ambrofbury*, *Wilts*, at which Place the Subject of our prefent Confideration receiv'd his vital Breath, on the 1ft Day of *May*, 1672.—— He was very early fent to School to *Ambrofbury*, being put under the Care of the Rev. Mr. *Naifh*, then Mafter of that School; from thence, as foon as he had received the firft Rudiments of Literature, he was removed to *Salifbury* School, taught by the Reverend

Mr.

Mr. *Taylor*, and after that to the *Charter-Houfe*, where he was under the Tuition of the learned Dr. *Ellis*.——Here he firft contracted an Intimacy with Mr. *Steele*, afterwards Sir *Richard*, which continued inviolable till his Death.——At about fifteen Years of Age he was enter'd of *Queen*'s College, *Oxford*, and in about two Years afterwards, thro' the Intereft of Dr. *Lancafter*, Dean of *Magdalen*'s, elected into that College, and admitted to the Degrees of Bachelor and Mafter of Arts.

While he was at the Univerfity, he was repeatedly folicited by his Father and other Friends to enter into Holy Orders, which, altho' from his extreme Modefty and natural Diffidence he would gladly have declined, yet, in Compliance with his Father's Defires, he was once very near concluding on ; when having, thro' Mr. *Congreve*'s Means, become a great Favorite with that univerfal Patron of Poetry and the polite Arts, the famous Lord *Halifax*, that Nobleman, who had frequently regretted that fo few Men of liberal Education and great Abilities applied themfelves to Affairs of public Bufinefs, in which their Country might reap the Advantage of their Talents, earneftly perfuaded him to lay afide this Defign, and as an Encouragement for him fo to do, and an Indulgence to an Inclination for Travel, which fhew'd itfelf in Mr. *Addifon*, procur'd him an annual Penfion of 3col. from the Crown, to enable him to make the Tour of *France* and *Italy*.

On this Tour then he fet out at the latter End of the Year 1699, did his Country great Honour by his extraordinary Abi-

lities, receiving in his Turn every Mark of Efteem that could be fhewn to a Man of exalted Genius, particularly from M. *Boileau*, the famous *French* Poet, and the Abbe *Salvini*, Profeffor of the *Greek* Tongue in the Univerfity of *Florence*, the former of whom declar'd that he firft conceived an Opinion of the *Englifh* Genius for Poetry from Mr. *Addifon*'s *Latin* Poems, printed in the *Mufæ Anglicanæ*, and the latter tranflated into elegant *Italian* Verfe, his Epiftolary Poem to Lord *Halifax*, which is efteemed a Mafter-Piece in it's Kind.

In the Year 1702, as he was about to return Home, he was informed from his Friends in *England*, by Letter, that King *William* intended him the Poft of Secretary to attend the Army under Prince *Eugene* in *Italy*.—This was an Office that would have been extremely acceptable to Mr. *Addifon* ; but his Majefty's Death, which happen'd before he could get his Appointment, put a Stop to that, together with his Penfion.—This News came to him at *Geneva* ; he therefore chofe to make the Tour of *Germany* in his Way Home, and at *Vienna* compos'd his Treatife on Medals, which however did not make it's Appearance till after his Death.

A different Set of Minifters coming to the Management of Affairs in the Beginning of Queen *Anne*'s Reign, and confequently the Intereft of Mr. *Addifon*'s Friends being confiderably weaken'd, he continued unemploy'd and in Obfcurity till 1704, when an Accident call'd him again into Notice.

The amazing Victory gain'd by the great Duke of *Marlborough* at *Blenheim*, exciting a Defire in the Earl of *Godolphin*, then Lord High Treafurer, to have it celebrated in Verfe, Lord *Hallifax*, to whom that Nobleman had communicated this his Wifh, recommended Mr. *Addifon* to him, as the only Perfon who was likely to execute fuch a Tafk in a Manner adequate to the Subject; in which he fucceeded fo happily, that when the Poem he wrote, *viz.* the *Campaign*, was finifhed no farther than to the celebrated Simile of the Angel, the Lord High Treafurer was fo delighted with it, that he immediately prefented the Author with the Place of one of the Commiffioners of Appeals in the Excife, in the Room of Mr. *Locke*, who had been juft promoted to the Board of Trade.

In the Year 1705, he attended Lord *Hallifax* to *Hanover*, and in the fucceeding Year was appointed Under Secretary to Sir *Charles Hedges*, then Secretary of State; nor did he lofe this Poft on the Removal of Sir *Charles*, the Earl of *Sunderland*, who fucceeded to that Gentleman, willingly continuing Mr. *Addifon* as his Under-Secretary.

In 1709, Lord *Wharton* being appointed Lord Lieutenant of *Ireland*, nominated our Author Secretary for that Kingdom, the Queen at the fame Time beftowing on him alfo the Poft of Keeper of the Records in *Ireland*.—But when, in the latter End of her Majefty's Reign the Miniftry was again changed, and Mr. *Addifon* expected no farther Employment, he gladly fubmitted to a Retirement, in which he had formed a Defign, which it is much to be regretted that he never had in his Power to put in Execution, *viz.* the compiling a Dic-

tionary to fix the Standard of the *English* Language upon the fame Kind of Plan with the famous *Dittionario della Crufca* of the *Italians*.—A Work in no Language fo much wanted as in our own, and which from fo mafterly, fo elegant and fo correct a Pen as this Gentleman's, could not have fail'd being executed to the greateft Degree of Perfection.—We have however the lefs Reafon to lament this Lofs, as the fame Defign has fince been carried on, and brought to a Maturity that reflects the higheft Honour on our Country in general, and it's Author in particular;—nor after this Character can I, I think, have need to enter into a farther Explanation, or even hint, that I mean Mr. *Samuel Johnfon*'s Dictionary of the *English* Language.

What prevented Mr. *Addifon*'s purfuing this Defign, was his being again called out into public Bufinefs; for on the Death of the Queen, he was appointed Secretary to the Lords Juftices; then again, in 1711, Secretary for *Ireland*, and on Lord *Sunderland*'s Refignation of the Lord Lieutenancy, he was made one of the Lords Commiffioners of Trade.

In 1716, he married the Countefs of *Warwick*, and in the enfuing Year was raifed to the high Dignity of one of her Majefty's principal Secretaries of State.—The Fatigues of this important Poft being too much for Mr. *Addifon*'s Conftitution, which was naturally not an extraordinary one, he was very foon obliged to refign it, intending for the Remainder of his Life to purfue the Completion of fome literary Defigns which he had planned out: but this he had no long Time allowed him for the doing, an Afthma, attended with a Dropfy,

 carrying

carrying him off the Stage of this World before he could finish any of his Schemes.——He departed this Life at *Holland* House, near *Kensington*, on the 17th of *June*, 1719, having then just entered into his 48th Year, and left behind him one only Daughter.

As a *Writer* we need say little of him, as the general Esteem his Works were, still are, and ever must, be held in, " *pleads*, " as *Shakespeare* says, *like Angels* " *Trumpet tongu'd*," in their Behalf.——As a Poet, his *Cato* in the *dramatic*, and his *Campaign* in the *heroic* Way, will ever maintain a Place among the first Rate Works of either Kind.——Yet I cannot help thinking even these excelled by the Elegance, Accuracy, and Elevation of his *Prose Writings*; among which his Papers in the *Tatlers*, *Spectators* and *Guardians* hold a foremost Rank, and must continue the Objects of Admiration, so long as the *English* Language retains its Purity, or any Authors who have written in it continue to be read.——As a *Man*, it is impossible to say too much, and it would even extend beyond our present Limits to say enough, in his Praise, as he was in every Respect truly valuable.--In private life he was amiable, in public Employment honourable; a zealous Patriot; faithful to his Friends and stedfast to his Principles; and the noble Sentiments which every where breathe thro' his *Cato*, are no more than Emanations of that Love for his Country, which was the constant Guide of all his Actions.——But last of all let us view him as a *Christian*, in which Light he will appear still more exalted than in any other.——And to this End nothing perhaps can more effectu-

ally lead us than the relating an Anecdote concerning his Death, in the Words of one of the *best Men* as well as the *best Writers* now living, who, in a Pamphlet written almost entirely to introduce this little Story, speaks of him in the following Manner.

" After a long and manly, but " vain Struggle with his Distem- " per," says he, " he dismissed " his Physicians, and with them " all Hopes of Life: but with " his Hopes of Life he dismissed " not his Concern for the Living, " but sent for a Youth nearly " related, and finely accomplish- " ed, but not above being the " better for good Impressions " from a dying Friend: he came; " but Life now glimmering in " the Socket, the dying Friend " was silent.——After a decent and " proper Pause, the Youth said, " *Dear Sir! you sent for me: I* " *believe, and I hope, that you* " *have some Commands; I shall hold* " *them most sacred.* — May distant " Ages," proceeds this Author, " not only *hear*, but *feel* the Re- " ply!——Forcibly grasping the " Youth's Hand, he softly said, " *See in what Peace a Christian* " *can die.*——He spoke with Diffi- " culty, and soon expired"——The Pamphlet from which this is quoted, is entitled, *Conjectures on original Composition*, and altho' published Anonymous, was written by the great Dr. *Edward Young*,——Nor can I with more Propriety close my Character of Mr. *Addison* than with this very Gentleman's Observations on the just-mentioned Anecdote, when, after telling us that it is to this Circumstance Mr. *Tickell* refers, where, in his Lines on this great Man's Death he has these Words,

He

*He taught us how to live; and,
   Ob! too high
A Price for Knowledge, taught
   us how to die.*

thus proceeds Dr. *Young*; " had
" not this poor Plank been thrown
" out, the chief Article of his
" Glory would probably have
" been funk for ever, and late
" Ages had received but a Frag-
" ment of his Fame.—A Frag-
" ment glorious indeed, for his
" Genius how bright! but to
" commend him for Compofition,
" tho' immortal, is Detraction
" *now*, if there our Encomium
" ends.—Let us look farther to
" that concluding Scene, which
" fpoke human Nature not unre-
" lated to the Divine.—To that
' let us pay the long and large
" Arrear of our greatly pofthu-
" mous Applaufe."

A little farther he thus termi-
nates this noble Encomium.——
" If Powers were not wanting, a
" Monument more durable than
" thofe of Marble, fhould proudly
" rife in this ambitious Page to
" the new and far nobler *Addifon*,
" than that which you and the
" Public have fo long and fo
" much admired :—nor this Na-
" tion only, for it is *Europe's*
" *Addifon* as well as ours; tho'
" *Europe* knows not half his Ti
" tles to her Efteem, being as
" yet unconfcious that the *dying*
" *Addifon* far outfhines her *Ad-*
" *difon* immortal."

Having thus given fome Account of the Life and Death of
this great Man, nothing more remains in this Place to be done,
but to give a Lift of his dramatic
Pieces, which were the following three.

  1. CATO. Trag.
  2. The *Drummer*. Com.
  3. ROSAMOND, Opera.

ALEXANDER, *William*. Vid.
STERLING, Earl of.

ARMIN, Mr. *Robert*.——This
Author lived in the Reign of
King *James* the firft, and was an
eminent Comedian of that Time,
as we may gather from the finding his Name among the Reft of
the Performers of Rank in the
original Drama of *Ben Jonfon's
Alchymift*, 1610.—I have in another Place ventur'd a Surmife in
Regard to his having been the
Author of one dramatic Piece,
from the Correfpondence of the
prefix'd Initials, (*Vid.* above, A.
R.) we are however affur'd in
Regard to another, to which he
has put his Name at Length,
viz.

The *Two Maids of* MOORE

  CLACKE. Hiftorical Play.
And it is very probable that he
belonged to the then Company of
Comedians, as in the Title Page
he writes himfelf *One of His Majefty's Servants.*—There was publifhed in the Year 1604, a Pamphlet entitled,

A Difcourfe of Elizabeth Armin, *who, with fome other Com-
plices, attempted to poifon her Hufband.*

Whether this Anecdote has
any Reference to our Author I
cannot pretend to affirm, but
think it by no Means improbable, from the Correfpondence of
the Date with the Time that he
flourifhed in.

ARNE, Dr. *Thomas Auguftine.*
—The Particulars of this Gentleman's Life having probably had
nothing extraordinary in them,
have no Claim to a Place here,
efpecially as he is ftill living,
and it may perhaps appear as a
Bufinefs of unneceffary Repetition to obferve to the Public what
almoft every individual of it well
knows already, *viz.* that he is

      one

one of the greateſt Maſters of Muſical Compoſition at preſent exiſting, either in this or any other Kingdom.——To him the World ſtands indebted for the Muſic of many of our beſt Oratorios, for the Accompanyments in others of our more regular theatrical Entertainments, and for the whole of one dramatic Piece, of which he is ſaid to be not only the Compoſer, but the Author, *viz.*

ARTAXERXES. Opera. *Vid.* APPENDIX.

ARROWSMITH, Mr.——This Gentleman was of *Cambridge*, and had the Degree of Maſter of Arts. *Langbaine* alone informs us that to him was aſcribed a Play, which however was publiſhed Anonymous, entitled,

The *Reformation*. Com.

ASTON, Mr. *Anthony*.—This Gentleman, according to the Teſtimony of the Author of the *Britiſh Theatre*, was an Actor in ſome of the travelling Companies, that perform in the Country Parts of this Kingdom.—— He is ſaid in that Work to have been Author of many humorous Scenes, acted, I ſuppoſe, by Way of Drolls or Interludes in the ſaid Company, and of a Piece which I imagine was never repreſented, called,

Love in a Hurry. Com.

AYRE, Mr. *William*.—Of this Gentleman I know nothing more than that he has favoured the Public with a Tranſlation of that celebrated dramatic Paſtoral of *Taſſo*, called;

AMINTAS.

and alſo with that of an *Italian* Tragedy, the original Text of which he has printed Page by Page with his Tranſlation, entitled,

MEROPE.

AYRES, Mr. *James*.——This Author is mentioned no where but in the *Britiſh Theatre*, where he is ſaid to be a Native of *Ireland* (probably yet living) and to have wrote one dramatic Piece, entitled,

Sancho at Court. Ballad Opera.

B.

B. P. or BELON, Mr. *Peter*.—— So does *Langbaine* interpret the two Letters prefixed to a Play, entitled,

The *Mock Duelliſt*. Com.

and tells us that the Gentleman whom he thus ſuppoſes the Author was at that Time living.

B. J.—Theſe Letters ſtand on the Title Page of a Play, called,

The *Amorous Gallant*. Com.

but none of the Writers have given the leaſt Hint of the Author's real Name.

B. T.—Theſe Letters only are prefixed to a Comedy, called,

The *Country Girl*.

The Writers in general however have attributed this Piece to *Anthony Brewer*.

B. W.——This Author ſtands in the ſame Predicament with the laſt-mentioned one; none of the Writers making any Mention of him but by the above Initials, which are prefixed to a little Piece which was never acted, but is printed by the Title of,

The *Juror*. Farce.

This Piece was publiſhed in 1717, nor do I meet with any Author nearer than the Year 1729, which is twelve Years afterwards, whoſe Name will correſpond to theſe Letters; at which Time I find a Tragedy, called *Injur'd Innocence*, written by *William Billers*, Eſq; and acted at *Drury Lane* with ſome Succeſs.——This is certainly

tainly not enough to authorize our *fixing* on him as the Author of the Farce before us, yet it is far from impoffible that it might be only the firft Effay of a Man, who afterwards afpir'd to fomewhat of more Importance.

BAILEY, Mr. *Abraham.*—— This Gentleman was a Member of the honourable Society of *Lincoln's-Inn*, and in the early Part of his Life wrote a Play, call'd,

The *Spightful Sifter.* Com.

BAILEY, Dr. *John.*——This Gentleman was a Phyfician.— During fome leifure Hours which he could fpare from Bufinefs, he amufed himfelf in compofing a dramatic Piece, called,

The *Married Coquet.* Com. It was never acted, and probably the Doctor never intended it for a public Reprefentation ; but being at his Deceafe, which was in the Year 1746, found among his Papers, it was publifhed by Subfcription for the Emolument of his Widow.

BAKER, Mr. *Thomas.* — This Gentleman was the Son of a very eminent Attorney in the City of *London.*—Whether he was himfelf bred up to any Bufinefs or not, I have not been able to trace, but it is apparent by the Pieces he has left behind him, that he muft have devoted fome Part of his Time to the Mufes.—His Turn was entirely to Comedy, and his Plays in general met with Succefs, and were held in good Eftimation.—Nor was that Approbation by any Means unjuft, notwithftanding the flighting Manner in which Mr. *Whincop* has fpoken of his Writings.—— His Plots are in general his own, his Conduct of them pleafing, his Characters ftrongly drawn, (which is certainly one of the greateft Perfections of Comedy) his Language eafy and agreeable, his Wit pure and genuine, and his Satire juft and poignant.—— I have the more readily entered into this Encomium, which I think his Writings deferve, to vindicate their Character, as well as the Judgment of the Public which gave them the Sanction of Applaufe, from the Contempt thrown on them by Mr. *Whincop*, who is the only Writer that has attempted to give them any Character at all, and who indeed contradicts himfelf in the Character he has given, fince he denies them both Wit and Humour, and yet allows them to poffefs the *Vis comica*, (or, as he calls it, " fomething to make one laugh") which certainly can never fubfift without one or the other of thefe two Properties ; but indeed Mr. *Whincop* feems on the whole to write with fome Degree of Prejudice againft him, throwing the fame Kind of Abufe on a periodical Paper which he was the Author of, called the *Female Tatler.*

The dramatic Pieces he has left behind him are five in Number, and their Titles as follow,

1. *Act at Oxford.* Com.
2. *Fine Ladies Airs.* Com.
3. *Hampftead Heath.* Com.
4. *Humours of the Age.* Com.
5. *Tunbridge Walks.* Com.

All of them have a confiderable Share of Merit, yet only one among the Number ftands on the prefent Lift of Acting Plays, viz. *Tunbridge Walks.*

There is an Anecdote in Regard to a Character in this Comedy, with Refpect to the Author's Character, which I might properly have taken Notice of here, but that the Reader will find

find it in the former Part of this Work in my Account of the Piece itfelf.

Whether the effeminate Turn of Difpofition there hinted at, or this Gentleman's Attachment to the Mufes, drew him from any Application to Bufinefs, or from what other Caufe I know not, but during the latter Part of his Life he ftood on but indifferent Terms with his Father, who allowing him but a very fcanty Income, he was obliged to retire into *Worcefterfhire*, where *Whincop* tells us he is reported to have died of that loathfome Diforder the *Morbus pediculofus*.

BANKS, Mr. *John*.——This Gentleman was bred an Attorney at Law, and belonged to the Society of *New-Inn*.——The dry Study of the Law however not being fo fuitable to his natural Difpofition as the more elevated Flights of poetical Imagination, he quitted the Purfuit of Riches in the Inns of Court, for the paying his Attendance on thofe ragged Jades the Mufes in the Theatre.——Here however he found his Rewards by no Means adequate to his Deferts. His Emoluments at the beft were precarious, and the various Succeffes of his Pieces too feelingly convinced him of the Error in his Choice.——This however did not prevent him from purfuing with Chearfulnefs the Path he had taken, his Thirft of Fame, and Warmth of poetic Enthufiafm alleviating to his Imagination many difagreeable Circumftances, which Indigence, the too frequent Attendant on poetical Purfuits, frequently threw him into.

His Turn was entirely to *Tragedy*.——His Merit in which is of a peculiar Kind.——For at the fame Time that his Language muft be confefs'd to be extremely unpoetical, and his Numbers uncouth and inharmonious; nay, even his Characters very far from being ftrongly marked or diftinguifhed, and his Epifodes extremely irregular; yet it is impoffible to avoid being deeply affected at the Reprefentation, and even at the reading of his tragic Pieces.——This is owing in the general to an happy Choice of his Subjects, which are all borrowed from Hiftory, either real or romantic, and indeed the moft of them from Circumftances in the Annals of our own Country, which, not only from their being familiar to our continual Recollection, but even from their having fome Degree of Relation to ourfelves, we are apt to receive with a Kind of partial Prepoffeffion, and a Pre-determination to be pleafed.——He has conftantly chofen as the Bafis of his Plays fuch Tales as were in themfelves and their well-known Cataftrophes moft truly adapted to the Purpofes of the Drama.——He has indeed but little varied from the Strictnefs of Hiftorical Facts, yet he feems to have made it his conftant Rule to keep the Scene perpetually alive, and never fuffer his Characters to droop.——His Verfe is not Poetry, but Profe run mad.——Yet will the falfe Gem fometimes approach fo near in Glitter to the true one, at leaft in the Eyes of all but the real *Connoiffeurs*, (and how fmall a Part of an Audience are to be ranked in this Clafs will need no Ghoft to inform us) that Bombaft will frequently pafs for the true Sublime, and where it is render'd the Vehicle of Incidents in themfelves affecting, and in which the Heart is apt to intereft itfelf, it will perhaps be found to

have

have a ſtronger Power on the human Paſſions than even that Property to which it is in Reality no more than a bare *Succedaneum*.—— And from theſe Principles it is that we muſt account for Mr. *Banks*'s Writings having in the general drawn more Tears from, and excited more Terror in, even judicious Audiences, than thoſe of much more correct and more truly poetical Authors.

The Tragedies he has left behind him are eight in Number, and are as follow,

1. *Albion Queens.*
2. CYRUS *the Great.*
3. *Deſtruction of* TROY.
4. *Innocent Uſurper.*
5. *Iſland Queens.* (This is only the *Albion Queens* alter'd.)
6. *Rival Kings.*
7. *Virtue betray'd.*
8. *Unhappy Favorite.*

Of theſe few have been performed for ſome Years paſt, excepting the *Unhappy Favorite*, or *Earl of* ESSEX, which continued till very lately a Stock Tragedy at both Theatres.—Mr. *Jones*'s Tragedy on the ſame Subject, which came out in 1753, and ſince that another by Mr. *Brooke*, (both which ſee an Account of in their proper Places) ſeem however to have baniſhed that alſo from the Stage ; at leaſt for a while.— Yet I cannot help obſerving, to the Honour of Mr. *Banks*'s Play, that altho' theſe two Writers, and another of Eminence, *viz.* Mr. *Ralph*, have all handled the ſame Story in ſomewhat a different Manner, yet they have all concurr'd in borrowing many Paſſages from his Tragedy ; and moreover, that whatever Advantages their Pieces may have over his in ſome Reſpects, yet in Point of *Pathos*, which ought to be one of the great Aims of Tragedy,

he ſtill ſtands ſuperior to them all.

The Writers on dramatic Subjects have not aſcertained either the Year of the Birth or that of the Death of this Author.—His laſt Remains however lie interr'd in the Church of St. *James's, Weſtminſter.*

BANCROFT, Mr. *John*.—— This Author was by Profeſſion a Surgeon ; and happening to have a good Deal of Practice among the young Wits and Frequenters of the Theatres, whom the warm Favours they had met with among the fair Devotees of the *Paphian* Goddeſs drove to ſeek his Advice and Aſſiſtance, he acquir'd from their Converſation a Paſſion for the Muſes, and an Inclination to ſignalize himſelf in their Service :—In Conſequence of which Inclination he made two Eſſays in the dramatic Way, neither of which are devoid of Merit, nor fail'd of meeting with ſome Degree of Succeſs, *viz.*

1. HENRY II. Trag.
2. SERTORIUS. Trag.

He died in the Year 1696, and lies interr'd in St. *Paul's, Covent-Garden.*—It is not improbable that he might be related to, or a Deſcendant from, Mr. *Thomas Bancroft, of Swanton* in *Derbyſhire*, whom Sir *Aſton Cockaine* has celebrated as a Poet of Eſteem.——See *Cockaine*'s Poems, 8vo. 1658. p. 103. 112. 116. 156.

Coxeter attributes another Play to this Author, which however he ſays he made a Preſent both of the Reputation and Profits of to *Mountfort* the Player.—It was entitled,

3. EDWARD III. Trag.

BARCLAY, Sir *William*.—Of this Gentleman I know no more than that he lived in the Reigns of K. *James* I. and K. *Charles* I. and that he was Author of one Play, entitled,

The *Loft Lady*, Tr.-Com.

BARFORD, Mr. *Richard*.—Of this Gentleman I meet with nothing more than the Name, and that he was Author of one dramatic Piece, called,

The *Virgin Queen*. Com.

BARKER, Mr.—A Gentleman of this Name is faid by all the Writers to have been the Author of two dramatic Pieces, whofe Titles are as follow,

1. *Beau defeated*. Com.

2. *Fidelia and Fortunatus*.

Neither of them have any Date; nor any Mention in the Title Page of their having been acted; yet the Author of the *Britifh Theatre* fixes the latter of them about 1690. and *Coxeter* in his MS. Notes fays, that the firft was acted at the new Theatre in *Lincoln's-Inn-Fields*; and moreover remarks that the Mr. *Barker*, who wrote *Fidelia and Fortunatus*, is a different Perfon from him who was Author of the *Beau defeated*.

BARKER, Mr. *Tho.*—On the Authority of *Coxeter*, who tells us that in fome of the old Catalogues this Name is inferted as Author of a Dramatic Piece, called,

The *Bloody Banquet*. Trag.

I have ventur'd to introduce him as fuch in this Place, altho' I cannot help thinking it attended with fome Degree of Improbability, as in two feveral Editions of this Play, *viz.* in 1620 and 1639 the Letters *T. D.* are affixed to the Title Page.

BARKSTED, *William.*—Neither this Gentleman nor the under-mentioned Play are taken Notice of, or even named either by *Langbaine*, *Jacob*, *Gildon*,

Whincop, or the Author of the *Britifh Theatre.* - Yet has *Coxeter* in a *MS.* Note mentioned him as Author of a Dramatic Piece, called,

HIREN. Trag.

In Vindication of this Affertion he quotes *Hyde's* Catalogue, p. 65. and by the Date of the Play, which he fets down as 1611, Mr. *Barkfted* appears to have been a Writer of *James* the firft's Reign.

BARNES, Mr. *Barnaby.*—All the Mention the Writers make of this Gentleman amounts to no more than that he lived in the Reign of King *James* the firft, and wrote one Play, entitled,

The *Devil's Charter*. Trag.

BARON, *Robert*, Efq; — This Author was a young Gentleman, who lived during the Reign of *Charles* I. and the Protectorfhip of *Oliver Cromwell.*——He received the earlier Parts of his Education at *Cambridge*, after which he became a Member of the honourable Society of *Gray's-Inn.*—— During his Refidence at the Univerfity, and indeed when he was no more than feventeen Years of Age, he wrote a Novel called the *Cyprian Academy*, in which he introduced the two firft of the dramatic Pieces mentioned below.—— The third of them is a much more regular and perfect Play, and was probably written when the Author had attained a riper Age.—— The Names of them are as follows,

1. *Deorum Dona*. Mafque.

2. *Gripus and Hegio*. Paftoral.

3. *Mirza*. Trag.

Phillips and *Winftanley* have alfo attributed fome other Plays to him, but on what Foundation I know not, *viz.*

Dick Scorner. Com.

Don QUIXOTE. Com.

Deftruction

Destruction of Jerusalem.
Marriage of Wit and Science.

Together with Masques and Interludes, all which however *Langbaine* denies to be his, as he also does *Phillips*'s Assertion that any of his Pieces were ever represented on the Stage.

Mr. *Baron* had a great Intimacy with the celebrated Mr. *James Howell*, the great Traveller, in whose Collections of Letters there is one to this Gentleman (See *Howell*'s Letters, *Vol.* III. *Letter* 418) who was at that Time at *Paris*.—To Mr. *Howell* in particular, and to all the Ladies and Gentlewomen of *England* in general, he has dedicated his Romance.

BARRY, *Lodowick*. Esq;—What this Gentleman's Rank in Life was seems somewhat difficult to determine.—The Writers on dramatic Subjects, viz. *Langbaine, Jacob, Gildon, Whincop,* &c. stiling him only Mr. *Lodowick Barry,* whereas *Anth. Wood,* in his *Athen. Oxon.* Vol. I. p. 629. calls him *Lodowick* Lord *Barry,* which Title *Coxeter* in his *MS.* has also bestowed on him.—This is however positively denied by *Whincop,* p. 91.—But let this be as it may, all Authors agree that he was of an ancient and honourable Family in *Ireland,* that he flourished about the Middle of K. *James* the first's Reign, and that he wrote one dramatic Piece, entitled,

Ram Alley. Com.

BASKER, Mr. *Thomas.*—To a Gentleman of this Name, *Langbaine* informs us some of the old Catalogues have attributed the being Author of a Play printed with the Letters *T. D.* in the Title Page, and called,

The *Bloody Banquet.* Trag.

BEAUMONT, *Francis,* and *John* FLETCHER.

As these two Gentlemen were, while living, the most inviolable Friends and inseparable Companions; as in their Works also they were united, the *Orestes* and *Pylades* of the poetical World, it would be a Kind of Injury done to the *Manes* of their Friendship, should we here, after Death, separate those Names which before it were found for ever join'd. —For this Reason we shall, under this single Article, deliver what we have been able to collect concerning both, yet, for the Sake of Order, it will be proper first to take some Notice of those Particulars which separately relate to each. First then, as his Name stands at the Head of this Article, we will begin with

Mr. *Francis* BEAUMONT.— This Gentleman was descended from a very ancient Family of that Name, seated at *Grace-Dieu* in *Leicestershire.*—His Grand-Father, *John Beaumont,* had been Master of the Rolls, and his Father, *Francis Beaumont,* one of the Judges of the Court of *Common Pleas.*—Nor was his Descent less honourable on the Side of his Mother, whose Name was *Anne,* the Daughter of *George Pierrepoint* of *Home Pierrepoint* in the County of *Nottingham,* Esq; and of the same Family from which the present Duke of *Kingston* derives his Ancestry.

Our Poet however appears to have been only a younger Son, *Jacob* mentioning a Brother of his by the Title of Sir *Henry Beaumont,* tho' *Cibber,* in his *Lives of the Poets,* Vol. I. p. 157. calls him Sir *John Beaumont.*—He was born in the Year 1585, and received his Education at *Cambridge,*
tho'

tho' in what Colledge is a Point which we have not been able to trace.——He afterwards was enter'd a Student in the *Inner Temple*.—It is not however apparent that he made any great Proficiency in the Law, that being a Study probably too dry and unentertaining to be attended to by a Man of his fertile and sprightly Genius.—And indeed, we should scarcely be surprised to find that he had given no Application to any Study but Poetry, nor attended on any Court but that of the *Muses*, but on the contrary our Admiration might fix itself in the opposite Extreme, and fill us with Astonishment at the extreme Assiduity of his Genius and Rapidity of his Pen, when we look back on the Voluminousness of his Works, and then enquire into the Time allowed him for them; Works that might well have taken up a long Life to have executed.—For altho', out of fifty-three Plays which are collected together as the Labours of these united Authors, Mr. *Beaumont* was concerned in much the greatest Part of them, yet he did not live to complete his thirtieth Year, the King of Terrors summoning him away in the Beginning of *March* 1615, on the 9th Day of which he was interr'd in the Entrance of St. *Benedict*'s Chapel in *Westminster-Abbey*.—He left behind him only one Daughter, Mrs. *Frances Beaumont*, who must then have been an Infant, as she died in *Leicestershire* since the Year 1700.—She had been possessed of several MS. Poems of her Father's Writing, but the envious *Irish* Seas, which robbed the World of that invaluable Treasure, the remaining Part of *Spencer*'s *Fairy Queen*, deprived it also of these Poems, which were

lost in her Voyage from *Ireland*, in which Kingdom she had resided for some Time in the Family of the Duke of *Ormond*.—Let us now proceed to our second Author,

Mr. *John* FLETCHER.—This Gentleman was not more meanly descended than his poetical Colleague.—His Father, the Reverend Dr. *Fletcher*, having been first made Bishop of *Bristol* by Queen *Elizabeth*, and afterwards by the same Monarch, in the Year 1593, translated to the rich and honourable See of *London*.——Our Poet was born in 1576, and was, as well as his Friend, educated at *Cambridge*, where he made a great Proficiency in his Studies, and was accounted a very good Scholar.——His natural Vivacity of Wit, for which he was remarkable, soon render'd him a Devotee to the Muses, and his close Attention to their Service and fortunate Connection with a Genius equal to his own, soon rais'd him to one of the highest Places in the Temple of poetical Fame.—As he was born near ten Years before Mr. *Beaumont*, so did he also survive him by an equal Number of Years.—The general Calamity of a Plague, which happened in the Year 1625, involving him in it's great Destruction, he being at that Time forty nine Years of Age.

During the joint Lives of these two great Poets, it appears that they wrote nothing separately, excepting one little Piece by each, which seem'd of too trivial a Nature for either to require Assistance in, viz. *The Faithful Shepherd*, a Pastoral, by *Fletcher*, and *The Masque of Gray's-Inn Gentlemen*, by *Beaumont*.——Yet what Share each had in the Writing or Designing of the Pieces thus
composed

compofed by them jointly, there is no Poffibility of determining. —It is however generally allowed that *Fletcher*'s peculiar Talent was *Wit*, and *Beaumont*'s, tho' much the younger Man, *Judgment.*— Nay, fo extraordinary was the latter Property in Mr. *Beaumont*, that it is recorded of the great *Ben Jonfon*, who feems moreover to have had a fufficient Degree of Self Opinion of his own Abilities, that he conftantly, fo long as this Gentleman lived, fubmitted his own Writings to his Cenfure, and, as it is thought, availed himfelf of his Judgment at leaft in the correcting, if not even in the contriving all his Plots.

It is probable therefore that the forming the Plots and contriving the Conduct of the Fable, the writing of the more ferious and pathetic Parts, and topping the redundant Branches of *Fletcher*'s Wit, whofe Luxuriance, we are told, frequently ftood in Need of Caftigation, might be in general *Beaumont*'s Portion in the Work, while *Fletcher*, whofe Converfation with the *Beau Monde* (which indeed both of them from their Births and Stations in Life had been ever accuftomed to) added to the volatile and lively Turn he poffeffed, render'd him perfectly Mafter of Dialogue and polite Language, might execute the Defigns formed by the other, and raife the Superftructure of thofe lively and fpirited Scenes which *Beaumont* had only laid the Foundation of; and in this he was fo fuccefsful, that tho' his Wit and Raillery were extremely keen and poignant, yet they were at the fame Time fo perfectly genteel, that they ufed rather to pleafe than difguft the very Perfons on whom they feem'd to reflect.—Yet that *Fletcher* was not intirely excluded

from a Share in the Conduct of the Drama, may be gather'd from a Story related by *Winftanley*, viz. that our two Bards having concerted the rough Draught of a Tragedy over a Bottle of Wine at a Tavern, *Fletcher* faid, he would undertake to *kill the King*, which Words being overheard by the Waiter, who had not happen'd to have been Witnefs to the Context of their Converfation, he lodged an Information of Treafon againft them.—But on their Explanation of it only to mean the Deftruction of a theatrical Monarch, their Loyalty moreover being unqueftioned, the Affair ended in a Jeft.

On the whole, the Works of thefe Authors have undoubtedly very great Merit, and fome of their Pieces defervedly ftand on the Lift of the prefent Ornaments of the Theatre.—The Plots are ingenious, interefting and well managed, the Characters ftrongly marked, and the Dialogue fprightly and natural, yet there is in the latter a Coarfenefs which is not fuitable to the Politenefs of the prefent Age, and a Fondnefs of Repartee, which frequently runs into Obfcenity, and which we may fuppofe was the Vice of that Time; fince even the delicate *Shakefpeare* himfelf is not entirely free from it.—But as thefe Authors have more of that Kind of Wit than the laft-mentioned Writer, it is not to be wondered if their Works were, in the licentious Reign of *Charles* II. prefer'd to his.—Now, however, to the Honour of the prefent Tafte be it fpoken, the Tables are entirely turned, and while *Shakefpeare*'s immortal Works are our conftant and daily Fare, thofe of *Beaumont* and *Fletcher*, tho' delicate in their Kind, are only occafionally ferved up, and even then great Pains is ever taken to clear them of that *Fumét*, which the *Haut Gout* of *their* Contemporaries confider'd as their fupremeft Relifh, but which the more undepraved Tafte of *ours*, has been juftly taught to look on as what it really is, no more than a corrupted and unwholfome Taint.

The Pieces they have left behind them are as follows.

1. *Beggar's Bufh.* C
2. *Bloody Brother.* T.
3. *Bonduca.* T.
4. *Captain.* T.
5. *Chances.* C.
6. *Coronation.* Tr.-C. (claim'd by *Shirley*)
7. *Coxcomb.* C.
8. *Cupid's Revenge.* T.
9. *Cuftom of the Country.* C.
10. *Double Marriage.* T.
11. *Elder Brother.* C.
12. *Faithful Shepherdefs.* Paft. (by *Fletcher* alone.)
13. *Fair Maid of the Inn.* Tragi-Com.
14. *Falfe One.* T.
15. *Four Plays in One.*
16. *Honeft Man's Fortune.* Tr.-Com.
17. *Humorous Lieutenant.* Tr.-Com.
18. *Ifland Princefs.* Tr.-Com.
19. *King and no King.* Tr.-C.
20. *Knight of* MALTA. Tr.-Com.
21. *Knight of the burning Peftle.* Com.
22. *Laws of* CANDY. Tr.-C.
23. *Little French Lawyer.* C.
24. *Love's Cure.* C.
25. *Love's Pilgrimage.* C.
26. *Lover's Progrefs.* Tr.-C.
27. *Loyal Subject.* C.
28. *Mad Lover.* Tr.-Com.
29. *Maid in the Mill.* Com.
30. *Maid's Tragedy.*
31. *Mafque of* Gray's-Inn *Gentlemen* (by *Beaumont* alone)
32. *Monfieur* THOMAS. (by *Fletcher* alone)
33. *Nice Valour.* Com.
34. *Night Walker.* Com. (by *Fletcher* alone.)
35. *Noble Gentleman.* C.
36. PHILASTER. Tr.
37. *Pilgrim.* C.
38. *Prophetefs.* Trag. Hift.
39. *Queen of* CORINTH. Tr.-Com.
40. *Rule a Wife and have a Wife.* C.
41. *Scornful Lady.* C.
42. *Sea Voyage.* C.
43. *Spanifh Curate.* C.
44. THIERRY *and* THEODORET. T.
45. *Two Noble Kinfmen.* Tr.-Com. (This Play was written by *Fletcher*, with fome Affiftance by *Shakefpeare.*)
46. VALENTINIAN. T.
47. *Widow.* Com. (Affifted by *Johnfon* and *Middleton*)
48. *Wife for a Month.* C.
49. *Wild Goofe Chace.* C.
50. *Wit at feveral Weapons.* C.
51. *Wit without Money.* C.
52. *Woman Hater.* Com. (by *Fletcher* alone.)
53. *Woman pleas'd.* C.
54. *Woman's Prize.* Com. (by *Fletcher* alone.)

BECKINGHAM, Mr. *Charles.* —This Gentleman was the Son of a Linnen-Draper in *Fleet-ftreet.* —He was educated at that great Nurfery of Learning *Merchant-Taylor's-School*, under the learned Doctor *Smith*, where he made a very great Proficiency in all his Studies, and gave the ftrongeft Teftimonials of very extraordinary Abilities.——In Poetry more particularly he very early difcover'd an uncommon Genius, two dramatic Pieces of his Writing being reprefented on the Stage before he had well compleated his twentieth

tieth Year.—And thofe not fuch as requir'd the leaft Indulgence or Allowance on Account of his Years, but fuch as bore Evidence to a Boldnefs of Sentiment, an Accuracy of Diction, an Ingenuity of Conduct, and a Maturity of Judgment, which would have done Honour to a much more ripened Age.—The Titles of his Plays, both of which were Tragedies, are,

1. *Henry* IV. *of France.*
2. *Scipio Africanus.*

At the Reprefentation of the laft-mentioned Piece, which indeed was the firft he wrote, his School-Mafter Dr. *Smith,* as a peculiar Mark of Diftinction and Regard to the Merit of his Pupil, gave all his Boys a Holiday on the Afternoon of the Author's Benefit, in order to afford an Opportunity, to fuch of them as pleafed, to pay their Compliments to their School-Fellow on that Occafion.

He was born in 1699, and befides thefe dramatic Pieces wrote feveral other Poems; but his Genius was not permitted any very long Period to expand itfelf in; for he died on the 18th of *Feb.* 1730, in the 32d Year of his Age.

BEDLOE, Capt. *William.*—— This Gentleman, at the Time he lived, made himfelf better known and more confidered on Account of his Actions than his Writings, having been a very principal and ufeful Evidence in the Difcovery of the Popifh Plot in the Reign of King *Charles* II.—The Particulars of that important Event may be feen by looking into any of the *Englifh* Hiftorians relating to that Period; and Captain *Bedloe*'s Life, which contained little extraordinary excepting what concerned the faid Plot, having been written by an unknown Hand,

and publifhed in 1681, 8vo. being the Year after his Death, we fhall refer our Readers to that Work, and only proceed to the Mention of one dramatic Piece, which he publifhed in his Life Time, altho' never acted.——It is entitled,

The *Excommunicated Prince.* Trag.

The Printer having, without the Author's Knowledge, added a fecond Title, and called it " *The Popifh Plot in a Play,*" greatly excited the Curiofity of the Public, who were however much difappointed when they found the Plan of the Piece to be founded on a quite different Story.——*Anth. à Wood,* in his *Athenæ Oxon.* Vol. 2. p. 884. will not allow the Captain the Merit of this Play, but afferts that it was written partly, if not entirely, by one *Tho. Walter,* M. A. of *Jefus* College, *Oxford.*

Capt. *Bedloe* died at *Briftol, Aug.* 20, 1680.

BEHN, Mrs. *Aphara,* or *Aphra.*—Some Kind of Difpute has arifen in Regard to this Lady's Chriftian Name, in Confequence of *Langbaine*'s having attributed that of *Aftræa* to her as a real Name, which was indeed no more than a poetical one, by which fhe was known and addreffed by her Contemporaries.—She was a Gentlewoman by Birth, being defcended from a very good Family, whofe Refidence was in the City of *Canterbury.*—She was born fome Time in *Charles* I's Reign, but in what Year is uncertain.— Her Father's Name was *Johnfon,* who, through the Intereft of the Lord *Willoughby,* to whom he was related, being appointed Lieutenant-Gen. of *Surinam,* and fix and thirty Iflands, undertook a Journey to the *Weft-Indies,* taking with

him

him his whole Family, among whom was our Poetefs, at that Time very young.—Mr. *Johnfon* died in the Voyage, but his Family reaching *Surinam*, fettled there for fome Years.

Here it was that fhe learned the Hiftory of, and acquired a perfonal Intimacy with, the *American* Prince *Oroonoko*, and his beloved *Imoinda*, whofe Adventures fhe has herfelf fo pathetically related in her celebrated Novel of that Name, and which Mr. *Southerne* afterwards made fuch an admirable Ufe of in making it the Ground-work of one of the beft Tragedies in the *Englifh* Language.——Her Intimacy with this Prince, and the Intereft fhe took in his Concerns, added to her own Youth and Beauty, afforded an Opportunity to the ill-natur'd and cenforious to accufe her of a nearer Connection with him than that of Friendfhip. — This, however, a Lady of her Acquaintance, who has prefixed fome Memoirs of her Life to an Edition of her Novels, takes great Pains, and I think very much to the Purpofe, to acquit her of.

On her Return to *London*, fhe became the Wife of one Mr. *Behn*, a Merchant, refiding in that City, but of *Dutch* Extraction.—How long he lived after their Marriage, is not very apparent, probably not very long; for her Wit and Abilities having brought her into high Eftimation at Court, King *Charles* II. fix'd on her as a proper Perfon to tranfact fome Affairs of Importance abroad during the Courfe of the *Dutch* War,——To this Purpofe fhe went over to *Antwerp*, where, by her Intrigues and Gallantries, fhe fo far crept into the Secrets of State, as to anfwer the Ends

propos'd by fending her over.— Nay, in the latter End of 1666, fhe, by Means of the Influence fhe had over one *Vander Albert*, a *Dutchman* of Eminence, whofe Heart was warmly attached to her, fhe wormed out of him the Defign form'd by *De Ruyter*, in Conjunction with the Family of the *De Wits*, of failing up the *Thames*, and burning the *Englifh* Ships in their Harbours, which they afterwards put in Execution at *Rochefter*.—This fhe immediately communicated to the *Englifh* Court, but tho' the Event proved her Intelligence to be well grounded, yet it was at that Time only laugh'd at, which together, probably, with no great Inclination fhewn to reward her for the Pains fhe had been at, determined her to drop all farther Thoughts of political Affairs, and during the Remainder of her Stay at *Antwerp*, to give herfelf up entirely to the Gaiety and Gallantries of the Place.—*Vander Albert* continued his Addreffes, and after having made fome unfuccefsful Attempts to obtain the Poffeffion of her Perfon on eafier Terms than Matrimony, at length confented to make her his Wife; but while he was preparing at *Amfterdam* for a Journey to *England* with that Intent, a Fever carried him off, and left her free from any amorous Engagements. —She was alfo ftrongly folicited by a very old Man, of the Name of *Van Bruin*, at whofe Expence fhe diverted herfelf for a Time, and then rejected him with that Ridicule which his abfurd Addreffes juftly merited.

In her Voyage back to *England*, fhe was very near being loft, the Veffel fhe was in being driven on the Coaft by a Storm, but happening to founder within Sight

Sight of Land, the Paſſengers were, by the timely Aſſiſtance of Boats from the Shore, all fortunately preſerved.

From this Period ſhe devoted her Life entirely to Pleaſure and the Muſes.—Her Works are extremely numerous, and all of them have a lively and amorous Turn.——It is no Wonder then that her Wit ſhould gain her the Eſteem of Mr. *Dryden, Southerne,* and other Men of Genius, as her Beauty of which in her younger Part of Life ſhe poſſeſſed a great Share, did the *Love* of thoſe of Gallantry.—Nor does ſhe appear to have been any Stranger to the delicate Senſations of that Paſſion, as appears from ſome of her Letters to a Gentleman, with whom ſhe correſponded under the Name of *Lycida,* and who ſeems not to have returned her Flame with equal Ardor, or received it with that Rapture her Charms might well have been expected to command.

Her Works, as I have before obſerved, were very numerous, conſiſting of Plays, Novels, Poems, Letters, &c.—But as our preſent Deſign only authorizes our taking Notice of her dramatic Pieces, we ſhall hereto ſubjoin a Liſt of them, amounting to ſixteen in Number, *viz.*

1. **Abdelazar.** T.
2. *Amorous Prince.* C.
3. *City Heireſs.* C.
4. *Dutch Lover.* C.
5. *Emperor of the Moon.* Far.
6. *Falſe Count.* C.
7. *Feign'd Courtezans.* C.
8. *Forc'd Marriage.* T. C.
9. *Lucky Chance.* C.
10. *Rover.* C. two Parts.
11. *Roundheads.* C.
12. Sir **Patient Fancy.** C.
13. *Town Fop.* C.
14. *Widow Ranter.* C.
15. *Younger Brother.* C.
16. *Young King.* T. C.

It will appear by this Catalogue that the Turn of her Genius was chiefly to Comedy. — As to the Character her Plays ſhould maintain in the Records of dramatic Hiſtory, it will be difficult to determine, ſince their Faults and Perfections ſtand in ſtrong Oppoſition to each other.—In all, even the moſt indifferent of her Pieces, there are ſtrong Marks of Genius and Underſtanding.——Her Plots are full of Buſineſs and Ingenuity, and her Dialogue ſparkles with the dazzling Luſtre of genuine Wit, which every where glitters among it.—But then ſhe has been accuſed, and that not without great Juſtice, of interlarding her Comedies with the moſt indecent Scenes, and giving an Indulgence in her Wit to the moſt indelicate Expreſſions.—To this Accuſation ſhe has herſelf made ſome Reply in the *Preface* to the *Lucky Chance;* but the retorting the Charge of Prudery and Preciſeneſs on her Accuſers, is far from being a ſufficient Exculpation of herſelf.—The beſt, and perhaps the only true Excuſe that can be made for it is, that altho' ſhe might herſelf have as great an Averſion as any One to looſe Scenes or too warm Deſcriptions, yet, as ſhe wrote for a Livelihood, ſhe was obliged to comply with the corrupt Taſte of the Times.—And, as ſhe was a Woman, and naturally, moreover, of an amorous Complexion, and wrote in an Age, and to a Court of Gallantry and Licentiouſneſs, the latter Circumſtances, added to her Neceſſities, compell'd her to indulge her Audience in their favorite Depravity, and the for-

mer,

mer, affifted by a rapid Flow of Wit and Vivacity enabled her fo to do; fo that both together have given her Plays the loofe Caft which it is but too apparent they poffefs.

Her own private Character I fhall give to my Readers in the Words of one of her own female Companions, who, in the Memoirs before-mentioned, prefixed to her Novels, fpoke of her thus, " She was," fays this Lady, " of " a generous humane Difpofition, " fomething paffionate, very fer- " viceable to her Friends in all " that was in her Power, and " could fooner forgive an Injury " than do one.—She had Wit, " Humour, Good - Nature, and " Judgment:—She was Miftrefs " of all the pleafing Arts of Con- " verfation:—She was a Woman " of Senfe, and confequently a " Lover of Pleafure.——For my " Part I knew her intimately, " and never faw ought unbecom- " ing the juft Modefty of our " Sex; tho' more gay and free, " than the Folly of the Precife " will allow."

After a Life intermingled with numerous Difappointments, which, as Mr. *Gildon* juftly obferves, a Woman of her Senfe and Merit ought never to have met with, and in the Clofe of a long Indif- pofition, Mrs. *Behn* departed from this World on the 16th of *April* 1689, and lies interr'd in the Cloyfter of *Weftminfter-Abbey*, un- der a blue Marble Stone, againft the firft Pillar in the Eaft Am- bulatory with the following In- fcription,

Mrs. *Aphra Behn.*
died *April* the 16th,
1689,
*Here lies a Proof that Wit can ne-
ver be
Defence enough againft Mortality.*

Revived by *Tho. Waine*, in Re fpect to fo bright a Genius.

BELCHIER, Mr. *Dawbridge-Court.*—This Gentleman was the eldeft Son of *William Belchier*, of *Gillefborough* in *Northamptonfhire*, Efq;—He was enter'd of *Chrift Church, Oxford*, where he took the Degree of Bachelor of Arts, *Feb.* 6, 1600, fome Years after which he went into the *United Provinces*, and fettled at *Utrecht*, where he wrote, or, as *Coxeter* terms it, *tranflated into Englifh* (from the *Dutch*, I fuppofe) one dramatic Piece, called,

HANS BEER POT's *Invifible Comedy.*

Phillips and *Winftanley*, how- ever, among the numerous Mif- takes they are guilty of, have at- tributed this Piece to *Thomas Nafh.*

Mr. *Belchier* died in the *Low Countries*, in 1621.

BELLAMY, Meffrs. *Daniel*, Sen. and Jun.—Thefe Gentle- men are Father and Son, and I believe are both ftill living.—— The Father, as we are informed in the Title Page to their Works, was fome Time fince of St. *John*'s College, *Oxford*, and the Son of *Trinity College, Cambridge.*—They are Authors in Conjunction, and in the Year 1746, publifhed a Collection of Mifcellanies in Profe and Verfe, in two vol. 12mo. in which, among other Pieces, are the following dramatic ones, all excepting the fecond-mentioned one, which is a mufical Inter- lude, and was publifhed by itfelf, but at what Time, or whether written by the Father or Son, I cannot pretend to determine.— The Names of the feveral Pieces are as follows,

1. *Innocence betray'd.*
2. *Languifhing Lover.*
3. *Love triumphant.*

4. *Perjur'd*

4. *Perjur'd Devotee.*
5. *Rival Nymphs.*
6. *Rival Priests.*
7. *Vanquished Love,* and
8. Three select Scenes of *Guarini's Pastor Fido.*

All these little Pieces (the 2d and 8th only excepted) were expressly written to be performed by the young Ladies of Mrs. *Bellamy*'s Boarding-School at *Chelsea*, at the stated Periods of breaking up for the Holidays, for the Improvement of themselves, and the Amusement of their Parents and Friends.—They are well adapted to the Purpose, being short and concise, the Plots simple and familiar, and the Language, tho' not remarkably poetical, nor adorn'd with any very extraordinary Beauty, yet, on the whole, far from contemptible.——They are calculated for the shewing the peculiar Talents of the young Ladies, who were to appear in them ; and to set forth the Improvements they had acquired in their Education, especially in Music, to which End Songs are pretty lavishly dispersed through them all.—In a Word, the Design on the whole is laudable, and it were to be wished that an Example of this Sort were to be followed in more of the Seminaries of Education both Male and Female, as these Kinds of public Exhibitions constantly excite a Degree of Emulation which awakens Talents that might otherwise have lain entirely buried in Obscurity, and rouzes to a greater Degree of Exertion those which have already been discovered.

BENNET, *Philip,* Esq; —— Who this Gentleman is I know not.—His Name, as the Author of a dramatic Piece, which however was never acted, I find in the Monthly Lists of Publica-

tions for the Year 1733, but both *Whincop* and the Author of the *British Theatre* have omitted taking any Notice of either the Author, or his Works ;—the Title of the latter, as it stands in the said literary Records, is,

The *Beau's Adventures.* Farce.

BENTLEY, Mr.—This Gentleman, who is now living, is the Son of the late well-known Dr. *Bentley,* the great Critic.—The present Author is possess'd of great literary Abilities, yet the Turn of his Genius seems not greatly adapted to dramatic Writings, by the Specimen he has given of them in a Piece which made it's Appearance at *Drury Lane* Theatre, in the Summer of 1761.—It was entitled,

The *Wishes.* Com.

It is attempted to be written after the Manner of the *Italian* Comedy, but tho' the Author has shewn great Knowledge of the World, an Accuracy of Judgment, and in some Passages of it a strong Poignancy of Satire, yet on the whole it is deficient in that Novelty of Plot, Variety of Incident, and Vivacity of Wit, which are essential to the very Existence of Comedy.—In short, the Author has written more like a Man of *Learning* than *Genius,* more to the *Closet* than the *Stage.* —It will not therefore perhaps be regretted if he should for the future employ that Learning he is Master of, for the Emolument of the Public on Subjects of more Importance, and quit the arduous, yet less valuable Talent of *amusing,* for the more useful one of *instructing.*

BERNARD, *Richard.* — As to the Particulars of this Gentleman's Life, none have been handed down to us, farther than that he flourished in the Reign of

Queen

Queen *Elizabeth*, aud that he lived at *Epworth* in *Lincolnſhire*.—In his literary Capacity only therefore we can ſpeak of him, in which Light we are to conſider him as the firſt Perſon who gave this Kingdom an entire Tranſlation of *Terence's Comedies*.——To the learned it would be needleſs to repeat their Names, but for the Sake of our Fair Readers, and others who may not be ſo well acquainted with the *Latin* Claſſics, it may not be improper to inform them that they were ſix in Number, and their Titles as follows,

1. *Adelphi.*
2. *Andria.*
3. *Eunuchus.*
4. *Heautontimorumenos.*
5. *Hecyra.*
6. *Phormio.*

Mr. *Bernard* has not, however, contented himſelf with giving a bare Tranſlation of theſe ſix Plays, but has alſo ſelected ſeparately and diſtinctly, in each Scene, all the moſt remarkable Forms of Speech, Theſes and moral Sentences, after the ſame Manner as had been done before him in an old *French* Tranſlation of the ſame Author, printed at *Paris* in 1574.——Theſe little Extracts are extremely uſeful and entertaining, and may not only be render'd ſerviceable to Boys at School in the more immediate Underſtanding of the Author, but are alſo of great Aſſiſtance to thoſe who read him with a more claſſical View, in the pointing out, and fixing on the Memory ſome of the moſt beautiful Paſſages, or ſuch as from the Importance of the Sentiment, or the peculiar Arrangement of the Phraſeology, may be the moſt deſirable to remember.

BETTERTON, Mr. *Thomas*.— Tho' in Purſuance of the Deſign of this Work we can inſert no Names but thoſe of dramatic *Writers*, yet the Gentleman who now comes under our Conſideration requires our ſpeaking of him not in that Light only, but alſo as an Actor, and that perhaps as the moſt capital one that this or any other Country has ever produced.—He was born in *Tothill-Street*, *Weſtminſter*, in the Year 1635, his Father being at that Time under Cook to K. *Charles* I. —He received the firſt Rudiments of a genteel Education, and ſhewed ſuch a Propenſity to Literature, that it was for ſome Time the Intention of his Family to have brought him up to one of the liberal Profeſſions.—But this Deſign the Confuſion and Violence of the enſuing Times diverted them from, or probably put it out of their Power to accompliſh.—His Fondneſs of Reading, however, induced him to requeſt of his Parents that they would bind him Apprentice to a Bookſeller, which was readily complied with, fixing on one Mr. *Rhodes*, near *Charing-Croſs*, for his Maſter.

This Gentleman, who had been *Wardrobe-Keeper* to the Theatre in *Black-Friars* before the Troubles, obtained a Licence in 1659, from the Powers then in being, to ſet up a Company of Players in the *Cock-pit* in *Drury-Lane*, in which Company Mr. *Betterton* enter'd himſelf, and tho' not much above twenty Years of Age, immediately gave Proof of the moſt capital Genius and Merit, and acquired the higheſt Applauſe in the *Loyal Subject*, the *Wild Gooſe Chace*, the *Spaniſh Curate*, and ſeveral other Plays of *Beaumont* and *Fletcher*, which were then the Pieces moſt in Vogue.

Preſently

Prefently after the Reftoration, two diftinct Theatres were
eftablifhed by Royal Authority,
the one in *Drury Lane*, in Confequence of a Patent granted to
Henry Killigrew, Efq; which was
called the *King*'s Company : The
other in *Lincoln's-Inn-Fields*, who
ftiled themfelves the Duke of
York's Servants, the Patentee of
which was the ingenious Sir *William Davenant* ;—which laft-mentioned Gentleman having long had
a clofe Intimacy with, and warm
Friendfhip for, Mr. *Rhodes*, engaged Mr. *Betterton*, and all who
had acted under Mr. *Rhodes*, into his Company, which opened
in 1662, with a new Play of Sir
William's, in two Parts, called
the *Siege of Rhodes*.

In this Piece, as well as in the
fubfequent Characters which Mr.
Betterton performed, he increafed
his Reputation and Efteem with
the Public, and indeed became fo
much in Favour with King
Charles II. that one of his Biographers afferts (Vid. *Cibber's
Lives of the Poets*, Vol. III.
p. 157.) that by his Majefty's
efpecial Command he went over
to *Paris*, to take a View of the
French Stage, that he might the
better judge what would contribute to the Improvement of our
own, and even goes fo far as to
fay, that he was the firft who introduced moving Scenes on the
Englifh Stage, the Honour of
which, however, the other Writers have given to Sir *William*
himfelf.

In the Year 1670, he married
one Mrs. *Saunderfon*, a female Performer on the fame Stage, who, both
as an Actrefs and a Woman, was
every Thing that human Perfection was capable of arriving at,
and with whom he, through the
whole Courfe of his remaining

Life, poffefs'd every Degree of
Happinefs that a perfect Union
of Hearts can beftow.

When the *Duke*'s Company removed to *Dorfet Gardens*, he ftill
continued with them, and on the
Coalition of the two Companies
in 1684, he acceded to the Treaty, and remained among them;
Mrs. *Betterton* maintaining the
fame foremoft Figure among the
Women, that her Hufband fupported among the Male Performers.—And fo great was the Eftimation they were both held in,
that in the Year 1675, when a
Paftoral, called *Califto*, or the
Chafte Nymph, written by Mr.
Crown, at the Defire of Queen
Catherine, Confort to *Charles* II.
was to be performed at Court by
Perfons of the greateft Diftinction, our *Englifh Rofcius* was employed to inftruct the Gentlemen, and Mrs. *Betterton* honoured
with the Tutorage of the Ladies,
among whom were the two Princeffes *Mary* and *Anne*, Daughters
of the Duke of *York*, both of
whom afterwards fucceeded to the
Crown of thefe Realms.——In
grateful Remembrance of which
the latter of them, when Queen,
fettled a Penfion of £ 100 *per
annum* on her old Inftructrefs.

In 1693, Mr. *Betterton* having
founded the Inclinations of a felect Number of the Actors whom
he found ready to join with him,
obtained, thro' the Influence of
the Earl of *Dorfet*, the Royal Licence for acting in a feparate
Theatre; and was very foon enabled, by the voluntary Subfcrip-
tions of many Perfons of Quality,
to erect a new Play-houfe within the Walls of the *Tennis* Court
in *Lincoln's-Inn-Fields*.

To this Step Mr. *Betterton* was
probably induced by two diftinct
Motives.—The firft was the ill
Treatment

Treatment he received from the Managers, who, exerting a defpotic Authority over their Performers, which he thought it his Duty to remonftrate againft, began to grow jealous of his Power; and therefore with a Hope of abating his Influence, gave away fome of his capital Parts to young and infufficient Performers. This Conduct however had the direct contrary Effect to that which they expected from it, by attaching to Mr. *Betterton* all the beft Players (who became apprehenfive of meeting with the fame Treatment themfelves) and at the fame Time exafperating the Town, which would not, as in our calmer Period, fubmit to be dictated to in it's Diverfions, or have it's moft rational Amufements damp'd by bungling and imperfect Performances, when it was apparently in the Power of the Managers to give them in the greateft Height of Perfection.

The other Motive probably was a pecuniary one, with a View to repair, by the more enlarged Profits of a Manager, the Lofs of his whole Fortune (upwards of two Thoufand Pounds) which he had undergone in the Year 1692, by adventuring it in a commercial Scheme to the *Eaft-Indies*.

Be this however as it will, the new Theatre open'd in 1695, with Mr. *Congreve's Love for Love*, the Succefs of which was amazingly great.—Yet in a few Years it appear'd that the Profits arifing from this Theatre, oppofed as it was by all the Strength of *Cibber's* and *Vanbrugh's* Writings at the other Houfe, were very infignificant; and Mr. *Betterton* growing now into the Infirmities of Age, and labouring under violent Attacks of the Gout, he gladly quitted at once the Fatigues of Management, and the Hurry of the Stage.

The Public, however, who retained a grateful Senfe of the Pleafure they had frequently received from this theatrical *Veteran*, and fenfible of the Narrownefs of his Circumftances, refolved to continue the Marks of their Efteem to him, by giving him a Benefit.——On the 7th of *April* 1709, the Comedy of *Love for Love* was performed for that Purpofe, in which this Gentleman himfelf, tho' then upwards of feventy Years of Age, acted the youthful Part of *Valentine*; as in the *September* following he did that of *Hamlet*, his Performance of which the Author of the *Tatler* has taken a particular Notice of.——On the former Occafion, thofe very eminent Performers Mrs. *Barry*, Mrs. *Bracegirdle* and Mr. *Dogget*, who had all quitted the Stage fome Years before, in Gratitude to one whom they had had fo many Obligations to, acted the Parts of *Angelica*, Mrs. *Frail* and *Ben*; and Mr. *Rowe* wrote an Epilogue for that Night, which was fpoken by the two Ladies, fupporting between them this once powerful Supporter of the *Englifh* Stage.

The Profits of this Night are faid to have amounted to upwards of £ 500, the Prices having been raifed to the fame that the Operas and Oratorios are at prefent, and when the Curtain drew up, almoft as large an Audience appearing behind as before it.

The next Winter, Mr. *Betterton* was prevailed on by Mr. *Owen M'Swinney*, then Manager of the *Opera* Houfe in the *Haymarket* (at which Plays were acted four Times a Week) to continue performing, tho' but feldom.—In Confequence of which, in the

enfuing

Spring, *viz.* on the 25th of *A-pril* 1710, another Play was given out for this Gentleman's Benefit, *viz.* the *Maid's Tragedy* of *Beaumont* and *Fletcher*, in which he himself performed his cele-brated Part of *Melantius.*—This however was the laſt Time he was to appear on the Stage.—For hav-ing been ſudden'y ſeized with the Gout, and being impatient at the Thoughts of diſappointing his Friends, he made Uſe of outward Applications to reduce the Swel-lings of his Feet, which enabled him to walk on the Stage, tho' obliged to have his Foot in a Slipper.—But altho' he acted that Day with unuſual Spirit and Briſkneſs, and met with univer-ſal Applauſe, yet he paid very dear for this Tribute he had paid to the Public; for the Fo-mentations he had made Uſe of occaſioning a Revulſion of the Gouty Humour to the nobler Parts, threw the Diſtemper up into his Head, and terminated his Life on the 28th of that Month.—On the 2d of *May*, his Body was interr'd with much Ce-remony in the Cloyſter of *Weſt-minſter*, and great Honour paid to his Memory by his Friend the *Tatler*, who has related in a very pathetic, and at the ſame Time the moſt dignified Manner, the Proceſs of the Ceremonial.

The Dramatic Pieces he has left behind him are as follows,

1. *Amorous Widow.* C.
2. *Diocleſian.* Dram. Opera.
3. *Maſque in the* Opera *of the* PROPHETESS.
4. *Revenge.* C.
5. *Unjuſt Judge.* T.
6. *Woman made a Juſtice.* C.

Of theſe I have not much more to ſay, than that thoſe which are properly his own are not devoid of Merit, and thoſe which he has only alter'd have received an Ad-vantage from his Amendment.—In both, however, he has pre-ſerved one Degree of Perfection, which is of great Conſequence to the Succeſs of any dramatic Piece, *viz.* an exact Diſpoſition of the Scenes, and the Preſervation of a juſt Length, abſolute Propriety, and natural Connections.

As an Actor, he was certainly one of the greateſt of either his own or any other Age, but to en-ter into particular Details in that Reſpect would only take up the Time of our Readers unneceſſa-rily, and fill up a greater Portion of Room in this Work than we have a Right to allot to any one Article.—I ſhall therefore refer thoſe who are deſirous of having him painted out in the moſt lively Colours to their Imagination, to the Deſcription given of him by his Contemporary and Friend Mr. *Colley Cibber*, in the Apology for his own Life.—And as a Man, it is ſcarcely poſſible to ſay more, and it would be Injuſtice to ſay leſs of him, than that he was as unblemiſhed a Pattern of private and ſocial Qualities, as he was a perfect Model of theatrical Ac-tion and dramatic Execution.

It was on the Death of Mr. *Betterton* that Queen *Anne* ſettled on his Widow the Penſion I have taken Notice of above, which however ſhe did not enjoy long, the Grief for the Loſs of ſo good a Huſband, with whom ſhe lived forty Years in the utmoſt Har-mony and Affection, wrought ſo ſtrongly on her delicate Frame, which was already enfeebled by old Age, and a long State of bad Health, that it very ſoon deprived her of her Reaſon, and at the End of about half a Year of her Life alſo.

BILLERS,

BILLERS, *William*, Efq;——
I do not find any Mention who this Gentleman was in the Writers on dramatic Subjects, more than his being the affured Author of one Play, called,

Injur'd Innocence. Trag.

For a Conjecture as to his having once before made an Attempt in the dramatic Way, (See above, under B. W.

BLADEN, *Martin*, Efq;——
This Gentleman was formerly an Officer in the Army, bearing the Commiffion of a Lieutenant-Colonel in Queen *Anne*'s Reign, under the great Duke of *Marlborough*, to whom he dedicated a Tranflation of CÆSAR's *Commentaries* which he had compleated, and which is to this Day a Book held in very good Eftimation.—— In 1714, he was made one of the Lords Commiffioners of Trade and Plantations, and in 1717 was appointed Envoy Extraordinary to the Court of *Spain*, in the Room of —— *Brett*, Efq; but declined it, chufing rather to keep the Poft he already had, which was worth a thoufand Pounds *per Annum*, and which he never parted with till his Death, which was in *May* 1746.——He was alfo for many Years Member of Parliament for the Town of *Portfmouth*, and *Coxeter* hints that he was Secretary of State in *Ireland*, but in this he feems not abfolutely certain, making a Quære in Regard to the Time when, which however muft, if at all, have been in Queen *Anne*'s Reign; for from the firft Year of *George* I. to the Time of his Death, he held his Place at the Board of Trade, and I believe was not out of *England*.

He wrote two dramatic Pieces, both of which (for the one is only a Mafque introduced in the

third Act of the other) were printed in the Year 1705, without the Author's Confent.——Their Names are,

1. ORPHEUS *and* EURIDICE. Mafque.
2. SOLON. T. C.

BLANCH, Rev. Mr. — This Gentleman is the Author of two Comedies, neither of which were ever acted, entitled,

1. *Beau Merchant.*
2. *Swords into Anchors.*

Coxeter fays he lived near *Gloucefter*.—By the Prologue to the laft-mentioned Piece he appears to have been a Cleryyman, and by his own Account in his Dedication, which is to the Princefs of *Wales*, afterwards Queen *Caroline*, he muft have been born about 1650, the Play being publifhed in 1725, at which Time he declares himfelf to have been feventy five Years of Age.—He appears in the Courfe of his Writings to have been a Man of Reading and Knowledge, and to be both zealous for, and well inftructed in, the Commercial Interefts of this Nation.—But as a dramatic Writer nothing can well be more contemptible than his Works.

BLESSINGTON, *Murrough Boyle*, Lord Vifcount.——This Right Honourable Author was a Peer of the Kingdom of *Ireland*, and is afferted by *Jacob* to have been the Writer of a Tragedy, called,

The *Loft Princefs.*

It was however printed without any Author's Name, nor can I find that it ever made an Appearance on the Stage.

BODENS, Capt. *Charles*.—— This Gentleman had a Commiffion in the Foot Guards, befides which he had the Honour of being for many Years one of the Gentlemen Ufhers to his late Majefty.

Majesty.——He was a Man of a gay Turn and lively Disposition, which he indulged by the composing one Piece for the Stage, which was far from being totally devoid of Merit, and yet did not meet with any very extraordinary Success.—It was entitled,

The *Modish Couple*. C.

This Play has been since cut down into a Farce, and acted three Years ago for Mr. *Yates*'s Benefit, by the Title of,

Marriage a-la-Mode.

It has not however made it's Appearance in Print under that Form.

BONONCINI, Sign. *Giovanni.* —This Gentleman was a very eminent Composer of Music, and for some Time divided the Opinions of the *Conoscenti* of this Kingdom with Respect to the comparative Merits of himself and the great *Handel*, which gave Occasion for the following Epigram, said to have been written by Dean *Swift*.

> Some say that Signior *Bononcini*
> Compar'd to *Handel*'s a meer
>   Ninny ;
> Others aver that to him *Handel*
> Is scarcely fit to hold the Can-
>   dle :
> Strange ! that such high Dis-
> putes should be
> 'Twixt *Tweedle Dum* and *Twee-*
> *dle Dee.*

There is one Opera published with his Name prefixed to it, entitled,

PHARNACES. Ital. Opera.

But whether the Words, or only the Music, are his Composition, I cannot pretend to determine, and indeed in the general the Language of those Pieces, written meerly for Musical Representation, is so extremely pal-

try and so opposite to every Thing that can be deemed Poetry, that the greatest Compliment can be paid to the Authors of them is to suffer their Names to lie buried in the Shades of Obscurity.

BOOTH, Mr. *Barton*. — This Gentleman, who was an Author, and also a very eminent Actor, was descended from a very ancient and honourable Family, which originally had a Settlement in the County Palatine of *Lancaster*.—— He was the third Son of *John Booth*, Esq; who was nearly related to the Earl of *Warrington*, and who, tho' his Fortune was not very considerable, was extremely attentive to the Education of his Children.—In Consequence of this parental Care, he put the Subject of our present Observations, as soon as he arrived at the Age of nine Years, to *Westminster*-School, where he was first under the Tuition of the famous Dr. *Busby*, and afterwards under that of his Successor, the no less famous Dr. *Knipe*.——Here he shew'd a strong Passion for Learning in general, and more particularly for an Acquaintance with the *Latin* Poets, the finest Passages in whose Works he used with great Pains and Liberty to imprint in his Memory ; and had besides such a peculiar Propriety and judicious Emphasis in the Repetition of them, assisted by so fine a Tone of Voice, and adorned with such a natural Gracefulness of Action, as drew on him the Admiration of the whole School, and, added to the Sprightliness of his Parts in general, strongly recommended him to the Notice of his Master Dr. *Busby*, who having himself, when young, obtain'd great Applause in the Performance of a Part in the *Royal Slave*, a Play written by

 William

William Cartwright, had ever after held theatrical Accomplishments in the higheſt Eſtimation.

In Conſequence of this extraordinary Talent, when, according to the Cuſtom of the School, a *Latin* Play was to be performed, Mr. *Booth* was fixed upon for the acting the capital Part.——The Play happened to be the *Andria*, and the Part aſſigned to him that of *Pamphilus*, the young *Bevil* of *Terence*, in which the muſical Sweetneſs of his Voice, his Elegance of Deportment, and Gracefulneſs of Action drew the univerſal Applauſe of all the Spectators; and he has himſelf confeſs'd that this Circumſtance was what firſt fir'd his young Breaſt with theatrical Ambition.——His Father intended him for the Pulpit, but his Mind and Inclinations were now ſo fixed on the Stage, that when he had arrived at the Age of ſeventeen, and the Time approached when he muſt have been taken from School in order to be ſent to the Univerſity, he determined to run any Riſque rather than enter on a Courſe of Life ſo unſuitable to the natural Vivacity of his Diſpoſition; and therefore becoming acquainted with one Mr. *Aſhbury*, Manager of the *Dublin* Theatre, who was then in *London*, probably on the recruiting Scheme, and was very glad to receive a Youth of ſuch promiſing Expectations and growing Genius, he immediately quitted all other Views, engaged himſelf to Mr. *Aſhbury*, ſtole away from School, and went over to *Ireland* with that Gentleman in *June* 1698.

His firſt Appearance on the Stage was in the Part of *Oroonoko*, in which he came off with every Teſtimonial of Approbation from the Audience.—From this

Time he continued daily improving, and after two ſucceſsful Campaigns in that Kingdom, conceived Thoughts of returning to his native Country, and making a Trial of his Abilities on the *Engliſh* Stage.—To this End he firſt by Letters reconciled himſelf to his Friends, and then, as a farther Step towards inſuring his Succeſs, obtained a Recommendation from Lord *Fitzharding* (one of the Lords of the Bedchamber to Prince *George* of *Denmark*) to Mr. *Betterton*, who, with great Candour and Good-Nature, took him under his Care, and gave him all the Aſſiſtance in his Power.

The firſt Part Mr. *Booth* appeared in at *London*, which was in 1701, was that of *Maximus*, in Lord *Rocheſter's Valentinian*, his Reception in which exceeded even his moſt ſanguine Expectations, and very ſoon after his Performance of *Artaban*, in *Rowe's Ambitious Stepmother*, which was a new Tragedy, eſtabliſhed his Reputation as ſecond at leaſt to his great Inſtructor.—*Pyrrhus*, in the *Diſtreſt Mother*, was another Part in which he ſhone without a Rival.—But he was indebted to a happy Coincidence of Merit and Chance for that Height of Fame which he at length attained, in the Character of *Cato*, as drawn by Mr. *Addiſon*, in 1712.—For this Play being conſidered as a Party one, the Whigs, in Favour of whoſe Principles it was apparently written, thought it their Duty ſtrongly to ſupport it, while at the ſame Time the Tories, who had too much Senſe to appear to conſider it as a Reflection on their Adminiſtration, were ſtill more vehement in their Approbation of it, which they carried to ſuch an Height, as even

to

to make a Collection of fifty Guineas in the Boxes during the Time of the Performance, and prefent them to Mr. *Booth*, with this Compliment, That it was a flight Acknowledgment *for his honeft Oppofition to a perpetual Dictator, and his dying fo bravely in the Caufe of Liberty;* befides which he had another Prefent of an equal Sum from the Managers, in Confideration of the great Succefs of the Play, which they attributed in good Meafure to his extraordinary Merit in the Performance; and certain it is, that no one fince that Time has ever equalled or even nearly approached his Excellence in that Character.

But thefe were not the only Advantages which were to accrue to Mr. *Booth* from his Succefs in this Part; for Lord *Bolingbroke*, then one of the Principal Secretaries of State, in a little Time after procured a fpecial Licence from Queen *Anne*, recalling all the former ones, and nominating Mr. *Booth* as joint Manager with *Wilks*, *Cibber* and *Dogget*, none of whom were pleafed at it, but the laft more efpecially took fuch Difguft, as to withdraw himfelf from any farther Share in the Management.

In 1704, Mr. *Booth* had married a Daughter of Sir *William Barkham*, of *Norfolk*, Bart. who died in 1710, without Iffue.——After her Death, he engaged in an Amour with Mrs. *Mountford*, who readily put her whole Fortune, which was confiderable, being not lefs than £ 8000, into his Hands.——This however he very honourably returned to her, when, on the Difcovery of her Intimacy with another Gentleman, he thought proper to break off his Connection with her.—— She had, however, great Reafon to repent of her Infidelity to him, for her new Lover not only embezzled and made away with all her Money, but even treated her in other Refpects extremely ill, and was guilty of Meanneffes greatly inconfiftent with the Title of a Gentleman.

Being now eftablifhed in the Management, he once more turned his Thoughts towards Matrimony, and in the Year 1719, united himfelf in that happy State to the celebrated Mifs *Hefter Santlow*, a Woman of a moft amiable Difpofition, whofe great Merit as an Actrefs, added to the utmoft Difcretion and prudential Oeconomy, had enabled her to fave up a confiderable Fortune, which was by no Means unacceptable to Mr. *Booth*, who, tho' a Man that had the ftricteft Regard to Juftice and Punctuality in his Dealings with every one, yet was not much inclined to the faving of Money.

With this valuable Companion, he continued in the moft perfect State of domeftic Happinefs, till the Year 1727, when he was attacked by a violent Fever, which lafted him for forty-fix Days without Intermiffion; and altho', thro' the Care and Skill of thofe great Phyficians Dr. *Friend* and Dr. *Broxholm*, by whom he was attended, he got the better of the prefent Diforder, yet from that Time to the Day of his Death, which was not till fix Years after, his Health was never perfectly re-eftablifhed. —Nor did he ever, during that Interval, appear on the Stage, excepting in the Run of a Play called the *Double Falfhood*, brought on the Theatre by Mr. *Theobald* in

1729, and afferted, but unjuftly, to be written by *Shakefpeare.*—In this Piece he was prevailed on to accept a Part on the fifth Night of it's Performance, which he continued to act till the twelfth, which was the laft Time of his theatrical Appearance, altho' he did not die till the 10th of *May* 1733, when having been attack-ed by a Complication of Difor-ders, he paid the laft Debt to Nature, leaving behind him no Iffue, but. only a difconfolate Widow, who immediately quitted the Stage, devoting herfelf en-tirely to a private Life, and who is I believe ftill living,—A Copy of his Will may be feen in the *London Magazine* for 1733, p. 126, in which he ftrongly tefti-fies his Efteem for this amiable Woman, and affigns his Reafons for bequeathing her the whole of his Fortune, which he acknow-ledges not to be more than two thirds of what he received from her on the Day of Marriage.

His Character as a Writer has not been eftablifhed by any Works of great Importance, yet he was undoubtedly a Man of confiderable Erudition, of good Claffical Knowledge, and though what he has written are trivial in Point of Bulk and Extent, yet they are far from being fo in Point of Merit.——He has left behind him only one dramatic Piece, which, tho' fuccefsful, was his only Attempt in that Way.—It is entitled,

D I D O *and* Æ N E A S. A Mafque.

With Refpect to his Abilities as an Actor, there is furely no great Occafion to expatiate on them, as they have never yet been call'd in Queftion; the Applaufe of the Public bore Witnefs to them in his Life Time; the Commendations of his Cotempo-raries have handed them down to Pofterity.——His Excellency lay wholly in Tragedy, not being a-ble to endure fuch Parts as had not ftrong Paffion to infpire him.—And even in this Walk Dig-nity, rather than Complacency, Rage rather than Tendernefs feemed to be his *Tafte.*——For a more particular Idea of him how-ever I fhall recommend to my Readers the Defcription Mr. *Cib-ber* has given of him in his Apo-logy, and the admirable Charac-ter drawn of him by that excel-lent Judge in dramatic Perfec-tion, *Aaron Hill*, Efq; in a poli-tical Paper publifhed by him, called the *Prompter,* which, tho' too long for our inferting in this Place, may be feen at length in *Theoph. Cibber's Lives of the Poets,* and in *Chetwood's Hiftory of the Stage.*——His Character as a Man was adorned with many amiable Qualities, among which a perfect Goodnefs of Heart, the Bafis of every Virtue was remarkably confpicuous.——He was a gay, lively, chearful Companion, yet humble and diffident of his own Abilities, by which Means he acquir'd the Love and Efteem of every one; and fo particularly was he diftinguifhed and careffed, and his Company fought by the great, that as *Chetwood* relates of him, altho' he kept no Equipage of his own, not one Nobleman in the Kingdom had fo many Sets of Horfes at Command as he had. —For at the Time that the Pa-tentees, jealous of his Merit, and apprehenfive of his Influence with the Miniftry, in order to prevent his Application to his Friends at Court, which was then kept at *Windfor,* took Care to give him conftant Employment in *London,* by giving out every Night

Night such Plays as he had principal Parts in, yet even this Policy could not avail them, as there was punctually every Night the Chariot and Six of some Nobleman or other waiting for him at the Conclusion of the Play, which carried him the twenty Miles in three Hours at farthest, and brought him back again next Night, Time enough for the Business of the Theatre.

BOOTHBY, Mrs. *Frances.*—This Gentlewoman lived in the Reign of King *Charles* II. and was related to Lady *Yate*, of *Harvington* in *Worcestershire*, as it appears from some Passages in the Dedication of a dramatic Piece, which she has addressed to that Lady, and which was performed with some Success at the Theatre Royal.—The Title of it is,

MARCELIA. T. C.

BOURNE, Mr. *Reuben.*—This Gentleman was of the *Middle Temple*, and has left behind him one Play, entitled,

The *Contented Cuckold.* C.

BOYDE, Mrs. *Elizabeth.*—— Who this Lady was I know not, but find her to have been a Devotee to the Muses, from a dramatic Piece published under her Name, entitled,

Don SANCHO. Farce.

BOYER, Mr. *Abel.*——This Gentleman was a *Frenchman*, and a *Refugié* to this Kingdom on the Account of his Religion.—— When here he applied himself so closely to the Study of the *English* Language, and made so great Proficiency in it, that he became an Author of considerable Note in it, being employed in the Writing of several periodical and political Works.——He was for many Years concerned in, and had the principal Management of, a News Paper, called

the *Post-Boy.*—He likewise published a Monthly Work, entitled, *The Political State of* GREAT-BRITAIN.—He wrote a *Life of Queen Anne,* in Folio, which is esteemed a very good Chronicle of that Period of the *English* History.——But what has render'd him the most known and established his Name to latest Posterity, are the very compleat Dictionary and Grammar of the *French* Language, which he compiled, and which have been, and still are, esteemed, the very best in their Kind.—Yet all these Works would not authorize our giving him a Place here, had he not enlisted himself under the Standard of the Buskin, by writing, or rather translating from the *French* of M. *de Racine,* the Tragedy of *Iphigenia,* which he published under the Title of,

The *Victim.* Trag. *Vid.* Vol. I. APPENDIX.

It was performed with some Degree of Success at the Theatre in *Drury Lane,* and is far from being a bad Play —Nor can there perhaps be a stronger Instance of the Abilities of it's Author than Success in such an Attempt, since writing with any Degree of Correctness or Elegance, even in Prose, in a Language which we were not born to the Speaking of, is an Excellence not very frequently attained; but to proceed so far in the Perfection of it, as to be even sufferable in Poetry, and more especially in that of the *Drama,* in which the Diction and Manner of Expression require a peculiar Dignity and Force, and in a Language so difficult to attain the perfect Command of as the *English,* is what has been very seldom accomplished but in the Instance of the Gentleman we are now speaking of; and indeed

deed

deed with Regard to the Piece itfelf, it is but Juftice to acknowledge, that notwithftanding the Reftraint which all Tranflation naturally undergoes, and the other Difadvantages which attended on it's Author, the Language, tho' not perhaps fo fublime or poetical, fo polifhed into Poetry as that of fome of our Native Writers, yet poffeffed fo great a Share of Correctnefs, and is fo entirely free from any Gallicifms, or even the leaft Veftige of the Foreigner in it, that it is even in that Refpect fuperior to many of our Modern Tragedies, (efpecially thofe written about the Time in which that appear'd) and fuch as no native *Englifhman* as a firft Attempt need be afham'd to confefs himfelf the Author of.—It is however remarkable, that notwithftanding the great Difficulty that moft Foreigners find in the acquiring our Languages; this is not the only Inftance of their having attained it in great Perfection, fince we meet with another Gentleman, a Countryman of our Author, who not only attempted, but even repeatedly fucceeded in dramatic Writing in it. —This Gentleman was Mr. *Motteux*, of whom I fhall make a fuller Mention hereafter.——And this feems a Kind of tacit Proof, not only of the native Beauty of the Language in itfelf, and it's Aptnefs for the Purpofes of the *Drama*, which could tempt even Foreigners to effay it's Powers, but alfo that it is not of fo difficult a Conftruction, nor of fo wild and ungovernable a Nature, fo hard to reduce within the Limits of grammatical Rules, as it has been contended to be.

BOYLE, *Roger*, Vid, ORRERY, *Earl of*.

BRADY, Dr. —This Gentleman was a Divine, and lived at *Richmond* in *Surry*, where I imagine his Benefice to have been, —This however is all I can gather of him, excepting that he wrote one Play, called,

The *Rape*. T.

BRANDON, Mr. *Samuel*.—— This Author wrote about the latter Part of Queen *Elizabeth*'s Reign, but of what Profeffion he was, or what Rank he held in Life, I have not been able to procure any Information concerning. —He appears however to have been poffefs'd of no fmall Share of Vanity and Self-fufficiency, from the *Italian* Verfe he has fubjoined to the only dramatic Piece he wrote, and which notwithftanding the high Opinions he, and perhaps fome of his partial Friends might entertain of it, he was never able to bring on the Stage, *viz.*

L'Acqua non temo dell' eterno Oblio.

which may thus be englifhed,

OBLIVION's *Powers I have no Caufe to fear;*
MY *Works her Waves* ETERNALLY *fhall fpare.*

The Title of the Play, which he thus defies either Time, Eternity, or Oblivion to eraze the Remembrance of, is,

The *Virtuous Octavia*. T. C.

BRERETON, Mr. *Thomas*.—— This Gentleman was the Son of Major *Thomas Brereton*, of the Queen's Dragoons, in the Reign of King *William* III. and was lineally defcended by a younger Branch from the very ancient and noble Family of the *Breretons*, of *Brereton* in *Chefhire*.—He received the firft Rudiments of

Learning

Learning at the Free-School at *Chester*, from which he was first removed to a Boarding-School in the same City, kept by one Mr. *Dennis*, a *French Refugié*, and afterwards to *Brazen-Nose* College in *Oxford*, of which he continued a Member for eight Years, and took the Degree of Batchelor of Arts.—About 1717, Sir *Robert Walpole*, then Prime Minister, and who had some Friendship for Mr. *Brereton*'s Family, presented him with a little Post in the Customs, in which his Station was very agreeable to himself, being in the Port of *Chester*, his own native Country.—To this then he retired, but did not long enjoy it, Death snatching him away in a few Years after his settling there.——The dramatic Pieces which he lived to finish were only two, and were never acted, viz.

1. ESTHER. Trag.
2. Sir *John Oldcastle*. Trag.

The first is little more than a Translation of the *Esther* of *Racine*, and the last a close Imitation of the *Policuéte* of *Corneille*, and indeed neither of them have any great Share of Merit in the Execution.—He had however begun two other Pieces, the one a Tragedy, called,

ATHALIAH,

which was to have been a Translation from *Racine*'s Play of that Name, and the other a Comedy, to which he intended to have given the Title of

The *Oxford Ladies*, or the *Nobleman*.

Neither of these however did he live to finish.

BRETON, Mr. *Nicholas*.—To this Gentleman have both *Jacob* and *Gildon* attributed the Honour of Authorship in Regard to an old dramatic Piece, entitled,

An *Old Man's Lesson*, or a *Young Man's Love*. Interl.

but one would be apt to imagine they neither of them had seen the Piece, and that the latter had implicitly copied the Error branch'd by the former, since in the Preface Mr. *Breton* acknowledges himself to have been only the Editor of this Interlude, nay, even declares that he is wholly ignorant who the Author was.—As such however I could not with Propriety avoid inserting his Name in this Place, since to him the World is at least obliged for the Knowledge of whatever Share of Merit may be found in the Piece.

BREVAL, Capt. *John Durant*.—This Gentleman was the Son of Dr. *Francis Durant Breval*, one of the Prebends of *Westminster* and *Rochester*.—He received a liberal Education, the early Parts of which he was initiated into at *Westminster* School.—From thence he went to the University of *Cambridge*, where he was elected into *Trinity* College, and obtained a Fellowship, which he kept for some Time ; but whether he found a College Life too confined and heavy for his Disposition, which probably had a more volatile Turn, or on what other Account I know not, but he at length quitted the University, and on so doing, attach'd himself to the Charms of a scarlet Coat and Cockade, and obtaining a Lieutenant's Commission, went into the Army.—Whether he met with any Advancement there, or at what Time he died, I have not been able to trace.——However, it is certain, that after the Period of his accepting the Commission, he made

made the Tour of *France* and *Italy*, in the Capacity of a fort of travelling Companion to fome young Nobleman, on the Return from which he publifhed his Obfervations during his Journey, compiled into a Volume in Folio.—He had moreover a poetical Turn, and wrote three or four Poems, which were not efteemed bad ones.——He alfo brought one dramatic Piece on the Stage, but which met with no great Succefs, entitled,

The *Play's the Plot*. C.

From it however have been extracted the Subftance of two Farces, which fucceeded tolerably well, *viz.*

The *Mock Princefs*, and

The *Strollers*.

Soon after the Appearance of that doughty Performance of a Club of Wits, called *Three Hours after Marriage*, which, tho' publifhed with only Mr. *Gay*'s Name to it, was undoubtedly the joint Offspring of that Gentleman, Mr. *Pope* and Dr. *Arbuthnot*, and which met with that Condemnation from the Public which it juftly merited, Capt. *Breval* under the affumed Name of *Joseph Gay* publifhed a Satire on that Piece, entitled,

The *Confederates*. A Farce.

On which Account Mr. *Pope*, who never could forgive the leaft Attempt made againft his reigning the unrival'd Sovereign on the Throne of Wit, has introduced this Gentleman into that poetical Pillory the *Dunciad*, among the various Authors whom he has fuppofed Devotees of the Goddefs of *Dullnefs*.

BREWER, Mr. *Anthony*.—— This Writer lived in the Reign of King *Charles* I. and appears to have been held in high Eftimation by the Wits of that Time,

as may be more particularly gather'd from an elegant Compliment paid to him in a Poem, called *Steps to Parnaffus*, wherein he is fuppofed to have a magic Power to call the Mufes to his Affiftance, and is even fet on an Equality with the immortal *Shakefpeare* himfelf.—There are however great Difputes among the feveral Writers as to the Number of his Works.—*Winftanley* and *Phillips* have made him Author of fix Plays.—The Author of the *Britifh Theatre*, and after him Mr. *Theoph. Cibber*, have given him the Credit of three only.—*Langbaine*, *Jacob* and *Gildon* allow him but two, and even of thofe, the firft of thefe Authors feems to doubt the Authenticity of more than one.

To come however to the beft Judgment I can collect, I fhall firft mention the Pieces which *Winftanley* has affigned to him and which are univerfally rejected.— Thefe are the following three.

1. LANDGARTHA. T. C.
2. *Love's Dominion*. Paftoral.
3. *Love's Loadftone*. C.

The Reafons for difallowing of thefe are all fubftantial Ones.— The firft being written by *Henry Burnell*, Efq; the fecond by Mr. *Flecknoe*, and the laft, tho' printed Anonym. (which leaves Scope for the afcribing it to any Body) is faid to be a pofthumous Work, and only publifhed by a Friend of the Author after his Deceafe. Now this being the Cafe, it is impoffible to have been *Brewer*'s, this *pofthumous* Publication happens to have been in 1630, five and twenty Years earlier than the Date of the *Lovefick King*, the only Piece which feems to be indifputably given to Mr. *Brewer*, and which was firft printed in 4to. 1655.

The

The two Plays, which all the Writers in general have set down to this Author, are,

1. *Country Girl.* C.
2. *Love-fick King.* T. C.

Langbaine's Objection to the first of these being only the Letters T. B. in the Title Page, which might have been only a typographical Error, proceeding, perhaps, from the Negligence or Carelessness of the Printer, who, not being certain of the Author's Christian Name, might chuse rather the inserting any Letter at a Venture, than delaying the working off the Sheet till he could obtain a more authentic Information.

And now the only Piece in Dispute is that, entitled,

LINGUA.

This *Langbaine* absolutely denies to be *Brewer*'s, yet assigns no other Reason for so doing but his own bare *ipse dixit*, neither does *Winstanley* shew any Cause for ascribing it to him.—Mr. *Theoph. Cibber*, however, as well as the Author of the *British Theatre*, has followed the Authority of the latter, as has also Mr. *Dodsley*, who, in the Course of his Business as a Bookseller, exclusive of his own admirable Judgment as a Poet, might have an Opportunity of knowing better than either of them; and who has republished the Piece with the Name of *Anthony Brewer*, in his Collection of old Plays.—To this I may add, that Probability is also in it's Favour, since, being of a much earlier Date than either of the other two, it is published anonymous, and may therefore be suppos'd to have been the Author's first Essay in this Kind of Writing.

Be the Author, however, whom he will, there is a remarkable Anecdote recorded by *Winstanley*, in Regard to the Piece itself, which points it out to have been in some Measure the innocent Cause of those Troubles which disturbed the Peace of these Realms in the Middle of the 17th Century.—He tells us, that when this Play was acted at *Cambridge*, *Oliver Cromwell* (then a Youth) performed a Part in it. —The Substance of the Piece is a Contention among the Senses for a Crown, which LINGUA had laid for them to find.—The Part allotted to young *Cromwell* was that of *Tactus*, or *Touch*, who, having obtained the contested Coronet, makes this spirited Declamation,

Roses, and Bays, pack hence! this Crown and Robe,
My Brows, and Body, circles and invests;
How gallantly it fits me!—sure the Slave
Measur'd my Head that wrought this Coronet.—
They lie that say, Complexions cannot change!
My Blood's ennobled, and I am transform'd
Unto the sacred Temper of a King.
Methinks I hear my noble Parasites
Stiling me Cæsar or great Alexander
Licking my Feet, &c.

It is said that he felt the whole Part so warmly, and more especially the above-quoted Speech, that it was what first fired his Soul with Ambition, and excited him, from the Possession of an *imaginary* Crown, to stretch his Views to that of a *real* one, for the Accomplishment of which he was contented to wade thro' Seas of Blood, and " shut the Gates of " Mercy on Mankind."

BROME,

Brome, *Alexander.*—This Author flourished in the Reign of King *Charles* I. and was an Attorney in the Lord Mayor's Court. —He was born in 1620, and died *June* 30th, 1666.—So that he lived thro' the whole of the Civil Wars and the Protectorship, during all which Time he maintain'd his Loyalty untainted.—He was a warm Cavalier, and tho' in his Profession of the Law he could do no Service to the Cause he lov'd, yet as he was a Devotee of the Muses, as well as an Attendant on the Courts, he frequently turned his Pen from the filling up of Writts, Pleas, and Demurrers, to the inditing of Odes, Sonnets and Dithyrambs, in the most of which he treated the Round-Heads with great Keenness and Severity.—In short he was Author of much the greatest Part of those Songs and Epigrams which were published in Favour of the Royalists, and against the *Rump,* as well in *Oliver Cromwell*'s Time as during the Rebellion.—These, together with his Epistles and Epigrams translated from different Authors, were all printed in one Vol. 8vo. after the Restoration.—He also published a Version of *Horace,* by himself and other Hands, which is very far from a bad one.—He left behind him only one Dramatic Piece, which is entitled,

The *Cunning Lovers.* C.

The World however is indebted to him for two Volumes of *Richard Brome's* Plays in Octavo, many of which, but for his Care in preserving and publishing them, would in all Probability have been entirely lost.

Brome, Mr. *Richard.*—This Author lived in the Reign of King *Charles* I. and was cotemorary with *Decker, Ford, Shirley,*

&c.—His Extraction was mean, he having originally been no better than a menial Servant to the celebrated *Ben Jonson.*—He wrote himself however into high Repute, as is testified not only by various Commendatory Verses written by his Cotemporaries, and prefix'd to many of his Plays, but also by some Lines which his quondam Master addres'd to him on account of his Comedy call'd the *Northern Lass,* in which, altho' *Ben Jonson* has given Way to that Kind of Vanity which is perpetually starting forth in all his Writings, and represents himself as the first who had instructed the Age in the *comic Laws,* and all the perfect Arts of the Drama, yet he pays great Commendation to *Richard Brome,* by acknowledging that he has made very good Use of the Improvements he had acquir'd during a long Apprenticeship under so skilful a Master.

Brome, in Imitation of his Master, laid it down as his first great point, to apply closely to the Study of Men and Manners. —His Genius was entirely turned to Comedy, and therefore his proper Province was Observation more than Reading.—His Plots are all his own, and are far from being ill-conducted; and his Characters, which for the most Part are strongly marked, were the Offspring of his own Judgment and Experience, and his close Attention to the Foibles of the human Heart.—In a word, his Plays in general are good ones, met with great Applause when first acted, and, as *Langbain* informs us, were thought by the Players worthy to be revived, to their own Profit and the Author's Honour, in that critical Age which he himself lived in.—

Nay

Nay we have had a Proof even in our own Time, of the Merit of one of his Comedies, which with a very little Alteration, has been lately revived and with great Succefs, viz. the *Jovial Crew*, which for no lefs than three Seafon paft has brought crowded Audiences to the Theatre-Royal in *Covent Garden*, at all the frequent Repetitions of its Performances.

The Comedies which the Author has left behind him are Fifteen in Number, Ten of which are collected together, as before-mentioned, under *Alexander Brome*, in two Volumes 8vo. Each Volume bearing the Title of *Five New Plays by* Richard Brome.—The whole Lift of his Pieces is as follows.

1. *Antipodes.* C.
2. *Afparagus Garden.* C.
3. *City Wit.* C.
4. *Covent Garden Weeded.* C.
5. *Court Beggar.* C.
6. *Damoifelle.* C.
7. *Englifh Moor.* C.
8. *Jovial Crew.* C.
9. *Lovefick Court.* C.
10. *Mad Couple well match'd.* C.
11. *New Academy.* C.
12. *Northen Lafs.* C.
13. *Novella.* C.
14. *Queen and Concubine.* C.
15. *Queen's Exchange.* C.

He joined alfo with *Thomas Heywood*, in a Play called the *Lancafhire Witches*, of which fee an Account in its proper Place.

BROOK, Sir *Fulk Greville*, Lord. —This Right Honourable Author was Son to Sir *Fulk Greville*, the Elder, of *Beauchamp Court* in *Warwickfhire*, and defcended from the ancient Family of the *Grevilles*, who in the Reign of *Edward* the IIId. were feated at *Cambden* in *Gloucefterfhire.*—He was born in 1554, the fame

Year with his Friend Sir *Philip Sidney*, and received his Education at *Trinity* Colledge *Cambridge*; from whom, on his Removal to Court, he foon grew highly in Favour with Queen *Elizabeth*, nor continued lefs in the Efteem of her Succeffor *James* I. who at his Coronation created him Knight of the *Bath*, in 1615 made him Chancellor of the Exchequer, and in the feventeenth Year of his Reign rais'd him to the Rank of the Peerage, with the Title of Baron *Brook* of *Beauchamp's Court*, and one of the Gentlemen of the Bed-Chamber.— He was equally eminent for his Learning and Courage, in both which he greatly diftinguifhed himfelf, and was one of the moft particular Intimates of the ingenious Sir *Philip Sidney*, whofe Life prefixed to his celebrated Romance the *Arcadia*, under the Name of *Philophilippos*, was written by this Gentleman.—Befides this he wrote a *Treatife of Human Learning*, a *Treatife of Wars*, and an *Inquifition upon Force and Honour*, all of which are compos'd in *Seftines*, or Stanzas of fix Lines each, the four firft of which are alternate, and the laft two rhyming to each other. His Title to a Place in this Work however is founded on two Dramatic Pieces (both Tragedies) which he wrote, entitled,

1. *Alaham.* T.
2. *Muftapha.* T.

Neither of thefe I believe were ever acted, they being written ftrictly after the Model of the Ancients, with *Chorufes*, &c. and entirely unfit for the Englifh Stage.

This amiable Man of Quality loft his Life in a tragical Manner on the 30th of September in the Year 1628, being then 74 Years of Age, by the Hands of one *Haywood*, who had spent the greatest and best Part of his Time in his personal Service, for which not thinking himself sufficiently rewarded, he expostulated with his Master on it, they two being alone in his Lordship's Bedchamber in *Brook* House in *Holborn*, (the Spot of Ground where *Brook* Street now stands).—His Remonstrances however being probably made with too much Peremptoriness and an Air of Insolence, he received a sharp Rebuke from his Lordship, which he immediately returned by giving him a mortal Stab in the Back, of which Wound he died, but whether instantly or not, does not appear.—The Assassin however conceiving his own Condition to be desperate, went into another Room, and having locked the Door fell on his own Sword.—Thus in order to evade the Sentence of the Law, he became himself the Executioner of Justice, receiving from his own Hand that Death which otherwise would have been inflicted on him by that of the common Hangman.

Lord *Brook* lies buried among the rest of his honourable Ancestors, in *Warwick* Church, under a Monument of black and white Marble, on the which he is stil'd,

Servant to Queen Elizabeth
Counsellor to King James,
and
Friend to Sir Philip Sidney.

He died without Issue, having never been married, and those who are desirous of reading his Character more at large, may be further satisfied by perusing the Account given of him by *Fuller*, in his *British Worthies.* (vid. *Warwickshire*, p. 127.)

BROOKE, *Henry*, Esq.—This Gentleman, who is still living, is a Native of *Ireland*, having, as I have been informed, a paternal Estate in the County of *Cavan*, and is besides Barrack Master of *Mullingar*, in the County of *Westmeath*.—He ga'n'd great Reputation as a Writer, by the *Farmer's Letters*, published in *Ireland*, in the Time of the Rebellion, and written after the Manner of Dean *Swift*'s *Drapers* Letters, which were universally ascribed to him.—His greatest Application however seems to have been to the Drama, for in the Year 1738, he had his Tragedy of *Gustavus Vasa*, rehearsed at the Theatre Royal in *Drury* Lane, the Actors were all ready in their Parts, and no Bar seem'd in the Way to its public Appearance, when an Order came from the Lord Chamberlain to prohibit it.—He met with the same Ill-success in *Dublin* with Regard to an Opera call'd *Jack the Giant Queller*, brought on soon after the Close of the Rebellion, which after the first Night's Representation was forbidden by the Government to be continued.—As to his first Play, however, the Prohibition did him no Kind of Injury, as he was immediately encouraged to publish it by a Subscription, which has been said to have amounted to eight hundred Pounds.—In 1741. His *Betrayer of his Country* was brought on the Stage in *Dublin*, and met with Success, and about 1752, at the same Theatre, his *Earl of Essex*.—This last Play however having never been printed, and being I believe the Property of Mr. *Sheridan*, late Manager of *Smock Alley* Theatre, when that Gentleman acted at *Drury Lane* in the Winter of 1761. his Emoluments being to arise from a
cer-

certain Proportion of the Profits of the House on thofe Nights in which he performed, he was allowed a Right of reviving or getting up fuch Plays as he imagined would turn out the moft to his and the Managers joint Advantages.—Among thofe which he fix'd on as his Choice, was Mr. *Brooke*'s *Earl of Effex*, which being licenced by the Lord Chamberlain was now brought on at *Drury Lane*, and met with good Succefs.

Thro' the whole of Mr. *Brooke*'s Writings there breathes a ftrong Spirit of Liberty, and patriotic Zeal, which, tho' the natural and inborn Principles of every Subject of thefe Realms, may have fubjected them to Mifreprefentation, and, what is far from an uncommon Cafe render'd general Sentiment fufpected as particular Reflection.——Yet thofe who have the Pleafure of knowing this Gentleman perfonally, muft be fo well affur'd of the Integrity of his Heart, and his firm Attachment to the prefent happy Succeffion, as will entirely clear him from the flighteft Suppofition of any Intent to excite Corruption or awaken Difcontent by any of his Writings.

His dramatic Pieces in themfelves are independent of thefe Kind of Confiderations, tho' not to be ranked in the firft Clafs, have undoubtedly a confiderable Share of Merit.—His Plots are ingenioufly laid and well conducted, his Characters not ill drawn, and his Language bold and nervous; tho' it muft be acknowledged in the laft Particular the Author at Times feems to pay too little Regard, to the Correctnefs of Meafure, to that Polifh which the Language of

Tragedy ought to receive from Harmony of Numbers.

His dramatic Pieces are as follow,

1. The *Betrayer of his Country*. T.—This was played at *Dublin* under the Title of the Earl of *Weftmorland*.
2. *Earl of Effex*. T.
3. *Guftavus Vafa*. T.—This was as I think (tho' prohibited in *London*, acted at *Dublin* by the Title of the *Patriot*.)
4. *Jack the Giant Queller*. F.

BROOKES, Mrs. This Lady, whofe Maiden Name was *Moore*, is the Daughter and Wife of a Clergyman, and a Lady of great Abilities.—She has written and publifhed one Play, which was never acted, entitled,

VIRGINIA. Trag.

BROWN, *Anthony*, Efq.—This Gentleman was a Member of the *Temple*, and wrote a Play entitled,

The *Fatal Retirement*. T.

This Play was damn'd, and indeed very defervedly, there being neither Plot, Incident, or Language in it that had by any Means a Right to recommend it to the public Regard.—Yet its Want of Succefs was the Occafion of fome Infults being fhewn to an Actor of great Confequence, whofe fpirited Behaviour on the Circumftance may be feen more at large in the Account of this Play in the former Part of this Work.

BROWNE, Dr.—This Gentleman is a Clergyman and Doctor in Divinity, and is poffeffed of fome Church Preferment in the Northern Part of this Kingdom. He has very juftly acquired a great Reputation by fome of his Profe Writings, more particularly by his *Eftimate of the Manners of the*

Times;

Times; and as a Poet, tho' he cannot be confider'd as the firft, yet he is undoubtedly very far from the leaft confiderable of our prefent Writers.——The Stage ftands indebted to him for two dramatic Pieces, the Succefs of which has been different, yet has not I think done any great Honour to public Tafte, fince his *Athelftan*, which I cannot help thinking much the more original and better executed Piece of the two, has never been performed fince the Seafon of its firft Appearance, while *Barbaroffa*, whofe Defign is much too nearly approaching to that of *Merope* and fome other of our modern Tragedies, ftill continues on the Lift of acting Plays.

His Tragedies, as I before obferved, are only two, *viz.*

1. ATHELSTAN.

2. BARBAROSSA.

BROWNE, Mr. *Mofes.*——Who this gentleman was, or whether yet living I know not, all the Information I can procure concerning him is, that he was Author of two Pieces, which were both reprefented together, and have pretty nearly an equal Degree of Merit. They are entitled,

1. *All bedevilled.* F.

2. *Polidus.* T.

The firft was acted by way of an Entertainment added to the fecond.——Neither of them however were performed at a Theatre Royal, or even by regular Actors, but only by fome Gentlemen of the Author's Acquaintance, for their own Diverfion and the Gratification of his Vanity, at a Place which in the Title Page is called the private Theatre in St. Alban's Street, but this I imagine to have been nothing more than fome School or Affembly Room

fitted up for the immediate Occafion of this Play, and other Reprefentations of that Kind.

BUCKHURST, *Thomas Sackville*, Lord.——This noble Author who from a private Gentleman was before his Death advanced to a very high Rank both in Honour, Fame, and Fortune, was Son of *Richard Sackville*, Efq; of *Buckhurft*, in the Parifh of *Withian* in *Suffex*, at which Place our Author was born in the Year 1536.—His Mother's Name was *Winifred*, the Daughter of Sir *John Bruges*, fome Time Lord Mayor of *London*.——From his Childhood he was diftinguifhed for a Livelinefs of Wit and Manlinefs of Behaviour.—He received the firft Part of his Univerfity Education at *Hart Hall Oxford*, yet took no Degree there, but removed to *Cambridge*, where he did not refide long; but had the Degree of Mafter of Arts conferred on him.—He afterwards enter'd himfelf a Student in the Temple, and at an early Time of Life was called to the Bar.—Here it was probably that his Friendfhip and Intimacy commenc'd with Mr. *Thomas Norton*, in Conjunction with whom he wrote a Tragedy entitled,

Ferrex and *Porrex*, the two Sons of *Gorboduc*, King of *Britain*.

Which Mr. *T. Cibber*, in his Life of this Nobleman, afferts, tho' I think falfely, to have been the firft Scenes written in Verfe in *England*, and which was afterwards alter'd by his Lordfhip, and republifhed under the Title of,

Gorboduc. Trag.

This Piece in its original Form, of which Mr. *Norton* wrote the three firft Acts, and Mr. *Sackville* the two laft, was performed by the Gentlemen of the *Inner Temple*

Temple at *Whiteball*, before Queen *Elizabeth*, on the 18th of January 1561. long before *Shakespeare* appear'd on the Stage, and when Mr. *Sackville* was only in his twenty sixth Year.

Altho' the Sprightliness of Mr. *Sackville's* Genius had thus induced him to dedicate some of his Hours to Poetry and Pleasure, yet History was his favorite Study, more especially that of his own Country, in Consequence of which he had formed a Design of a Kind of *Biographia illustrium Virorum*, or the Lives of several great Personages in Verse, of which some specimens are printed in a Book published in 1610. called the *Mirrour of Magistrates*, the Induction to which is wholly his, and is perhaps the earliest Attempt in allegorical Poetry that we have extant in our Langage.

This Design however Mr. *Sackville* had not Leisure or Opportunity to pursue, for his great Abilities being distinguished at Court, he was called forth into such a continued Connexion with public Affairs, as left him no Time for the Execution of any of his literary Plans. In the 4th and 5th Years of Queen *Mary* we find his Name on the Parliamentary Lists; and in the 5th of Queen *Elizabeth*, Anno 1564, when his Father was elected Knight of the Shire for *Suffex*, he was returned as one of the Members for *Buckinghamshire.*— Not long after this however he went abroad to travel, and was detain'd for some Time Prisoner at *Rome*, but his Liberty being procur'd him, he return'd to *England*, to take Possession of a very large Inheritance, which by his Father's Death in 1566 was devoted to him.

On his Return he was knighted in 1567, in the Queen's Presence, by the Duke of *Norfolk*, and at the same Time promoted to the Dignity of the Peerage by the Title of Baron *Buckhurst.*— His Lordship was of so profuse a Temper that tho' his Income was a very large one, yet his Fondness of Magnificence and Expence would not permit him to live within it, and sometimes subjected him to considerable Inconveniencies.—The Queen's frequent Admonitions on this Subject, however, at length made some Impression on him, and induced him to become more careful of his Affairs.

In 1573 his Royal Mistress sent him Ambassador to *Charles* IX. King of *France*, to congratulate that Prince on his Marriage with the Emperor *Maximilian's* Daughter, and on other important Affairs; where he was received and entertained with all those Honours which were due to his own Merit, and the Dignity of his Sove eign.

In 1574 we find his Name mentioned as one of the Peers who sat on the Trial of *Thomas Howard*, Duke of *Norfolk*, who was condemned and executed for being concerned in a Plot for recovering the Liberty of *Mary* Queen of *Scots*, at which Time he was also in the Privy-Council, he was nominated one of the Commissioners for the Trial of that unhappy Queen herself, and tho' it does not appear that he was present at her Condemnation at *Fotheringay* Castle, yet after the Confirmation of her Sentence he was the Person made Choice of on Account of his Address and Tenderness of Disposition to bear the unhappy Tidings

to

to her, and fee the Decree put in Execution.

In 1567 he went Ambaffador to the States-General, to accommodate Differences in Regard to fome Remonftrances they had made againft the Conduct of the Earl of *Leicefter*.—This Commiffion he executed with the utmoft Fidelity and Honour, yet by it he incurr'd the Difpleafure of Lord *Burleigh*, whofe Influence with the Queen occafioned him not only to be recalled, but confined to his Houfe for nine Months.—On the Death of Lord *Leicefter* however, his Intereft at Court was renew'd; he was made Knight of the Garter, was one of the Peers who fat on the Trial of the Earl of *Arundel*, and was joined with Lord *Burleigh* in the promoting a Peace with *Spain*; in Confequence of which a Treaty was renewed with the States-General, which, as Lord *Burleigh* then lay fick, was negotiated folely by Lord *Buckhurft*; whereby the Queen, befides other Advantages, was eafed of a Charge of at leaft 120,000*l. per Annum*; which, according to the Value of Money then, was not much lefs than equal to half a Million now.

On *Dec.* 17th 1591, he was, in Confequence of feveral Letters from the Queen in his Favour, elected Chancellor of the Univerfity of *Oxford*, in Oppofition to the Earl of *Effex*, and incorporated Mafter of Arts; and on Lord *Burleigh*'s Death the Queen as a juft Reward for his Merits, for the Service he had done his Country, and the vaft Sums he had expended, was pleafed to conftitute him Lord High Treafurer.

In the fucceeding Year he was joined in a Commiffion with Sir *Thomas Egerton* and Lord *Effex* for negotiating Affairs with the Senate of *Denmark*.—When the laft named Nobleman and his Faction difperfed Libels againft the Queen concerning the Affairs of *Ireland*, Lord *Buckhurft* engaged in her Majefty's Vindication, and when at laft that poor, mifguided, rafh, unhappy Favorite was, with his Friend *Southampton*, brought to Trial, this Nobleman was conftituted Lord High Steward on the Occafion.

After the Death of the Queen, her Succeffor King *James* I. who had the higheft Senfe of his Services and great Abilities, even before his Arrival in *England*, renewed his Patent for Life as Lord High Treafurer, and in the enfuing Year created him Earl of *Dorfet*, and appointed him one of the Commiffioners for executing the Office of Earl Marfhal.

He did not however very long enjoy thefe additional Honours, for on the 19th of *April* 1608, he died fuddenly, at the Council Table *Whitehall*, and on the 26th of *May* following was interr'd with great Solemnity at *Weftminfter Abbey*, his Funeral Sermon being preached by the famous Dr. *Abbot*, at that Time his Chaplain, but afterwards Archbifhop of *Canterbury*.

The Suddennefs of his Death afforded fome little Grounds for Conjecture and Sufpicion, but thofe were immediately put a Stop to, when on opening his Head, the Caufe of his Deceafe was found to be a *Hydrocephalus*, or little Bags of Water collected about the Brain, which by this fudden burfting muft neceffarily occafion the Cataftrophe that followed.

His Character as a Statefman and a Man we need not expatiate

on,

on, as the Chronicles of our own National Affairs during his Time are all lavifh in his Praife.—As a Writer, in which Light however it is probable he would have fhone with fuperior Brilliance, had not Matters of much more material Importance ftopped his Pen, we have but few Remains left; yet, concerning what we have, I cannot better guide the Judgment of our Readers with refpect to them, than by repeating the Character given of his *Gorboduc*, by that elegant Writer and acknowledged Judge of Literature, Sir *Philip Sidney*.—" It " is," fays he, " full of ftate- " ly Speeches, well - founding " Phrafes, climbirg to the Height " of *Seneca*'s Stile, and as full of " notable Morality, which it doth " moft delightfully teach, and fo " obtain the very End of Po- " etry."

From this great Man is lineally defcended his Grace the prefent Duke of *Dorfet*, whofe great Abilities, as well as thofe of his intermediate Anceftry, all of whom have been eminent for their great Virtues, extraordirary Talents, and their Patronage of polite Literature, befpeak him the genuine Offspring of our illuftrious *Sackville*.

Wood fays, he was buried at *Withiam* above-mentioned, but is under a miftake.

BUCKINGHAM, *John Shrffield*, Duke of.—This great Nobleman, whofe Character was confpicuous in the Age he lived in, in the feveral Capacities of a Soldier, a Statefman and a Writer, was born in the Year 1645. —At nine Years of Age he loft his Father, and his Mother marrying again foon after, the Care of his Education was left entirely to the Conduct of a Governor, who,

tho' himfelf a Man of Learning, had not that happy Manner of communicating his Knowledge, whereby his Pupil could reap any great Improvement under him.— In Confequence of which, when he came to part from his Governor, after having travelled with him into *France*, he quickly difcover'd in the Courfe of his Converfation with Men of Genius, that tho' he had acquired the politer Accomplifhments of a Gentleman, yet that he was ftill greatly deficient in every Part of Literature, and thofe higher Excellencies, without which it is impoffible to rife to any confiderable Degree of Eminence.

Piqued at this Reflection, and refolved by his own Application to make Amends for the Fault of his Governor, and recal the Time he had loft, he determined, tho' in the Height of ycuthful Blood, and in Poffeffion of an ample Fortune, two ftrong Allurements to Diffipation, to lay a Reftraint on his Appetites and Paffions, and dedicate for fome Time a certain Number of Hours every Day to Study.——By this Means he made an amazing Progrefs, and very foon acquir'd a Degree of Learning, which very juftly entitled him to the Character he ever after maintained, of a very fine Scholar.

Not contented however with this Acquifition, but as eager in the Purfuit of Martial as of Literary Glory, he again obtain'd a Maftery over even the moft irrefiftable of all the Paffions, and tho' engaged in an Attachment of Love to a Lady, by whom, from his own Account, he met with an equal Return of Affection, yet even this Tie could not keep him at Home, when the Call of Honour fummon'd him abroad.

abroad.——In ſhort, he enter'd himſelf a Volunteer with the Earl of *Oſſory*, in the ſecond *Dutch* War, and was preſent in that famous and bloody Naval Engagement at *Soldbay*, where the Duke of *York*, afterwards *James* II. commanded as Admiral.—— And tho' this was at a Time of Life when moſt young Gentlemen are ſcarcely out of the Hands of their Dancing Maſters, our youthful Hero exerted ſo much Gallantry of Behaviour, that he was immediately appointed Commander of the *Royal Catharine*, a ſecond Rate Man of War.

After this our Author made a Campaign in the *French* Service, and when *Tangier* was in Danger of being taken by the *Moors*, he was, in Conſequence of his own Offer to head the Forces which were to defend it, appointed Commander of them.—He was then Earl of *Mulgrave*, one of the Lords of the Bed-Chamber to King *Charles* II. and had been, on the 28th of *May* 1674, inſtalled Knight of the Garter.— But now a moſt wicked Machination againſt his Life was concerted at Court, in which the King himſelf has been ſuſpected to have acted a very principal Part, and for which Hiſtorians aſſign different Cauſes.—Some of the Writers have imagined that the King had diſcovered an Intrigue between Lord *Mulgrave* and one of his own Miſtreſſes, and was therefore determined to put his Rival out of the Way at any Rate.—But Mrs. *Manley*, in her *Atalantis*, and Mr. *Boyer* in his Hiſtory of Queen *Anne*, attributes it to the Diſcovery of certain Overtures towards Marriage, which this Nobleman was bold enough to make to the Princeſs *Anne*, and which ſhe herſelf

ſeem'd not inclinable to diſcourage.

Be the Cauſe what it would, however, it is apparent that it was intended Lord *Mulgrave* ſhould be loſt in the Paſſage ; a Veſſel being provided to carry him over, which had been ſent Home as unſerviceable, and was in ſo ſhatter'd a Condition, that the Captain of her declar'd he was afraid to make the Voyage.—On this his Lordſhip applied not only to the Lord High Admiral, but to the King himſelf.—Theſe Remonſtrances, however, were in vain ; no Redreſs was to be had, and the Earl, who ſaw the Trap laid for him by his Enemies, was compelled to throw himſelf into almoſt inevitable Danger, to avoid the Imputation of Cowardice, which of all others he had the greateſt Deteſtation of.—He however diſſuaded ſeveral Volunteers of Quality from accompanying him in the Expedition ; only the Earl of *Plymouth*, the King's natural Son, piqued himſelf on running the ſame Hazard with a Man, who, in ſpite of the ill Treatment he met with from the Miniſtry, could ſo valiantly brave every Danger in the Service of his Father.

Providence, however, defeated this malicious Scheme, by giving them remarkably fine Weather thro' the whole Voyage, which laſted three Weeks, at the Termination of which, by the Aſſiſtance of pumping the whole Time to diſcharge the Water, which leaked in very faſt, they arrived ſafe at *Tangier*.——And perhaps there cannot be a more ſtriking Inſtance of innate Firmneſs and Magnanimity than in the Behaviour of this Nobleman during the Voyage.—For though he was fully convinced of the hourly

dangers

Dangers they were in, yet was his Mind so calm and undisturbed, that he even indulged his Passion for the Muses amidst the Tumults of the tempestuous Elements, and during this Voyage, compos'd a Poem, which is to be met with among his other Works.

The Consequence of this Expedition was the Retreat of the *Moors*, and the blowing up of *Tangier*.——On his Return, the King becoming appeased, and the Earl forgetting the ill Offices done him, a mutual Reconciliation ensued, and he enjoyed his Majesty's Favour to the last.

During the short Reign of King *James* II. he held several considerable Posts, particularly that of Governor of *Hull*, in which he succeeded the degraded Duke of *Monmouth*, and the high Office of Lord Chamberlain, which, altho' latterly that Monarch grew cooler towards him on Account of the zealous and honest Remonstrances he frequently made to him against those Measures by which he afterwards lost the Crown, yet he did not think proper to take from him. —His Lordship was no Friend to, or Promoter of, the Revolution ; and when King *James*, in Opposition to that Nobleman's Advice and that of others of his Friends, did quit the Kingdom, he appears to have been one of the Lords who wrote such Letters to the Fleet, the Army and all the considerable Garrisons in *England*, as persuaded them to continue in proper Order and Subjection.—To his Humanity, Direction and spirited Behaviour in Council also, his Majesty stood indebted for the Protection he obtained from the Lords in *London*, upon his being seiz'd and in-

sulted by the Populace at *Feversham* in *Kent*.

When the Revolution was brought about, Lord *Mulgrave* was guilty of no mean Compliances to King *William*, and tho' he voted and gave his Reasons strongly in Parliament for the Prince of *Orange*'s being proclaimed King, together with the Princess his Wife, and afterwards went to Court to pay his Addresses, where he was very graciously received, yet he accepted of no Post under that Government till some Years afterwards.

In the latter Part of King *William*'s Reign, however, he enjoyed several high Offices, and on the Accession of Queen *Anne*, that Princess, who had ever had a great Regard for him, loaded him with Employments and Dignities.—In *April* 1702, he was sworn Lord Privy Seal, made Lord Lieutenant and Custos Rotulorum for the North Riding of *Yorkshire*, and one of the Governors of the *Charter house*, and the same Year was appointed one of the Commissioners to treat of an Union between *England* and *Scotland*.——On the 9th of *March*, 1703, he was created Duke of *Normanby* (of which he had been made Marquis by King *William)* and on the 19th of the same Month Duke of *Buckingham*.

In the Year 1712, the Whig Ministry beginning to give Ground, and his Grace, who was strongly attached to Tory Principles, joined with Mr. *Harley*, afterwards Earl of *Oxford*, in such Measures as brought about a Change in the Ministry, shook the Power of the Duke and Dutchess of *Marlborough*, and introduced Mr. *Harley*, the Earl of *Shrewsbury*, Lord *Bolingbroke*, &c. into the Administration.

ſtration.—Her Majeſty now offer'd to make him Chancellor, which he refuſed, but in 1711, was appointed Steward of her Majeſty's Houſhold, and Preſident of the Council, and on her Deceaſe in 1713, was nominated one of the Lords Juſtices in *Great Britain*, till the Arrival of King *George* I. from *Hanover*.

His Grace died on the 24th of *February* 1720, in the 75th Year of his Age, and after lying in State for ſome Days at *Buckingham* Houſe, was interr'd with great Solemnity in *Weſtminſter-Abbey*, where a handſome Monument has ſince been erected to his Memory, with an Epitaph written by himſelf, and directed by his Will to be engraved on it.—He left only one legitimate Son behind him, named *Edmund*, but that young Nobleman dying in the very Bloom of Youth, with him the Titles of the *Sheffield* Family expired.

His Grace's Valour was on many Occaſions ſufficiently proved, nor were his other Abilities confined to Letters only, and the Encouragement of Learning, for by the Accounts given of him by all his Biographers, he appears to have been a moſt accompliſhed Nobleman, whether we view him in the Light of an excellent Poet, a ſhining Orator, a polite Courtier, or a conſummate Stateſman. —But as Talents ſo ſuperior, and a Diſpoſition ſo enterprizing as the Duke of *Buckingham's* never fail to excite Envy and Malevolence, it is not to be wonder'd at that his Character ſhould have been attacked with Severity by ſome of his Enemies.—The principal Faults they have laid to his Charge are Avarice, Pride and Ill-Nature.—As to the firſt, every one who is in the leaſt acquainted with the human Heart, muſt be

perfectly convinced that Covetouſneſs is abſolutely incompatible with Indolence, and yet it is well known that his Grace loſt very conſiderably for a Courſe of forty Years together, from his not taking the Pains to viſit thoſe Eſtates he poſſeſſed at ſome Diſtance from *London*.—And as to the latter Part of the Accuſation, thoſe who were moſt intimate with him have declar'd him to be of a tender compaſſionate Diſpoſition.—He is indeed allowed to have been paſſionate, but when his Rage ſubſided, his Concern for having given Way to that Infirmity, ever teſtified itſelf in peculiar Acts of Kindneſs and Beneficence towards thoſe on whom his Paſſion had vented itſelf.— An intrepid Magnanimity and Perſeverance in whatever he undertook, ſeems to have been his ſtrongeſt Characteriſtic, and altho' a natural Gaiety of Diſpoſition, back'd by Affluence of Fortune, led him into ſome Acts of Libertiniſm in his Youth, eſpecially with Regard to the Fair Sex, which in the latter Part of his Life he frequently expreſſed Concern for, yet over his Paſſions he ſeems to have had the ſtrongeſt Command, whenever Motives of greater Importance called on him to lay a Reſtraint upon them.

With Reſpect to Genius and thoſe Talents which were adapted to the polite Arts, it is evident from his Works that he poſſeſſed them in an eminent Degree.—— He was perhaps one of the moſt elegant Proſe Writers of his Time, and is inferior to few even in the ſublime Flights of Poetry. —He has left behind him two dramatic Pieces, which, though never acted, were intended for the Stage, and to be performed

aft

after the Manner of the Ancients, with mufical Choruffes between the Acts.——They are both taken from the Tragedy of *Julius Cæfar*, as written by *Shakefpeare*, but great Alterations made in them by our Author.——The Titles of them are,

The Death of MARCUS BRUTUS. Trag.

JULIUS CÆSAR. Trag.

BUCKINGHAM, *George Villiers*, Duke of.——This ingenious and witty Nobleman, whofe mingled Character render'd him at once the Ornament and Difgrace, the Envy and Ridicule of the Court he lived in, was Son to that famous Statefman and Favourite of King *Charles* I. who loft his Life by the Hands of Lieutenant *Felton*.——Our Author was born at *Wallingford* Houfe, in the Parifh of St. *Martins* in the Fields, on the 30th of *Jan.* 1627, which being but the Year before the fatal Cataftrophe of his Father's Death, the young Duke was left a perfect Infant; a Circumftance which is frequently prejudicial to the Morals of Men born to high Rank and Affluence of Fortune.——The early Parts of his Education he received from various domeftic Tutors, after which he was fent to the Univerfity of *Cambridge*, where having compleated a Courfe of Studies, he, with his Brother Lord *Francis*, went abroad, under the Care of one Mr. *Aylefbury*.——Upon his Return, which was not till after the breaking out of the Civil Wars, the King being at *Oxford*, his Grace repair'd thither, was prefented to his Majefty, and enter'd of *Chrift Church* College.——Upon the Decline of the King's Caufe, he attended Prince *Charles* into *Scotland*, and was with him at the

Battle of *Worcefter* in 1651, after which, making his Efcape beyond Sea, he again joined him, and was foon after, as a Reward for this Attachment, made Knight of the Garter.

Defirous, however, of retrieving his Affairs, he came privately to *England*, and in 1657 married *Mary*, the Daughter and fole Heirefs of *Thomas* Lord *Fairfax*, thro' whofe Intereft he recover'd the greateft Part of the Eftate he had loft, and the Affurance of fucceeding to an Accumulation of Wealth in the Right of his Wife.

We do not find however that this Step loft him the Royal Favour, for, after the Reftoration, at which Time he is faid to have poffefs'd an Eftate of twenty thoufand Pounds *per Annum*, he was made one of the Lords of the Bed-Chamber, called to the Privy Council, and appointed Lord Lieutenant of *Yorkfhire*, and Mafter of the Horfe.——All thefe high Pofts however he loft again in the Year 1666.——For having been refus'd the Poft of Prefident of the North, he became difaffected to the King, and it was difcovered that he had carried on a fecret Correfpondence by Letters and other Tranfactions with one Dr. *Heydon* (a Man of no Kind of Confequence, but well fitted to be made the Implement of any Kind of Bufinefs) tending to raife Mutinies among his Majefty's Forces, particularly in the Navy, to ftir up Sedition among the People, and even to engage Perfons in a Confpiracy for the feizing the *Tower* of *London*.——Nay, to fuch bafe Lengths had he proceeded, as even to have given Money to Villains to put on Jackets, and, perfonating Seamen, to go about the Country begging,

and

and exclaiming for Want of Pay, while the People oppress'd with Taxes were cheated of their Money by the great Officers of the Crown.—Matters were ripe for Execution, and an Insurrection, at the Head of which the Duke was openly to have appear'd, on the very Eve of breaking out, when it was discover'd by Means of some Agents whom *Heydon* had employed to carry Letters to the Duke.—The Detection of this Affair so exasperated the King, who knew *Buckingham* to be capable of the blackest Designs, that he immediately order'd him to be seiz'd, but the Duke finding Means, having defended his House for some Time by Force, to make his Escape, his Majesty struck him out of all his Commissions, and issued out a Proclamation, requiring his Surrender by a certain Day.

This Storm, however, did not long hang over his Head; for on his making an humble Submission, King *Charles*, who was far from being of an implacable Temper, took him again into Favour, and the very next Year restor'd him both to the Privy-Council and Bed-Chamber.—But the Duke's Disposition for Intrigue and Machination could not long lie idle, for having conceived a Resentment against the Duke of *Ormond*, for having acted with some Severity against him in Regard to the last-mentioned Affair, he, in 1670, was supposed to be concerned in an Attempt made on that Nobleman's Life by the same *Blood*, who afterwards endeavour'd to steal the Crown.—Their Design was to have conveyed the Duke to *Tyburn*, and there have hanged him; and so far did they proceed towards the putting it in Execution, that *Blood*

and his Son had actually forced the Duke out of his Coach in St. *James*'s Street, and carried him away beyond *Devonshire* House, *Piccadilly*, before he was rescued from them.

That there must have been the strongest Reasons for suspecting the Duke of *Buckingham* of having been a Party in this villainous Project, is apparent from a Story Mr. *Carte* relates from the best Authority in his Life of the Duke of *Ormond*, of the public Resentment and open Menaces thrown out to the Duke on the Occasion, by the Earl of *Ossory*, the Duke of *Ormond*'s Son, even in the Presence of the King himself.—But as *Charles* II. like most other Men, was more sensible of Injuries done to himself than others, it does not appear, that this Transaction hurt the Duke's Interest at Court, for in 1671 he was installed Chancellor of the University of *Cambridge*, and sent Ambassador to *France*; where he was very nobly entertained by *Lewis* XIV. and presented by that Monarch at his Departure with a Sword and Belt set with Jewels, to the Value of forty thousand Pistoles; and the next Year he was employed in a second Embassy to that King at *Utrecht*.——However, in *June* 1674, he resigned the Chancellorship of *Cambridge*, and about the same Time became a zealous Partizan and Favourer of the Nonconformists.—On the 16th of *Feb.* 1676, his Grace, with the Earls of *Salisbury* and *Shaftesbury* and Lord *Wharton*, were committed to the *Tower* by Order of the House of Lords, for a Contempt, in refusing to retract the Purport of a Speech which the Duke had made concerning a Dissolution of the Parliament.—

This

This Confinement did not, I suppose, last long, yet I find no material Transactions of this Nobleman's Life recorded after it, till the Time of his Death, which happened on the 16th of *April* 1687.—*Wood* tells us that he died at his House in *Yorkshire*; but Mr. *Pope*, who must certainly have had very good Information, and it is to be imagined would not have dared to advance an injurious Falshood of a Person of his Rank, has, in his Epistle to Lord *Bathurst*, given us a most affecting Account of the Death of this ill-starr'd Nobleman, who, after having been Master of near fifty thousand Pounds *per Annum*, he describes as reduced to the deepest Distress by his Vice and Extravagance, and breathing his last Moments in a mean Apartment at an Inn.—Be this particular Circumstance, however, as it will, it is certain that he had greatly reduced his Fortune before his Death, and that his natural Turn for Gallantry and Dissipation, encouraged and supported by the Fashion of the Age, and the Countenance that Vice of all Kinds met with at Court, threw him into Expences that would have been, as *Shakespeare* says,
" *enough to press a* Royal *Merchant*
" *down.*"

As to his personal Character, it is impossible to say any Thing in it's Vindication, for tho' his severest Enemies acknowledge him to have possess'd great Vivacity and a Quickness of Parts peculiarly adapted to the Purposes of Ridicule, yet his warmest Advocates have never attributed to him a single Virtue.—His Generosity was Profuseness, his Wit Malevolence, the Gratification of his Passions his sole Aim through

Life, his very Talents Caprice, and even his Gallantry the meer Love of Pleasure.—But it is impossible to draw his Character with equal Beauty, or with more Justice than in that given of him by *Dryden*, in his *Absalom* and *Achitophel*, under the Name of *Zimri*, which is too well known to authorize my inserting it here, and to which therefore I shall refer my Readers.

How greatly is it to be lamented that such Abilities should have been so shamefully misapplied.—For to sum up his Character at once, if he appears inferior to his Father as a Statesman, he was certainly superior to him as a Wit, and wanted only Application and Steadiness to have made as conspicuous a Figure in the Senate and the Cabinet as he did in the Drawing-Room.—But his Love of Pleasure was so immoderate, and his Eagerness in the Pursuit of it so ungovernable, that they were perpetual Bars against the Execution of even any Plan he might have formed solid or praise-worthy.—In Consequence of which, with the Possession of a Fortune that might have enabled him to render himself an Object of almost Adoration, we do not find him on Record for any one deservedly generous Action.——As he had liv'd a Profligate, he died a Beggar, and as he had raised no Friend in his Life, he found none to lament him at his Death.

As a Writer, however, he stands in a quite different Point of View.—There we see the Wit and forget the *Libertine*.——His Poems, which indeed are not very numerous, are capital in their Kind, but what will immortalize his Memory while Language

guage fhall be underftood, or true Wit relifhed, is his celebrated Comedy of

The *Rehearfal.*

A Comedy, which is fo perfect a Mafter-Piece in it's Way, and fo truly an Original, that notwithftanding it's prodigious Succefs, even the Tafk of Imitation, which moft Kinds of Excellence have excited inferior Geniuffes to undertake, has appear'd as too arduous to be attempted with Regard to this, which through an whole Century ftill ftands alone, notwithftanding that the very Plays it was written exprefsly to ridicule are forgotten, and the Tafte it was meant to expofe totally exploded, and altho' many other Pieces as abfurd and a Tafte as deprav'd have fince at Times fprung up, which might have afforded ample Materials in the Hands of an equal Artificer.

There is alfo another Play publifhed under the Duke's Name, called,

The *Chances.* Com.

This however is no more than a profeffed Alteration of the Comedy of the fame Name, written by *Beaumont* and *Fletcher.*

BULLOCK, Mr. *Chriftopher.*— This Author was a Player by Profeffion, and the Son of Mr. *Wm. Bullock,* whom we find to have ftood in very good Eftimation in his theatrical Capacity, nor was this Son of his by any Means deficient in Point of Merit as an Actor.——At what Place, or in what Year our Author was born, I have not been able to trace.— He became joint Manager with Mr. *Keene,* and another Actor, of the Theatre in *Lincoln's-Inn-Fields.*——In the Year 1717 he married a natural Daughter of that great Performer Mr. *Wilks,* by Mrs. *Rogers* the Actrefs.——

This Lady was bred up to the Stage, but altho', from the Advantage of an agreeable Figure, fhe pleas'd tolerably well in feveral dramatic Characters, yet fhe was far from inheriting the capital Merit of either her Father or Mother.—Mr. *Bullock* died in 1724, not much advanced in Life, for Mr. *Chetwood,* who muft have perfonally known him, fays he was then only in the Road to Excellence.—He had a great Deal of natural Sprightlinefs, which was of Advantage to him on the Stage, he performing for the moft Part the fame Caft of Characters at the one Houfe that Mr. *Colley Cibber* fupported at the other, which were the Fops, pert Gentlemen, *&c.* in which Livelinefs and Eafe are moft effentially neceffary.

The dramatic Pieces Mr. *Bullock* left behind him were fix in Number, and are as follows,

1. *Adventures of half an Hour.* Farce.
2. *Cobler of Prefton.* F.
3. *Perjuror.* F.
4. *Slip.* F.
5. *Woman's a Riddle.* C.
6. *Woman's Revenge.* C.

As to the Comedy of *Woman's a Riddle,* he has been accufed of fome unfair Dealing about it, with Regard to Mr. *Savage* ; but that is a Point I fhall endeavour more fully to explain when we come to the Life of that Gentleman.

BURKHEAD, Mr. *Henry.*—— This Gentleman was a Merchant of *Briftol,* and lived in the Reign of King *Charles* I.—He feems to have been a Man of ftrong Party Principles, and wrote a Play which was never acted, nor probably even intended fo to be, entitled,

Cola's Fury. Trag.

The

the Subject of it being the *Irish Rebellion,* which broke out in *October* 1641.——In it he has characterized all the principal Persons concerned in the Affairs of that Time, under feign'd Names.—And even the second Title to the Piece, viz. *Lirenda's Misery,* is expressive of the Subject aimed at, *Lirenda* being no more than an Anagram (which was a Kind of Quibble then much in Vogue) formed from the Letters which compose the Name of *Ireland.*

BURNABY, *Charles,* Esq;—— This Gentleman had a liberal Education, having been bred up at the University, and afterwards enter'd a Member of the *Inner Temple.*——He wrote four Plays, the Names of which are as follow,

1. The *Ladies Visiting Day.* C.
2. *Love betray'd.* C.
3. The *Modish Husband.* C.
4. The *Reformed Wife.* C.

BURNEL, *Henry,* Esq;—All I can gather in Regard to this Gentleman is, that he was a Native of *Ireland,* and wrote a Play, which was acted with Applause at the Theatre in *Dublin,* called,

LANDGARTHA. T. C.

It appears that he had before this made an Attempt in the dramatic Way, which had miscarried, but what the Name of that former Play was I cannot trace, nor is it at all improbable that it might never make its Appearance in Print.

BUSH, *Amyas,* Esq;—Of this Gentleman I know nothing more than the finding his Name in the Monthly Lists of Publication as the Author of one dramatic Piece, not I believe intended for the Stage, entitled,

SOCRATES, Dram. Poem.

C.

C J.—These two Letters are prefixed to a Comedy, entitled,

The *Two Merry Milkmaids.* C. but I cannot, either from these Letters, from the Date, or from any other Circumstance belonging to his Piece, attribute it to any known Author.

C. R.—These Letters stand in the Title Page to a Translation of a *Latin* Play, written by *R. Ruggles,* entitled,

IGNORAMUS. C. translated by *R. C.* who is there said to have been some Time Master of Arts in *Magdalen* College in *Oxford,* and which Letters *Coxeter* in a MS. Note explains to stand for *Robert Codrington.*

The Writers however have made a strange Jumble of Errors in Regard to this Translator and the Author of an historical Play called,

ALPHONSUS, *King of Arragon.,* *Langbaine* and *Gildon* having equally run into the Error of ascribing both these Plays to the same Author, with this only Difference, that the first has distinguished his Name by the Letters *R. C.* and the latter by those of *R. G.*—But as the Date of Publication of these two Pieces has a Difference of upwards of sixty Years, *Alphonsus* being published in 1599, and *Ignoramus* not till 1662, it is not very probable they should both be the Work of one Person.—I have therefore thought it most reasonable to follow the Authority of *Langbaine,* as explained by *Coxeter,* for the Translator of the latter; and that of *Gildon,* which *Jacob* likewise acquiefces with, for the Author of the former.

CARELL, Mr. *John*.—Of this Gentleman I know nothing more than his being mentioned by *Langbaine* and *Coxeter*, as the fuppofed Author of a dramatic Piece, entitled,

Sir *Salomon*. C.

which however *Jacob*, *Whincop*, *Gildon*, and the Author of the *Britifh Theatre* have all afcribed to Mr. *Lodowic Carlell*, and that with the fame fecond Title of the *Cautious Coxcomb*.

To this Gentleman alfo has been afcribed another dramatic Piece, called,

The *Englifh Princefs*. T.

CAREW, Lady *Elizabeth*.——This Lady flourifhed in the Reign of Queen *Elizabeth*, and muft have been of Diftinction in her Time; but from what Family fhe was defcended, or what Part of the Kingdom claim'd the Honour of her Birth I have not been able to difcover.—We find, however, fome of her Cotemporaries dedicating their Works to her, and fhe herfelf has written one dramatic Piece, entitled,

MARIAM, *the fair Queen of* JEWRY. Trag.

CAREW, *Thomas*, Efq;—This Gentleman was defcended from a very ancient and honourable Family of the Name, whofe Eftablifhment had long been in the County of *Devon*.—He flourifhed in the Reign of King *Charles* I. and was Brother to *Mathew Carew*, who, in the Time of the Rebellion, appear'd to have been very ftrongly attached to the Caufe of that unfortunate Prince.—Our Author received the Rudiments of his Education in *Corpus Chrifti* College, *Cambridge*, but it does not appear that he either took any Degree there, or was even matriculated as a Member.—Afterwards, however, having greatly improved himfelf by travelling abroad, and by the Converfation of ingenious Men at Home, he acquired a great Reputation for his Wit and poetical Abilities, which being taken Notice of at Court, he was made a Gentleman of the Privy Chamber, and Sewer in Ordinary to the King, with whom he ftood very high in Favour, infomuch that to the laft he efteemed him as one of the moft deferving Wits about his Court.—Nay, fo favourable an Opinion did he entertain of his Abilities in that Refpect, that it was by his Majefty's peculiar Command that he undertook the only dramatic Piece he appears to have written, and which is entitled,

Cœlum Britannicum. A Mafque.

With a Reference to which Circumftance he has prefixed to it the following modeft Diftich.

Non habet ingenium; Cæfar fed juffit; habebo:
Cur me poffe negem, poffe quod ille putat?

He was very much efteem'd and refpected by his cotemporary Poets, particularly by *Ben Jonfon*.—Yet, from a Stanza relating to him in Sir *John Suckling*'s Seffion of the Poets, he appears to have been a ftudied laborious Writer.—For though that Gentleman was his Friend, and had much Kindnefs for him, yet he could not help characterizing him as follows,

TOM CAREW *was next, but he had a Fault,*
That would not well ftand with a Laureat;

His

*His Muse was hide-bound, and
    the Issue of 's Brain
Was seldom brought forth but
    with Trouble and Pain.*

In what Year this Author was born I know not, but he appears to have died very much regretted in the Year 1639.

CAREY, Mr. *Henry.*——This Writer was by Profession a Master of Music, his Acquaintance with which Science, added to a Passion for it's Sister Poetry, not only inspir'd him with the Inclination, but also afforded him the Ability, to form several little dramatic Pieces, most of them of the humorous Kind, and almost all of them musical Entertainments.——On the whole they met with good Success, some of them still standing on the theatrical List for frequent Repetition.——The Titles of all his dramatic Works are as follow,

1. AMELIA. C.
2. BETTY. Ballad F.
3. CHRONONHOTONTHOLO-GOS. Mock Tra.
4. *Contrivances.* Ballad Farce.
5. *Dragon of* WANTLEY. Burlesque Opera.
6. *Hanging and Marriage.* Far. *Vid.* APPENDIX.
7. *Honest Yorkshire Man.* Ballad Farce.
8. MARGERY. Ballad Opera.
9. NANCY. Musical Interl.
10. TERAMINTA. English Opera.
11. *Wife well managed.* Far.

By a Hint given by the Author of the *British Theatre*, I am apt to imagine that this Gentleman hastened his own End; for that Writer, in his Account of Mr. *Odingsells*, has this remarkable Expression.——" This " Gentleman (says he) put an " End to his own Life in the " same Manner as *Creech* had done " before and *Carey* since."——The Manner that *Creech* ended his Life was by a Halter.

CAREY, *Henry.* Vid. FAULKLAND, Lord.

CARLELL, *Lodowic,* Esq;——This Gentleman was a Courtier, who lived in the Reigns both of King *Charles* the first and second.——He had various Places at Court, being Gentleman of the Bows to King *Charles* I. Groom of the King's and Queen's Privy Chamber, and served the Queen Mother many Years.——He wrote several dramatic Pieces, the most of which were acted with considerable Applause.——Their Titles are as follow,

1. *Arviragus and Philicia.* T.-Com. in two Parts.
2. *Deserving Favourite.* T. C.
3. *Fool would be a Favourite.* Com.
4. HERACLITUS. T.
5. OSMOND *the Great Turk.* Trag.
6. *Passionate Lover.* T. C. in two Parts.
7. *Spartan Ladies.* C.

The six first of these Plays only in general are ascribed to this Author; as to the last-mentioned one it is named only in a Catalogue at the End of an Edition of *Middleton's More Dissemblers besides Women.*——But *Winstanley*, who has omitted the *Heraclius*, which undoubtedly was Mr. *Carlell's*, has as erroneously attributed to him a Tragedy, written by Dr. *Loage*, entitled,

MARIUS and SYLLA.

CARLISLE, Mr. *James.* This Gentleman was a Native of *Lancashire*, and in the earlier Parts of his Life followed the Profession of a Player, but afterwards prefering the active Stage of the real World to the feign'd Affairs of

 the

the theatrical one, and chusing rather to *be*, than to *perfonate* a Hero, he quitted that Employment, and took up Arms in the Defence of his Country's Religion and Liberties in the *Irifh* Wars under King *William* III. to which glorious Caufe he refigned himfelf a willing Sacrifice, dying in the Bed of Honour at the famous Battle of *Aughrim* on the 11th of *July* 1691.—He left behind him one dramatic Piece which had been well received, entitled,

The *Fortune Hunters*. Com.

CARPENTER, Mr. *Richard*. —This Gentleman, who from the general Tenor of his Writings, and from fome Sermons publifhed under the fame Name, in the Year 1623, it is reafonable to conclude was a Divine, was born about the beginning of King *James* I's Reign, and lived till towards the End of *Charles* II's, being alive at *Aylefbury* in *Bucks*, in 1670.—He received his firft Rudiments of Education at *Eton* School, from whence he was removed to *Cambridge*, and was elected a Scholar of *King's* College in that Univerfity, Anno 1622. Here he ftaid two or three Years, after which he not only quitted that, but alfo his Country and Friends, went abroad, and ftudied in *Flanders*, *France*, *Spain*, and *Italy*, and at length took Orders in the *Romifh* Church from the Hands of the *Pope's* Subftitute at *Rome*, and becoming a Monk of the *Benedictine* Order, was foon after fent into *England* in Order to gain Profelytes.——But he had fcarcely been a Year and half in this Employment before he returned to the Proteftant Religion, and accepted of the Vicarage of *Poling*, near *Arundel* Caftle in *Suffex*; on which Account he received many Affronts from the Romifh Priefts who refided in thofe Parts, notwithftanding which in the Time of the Civil War, he went over to *Paris*, and there commenced a Railer againft the Proteftants.—On his Return to *England* he again became a Proteftant, but revolted once more before his Death to Popery, in which Perfuafion he died.—The great Antiquary *Anth. à Wood*, who was perfonally acquainted with him fays of him, " That " he was a fantaftical Man, that " changed his Mind with his " Cloaths, and that for his Juggles " and Tricks in Matters of Reli- " gion, he was efteemed a Theo- " logical Mountebank."—And indeed the Account I have already given of his leaving both Country and Religion, of his returning to them both, and again forfaking them, feems I think perfectly to juftify that Character of him (*Vid. Athen. Oxonienf.* Vol. I. p. 439.)

He has moreover left behind him one dramatic Piece, which from its very Title conveys to us an Idea of its having been written by one who, if not an Enthufiaft, muft at leaft have been a warm Controvertift in Religion, fince he could be induc'd to make fuch Controverfy the Bafis of a Work, which notwithftanding the Propriety of blending Inftruction with Amufement in the Superftructure, is ever expected to have its Foundation laid in the latter. —It is called,

The *Pragmatical Jefuit new leaven'd*. Com.

and is faid in the Title Page to be a Play tending to Morality and Virtue.—To this Comedy his Picture is prefixed, in a very genteel Lay Habit, whereas before another Work publifhed by him he is reprefented as a formal Clergyman,

gyman, and with a very grave and mortified Countenance.

CARTWRIGHT, Mr. *George.*—Of this Gentleman I know nothing more than that he lived at *Fulham*, and has obliged the World with one Play, entitled,

The *Heroic Lover.* Tragedy.

Langbaine has omitted any Mention of this Piece or its Author.

CARTWRIGHT, Mr. *William.*—There is some Degree of Contest among the Biographers concerning the Place of this Author's Nativity, and the Name of his Father.—*Lloyd*, in his *Memoires*, declaring him to be the Son of *Thomas Cartwright* of *Burford* in *Oxfordshire*, and born *Aug.* 16, 1615.—Whereas *Wood*, in his *Athen. Oxon.* (which I must confess I look as the better Authority) tell us that he was born at *Northway* near *Tewksbury* in *Gloucestershire*, in *Sept.* 1611. and that his Father's Name was *William*; and adds, that the Father having dissipated a fair Inheritance he knew not how, was at last reduced to turn Innkeeper at *Cirencester.*—By this Way of Life, however, it is probable he healed his broken Fortune, as we find him afterwards bestowing a liberal Education on this Son, who being a Lad of a promising Genius, he procured first to be initiated into Learning by Mr. *Topp*, Master of the Free School at *Cirencester.*—From thence he was removed to *Westminster*, as a King's Scholar, and studied under the learned Dr. *Osbaldiston.*—From thence, in 1628, he went to the University of *Oxford*, where he was chosen a Student of *Christ Church*, and plac'd under the Care of Mr. *Tarrent.*—Here he pursued his Studies with unwearied Diligence and Rapidity, went thro' the Classes of Logic

and Philosophy, took the Degree of Batchelor and Master of Arts, enter'd into holy Orders, in which he soon became eminent for his Preaching, and was made Metaphysical Reader in the Room of Mr. *Thomas Barlow* of *Queen's* Colledge, who afterwards became Bishop of *Lincoln.*—In this Office also he acquir'd great Reputation both for his Literary Knowledge and his Oratorical Endowments.

In 1642 he was promoted to the Place of Succentor to the Cathedral of *Salisbury*, and on the 12th of *April* 1643 was elected junior Proctor of the University.—Yet, as if he had in so short a Period run the full Race of Learning, and reach the Goal of Perfection, beyond which he could go no farther, he was taken out of this World on the 29th of *November* following, 1643, by a Malignant Fever which then reign'd at *Oxford*, was known by the Name of the *Camp Disease*, and was fatal to Numbers besides.

No Man perhaps ever acquir'd an earlier Fame than this amiable Youth, or, leaving the World at a Time of Life when Men in general begin but to be known, had obtain'd so universal a Homage to his Memory from his Cotemporaries.—For tho' according to the earliest Account of his Birth he could but have enter'd into his thirty-third Year (and the Publisher of his Poems says, as *Wood* also implies, that he died at thirty) he was most universally lamented, and even the King and Queen, who were then at *Oxford*, shew'd great Anxiety during his Illness, and were greatly afflicted at his Death.

The Character given of him by the Writers of his Time is

almost

almoſt beyond Belief.—*Ben Jon-ſon*, who gave him the Title of his Son, valued him ſo highly that he ſaid of him, *My Son* CARTWRIGHT *writes all like a Man.*—The Editor of his Works applies to him the Saying of *Ariſtotle* concerning *Æſchron* the Poet, *that he could not tell what Æschron could not do.*—*Lang-baine* ſays of him that " He was " extreamly remarkable both for " his outward and inward En-" dowments; his Body being as " handſome as his Soul.—He " was an expert Linguiſt, under-" ſtanding not only *Greek*, and " *Latin*, but *French* and *Italian*, " as perfectly as his Mother " Tongue.—He was an excellent " Orator, and yet an admirable " Poet; a Quality which *Cicero* " with all his Pains could not " attain to; nor was *Ariſtotle* leſs " known to him than *Cicero* and " *Virgil*."

In a Word he was of ſo ſweet a Diſpoſition, and ſo replete with all Virtues, that he was beloved of all learned Men that knew him, and admir'd by all Stran-gers.—And when after his Death his Plays and Poems were pub-liſhed together, we find them ac-companied by above fifty Copies of Verſes written by the moſt eminent Wits of the Univerſity, every one being deſirous to appear in the Number of his Friends, and to give Public Teſtimony to the World of the Value they had for his Memory.—It is im-poſſible however to cloſe his Cha-racter with any Thing ſtronger or more conciſe than the Men-tion made of him by the learned and pious Dr. *Fell*, Biſhop of *Oxford*, Who ſaid of him, " Cart-" wright *was the utmoſt Man could come to.*"
"

His Dramatic Pieces are only four, viz.

1. *Lady Errant*, T. C.
2. *Ordinary*. C.
3. *Royal Slave*, T. C.
4. *Siege.* Tr.-Com.

CAVENDISH, *William*. Vid. NEWCASTLE, Duke of.

CENTLIVRE, Mrs. *Suſanna.* This Lady was Daughter of one Mr. *Freeman* of *Holbeach* in *Lin-colnſhire*, who altho' he had been poſſeſs'd of no inconſiderable Eſ-tate, yet being a Diſſenter, and a zealous Parliamentarian, was at the Time of the Reſtoration ex-tremely perſecuted, as were alſo the Family of his Wife, who was Daughter of Mr. *Markam*, a Gentleman of a good Eſtate at *Lynn Regis* in *Norfolk*, but of the ſame political Principles with Mr. *Freeman*, ſo that his Eſtate was confiſcated, and he himſelf com-pelled to fly to *Ireland*.—How long he ſtaid there I have not been able to trace, nor whether our Authoreſs, who from a Com-pariſon of concurrent Circum-ſtances I imagine muſt have been born about 1680, drew her firſt Breath in that Kingdom or in *England*.—Theſe are Particulars all her Hiſtorians have been ſilent in Regard to, yet I am apt to conjecture that ſhe was born in *Ireland*, as I think it probable her Mother might not return to her native Country till after the Death of her Huſband, which happened when this Girl was only three Years old.—Be this as it will, we find her left to the wide World by the Death of her Mo-ther alſo, before ſhe had com-pleated her twelfth Year.—*Whin-cop* relates a romantic Story of her in a very early Period of her Life, which although he ſeems miſtaken in ſome Parts of her Hiſ-tory,

tory, (at leaft either he or *Jacob*
muft have been fo) having made
her Father furvive the Mother,
and even to have married again
before his Death, yet as he feems
to have taken Pains in collecting
many Circumftances of her Life
which are no where elfe related,
I cannot think myfelf authorized
entirely to omit it.—He tells us
that after her Father's Death,
finding herfelf very ill treated by
her Stepmother, fhe determined,
tho' almoft deftitute of Money
and every other Neceffary, to go
up to *London* to feek a better
Fortune than what fhe had hitherto experienced.—That as fhe
was proceeding on her Journey on
Foot, fhe was met by a young
Gentleman from the Univerfity
of *Cambridge*, (whofe Name, by
the Way he informs us of, and
was no other than the afterwards
well-known *Anthony Hammond*,
Efq;) who was fo extremely ftruck
with her Youth and Beauty, and
fo affected with the Diftrefs which
her Circumftances naturally declar'd in her Countenance, that
he fell inftantly in Love with her,
and enquiring into the Particulars
of her Story, foon prevailed on
her inexperienced Innocence to
feize on the Protection he offer'd
her, and go with him to *Cambridge*, where, equipping her in
Boy's Cloaths, he introduc'd her
to his Intimates at Colledge as a
Relation who was come down to
fee the Univerfity, and pafs fome
Time with him there; and that
they continued this Intercourfe for
fome Months, till at length, fated
perhaps with Poffeffion, or perhaps afraid that the Affair would
be difcover'd at the Univerfity,
he perfuaded her to come to *London*, providing her however with
a confiderable Sum of Money, and
a Letter of Recommendation to

a Gentlewoman of his Acquaintance in Town, fealing the whole
with a Promife, which however
it does not appear he ever performed, of fpeedily following her
to *London*, and there renewing
their amorous Intercourfe.—If
this Story is true, it muft have
happen'd when fhe was extremely
young; *Whincop*, as well as the
other Writers acknowledging that
fhe was married in her fixteenth
Year to a Nephew of the late Sir
STEPHEN FOX. But that Gentleman not living with her above
a Twelve Month, her Wit and
Beauty foon procur'd her a fecond
Hufband, whofe Name was *Carrol*,
and who was an Officer in the
Army, but he having the Mif-
fortune to be killed in a Duel
within about a Year and half after their Marriage, fhe became a
fecond Time a Widow. This Lofs
was a fevere Affliction to her, as
fhe appears to have fincerely loved
this Gentleman.—Partly perhaps
to divert her Melancholy, but
chiefly it is probable for the Sake
of a Support, fhe now applied to
her Pen, and became a Votary to
the Mufes, and it is under this
Name of *Carrol* that fome of her
earlier Pieces were publifhed.—
Her firft Attempt was in Tragedy, in a Play called the *Perjur'd Hufband*; yet her natural
Vivacity leading her afterwards
more to Comedy, we find but
one more Attempt in the Bufkin
among eighteen dramatic Pieces
which fhe afterwards wrote.

Such an Attachment fhe feems
to have had to the Theatre, that
fhe even became herfelf a Performer, tho' it is probable of no
great Merit, as fhe never rofe
above the Station of a Country
Actrefs.—However fhe was not
long in this Way of Life, for in
1706, performing the Part of

Alexander the Great in *Lee's Rival Queens*, at *Windsor*, where the Court then was, she wounded the Heart of one Mr. *Joseph Centlivre*, Yeoman of the Mouth, or in other Words principal Cook to her Majesty, who soon after married her, and after passing several Years happily together, she died at his House in *Spring Garden*, *Charing-Cross*, on the First of *December* 1723, and was buried in the Parish of St. *Martin's* in the Fields.

Thus did she at length happily close a Life, which at its first setting out was overclouded with Difficulty and Misfortune.—She for many Years enjoy'd the Intimacy and Esteem of the most eminent Wits of the Time, viz. Sir *Richard Steele*, Mr. *Rowe*, *Budgell*, *Farquhar*, Dr. *Sewell*, &c. and very few Authors received more Tokens of Esteem and Patronage from the Great; to which however the Consideration of her Sex, and the Power of her Beauty, of which she possess'd a considerable Share might, in some Degree, contribute.

Her Disposition was good-natur'd, benevolent and friendly, and her Conversation if not what could be called witty, was at least sprightly and entertaining. —Her Family had been warm Party Folks, and she seem'd to inherit the same Disposition from them, maintaining the strictest Attachment to Whig Principles, even in the most dangerous Times, and a most zealous Regard for the illustrious House of *Hanover*. —This Party Spirit, however, which breathes even in many of her dramatic Pieces, procur'd her some Friends and many Enemies.

As a Writer, it is no very easy Thing to estimate her Rank.—

It must be allowed that her Plays do not abound with Wit, and that the Language of them is sometimes even poor, enervate, incorrect and puerile, but then her Plots are busy and well conducted, and her Characters in general natural and well marked. —But as Plot and Character are undoubtedly the Body and Soul of Comedy; and Language and Wit, at best, but the Cloathing and external Ornaments, it is certainly less excusable to shew a Deficiency in the former, than in the latter.—And the Success of some of Mrs. *Centlivre's* Plays plainly evince that the first will strike the Minds of an Audience more powerfully than the last, since her Comedy of the *Busy Body*, which all the Players had decried before its Appearance, which Mr. *Wilks* had even for a Time absolutely refused to play in, and which the Audience came prejudiced against, rouz'd their Attention in Despite of that Prejudice, and forced a Run of thirteen Nights, while Mr. *Congreve's* *Way of the World*, which perhaps contains more true intrinsic Wit, and unexceptionable Accuracy of Language than any dramatic Piece ever written, brought on the Stage with every Advantage of Recommendation, and when the Author was in the Height of Reputation, could scarcely make its Way at all.— Nay, I have been confidently assured, that the very same great Actor I mentioned just now, made Use of this remarkable Expression with Regard to her *Bold Stroke for a Wife*, viz. *that not only her Play would be damn'd, but she herself be damn'd for writing it.* —Yet we find it still standing on the List of acting Plays, nor is it ever performed without meeting with the Approbation of the Audience, as do also her *Busy Body, Wonder,* and *Artifice.*

That Mrs. *Centlivre* was very perfectly acquainted with Life, and closely read the Minds and Manners of Mankind, no one I think can doubt who reads her Comedies; but what appears to me the most extraordinary, is, when we consider her History, the Disadvantages she must have labour'd under by being so early left to bustle with the World, and that all the Education she could have had must have been owing to her own Application and Assiduity, when I lay we consider her as an absolutely self-cultivated Genius, it is astonishing to find the Traces of so much Reading and Learning as we meet with in many of her Pieces, since for the drawing of the various Characters she has presented us with, she must have perfectly well understood the *French, Dutch* and *Spanish* Languages, all the provincial Dialects of her own, and somewhat even of the *Latin,* since all these she occasionally makes Use of, and whenever she does so, it is constantly with the utmost Propriety and the greatest Accuracy. In a Word, I cannot help giving it as my Opinion, that if we do not allow her to be the very first of our Female Writers, she has but one above her, and may justly be plac'd next to her Predecessor in dramatic Glory the great Mrs. *Behn.*

1. *Artifice.* Com.
2. *Basset Table.* Com.
3. *Beau's Duel.* Com.
4. *Bickerstaff's Burying.* F.
5. *Bold Stroke for a Wife.* C.
6. *Busy Body.* Com.
7. *Cruel Gift.* Trag.
8. *Gamester.* Com.
9. *Gotham Election.* Farce.
10. *Love at a Venture.* Com.
11. *Love's Contrivances.* Com.
12. *Man's bewitch'd.* Com.
13. MARPLOT. Com.
14. *Perjur'd Husband.* Trag.
15. *Perplex'd Lovers.* Com.
16. *Platonic Lady.* Com.
17. *Stolen Heiress.* Com.
18. *Wife well managed.* Farce.
19. *Wonder.* Com.

CHAMBERLAIN, Mr. *Robert.*—This Author lived in the Time of King *Charles* I. being born in 1607, at *Standish* in *Lincolnshire.*—He lived for some Years as Clerk to *Peter Ball,* Esq; who was Solicitor-General to King *Charles* Ist's Queen.—By this Gentleman he was at the Age of thirty sent to *Exeter* College *Oxford,* where he pursued his Studies, and probably was bred to the Pulpit, as we find a Book written by him, entitled, *Nocturnal Lucubrations,* or *Meditations Divine and Moral.*—He wrote a Play called,

The *Swaggering Damsel.* C. *Winstanley* has also attributed to him a Pastoral called,

Sicelides.

But as he has a few Pages farther given a *Piscatory* of the same Title to *Phineas Fletcher,* I own myself rather inclinable to look on this as one of the numerous Mistakes with which that Author abounds; and yet as *Wood* has mentioned both these Pieces, attributing the former to our Author, and telling us that the latter was several Times acted at *King's* Colledge *Cambridge,* and therefore was probably written by one of that House, it is not impossible that *Winstanley* may in this Particular be in the Right.

CHAMBERLAINE, Dr. *William.*—This Gentleman was a Physi-

Phyſician, and I imagine was Son of Dr. *Peter Chamberlaine.*—He lived at *Shaftſbury* in *Dorſetſhire* in the Reigns of King *Charles* I. and King *Charles* II. and was a very zealous Cavalier.—He wrote but one Play, entitled,

Love's Victory. Tr. Com. which, being compoſed during the inteſtine Troubles, at which Time the Play-houſes were ſuppreſſed, could not then be acted, but ſome Years after the Reſtoration was brought on the Stage under the Title of,

Wits led by the Noſe. C.

CHAPMAN, Mr. *George.*—Of this voluminous and ingenious Writer we are at a Loſs to trace ſome material Particulars.—Viz. The Family from whence he was deſcended, the Place where he was born, and the School at which he imbibed the earlieſt Rudiments of his Erudition.—It is known however that he firſt drew Breath in the Year 1557, and that in 1574, being then only in his ſeventeenth Year, yet well grounded in Grammar Learning, he was ſent to the Univerſity; but here again ſome Difficulty ariſes as to whether *Oxford* or *Cambridge* had the Honour of compleating his Studies.—For tho' it is certain that he was ſome Time at *Oxford,* and made a Figure there in the *Greek* and *Latin* Languages, yet it does not appear that he ſhone there either in Logic or Philoſophy, or took any Degree.—On his Return to *London* he was warmly patronized by Sir *Thomas Walſingham,* and after his Death by his Son.—He was alſo held in high Eſtimation by *Henry* Prince of *Wales,* and the Earl of *Somerſet;* but the firſt dying, and the other being diſgraced, *Chapman's* Hopes of Preferment were fruſtrated; to which

Diſappointments perhaps the Umbrage taken by King *James* at ſome Reflections caſt on the *Scots* Nation in a Comedy call'd *Eaſtward Hoe,* wherein this Author had a Hand, might be no ſmall Addition.—He appears however to have had ſome Place at Court under that Monarch, or his Queen *Anne.*—But what became of him during the Troubles which he lived to ſee, but not to be Witneſs to their entire Termination, I know not.—He paſſed however thro' a long Life, dying on the 12th of *May,* 1654. *Æt.* 77. and was buried on the South Side of the Church of St. *Giles's* in the Fields, a Monument being erected over his Grave at the Expence and according to the Invention of that great Architect *Inigo Jones,* who had been his peculiar Friend and Intimate.

He was undoubtedly a Man of very great Learning, and altho' Tranſlation has within our latter Ages reach'd a greater Degree of Perfection than it had then attained, a due Honour ought to be paid to the Induſtry of this Writer, who tranſlated, and that in a Manner far from contemptible, the whole *Iliad, Odyſſey,* and *Batryomyomachia* of *Homer,* ſome Parts of *Heſiod,* and *Muſæus's Erotopægnion.*—As to his dramatic Works, they are ſome of them unequal, nor has he in any of them paid much Attention to Regularity, the which he has ſo greatly infringed, as to extend his Number of Acts in one Piece, viz. *Two Wiſe Men and all the reſt Fools,* to two beyond the ſettled Standard.—His Maſter Pieces in the dramatic Way are his *Buſſy D'Amboiſe* in Tragedy, his *Widow's Tears* in Comedy, and his Maſque of the Inns of Court.— In his private Character he was truly

truly amiable, and maintained a very cloſe Acquaintance with the firſt Rate Writers of his Time, viz. *Shakeſpeare, Johnſon, Sidney, Spenſer* and *Daniel.*——Yet ſuch was *Jonſon's* natural Enviouſneſs of Diſpoſition and Haughtineſs of Temper, that as *Chapman* began to grow into Reputation he is ſaid to have grown jealous of him, and being, by the Death of *Shakeſpeare,* left without a Rival, ſtrove to continue ſo, by endeavouring to ſuppreſs as much as poſſible the riſing Fame of this his Friend.

The Plays *Chapman* has left behind him are as follow,

1. *All Fools.* C.
2. ALPHONSUS *Emperor of* GERMANY. T.
3. *Blind Beggar of* ALEXANDRIA. C.
4. BUSSY D'AMBOIS. T.
5. BUSSY D'AMBOIS's *Revenge.* T.
6. CÆSAR *and* POMPEY. T.
7. *Conſpiracy of* BIRON. T. two Parts.
8. *Eaſtward Hoe.* C. (Aſſiſted by *Ben Jonſon* and *Marſton.*)
9. *Gentleman Uſher.* C.
10. *Humourous Day's Mirth.* C.
11. *Maſque of the* Middle Temple *and* Lincoln's-Inn.
12. *May Day.* C.
13. *Monſieur* D'OLIVE. C.
14. *Revenge for Honour.* T.
15. *Two wiſe Men and all the reſt Fools.* Comical Moral.
16. *Widow's Tears.* C.

CHARKE, Mrs. *Charlotte.*—— This Lady on the Score of an Author has, I muſt confeſs, but barely a Right to a Place in this Work, having only produced one little Piece in the dramatic Kind, entitled,

The *Art of Management.* Far. But as ſhe was a Daughter of the celebrated *Colley Cibber,* Eſq; and Siſter to Mr. *Theophilus Cibber,* Comedian, ſhe ſeems to have a Kind of hereditary Claim to ſome particular Notice in a Work profeſſedly intended for the recording of ſuch Perſonages and Things as have any cloſe Connection with, or Reference to, the Affairs of the Theatre.——And although ſhe cannot be conſidered of equal Conſequence to the Public with either of theſe her before-nam'd Relations, yet as by a Courſe of ſtrange Occurrences, and a Diſpoſition apparently of the moſt romantic and inconſiderate Nature, ſhe rendered herſelf the Subject of much Converſation and Cenſure, and as, like her Father and Brother, ſhe has thought proper to publiſh to the World ſome of the Adventures of her Life, with a View, as it ſhould ſeem, to apologize for Part of her Conduct, it would certainly be an Omiſſion that I could ſcarcely be forgiven for, was I not to oblige my Readers with a ſhort Summary of thoſe Adventures which, diveſted from the Number of very trifling Incidents which ſhe had interlarded them with, in order to ſwell out her Life to the Bulk of a Volume, may not perhaps be totally unentertaining.

She informs us that ſhe was the youngeſt Child of the celebrated Laureat, born at a Time when her Mother was forty-five Years of Age, and having borne no Children for ſome Years before, began to imagine that without this additional Bleſſing ſhe had fully anſwered the End of her Creation, and therefore ſeems to conclude that (excluſive of her Parents, by whom ſhe confeſſes ſhe was treated with the utmoſt Tenderneſs and Affection) ſhe

came

came not only an unexpected but an unwelcome Guest into the Family.—To this Dislike of her other Relations she attributes a very considerable Share of her following Misfortunes, but indeed it must be confessed that she very early seem'd to shew a Disposition so wild, so dissipated, and so unsuitable to her Sex, that it is scarcely to be wonder'd should give Disgust to those of her Friends, whose Wishes were even the most favourable towards her. In short, from Infancy she owns she had more of the Male than Female in her Inclinations, and relates two or three droll Adventures of her dressing herself up in her Father's Cloaths; her riding out on the Back of an Ass's Foal, when not above four or five Years old, &c. that seem an evident Foretaste of the like masculine Conduct which she pursued thro' Life.—At eight Years old she was put to School, but had an Education bestowed on her more suitable to a Boy than to one of the opposite Sex; and as she grew up she followed the same plan, being much more frequently in the Stable than in the Bed-Chamber, and fully Mistress of the handling of a Curry-Comb, tho' totally ignorant of the Use of a Needle.—Her very Amusements all took the same Masculine Turn, Shooting, Hunting, riding Races, and digging in a Garden being ever her favorite Exercises.—She also relates an Act of her Prowess when a meer Child, in protecting the House, when in Expectation of an Attack from Thieves, by the firing of Pistols and Blunderbusses out at the Windows.——All her Actions seem to have had a boyish Mischievousness in them, and she sometimes appears to have run

great Risque of ending them with the most fatal Consequences.

This Wildness, however, was put some Check to by her Marriage, when very young, with Mr. *Richard Charke*, an eminent Performer on the Violin, immediately after which she launched into the Billows of a stormy World, in which she was, thro' the whole Remainder of her Life, buffeted about without ever once reaching a peaceful Harbour.—Her Husband's insatiable Passion for Women very soon gave her just Cause of Uneasiness, and in a short Time appears to have occasioned a Separation.—She then applied to the Stage, apparently from Inclination as well as Necessity, and opened with the little Part of *Mademoiselle* in the *Provoked Wife*, in which she met with all the Success she could expect.—From this she rose in her second and third Attempts to the capital Characters of *Alicia* in *Jane Shore*, and *Andromache* in the *Distress'd Mother*, in which, notwithstanding the Remembrance of Mrs. *Porter* and Mrs. *Oldfield*, she met with great Indulgence from the Audience, and being remarkable for reading well, was suffer'd to go on upon sudden Emergences to read Characters of no less Importance than those of *Cleopatra* and Queen *Elizabeth*.—She was after this engaged at a very good Salary and a sufficient Supply of very considerable Parts, at the Theatre in the *Haymarket*, and after that at *Drury-Lane*.—In a Word, she seem'd well settled, and likely to have made no inglorious Figure in theatrical Life, had not that Want of Consideration and ungovernable Impetuosity of Passions which run thro' all her Actions, induced her to quarrel with Mr. *Fleetwood*,

wood, the then Manager, whom she not only left on a Sudden without any Notice given, but even vented her Spleen against him in public, by the writing of the little dramatic Piece I have spoken of above; and tho' that Gentleman not only forgave her this Injury and restored her to her former Station, yet she acknowledges that she afterwards very ungratefully left him a second Time, on a Cause in which he could incur no Share of Blame.

Thus having thrown herself out of Employment in a Profession in which she had a fair apparent Prospect of Success, she next enter'd on a Business, which, by knowing nothing of, she must be certain to fail in;———in a Word, she commenced Trader, and set up as a Grocer and Oil-woman in a Shop in *Long-Acre*.

In this Station she, with a great Deal of Humour, describes and rallies her sanguine Expectations and absurd Proceedings, till between her own Ignorance, and the Tricks of Sharpers, some of whom cheated, and others robbed her, she was, after having kept Shop about three Months, forced to throw it up, and set up a great Puppet-Shew, over the *Tennis-Court*, in *James*-Street, near the *Haymarket*.—But after some little Course of Success in this Design it began to fail, and she was reduced to sell for twenty Guineas what she says had cost her near five hundred Pounds.

During the Course of these Transactions, Mrs. *Charke* informs us, that she had highly offended her Father, but by what Action of her own she does not inform us.—She confesses indeed that she had in some Respects justly incurred his Displeasure, but is desirous of having it appear

that it had been greatly aggravated and occasioned to hang with a heavier Load on her than it would otherwise have done, thro' the Ill Offices of an elder Sister. —However, I cannot help imagining the Offence to have been of a very heinous Nature, since it is evident Mr. *Cibber* never after forgave her, nor in her greatest Distresses seems to have at all assisted her; a Conduct entirely opposite to that Humanity and universal Benevolence, which were so well known to be the Characteristics of that Gentleman's Disposition; and indeed, whatever was the first Cause of his abandoning her, it is apparent she took no great Care to avoid a farther Occasion of Resentment: for in a Piece called the *Battle of the Poets*, in which was a Character most abusively and scurrilously aimed at the Laureat, Mrs. *Charke*, who happened to be a Member of the Company who performed it, was herself the very Person by whom that Character was represented; a Step which she could not have been compelled to take, but which must have been a voluntary Act of her own in the Exertion of her Resentment, somewhat of the same Nature with her Conduct towards Mr. *Fleetwood*; but which, in Consequence of the Relation she stood in to Mr. *Cibber*, must apparently be the Means of throwing an insuperable Bar in the Way of any Reconciliation between them.

But to proceed.—During the Course of these Transactions, Mr. *Charke*, whom I have before mentioned, had been for some Time parted from his Wife, and had engaged himself to go over to *Jamaica* with a Gentleman in the mercantile Way, where, in about twenty Months after his Arrival,

he

he died, leaving our Heroine once more at Liberty to unite herself by the Matrimonial Tie where-ever she should think proper.——She therefore informs us, that soon after her parting with her Property as above-related, she was very closely addressed by a worthy Gentleman, whose Name she seems very carefully to conceal, in Consequence of a strict Vow she had taken never to discover it.—To this Gentleman she gives us to understand she was united by a secret Marriage; but as he did not long survive that Union, she was once again left destitute and friendless; nay, even prejudiced in her Affairs from a false Report of her having by his Death come into a very considerable Fortune.—In short, she was soon after arrested for a small Sum; in Consequence of which she was compelled to remain for some Hours in a Bailiff's House.—The Description she gives of her Sensations on this Occasion, and the Disappointment she met with in her various Applications for Relief, are natural, but not new, and I cannot say she has done any great Honour to the apparent Choice she must have made of Acquaintance, as she informs us that she had not been half an Hour in Custody before she was surrounded by all the Ladies who kept Coffee-Houses in and about *Covent-Garden*; and that we find her Discharge at last was brought about entirely by a Subscription, formed among a Number of well-known Prostitutes and public Brothel-Keepers.

Being now released, her sole Means of procuring a Livelihood was by seeking out for the lowest Kind of theatrical Employment, in filling up occasionally such Parts as chanced to be deficient

in the private Exhibitions, or rather Butcheries of some of our dramatic Pieces at the *Tennis-Court*, or elsewhere: in which Business she seems generally to have chosen the Male Characters; and indeed she most commonly used to be dressed in Man's Cloaths even in private Life, the Reason of which she affects to make a Mystery of, and to imply as if that Mystery had some Reference to her Connection with the Gentleman above-mentioned.

Be this as it will, we are informed that in the Progress of her theatrical Adventures of this Kind, she met with one whereby she was for a short Time not a little embarrassed, which was no other than her becoming the Object of a tender Passion in the Bosom of a young Lady, who, having an immense Fortune in her own Possession, thought herself at Liberty to make an open Profession of her Love, and even to offer Proposals of Matrimony. —This Circumstance, however, obliged her to a Declaration of her Sex, to the no small Disappointment of the Lady; and the Company of Actors she belonged to soon quitting the Town, the Affair was hushed up, and the Report of it silenced.

In this uncertain Kind of Employment she continued till, thro' the Recommendation of her Brother, she was received into the Family of a certain Nobleman, in the Character of a *Valet de Chambre* or Gentleman.—In this Situation she describes herself as being very happy, till some Friends of his Lordship's remarking an Impropriety in the entertaining one of her Sex in that Character, she was again discharg'd and left to the wide World.

Her

Her next Employment was the making and selling of Sausages for the Support of herself and Child.——But this failing, she became a Waiter at the *King's-Head* Tavern at *Marybone*; commenced afterwards Manager of a strolling Company of Players, and pass'd thro' several trivial Adventures, but most of them distressful ones, till at length, by the Assistance of an Uncle, she was enabled to open a Public House, the Situation of which she imprudently fixed in *Drury Lane*; and here, notwithstanding the Experience her long Acquaintance with Misfortune might, one would think, have given her, the same Indiscretion and Mismanagement which before had ruined her still continued to direct her Actions, and forced her in a very short Time to shut up her House, and dispose of all her Effects.——She then engaged herself in the *Haymarket* Theatre, under her Brother Mr. *Theophilus Cibber*; but this Provision did not long continue, that Gentleman and his Company being soon after obliged to desist by Virtue of an Order from the Lord Chamberlain.

Her next Engagement was with the celebrated Mr. *Russel*, the Puppet-Shew Man, by whom she tells us she was employed at a Guinea *per* Day to move his Figures during his Exhibition at *Hickford*'s Great Room in *Brewer*'s Street.——But after his Death, the distressful and wretched Circumstances of which she has not badly related, she again joined Fortunes with different Sets of strolling Players, among whom she remained for very near nine Years.

Her Adventures during the Course of that Time being nothing but one variegated Scene of pitiable Distresses, of a Kind which no one can be a Stranger to who has either seen or read the Accounts of those most wretched of all human Beings, the Members of a meer strolling Company of Actors, I shall be excused the entring into Particulars, and be permitted to proceed to her coming to *London* in 1755, where she published that Narrative of her own Life, from which this Account is abstracted, and which therefore proceeds so far as to that Year.——Whether the Profits of her Book enabled her to subsist for the short Remainder of her Life without the seeking for farther Adventures I know not. ——Death, however, put a Period to it, and thereby to one continued Course of Misery, the evident Consequence of Folly, Imprudence and Absurdity, some Time in the Year 1759; having not long survived her Father and Brother; some Account of whose Lives our Reader will find a little further in this Work.

CHAVES, Mr. *A.*——Of this Author I can trace nothing farther than that he wrote one Play, called,

The *Lover's Cure*. C.

He does not however appear to have been a Person of any considerable Note, by his Piece being dedicated to Sir *William Read* the Mountebank.

CHEEKE, Mr. *Henry.*——Of this Gentleman I know nothing more than the finding his Name in *Coxeter*'s MS. Notes, as Author, as rather Translator from the *Italian*, of a Play, called,

Free Will. Trag.

CHETWOOD, Mr. *William Rufus.*——This Author for some Time kept a Bookseller's Shop in *Covent Garden*.——He was also for twenty Years Prompter to *Drury*

Lane Theatre, and in that very laborious and useful Office was esteem'd to have great Excellence. —Tho' no Actor himself, yet, from being so conversant with the Stage, and with the various Manners of different eminent Performers, he became no bad theatrical Instructor; and to the Pains he has taken in that Business some considerable Actors now living, perhaps, stand indebted for Part at least of their early Approbation.——I have in particular heard it asserted, not only by Mr. *Chetwood* himself, but others, that Mr. *Barry* received his first Rudiments of theatrical Execution from this Gentleman, as did also a Lady, who has for a few Years past stood in high Estimation with the Audiences of *Dublin*, viz. Mrs. *Fitzhenry*, formerly Mrs. *Gregory*.

Mr. *Chetwood* by his first Wife had a Daughter, who was bred up to the theatrical Life, and was married to one Mr. *Gemea*.—His second Wife, who I believe is still living, was a Grand-Daughter of Mr. *Colley Cibber*.—Mr. *Chetwood* himself also is living, and I think in *Dublin*, but in a very advanced Age.—He has wrote some Pieces in the Novel Way, and a Work call'd A *General History of the Stage*, which however has very little, or rather indeed no Merit. —He has also written the following dramatic Pieces,

   1. *Generous Free Mason.* T.- C. F. B. Opera.
   2. *Humours of Exchange-Alley.* Farce.
   3. *Lover's Opera.* Ballad Far. *Vid.* Vol. I. APPENDIX.
   4. *South-Sea.* Farce.

CIBBER, *Colley*, Esq;—This Gentleman, to whom the English Stage has been in many Respects greatly obliged, both as an Actor and a Writer; and in the latter Character doubly so by being not only greatly assistant in supporting it by his numerous and entertaining dramatic Pieces, but also its Historiographer thro' a very long and important Period, has given us so very pleasing and impartial a Detail of the most material Circumstances of his Life, that I cannot apply to a more perfect Source of Intelligence concerning it than what that Work will afford me, more especially as in it he has drawn the most candid Portrait of the Features of his Mind, as well as the clearest Narrative of the Effects produced by the different Combinations of the several Parts of his natural Disposition.—From that therefore the greatest Part of the following Account will, in as concise a Manner as possible, be extracted.

Mr. *Cibber* then was born on the 6th of *November*, O. S. 1671. in *Southampton* Street, *Covent* Garden.—His Father *Caius Gabriel Cibber* was a Native of *Holstein*, and came into *England* to follow his Profession of a Statuary sometime before the Restoration of King *Charles* II.—The Eminence he attain'd to in his Art may be judged from the two celebrated Images of raging and melancholy Madness on the two Piers of the great Gate of *Bethlehem* Hospital, and also by the Basso Relievo on the Pedestal of that stupendous Column called the Monument, erected in Commemoration of the great Fire of *London* in 1666.— His Mother was the Daughter of *William Colley*, Esq; of *Glaiston* in *Rutlandshire*, whose Father, Sir *Anthony Colley*, by his steady Attachment to the Royal Cause, during the Troubles of King *Charles* Ist's Reign reduced his

Estate

Eſtate from three thouſand to about three hundred Pounds *per Annum.*—The Family of the *Colleys*, tho' extinct by the Death of our Laureat's Uncle *Edward Colley*, Eſq; from whom our Author received his Chriſtian Name, and who was the laſt Heir Male of it, had been a very ancient one, it appearing from *Wright*'s Hiſtory of *Rutlandſh re*, that they had been Sheriffs and Members of Parliament from the Reign of *Henry* VII. to the latter End of King *Charles* I.——In 1682 he was ſent to the Free-School of *Grantham* in *Lincolnſhire*, where he ſtaid till he got through it, from the loweſt Form to the uppermoſt, and ſuch Learning as that School could give him, is, as he himſelf acknowledges, the moſt he could pretend to: About 1689 he was taken from School to ſtand for the Election of Children into *Wincheſter* Colledge, but having no farther Intereſt or Recommendation than that of his own naked Merit, and the being deſcended by the Mother's Side from *William* of *Wickham* the Founder, it is not to be wonder'd at that he was unſucceſsful.—Rather pleas'd with what he look'd on as a Reprieve from the confined Life of a School-Boy, than piqued at the Loſs of his Election, he returned to *London*, and there even thus early conceived an Inclination for the Stage, which however he, on more Conſiderations than one, thought proper to ſuppreſs; and therefore wrote down to his Father, who was at that Time employed at *Chatſworth* in *Derbyſhire*, by the Earl (afterwards Duke) of *Devonſhire* in the raiſing that Seat to the Magnificence it has ever ſince poſſeſs'd, to intreat of him that he might be ſent as

ſoon as poſſible to the Univerſity.—This Requeſt his Father ſeem'd very inclinable to comply with, and aſſur'd him in his Anſwer, that as ſoon as his own Leiſure would permit, he would go with him to *Cambridge*, at which Univerſity he imagin'd he had more Intereſt to ſettle him to Advantage than at *Oxford*; but in the mean Time ſent for him down to *Cha ſworth*, that he might in the Interim be more immediately under his own Eye.

Before young *Cibber*, however, could ſet out on his Journey for that Place, the Prince of *Orange*, afterwards King *William* III. had landed in the Weſt, ſo that when our Author came to *Nottingham*, he found his Father in Arms there among the Forces which the Earl of *Devonſhire* had raiſed to aid that Prince.——The old Man conſidering this as a very proper Seaſon for a young Fellow to diſtinguiſh himſelf in, and being beſides too far advanced in Years to endure the Fatigue of a Winter Compaign, entreated the Earl of *Devonſhire* to accept of this Son in his Room, which his Lordſhip not only conſented to, but even promiſed, that when Affairs were ſettled he would farther provide for him.—Thus all at once was the Current of our young Hero's Fortune entirely turned into a new Channel, his Thoughts of the Univerſity were ſmother'd in Ambition, and the intended Academician converted, to his inexpreſſible Delight, into a Campaigner.

They had not been many Days at *Nottingham* before they heard that Prince *George* of *Denmark*, with ſome other great Perſons, were gone off from the King to the Prince of *Orange*, and that the Princeſs *Anne*, fearing

her

he Father's Refentment, in Confequence of this Step of her Confort, had withdrawn herfelf from *London* in the Night, and was then within half a Day's Journey of *Nottingham*; and moreover, that a Thoufand of the King's Dragoons were in Purfuit of her, in order to bring her back Prifoner to *London*.—Altho' this laft Article was no more than a falfe Alarm, being one of the Stratagems made Ufe of over the whole Kingdom, in order to excite and animate the People to their common Defence; yet it obliged the Troops to fcramble to Arms in as much Order as their Confternation would admit of, to haften to her Affiftance or Refcue; but they had not advanced many Miles on the *London* Road, before they met the Princefs in a Coach, attended only by Lady *Churchill* and Lady *Fitzharding*, whom they conducted thro' the Acclamations of the People to *Nottingham*, where they were that Night entertain'd at the Charge of the Earl of *Devonfhire*. On this Occafion Mr. *Cibber* being defir'd by his Lordfhip's *Maitre D'Hotel* to attend, the Poft affign'd him was to obferve what the Lady *Churchill*, afterwards Dutchefs of *Marlborough*, might call for; and from the Manner in which he has made Mention of that Lady, it is apparent that her Charms at that Time made fuch an Impreffion on his young Heart, as, tho' the immenfe Diftance of her Rank obliged, and at the fame Time perhaps enabled him to fupprefs, yet even a Courfe of fifty Years which paffed between that Period and the Time of his writing his Apology could not entirely efface.

From *Nottingham* the Troops marched to *Oxford*, where the Prince and Princefs of *Denmark* met.—Here the Troops continued in quiet Quarters till on the fettling of the publick Tranquility, when they were remanded back to *Nottingham*, and thofe who chofe it were granted their Difcharge, among whom was our Author, who now quitted the Field and the Hopes of Military Preferment, and return'd to his Father at *Chatfworth*.—And now his Expectations of future Fortune, in a great Meafure, depended upon the Promifes of Patronage he had receiv'd from the Earl of *Devonfhire*, who, on being reminded of them, was fo good as to defire his Father to fend him to *London* in the Winter, when he would confider of fome Provifion for him; and our Author, with equal Honour and Candour, acknowledges that it might well require Time to confider it, for that it was then much harder to know what he was really fit for, than to have got him any Thing he was not fit for. During his Period of Attendance on this Nobleman, however, a frequent Application to the Amufements of the Theatre, awakened in him his Paffion for the Stage, which he feem'd now determin'd on purfuing as his *Summum Bonum*, and in fpite of Father, Mother, or Friends to fix on as his *Ne plus Ultra*.

Previous however to our proceeding to the theatrical Anecdotes of his Life, it may be proper to mention one Circumftance which tho' it happen'd fomewhat later than his firft commencing Actor, I cannot without an improper Interruption introduce with any Chronological Exactnefs without breaking into the Thread of my Narrative hereafter; yet which is an Event conftantly of Importance

ance in every Man's Hiftory, and which he himfelf mentions as an Inftance of his Difcretion more defperate than that of preferring the Stage to any Views of Life. —This is no other than his Marriage, which he enter'd into before he was quite twenty-two Years of Age, merely on the Plan of Love, at a Time when he himfelf informs us he had no more than twenty Pounds a Year, which his Father had affur'd to him, and twenty Shillings *per* Week from the Theatre, which could not amount to above thirty Pounds *per Ann.* more.—The Lady he married was Sifter to *John Shore,* Efq; who for many Years was Serjeant-Trumpet of *England,* to which Gentleman as Mr. *Cibber* was one Day paying a Vifit, his Ear was charmed with the Harmony of a Female Voice, accompanied by a Finger which performed in a mafterly Manner on a Harpfichord; being informed, on an Enquiry which an unufual Curiofity urged him to make, that both the Voice and Hand belong'd to the Sifter of his Friend, he begg'd to be introduc'd, and at firft Sight was captivated with the View of every perfonal Charm that could render a Female amiable and attractive.—Nor was fhe lefs delighted with the Sprightlinefs of his Wit, and the eafy Gaiety of his Addrefs.—In fhort a Courtfhip quickly commenc'd on the Foundation of a mutual Paffion, and terminated in a Marriage contrary to the Confent of the young Lady's Father, who, tho' he afterwards thought proper to give her fome Fortune, yet in the Suddennefs of his Refentment put it out of his own Power to beftow on her all that he had originally intended her, by appropriating great Part of what he

had fo defigned her, to the building of a little Retirement on the *Thames,* which he called *Shore's Folly,* and which has been demolifhed for many Years paft.

But to proceed to his dramatic Hiftory.—It appears to have been about *February* 1689, when our Author firft became a Dangler about the Theatre, where for fome Time he confider'd the Priviledge of every Day feeing Plays a fufficient Confideration for the beft of his Services; fo that he was full three Quarters of a Year before he was taken into a Salary of ten Shillings *per* Week.—The Infufficiency of his Voice, and the Difadvantages of a meagre uninformed Perfon, were Bars to his fetting out as a Hero; and all that feem'd promifing in him was an Aptnefs of Ear, and in Confequence of that a Juftnefs in his Manner of fpeaking.—The Parts he play'd were very trivial; that which he was firft taken any confiderable Notice of being of no greater Confequence than the Chaplain in the *Orphan;* and he himfelf informs us, that the Commendations he received on that Occafion from *Goodman,* a Veteran of Eminence on the Stage, which he had at that Time quitted, filled him with a Tranfport which could fcarcely be exceeded by thofe of *Alexander* or *Charles* XII. at the Head of their victorious Armies.——His next Step to Fame was in Confequence of Queen *Mary's* having commanded the *Double Dealer* to be acted, when Mr. *Kynafton,* who originally play'd Lord *Touchwood,* being fo ill, as to be entirely incapable of going on for it, Mr. *Cibber,* on the Recommendation of *Congreve,* the Author of the Play, undertook the Part, and at that very fhort Notice, performed it fo well, that Mr. *Congreve*

greve not only paid him some very high Complements on it, but recommended him to an Enlargement of Salary from fifteen to twenty Shillings *per* Week.—But even this Success did not greatly elevate the Rank of Estimation in which he stood with the Patentees as an Actor; for on the opening of *Drury-Lane* Theatre in 1693, with the Remainder of the old Company, on the Revolt of *Betterton* and several of the principal Performers to *Lincolns-Inn* Fields, an Occasional Prologue which he had written, altho' acknowledged the best that had been offer'd, and very readily paid for, yet would not be admitted to an Acceptance on any other Terms than his absolutely relinquishing any Claim to the speaking it himself.

Soon after his accepting of the Part of *Fondlewife* in the *Old Batchelor* on a sudden Emergency, in which, by the closest Imitation of *Dogget*, who had been an original Performer of it, not only in Dress, but in Voice and Manner, he obtained an almost unbounded Plaudit from the Audience, gave him some little Flight of Reputation; yet not only this, but even the Applause which in the ensuing Year he obtained, both as an Author and Actor, by his first Comedy, called *Love's Shift*, or the *Fool in Fashion*, were insufficient to promote him to any considerable Cast of Parts, till the Year 1696, when Sir *John Vanbrugh* did him a double Honour, *viz.* first, by borrowing the Hint of his Comedy for the writing of his *Relapse*, by Way of Sequel to it; and secondly, by fixing on him for the Performance of his favorite Character in it of Lord *Foppington*.—In 1706, however, we find him considered by Mr. *Rich* the Patentee, as of

some Consequence, by his excepting him from the Number of the Performers whom He permitted Mr. *Swiney* to engage with for his Theatre in the *Haymarket*, (tho' our Author, on finding himself slightly us'd by this Manager, paid no Regard to that Exception, but joined *Swiney*) and in the ensuing Year, when his Friend Colonel *Brett* obtained a fourth Share in the Patent, and that the Performers formed a Coalition, and returned to *Drury Lane*, Mr. *Cibber* also conceded to the Treaty, and returned with them; but on the silencing of the Patent in 1709, he, together with *Wilks*, *Dogget* and Mrs. *Oldfield*, went over again to Mr. *Swiney*.

In 1711, he became united as joint Patentee with *Collier*, *Wilks* and *Dogget*, in the Management of *Drury Lane* Theatre.—And afterwards in a like Partnership with *Booth*, *Wilks* and Sir *Rich. Steele*.—During this latter Period, which continued till 1731, the *English* Stage was perhaps in the most flourishing State it ever enjoy'd.——But the Loss of *Booth*, Mrs. *Oldfield*, Mrs. *Porter* and Mr. *Wilks*, lopping off it's principal Supports, Mr. *Cibber* sold out his Share of the Patent, and retired from the public Business of the Stage, to which however he at a few particular Periods occasionally returned, performing at no less a Salary, as I have been informed, than fifty Guineas *per* Night; and in the Year 1745, tho' upwards of seventy-four, he appear'd in the Character of *Randolph* the Pope's Legate, in his own Tragedy, called *Papal Tyranny*, which he performed; notwithstanding his advanced Age, with great Vigour and Spirit.

What might perhaps be an additional

pitional Inducement to this Gentleman to leave the Stage at the Time he did, when, as he himself tells us, though it began to grow late in Life with him, yet, still having Health and Strength enough to have been as useful on the Stage as ever, he was under no visible Necessity of quitting it, might be his having, in the Year 1730, on the Death of Mr. *Eusden*, been promoted to the vacant Laurel, the Salary annexed to which, together with what he had saved from the Emoluments of the Theatre, and the Sale of his Share in the Patent, set him above the Necessity of continuing on it.—And after a Number of Years pass'd in the utmost Ease, Gaiety and Good-Humour, he departed this Life towards the latter End of the Year 1757, having just compleated his 86th Year.

Mr. *Cibber* has, in his own Apology for his Life, drawn so open and candid a Portrait of himself in every Light in which we can have occasion to consider him, that I can by no Means do more justice to his Character than by taking separately the several Features of that Portrait to enable the Reader to form an Idea of him in the several Points of View, of a *Man*, an *Actor*, and a *Writer*.

As a *Man* he has told us, that even from his School-Days there was ever a Degree of Inconsistency in his Disposition; that he was always in full Spirits; in some small Capacity to do right, but in a more frequent Alacrity to do wrong; and consequently often under a worse Character than he wholly deserved.—A giddy Negligence always possess'd him, insomuch that he tells us he remembers having been once whipp'd for his Theme, tho' his

Master told him at the same Time that what was good of it was better than any Boy's in the Form.—The same odd Fate frequently attended the Course of his later Conduct in Life, for the Indiscretion, or at least unskilful Openness with which he always acted, drew more Ill-Will towards him, than Men of worse Morals and more Wit might have met with; whilst his Ignorance and Want of Jealousy of Mankind was so strong that it was with Reluctance he could be brought to believe any Person he was acquainted with capable of Envy, Malice, or Ingratitude.—In short, a Degree of Vanity sufficient to keep him ever in Temper with himself; blended with such a Share of Humility as made him sensible of his own Follies, ready to acknowledge them, and as ready to laugh at them; a sprightly Readiness of Wit and Repartee, which frequently enabled him to keep the Laugh in his Favour, with a Fund of Good-Nature which was not to be ruffled when the Jest happened to run against him; together with a great natural Quickness of Parts, and an intimate Acquaintance with elegant and polite Life seem to be the principal Materials of which his Character was compos'd.—Few Men had more personal Friends and Admirers, and few Men perhaps a greater Number of undeserved Enemies.—A steady Attachment to those Revolution Principles which he first set out with in Life, though not pursued by him with Virulence or Offence to any one, created a Party against him which almost constantly prevented his receiving those Advantages from his Writings, or that Applause for his Acting, which both justly merited.

merited.—Yet, that the Malevolence of his Opponents had very little Effect on his Spleen, is apparent through the whole Course of his Difputes with Mr. *Pope*, who, tho' a much fuperior Writer with Refpect to Sublimity and Correctnefs, yet ftood very little Chance when obliged to encounter with the Keennefs of his Raillery, and the eafy unaffected Nonchalance of his Humour.—In a Word, he feem'd moft truly of Sir *Harry Wildair*'s Temper, whofe Spleen nothing could move but Impoffibilities.—Nor did it feem within the Power of even Age and Infirmity to get the better of this Self-created Happinefs in his Difpofition, for even in the very latter Years of his Life I remember to have feen him, when, amidft a Circle of Perfons, not one of whom perhaps had attained to the third Part of his Age, yet has Mr. *Cibber*, by his eafy Goodhumour, Livelinefs of Converfation, and a peculiar Happinefs he had in telling a Story, been apparently the very Life of the Company, and, but for the too evident Marks of the Hand of Time on his Features, might have been imagined the youngeft Man in it. —Add to this, that befides thefe fuperficial *Agremens*, he was poffefs'd of great Humanity, Benevolence and univerfal Philanthropy, and by continued Actions of Charity, Compaffion and Beneficence, ever bore the ftrongeft Teftimonial to his being Mafter of that brighteft of all fublunary Gems, a truly good Heart.

As an *Actor* nothing can furely be a ftronger Proof of his Merit than the Eminence which he attained to in that Profeffion, in Oppofition to all the Difadvantages which, by his own Account, we find he had to ftruggle with. For, exclufive of the Pains taken by many of his Cotemporaries to keep him below the Notice of the Public, Nature feem'd herfelf to oppofe his Advancement.

His Perfon at firft, though not ill-made, was, he tells us, meagre and uninformed; (but this Defect was probably foon amended, as he latterly had a Figure of fufficiently Fulnefs and Weight for any Part) his Complexion was pale and difmal, and his Voice weak, thin, and inclining to the Treble.—His greateft Advantages feem to have been thofe of a very accurate Ear, and a critical Judgment of Nature.— His chief Excellency lay in the Walk of Fops and feeble old Men in Comedy, in the former of which he does not appear ever to have been excelled in any Period before him, or nearly equalled in any fince.—Yet, it is apparent, that he frequently acted Parts of Confequence in Tragedy, and thofe too, if not with the Admiration, yet with the patient Sufferance of the Audience; and the Rank of Eftimation he ftood in with Refpect to the Public in the oppofed Lights of a Tragedian and a comic Performer, cannot be better defcribed than in his own Words.——" I was vain e-" nough to think," fays he, " that I had more Ways than " one to come at Applaufe, and " that in the Variety of Cha-" racters I acted, the Chances to " win it were the ftrongeft on my " Side.—That if the Multitude " were not in a Roar to fee me " in Cardinal *Wolfey*, I could be " fure of them in Alderman *Fon-*" *dlewife*.—If they hated me in " *Iago*, in Sir *Fopling* they took " me for a fine Gentleman.—If " they were filent at *Syphax*, no " *Italian-*

" *Italian* Eunuch was more ap-
" plauded than when I fung in
" Sir *Courtly.*——If the Morals of
" *Æfop* were too grave for them,
" Juftice *Shallow* was as fimple
" and as merry an old Rake as
" the wifeft of our young ones
" could wifh me.——And though
" the Terror and Deteftation
" rais'd by King *Richard* might
" be too fevere a Delight for
" them, yet the more gentle and
" modern Vanities of a Poet *Bayes*,
" or the well-bred Vices of a Lord
" *Foppington*, were not at all more
" than their merry Hearts, or
" nicer Morals could bear."

Tho' in this Account, Mr. *Cibber* has fpoken with great Moderation of himfelf, yet it is apparent that he muft have had great Merit in Tragedy as well as Comedy, fince the Impreffion he made on the Audience was nearly the fame in both; for as it is well known that his Excellence in re-prefenting the Fops, induced many to imagine him as great a Cox-comb in real Life as he appear'd to be on the Stage, fo, he informs us, that from the Delight he feem'd to take in performing the villainous Characters in Tragedy, half his Auditors were per-fuaded that a great Share of the Wickednefs of them muft have been in his own Nature.——But this he confeffes that he look'd on in the very Light I mention it in this Place, rather as a Praife than a Cenfure of his Perform-ance, fince Averfion in that Cafe is nothing more than an Hatred incurr'd for being like the Thing one *ought* to be like.

The third and laft View in which we are to confider him is that of a *Writer.*——In this Cha-racter he was at Times very fe-verely handled by fome of his co-

temporary Critics; but by none with more Harfhnefs than Mr. *Pope.*——Party Zeal, however, feems to have had a large Share in exciting the Oppofition againft him, as it is apparent, that when uninfluenced by Prejudice, the Audience has, through a Courfe of upwards of fixty Years, receiv-ed great Pleafure from many of his Plays, which have conftantly formed Part of the Entertainment of every Seafon, and many of them repeatedly performed with that Approbation they undoubt-edly merit.——The moft impor-tant Charge againft him feems to have been that his Plots were not always his own, which Reflexion would have been juft, had he pro-duced no Plays but fuch as he had alter'd from other Authors, but in his firft Letter to Mr. *Pope* he affures us, and with great Truth, that his *Fool in Fafhion* and *Care-lefs Hufband*, in particular, were *as much* (if not *fo valuable*) Ori-ginals, as any Thing his Anta-gonift had ever written.——And in Excufe for thofe which he did only alter, or indeed compile from others, it is evident that they were for the moft Part compofed by collecting what little was good in perhaps feveral Pieces which had had no Succefs, and were laid afide as theatrical Lumber.——On this Account he was fre-quently treated as a Plagiary, yet it is certain, that many of thofe Plays which had been dead to the Stage out of all Memory, have, by his affifting Hand, not only been reftor'd to Life, but have even continued ever fince in full Spirit and Vigour.——On this Account furely the Public and the original Authors are greatly in-debted to him, that Sentiment of
the

the Poet being certainly true,

*Chi trae l'Uom del Sepolcro, ed
in Vita lo ferba.*
Petrarch.

Nor have other Writers been fo violently attacked for the fame Fault.—Mr. *Dryden* thought it no Diminution of his Fame to take the fame Liberty with the *Tempeft* and the *Troilus and Creffida* of *Shakefpeare*. Nor do thefe alter'd Plays, as Mr. *Cibber* juftly pleads, take from the Merit of thofe more fuccefsful Pieces, which were entirely his own.—A Taylor that can make a new Coat well is not furely the worfe Workman becaufe he can mend an old one; a Cobler may be allowed to be ufeful, tho' no one will contend for his being famous; nor is any Man blameable for doing a little good, tho' he cannot do as much as another.——Befides, Mr. *Cibber* candidly declares, that whenever he took upon him to make fome dormant Play of an old Author fit for the Stage, it was honeftly not to be idle that fet him to work, as a good Houfewife will mend old Linen when fhe has not better Employment.—But that, when he was more warmly engaged by a Subject entirely new, he only thought it a good Subject, when it feem'd worthy of an abler Pen than his own, and might prove as ufeful to the Hearer as profitable to himfelf.—And indeed, this effential Piece of Merit muft be granted to his own original Plays, *viz.* that they always tend to the Improvement of the Mind as well as the Entertainment of the Eye; that Vice and Folly, however pleafingly habited, are conftantly lafhed, ridiculed or reclaimed in

them, and Virtue as conftantly rewarded.

There is an Argument, indeed, which might be pleaded in Favour of this Author, were his Plays poffefs'd of a much fmaller Share of Merit than is to be found in them, which is, that he wrote, at leaft in the early Part of his Life, thro' Neceffity, for the Support of his encreafing Family; his precarious Income as an Actor being then too fcanty to fupply it, with even the Neceffaries of Life: and with great Pleafantry he acquaints us, that his Mufe and his Spoufe were equally prolific; that the one was feldom Mother of a Child, but in the fame Year the other made him the Father of a Play; and that they had had a Dozen of each Sort between them, of both which Kinds fome died in their Infancy, and near an equal Number of each were alive when he quitted the Theatre.—No Wonder then, when the Mufe is only called upon by Family Duty, that fhe fhould not always rejoice in the Fruit of her Labour.—This Excufe, I fay, might be pleaded in Mr. *Cibber*'s Favour: but I muft confefs myfelf of the Opinion that there is no Occafion for the Plea; and that his Plays have Merit enough to fpeak their own Caufe, without the Neceffity of begging Indulgence.—His Plots, whether original or borrowed, are lively and full of Bufinefs, yet not confufed in the Action nor bungled in the Cataftrophe.—His Characters are well drawn, and his Dialogue eafy, genteel and natural.—And if he has not the intrinfic Wit of a *Congreve* or a *Vanbrugh*, yet there is a Luxuriance of Fancy in his Thoughts which gives an almoft
equal

equal Pleasure, and a Purity in his Sentiments and Morals, the Want of which in the above-named Authors has so frequently and so justly been censur'd.—In a Word, I think the *English* Stage more obliged to Mr. *Cibber* for a Fund of rational Entertainment, than to any dramatic Writer this Nation has produced, *Shakespeare* only excepted,—And one unanswerable Evidence has been borne to the Satisfaction the Public have received from his Plays; and such an one as no Author besides himself can boast, *viz.* that altho' the Number of his dramatic Pieces is very extensive, half of them at least are now, and seem likely to continue, on the List of acting and favorite Plays.

As a Writer, exclusive of the Stage, his two Letters to Mr. *Pope*, and his *Apology for his own Life*, are too well known, and too justly admired, to leave me any Room to expatiate on their Worth.——His dramatic Pieces are,

1. CÆSAR *in* EGYPT. Tr.
2. *Careless Husband.* C.
3. *Chuck.* Opera. (attributed to this Gentleman by the Editor.)
4. *Comical Lovers.* C.
5. DAMON *and* PHILLIDA. Ballad Past.
6. *Double Gallant.* C.
7. HOB. Ballad Farce.
8. *Lady's last Stake.* C.
9. *Love in a Riddle.* Pastoral Ballad Opera.
10. *Love makes a Man.* C.
11. *Love's last Shift.* C.
12. MYRTILLO. Pastoral Interlude.
13. *Nonjuror.* C.
14. *Papal Tyranny in the Reign of King* JOHN. T.
15. PEROLLA *and* IZADORA. Trag.
16. *Provok'd Husband.* Com. (Part by Sir *John Vanbrugh.*)
17. *Refusal.* C.
18. *Rival Fools.* C.
19. *Rival Queans.* Burlesque Tragedy.
20. *School-Boy.* Farce.
21. *She wou'd and She wou'd not.* C.
22. VENUS *and* ADONIS. Masque.
23. *Woman's Wit.* C.
24. XERXES. T.
25. XIMENA. T.

CIBBER, Mrs. *Susanna Maria.* This Lady, whose Maiden Name was *Arne*, and whose Merit as an Actress is so well known, and has been so long established, was the Daughter of an eminent Upholsterer in *Covent Garden*, and is Sister to that great Musical Composer Dr. *Thomas Augustine Arne.* ——Her first Appearance on the Stage was as a Singer; in which Light the Sweetness of her Voice and the Strength of her Judgment render'd her very soon conspicuous.——In the Year 1736, however, she made her first Attempt as a speaking Performer, in the Character of *Zara*, in Mr. *Hill*'s Tragedy of that Name, being it's first Representation; in which Part she gave both Surprize and Delight to the Audience, who were no less charmed with the Beauties of her present Performance, than with the Prospect of future Entertainment from so valuable an Acquisition to the Stage.—A Prospect which has ever since been perfectly maintained, and a Meridian Lustre shone forth fully equal to what was promised from the Morning Dawn.—And though it may not appear to have any immediate Relation with our present Design, yet I cannot, with

Juftice to her Merits, difpenfe with the tranfmitting down to Pofterity, by this Opportunity, fome flight Idea of this capital Ornament of our prefent Stage. —Her Perfon is ftill perfectly elegant; for although fhe is fomewhat declined beyond the Bloom of Youth, and even wants that *Embonpoint*, which fometimes is affiftant in concealing the Impreffion made by the Hand of Time, yet there is fo compleat a Symmetry and Proportion in the different Parts which conftitute this Lady's Form, that it is impoffible to view her Figure and not think her young, or look in her Face and not confider her handfome.—Her Voice is beyond Conception plaintive and mufical, yet far from deficient in Powers for the Expreffion of Refentment or Difdain, and fo much equal Command of Feature does fhe poffefs for the Reprefentation of Pity or Rage, of Complacence or Difdain, that it would be difficult to fay whether fhe affects the Hearts of an Audience moft, when playing the gentle, the delicate *Celia*, or the haughty, the refenting *Hermione*; in the innocent love-fick *Juliet*, or in the forfaken, the enrag'd *Alicia*.—In a Word, thro' every Caft of Tragedy fhe is excellent, and, could we forget the Excellence of a *Pritchard*, we fhould be apt to fay, inimitable.——She has of late made fome Attempts in Comedy. — They have, however, been in no Degree equal to her Excellence in the oppofite Walk, and indeed, after the Mention I have juft made of another Lady, it will be fufficient to remind my Reader, that *one Actor* and *one Actrefs univerfally capital*, is as much as can be expected to be the Produce of a fingle Century.——But to drop this Digref-

fion. Mrs. *Cibber* was fecond Wife to Mr. *Theophilus Cibber*, whofe Life I fhall immediately relate fome of the Circumftances of.—In what Year they were married I do not exactly know, but imagine it to have been no very long Time before her Appearance in *Zara*, that being by his own Account in 1736, and in the Year 1733 his Comedy of the *Lover* came firft on the Stage, a principal Part in which was performed by his firft Wife.—What were the Confequences of their Union is too well known to render my entering into any Particulars in Relation to them neceffary.

Mrs. CIBBER has a Right to a Place in this Work as a dramatic Writer, having brought a very elegant little Piece on the Stage, taken from the *French*, called,

The *Oracle*. Com. of one Act.

CIBBER, Mr. *Theophilus*.—— This Gentleman was Son of the celebrated Laureat, and Hufband to the Lady mentioned in the preceding Article.——As if the very Beginning of his Life was intended a Prefage of the Confufion and Perplexities which were to attend the Progrefs of it, and of the dreadful Cataftrophe which was to put the clofing Period to it, he was born on the Day of the violent and deftructive Storm, in the Year 1703, whofe Fury rang'd over the greateft Part of *Europe*, but was particularly fatal to this Kingdom.—In what Degree of Elderfhip he ftood among the Children of the Laureat I know not, but as it is apparent that Mrs. *Cibber* was very prolific, and as our Hero did not come into the World till ten Years after his Father's Marriage, it is probable he had many Seniors.——

About

About the Year 1716 or 1717 he was sent to *Winchester* School, where he received all the Education he had to boast of, and I believe very soon after his Return from thence came on the Stage. —Inclination and Genius probably induced him to make this Profession his Choice, and the Power his Father possess'd as one of the Managers of the Theatre-Royal, together with the Estimation he stood in as an Actor, enabled this his Son to pursue it with considerable Advantages, which do not always so favourably attend the first Attempts of a young Performer.—In this Profession, however, he quickly gave Proofs of great Merit, and soon attained a considerable Share of the public Favour.—His Manner of acting was in the same Walk of Characters which his Father had with so much and so just a Reputation supported.——In his Steps he trod, and tho' not with equal Excellence, yet with sufficient to set him on a Rank with most of the rising Generation of Performers, both as to present Worth and future Prospect of Improvement.

The same natural Imperfections which were so long the Bars to his Father's theatrical Advancement, stood still more strongly in his Way.—His Person was far from pleasing, the Features of his Face rather disgustful.—His Voice had the same shrill Treble, but without that Musical Harmony which Mr. *Colley Cibber* was Master of.—Yet still an apparent good Understanding and Quickness of Parts; a perfect Knowledge of what he ought to represent; together with a Vivacity in his Manner, and a Kind of *Effronterie* which was well adapted to the Characters he was to represent,

pretty amply counterballanced those Deficiencies.—In a Word, his first setting out in Life seem'd to promise the Assurance of future Happiness to him both as to Ease, and even Affluence of Circumstances, and with Respect to Fame and Reputation; had not one Foible overclouded his brightest Prospects, and at length led him into Errors, the Consequences of which it was almost impossible he should ever be able to retrieve. —This Foible was no other than Extravagance and Want of Occonomy.—A Fondness for Indulgences which a moderate Income could not afford, probably induced him to submit to Obligations which it had the Appearance of Meanness to accept of; the Consciousness of those Obligations, and the Use he imagined they might be made of against him, perhaps might at first prevail on him to appear ignorant of what it was but too evident he could not avoid knowing, and afterwards urge him to Steps, in the Pursuance of which, without his by any Means avenging his Wrongs, his Fame, his Peace of Mind, his Credit, and even his future Fortunes were all wrecked at once.——The real actuating Principles of the human Heart it is impossible to dive into, and the charitably dispos'd Mind will ever be inclinable to believe the best; especially with Regard to those who are no longer in a Condition to defend themselves.—Let then his Ashes rest in Peace, and avoiding any minute Investigation of those Circumstances which cast a low'ring Cloud over his Character while living, proceed we to those few Particulars which immediately come within our Notice as his Historiographers.

Mr. *Theophilus Cibber* then seems

to have enter'd firſt into the Matrimonial State pretty early in Life.——His firſt Wife was one Miſs *Jenny Johnſon*, who was a Companion and Intimate of Miſs *Rafter*'s (now Mrs. *Clive*) and in her very earlieſt Years had a ſtrong Inclination for the Stage. This Lady, according to her Huſband's own Account of her, ſeem'd likely to have made a very conſpicuous Figure in the Theatre, had not Death put a Stop to her Career in the very Prime of Life.—She left behind her two Daughters, *Jane* and *Elizabeth*, both of whom are, I believe, ſtill living.—The firſt-mentioned of theſe Ladies made two or three Attempts on the Stage; but tho' agreeable in her Perſon and elegant in her Manner, yet, from the Want of ſufficient Spirit, and the Defect of but an indifferent Voice, ſhe met with no extraordinary Succeſs.

After the Death of Mrs. *Jane Cibber*, Mr. *Cibber*, in the Year 1734 or 1735, paid his Addreſſes to Miſs *Suſanna Maria Arne*, whoſe amiable and virtuous Diſpoſition, he himſelf informs us, were the Conſiderations that induced him to make her his Wife.—She was at that Time remarkable on the Stage only for her muſical Qualifications; but ſoon after their Marriage made her firſt Attempt as an Actreſs, her Succeſs in which I have taken Notice of under the laſt Article.—Mr. *Cibber*'s Pecuniary Indiſcretions, however, not permitting him to reſtrain his Expences within the Limits of his own and his Wife's Salaries and Benefits, tho' their Amount was very conſiderable, he took a Journey to *France* for ſome ſhort Time in the Year 1738, on his Return from which he appears firſt to

have taken Notice of too cloſe an Intimacy between his Wife and a certain young Gentleman of Fortune, with whom he had united himſelf apparently by all the cloſeſt Ties of Friendſhip.—How far he was or was not guilty of the Meanneſs changed on him of being acceſſary to their Correſpondence is a Point I ſhall not here enter into the Diſcuſſion of.—A Suit was commenced for Criminal Converſation, he laying his Damage at 5000l. the Verdict on which of only ten Pounds Damages, too plainly evinces the Senſe of the Adminiſtrators of Juſtice in the Caſe to need any farther Comment.

After this Event Mr. *Cibber*'s Creditors, who were numerous, and had perhaps been ſomewhat appeaſed from the Proſpect of the pecuniary Advantages that might accrue to their Debtor in Conſequence of the Trial, became more impatient than ever, and not long after Mr. *Cibber* was arreſted for ſome conſiderable Sums, and thrown into the King's Bench Priſon.—By the Means of Benefit Plays, however, and other Aſſiſtances, he obtained his Liberty; but as the Affair relating to his Wife, who was now become an Actreſs of the firſt Conſequence, and in the higheſt Favour with the Town, had greatly prejudiced him, not only in the Opinion of the Public, but even by ſtanding as a Bar to his theatrical Engagements; and as his natural Paſſion for Diſſipation could not be kept within Bounds, theſe Difficulties repeatedly occur'd to him, and he was frequently excluded entirely from any Theatre for a whole Seaſon together.—In theſe Diſtreſſes he was ever ready to head any theatrical Mutiny that might put it

in

in his Power to form a separate Company, which he more than once attempted to fix at the Theatre in the *Haymarket*, but in vain ; the Legiflative Power urged to Exertion by the Interefts of the eftablifhed and patent Theatres, conftantly putting a Stop to his Proceedings after a few Night's Performance.—In one continual Series of Diftrefs, Extravagance and Perplexity of this Kind, did he continue till the Winter of 1757, when he was engaged by Mr. *Sheridan* to go over to *Dublin* to affift him in making a Stand againft the new Theatre juft then opened in Oppofition to him in *Crow-Street.*—On this Expedition Mr. *Cibber* embarked at *Park-Gate*, (together with Mr. *Maddox* the celebrated Wire Dancer, who had alfo been engaged as an Auxiliary to the fame Theatre) on board the *Dublin Trader*, fome Time in the Month of *October*; but the high Winds, which are frequent at that Time of the Year in St. *George's* Channel, and which are fatal to many Veffels in the Paffage from this Kingdom to *Ireland*, proved particularly fo to this.—The Veffel was driven to the Coaft of *Scotland*, where it was caft away, every Soul in it (and the Paffengers were extremely numerous) perifhing in the Waves, and the Ship itfelf fo entirely loft, that fcarcely any Veftiges of it remained to indicate where it had been wreck'd, excepting a Box containing Books and Papers, which were known to be Mr. *Cibber's*, and which were caft up on the Weftern Coaft of *Scotland*.

Thus fell the well-known Mr. *Theophilus Cibber*, whofe Life was begun, purfued and ended in a Storm.—Poffeffed of Talents that might have made him happy, and Qualities that might have render'd him beloved, yet thro' a too infatiable Thirft of Pleafure, and a Want of Confideration in the Means of purfuing it, his Life was one Scene of Mifery, and his Character made the Mark of Cenfure and Contempt.——Now, however, let his Virtues, which were not a few, remain on Record, and for his Indifcretions,

> Let them be buried with him in the Grave,
> But not remember'd in his Epitaph.

As a Writer, he has not render'd himfelf very confpicuous excepting in fome Appeals to the Public on peculiar Circumftances of his own diftreffed Life.—He was indeed concerned in, and has put his Name to, an Account of the Lives of the Poets of *Great-Britain* and *Ireland*, in five Vol. 8vo.—But in this Work his own peculiar Share was very inconfiderable, many other Hands having been concerned with him in it.—In the dramatic Way he has altered for the Stage three Pieces of other Authors, and produced one Original of his own.—Their Titles will be found in the enfuing Lift.

1. *Henry* VI. Trag. from *Shakefpeare*.
2. *Lover.* Com.
3. *Patie and Peggy.* Ballad Op. and
4. An Alteration of *Shakefpeare's Romeo and Juliet.*

CLANCY, Dr. *Michael.*—This Gentleman, who I believe is ftill living, was a Phyfician, and, as I imagine, a Native of *Ireland*, one of his Plays having been originally acted in that Kingdom.— He had the Misfortune to lofe his Sight, in Confideration of

which his late Majefty was pleafed to beftow on him a Penfion
of forty Pounds *per Annum* during
Life ; and in the Year 1746, the
Manager of *Drury* Lane gave him
a Benefit in that Theatre.—The
Play he made Choice of was
Oedipus, King of *Thebes*, in which
the Doctor himfelf performed the
Part of *Tirefias* the blind Pro-
phet, the Novelty of which, to-
gether with Dr. *Clancy*'s great
Perfonal Intereft, brought a very
numerous Audience.—He is Au-
thor of a Latin Poem, entitled,
*Templum Veneris, five Amorum
Rhapfodiæ*, and of two dramatic
Pieces, whofe Titles are,

 1. HERMON, *Prince of* CHO-
  RÆA. T.
 2. *Sharper.* C.

CLAYTON, Mr. *Thomas.*—Of
this Gentleman I find no more
than his Name mentioned by *Coxeter* as the Author of an *Englifh*
Opera, after the *Italian* Manner,
entitled,

ARSINOE, *Queen of Cyprus.*
notwithftanding which both *Whincop* and the Author of the *Britifh
Theatre* have afcribed an Opera
of that Name to Mr. *Motteux.*

CLELAND, *John*, Efq;—This
Gentleman, who is ftill living,
is a Son of the Colonel *Cleland*,
who was fo clofe an Intimate
with, and fo zealous an Advocate for, Mr. *Pope.*—What this
his Son was originally bred to I
know not, but he paffed many
Years of the early Part of his
Life abroad, where he acquired
a very perfect Aequaintance with
moft of the Modern Languages,
and feems to have imbibed no
fmall Share of the Luxury of the
Eaft, if we may form a Judgment from his celebrated Novel,
entitled, the *Memoirs of a Woman
of Pleafure*, which tho' a Book
of the moft pernicious Tendency,

and juftly cenfured by every one
who has the leaft Regard to Virtue or Decency, yet contains an
Elegance of Manner, and a Luxuriancy of Fancy, that would do Honour to the Author, if made Ufe
of in a better Caufe.—His *Memoirs
of a Coxcomb*, however, have great
Merit; nor are his political Writings, tho' warm and enthufiaftically
bigotted to one Syftem, devoid of
great Perfpicuity, Penetration and
Depth of Reafoning. In the dramatic Way he has publifhed two
Pieces, neither of which however have made an Appearance on
the Stage, *viz.*

 1. TITUS VESPASIAN. T.
 2. TOMBO-CHIQUI. Dram.-
  Ent. in three Acts.

CLIVE, Mrs. *Catharine.*—This
Lady, whofe Name as a dramatic
Writer we are obliged to mention
here, is however much better
known for her unequalled Merit
as a Comedian, in which Light,
while any theatrical Records are
remaining, her Memory muft
ever be held in the higheft Eftimation.—She was the Daughter
of Mr. *William Raftor*, a Gentleman who was a Native of the
City of *Kilkenny* in *Ireland*, and
bred to the Law ; but being
ftrongly attached to the Interefts
of the unfortunate King *James* II.
when that Monarch was in *Ireland*, he enter'd into his Service ;
on which Account a confiderable
paternal Eftate in the County of
Kilkenny, which he would otherwife have inherited, became for-
feit to the Crown.——After the
decifive Battle of the *Boyne*, however, he ftill followed his Mafter's Fortunes, and through that
Intereft and his own Merit, obtain'd a Captain's Commiffion in
the Service of *Louis* XIV.—But
afterwards, procuring a Pardon
        from

from the *English* Court, he came to this Metropolis, where he married the Daughter of an eminent Citizen on *Fishstreet - Hill*, by whom he had several Children, and, among the rest, the Subject of our present Memoirs.

Miss *Raftor* was born in 1711, and shewed a very early Inclination and Genius for the Stage.—Her natural Turn of Humour, and her pleasing Manner of singing Songs of Spirit, induced some Friends to recommend her to the late Mr. *Colley Cibber*, then one of the Managers of *Drury Lane* Theatre, who immediately engaged her at a small Salary.—Her first Appearance was in Boy's Cloaths, in the Character of a Page, in the Tragedy of *Mithridates* King of PONTUS, in which she was introduced only to sing a Song.—Yet even in this she met with great Applause.—This was in 1728, at which Time she was but seventeen Years of Age; and in the very same Season we find that the Audience paid so great Attention to her Merit in the Part of *Phillida*, in *Cibber's Love in a Riddle*, which Party-Prejudice had determined to damn, right or wrong, on Account of the Author, as to suffer their riotous Clamours to subside whenever she was on the Stage; a Compliment which they even denied to the Blood Royal itself on the ensuing Night.——In 1730, however, she had an Opportunity afforded her, which she did not permit to pass unemployed, of breaking forth on the Public in a full Blaze of Comic Brightness.—This was in the Part of *Nell*, in the *Devil to pay*, or *the Wives Metamorphos'd*, a Ballad Farce, written by *Coffey*, in which she threw out a full Exertion of those

comic Powers, which every Frequenter of the Theatre must since have received such infinite Delight from.—Her Merit in this Character occasioned her Salary to be doubled, and not only established her own Reputation with the Audience, but fixed the Piece itself on the constant List of acting Farces, an Honour which perhaps it would never have arrived at, had she not been in it, nor may long maintain when her Support in it is lost.——In the Year 1732, she was married to G. *Clive*, Esq; a Son of the late Mr. Baron *Clive*, which Gentleman is still living.—They did not however cohabit long together; yet, notwithstanding the Temptations to which a Theatre is sometimes apt to expose young Persons of the Female Sex, and the too great Readiness of the Public to give Way to unkind Suppositions in Regard to them, Calumny itself has never seem'd to aim the slightest Arrow at her Fame.

To expatiate on her Merit as an Actress (while she keeps within the very extensive Walk which is adapted to her Excellence) would far exceed our Limits, and be wholly unnecessary.—As an Author, I imagine, she does not aim at Immortality, yet she has, at different Benefits of her own, introduced three several *petite Pieces* on the Stage, neither of which is totally devoid of Merit.—Their Titles are as follow,

1. BAYES *in Petticoats*.
2. *Every Woman in her Humour*.
3. *Island of Slaves*.

Only the first of these, however, has yet appear'd in Print, and as to the last it is no more than an almost literal Translation of *Marivaux's*

rivaux's Ifle des Efclaves, executed, as fhe herfelf confeffes, by
a Gentleman at her Requeft.

CockAIN, Sir *Afton*. — This
Gentleman lived in the Reign of
Charles I —He was Son to *Thomas
Cockain*, Efq; and was born in the
Year 1706 at *Afhbourne*, in the
Peak of *Derbyfhire*, where his
Father had a fine Seat, and where
fome of his Predeceffors had refided ever fince the Reign of *Edward* I. — His Family, however,
appears to have been ftill more
ancient, tracing back their Origin as far as *William* the Conqueror, to whom they were al-
lied, and in whofe Reign they
lived at *Hemmington* Caftle in *Effex*.—Our Author had a liberal
Education, having been fent to
both the Univerfities of *Oxford*
and *Cambridge*, at the latter of
which he was a Fellow Commoner of *Trinity* College.—From
the Univerfities he for a Time
was enter'd in the Inns of
Court, where he feems to have
continued more for Fafhion's
Sake than from any other Motive.——In 1632 he fet out on a
Tour of *Europe*, and travelled
thro' *France, Italy, Germany*, &c.
—Here however there appears an
effential Difference in the Biographers of his Life, *Cibber* in
his Lives of the Poets, Vol. II.
p. 216. pofitively declaring that
he went abroad with Sir *Kenelm
Digby*, and was abfent for the
Space of twelve Years, and *Langbaine* and all the other Writers
making him compleat his Tour
in as many Months.——Befides
which *Coxeter* in his MS. Notes
has beftowed on him as a travelling Tutor one Dr. *Rob. Creich-
ton*.—The latter Accounts however appears moft probable.——
During the Civil Wars he fuffer'd greatly for his Religion,

which was that of the Church of
Rome, and for his attachment to
the King's Caufe, under whom
he claim'd the Title of a Baronet ; yet, as there was no Record
or proper Enrollment of a Patent
to that Effect, he was not univerfally allowed the Title.—He
was ftrongly addicted to Books
and the Study of Poetry, in which
he indulged himfelf in a retired
Life, refiding moftly at a Lordfhip belonging to him, called
Pooley, in the Parifh of *Polefworth*
in *Warwickfhire*.——He died at
Derby upon the breaking of the
great Froft in *Feb.* 1684, in the
78th Year of his Age, and was
privately buried in the Chancel of
Polefworth Church.

Sir *Afton* is univerfally acknowledged to have been a great
Lover of the polite Arts, and by
fome is efteemed a confiderable
Poet. In his private Tranfactions
he was greatly deficient in Point of
Oeconomy, by which Means, together with his Loffes during the
Civil Wars, he was obliged to
difpofe of all his Patrimony during his Life-Time ; the Lordfhip
of *Afhbourne* being fold to Sir
William Boothby, Bart. and that
of *Pooley* above-mentioned, which
had belonged to the Family ever
fince *Richard* II's Time, he parted with to one *Humphrey Jen-
nings*, Efq; with the Refervation
of an Annuity for his own Life.

The dramatic Pieces he has
left behind him are as follow,

1. *Obftinate Lady.* C.
2. Ovid's *Tragedy.*
3. Trappolin *fuppos'd a
Prince.* T. C.
4. *A Mafque for Twelfth-
Night.*

Phillips and *Winftanley* have omit-
ed the fecond and laft of thefe in
their Account of his Writings,
and attributed to him two anonymous

nymous Pieces which are certainly none of his, entitled,

THERSITES. Interlude. and *Tyrannical Government*. T. C. *Coxeter* in his MS. Notes contradicts the Place of his Birth, fixing it at *Elveston* in *Derbyshire*, and adds moreover, that he was Nephew to *Philip*, the first Earl of *Chesterfield*, to whom and his Countess he has dedicated his *Masque for Twelfth Night*, which was performed at their Country Seat, two of their Sons acting in it.

CODRINGTON, *Robert*, A. M. This Writer was descended from an ancient and estimable Family in *Gloucestershire*, in which County he was born in the Year 1601, and at seventeen Years of Age, *viz.* on *July* 20, 1619, he was elected Dean of *Magdalen* College, *Oxford*, being then some Months standing in t at House. —Here he took the Degrees in Arts, that of Master being compleated in 1626.—He afterwards went abroad on his Travels, on his Return from which, being possess'd of an independent Fortune, he lived for several Years in *Norfolk*, and there remained. —At length, however, he went to *London*, where he settled for the Remainder of his Life, which was put a Period to in the general great Calamity of the Plague in that City, in 1665.—He was a rank Parliamentarian, as appears in the Life of the Earl of *Essex*, which he has written.— He was a voluminous Writer, but seems principally to have employed himself in Compilement and Translation, among the latter of which he has left a Translation of one *Latin* Play, written by R. *Ruggles*, of *Clare-Hall*, *Cambridge*, entitled,

IGNORAMUS. C.

COFFEY, Mr. *Charles*.—This Author was a Native of *Ireland*. —He had no very great Share of original Genius; his Turn was Humour, and having met with some Success in altering and patching up an old Farce of *Jevon*'s, called the *Devil of a Wife*, he pursued the same Kind of Plan with some other dramatic Pieces, but with very little Success; most of them having been very justly damned.—The Numbers and Names of them may however be seen in the following List,

1. *Beggar's Wedding*. Ballad Opera.
2. *Boarding-School Romps*. Bal. Farce.
3. *Devil to pay*. Ball. Farce.
4. *Devil upon two Sticks*. Ball. Farce.
5. *Female Parson*, Ball. Opera.
6. *Merry Cobler*. Farce.
7. *Southwark Fair*. C.
8. *Wife and no Wife*. Farce.

Mr. *Coffey* was in his Person considerably deformed; yet no Man was more ready to admit of, and even join in any Raillery on himself.—One remarkable Instance of which was his performing the Character of *Æsop* for his own Benefit in *Dublin*.—He died on the 13th of *May* 1745, and was buried in the Parish of St. *Clement's Danes*.

COLMAN, *George*, Esq;—This Gentleman is a living Writer, and but of an Age advancing towards that in which Perfection is to be expected.—He is Nephew to the late Countess of *Bath*, and has been warmly patronised by her noble Lord.—His Genius leads him to Works of Humour, a considerable Fund of which appears in some of the Essays which he has written in the Course of a periodical Paper, called the *Connoisseur*.

neilleur.——He feems at prefent however to pay his Court folely to the Comic Mufe, by whofe Infpiration he has already produced three dramatic Pieces, *viz.*

1. *Jealous Wife.* C.
2. *Mufical Lady.* Farce.
3. POLLY HONEYCOMBE. Farce.

Thefe Pieces, tho' not abfolutely perfect, have neverthelefs confiderable Merit.—In his *Petite Pieces* the Plots are fimple, and no great Matter of Incident introduced into them.—Yet they contain ftrong Character, and are aimed at the ridiculing of fafhionable and prevailing Follies, which ought to be made effential Points of Confideration in every Production of the Sock.—His more regular Comedy has the fame Merit with the others as to the Prefervation of Character; and it's Plot, tho' profeffedly borrowed, receives Advantages from the Conduct of it, which reflect Honour on the Author; and afford us the pleafing Profpect, amidft the prefent Dearth of comic Writers, of an ample Contribution from this Quarter to the Variety of our dramatic Entertainments of this more difficult Kind.—This Gentleman has been alfo fuppofed to be the Author of fome Effays, under the Title of the *Genius*, lately publifhed in the St. *James's Evening Poft.*

CONCANEN, *Mathew*, Efq;—This Gentleman was a Native of *Ireland*, and defcended from a good Family in that Kingdom.—He had a liberal Education beftowed on him by his Parents, and was bred to the Law.—His Wit and literary Abilities recommended him to the Favour of his Grace the Duke of *Newcaftle*, thro' whofe Intereft he obtained the Poft of Attorney-General of the Ifland of *Jamaica*, which Office he filled with the utmoft Integrity and Honour, and to the perfect Satisfaction of the Inhabitants, for upwards of twenty Years; 'when having acquir'd an ample Fortune, he was defirous of paffing the Clofe of his Life in his Native Country; with which Intention he quitted *Jamaica* and came to *London*, propofing to pafs fome little Time there before he went to fettle entirely in *Ireland*.—But the Difference of Climate between that Metropolis and the Place he had fo long been accuftomed to, had fuch an Effect on his Conftitution, that he fell into a galloping Confumption, of which he died in a few Weeks after his Arrival in *London*.

The World is obliged to him for a very elegant Tranflation of *Vida*'s Art of Poetry; for feveral original Poems, which, tho' fmall, have confiderable Merit; and for one Play, entitled,

WEXFORD *Wells.* Com.
He was alfo concerned with Mr. *Roome* and another Gentleman in altering *Richard Brome's Jovial Crew* into a Ballad Opera, in which Form it is now frequently performed.——As to his Profe Writings they are moftly political, or critical; in the latter of which, having pretty feverely attacked Mr. *Pope* and Dean *Swift*, the former of whom, whofe Difpofition was on no Occafion of the moft forgiving Nature, has handled him very feverely in the *Dunciad.*

CONGREVE, *William*, Efq;—This Gentleman was defcended from the ancient Family of the *Congreves*, of *Congreve* in *Staffordfhire*, his Father being fecond Son to *Richard Congreve*, of that Place.

——Some

—Some Authors, and in particular Sir *James Ware*, contend for his having been born in *Ireland*, but as *Jacob*, who was particularly acquainted with him, and who in his Preface acknowledges his Obligations to Mr. *Congreve* for his Communication of what related to himself, has absolutely contradicted that Report, I shall on his Authority, which I consider to be the same as Mr. *Congreve*'s own, fix the Spot of his Nativity at a Place called *Bardsa*, not far from *Leeds* in *Yorkshire*, being Part of the Estate of Sir *John Lewis*, his Great-Uncle by his Mother's Side.—It is certain, however, that he went over to that Kingdom very young.—For his Father being only a younger Brother, and provided for in the Army by a Commission on the *Irish* Establishment, was compelled to undertake a Journey thither in Consequence of his Command; which he afterwards parted with to accept of the Management of a considerable Estate belonging to the *Burlington* Family, which fix'd his Residence there.—However, tho' he suffer'd this Son to receive his first Tincture of Letters in the great School at *Kilkenny*, and afterwards, to compleat his Classical Learning under the Direction of Dr. *Ash*, in the University of *Dublin*, yet being desirous that his Studies should be directed to Profit as well as Improvement, he sent him over to *England* soon after the Revolution, and placed him as a Student in the *Temple*.—The dry, plodding Study of the Law, however, was by no Means suitable to the sprightly volatile Genius of Mr. *Congreve*, and therefore, tho' he did not want Approbation in those Studies to which his Genius led him, yet he did not even attempt to make any Proficiency in a Service which he was probably conscious he should make no Figure in.—Excellence and Perfection were what, it is apparent, he laid it down as his Principle from the very first, to make it his Aim the acquiring; for in the very earliest Education of his Genius, and a very early one indeed it was, *viz.* his Novel, call'd *Love and Duty reconciled,* written when he was not above seventeen Years of Age, he had not only endeavoured at, but indeed succeeded in, the presenting to the World not a meer Novel according to Taste and Fashion then prevailing, but a Piece which should point out, and be in itself a Model of, what Novels ought to be. —And tho' this cannot itself be called with Propriety a dramatic Work, yet he has so strictly adher'd to dramatic Rules in the Composition of it, that his arriving at so great a Degree of Perfection in the regular Drama, in so short a Time afterwards, is hardly to be wonder'd at.——His first Play was the *Old Batchelor,* and was the Amusement of some leisure Hours during a slow Recovery from a Fit of Illness, soon after his Return to *England,* and was in itself so perfect, that Mr. *Dryden,* on it's being shewn to him, declar'd he had never in his Life seen such a first Play; and that great Poet having, in Conjunction with Mr. *Southerne* and *Arthur Manwaring,* Esq; given it a slight Revisal, Dr. *Davenant,* who was the Manager of *Drury Lane* Theatre, and was delighted both with the Piece and it's Author, brought it on the Stage in 1693, where it met with such universal Approbation, that Mr. *Congreve,* tho' he was but nineteen Years of Age at the Time

of

of his writing it, became now consider'd as a Prop to the declining Stage, and a rising Genius in dramatic Poetry.—The next Year he produced the *Double Dealer*, which, for what Reason however I know not, did not meet with so much Success as the former.——The Merit of his first Play, however, had obtain'd him the Favour and Patronage of Lord *Hallifax*, and some peculiar Marks of Distinction from Queen *Mary*, on whose Death, which happened in the Close of this Year, he wrote a very elegant elegiac Pastoral.—In 1695, when *Betterton* opened the new House in *Lincoln's-Inn-Fields*, Mr. *Congreve* joining with him, gave him his Comedy of *Love for Love*, with which the Company opened their Campaign, and which met with such Success, that they immediately offer'd the Author a Share in the Management of the House, on Condition of his furnishing them with one Play yearly.——This Offer he accepted of; but whether thro' Indolence, or that Correctness which he look'd on as necessary to his Works, his *Mourning Bride* did not come out till 1697, nor his *Way of the World* till two Years after that.—The indifferent Success this last-mentioned Play, tho' an exceeding good one, met from the Public, compleated that Disgust to the Theatre, which a long Contest with *Jeremy Collier*, who had attacked the Immoralities of the *English* Stage, and more especially some of his Pieces, had begun, and he determined never more to write for the Stage.——This Resolution he punctually kept, and Mr. *Dennis's* Observation on that Point will, I am afraid, be found but too true, when he said, "that Mr. *Con-*

"*greve* quitted the Stage early, "and that Comedy left it with "him."—Yet, tho' he quitted dramatic Writing, he did not lay down the Pen entirely; but occasionally wrote many little Pieces both in Prose and Verse, all of which stand on the Records of literary Fame.

It is very possible, however, that he might not so soon have given Way to this Disgust, had not the Easiness of his Circumstances render'd any Subservience to the Opinions and Caprice of the Town absolutely unnecessary to him.—For his Abilities having very early in Life raised him to the Acquaintance of the Earl of *Halifax*, who was then the *Mæcenas* of the Age, that Nobleman, desirous of raising so promising a Genius above the Necessity of too hasty Productions, made him one of the Commissioners for licensing Hackney-Coaches, or, according to *Coxeter*, a Commission of the *Wine Licence.*—He soon after bestow'd on him a Place in the *Pipe-Office*, and not long after that gave him a Post in the Customs, worth six hundred Pounds *per Annum*.

In the Year 1718, he was appointed Secretary of *Jamaica*, so that, with all together, his Income towards the latter Part of his Life was upwards of twelve hundred Pounds a Year.—Thus rais'd above Dependance, it is no Wonder he would no longer render himself subject to the capricious Censures of impotent Critics.—And had his poetical Father, Mr. *Dryden*, ever been rais'd to the same Circumstances, it is probable that his *All for Love* would not now have been esteemed the best of his dramatic Pieces, nor would he have been compell'd for a bare Livelihood to the

Drudgery

Drudgery of producing four Plays in a Space of Time scarce more than sufficient for forming the Plot of one.

But to return to *Congreve*.—— The greatest Part of the last twenty Years of his Life were spent in Ease and Retirement, and he either did not, or affected not to give himself any Trouble about Reputation.——Yet some Part of that Conduct might proceed from a Degree of Pride; *T. Cibber*, in his Lives of the Poets, Vol. IV. p. 93. relates an Anecdote of him, which I cannot properly omit here,—" When the " celebrated *Voltaire*, says he, was " in *England*, he waited upon " *Congreve*, and pass'd him some " Compliments as to the Reputa- " tion and Merit of his Works. " —*Congreve* thank'd him, but " at the same Time told that in- " genious Foreigner, *be did not* " *chuse to be consider'd as an Au-* " *thor, but only as a* private Gen- " tleman, *and in that Light ex-* " *pected to be visited.—Voltaire* an- " swered, *That if be bad never* " *been any Thing but a private* " *Gentleman, in all Probability be* " *bad never been troubled with* " that *Visit.*——And observes in " his own Account of the Trans- " action, that he was not a little " disgusted with so unseasonable " Name.

Towards the Close of his Life he was much afflicted with the Gout, and making a Tour to *Bath*, for the Benefit of the Waters, was unfortunately overturned in his Chariot, by which it is suppos'd he got some inward Bruise, as he ever after complained of a Pain in his Side, and on his Return to *London*, continued gradually declining in his Health, till the 19th of *Jan.* 1729, when he died, aged 57, at his House in *Surry-Street*, in the *Strand*, and on the 26th following was buried in *Westminster-Abbey*, the Pall being supported by Persons of the first Distinction.

His dramatic Pieces are seven in Number, and their Titles as follow,

1. *Double Dealer.* C.
2. *Judgment of* PARIS. Masq;
3. *Love for Love.* C.
4. *Mourning Bride.* T.
5. *Old Batchelor.* C.
6. SEMELE. Oratorio.
7. *Way of the World.* C.

CONOLLY, Mr.—This Gentleman was of the Kingdom of *Ireland*, and a Student in the *Temple.*——He wrote one unsuccessful Play, entitled,

The *Connoisseur.* C.

Coxeter in his Notes calls him *Connol*, but on what Authority I know not.

CONSTABLE, Mr. *Francis.*—— This Gentleman was the Editor of an anonymous Piece, entitled

PATHOMACHIA.

which however was not published till some Time after the Death of the Author, who appears to have been a Friend of Mr. *Constable*'s, tho' that Gentleman has not obliged the World with informing it what was his Name.

Phillips and *Winstanley* have, among their innumerable Mistakes, ascribed this Piece to *Anthony Brewer.*

COOK, Mr. *John.*——Of this Author no farther Account is extant, than that he wrote in King *James* I's Time, and obliged the World with one Play, entitled,

GREEN'*s tu quoque.* C.

COOKE, *Edward*, Esq;——Of this Gentleman *Langbaine, &c.* make no farther Mention than

 that

that he wrote in King *Charles* II's Time, and was Author of one dramatic Piece, *viz.*

Love's Triumph. T. C.

Coxeter, in his MS. takes Notice of a Tranflation of *le Grand's Divine Epicurus*, or the *Empire of Pleafure over the Virtues*, by one *Edward Cooke*, Efq; from the Date of which, being publifhed in 1676, it is probably the Work of this Author.

COOKE, Mr. *Thomas.*—This Gentleman, who for any thing I know to the contrary, is ftill living, was born at *Braintree* in *Effex*, and educated at *Felfted* School in the fame County, about the Year 1707.—He muft have made a very rapid Progrefs in Literature, for in 1726, at which Time he was only nineteen Years of Age, he gave the World a very correct Edition of the Works of the famous *Andrew Marvel*, prefixed to which is a Life of the Author.—This Work he dedicated to the Earl of *Pembroke*, who being much delighted with the Learning and Abilities of fo young a Writer, became a very warm Patron to him (as he had before been to the great Mr. *Locke*,) and even wrote feveral of the Notes to his Tranflation of *Hefiod*, which he publifhed 1728.—Befides thefe Mr. *Cooke* has obliged the Public with a Tranflation of *Cicero de Natura Deorum*, and of the Comedies of *Terence*, and prepared an Edition and Tranflation of *Plautus* alfo, the *Amphytrion* only of whom however he has hitherto publifhed.—His Reputation and Merit therefore as a claffical Writer are apparently great —Which is more than I can venture to fay of him as a dramatic Author.—Yet as he has launched into that Path we cannot refufe his Pieces a Place

here, tho' they met with no Succefs at the Time they appeared. —Their Titles are as follow,

1. ALBION. Mafque.
2. *Eunuch.* F.
3. *Love the Caufe and Cure of Grief.* T.
4. *Mournful Nuptials.* T.
5. *Triumphs of Love and Honour.* T.

He was alfo concerned with Mr. *Mottley*, in writing a Farce, called, *Penelope.*

of which fee more particularly in its proper Place, in the former Part of this Work.

COOPER, Mrs.—Of this Lady, who is ftill living, and whom we muft rank among the Female Geniufes of this Kingdom, I can trace nothing farther than that fhe is the Widow of one Mr. *Cooper*, an Auctioneer, that fhe was the Editor of a Work, entitled the *Mufes Library*, and Author of one Comedy, entitled

Rival Widows. C.

COREY, Mr. *John.*—All that is recorded of this Gentleman is that he lived in King *Charles* II's Reign, and fent forth into the World a dramatic Piece, which is entirely a Compilement, or rather Plagiary from other Authors.—The Title of it is,

The Generous Enemies. C.

COREY, *John.*—This Gentleman has been, by fome of the Writers, confounded with the laft-mentioned one.—But is indeed quite another Perfon, having flourifhed in Queen *Anne*'s and King *George* Ift's Reigns.—He was defcended from an ancient Family in *Cornwall*, but was himfelf born at *Barnftaple* in *Devonfhire*.—He was intended for the Study of the Law, and to that Purpofe was enter'd of *New-Inn*; but having a theatrical Turn, and preferring the Oratory of the

Stage

Stage to that of the Bar, he did not long continue there, before he turned Player, which Profeſſion he followed for twenty Years, to the Time of his Death, which happened about 1721.——Yet it is probable he might have made a more conſpicuous Figure in the Walk of his firſt Deſtination; for tho' he was ackuowledged to be a juſt and ſenſible Speaker, yet being but low in Stature, and his Voice none of the beſt, he was ever obliged to work againſt the Stream, and labour with Difficulties which prevented his being held in any very high Eſtimation in a Profeſſion which, of all others, requires the greateſt Number of Perfeₓtions, and to arrive at Excellence in which a Perſon ought not to be deficient in any one Advantage that either Nature or Art can beſtow.——He brought two dramatic Pieces on the Stage, whoſe Titles are as follow,

1. *A Cure for Jealouſy.* C.
2. *The Metamorphoſis.* C.

CORI, Sign. *Angelo.*—Of this Gentleman I know nothing more than that he was an *Italian* Muſician, and that I have met with two *Italian* Operas, with his Name prefixed to them, performed at the King's Theatre in the *Hay-market.*—Their Titles are,

Conqueſt of the Golden Fleece. Ital.-Opera.

HYPSIPILE. Ital.-Op.

COTTON, *Charles,* Eſq;—This Gentleman lived in the Reigns of *Charles* II. and *James* II. and reſided for the greateſt Part of his Life at *Bereſford* in *Stafford-ſhire.*—He wrote one dramatic Piece, or rather tranſlated it from the *French* of *Corneille,* for the Uſe of his Siſter Mrs. *Stanhope Hutchinſon,* to whom, when it was publiſhed, which was not till many Years after the Writing of it, he thought proper to dedicate it.——It is entitled,

HORACE. T.

yet tho', on Account of this Piece, I have a Right to mention him as a dramatic Writer, yet his principal Fame was founded on his Merit as a burleſque Writer, in which Light he is ſo conſiderable as to ſtand even in Competition with the celebrated Author of *Hudibraſs* himſelf.—His moſt celebrated Poem of this Kind is his *Scarronides,* or Traveſtie of his firſt and fourth Books of the *Æneid.*—But altho' from the Title one would be apt to imagine it an Imitation of *Scarron*'s famous Traveſtie of the ſame Author, yet, on an Examination, it will be found greatly to excel not only that, but every Attempt of that Kind hitherto made in any Language.—He has alſo tranſlated ſeveral of *Lucian*'s Dialogues in the ſame Manner, under the Title of the *Scoffer ſcoff'd.*——And written another Poem of a more ſerious Kind, called the *Wonders of the Peak.*—— The exaₓt Period of either Mr. *Cotton*'s Birth or his Death, are not any where to my Knowledge recorded, but it is probable the latter happen'd about the Time of the Revolution.—Neither is it better known what his Circumſtances were with reſpeₓt to Fortune; they appear however to have been eaſy, if one may form any Judgment from the Turn of his Writings, which ſeems to be ſuch as it is ſcarcely poſſible any one could indulge in, whoſe Mind was not perfeₓtly at Eaſe.—Yet there is one Anecdote in relation to him, which I cannot avoid relating, and which ſeems to ſhew that his Vein of Humour could not reſtrain itſelf on any Conſideration, viz. that in Confequence of a fingle Couplet in his *Virgil traveftie*, wherein he has made mention of a pecular Kind of Ruff worn by a Grandmother of his, who lived in the Peak, he loft an Eftate of four hundred Pounds *per Annum*, the old Lady, whofe Humour and tefty Difpofition he could by no Means have been a Stranger to, never being able to forgive the Liberty he had taken with her, and having her Fortune wholly in her own Difpofal, altho' fhe had before made him her fole Heir, alter'd her Will, and gave it all away to an abfolute Stranger.

COWLEY, Mr. *Abraham.* — This excellent Poet was the Son of a Grocer near the End of *Chancery-Lane*, in *Fleet-Street*, *London*, at which Place our Author was born in the Year 1618. —His Mother, thro' the Intereft of fome Friends, procur'd him to be admitted a King's Scholar in *Weftminfter* School, where his Inclination and Genius for Poetry fhewed itfelf very early, for *Langbaine*, *Jacob*, *Gilden*, and all the other Writers fay that he wrote the tragical Hiftory of *Pyramus* and *Thifbe* at ten Years old, at twelve that of *Conftantia*, and that at thirteen he publifhed a Collection of Poems under the Title of *Poetical Bloffoms*; *Cibber* however, in Oppofition to them all, does not fpeak of the Publication of this Collection till his fixteenth Year, which I cannot help thinking the moft probable Account. —But one Thing extreamly remarkable in him was, that with fo extraordinary a natural Genius, he had fo very bad a Memory that his Teachers could never bring him to retain even the common Rules of Grammar. So that had he not formed the moft

intimate Acquaintance with the Books themfelves from which thofe Rules are drawn, he could never have been Mafter of them. —In 1636 he was elected a Scholar of *Trinity Colledge, Cambridge,* and removed to that Univerfity. —Here he went thro' all his Exercifes with a remarkable Degree of Reputation, and at the fame Time muft have purfued his Poetical Turn with great Eagernefs, as it appears that the greateft Part of his Poems were written before he left the Univerfities. —He had taken his Degree of Mafter of Arts before 1643, when in Confequence of the turbulent Times, he, among many others, was ejected from the College; whereon retiring to *Oxford*, he enter'd himfelf of St. *John*'s College, and that very Year, under the Denomination of a *Scholar of Oxford*, publifhed a Satire called *the Puritan and the Papift.*—It is apparent however, that he did not remain very long at *Oxford*, for his Zeal to the Royal Caufe engaging him in the Service of the King, who was very fenfible of his Abilities, and by whom he was frequently employed, he attended his Majefty in many of his Journies and Expeditions, and gain'd not only that Prince's Efteem, but that of many other great Perfonages, and in particular of Lord *Falkland*, one of the principal Secretaries of State.

During the Heat of the Civil War he was fettled in the Earl of St. *Alban*'s Family, and when the Queen Mother was obliged to retire into *France* he accompanied her thither, labour'd ftrenuoufly in the Affairs of the Royal Family, undertook feveral very dangerous Journeys on their Account, and was the principal Inftrument

in

in maintaining an epistolary Correspondence between the King and Queen.

In the Year 1656 it was judged proper that Mr. *Cowley* should come over to *England*, and under Pretence of Privacy and Retirement give Notice of the Situation of Affairs in this Kingdom to those by whom he was employed. —Soon after his Arrival however he was seiz'd, in the Search after another Gentleman of considerable Note in the King's Party; but altho' it was thro' Mistake that he was taken, yet when the Republicans found all their Attempts of every Kind to bring him over to their Cause proved ineffectual, he was committed to a severe Confinement, and it was even with considerable Difficulty that he obtained his Liberty, when, venturing back to *France*, he remained there in his former Situation, till near the Time of the King's Return.

Soon after the Restoration he became possess'd of a very competent Estate, thro' the Favour of his principal Friends the Duke of *Buckingham*, and the Earl of St. *Albans*, and being now upwards of forty Years of Age, he took up a Resolution to pass the Remainder of a Life, which had been a Scene of Tempest and Tumult, in that Situation which had ever been the Object of his Wishes, a studious Retirement.— His Eagerness to get out of the Bustle of a Court and City, made him less careful than he might have been in the Choice of a healthful Habitation in the Country, by which Means he found his Solitude from the very Beginning, suit less with the Constitution of his Body than with his Mind.—His first Rural Residence was at *Barn Elms*, a Place

which lying low, and being near a large River was subject to variety of Breezes, from Land and Water, and liable in the Winter Time to great Inconvenience from the Dampness of the Soil.—The Consequences of this Mr. *Cowley* too soon experienced, by being seized with a dangerous and lingering Fever.—On his Recovery from this he removed to *Chertsey*, a Situation not much more healthful, where he had not long been before he was seized with another consuming Disease.—Having languish'd under this for some Months, he at length got the better of it, and seem'd pretty well recover'd from its bad Symptoms; when one Day, in the Heat of Summer of 1667, staying too long in the Fields to give some Directions to his Labourers, he caught a most violent Cold, which was attended with a Defluxion and Stoppage in his Breast, which for Want of timely Care, by treating it as a common Cold, and refusing Advice till it was past Remedy, took him off the Stage of Life on the 28th of *July* in that Year, being the 49th of his Age, and on the 3d of *August* following he was interr'd in *Westminster-Abbey*, near the Ashes of *Chaucer* and his beloved *Spencer*.

Mr. *Cowley*, as a Writer, had perhaps as much Fire and Imagination as any Author of the *English* Nation; his Wit is genuine and natural; but then his Versification is frequently irregular, rough and incorrect, and the Redundancy of his Fancy outrunning the Power of his Expression; this latter appears sometimes puerile, and even flat and insipid.——Yet these Faults are certainly excusable, when we consider at how early a Time of Life

almoſt all his Pieces were written.
—Had he lived in a leſs perplexed
Period of our Hiſtory, or been
himſelf leſs principally concerned
in the Tranſactions of the Period
he did live in, we perhaps might
have met with greater Pleaſure
from thoſe Writings which he
might have produced at a more
advanced Age, when the Judgment, being arriv'd at greater Maturity, could have held a tighter
Rein over the rapid and unruly
Courſers of Imagination.—It is
evident that *Fancy* was his principal Directreſs, and by a kind of
Sympathy with Writers of the
ſame Diſpoſition, he became involuntarily a Poet.—He tells us
himſelf, that his Admiration of
Spencer, whom he had read over
before he was twelve Years old,
firſt inſpir'd him with an Inclination for Poetry; and what Writer has Imagination equal to *Spencer?* And we are alſo told that
his accidentally meeting with the
Works of *Pindar*, the moſt exalted Genius for the Flights of
Fancy among the Ancients, led
him into that *Pindarique* Way of
Writing, in which, however faulty
he may ſometimes be in Reſpect
to Numbers, he has never yet
been excelled in the Force of his
Figures, and the Sublimity of his
Stile and Sentiments.

As a Man, in his public Capacity, he was active and diſcerning, of the ſtricteſt Integrity,
and moſt unſhaken Loyalty.—In
his private Life, he was eaſy of
Acceſs, gentle, polite and modeſt,
generous in his Diſpoſition, temperate in his Life, devout and
pious in his Religion, a ſocial
Companion and a ſincere Friend.
—Or, to ſum up his Character in
a few Words, we need only repeat the Words of his Maſter
King *Charles* II. who on the

" News of his Death declar'd that
" Mr. *Cowley* had not left a bet-
" ter Man behind him in *Eng-*
" *land*."—It is moreover one of
the peculiar Advantages of exalted Virtue, that even bad Men
reverence it, and are pleaſed to
draw ſome Honour to themſelves
by paying Tribute to it: A Monument therefore was erected to the
Memory of *Cowley*, by *George
Villers*, Duke of *Buckingham*, in
1675.——His dramatic Works,
which however are thoſe of all
his Writings the leaſt eſteem'd,
are four in Number, their Titles
are as follow,

  1. *Cutter of* COLEMAN *Street*.
    Com.

  2. *Guardian*.   C.
  3. *Love's Riddle*.   Paſt.-C.
  4. *Naufragium Joculare*. C.

Cox, Mr. *Robert*.—This Author, if he has a Right to be
called by that Title, was an excellent Comedian, who lived in
the Reign of King *Charles* I.—
But when the Ringleaders of the
Rebellion, and the pretended Reformers of the Nation, among
other Acts of puritanical Zeal
ſuppreſs'd the Repreſentations of
the Theatre, this Performer was
compelled for a Livelihood to
betake himſelf to the making
of Drolls or Farces, which were
in general nothing more than ſelect Scenes of Humour from ſome
of the Plays which had been the
greateſt Favorites, put together
without any Order, Regularity or
apparent Deſign.—Theſe Drolls
he found Means of getting licenced, or rather connived at by
the Legiſlature, and perform'd, as
it were by Stealth, under the
Sanction of Ropedancing, at the
Red-Bull Playhouſe, and in Country Towns at Wakes and Fairs.—
A large Collection of them were
publiſhed after the Reſtoration by
Kirk-

Kirkman; for some Account of which, and the Plays they were selected from, see the first Volume of this Work under the Title of WITTS, or *Sport upon Sport.*——There is another Collection published, as a second Part to the former, the Pieces in which are supposed by *Kirkman* to have been originally written by *Cox*, and which consists of the following Interludes, excepting only the first, which I believe is known to be his, viz.

  1. ACTÆON *and* DIANA. Interl.
  2. AHASUERUS *and* ESTHER.
  3. *Black Man.* Inter.
  4. DIPHILO *and* GRANIDA. Ditto.
  5. *King* SOLOMON's *Wisdom.*
  6. PHILETUS *and* CONSTANTIA.
  7. VENUS *and* ADONIS.

In these Kind of Drolls he used to perform the principal Parts himself, and that so well, that he was a great Favourite, not only in the Country, but also at *London*, and in the Universities themselves. And *Langbaine* relates the following humourous Anecdote of him, (which proves him to have been a very natural Performer,) that once after he had been playing the Part of *Simpleton* the Smith, in his own *Diana* and *Actæon*, a *real* Smith of some Eminence in those Parts who saw him act. came to him, and offer'd to take him as his Journeyman, and even to allow him Twelve-pence a Week more than the customary Wages.

CRAUFURD, *David*, Esq;——This Gentleman was a *North Briton*, of *Dumfoy* in the Western Part of *Scotland*, and was Historiographer for that Kingdom to Queen *Anne.*——He wrote two Plays, whose Titles were as follow,

  1. *Courtship Alamode.* Com.
  2. *Love at first Sight.* Com.

The first of these Pieces he left to the Care of Mr. *Pinkethman* the Comedian to publish, his Affairs calling him into his own Country just as it was about to be acted.

His other Writings are, a Set of Love Epistles in Verse, in Imitation of *Ovid*, and intitled *Ovidius Britannicus*, being an Intrigue between two Persons of Quality ; *Three Novels*, in one Volume 8vo. and some *Memoirs of the Affairs and Revolutions of Scotland.*

CRISP, Mr.——I know nothing farther of this Gentleman than that he is a living Writer, to whom *Victor*, in his History of the Stage, has attributed a Tragedy, which was acted in 1754 at *Drury Lane* Theatre, but published without any Author's Name, entitled,

VIRGINIA. T.

CROWNE, Mr. *John.*——This Gentleman was the Son of an independant Minister in that Part of *America* called *Nova Scotia*, but whether born there or not is not apparent.——He received his Education however in that Climate, the rigid Manners of which however not altogether suiting with the Vivacity of his Genius, he determined to quit that Country and seek his Fortune in *England.*——At his first Arrival here, his Necessities compell'd him to accept of an Office still more formal and disgustful than even his Situation in *America.*——This was no other than the being Gentleman-Usher to an old Independent Lady of Quality.——Soon weary of this disagreeable Drudgery, he had Recourse to his Pen.

for Support; and as neither the Precifenefs of his Education, nor the Diftrefs of his Circumftances could fupprefs the Fire of his Genius, his Writings, which were in the dramatic Way, foon render'd his Abilities known to the Town and Court.—When, as it appears, fortunately for him, the Earl of *Rochefter*, whofe Enmity to *Dryden* made him readily fnatch at any Opportunity of mortifying him, prevail'd on the Queen to lay her Commands on *Crowne*, in Preference to that Poet, for the writing of a Mafque, to be performed at Court, which he executed under the Title of *Califto*.

That it was not from any peculiar Regard to our Author himfelf that Lord *Rochefter* urged this Nomination is very evident, for at no greater Diftance than two Years afterwards, the great Succefs of Mr. *Crowne*'s two Tragedies of the *Deftruction of Jerufalem*, excited the Envy of that Nobleman fo far, as to make him as fevere an Enemy as he had appeared to be a warm Friend to him; nay he even endeavour'd to do him Prejudice at Court, by informing the King of his Defcent and Education, which however his Majefty was fo far from paying any Regard to, that he even treated the Informer with that Contempt. fo mean an Infinuation juftly merited.——Mr. *Crowne* was now highly in Favour at Court, and particularly with the King, as indeed any one might be who contributed to his Pleafures, and it is well known that *Charles* II. was ever peculiarly fond of theatrical Amufements. —The Favours he received from this Monarch, added to the natural Gaiety of his Temper, induced him to join with the *Tory*

Party; in Confequence of which he wrote a Comedy called the *City Politics*, in which the *Whigs* were feverely fatirized.——When written he found much Difficulty in getting it reprefented, the oppofite Party, and particularly Lord *Arlington*, the Lord Chamberlain, who was fecretly in the Whig Intereft, endeavouring all they could to get it fupprefs'd.—At laft, however, by the immediate Command of the King himfelf it was brought on the Stage, but tho' even the contrary Party acknowledged it to be a good Play, it created Mr. *Crowne* a great many Enemies, which Circumftance, added to the Precarioufnefs of theatrical Emoluments induced him to apply to the King for fome Poft that might fecure him from Diftrefs for the Remainder of his Life.—This his Majefty readily promifed him, but infifted on our Author's writing one Comedy more before he took Leave of the Mufes, and to obviate all Objections which he made of being at a Lofs for a Plot, &c. put into his Hands, by Way of a Ground Work, a *Spanifh* Play called *Non puede effer*.—On this Mr. *Crowne* immediately fet to work, and altho', when he had proceeded fome Length in it, he found that it had been before tranflated, under the Title of *Tarugo*'s *Wiles*, by Sir *Thomas St. Serfe*, and had even been damn'd in the Reprefentation, yet he proceeded in his Plan, and produc'd his very excellent Comedy of Sir *Courtly Nice*.—And now he feem'd to be at the very Summit of his Hopes being gratified in the Performance of the King's Promife, when lo! in an Inftant an unfortunate Accident intervened to dafh them all at once, and tumble down the Fabric

bric which he had been rearing ! —This was no lefs than the fudden Death of the King, who was feized with an Apopletic Fit, on the Day of its laft Rehearfal, and tho' he did indeed revive from it, died in three Days afterwards, leaving our unfortunate Bard plung'd in the Depth of Diftrefs and Difappointment.

What were the particular Occurrences of Mr. *Crowne*'s Life after this great Lofs, I have not been able to trace; but it is moft probable that writing for the Stage became his fole Support, as we find befides the Play on which his Expectations were thus fix'd, and which was play'd at that Time with great Succefs, (as indeed it has ever fince been on every Revival of it) that he wrote five others, the laft of which made its firft Appearance in 1698. How long he lived afterwards is uncertain, for altho' *Coxeter*, in his Notes, informs us that he was living in 1703, no Writer has pretended to affign the abfolute Date of his Death.—It is probable however, that he did not long furvive that Period, and we are told by *Jacob* that he was buried in St. *Giles*'s in the Fields.

As a Man he feems to have poffefs'd many amiable and focial Virtues, mingled with great Vivacity and Eafinefs of Difpofition.—As a Writer his numerous Works bear fufficient Teftimony of his Merit.—His chief Excellence lay in Comedy, yet his Tragedies are far from contemptible. —His Plots are for the moft Part his own Invention, his Characters are in general ftrongly colour'd and highly finifhed, and his Dialogue lively and fpirited, attentively diverfified, and well adapted to the feveral Speakers.

So that on the whole he may affuredly be allowed to ftand at leaft in the third Rank of our dramatic Writers.

The Pieces he has left behind him are feventeen in Number, and their Names are as follow.

1. *Ambitious Statefman.* T.
2. ANDROMACHE. T.
3. CALIGULA. T.
4. CALISTO. Mafque.
5. CHARLES *the Eighth of France.* Trag.
6. *City Politicks.* C.
7. *Country Wit.* C.
8. DARIUS, *K. of Perfia.* T.
9. *Deftruction of Jerufalem.* T. in two Parts.
10. *English Fryars.* C.
11. HENRY VII. Tr. two Parts.
12. JULIANA, *Princefs of Po-* LAND. T. C.
13. *Married Beau.* C.
14. REGULUS. T.
15. Sir COURTLY NICE. C.
16. THYESTES. T.
17. TITUS ANDRONICUS. Trag.

CUMBERLAND, *Richard*, Efq; —Of this Gentleman I know nothing further than that he is ftill living, and enjoys fome Poft under the Government.——He wrote the Prologue and Epilogue to Mr. *Bentley*'s Comedy of the *Wifhes*, and has publifhed in a very pompous Manner in Quarto, a Tragedy of his own writing, but which was never acted, entitled,

The *Banifhment of* CICERO. Trag. *Vid.* Vol. I. APPENDIX.

CUTTS, *John.*—Of this Gentleman I know nothing further than that his Name ftands as an Author in the Title Page of one dramatic Piece, entitled,

Rebellion defeated. Trag.

D. D.

D.

D. Gent.—These Initials I find no where but in the *British Theatre*, the Author of which, has attributed them to a Translator of *Guarini's Pastor Fido* some time in the seventeenth Century, tho' without any particular Date, the Translation has assign'd to it the *English* Title of,

The *Faithful Shepherd*. Past. Com.

D. I.—These Initials stand equally in the Title Pages of two several dramatic Pieces; but as they are of very different Kinds, and thirteen Years Distance in their Dates, it is scarcely probable they should be both the Work of the same Author. Their Titles are,

1. *Hell's High Court of Justice*.
2. The *Mall*. C.

Langbaine tells us that the last was ascribed by Dr. *Hyde*, the *Proto-bibliothecarius*, or upper Librarian of one of the Universities, to Mr. *Dryden*, but as it is probable the Doctor might have no stronger Foundation for his Conjecture than the mere Correspondence of the Letters I. D. with the Words *John Dryden*; I am apt to join in Opinion with *Langbaine*, that the Dissimilarity of Stile, especially in the Epistle Dedicatory, in which Mr. *Dryden*'s Manner was in general very characteristic, is an Argument sufficiently strong against the too peremptorily giving the Honour or ascribing the Disgrace of being the Author of it to that very celebrated Writer.

D. R. Gent.—These two Letters are prefixed to a Play written in King *Charles* Ist's Time, entitled,

A New Trick to cheat the Devil. C.

D. T.—Under these Letters there is a Play in Print, call'd,

The *Bloody Banquet*. T.

In some of the old Catalogues however, the same Play is attributed to one *Thomas Barker*.

DALTON, The Rev. Dr.—— This ingenious Gentleman is, I believe, still living.——He was formerly Tutor or Governor to the only Son of *Algernon Seymour* late Duke of *Somerset*, a very hopeful and promising young Gentleman, whose Death in the Bloom of Youth and Expectation stand on Record in a very affecting Manner, in two Letters on that Occasion, written by his afflicted Mother the Countess of *Hertford* afterwards Duchess of *Somerset* and which have since her Death been published in some of the periodical Papers.—But to return to Dr. *Dalton*; his Claim to a Mention in this Work is his having alter'd and rendered more fit for dramatic Execution, *Milton*'s admirable Masque at *Ludlow* Castle, which this Gentleman has considerably extended and rendered dramatical not only by the Insertion of several Songs and different Passages selected from other of *Milton*'s Works, but also by the Addition of several Songs and Improvements of his own, so ably adapted to the Manner of the original Author of the Masque as by no Means to disgrace the more genuine Parts. but on the contrary must greatly exalt our Ideas of Dr. *Dalton*'s poetical Abilities. — It has moreover had the Advantage of being most excellently set to Music by Dr. *Arne* and stands now on the regular List of our dramatic Entertainments, under the Title of

COMUS. Masque.

I can

I cannot omit mentioning, to this Gentleman's great Honour, that, during the Run of this Piece, he induſtriouſly ſought out a Daughter of *Milton*, whom he heard was not only in very low Circumſtances, but of ſo advanced an Age as to be incapable of providing for herſelf, and procured her a Benefit from this Play, the Profits of which to her it is ſaid amounted to upwards of one hundred and twenty Pounds.

DANCER, Mr. *John*.—This Author, who lived in the Reign of *Charles* II. is ſaid to have been born in *Ireland*, but whether he was ſo or not, it is certain that he lived a great Part of his Time in that Kingdom.——About the Year 1670 he came over into *England*, and being perfect Maſter of the *French* and *Italian* Languages, he tranſlated three dramatick Pieces from the Originals of three eminent Poets, viz. *Taſſo*, *Corneille*, and *Quinault*.—The Pieces are as follow,

   1. AGRIPPA, King of ALBA. Trag.

   2. AMYNTA. Paſt.

   4. NICOMEDE. T. C.

Langbaine has given us this Author's Name DANCER, *alias*, DAUNCY, but whence the Doubt concerning his Name ariſes I know not, unleſs from the Irregularity of Spelling which was given way to at the Time this Gentleman wrote.

DANIEL, Mr. *Samuel*.—This Gentleman, who ſtands in high Eſtimation among the Writers of the Age he liv'd in, both as a Poet and an Hiſtorian, flouriſhed in the Reigns of Queen *Elizabeth* and King *James* I.—He was the Son of a Muſic Maſter, and born near *Taunton* in *Somerſetſhire*, in the Year 1562.—At 17 Years

of Age he was admitted a Commoner of *Magdalen* Hall *Oxford*, at which Place he continued for about the Space of three Years, during which Time, by the Aſſiſtance of an excellent Tutor and the Dint of great Aſſiduity and Application on his own Side, he made a very conſiderable Progreſs in all Branches of Academical Learning.—Thoſe which were of a graver Turn however not ſo well ſuiting his Genius, he aplied himſelf principally to Hiſtory and Poetry, which continued to be his Favourites during the Remainder of his Life.—At the Expiration of the abovementioned Term he quitted the Univerſity, and came up to *London*, where his own Merit, and the Intereſt of his Brother-in-law, *John Florio*, the celebrated Author of an *Italian* Dictionary, recommended him to the Favour of Queen *Anne*, King *James* Iſt's Conſort, who was pleaſed to confer on him the Honour of being firſt Gentleman extraordinary and afterwards one of her Grooms of the Privy Chamber ; which being a Poſt of very little Employment, the Income of it enabled him to rent a Houſe at a little Diſtance from *London*, which had a very fine Garden belonging to it, amongſt the ſolitary Amuſements of which he is ſaid to have compoſed the moſt of his Plays. Towards the latter Part of his Life he quitted *London* entirely, and retired, according to Dr. *Fuller*, to a Farm near the *Deviſes* in *Wiltſhire*, but *Wood* fixes the Place of his Retreat at *Beckington* near *Philips Norton* in *Somerſetſhire*, where he commenc'd Farmer, and after ſome Years ſpent in a healthful Exerciſe of that Employment, in the

Service

Service of the Mufes and in religious Contemplation he died in the Year 1619.

Such is the Sum of the Accounts given by different Authors of this Writer's Life.—Yet there is an evident Confufion in it which I cannot fay I well know how to clear up with refpect to his Age at the Time of his Death, all the Authors feeming to be agreed in the Year when he died ; nay, *Wood* has even given us a Copy of his Monumental Infcription, which affixes a Date to his Death : and yet *Langbaine, Gildon,* and *Jacob,* have all pofitively declared that he lived till near eighty Years of Age.—Nor can I account for this any otherwife, than by fuppofing that the two laft have, without any Examination or even Reflection, copied the grofs Errors of the firft, who has, in Concurrence with the Account given of him by *Wood,* abfolutely fixed his Birth in 1562, and his Death in 1619, at which Time he could have been only Fiftyfeven, and yet immediately after afferted that he lived to fourfcore Years of Age.—And even after all there is fome Difficulty remaining, as we find a corrected Edition of his *Cleopatra* greatly altered, and alfo one of the *Vifion of the twelve Goddeffes,* which is faid to be publifhed by the Author from his own Copy, in Juftification of himfelf, from a fpurious Edition before printed without his Knowledge ; both of which are dated in 1623.—But as the general Edition of his Works in 1623 were publifhed by his Brother Mr. *John Daniel,* it is poffible thefe Alterations may have been from MS. Copies which he had himfelf prepared for the Prefs before his Death, fince it is fcarcely

poffible that *Wood,* who had feen his Monument, could have miftaken the Date infcribed upon it. —The abovenamed Monument was erected to his Memory by the Lady *Anne Clifford,* afterwards Countefs of *Pembroke,* to whom he had formerly been Tutor, and who was a very great Lover and Encourager of Learning and learned Men.

His dramatic Pieces, which however are not equal to fome other of his Poetical Works, and ftill lefs fo to his Hiftories, which are yet held in very high Eftimation, are the following Five, *viz.*

1. CLEOPATRA. T.
2. HYMEN's *Triumph.* Paft. Trag-Com.
3. PHILOTAS. T.
4. *Queen's* ARCADIA. Paft.
5. *Vifion of the twelve Goddeffes.*

He was alfo Poet Laureat to King *James* I. in which Honour he was fucceeded by the celebrated *Ben Jonfon,* but in what Year he himfelf was firft promoted to the Laureat, I do not find any Account recorded.

DARCY, *James,* Efq;—This Gentleman was a Native of the County of *Galway* in *Ireland,* whether yet living or not I cannot pretend to affert.—But he has obliged the Public with two dramatic Pieces, both of them performed at the Theatre Royal in *Dublin.*—Their refpective Titles are,

1. *Love and Ambition.* T.
2. *Orphan of* VENICE. T.

DAUBORN, alias DABORN, The Rev. Mr. *Robert.*——Tho' the fame Difference appears in the Spelling of this Author's Name as in Mr. *Dancers,* beforementioned, the laft is certainly right.—He lived in the Reign of King

King *James* I. and had a liberal Education, being Mafter of Arts, but in what Univerfity he took his Degree appears uncertain.— He was alfo in holy Orders, and it is probable had a Living in *Ireland*.—At leaft it is apparent he was in that Kingdom, from a Sermon publifhed by him on *Zech*. ii. 7. in the Year 1618. which is faid in the Title-Page to have been preached at *Waterford*—He wrote the two following Plays,

1. *Chriftian turn'd Turk.* T.
2. *Poor Man's Comfort.* T. C.

D'AVENANT, *Charles,* LL. D. —This Gentleman was eldeft Son of Sir *William D'Avenant,* the Poet Laureat, whom we are juft about to mention.—He was educated at *Baliol* Colledge, *Oxford,* where he was enter'd a Gentleman-Commoner, but leaving it without taking a Degree there, had afterwards the Degree of Doctor of Civil Law conferr'd on him elfewhere.—At his Father's Death, which happen'd in 1668, he fucceeded to the Management of the Theatre Royal in *Drury* Lane, in which however he did not long continue.—In 1685, he was elected Burgefs of St. *Ives* in *Cornwall,* and was at the Time of his Death *Infpector General of the Exports and Imports of the Cuftoms.* —He wrote one dramatic Piece, entitled,

CIRCE. Dram.-Op.

Coxeter, in his Notes, has afferted that he was enter'd Gentleman Commoner at *Baliol* Coll. in 1671, that befides the above-mentioned Place, he was a Commiffioner of the *Excife* from 1679 to 1688, and that he died *Nov.* 6, 1714. ——Yet thefe Particulars are not only contradictory to fome known Facts, but even diffonant to each other,—For befides that the Death of his Father, the Period of which is perfectly well known, and at which Time he became Manager of the Theatre, (a Poft which requires the moft ripened Judgment) was in 1668, three Years before the Time affigned for his going firft to the Univerfity, it is moreover extremely improbable, that a Poft of fo much Confequence and Dignity as that of Commiffioner of the Excife fhould be beftowed on a Youth who, by that Account, could be but juft returned from Colledge.——It is moft likely therefore, the Date there mentioned might be that of his receiving the Dignity of Doctor of Laws.—Whether or not he was Commiffioner of *Excife* I know not, fince it is not improbable that *Charles* II. might beftow that Place on the Son of one who had been fo faithful a Servant to his Family as Sir *William;* nor more unlikely that at the Revolution it might be taken from him for the very fame Reafon ; if fo, it is not unreafonable to imagine if *Coxeter's* Date of Dr. *Davenant's* Death is right (tho' *Whincop,* and after him *Chetwood,* in his *Britifh Theatre,* have placed it about 1700) that, on Queen *Anne's* Acceffion to the Throne, the Poft he enjoyed in the Cuftoms might have been beftowed on him by Way of Recompence for the Lofs of the other.

DAVENANT, Sir *William,* Knt.—To this Gentleman, whofe variegated Life I am now about to relate the Circumftances of, the *Englifh* Stage perhaps ftands more deeply indebted than to any other Writer of this Nation, with Refpect to the Refinement of Poetry, and his zealous Application to the promoting and contributing towards thofe rational

tional Pleafures, which are fitteft for the Entertainment of a civilized People.—And the greater fhould his Merit be efteemed in this Particular, fince not only the important Affairs of the State, whofe Neceffities demanded his Affiftance, and of which he was no unactive Member at a Period of great Confufion and Perplexity, but even Confinement, and the Profpect of Death itfelf, were infufficient to abate his Ardor or leffen his Diligence in the Caufe of his darling Miftreffes the Mufes : For it is recorded of him, that when he was Prifoner in *Cowes* Caftle, and on a pretty near Certainty (according to his own Expreffion) of being hanged within a Week, he ftill purfued the Compofition of his celebrated Poem of *Gondibert*, and even was Mafter enough of his Temper and Abilities to write a Letter to his Friend *Hobbes*, giving fome Account of the Progrefs he had made in it, and offering fome Criticifms on the Nature of that Kind of Poetry.—But to proceed more regularly in his Hiftory.

Our Author was a younger Son of Mr. *John D'Avenant*, who was a Citizen of *Oxford*, being a very fubftantial Vintner, and keeping a large Tavern, afterwards known by the Name of the *Crown* in that City ; where he moreover, in 1621, attained to the Honour of being elected Mayor.—This Son was born at *Oxford*, in *Feb*. 1605, and very early in Life gave Tokens of a lively and promifing Genius.—He received the Rudiments of Grammatical Learning from Mr. *Edward Sylvefter*, who kept a School in the Parifh of *All - Saints*, *Oxford*, and in the Year 1621, being that of his Father's Mayoralty, he was enter'd a Member of *Lincoln* College in

that Univerfity, in order to compleat his academical Studies under Mr. *Daniel Hough*.——Here however he took no Degree, nor, according to *Wood*'s Opinion, made any long Refidence, that Writer abfolutely informing us, at the fame Time, that he acknowledges the Strength of his Genius, and even diftinguifhes him by the Title of the *Sweet Swan of Ifis*, that he was neverthelefs confiderably deficient in Univerfity Learning.

On his quitting the Univerfity, he became one in the Retinue of the magnificently difpofed *Frances* Dutchefs of *Richmond*, out of whofe Family he removed into that of the celebrated Sir *Fulke Greville*, Lord *Brook*, whofe Hiftory I have already recorded in it's proper Place.—But after the unhappy Death of that Nobleman in 1628, being now left without a Patron, altho' not in diftrefs'd Circumftances, it is probable that Views of Profit as well as Amufement might induce him to an Exertion of his Genius, as he in the enfuing Year produced his firft Play, called *Albovine, King of the Lombards*, which met with great Succefs.

For the eight fucceeding Years he paft his Time in the Service of the Mufes, and a conftant Attendance at Court, where he was very much careffed by all the great Wits there, among whom we find him in the clofeft Intimacy with the Earl of *Dorfet*, Lord Treafurer *Wefton*, and the accomplifhed *Endymion Porter*, Efq;—In Confequence of this extenfive perfonal Intereft, and the peculiar Patronage of the Queen, he was in the Year 1637 promoted to the Laurel, which was vacant by the Death of *Ben Jonfon*, and for which *Thomas May*

stood

ftood as his Competitor.——In the Life of that Poet the Reader will find related the Refentment he fhewed on the Lofs of this Election; and it will equally appear in the Courfe of this Gentleman's Hiftory, with what ardent Gratitude and unfhaken Zeal for the Caufe of the Royal Family he repaid this Mark of their Efteem for him.——For as foon as ever the Civil War broke out, he demonftrated his Loyalty to the King, not only in Word but Actions.

In *May* 1641, he was accufed by the Parliament, of being concerned in a Defign for feducing the Army from their Adherence to the Parliamentary Authority; and a Proclamation being iffued for the apprehending him and others engaged in that Defign, he was ftopped at *Feverfham,* fent up to *London,* and put under the Cuftody of the Serjeant at Arms. ——From hence, in the Month of *July* following, he was bailed, and foon after found it neceffary for him to withdraw to *France.*—— In this Attempt to fly, however, he was not much more fuccefsful than in the former, reaching no farther than *Canterbury* before he was again feized by the Mayor of that City, and obliged to undergo a very ftrict Examination.—— Whether he was put into Confinement on this Occafion, or fuffered to proceed on his Journey, is a Point that his Biographers have not render'd extremely clear, but it is pretty evident that the Delay arifing from it was not a very long one; as we find that he did at length join the Queen in *France,* where he ftaid for fome Time, till, accompanying fome military Stores which that Princefs fent over for the Ufe of the Earl of *Newcaftle,* he was

entertained by his Lordfhip, who had been his old Friend and Patron, in the Station of Lieutenant-General of the Ordnance.

In his military Capacity he appears to have behaved well, for, at the Siege of *Gloucefter* in *Sept.* 1643, he received the Honour of Knighthood from the King, as an Acknowledgment of his Bravery and fignal Services.——But on the Declining of the King's Affairs, fo far as to be beyond Retrieval, Sir *William* once more retired to *France* , where he changed his Religion for that of the Church of *Rome,* and remained for a confiderable Time with the Queen and Prince of *Wales.* ——By them he was held in high Efteem, and appears to have been entrufted with fome important Negociations in 1646, and particularly employed by the Queen in an Attempt, tho' an unfuccefsful one, to prevail on King *Charles* I. to comply with fome temporizing Steps which fhe confidered as neceffary to his Interefts.

In 1650, an ingenious Project having been formed for fending a felect Number of Artificers (particularly Weavers) from *France* to *Virginia,* for the Improvement of that Colony, our Author, encouraged to it by the Queen-Mother, undertook the Conduct of this Expedition, and abfolutely embarked in the Profecution of it from one of the Ports of *Normandy.*——But Fortune not being inclined to favour him, the Veffel had fcarcely got clear of the *French* Coaft, before fhe fell in with, and was taken by, a Ship of War belonging to the Parliament, who carried her into the Ifle of *Wight.*

Sir *William D'Avenant* on this Occafion was confined for fome

Time clofe Prifoner to *Cowes* Caftle, and in the enfuing Year was fent up to the *Tower* of *London*, in Order to take his Trial before the High Court of Juftice.

During his Confinement, his Life was for a long Time kept in the utmoft Sufpence and Danger; yet what is very remarkable, it had fo little Effect on his natural Vivacity and Eafinefs of Difpofition, that he ftill with great Affiduity purfued his Poem of *Gondibert*, two Books of which he had written while in *France*.—By what Means he efcaped this impending Storm is not abfolutely apparent.—Some have attributed it to the Interpofition of two Aldermen of *York*, to whom he had fhewn fome peculiar Civilities when they had been taken Prifoners in the North by the Earl of *Newcaftle*'s Forces; and others afcribe his Safety to the Mediation of the great *Milton*.—Tho' the former of thefe Particulars may have fome Foundation, and might be a concurrent Circumftance in his Prefervation, yet I cannot help thinking the latter moft likely to have been the principal Inftrument in it; as the immortal Bard was a Man whofe Intereft was moft potent at that Time; as it is reafonable to imagine a fympathetic Regard for a Perfon of Sir *William*'s poetical Abilities, muft plead ftrongly in his Favour in fo humane a Breaft as that of *Milton*, and point out to him that true *Genius* ought to be confider'd of *no* Party, but claims the Protection of *all*: And what feems to confirm this is, that we find ten Years afterwards, when the latter was exactly in the fame Predicament, he ftood indebted for the fame Protection to Sir *William*, to whom therefore Mankind ought

to confider themfelves as under double Obligations, fince, but for his Interceffion for the Life of *Milton*, it is more than probable the World would never have been enrichd with the nobleft Poem in it.

Be this however as it will, he was at length admitted to his Liberty as a Prifoner at large; yet his Circumftances being now confiderably reduced, he made a bold Effort towards at once redreffing them, and redeeming the Public from that cynical and aufere Gloom which had long hung over it, occafioned by the Suppreffion of theatrical Amufements.——He well knew that a Theatre, if conducted with Skill and Addrefs, would ftill find a fufficient Number of Partizans to fupport it; and having obtained the Countenance of Lord *Whitlocke*, Sir *John Maynard*, and other Perfons of Rank, who were in Reality no Friends to the Cant and Hypocrify which then fo ftrongly prevailed, he got Permiffion to open a Sort of Theatre at *Rutland* Houfe in *Charter-Houfe* Yard, where he began with a Reprefentation which he called an Opera, but was in Reality quite a different Thing.—This meeting with Encouragement, he ftill proceeded, till at length growing bolder by Succefs, he wrote, and caufed to be acted, feveral regular Plays, which, by the great Profits arifing from them, perfectly anfwer'd the more important Part of his Defign, that of amending his Fortunes.—Immediately after the Reftoration of King *Charles* II. however, which brought with it that of the *Britifh* Stage in a State of unreftrained Liberty, Sir *William D'Avenant* obtained a Patent for the Reprefentation of dramatic Pieces,

Pieces, under the Title of the *Duke*'s Theatre in *Lincoln's-Inn-Fields.*—The firſt Opening of this Theatre was with a new Play of his own, entitled the *Siege of Rhodes*, in which he introduced a great Variety of fine Scenes and beautiful Machinery.—And here it is neceſſary to obſerve, that Sir *William D'Avenant* was the firſt Perſon to whom the *Engliſh* Stage is indebted for thoſe Decorations ; which he brought over the Idea of from the Theatres in *France*, his long Reſidence in which Country had greatly improved his Taſte, and induced him to endeavour at a greater Regularity in the Conduct, and a greater Correctneſs in the Language of his Pieces, than the Manner of the dramatic Writers of his own Country had hitherto attained.—Nor could he, among other Improvements, omit thoſe of Decoration and Scenery, ſo neceſſary for heightening the Deception, on which ſo great a Part of our Pleaſure in this Kind of Entertainments conſtantly depends ; in which we now even greatly exceed our Neighbours ; but which at that Time the *Engliſh* Stage was ſo barbarouſly deficient in ; for altho' it is true that, in the Reign of King *Charles* I. we read of many dramatic Entertainments, which were accompanied with very rich Scenery, curious Machines and other elegant Embelliſhments, and the greateſt Part of them even conducted by that great Architect *Inigo Jones*, yet theſe were employed only in the Maſques and Plays repreſented at Court, and were much too expenſive for the little Theatres in which Plays were then acted for Hire.—Theſe Theatres were ſo numerous, there being generally ſix or ſeven open

at once, and, (if I miſtake not, we are ſomewhere told, that there were at one Time no leſs than ſeventeen Playhouſes ſubſiſting in *London*, ſmall as it then was in Compariſon to it's preſent Extent) and the Prices ſo extremely low, that they could afford no farther Decorations to aſſiſt the Actor's Performance, or elevate the Spectator's Imagination, than bare Walls, coarſely matted, or at the beſt cover'd with Tapeſtry, and nothing more than a Blanket or a Piece of coarſe Cloth by Way of a Curtain.—In this Situation were they in *Shakeſpeare*'s Time, who, in ſome of his Choruſſes, ſeems to have had an apparent Reference to it ; and not much better does it appear to have been at any Period before the Reſtoration, at which Time Taſte and Luxury, Genius and Gallantry, Elegance and Licentiouſneſs, ſeem to have made a mingled Entry into theſe Kingdoms, under the Auſpices of a witty and wicked, a merry and miſchievous, Monarch.—— But to quit this Digreſſion.

Sir *William D'Avenant* continued at the Head of his Company, which he afterwards removed to a ſtill larger and more magnificent Theatre built in *Dorſet* Gardens, till the Time of his Death, which happened on the 17th of *April*, 1668, in the 64th Year of his Age ; and in two Days afterwards was interred in *Weſtminſter-Abbey*, very near his Rival for the Laurel, *Tho. May*, leaving his Son Dr. *Charles D'Avenant*, mentioned in the laſt Article, his Succeſſor in the Management of the Theatre.—On his Grave-Stone is inſcribed, in Imitation of *Een Jonſon*'s ſhort Epitaph, the following Words,

O rare Sir William Davenant !

 Thus,

Thus, after paffing thro' many Storms of Difficulty and Adverfity, he at length fpent the Evening of his Days in Eafe and Serenity. —While living he had the Happinefs of being univerfally beloved, and at his Death was as univerfally lamented.

As a Man, his Character appears to have been in every Refpect perfectly amiable.—Honour, Courage, Gratitude, Integrity, Genius and Vivacity having apparently been the predominant Features of his Mind; and all the Hiftorians feem to allow, that he was poffefs'd of an agreeable Perfon and handfome Face, till, in Confequence of fome amorous Dalliances, whereby his Nofe had greatly fuffered, the Symmetry of the latter was confiderably disfigured, and became the Subject of much Wit among his Cotemporary Poets.—Sir *John Suckling* in particular, tho' his Friend, could not avoid touching on it in his *Seffion of the Poets,* in which he has the following Lines,

> Will D'Avenant, *afham'd of a*
> *   foolifh Mifchance*
> *That he had got lately travelling*
> *   in* France,
> *Modeftly kop'd the Handfcmenefs*
> *   of his Mufe*
> *Might any Deformity about him*
> *   excufe.*
>
> *Surely the Company had been con-*
> *   tent*
> *If they could have found any*
> *   Precedent,*
> *But in all their Records in Verfe*
> *   or in Profe,*
> *There was none of a Laureat that*
> *   wanted a Nofe.*

Altho' it is far from my Inclination to propagate Slander, or add to the perpetuating any Tale

of private Calumny, yet I might, as a Biographer, be thought guilty of an Omiffion, fhould I not take Notice in this Place, that, in Confequence of the extraordinary Beauty of Mrs. *D'Avenant,* our Author's Mother, and the Frequency of the Vifits of *Shakefpeare,* who, in the Courfe of his Journeys into *Oxfordfhire,* ufed moft generally to refide at the Houfe of her Hufband, who, as I have before obferved, kept an Inn in the City of *Oxford,* there have not been wanting thofe who have conjectur'd Sir *William D'Avenant* to have been not only the poetical, but even the natural Son of that inimitable Bard.— And, as a farther Corroboration of the Surmife, would infinuate a Refemblance of Feature, and urge the Vivacity of Sir *William's* natural Difpofition, which was diametrically oppofite to the gloomy faturnine Complexion of Mr. *D'Avenant,* his fuppofed and legal Parent.—Was the Fact certain, how greatly would this Author appear the Favorite of the Mufes, firft to receive his Exiftence, and afterwards to owe the Continuance of it, to the two moft exalted Geniufes that ever lived! —But, as the Circumftances on which the Suppofition is founded, are by no Means fuch as are adequate to a Proof; as Gallantry, and more efpecially Adultery, were far from the reigning or fafhionable Vices of that Age; and moreover, as *Shakefpeare* more particularly feems remarkable for the Chaftity and amiable Purity of his Morals; I cannot think, that the cafting a Stain on the Virtue of a Lady of Reputation, and fixing a Blot on the moral Conduct of fo valuable a Man, are fufficiently authorized by the mere Suggeftions of Fancy, or

the

the Inclination of tracing out a Baſtard Pedigree in the poetical Line, for a Writer, whoſe own Merit is ſufficient to enſure him the Remembrance of Ages yet to come.

As a Poet, Sir *William*'s Rank ſeems as yet undetermined.—His celebrated Epic of *Gondibert* was render'd at the ſame Time the Subject of the higheſt Commendation and the ſevereſt Criticiſm; tho', I muſt confeſs, that Envy appears to me to have had a much greater Share in the latter than Juſtice; for, tho' the Story of it may not perhaps be ſo intereſting, (and that too in great Meaſure from it's not being ſo well known) as thoſe of the *Iliad* and *Æneid*, and that the Fetters of Rhime, and ſtill more ſo thoſe of Stanza Poetry, lay it under very great Reſtraint, yet it muſt be acknowledged, even by it's ſtrongeſt Opponents, that there runs thro' the whole of it a Sublimity in the Sentiments, a Nobleneſs in the Manners, a Purity in the Diction, and a Luxuriancy in the Conceptions, that would have done Honour to any Writer of any Age or Country whatſoever.—But to ceaſe any farther Eulogium on this Poem, as no Teſtimony of his poetical Merits can be, conſider'd more valid than that of Mr. *Dryden*, who was not only his Cotemporary, but even wrote in Conjunction with him, and as Nothing can be ſtronger or more ample than the Commendation that Gentleman has given him, I ſhall with his Words cloſe the preſent Account of Sir *William D'Avenant* and his Abilities.

" I found him (ſays that Author, in his Preface to the *Tempeſt*) of ſo quick a Fancy, " that nothing was propoſed to

" him on which he could not " quickly produce a Thought ex- " tremely pleaſant and ſurpriſing; " and thoſe firſt Thoughts of his, " contrary to the old *Latin* Pro- " verb, were not always the leaſt " happy; and as his Fancy was " quick, ſo likewiſe were the " Products of it remote and new. " He borrowed not of any other, " and his Imaginations were ſuch " as could not eaſily enter into " any other Man.—His Correc- " tions were ſober and judicious, " and he corrected his own Wri- " tings much more ſeverely than " thoſe of another Man; be- " ſtowing twice the Labour and " Pains in poliſhing which he " uſed in Invention."

Sir *William D'Avenant*'s dramatic Works are numerous, yet not one of them is at preſent on the Liſt of acting Plays, which I cannot help ſometimes regretting, as there are certainly ſome among them that much better deſerve that Honour, than many Pieces which are very frequently and ſucceſsfully repreſented.——— The Titles of them all may be ſeen in the following Liſt.

1. ALBOVINE, *King of the* LOMBARDS. T.
2. *Britannia Triumphans.* Maſque.
3. *Cruel Brother.* T.
4. *Diſtreſſes.* T. C.
5. *Entertainment at* Rutland Houſe.
6. *Fair Favorite.* T. C.
7. *Juſt Italian.* T. C.
8. *Law againſt Lovers.* T.C.
9. *Love and Honour.* T. C.
10. *Man's the Maſter.* C.
11. *Platonic Lovers.* C.
12. *Playhouſe to be lett.*
13. *Rivals.* T. C. (attributed by *Langbaine* to this Author.)
14. *Siege.* T. C.

15. *Siege of* RHODES. Play, two Parts.
16. *Temple of Love.* Masque.
17. *Tempest.* (alter'd from *Shakespeare* by *Dryden* and this Author.)
18. *Triumphs of the Prince* D'AMOUR. Masque.
19. *Unfortunate Lovers.* T.
20. *Wits.* C.

DAVENPORT, Mr. *Robert.*—An Author who lived in the Reign of *Charles* I. and during the Troubles of that Reign wrote two Plays, which however, on Account of the Suppression of the Theatre under the Commonwealth, did not make their Appearance till after the Restoration.—Their Names are,

1. *The City Night Cap.* T. C.
2. *King* JOHN *and* MATILDA. T.

DAUNCEY. *Vid.* DANCER.

DAVY, *Samuel.*—This Author is mentioned no where but in the *British Theatre,* he was born in *Ireland,* and I imagine it was in that Kingdom that he brought the following Piece on the Stage, *viz.*

The *Treacherous Husband.* T.

DAVYS, or DAVIS, Mrs. *Mary.*—This female Author was born in *Ireland,* she was married to a Clergyman, whom she survived, and wrote two dramatic Pieces, both in the comic Walk, entitled,

1. The *Northern Heiress.* C.
2. *Self Rival.* C.

Besides these she wrote some Novels, Poems, and Familiar Letters, which, together with the above, are published in two Vol. 8vo. 1725. under the Title of The Works of Mrs. *Davis.*

DAY, Mr. *John*—This Author, by the Date of his Works, must have flourished in the Reigns of King *James* I. and King *Charles* I. and wrote the following dramatic Pieces.

1. *Blind Beggar of* BETHNAL *Green.* C.
2. *Humour out of Breath.* C.
3. *Isle of Gulls.* C.
4. *Law Tricks.* C.
5. *Parliament of Bees.* Masque. (The Author was assisted in this by *William Rowley* and *George Wilkins.*)
6. *Travels of three English Brothers.* Historical Play.

The precise Time of his Birth and Death, however, are not known, nor any farther Particulars recorded concerning him, excepting that he had Connection with some of his cotemporary Poets of Note, and had been for some Time Student in *Caius* Colledge, *Cambridge.*

DECKER, Mr. *Thomas.*—This Gentleman was a Writer in the Reign of King *James* I. and being a Cotemporary with *Ben Jonson,* became more eminent by having a Quarrel with that great Poet, than he would perhaps otherwise have done from the Merit of his own Works, which are but of a very moderate Rank of Excellence.—What the original Occasion of their Contest was, I know not, but *Jonson,* who certainly could never " bear a " Rival near the Throne" has, in his *Poetaster,* the *Dunciad* of that Author, among many other Poets whom he has satyriz'd, been peculiarly severe on *Decker,* whom he has characteris'd under the Name of *Crispinus.*——This Compliment *Decker* has amply repaid in his *Satyromastix,* or the *Untrussing a humorous Poet,* in which, under the Title of young *Horace* he has made *Ben,* the Hero of his Piece.—As great Wits, and especially those of the Satyrical Kind,

Kind, will always have numerous Enemies, befides the general Fondnefs the Public have of feeing Men of Abilities abufe each other, this Play was extremely followed, and as it appears to have been one of our Authors firft Pieces, it probably laid the Foundation of his Fame as a Writer.—Altho', as I have before obferved, *Decker* was but a middling Poet, yet he did not want his Admirers, even among the Poets of his Time ; fome of whom thought themfelves not difgraced by writing in Conjunction with him ; *Webfter* having a Hand in three of his Plays, and *Rowley* and *Ford* joining with him in another.—*Richard Brome* in particular ufed always to call him Father, which is fomewhat the more extraordinary, confidering the Oppofition fubfifting between him and *Jonfon*, as *Brome* had been Servant to, and was a particular Favorite with, the Laureat.—Mr. *The. Cibber* obferves, on this Occafion, that it is the Misfortune of little Wits, that their Admirers are as inconfiderable as themfelves, and that *Brome*'s Applaufes confer no great Honour on thofe who enjoy them. —Yet I think in this Cenfure he has been fomewhat too fevere on both, for *Brome*'s Merit was certainly not inconfiderable, fince it could force Admiration and even public Praife from the envious *Ben* himfelf.—And altho' *Langbaine*, who writes with Partiality to *Ben Jonfon*, has given the Preference in fo fuperlative a Degree to thofe Plays in which our Author was united with others, againft thofe which were entirely his own, yet I cannot help thinking that in his *Honeft Whore*, and the Comedy of *Fortunatus*, both which

are allow'd to be folely his, there are Beauties, both as to Character, Plot, and Language, equal to the Abilities of any of thofe Authors that he was ever affifted by, and indeed in the latter equal to any dramatic Writer *(Shakefpeare* excepted) that this Ifland has produced.

The dramatic Pieces he was concerned in are twelve in Number, and may be feen in the enfuing Catalogue.

1. FORTUNATUS. C.
2. *Honeft Whore.* Com. two Parts.
3. *If this ben't a good Play the Devil's in't.* C.
4. *Match me in London.* Tr.-Com.
5. *Northward Hoe.* C. (Affifted by *Webfter*.)
6. *Satyromaftix.* Com.-Satire.
7. *Sun's Darling.* Mafque. (Affifted by *Ford*).
8. *Weftward Hoe.* C. (Affifted by *Webfter*.)
9. *Whore of* BABYLON. Hiftory.
10. *Witch of* EDMONTON. C. (Our Author, in Conjunction with *Ford*, greatly affifted *Rowley* in the Writing of this Comedy, altho' it paffes under *Rowley*'s Name.)
11. *Wonder of a Kingdom.* C.
12. WYAT's *Hiftory.* (Affifted by *Webfter*.)

Befides thefe *Phillips* and *Winftanley*, have afcribed four other Plays to this Author in Conjunction with *Webfter*, viz.

New Trick to cheat the Devil. C.
Noble Stranger. C.
Weakeft goes to the Wall. Tr.-Com.
Woman will have her Will. C.
in this however they are miftaken, the *Noble Stranger* having been

written

written by *Lewis Sharpe*, and the other three by anonymous Authors.

The precife Time of this Author's Birth and Death are not recorded, yet he could not have died young, as the firft Play we find of his writing was publifhed in 1600, and the lateft Date we meet with to any other is in 1638. excepting the *Sun's Darling*, which *Langbaine* obferves was not publifhed till after the Death of its Authors.

DELAP, Mr.—Of this Gentleman I know no more than the having heard that he is a *North-Briton*, and a Clergyman, but whether of the Church of *England* or that of *Scotland* I am not thoroughly informed, tho' moft probably of the latter,—He is a living Writer, and has lately brought on the Stage one dramatic Piece, entitled,

HECUBA. Tr.

DENHAM, Sir *John*.——This elegant Writer was the only Son of Sir *John Denham*, Knight, of little *Horfley*, who was, at the Time of our Author's Birth, which happened in 1615, Lord Chief Baron of the Exchequer in *Ireland*, and one of the Lords Juftices of that Kingdom : In Confequence of which our Author was born in *Dublin*, but was brought over from thence at two Years old, on the Promotion of his Father to the Rank of a Baron of the Exchequer in *England*.

His grammatical Learning he received in *London*, and in *Michaelmas* Term 1631, was removed from thence to *Oxford*, where he was enter'd a Gentleman Commoner of *Trinity* College; but inftead of fhewing any early Dawnings of that Genius which afterwards fhone forth in him, he appear'd a flow dreaming young Man, and one whofe darling Paffion was Gaming.—Here he continued for three Years, when, having pafs'd his Examinations, and taken a Degree as Batchelor of Arts, he came to *London*, and enter'd himfelf at *Lincoln's-Inn*, where he applied pretty clofely to the Study of the Law.—Yet his darling Vice was ftill predominant, and he frequently found himfelf ftripped to his laft Shilling, by which he fo greatly difpleas'd his Father, that he was obliged, in Appearance at leaft, to reform, for fear of being abfolutely abandoned by him.— On his Death, however, being no longer reftrained by parental Authority, he again gave Way to it, and being a Dupe to Sharpers, foon fquander'd away feveral thoufand Pounds.

In the latter End of 1641, however, to the Aftonifhment of every one, his Genius broke forth in a full Blaze of Meridian Brightnefs, in that juftly celebrated and admir'd Tragedy the *Sophy*, and foon after fhone out again in his Poem of *Cooper*'s Hill.—In the fame Year he was prick'd for High Sheriff for the County of *Surry*, and made Governor of *Farnham* Caftle, for the King.— But being poffefs'd of no great Share of military Knowledge, he prefently quitted that Poft, and retired to his Majefty at *Oxford*.

And now the grand Rebellion being broke out in its full Force, he fhewed the warmeft Attachment to the Royal Family, and in the Courfe of their unhappy Affairs, became of fignal Service to them.—In the Year 1647, when the King had been deliver'd into the Hands of the Army, he undertook, on the Behalf of the Queen Mother, to gain Accefs to his Majefty, which

which he found Means to do by the Affiſtance of *Hugh Peters*.—On this Occaſion the King converſed with him in an unreſerved Manner, with Regard to his Affairs, and entruſting him with nine Cyphers, commanded him to ſtay privately in *London*, in order to receive all his Letters to and from his Correſpondents, all which were conſtantly decypher'd and undecyphered by Mr. *Cowley*, at that Time with the Queen Mother in *France*. This Truſt he performed with great Punctuality and Safety for ſome Time, till at length Mr. *Cowley*'s Hand being known, this Affair was diſcovered, and Mr. *Denham* obliged to make his Eſcape to *France*.—In 1648 he was ſent Ambaſſador, together with Lord *Crofts*, to *Poland*, where he ſucceeded ſo well as to bring back ten thouſand Pounds for the King, levied there on his Majeſty's *Scottiſh* Subjects.

About 1652 he return'd to *England*, and reſided about a Year at the Earl of *Pembroke*'s at *Wilton*, having quite exhauſted his own Fortune, by his Paſſion for Gaming, and the Expences he had been at during the Civil War. —It does not clearly appear what became of him between that Time and the Reſtoration, tho' it is moſt probable he went over again to *France*, and reſided there till King *Charles* II's Return from St. *Germain*'s to *Jerſey*, when he was immediately appointed, without any Solicitation, Surveyor General of all his Majeſty's Buildings, and at the Coronation of that Monarch made Knight of the *Bath*.

On ſome Diſcontent ariſing from a ſecond Marriage, he for a little Time loſt his Senſes, but on his Recovery, continued in

great Eſteem at Court for his Poetical Abilities, eſpecially with the King, who was fond of Poetry, and during his Exile us'd frequently to give Mr. *Denham* Arguments to write on.

This ingenious Gentleman died at an Office he had built for himſelf near *Whitehall*, *March* 10, 1668, Ætatis 53. and was buried in *Weſtminſter Abbey*, leaving behind him among the ſeveral Works whereby his Poetical Fame ſtands eſtabliſhed, only one dramatic one, *viz.*

The *Sophy*. T.

As a Poet we need only refer to the Teſtimonials of many Writers, particularly *Dryden* and *Pope*, in his Favour.—As to his moral Character, he has had no Vice imputed to him but that of Gameing, and altho' Authors have been ſilent as to his Virtues, yet if we may judge from his Works, he was a good-natur'd Man and an eaſy Companion; and from his Actions it appears that he was one of ſtrict Honour and Integrity, and in the Day of Danger and Tumult of unſhaken Loyalty to the ſuffering Intereſt of his Sovereign.

DENNIS, Mr. *John*.—This Gentleman who, tho' he has left many dramatic Pieces behind him, was much leſs celebrated for them than for his critical Writings, was the Son of an eminent Sadler, a Citizen of *London*, in which Metropolis our Author was born in the Year 1657.

He received the firſt Branches of Education under Dr. *Horn*, at the great School at *Harrow on the Hill*, where he commenced Acquaintance and Intimacy with many young Noblemen and Gentlemen, who afterwards made conſiderable Figures in public Affairs; whereby he laid the Foundation of a very ftrong and extenfive Intereft, which might, but for his own Fault, have been of infinite Service to him in future Life.

From *Harrow* he went in 1675 to *Caius* College, *Cambridge*, where, after his proper Standing, he took the Degree of Batchelor of Arts. —When he quitted the Univerfity he made the Tour of *Europe*, in the Courfe of which he con ceived fuch a Deteftation for Defpotifm, as confirmed him ftill more ftrongly in thofe Whig Principles which he had from his Infancy imbibed.

On his Return to *England* he became early acquainted with *Dryden*, *Wycherley*, *Congreve*, and *Southerne*, whofe Converfation infpiring him with a Paffion for Poetry, and a Contempt for every Attainment that had not fome Relation to the *Belles Lettres*, diverted him from the Acquifition of any profitable Art, or the Exercife of any Profeffion.

This to a Man who had not an Independent Income, was undoubtedly a Misfortune. However, the Zeal he fhew'd for the Proteftant Succeffion having recommended him to the Patronage of the Duke of *Marlborough*, that Nobleman procur'd him a Place in the Cuftoms, worth 120 *l. per Ann.* which he enjoy'd for fome Years, till from Profufenefs and Want of Occonomy he was reduced to the Neceffity of difpofing of it to fatisfy fome very preffing Demands.—By the Advice of Lord *Hallifax*, however, he referved to himfelf, in the Sale of it, an Annuity for a Term of Years, which Term he outlived, and was, in the Decline of his Life, reduced to extreme Neceffity.—Mr. *Theo. Cibber* relates an Anecdote of him which I cannot avoid repeating, as it is not

only highly Characteriftic of the Man whofe Affairs we are now confidering; but alfo a ftriking and melancholy Inftance among Thoufands, of the diftrefsful Predicaments into which Men of Genius and literary Abilities are perhaps apter than any others to plunge themfelves into, by paying too flight an Attention to the common Concerns of Life, and their own moft important Interefts.

"After he was worn out," fays that Author, " with Age " and Poverty, he refided within " the Verge of the Court, to pre- " vent Danger from his Creditors. " —One *Saturday* Night, he hap- " pen'd to faunter to a Public " Houfe, which, in a fhort Time, " he difcovered to be out of the " Verge.—He was fitting in an " open drinking Room, and a " Man of a fufpicious Appear- " ance happened to come in.— " There was fomething about the " Man which denoted to Mr. " *Dennis*, that he was a Bailiff. " This ftruck him with a Panic ; " he was afraid his Liberty was " now at an End ; he fat in the " utmoft Solicitude, but durft not " offer to ftir, left he fhould be " feiz'd upon.—After an Hour " or two had paft in this painful " Anxiety, at laft the Clock " ftruck Twelve, when Mr. *Den-* " *nis*, in an Extafy, cried out, " addreffing himfelf to the fuf- " pected Perfon, *Now, Sir, Bai-* " *liff or no Bailiff, I don't care a* " *Farthing for you, you have no* " *Power now.*—The Man was " aftonifhed at his Behaviour, and " when it was explained to him, " was fo much affronted with " the Sufpicion, that had not " Mr. *Dennis* found his Protection " in Age, he would probably " have fmarted for his miftaken " Opinion

" Opinion of him."—A ftrong Picture of the Effects of Fear and Apprehenfion, in a Temper naturally fo timorous and jealous as Mr. *Dennis's*, of which the Reader may fee two more whimfical Inftances in the firft Part of this Work, under the Tragdy of Liberty Asserted.

Mr. *Dennis* partly thro' a natural Peevifhnefs and Petulance of Temper, and partly perhaps for the Sake of procuring the Means of Subfiftence, was continually engaged in a Paper War with his Cotemporaries, whom he ever treated with the utmoft Severity; and tho' many of his Obfervations were judicious, yet he ufually conveyed them in Language fo fcurrilous and abufive as deftroyed their intended Effect; and as his Attacks were almoft always on Perfons of fuperior Abilities to himfelf, viz. *Addifon*, *Steele*, and *Pope*, their Replies ufually turned the popular Opinion fo greatly againft him, that by irritating his tefty Temper the more, it render'd him a perpetual Torment to himfelf; till at length, after a long Life of Viciffitudes, Difappointments and Turmoils, render'd wretched by Indifcretion, and hateful by Malevolence, having out-lived the Reverfion of his Eftate, and reduced to Diftrefs, from which his having been daily erecting Enemies had left him fcarcely any Hope of Relief, he was compelled to, what muft be the moft irkfome Station that can be conceived in human Life, the receiving Obligations from thofe whom he had been continually treating ill.—In the very clofe of his Days a Play was acted for his Benefit at the little Theatre in the *Haymarket*, procured thro' the united Interefts of Meffrs. *Thomfon*, *Mallet* and *Pope*, the laft of whom, notwithftanding the grofs Manner in which Mr. *Dennis* had on many Occafions us'd him, and the long Warfare that had fubfifted between them, interefted himfelf very warmly for him, and even wrote an occafional Prologue to the Play, which was fpoken by Mr. *Cibber* jun.

Not long after this, *viz.* on the 6th of *Jan.* 1733. Mr. *Dennis* died, being then in the 77th Year of his Age.

His Character as a Man may be fufficiently gather'd from the Circumftances we have related of him.—As a Writer, he certainly was poffefs'd of much Erudition and a confiderable Share of Genius; and had not his Self Opinion, of which perhaps no Man ever poffefs'd a larger Share, induced him to aim at the Empire of Wit, for which he was by no Means qualified, and in Confequence thereof led him to treat every one as a Rebel who did not fubfcribe to his pretended Right, he would probably have been allowed, and from the Enjoyment of an eafy Mind, poffibly poffefs'd, more Merit than appears in many of his Writings.——In Profe, he is far from a bad Writer, where Abufe and perfonal Scurrility does not mingle itfelf with his Language.—In Verfe, he is extremely unequal, his Numbers being at fome Times fpirited and harmonious, and his Subjects elevated and judicious, and at others flat, harfh, and puerile.—As a dramatic Author he certainly deferves not to be held in any Confideration.—His Plots, excepting that of his *Plot and no Plot*, which is a political Play, are all borrowed, yet in the general not ill-chofen. But his Characters are ill-defign'd and unfi-

nifhed,

nifhed, his Language profaical, flat, and undramatic, and the *Conduct of his principal Scenes heavy, dull, and unempaffioned. —In fhort, tho' he certainly had Judgment, it is evident he had no Execution, and fo much better a Critic is he than a Dramatift, that I cannot help fubfcribing to the Opinion of a Gentleman, who faid of him, that he was the moft compleat Inftructor for a dramatic Poet, fince he could teach him to diftinguifh *good* Plays by his *Precepts*, and *bad* ones by his *Examples*.

His dramatic Pieces are nine in Number, as may be feen in the following Lift,

1. Appius *and* Virginia. Trag. *Vid.* Vol. I, Appendix.
2. *Comical Gallant.* C.
3. Coriolanus. T.
4. Gibraltar. C.
5. Iphigenia. T.
6. *Liberty afferted.* T.
7. Orpheus *and* Euridice. Mafque.
8. *Plot and no Plot.* C.
9. Rinaldo *and* Armida. Trag.

Derrick, Mr. —— Of this Gentleman I know little more than that he is an Author now living, is I believe a Native of *Ireland*, and, as I have been informed, was formerly in the Army.—He has tranflated one little Piece from the *French*, intitled,

Sylla. Dram. Entert.

Digby, Lord.—Of this Nobleman I know nothing more than that he is faid by *Jacob* to have been the fuppofed Author of one very good Play, entitled,

Elvira. Com.

Dilke, *Thomas*, Efq;—This Gentleman lived in the Reign of *William* III. and was the Son of Mr. *Samuel Dilke*, of an ancient

Family at *Litchfield*, where our Author was born. — He had a Univerfity Education, having been fome Time a Student at *Oriel* College, *Oxford*.—When he quitted the Univerfity he went into the Army, and had a Lieutenant's Commiffion under Lord *Raby*, afterwards Earl of *Strafford*, to which Nobleman he dedicated one of his Plays, of which he has left three behind him, whofe Titles are as follow,

1. *City Lady.* C.
2. *Lover's Luck.* C.
3. *Pretenders.* C.

Dodsley, Mr. *Robert.*—This ingenious Author is now living. In what Year, or at what Place he was born, I am not certain, though I have heard the latter to have been either in *Warwickfhire* or *Nottinghamfhire*; his firft fetting out in Life was in a fervile Station, which however his Abilities very foon raifed him from; for having written the *Toyfhop*, and that Piece being fhewn to Mr. *Pope*, the Delicacy of Satire which is confpicuous in it, tho' cloath'd with the greateft Simplicity of Defign, fo ftrongly recommended it's Author to the Notice of that celebrated Poet, that he continued from that Time to the Day of his Death a warm Friend and zealous Patron to Mr. *Dodfley*, and altho' he had himfelf no Connection with the Theatres, yet procured him fuch an Intereft as infur'd it's being immediately brought on the Stage, where it met with the Succefs it merited: as did alfo a Farce called the King and Miller of *Mansfield*, which made it's Appearance in the enfuing Year, *viz.* 1736.— From the Succefs of thefe Pieces he enter'd into that Bufinefs which of all others has the clofeft Connection with, and the moft immediate Dependance on, Perfons

fons of Genius and Literature, *viz.* that of a Bookſeller.—In this Station Mr. *Pope*'s Recommendation, and his own Merit, ſoon obtained him not only the Countenance of Perſons of the firſt Abilities, but alſo of thoſe of the firſt Rank, and in a few Years rais'd him to great Eminence in his Profeſſion, in which he is now almoſt, if not altogether, at the Head.—Yet, neither in this Capacity, nor in that of a Writer, has Succeſs had any improper Effect on him.—In one Light he has preſerved the ſtricteſt Integrity, in the other the moſt becoming Humility.—Mindful of the early Encouragement his own Talents met with, he has been ever ready to give the ſame Opportunity of Advancement to thoſe of others, and has on many Occaſions been not only the Publiſher but the Patron of Genius.——But there is no Circumſtance which adds more Luſtre to his Character, than the grateful Remembrance he retains, and ever expreſſes, to the Memory of thoſe to whom he owed the Obligation of his firſt being taken Notice of in Life.—A remarkable Inſtance of which ſhew'd itſelf ſome Years ago, in the Zeal and Ardour which he ſhew'd in Vindication of the Character of his great Patron and Friend Mr. *Pope*, from an Accuſation brought againſt him by a late noble Lord ; in which, what Juſtice or Falſhood there was in the Charge, or how far the Partiality of Friendſhip might or might not paint the Circumſtance itſelf in a more favourable Light than it deſerved, I ſhall not here pretend to decide; but it was certainly the Office of a ſincere Friend to ſtand up in Defence of the Memory of one, who no

longer had it in his Power (from the ſilent Grave) to anſwer any Accuſation whatſoever.—I ſhall not, however, dwell any longer on the Amiableneſs of Mr. *Docſley*'s Character as a Man, ſince many beſides myſelf are well acquainted with it.—As a Writer, there is an Eaſe and Elegance that runs thro' all his Works, which ſometimes is more pleaſing than a more laboured and ornamented Manner.—In Verſe, his Numbers are flowing, if not ſublime, and his Subjects conſtantly well choſen and entertaining.——In Proſe he is familiar, yet chaſte ; and in his dramatic Pieces he has ever kept in his Eye the one great Principle, *delectando pariterque monendo* ;—ſome general Moral is conſtantly conveyed in the general Plan, and particular Inſtruction diſperſed in the particular Strokes of Satire.—The Dialogue moreover is eaſy, the Plots are ſimple, and the Cataſtrophes intereſting and pathetic.

After what I have ſaid of them I ſhall now take leave of this Author, by enumerating his Pieces as follow,

1. *Blind Beggar of Bethnal Green.* Farce.
2. *Cleone.* Trag.
3. *King and Miller of Mansfield.* Farce.
4. *Sir John Cockle at Court.* Farce.
5. *Toyſhop.* Dram. Satire.
6. *Triumph of Peace.* Maſque.

Beſides theſe, he has publiſhed a little Collection of his own Works in one Volume 8vo. under the modeſt Title of *Trifles* and a Poem of conſiderable Length, entitled, *Public Virtue*, in 4to. 1754.

He has alſo performed two Works of great Service to the Cauſe of Genius, as they are the Means of preſerving Pieces of

Merit, that might otherwife fink into Oblivion, *viz.* the Publication of a Collection of Poems by different eminent Hands, in fix Vol. 12mo. and a Collection of Plays by old Authors, in twelve Volumes of the fame Size.

DOGGET, Mr. *Thomas.*—This Author was alfo an Actor.—He was born in *Caftle-Street, Dublin,* and made his firft theatical Attempt on the Stage of that Metropolis; but not meeting with the Encouragement there that his Merit undoubtedly had a Right to, he came over to *England,* and enter'd himfelf in a travelling Company, but from thence very foon was remov'd to *London,* and eftablifhed in *Lincoln's-Inn-Fields* Theatre, where he was univerfally liked in every Character he performed, but fhone in none more confpicuoufly than in thofe of *Fondcwife* in the *Old Batchelor,* and *Ben* in *Love for Love,* which Mr. *Congreve,* with whom he was a very great Favorite, wrote in fome Meafure with a View to his Manner of acting.

In a few Years after he removed to *Drury Lane* Theatre, where he became joint Manager with *Wilks* and *Cibber,* in which Situation he continued till, on a Difguft he took in the Year 1712, at Mr. *Booth's* being forced on them as a Sharer in the Management, he threw up his Part in the Property of the Theatre, tho' it was look'd on to have been worth a Thoufand Pounds *per Annum.* — He had, however, by his Frugality, faved a competent Fortune to render him eafy for the Remainder of his Life, with which he retir'd from the Hurry of Bufinefs in the very Meridian of his Reputation.—As an Actor he had great Merit, and his Co-

temporary *Cibber* informs us that he was the moft an original, and the ftricteft Obferver of Nature of any Actor of his Time.—His Manner was original, and tho' borrowed from none, frequently ferved for a Model to many; and he poffeffed that peculiar Art which fo very few Performers are Mafters of, *viz.* the arriving at the perfectly ridiculous, without ftepping into the leaft Impropriety to attain it.—And fo extremely careful and fkilful was he in the dreffing his Characters to the greateft Exactnefs of Propriety, that the leaft Article of what he wore feem'd in fome Meafure to fpeak and mark the different Humour he prefented; a neceffary Care in a Comedian, in which many Performers are but too remifs.

Mr. *Dogget* lived fome Years after his quitting the Stage, having, as I before obferv'd, made himfelf independent of Bufinefs, by his Care and Oeconomy while he was in it.——In his political Principles he was, in the Words of Sir *Richard Steele,* a *Whig up to the Head and Ears;* and fo ftrictly was he attached to the Interefts of the Houfe of *Hanover,* that he never let flip any Occafion that prefented itfelf, of demonftrating his Sentiments in that Refpect.—One Inftance among others is well known, which is, that the Year after King *George* I. came to the Throne, this Performer gave a Waterman's Coat and Silver Badge, to be rowed for by Six Watermen, on the firft Day of *Auguft,* being the Anniverfary of that King's Acceffion to the Throne.—And at his Death bequeathed a certain Sum of Money, the Intereft of which was to be appropriated annually, for

ever,

ever, to the Purchase of a like Coat and Badge, to be rowed for in Honour of the Day.—Which Ceremony is every Year performed on the first of *August*, the Claimants setting out on a Signal given at that Time of the Tide when the Current is strongest against them, and rowing from the *Old Swan* near *London* Bridge to the *White Swan* at *Chelsea*.

As a Writer, Mr. *Dogget* has left behind him only one Come'dy, which has not been performed in it's original Form, for many Years, entitled,

The *Country Wake*. C.
It has been alter'd however into a Ballad Farce, which frequently makes its Appearance under the Title of,

FLORA, or *Hob in the Well*.

DORMAN, Mr.—This Gentleman did, and perhaps still does, live at *Hampstead*.—I know however nothing more of him than that he is the Author of one Play, entitled,

Sir ROGER DE COVERLEY, Com.

DORSET, Earl of, *Vid.* BUCKHURST, Lord.

DOVER, Mr. *John*.——This Gentleman was the Son of Mr. *Robert Dover*, an eminent Attorney at Law, at a Place call'd *Boston on the Heath*, in *Warwickshire*, and the chief Director and Manager of an Assembly called the *Olympic Games*, which were annually celebrated upon *Cotswold* Hill, in *Gloucestershire*.—Our Author received his Education at *Magdalen* College, *Oxon.* from whence, being intended by his Father for the Law, he removed to *Gray's-Inn*, and was called to the Bar.——The Oratory of the Courts, however, not suiting his Inclination so well as that of the Pulpit, he soon quitted the Law,

and took Orders; and *Coxeter* tells us, that at the Time his Notes were written, Mr. *Dover* was a Minister of the Gospel at *Drayton*, in *Oxfordshire*.——The exact Period of his Birth I find no where recorded, but imagine he must have lived to a considerable Age, as the Time of *Coxeter*'s Writing, when he mentions him as living, could not at the earliest be sooner than 1720, and a Play which he published, and which he declares to have been his Amusement after the Fatigues of the Law, was published according to *Langbaine* in 1677, and according to *Coxeter*'s MS. there was an Edition still ten Years earlier, *viz.* in 1667.—The Title of it is,

The ROMAN *Generals*. T.

DOWER, E.——Who, or of what Profession this Author was, I know not; but he seems by his Writings to have been the most perfect Professor of Poverty that ever devoted himself to the tatter'd Sisters of *Parnassus*; for the few Poems he has published breathe nothing but Complaints of his destitute and distress'd Condition; and indeed, his Brain seems to have been quite as empty as his Pockets.—He has printed the Poems above-mentioned, together with a Narrative, in which he casts the most severe Condemnations on the Manager of one of the Theatres, and on the late Dutchess Dowager of *Marlborough*, for not having given him Money, as a Reward for his having deprived the Community of perhaps a good Porter or Cobler, in the Attempt to make a most execrable Scribbler.—With these he has published a dramatic Piece, which, tho' far from having any Merit in Point of Plot or Character, yet is so far tolerable

 rable

rable with Respect to the Language, and so far superior to any of the other Specimens he has given us of his Writing, that, notwithstanding the Abuse he has dar'd to vent against Mr. *Fl—t-w—d* for not accepting it, I can scarcely believe it to have been his own.—It is called

The SALOPIAN *Squire*. Dramatic Tale.

DRAKE, Dr. *James*.——This Gentleman was born at *Cambridge* in 1667.——He was educated at *Gonville* and *Caius* College, *Cambridge*, where he took his Degrees in Physic.—He became afterwards a Fellow of the College of Physicians, and attained to considerable Eminence in that Profession.—He wrote one dramatic Piece, entitled,

The *Sham Lawyer*. C.

DRAYTON, Mr. *Michael*.—— This Gentleman, who was a Poet of great Renown in the Reigns of Queen *Elizabeth*, *James* I. and *Charles* I. was of a very ancient Family, originally descended from the Town of *Drayton* in *Leicestershire*; but his Parents removing into *Warwickshire*, he was born at a little Village, called *Harful*, in that County, in 1563. Whilst he was extremely young, he gave such Proofs of a growing Genius, as render'd him a Favorite with his Tutors, and procur'd him the Patronage of some Persons of Distinction; for from his own Words we may gather, that even at ten Years of Age he had made a considerable Proficiency in the *Latin* Tongue, and was Page to some Person of Quality.—Sir *Aston Cockain* mentions his having been for some Time a Student at *Oxford*, tho' it is most probable that he compleated his Studies at the other University. —His Propensity to Poetry was

extremely strong, even from his Infancy, and we find the most of his principal Poems published, and himself highly distinguished as a Poet, by the Time he was about thirty Years of Age. — It appears, from his Poem of *Moses's Birth and Miracles*, that he was a Spectator at *Dover* of the famous *Spanish* Armada, and it is not improbable, that he was engaged in some military Employment there.—It is certain, that not only for his Merit as a Writer, but his valuable Qualities as a Man, he was held in high Estimation, and strongly patronized by several Personages of Consequence; particularly by Sir *Henry Goodere*, Sir *Walter Aston*, and the Countess of *Bedford*, to the first of whom he owns himself indebted for great Part of his Education, and by the second he was for many Years supported.

At the Coronation of King *James* I. Sir *Walter Aston* fixed on Mr. *Drayton* as one of the 'Squires to attend him at his Creation of Knight of the *Bath*, and it has been alledged that, during King *James*'s Ministry, our Poet was instrumental in a Correspondence carried on between that Prince and Queen *Elizabeth*. —This Assertion, however, wants Confirmation, and the rather, as we find that, tho' *Drayton* did unquestionably stoop to gross Flattery to that Monarch, in some Poems written on his Accession, yet he met with no Preferment from him, and even his Poems themselves met with a very cool and unfavourable Reception.

His Poems are very numerous, and so elegant, that his Manner has been copied by many modern Writers of Eminence since.—— Among these the most celebrated one is the *Poly-Olbion*, which is
a De-

a Defcription of the feveral Parts of this Ifland, in twelve Foot Verfe, and contained in thirty Books, or, as the Author has himfelf called them, Songs.

Neither *Langbaine*, *Jacob*, nor any of the other Writers have mentioned him as a Dramatift, but *Coxeter* tells us, that he has feen an old MS. to the Play, called,

The *Merry Devil of Edmonton.* Com.

which declares it to have been written by *Michael Drayton*, Efq; and as the earlieft Edition of that Piece is dated in 1612, at which Time our Author was in very high Eftimation, it is moft prcbable to have been his.

This celebrated Bard died in 1631. being 68 Years of Age, and was buried amcng the Poets in *Weftminfter-Abbey.*—Over his Grave is erected a handfome Table Monument of Blue Marble, adorned with his Effigies in Bufto laureated.

DRURY, *Thomas.*——Of this Gentleman I know nothing more, than that he was an Attorney at Law, and wrote the three following Farces, *viz.*

 1. *Devil of a Duke.* Ballad Farce.
 2. *Mock Captain.* F.
 3. *Rival Milliners.* F.

DRYDEN, *John*, Efq;——As this very eminent Poet had but little Concern with public Affairs, any farther than by his Writings, and as the Incidents of his Life had no great Variety in them, or at leaft very few of them are on Record, I fhall moftly confine myfelf in this Detail of his Hiftory, to his Proceedings and Progrefs in literary ard poetical Fame.—It will therefore be fufficient to inform my Readers, that he was the Son of *Erafmus*

Dryden, Efq; of *Tichmarfh*, and Grandfon of Sir *Erafmus Dryden*, of *Canonfbury*, both in *Northamptonfhire*, and that he was born fome Time in the Year 1631, at *Oldwincle*, or *Aldwincle* near *Oundle*, in the faid County; a Village, which, as he himfelf informs us, belonged to the Earl of *Exeter*, and which was alfo famous for giving Birth to the celebrated Dr. *Thomas Fuller*, the Hiftorian.

He received the Rudiments of his Grammar Learning at *Weftminfter* School, under the learned Dr. *Bufby*, and from thence was removed in 1650 to *Cambridge*, being elected Scholar of *Trinity* College, of which he appears, by his *Latin* Verfes in the *Epithalamia. Cantabrigienf.* 4to. 1662. to have been afterwards a Fellow.—Yet. in his earlier Days he gave no very extraordinary Indications of Genius, for, even the Year before he quitted the Univerfity, he wrote a Poem on the Death of Lord *Haftings*, which was by no Means a Prefage of that amazing Perfection in poetical Powers which he afterwards poffefs'd.—His firft Play, *viz.* the *Wild Gallants*, did not appear till he was not much lefs than forty Years of Age, and then met with fuch indifferent Succefs, that had not Neceffity afterwards compelled him to purfue the arduous Tafk, the *Englifh* Stage had perhaps never been favoured with fome of it's brighteft Ornaments.

But to proceed more regularly.—On the Death of *Oliver Cromwell* he wrote fome heroic Stanzas to his Memory; but on the Reftoration, being defirous of ingratiating himfelf with the new Court, he wrote, firft, a Poem entitled *Aftræa redux*, and afterwards a Panegyrick to the King on his Coronationr—In 1662, he addreſſed a Poem to the Lord Chancellor *Hyde*, preſented on *New-Year*'s Day ; and in the ſame Year a Satire on the *Dutch*. —In 1668 appear'd his *Annus Mirabilis*, which was an hiſtorical Poem in Celebration of the Duke of *York*'s Victory over the *Dutch*. —Theſe Pieces at length obtained him the Favour of the Crown, and Sir *William D'Avenant* dying the ſame Year, Mr. *Dryden* was appointed to ſucceed him as Poet-Laureat.—About this Time alſo his Inclination for writing for the Stage ſeems firſt to have ſhewn itſelf, for, beſides his Concern with Sir *William D'Avenant* in the Alteration of *Shakeſpeare's Tempeſt*, which was the laſt Work that Gentleman was engaged in, Mr. *Dryden* in 1669 produced his *Wild Gallants*, a Comedy.— This, as I have before obſerved, met with very indifferent Succeſs ; yet the Author, not being diſcouraged by it's Failure, ſoon after gave the Public his *Indian Emperor*, which finding a more favourable Reception, encouraged him to proceed, and that with ſuch Rapidity that, in the Key to the Duke of *Buckingham's Rehearſal*, he is recorded to have engaged himſelf by Contract for the writing of four Plays *per* Year ; and indeed, in the Years 1679 and 1680, he appears to have fulfilled that Contract.—To this unhappy Neceſſity that our Author lay under, are to be attributed all thoſe Irregularities, thoſe bombaſtic Flights, and ſometimes even puerile Exuberances, which he has been ſo ſeverely criticized on for, and which, in the unavoidable Hurry in which he wrote, it was impoſſible he ſhould find Time to reviſe, either

for the lopping away or correcting.—This alſo is ſurely a ſufficient Excuſe for his borrowing many Things both with Regard to his general Plots, and the particular Incidents of ſome of his Plays, from other Authors; and indeed, it is much leſs to be wonder'd, that under all theſe Diſadvantages he was obliged to apply to thoſe Reſources which his Enemies have affixed the Charge of Plagiariſm on him for, than that he ſhould produce ſo many admirable Originals as in Deſpite of them all he has done ; for even at the very Period I have mentioned, we find two of the beſt Plays our Language has been honour'd with, *viz.* The *Spaniſh Fryar* and *All for Love*, in the Number of thoſe Publications.

In 1675, the Earl of *Rocheſter*, whoſe envious and malevolent Diſpoſition would not permit him to ſee growing Merit meet with it's due Reward, and was therefore ſincerely chagrin'd at the very juſt Applauſe which Mr. *Dryden*'s dramatic Pieces had been received with, was determined, if poſſible, to ſhake his Intereſt at Court, and ſucceeded ſo far as to recommend Mr. *Crowne*, an Author by no Means of equal Merit, and at that Time of an obſcure Reputation, to write a Maſque for the Court, which certainly belonged to Mr. *Dryden*'s Office as Poet Laureat ———Nor was this the only Attack, nor indeed the moſt potent one, that Mr. *Dryden*'s juſtly acquired Fame drew on him, for ſome Years before the Duke of *Buckingham*, a Man of not much better a Character than Lord *Rocheſter*, had moſt ſeverely ridiculed ſeveral of our Author's Plays, in his admired Piece called

called the *Rebearfal.*—But though the intrinfic Wit which runs through that Performance cannot even to this Hour fail of exciting our Laughter, yet at the fame Time it ought not to be the Standard on which we fhould fix Mr. *Dryden*'s poetical Reputation, if we confider that the Pieces there ridicu'ed are not any of thofe which are look'd on as the *Cref D'Oeuvres* of this Author, that the very Paffages burlefqued, are frequently, in their original Places, much lefs ridiculous, than when thus detached, like a rotten Limb, from the Body of the Work, and expofed to View with additional Diftortions, and divefted of that Connection with the other Parts, which, while it preferved, gave it not only Symmetry but Beauty; and laftly, that the various inimitable Beauties, which the Critic has funk in Ob livion, are infinitely more numerous than the Deformities which he has thus induftrioufly brought forth to our more immediate Infpection.

Mr. *Dryden*, however, did not fuffer thefe Attacks to pafs with Impunity, for in 1679 there came out an *Effay on Satire*, faid to be written jointly by that Gentleman and the Earl of *Mulgrave*, containing fome very fevere Reflections on the Earl of *Rochefter* and the Dutchefs of *Portfmouth*, who, it is not improbable, might be a joint Inftrument in the above-mentioned Affront fhewn to Mr. *Dryden*, and in 1681 he publifhed his *Abfalom* and *Ackitophel*, in which the well-known Character of *Zimri*, drawn for the Duke of *Buckingham*, is certainly fevere enough to repay all the Ridicule thrown on him by that Nobleman in the Character of *Bayes*. —— The Refentment

shewn by the different Peers was very different; Lord *Rochefter*, who was a Coward as well as a Man of the moft depraved Morals, bafely hired three Ruffians to cudgel *Dryden* in a Coffeehoufe; but the Duke of *Buckingham*, as we are told, in a more open Manner, took that Tafk on himfelf, and at the fame Time prefented him with a Purfe containing no very trifling Sum of Money, telling him that he gave him the Beating as a Punifhment for his Impudence, but beftowed the Gold on him as a Reward for his Wit.

In 1680 was publifhed a Tranflation of *Ovid's Epiftles* in *Englifh* Verfe, by feveral Hands, two of which, together with the Preface, were by Mr. *Dryden*.—In 1682, came out his *Religio Laici*, defigned as a Defence of revealed Religion, againft Deifts, Papifts, &c. and in 1634. he publifhed a Tranflation of M. *Al.imbourg*'s Hiftory of the League, which he had undertaken by the Command of King *Charles* II.——On the Death of that Prince he wrote a Poem facred to his Memory, entitled *Threnodia Augustalis*.

Soon after the Acceffion of King *James* II. our Author changed his Religion for that of the Church of *Rome*, and wrote two Pieces in Vindication of the *Romifh* Tenets, *viz. A Defence of the Papers*, written by the late King, of blefled Memory, found in his ftrong Box, and the celebrated Poem, afterwards anfwered by Lord *Hallifax*, entitled the *Hind and the Panther.*—By this extraordinary Step he not only engaged himfelf in Controverfy, and incurred much Cenfure and Ridicule from his Cotemporary Wits, but, on the Completion of the Revolution, being, on Account

of

of his newly-chofen Religion, difqualified from bearing any Office under the Government, he was ftripped of the Laurel, which to his ftill greater Mortification was beftowed on *Richard Flecknoe*, a Man to whom he had a moft fettled Averfion.——This Circumftance occafioned his writing the very fevere Poem, called *Mac Flecknoe*.

Mr. *Dryden*'s Circumftances had never been affluent, but now being deprived of this little Support, he found himfelf reduced to the Neceffity of writing for meer Bread.——We confequently find him from this Period engaged in Works of Labour as well as Genius, *viz.* in tranflating Works of others ; and to this Neceffity perhaps our Nation ftands indebted for fome of the beft Tranflations extant.——In the Year he loft the Laurel he publifhed the Life of St. *Francis Xavier*, from the *French*.——In 1693, came out a Tranflation of *Juvenal* and *Perfius*, in the firft of which he had a confiderable Hand, and of the latter the entire Execution.——In 1695 was publifhed his Profe Verfion of *Frefnoy*'s *Art of Painting*, and the Year 1697 gave the World that Tranflation of *Virgil*'s Works entire, which ftill does, and perhaps ever will, ftand foremoft among the Attempts made on that Author.—— The *Petite Pieces* of this eminent Writer, fuch as Prologues, Epilogues, Epitaphs, Elegies, Songs, *&c.* are too numerous to fpecify here, and too much difperfed to direct the Reader to.——The greateft Part of them however are to be found in a Collection of Mifcellanies, in fix Vol. 12mo.—— His laft Work is what is called his *Fables*, which confift of many of the moft interefting Stories in

Homer, *Ovid*, *Boccace* and *Chaucer*, tranflated or modernized in the moft elegant and poetical Manner, together with fome original Pieces, among which is that amazing Ode on St. *Cæcilia*'s Day, which, tho' written in the very Decline of it's Author's Life, and at a Period when Old Age and Diftrefs confpired as it were to damp his poetic Ardor and clip the Wings of Fancy, yet poffeffes fo much of both, as would be fufficient to have render'd him immortal, had he never written a fingle Line befides.

Dryden married the Lady *Elizabeth Howard*, Sifter to the Earl of *Berkfhire*, who furvived him eight Years, though for the laft four of them fhe was a Lunatic, having been deprived of her Senfes by a nervous Fever.——By this Lady he had three Sons, who all furvived him.——Their Names were *Charles*, *John* and *Henry*.—— Of the laft of thefe I can trace no Particulars.——The fecond fome little Account will be given of in the fucceeding Article, and with Refpect to the eldeft there is a Circumftance related by *Charles Wilfon*, Efq; in his Life of *Congreve*, which feems fo well attefted, and is itfelf of fo very extraordinary a Nature, that I cannot avoid admitting it to a Place here.——The Event is as follows.

Dryden, with all his Underftanding, was weak enough to be fond of Judicial Aftrology, and ufed to calculate the Nativity of his Children.——When his Lady was in Labour with his Son *Charles*, he being told it was decent to withdraw, laid his Watch on the Table, begging one of the Ladies then prefent, in a moft folemn Manner, to take exact Notice of the very Minute the Child was born, which fhe did,

and

and acquainted him with it.——
About a Week after, when his
Lady was pretty well recovered,
Mr. *Dryden* took Occafion to tell
her that he had been calculating
the Child's Nativity, and obferved, with Grief, that he was born
in an evil Hour, for *Jupiter*, *Venus* and the Sun, were all under
the Earth, and the Lord of his
Afcendant afflicted with a hateful Square of *Mars* and *Saturn*.——
If he lives to arrive at the 8th
Year, fays he, " he will go near
" to die a violent Death on his
" very Birth-Day, but if he
" fhould efcape, as I fee but fmall
" Hopes, he will in the 23d
" Year be under the very fame
" evil Direction, and if he fhould
" efcape that alfo, the 33d or
" 34th Year is, I fear"——here
he was interrupted by the immoderate Grief of his Lady, who
could no longer hear Calamity
prophecied to befall her Son.——
The Time at laft came, and *Auguft* was the inaufpicious Month
in which young *Dryden* was to
enter into the eighth Year of his
Age.——The Court being in Progrefs, and Mr. *Dryden* at leifure,
he was invited to the Country-
Seat of the Earl of *Berkfhire*, his
Brother-in-Law, to keep the long
Vacation with him in *Charlton* in
Wilts; his Lady was invited to
her Uncle *Mordaunt*'s, to pafs
the Remainder of the Summer.——
When they came to divide the
Children, Lady *Elizabeth* would
have him take *John*, and fuffer
her to take *Charles*; but Mr.
Dryden was too abfolute, and
they parted in Anger; he took
Charles with him, and fhe was
obliged to be content with *John*.
When the fatal Day came, the
Anxiety of the Lady's Spirits oc-
cafioned fuch an Effervefcence of
Blood, as threw her into fo vio-

lent a Fever, that her Life was
defpaired of, till a Letter came
from Mr. *Dryden*, reproving her
for her Womanifh Credulity, and
affuring her that her Child was
well, which recovered her Spirits,
and in fix Weeks after fhe received an Ecclairciffement of the
whole Affair. — Mr. *Dryden*, either through Fear of being reckoned fuperftitious, or thinking it
a Science beneath his Study, was
extremely cautious of letting any
one know that he was a Dealer
in Aftrology; therefore could not
excufe his Abfence, on his Son's
Anniverfary, from a general
Hunting Match Lord *Berkfhire*
had made, to which all the adjacent Gentlemen were invited.
When he went out, he took Care
to fet the Boy a double Exercife
in the *Latin* Tongue, which he
taught his Children himfelf, with
a ftrict Charge not to ftir out of
the Room till his Return; well
knowing the Tafk he had fet
him would take up longer Time.
Charles was performing his Duty,
in Obedience to his Father, but
as ill Fate would have it, the
Stag made towards the Houfe;
and the Noife alarming the Servants, they hafted out to fee the
Sport.——One of them took young
Dryden by the Hand, and led him
out to fee it alfo, when, juft as
they came to the Gate, the Stag
being at Bay with the Dogs, made
a bold Pufh, and leaped over the
Court Wall, which was very low,
and very old; and the Dogs following, threw down a Part of the
Wall ten Yards in Length, under which *Charles Dryden* lay buried.——He was immediately dug
out, and after fix Weeks languifhing in a dangerous Way he
recovered; fo far *Dryden*'s Pre-
diction was fulfilled : In the
twenty-third Year of his Age,
Charles

Charles fell from the Top of an old Tower belonging to the Vatican at *Rome*, occasioned by a Swimming in his Head, with which he was seized, the Heat of the Day being excessive.—He again recovered, but was ever after in a languishing sickly State. In the thirty-third Year of his Age, being returned to *England*, he was unhappily drowned at *Windsor*.—He had with another Gentleman swam twice over the *Thames*; but returning a third Time, it was supposed he was taken with the Cramp, because he called out for Help, tho' too late.—Thus the Father's Calculation proved but too prophetical.

At last, after a long Life, harrass'd with the most laborious of all Fatigues, *viz.* that of the Mind, and continually made anxious by Distress and Difficulty, our Author departed this Life on the first of *May* 1701, and was interred in *Westminster-Abbey*.— On the 19th of *April* he had been very bad with the Gout and Erisipelas in one leg; but he was then somewhat recovered, and designed to go abroad; on the *Friday* following he eat a Partridge for his Supper, and going to take a Turn in the little Garden behind his House in *Gerard-Street*, he was seized with a violent Pain under the Ball of the great Toe of his right Foot; that, unable to stand, he cried out for Help, and was carried in by his Servants, when, upon sending for Surgeons, they found a small black Spot in the Place affected; he submitted to their present Applications, and when gone called his Son *Charles* to him, using these Words. — " I know this " black Spot is a Mortification : " I know also, that it will seize " my Head, and that they will

" attempt to cut off my Leg; " but I command you my Son, " by your filial Duty, that you " do not suffer me to be dismem- " bered :" As he foretold, the Event proved, and his Son was too dutiful to disobey his Father's Commands.

On the *Wednesday* Morning following, he breathed his last, under the most excruciating Pains, in the 69th Year of his Age.

The Day after Mr. *Dryden*'s Death, the Dean of *Westminster* sent Word to Mr. *Dryden*'s Widow, that he would make a Present of the Ground, and all other Abbey-Fees for the Funeral :— The Lord *Halifax* likewise sent to the Lady *Elizabeth*, and to Mr. *Charles Dryden*, offering to defray the Expences of our Poet's Funeral, and afterwards to bestow 500 l. on a Monument in the *Abbey*; which generous Offer was accepted.—Accordingly, on *Sunday* following, the Company being assembled, the Corpse was put into a Velvet Hearse, attended by eighteen mourning Coaches.—When they were just ready to move, Lord *Jefferys*, Son of Lord Chancellor *Jeffreys*, a Name dedicated to Infamy, with some of his rakish Companions riding by, asked whose Funeral it was; and being told it was Mr. *Dryden*'s, he protested he should not be buried in that private Manner, that he would himself, with the Lady *Elizabeth*'s Leave, have the Honour of the Interment, and would bestow a thousand Pounds on a Monument in the *Abbey* for him.—This put a Stop to their Procession; and the Lord *Jefferys*, with several of the Gentlemen, who had alighted from their Coaches, went up Stairs to the Lady, who was sick in Bed.—His Lordship repeated
the

the Purport of what he had said below; but the Lady *Elizabeth* refusing her Consent, he fell on his Knees, vowing never to rise till his Request was granted.—The Lady under a sudden Surprise fainted away, and Lord *Jefferys* pretending to have obtained her Consent, ordered the Body to be carried to Mr. *Russel's* an Undertaker in *Cheapside*, and to be left there till further Orders.—In the mean Time the *Abbey* was lighted up, the Ground opened, the Choir attending, and the Bishop waiting some Hours to no Purpose for the Corpse.—The next Day Mr. *Charles Dryden* waited on my Lord *Halifax*, and the Bishop; and endeavoured to excuse his Mother, by relating the Truth. Three Days after the Undertaker having received no Orders, waited on the Lord *Jefferys*; who pretended it was a drunken Frolic, that he remembered nothing of the Matter, and he might do what he pleased with the Body. Upon this, the Undertaker waited on the Lady *Elizabeth*, who desired a Day's Respite, which was granted.—Mr. *Charles Dryden* immediately wrote to the Lord *Jefferys*, who returned for Answer, that he knew nothing of the Matter, and would be troubled no more about it.—Mr. *Dryden* hereupon applied again to the Lord *Halifax*, and the Bishop of *Rochester*, who absolutely refused to do any Thing in the Affair.

In this Distress, Dr. *Garth*, who had been Mr. *Dryden's* intimate Friend, sent for the Corpse to the College of Physicians, and proposed a Subscription; which succeeding, about three Weeks after Mr. *Dryden's* Decease, Dr. *Garth* pronounced a fine *Latin* Oration over the Body, which

was conveyed from the College, attended by a numerous Train of Coaches to *Westminster-Abbey*, but in very great Disorder.—At last the Corpse arrived at the *Abbey*, which was all unlighted.——No Organ played, no Anthem sung; only two of the singing Boys preceeding the Corpse, who sung an Ode of *Horace*, with each a small Candle in their Hand.—When the Funeral was over, Mr. *Charles Dryden* sent a Challenge to Lord *Jefferys*, who refusing to answer it, he sent several others, and went often himself; but could neither get a Letter delivered, nor Admittance to speak to him; which so incensed him, that finding his Lordship refused to answer him like a Gentleman, he resolved to watch an Opportunity, and brave him to fight, though with all the Rules of Honour; which his Lordship hearing, quitted the Town, and Mr. *Charles* never had an Opportunity to meet him, tho' he sought it to his Death, with the utmost Application.

Mr. *Dryden* had no Monument erected to him for several Years; to which Mr. *Pope* alludes in his Epitaph intended for Mr. *Rowe*, in this Line.

Beneath a rude and nameless Stone
he lies.

In a Note upon which we are informed, that the Tomb of Mr. *Dryden* was erected upon this Hint, by *Sheffield* Duke of *Buckingham*, to which was originally intended this Epitaph.

This Sheffield *raised.—The sacred*
Dust below,
Was Dryden *once; the rest who*
does not know.

Which

Which was fince changed into the plain Infcription now upon it, *viz.*

J. D R Y D E N,
Natus Aug. 9, 1631.
Mortus Maii 1. 1701.
*Johannes Sheffield, dux Buckingha-
mienfis fecit.*

Mr. *Dryden*'s Character has been very differently drawn by different Hands, fome of which have exalted it to the higheft Degree of Commendation, and others debafed it to the fevereft Cenfure.—The latter, however, we muft charge to that ftrong Spirit of Party which prevailed during great Part of *Dryden*'s Time, and ought therefore to be taken with great Allowances.—Were we indeed to form a Judgment of the Author from fome of his dramatic Writings, we fhould perhaps be apt to conclude him a Man of the moft licentious Morals, many of his Comedies containing a great Share of Loofenefs, even extending to Obfcenity; but if we confider that, as the Poet tells us,

*Thofe who live to pleafe, muft pleafe
to live,*

if we then look back to the fcandalous Licence of the Age he lived in, the Indigence which at Times he underwent, and the Neceffity he confequently lay under of complying with the public Tafte however deprav'd, we fhall furely not refufe our Pardon to the compelled Writer, nor our Credit to thofe of his Cotemporaries, who were intimately acquainted with him, and who have affur'd us there was nothing remarkably vicious in his perfonal Character.

From fome Parts of his Hiftory he appears unfteady, and to have too readily temporized with the feveral Revolutions in Church and State.—This however might in fome Meafure have been owing to that natural Timidity and Diffidence in his Difpofition, which almoft all the Writers feem to agree in his poffeffing.—*Congreve,* whofe Authority cannot be fufpected, has given us fuch an Account of him, as makes him appear no lefs amiable in his private Character as a Man, than he was illuftrious in his public one as a Poet.——In the former Light, according to that Gentleman, he was humane, compaffionate, forgiving, and fincerely friendly.—Of an extenfive Reading, a tenacious Memory, and a ready Communication.—Gentle in the Correction of the Writings of others, and patient under the Reprehenfion of his own Deficiencies.—Eafy of Accefs himfelf, but flow and diffident in his Advances to others; and of all Men the moft modeft and the moft eafy to be difcountenanced in his Approaches, either to his Superiors or his Equals.—As to his Writings, he is perhaps the happieft in the Harmony of his Numbers, of any Poet who ever lived either before or fince his Time, not even Mr. *Pope* himfelf excepted.—His Imagination is ever warm, his Images noble, his Defcriptions beautiful, and his Sentiments juft and becoming.—In his Profe he is poetical without Bombaft, concife without Pedantry, and clear without Prolixity.—As a Dramatift he has, perhaps, the leaft Merit of all his Writings; and indeed the fair Confeffion which he has made of his Unfitnefs for the writing of Comedy, (and his comic Pieces

it

it is that have been the moft feverely handled by the Critics) would, one might imagine, have been fufficient to filence the Clamour of that fnarling Band.——— The Paffage is in his admirable Effay on Dramatic Poetry.——" I " want, (fays he) that Gaiety of " Humour that is required in it. " ——My Converfation is flow and " dull, my Humour faturnine " and referved.——In fhort, I am " none of thofe who endeavour " to break Jefts in Company, and " make Repartees; fo that thofe " who decry my Comedies, do " me no Injury, except it be in " Point of Profit.——Reputation " in them is the laft Thing to " which I fhall pretend."

In Tragedy alfo he feems to have been very diffident of his own Merit, and confcious of the Difadvantages he lay under from his compelled Neceffity of rendering his Pieces popular; and tho' there are many of them which are truly excellent, yet he tells us that he never wrote any Thing in the dramatic Way to pleafe himfelf but his *All for Love.*———I fhall, however, clofe my Account of this celebrated Author with the Words of Mr. *Congreve,* who has borne the following ftrong Teftimonial to his poetical Merit.

" I may venture (fays that Gentleman) to fay in general Terms, that no Man has written in our Language, fo much, and fuch various Matter; and in fo various Manners fo well.——Another Thing, I may fay, was very peculiar to him, which is, that his Parts did not decline with his Years, but that he was an improved Writer to the laft, even to near feventy Years of Age; improving even in Fire and Imagination as well as in Judgment;

witnefs his Ode on St. *Cæcilia's* Day, and his Fables, his lateft Performance.——He was equally excellent in Verfe and Profe.—— His Profe had all the Clearnefs imaginable, without deviating to the Language or Diction of Poetry.——In his Poems, his Diction is, whenever his Subject requires it, fo fublime, and fo truly poetical, that it's Effence, like that of pure Gold, cannot be deftroyed.——Take his Verfes, and diveft them of their Rhimes, disjoint them of their Numbers, tranfpofe their Expreffions, make what Arrangement or Difpofition you pleafe in his Words; yet fhall there eternally be Poetry, and fomething which will be found incapable of being reduced to abfolute Profe.——What he has done in any one Species or diftinct Kind of Writing, would have been fufficient to have acquired him a very great Name.——If he had written nothing but his Prefaces, or nothing but his Songs and his Prologues, each of them would have entitled him to the Preference and Diftinction of excelling in it's Kind.

Befides his other numerous Writings, he was Author of, and concerned in, the following dramatic Pieces, *viz.*

1. ALBION *and* ALBANIUS. Oratorio.
2. ALEXANDER'S *Feaft.* Oratorio.
3. *All for Love.* T.
4. AMBOYNA. T.
5. AMPHYTRION. C.
6. *Affignation.* C.
7. AURENGE-ZEBE. T.
8. CLEOMENES. T.
9. *Conqueft of* GRANADA. T. two Parts.
10. *Don* SEBASTIAN. T.
11. *Duke of* GUISE. T. (affifted by *Lee.*)

12. *Eve-*

12. *Evening's Love.* C.
13. INDIAN *Emperor.* T. C.
14. *Kind Keeper.* C.
15. *King* ARTHUR. Dram. Opera.
16. *Love triumphant.* T. C.
17. *Mall.* C. (afcribed to him, but not probable to be his.)
18. *Marriage a-la-Mode.* C.
19. *Miftaken Hufband.* C. (only adopted by him and improved by the Addition of a Scene.)
20. OEDIPUS *King of* THEBES. T. (affifted by *N. Lee.*)
21. *Rival Ladies.* C.
22. *Secret Love.* T. C.
23. *Sir* MARTIN MARRALL. C.
24. SPANISH *Fryar.* T. C.
25. *State of Innocence.* Opera.
26. *Tempeft.* C. (alter'd from *Shakefpeare,* with the Affiftance of Sir *William D'Avenant.)*
27. TROILUS *and* CRESSIDA. Trag.
28. *Tyrannic Love.* T.
29. *Wild Gallant.* C.

DRYDEN, Mr. *John,* jun.——This Gentleman was fecond Son to the great Poet laft-mentioned.——He went early to *Rome,* where he was entertain'd by the Pope as one of the Gentlemen of his Bed-Chamber, and at which Place he died; but I cannot trace in what Year that Event happened.——While he was abroad he wrote one Play, which he fent over to his Father, who at length brought it on the Stage, though not till fome Years after it was written.——It is entitled,

The *Hufband his own Cuckold.* Com.

DUFFET, Mr. *Thomas,*——This Author was a Milliner in the *New Exchange,* but his Genius leading him to dramatic Poetry, he wrote feveral Pieces for the Stage, which at firft met with good Succefs, but afterwards funk into Contempt and Oblivion.—— And indeed, the favourable Reception they found at their firft Appearance feems not to have been fo much owing to the Genius of their Author, which was but of a very moderate Rank, as to that Fondnefs of Abufe and Scurrility which has been almoft at all Times prevalent with the Public; and Mr. *Duffet* ftood more indebted to the great Names of thofe Authors whofe Works he attempted to burlefque and ridicule, viz. *Dryden, Shadwell* and *Settle,* than to any Merit of his own.——Traveftie and Burlefque will ever create a Laugh; but, however intended, can never do any effential Hurt to Performances of real Worth; nor could the Mock *Tempeft, Pfyche* or *Emprefs of Morocco* leffen, in the Opinion of the judicious, the Value of the Originals on which they are founded.——And altho' now and then a great Genius and a true Fund of Humour may ftamp Immortality on a Burlefque, as in the Cafe of *Scarron's Virgil traveftie,* and *Cotton's Scarronides,* yet, where a Deficiency of thofe brilliant Qualities is apparent, and a Vein of Scurrility and perfonal Ill-Nature indulged, as in the above nam'd Works of Mr. *Duffet,* tho' they may for a fhort Period draw in the Public to join in the Laugh *with* them, yet it will conftantly be found, in a little Time, to exchange it for laughing *at* them, and at length to condemn them to a perpetual Obfcurity and Contempt.

The Pieces Mr. *Duffet* has left behind him, the beft of which were thofe which met with the worft worſt Succeſs, are ſix in Number, *viz.*

1. *Amorous old Woman.* C.
2. *Beauty's Triumph.* Maſque.
3. *Empreſs of* MOROCCO. F.
4. *Mock Tempeſt.* F.
5. PSYCHE *Debauch'd.* Mock Opera.
6. *Spaniſh Rogue.* C.

Among theſe, however, the firſt is every where mentioned as by an unknown Author, excepting by *Langbaine*, who attributes it to this Writer.

DUNCOMBE, Mr. *William.*— This very ingenious and worthy Gentleman is ſtill living, and has favour'd the World with many little Pieces of Eſtimation in the poetical Way.—He has alſo publiſhed very good Tranſlations of two celebrated *French* Tragedies, the one of *Racine*, the other of *Voltaire*, the firſt of which, however, was never acted, or, I believe, intended for the Stage, *viz.*

ATHALIAH. Trag.
LUCIUS JUNIUS BRUTUS. Trag.

D'URFEY, Mr. *Thomas.*—— Altho' this Author's Name is perhaps as well known as that of any Writer extant, yet there are very few Particulars that can be traced concerning him, more than that he was born in *Devonſhire*; but of what Family, or in what Year, ſeems uncertain.—He was originally bred to the Law, but ſoon finding that Profeſſion too ſaturnine for his volatile and lively Genius, he quitted it, to become a Devotee of the Muſes; in which he met with no ſmall Succeſs.——His dramatic Pieces, which are very numerous, were in general well received; yet, tho' he has not been dead above forty Years, there is not one of them now on the Muſter Roll of

acting Plays; that Licentiouſneſs of Intrigue, Looſeneſs of Sentiment, and Indelicacy of Wit, which were their ſtrongeſt Recommendations to the Audiences for whom they were written, having very juſtly baniſhed them from the Stage in this Period of purer Taſte.—Yet are they very far from being totally devoid of Merit.—The Plots are in general buſy, intricate and entertaining; the Characters not ill drawn, altho' rather too farcical, and the Language, if not perfectly correct, yet eaſy and well adapted for the Dialogue of Comedy.—But what Mr. *D'Urfey* obtained his greateſt Reputation by, was a peculiarly happy Knack he poſſeſſed in the writing of Satires and irregular Odes.—Many of theſe were upon temporary Occaſions, and were of no little Service to the Party in whoſe Cauſe he wrote; which, together with his natural Vivacity and Good-Humour, obtained him the Favour of great Numbers of Perſons of all Ranks and Conditions, Monarchs themſelves not excluded.—He was ſtrongly attached to the Tory Intereſt, and in the latter Part of Queen *Anne's* Reign had frequently the Honour of diverting that Princeſs with witty Catches and Songs of Humour, ſuited to the Spirit of the Times, written by himſelf, and which he ſung in a lively and entertaining Manner. —— And the Author of the *Guardian*, who in No. 67 has given a very humorous Account of Mr. *D'Urfey*, with a View to recommend him to the public Notice for a Benefit Play, tells us, that he remember'd King *Charles* II. leaning on *Tom D'Urfey's* Shoulder more than once, and humming over a Song with him.

He was certainly a very diverting Companion, and a chearful, honeſt, good-natur'd Man, ſo that he was the Delight of the moſt polite Companies and Converſations from the Beginning of *Charles* II's to the latter Part of King *George* I's Reign, and many an honeſt Gentleman got a Reputation in his Country by pretending to have been in Company with *Tom D'Urfey.*—Yet, ſo univerſal a Favorite as he was, it is apparent, that towards the latter Part of his Life he ſtood in Need of Aſſiſtance to prevent his paſſing the Remainder of it in a Cage like a ſinging Bird, for, to ſpeak in his own Words, as repeated by the above-named Author, " after having written more " Odes than *Horace,* and about " four Times as many Comedies " as *Terence,* he found himſelf " reduced to great Difficulties by " the Importunities of a Set of " Men, who of late Years had " furniſhed him with the Ac- " commodations of Life, and " would not, as we ſay, be paid " with a Song."—Mr. *Addiſon* then informs us, that in order to extricate him from theſe Difficulties, he himſelf immediately applied to the Directors of the Playhouſe, who very generouſly agreed to act the *Plotting Siſters,* a Play of Mr. *D'Urfey*'s, for the Benefit of it's Author.—What the Reſult of this Benefit was does not appear, but it was probably ſufficient to make him eaſy, as we find him living and continuing to write with the ſame Humour and Livelineſs to the Time of his Death, which happened on the 26th of *Feb.* 1723.—What was his Age at this Time is not certainly ſpecified any where, but he muſt have been conſiderably advanced in Life, his firſt Play, which could ſcarcely have been written before he was twenty Years of Age, having made it's Appearance forty ſeven Years before.——He was buried in the Church-Yard of St. *James's, Weſtminſter.*

Thoſe who have a Curioſity to ſee his Ballads, Sonnets, *&c.* may find a large Number of them brought together in a Collection in three Volumes in Duodecimo, intitled *Laugh and be fat,* or *Pills to purge Melancholy,* of which the *Guardian,* in No. 29, ſpeaks in very favorable Terms.—The Titles of his dramatic Pieces may be found in the enſuing Liſt.

1. ARIADNE. Paſt. Opera. *Vid.* Vol. I. APPENDIX.
2. *Banditti.* C.
3. BATH. C.
4. BUSSY D'AMBOIS. T.
5. *Campaigners.* C.
6. *Commonwealth of Women.* Trag.-Com.
7. CYNTHIA *and* ENDYMION. Opera.
8. *Don* QUIXOTE. Com. in three Parts.
9. *Fond Huſband.* C.
10. *Fool's Preferment.* C.
11. *Fool turn'd Critic.* C.
12. GRECIAN *Heroine.* T.
13. *Injur'd Princeſs.* T. C.
14. *Intrigue at* VERSAILLES. Com.
15. *Love for Money.* C.
16. *Madam* FICKLE. C.
17. *Marriage hater match'd.* C.
18. MASSANIELLO. Play. in two Parts.
19. *Modern Prophets.* C.
20. *Old Mode and the New.* C.
21. *Queens of* BRENTFORD. Ball. Opera.
22. RICHMOND *Heireſs.* C.
23. *Royaliſt.* C.
24. *Siege of* MEMPHIS. T.

25. Sir

25. *Sir* BARNABY WHIG. Com.
26. *Squire* OLD SAP. C.
27. *Trick for Trick.* C.
28. *Virtuous Wife.* C.
29. *Wonders in the Sun.* Com. Opera.

———————

E.

E. K. *Vid.* K. F.

ECCLESTON, Mr. *Edward.*——Of this Gentleman I know no more than that he was Author of one dramatic Piece, entitled,

Noah's Flood. Opera.

It was afterwards republished by two different Titles, *viz.*

The *Cataclijm* and

The *Deluge.*

ECHARD, The Rev. Mr. *Lawrence.*—This Gentleman was, I believe, the only Son of a Clergyman, who was possess'd of a good Estate in *Suffolk.*—I do not find it recorded in what Year he was born, but one of his Translations from *Plautus,* viz. that of the *Amphitryo,* was published in 1694.—He received his Education at the University of *Cambridge,* and soon after his quitting College, having taken Orders, was presented to the Living of *Welton* and *Elkington* in *Lincolnshire,* where he past about twenty Years of his Life.—In the Year 1712, he was installed Archdeacon of *Stowe* and Prebend of *Lincoln.*—He acquired a great Reputation by his Writings, more especially his History of *England,* which, tho' violently attacked by *Oldmixon,* is still held in considerable Estimation.—In the dramatic Way he has produced nothing

original, nor any thing intended for theatrical Representation, but has, however, favoured the World with very good Translations, from *Plautus* and *Terence,* of the nine following Comedies, *viz.*

1. *Adelphi.* C.
2. AMPHYTRION. C.
3. *Andria.* C.
4. EPIDICUS. C.
5. *Eunuchus.* C.
6. *Heautontimorumenos.*
7. *Hecyra.*
8. PHORMIO.
9. *Rudens.*

Mr. *Echard* died in 1730.

EDWARDS, Mr. *Richard.*—— This very early Writer was born in *Somersetshire* in 1523, was admitted a Scholar of *Corpus Christi* College in *Oxford,* under the Tuition of *George Etheridge, May* 11, 1540.——In the Beginning of 1547, being only twenty four Years of Age, he was elected a Student of the upper Table of *Christ* Church, at its Foundation by King *Henry* VIII. and the same Year took his Degree as Master of Arts.—In the Beginning of Queen *Elizabeth* he was made one of the Gentlemen of her Chapel, and Teacher of Music to the Children of the Choir.—*Chetwood* asserts, but on what Foundation I know not, that he had a Licence granted him by that Monarch to superintend the Children of the Chapel as her Majesty's Company of Comedians; or, in other Terms, had a Patent as Manager of a Theatre Royal in that Reign. Be that as it will, it is certain that he was esteemed both an excellent Poet and Musician, as many of his Compositions in Music (for he was not only skilled in the executive, but also in the theoretical Part of that Science) and his Works in Poetry do shew; for which he was highly

valued

valued by thofe that knew him, efpecially his Affociates. in *Lincoln's-Inn*, of which Society he was not only a Member, but in fome Refpects an Ornament.

He is almoft one of our firft dramatic Writers, having left behind him three Pieces, which were reprefented on the Stage, the earlieft of which is dated as foon as 1562.—Their Titles are,

 1. DAMON *and* PYTHYAS. Com.

 2. PALÆMON *and* ARCYTE. Com. in two Parts.

The firft of thefe was acted at Court and in the Univerfity, and is reprinted in the firft Vol. of *Dodfley's* Collection of old Plays. —Of the latter *Wood* has furnifhed us with the following Anecdote, *viz.* that being acted in *Chrift* Church Hall, 1566, before Queen *Elizabeth*, her Majefty was fo much delighted with it, that fending for the Author to her, fhe was pleafed to give him many Thanks, with Promife of Reward for his Pains. —He alfo tells us, that in the faid Play was acted a Cry of Hourds in the Quadrant upon the Train of a Fox in the hunting of *Thefeus*; with which the young Scholars, who ftood in the remoter Parts of the Stage and in the Windows, were fo much taken and furprized, fuppofing it had been real, that they cried out, *there, there—he's caught, he's caught.*—All which the Queen, merrily beholding, faid, *Oh! excellent! thofe Boys in very Truth are ready to leap out of the Windows to follow the Hounds.*—He adds moreover, that at a Sort of private Rehearfal of this Piece before the Queen's Arrival at *Oxford*, in the Prefence of certain Courtiers, it was fo well liked by them, that they faid it far fur-

paffed *Damon and Pythyas*, than which they thought nothing could be better; nay, fome even faid, that if the Author proceeded to write any more Plays before his Death, he would certainly run mad.—This however was never put to the Teft, for tho' he began fome other dramatic Pieces, he never finifhed any but the above, Death taking him away, much lamented by all the ingenious Men of his Time, that very Year 1566.—He wrote feveral Poems, which were publifhed after his Death, together with thofe of fome other Authors, in a Collection entitled, *A Paradife of dainty Devifes*, 1578. —And when he was in the Extremity of his laft Sicknefs, he wrote a Poem on that Occafion, which was efteemed a good Piece, entitled, *Edwards's Soulknil*, or *the Soules Knell*.

ELIZABETH, Queen.—Our Readers may perhaps be furprized to find the Name of this illuftrious Princefs among the Catalogue of our dramatic Writers, as it is well known that there is no Piece extant as hers.——Yet it would be an inexcufable Omiffion in a Work of this Nature, were we to pafs over unnoticed the Information which Sir *Robert Naunton* and others have given us, that this Princefs, for her own private Amufement, tranflated one of the Tragedies of *Euripides* from the *Greek*; tho' which particular Play it was they have none of them fpecified.—To attempt any Account of the Events of the Life and Reign of this illuftrious Sovereign, befides that it would far o'erleap the Bounds of this Work, would be an Act of abfolute Superfluity, as it has been fo well and amply executed by many Hiftorians of great Abilities.—We

fhall

ſhall only here obſerve, that the Circumſtance on which we have here had Occaſion to mention her, is one Teſtimonial among many of that Eminence in Learning which ſhe maintained, and that ſhe not only was perfect Miſtreſs of moſt of the living Languages, but was alſo equally well acquainted with the dead ones, and converſant with the Labours of the Ingenious in Ages far remote.

ESTCOURT, Mr. *Richard*.— This Gentleman was an Actor as well as a Writer.—He was born at *Tewkſbury* in *Glouceſterſhire*, according to *Chetwood*, (General Hiſt. of the Stage, p. 140) in 1668, and received his Education at the *Latin* School of that Town, but having an early Inclination for the Stage, he ſtole away from his Father's Houſe at fifteen Years of Age, and joined a travelling Company of Comedians then at *Worceſter*, where, for fear of being known, he made his firſt Appearance in Woman's Cloaths, in the Part of *Roxana* in *Alexander the Great*.—But this Diſguiſe not ſufficiently concealing him, he was obliged to make his Eſcape from a Purſuit that was made after him, and, under the Appearance of a Girl, to make the beſt of his Way to *Chipping Norton*.—Here however being diſcover'd, and overtaken by his Purſuers, he was brought back to *Tewkſbury*, and his Father, in order to prevent ſuch Excurſions for the future, ſoon after carried him up to *London*, and bound him Apprentice to an Apothecary in *Hatton Garden*.—— From this Confinement Mr. *Chetwood*, who probably muſt have known him, and perhaps had theſe Particulars from his own Mouth, tells us, that he broke

away, and paſſed two Years in *England* in an itinerant Life; but *Jacob*, and *Whincop* after him, ſay that he ſet up in Buſineſs, but not finding it ſucceed to his Liking, quitted it for the Stage.— Be this however as it will, it is certain that he went over to *Ireland*, where he met with good Succeſs on the Stage, from whence he came back to *London*, and was received in *Drury Lane* Theatre.—His firſt Appearance there was in the Part of *Dominic* the *Spaniſh Fryar*, in which, altho' in himſelf but a very midling Actor, he eſtabliſhed his Character by a cloſe Imitation of *Leigh*, who had been very celebrated in it.—And indeed, in this and all his other Parts, he was moſtly indebted for his Applauſe to his Powers of Mimickry, in which he was inimitable, and which not only at Times afforded him Opportunities of appearing a much better Actor than he really was, by enabling him to copy very exactly ſeveral Performers of capital Merit, whoſe Manner he remember'd and aſſum'd, but alſo by recommending him to a very numerous Acquaintance in private Life, ſecur'd him an Indulgence for Faults in his public Profeſſion, that he might otherwiſe perhaps never have been pardoned ; among which he was remarkable for the Gratification of that "*pitiful Ambition*," as *Shakeſpeare* juſtly ſtiles it, and for which he condemns the low Comedians of his own Time, of imagining he could help his Author, and for that Reaſon frequently throwing in Additions of his own, which the Author not only had never intended, but perhaps would have conſidered as moſt oppoſite to his main Intention.

Eſtcourt

Eſtcourt however, as a Companion, was perfectly entertaining and agreeable, and Sir *Richard Steele*, in the *Spectator*, records him to have been not only a ſprightly Wit, but a Perſon of eaſy and natural Politeneſs.—In a Word, his Company was extremely courted by every one, and his Mimickry ſo much admir'd, that Perſons of the firſt Quality frequently invited him to their Entertainments, in order to divert their Friends with his Drollery, on which Occaſions he conſtantly received very handſome Preſents for his Company.—Among others he was a great Favourite with the great Duke of *Marlborough*, and at the Time that the famous *Beef Steak Club* was erected, which conſiſted of the chief Wits and greateſt Men in the Kingdom, Mr. *Eſtcourt* had the Office aſſign'd him of their *Providore*, and as a Mark of Diſtinction of that Honour, he us'd, by Way of a Badge, to wear a ſmall Gridiron of Gold, hung about his Neck with a Green Silk Ribband.—He quitted the Stage ſome Years before his Death, which happened in 1713, when he was interred in the Pariſh of St. *Paul's, Covent Garden*, where his Brother Comedian, *Joe Haines*, had been buried a few Years before.—He left behind him two dramatic Pieces, *viz.*

   1. *Fair Example.* C.

   2. Prunella. Interlude. The latter of theſe was only a Ridicule on the Abſurdity of the *Italian* Operas, at that Time, in which not only the unnatural Circumſtance was indulged of Muſic and Harmony attending on all, even the moſt agitating Paſſions, but alſo the very Words themſelves which were to accompany that Muſic, were written in different Languages, according as the Performers who were to ſing them happened to be, *Italians* or *Engliſh*.

ETHEREGE, Sir *George*, Knt. —This Gentleman, ſo remarkable for his Wit and Gallantry, flouriſhed in the Reigns of *Cha.* II. and *James* II.—He was deſcended from a very good and ancient Family in *Oxfordſhire*, and was born about the Year 1636.——It is ſuppoſed that he received the early Parts of his Education at the Univerſity of *Cambridge*, tho' it does not appear that he made any long Reſidence there, an Inclination for ſeeing the World having led him to travel into *France* when he was very young. —On his Return, he for ſome Time ſtudied the Municipal Laws of this Kingdom at one of the Inns of Court, but finding that Kind of Study too heavy for his volatile and airy Diſpoſition, and conſequently making but little Progreſs in it, he ſoon quitted it for Pleaſure and the Purſuit of gayer Accompliſhments.

In 1664, he brought on the Stage his Comedy of the *Comical Revenge*, or *Love in a Tub*, which met with good Succeſs, and introduced him to the Intimacy of the Earl of *Dorſet*, with whom, as well as other leading Wits, ſuch as the Duke of *Buckingham*, Lord *Rocheſter*, Sir *Charles Sedley*, &c. his eaſy unreſerved Converſation and happy Addreſs render'd him a very great Favourite.—— The Succeſs of this inſpir'd him to the Writing of a ſtill better Comedy, viz. *She wou'd if ſhe cou'd.*—This Piece rais'd great Expectations of frequent Additions to the Amuſements of the Theatre from ſo able a Pen; but Mr. *Etherege* was too much addicted to Pleaſure, and had too

few

few Incitements from Neceffity, for him to give any conftant Application to the *Belles Lettres*, which he made only the Amufement of a few leifure Moments. —So that he produced but one Play more, and that not till eight Years after the preceding one.— This was the *Man of Mode*, which is perhaps the moft elegant Comedy, and contains more of the real Manners of high Life than any one the *Englifh* Stage was ever adorned with.—This Piece he has dedicated to the beautiful Duchefs of *York*, in whofe Service he then was, and who had fo high a Regard for him, that when, on the Acceffion of King *James* II. fhe came to be Queen, fhe procur'd his being fent Ambaffador firft to *Hamburg* and afterwards to *Ratifbon*, where he continued till after his Majefty quitted this Kingdom.—Our Author was addicted to certain gay Extravagances, fuch as Gaming, and a moft unbounded Indulgence in Wine and Women, and as by the latter of thefe Intemperances he had greatly damaged his Countenance (for otherwife he was a handfome Man, being fair, flender and genteel) fo by the former he had greatly impaired his Fortune ; to retrieve which he paid his Addreffes to a rich Widow ; but fhe being an ambitious Woman, had determined not to condefcend to a Marriage with any Man who could not beftow a Title on her, on which Account he was obliged to purchafe a Knighthood.—It does not appear whether he had any Iffue by this Lady, but by Mrs. *Barry* the Actrefs, with whom he lived for fome Time, he had one Daughter, on whom he fettled a Fortune of five or fix thoufand Pounds ; fhe however died very young.

None of the Writers have exactly fixed the Period of Sir *George*'s Death, tho' all feem to place it not long after the Revolution.—Some fay that on that great Event he followed his Mafter King *James* into *France*, and died there.—But the Authors of the *Biographia Britannica* mention a Report that he came to an untimely Death, by an unlucky Accident at *Ratifbon* ; for that, after having treated fome Company with a liberal Entertainment at his Houfe there, where he had taken his Glafs too freely, and being, thro' his great Complaifance, too forward in waiting on his Guefts at their Departure, flufhed as he was, he tumbled down Stairs, and broke his Neck, and fo fell a Martyr to Jollity and Civility.

Sir *George Etherege* feems to have been perfectly formed for the Court and Age he lived in.— By the Letters which pafs'd between him and the Duke of *Buckingham*, the Earl of *Rochefter* and Sir *Charles Sedley*, he appears to have been thoroughly a Libertine in Speculation as well as Practice, yet poffefs'd all that Elegance of Sentiment, and eafy Affability of Addrefs, which are ever the Characteriftics of true Gallantry, but which the Libertines of the prefent Age feem to have very little Idea of. As a Writer, he certainly was born a Poet, and feems to have been poffeffed of a Genius whofe Vivacity needed no Cultivation ; for we have no Proofs of his having been a Scholar.—His Works have not, however, efcaped Cenfure, on Account of that Licentioufnefs which in the general runs thro' them, which render them dangerous to young unguarded Minds, and the more fo for the lively and
genuine

genuine Wit with which it is gilded over, and which has therefore juftly banifhed them from the Purity of the prefent Stage.

Sir *George* left behind him only the three dramatic Pieces we have before-mentioned, *viz.*

1. *Comical Revenge.* C.
2. *Man of Mode.* C.
3. *She wou'd if fhe cou'd.* C.

F.

FABIAN, Mr. *Thomas.*—All I find mentioned of this Author is, that he was fometime one of the Footmen to K. *George* the fecond, when Prince of *Wales*, and that he wrote one dramatic Piece, which was acted without Succefs, called,

Trick upon Trick. Farce.

FANE, Sir *Francis*, jun. Knt. of the *Bath.*——This honourable Author lived in the Reign of King *Charles* II.—He was Grandfon to the Earl of *Weftmoreland*, (his Father being one of that Nobleman's younger Sons) and refided for the moft Part at *Fulbeck* in *Lincolnfhire.*—He was appointed, by the Duke of *Newcaftle*, Governor, firft of *Doncafter*, and afterwards of *Lincoln.* *Langbaine* gives the higheft Commendations of his Wit and Abilities, and indeed other of his Cotemporaries have paid him high Compliments. —— Befides fome Poems he has left the following dramatic Pieces, *viz.*

1. *Love in the Dark.* C.
2. *Mafque for Lord* ROCHESTER'S VALENTINIAN.
3. *Sacrifice.* Trag.

FANSHAW, Sir *Richard*, Bart.—This Gentleman was the tenth

and youngeft Son of Sir *Henry Fanfhaw*, of *Ware-Park* in *Hertfordfhire* (who had been created a Baronet by King *Charles* I. at the Siege of *Oxford*) and Brother to the Right Honourable *Thomas* Lord Vifcount *Fanfhaw.*——He was born in 1607, and received the firft Rudiments of Learning from that famous Grammarian and Critic *Thomas Farnaby*, and compleated his Studies at the Univerfity of *Cambridge*, from whence he fet out on his Travels for the Attainment of farther Accomplifhments.—At his Return, his promifing Abilities recommended him to the Favour of King *Charles* I. who, in the Year 1635, appointed him Refident at the Court of *Spain*, for the adjufting of fome Points in Difpute between the two Powers.

On the breaking out of the Rebellion he returned to *England*, and attaching himfelf with great Firmnefs to the Royal Caufe, became intrufted in many very important Affairs, particularly the Truft of Secretary to the Prince of *Wales*, whom he attended in many of his Journeys.

In 1648 he was made Treafurer of the Navy under Prince *Rupert*, which Poft he kept till *Sept.* 2, 1650, when he was created a Baronet, and fent an Envoy Extraordinary to *Spain.*—— From thence being recalled to *Scotland*, where the King was, he ferved as Secretary of State till the fatal Battle of *Worcefter*, in which he was taken Prifoner, and committed for a long Time to clofe Confinement in *London*, till at length, on Account of his Health, he was admitted to Bail.

In *Feb.* 1659 he repair'd to the King at *Breda*, and returning to *England* at the Reftoration, it was expected he would have been appointed

appointed Secretary of State.—— He was, however, only made Master of Requests, an honourable and lucrative Employment, and Secretary for the *Latin* Tongue.

In 1661, at which Time he was one of the Burgesses in Parliament for the University of *Cambridge*, he was sworn a Privy Counsellor for *Ireland*, and sent first as Envoy Extraordinary, but afterwards endowed with a Plenipotentiary Commission to the Court of *Portugal*, where he negotiated a Marriage between his Master King *Charles* II. and the Infanta Donna *Catharina*, Daughter to King *John* VI.——Being recalled in 1663, he was sworn of the Privy Council, and, in *February* 1661, sent Ambassador to the Court of *Madrid*, to negotiate a Treaty of Commerce.—— During his Residence there King *Philip* died, and Sir *Richard*, availing himself of the Minority of his Son and Successor, put the finishing Hand to a Peace with *Spain*, a Treaty for which was signed at *Madrid*, *Dec.* 6. 1665. ——Having thus fully executed his Commissions, he was preparing for his Return to *England*, when, on the 14th of *June* 1666, he was seized at *Madrid* with a violent Fever, which, on the 26th of the same Month, the very Day he had appointed for setting out on his Journey, put an end to his valuable Life, in the 59th Year of his Age.——His Body being embalmed, was conveyed by Land to *Calais*, and so to *London*, from whence, being carried to *Allhallows* Church in *Hertford*, his Lady and all his surviving Children attending, it was deposited in the Vault of his Father-in-Law, Sir *John Harrison*, by whose

eldest Daughter Sir *Richard* had six Sons and eight Daughters, of whom however he left only one Son and four Daughters behind him.

Here it remained till the 18th of *May* 1671, on which Day it was removed into the Parish Church of *Ware*, in the said County, and there laid in a new Vault made or purchased on Purpose for him and his Family, over which was erected an elegant Monument for him and his Lady; being near the old Vault where all his Ancestors of *Ware* Park lay interred.

His General Character is very concisely conveyed by the Author of the short Account of his Life prefixed to his Letters, who says of him, " That he was remark- " able for his Meekness, Since- " rity, Humanity and Piety, and " was also an able Statesman and " a great Scholar, being in par- " ticular a compleat Master of " several Modern Languages, es- " pecially the *Spanish*, which he " spoke and wrote with as much " Advantage as if he had been a " Native."

As to his Writings, there are few excepting his Letters during his Embassies (and which were not published till 1702, in 8vo) that are original.——The most being Translations, and written, as it should seem, by Way of Amusement and Relaxation during his Confinement.——One of these Translations is from the *Italian* of the celebrated *Guarini*, the other from the *Spanish* of *Antonio de Mendoza*.—Their Names are as follow,

1. *Il Pastor Fido*. Pastoral.

2. *Querer per solo querer*. Play of three Acts.

N. B. To this Piece is added

another,

another, a Tranflation from the fame *Spanifh* Author, entitled,

3. *Fieftes de Aranjuez.*

Befides thefe he tranflated into *Latin* Verfe a Paftoral, written by *Fletcher*, entitled

The *Faithful Shephcrdefs*,

to which he has prefix'd the *Italian* Title of

4. *La Fida Paftora.*

FALKLAND, *Henry Carey,* Lord Vifcount.—This learned Nobleman, whom we find fo juftly celebrated by Mr. *Cowley*, was the only Son of Sir *Lucius Carey*, the great Lord *Falkland*, who died glorioufly in the Field of Honour and in the Support of his King, at the famous Battle of *Newbury*, *Sept.* 20, 1643.—His Mother's Name was *Lettice*, a Daughter of Sir *Richard Morifon*.—In what Year he was born I have not been able to trace, but find him to have married a *Margaret*, Daughter of *Anthony Hungerford*, Efq; and that he died in 1663.— He feems to have inherited the Virtues of his Father, having render'd himfelf eminent and very greatly refpected both at Court, in the Senate, and in his County of *Oxfordfhire*, of which he was Lord Lieutenant, not only for his extraordinaryParts, but alfo for his heroic Spirit.—*Langbaine* tells us that he was cut off in the Prime of his Years (which indeed he muft have been, his Father having been no more than 34 Years of Age when he was kill'd, and this Son furviving him only by twenty Years) and that he was as much mifs'd and regretted when dead, as he had been beloved and refpected while living. —He left one Play behind him, which, altho' it contains a great Deal of true Wit and Satire, yet it feems dubious whether it was ever reprefented or not, as the Date of it's Publication is fubfequent to that of it's Author's Death.—It is entitled,

The *Marriage Night.* T. This Play is republifhed in *Dodfley's* Collection of old Plays, Vol. X.

FARQUHAR, Mr. *George.*—— This Gentleman was defcended from a Family of no inconfiderable Rank in the North of *Ireland*, his Father being a Clergyman, and, according to fome, Dean of *Armagh.*—Our Author was born at *Londonderry* in 1678, where he received the Rudiments of Erudition, and from whence, as foon as he was properly qualified, he was fent to the Univerfity of *Dublin*, in 1694.—He had given very early Teftimony of a promifing Genius, and difcover'd even at ten Years of Age a ftrong Inclination for the Service of the Mufes.—By the Progrefs he made in his Studies at the Univerfity, he acquired a confiderable Reputation, but does not appear to have taken any Degree there, for the natural Livelinefs and Volatility of his Difpofition foon render'd him weary of an Academic Life.—The polite Entertainments of the Town more forcibly attracted his Attention, but among them all none feem'd to fix fo ftrong a Claim on his Regards as the Theatre, of which he foon found in himfelf a Propenfity for being not only a Spectator but a Performer.—His Intimacy with the celebrated Mr. *Wilks* might probably ftrengthen that Inclination in him, and when that Gentleman engaged himfelf to Mr. *Afhbury*, the Manager of the *Dublin* Theatre, Mr. *Farquhar* was foon introduced on the Stage thro' his Means.—In this Situation he continued no longer than

Part

Part of one Seafon, nor made any very confiderable Figure.—For tho' his Perfon was fufficiently in his Favour, and that he was poffeffed of the Requifites of a ftrong retentive Memory, a juft Manner of fpeaking, and an eafy and elegant Deportment, yet his natural Diffidence and Timidity, or what is ufually termed the *Stage-Terror*, which he was never able to overcome, added to a thin Infufficiency of Voice, were ftrong Bars in the Way of his Succefs, more efpecially in Tragedy.——However, notwithftanding thefe Difadvantages, it is not improbable, as from his amiable private Behaviour he was very much efteemed, and had never met with the leaft Repulfe from the Audience in any of his Performances, that he might have continued much longer on the Stage, but for an Accident which determined him to quit it on a fudden; for being to play the Part of *Guyomar* in *Dryden's Indian Emperor*, who kills *Vafquez*, one of the *Spanifh* Generals, Mr. *Farquhar*, by fome Miftake, took a real Sword inftead of a Foil on the Stage with him, and in the Engagement wounded his Brother Tragedian, who acted *Vafquez*, in fo dangerous a Manner, that, altho' it did not prove mortal, he was a long Time before he recovered it; and the Confideration of the fatal Confequences that might have enfued, wrought fo ftrongly on our Author's humane Difpofition, that he took up a Refolution never to go on the Stage again, or fubmit himfelf to the Poffibility of fuch another Miftake.

Thus did Mr. *Farquhar* quit the Stage, at a Period of Life when few have even attempted to go on it, for at this Juncture he

could not have been much more than feventeen Years of Age, fince fome Time afterwards, when Mr. *Wilks*, being engaged again to *Drury Lane* Theatre, left *Dublin*, Mr. *Farquhar* accompanied him to *London*; and this Event happened no later than in the Year 1696, at which Time he was but eighteen.—Here his Abilities and agreeable Addrefs met with confiderable Encouragement, and in particular recommended him to the Patronage of the Earl of *Orrery*, who gave him a Lieutenant's Commiffion in his own Regiment, then in *Ireland*, which he held feveral Years, and in his military Capacity conftantly behaved without Reproach, giving on many Occafions Proofs of great Bravery and Conduct.

But thefe were not all the Perfections which appear'd in Mr. *Farquhar*; and Mr. *Wilks*, who well knew his Humour and Abilities, and was convinced that he would make a much more confpicuous Figure as a dramatic Writer than as a theatrical Performer, never ceafed his Solicitations on that Head, till he had prevailed on him to undertake a Comedy, which he compleated and brought on the Stage in 1698.—This was his *Love and a Bottle*, a Comedy, which, tho' written by it's Author when under twenty Years of Age, yet contains fuch a Variety of Incidents and Character, and fuch a Sprightlinefs of Dialogue, as muft convince us, that even then he had a very confiderable Knowledge of the World, and a very clear Judgment of the Manners of Mankind; and the Succefs of it, even notwithftanding that Mr. *Wilks*, the Town's great Favorite in Comedy, had no Part in it, was equal to it's Defert.—Whe-

 ther

ther this Play made it's Appearance before or after he received his Commiffion, does not feem very clear, but it is evident that his military Avocations did not check his dramatic Talents, but on the contrary rather improved them, fince in many of his Plays, more efpecially in his *Recruiting Officer*, he has admirably availed himfelf of the Obfervations of Life and Character, which the Army was able fo amply to fupply him with.—And with fuch an eafy Pleafantry, and yet fo fevere a critical Juftice, has he rallied the Foibles, Follies and Vices even of thofe Characters that he might have been fuppofed the moft partial to, that it has been obferved, if he had not been himfelf an *Irifhman* and an Officer, it would have been almoft impoffible for him to have avoided the Refentments which would probably have fallen on him for the Liberty he has taken in fome of his Pieces with the Characters of fome of the Gentlemen of the Army, as well as with thofe of a neighbouring Kingdom.

The Succefs of his firft Play eftablifhed his Reputation, and encouraged him to proceed, and the Winter Seafon of the Jubilee Year 1700, gave the Public his favorite Play of the *Conftant Couple*, in which the gay airy Humour thrown into the Character of Sir *Harry Wildair*, were fo well fuited to Mr. *Wilks's* Talents, that they gave him fuch an Opportunity of Exertion, as greatly heightened his Reputation with the Public, and in great Meafure repaid thofe Acts of Friendfhip which he had ever beftowed on Mr. *Farquhar*.—This Piece was played fifty-three Nights in the firft Seafon, and has juftly conti-

nued in high Efteem ever fince. The following Year produced a Sequel to it; which, tho' much the moft indifferent of all his Plays, yet met with tolerable Succefs, and indeed with much better than the Comedy of the *Inconftant*, which he gave to the Public two Years afterwards, *viz.* in 1703, and which vaftly excelled it in Point of intrinfic Merit.—But the Failure of the laft-mentioned Piece was entirely owing to the Inundation of Foreign Entertainments of Mufic, Singing, Dancing, *&c.* which at that Time broke in upon the *Englifh* Stage in a Torrent, feem'd with a Magical Infatuation at once to take Poffeffion of *Britifh* Tafte, and occafion'd a total Neglect of the more valuable and intrinfic Productions of our own Countrymen.

This little Difcouragement, however, did not put a Stop to our Author's Ardor for the Entertainment of the Public, fince we find him ftill writing till almoft the Hour of his Death; his *Beaux Stratagem* having been written during his laft Illnefs, and his Death happening during the Run of it.—Thus far I have had Occafion to mention the Dates of fome of his Pieces, but as the chronological Order of them is not a Point of our Confideration in this Part of our Work, I fhall only in this Place compleat my Account of his Plays, by giving an entire Lift of them as ufual, in Alphabetical Order, as follows.

1. *Beau's Stratagem.* C.
2. *Conftant Couple.* C.
3. *Inconftant.* C.
4. *Love and a Bottle.* C.
5. *Recruiting Officer.* C.
6. *Sir* HARRY WILDAIR. C.
7. *Stage*

7. *Stage Coach.* F. (affisted by *Motteux.*)

8. *Twin Rivals.* C.

As it has been generally imagined that in all his Heroes, he has intended to sketch out his own Character, it is reasonable to conjecture that his own Character must have born a strong Resemblance to that of those Heroes; who are in general a Set of young, gay, rakish Sparks, guilty of some Wildnesses and Follies, but at the same Time blessed with Parts and Abilities, and adorned with Courage and Honour. —It is not therefore to be wondered that from the few Letters of his which are extant in Print, we find him strongly susceptible of the tenderer Passions, and at the same Time treating them with great Vivacity and Levity.—His warmest Attachment, however, appears to have been to her whom he constantly stiles his *dear Penelope,* who is supposed to have been the celebrated Mrs. *Oldfield.*—— Nor is it at all wonderful, that he should find his Heart engaged by a Lady who possessed every Attraction both of Person and Conversation, and to whose Excellence in her Profession he owed much of the Success of his Pieces.—Nor that she should entertain a very peculiar Regard for a young Gentleman of Wit, Spirit and Gallantry, to whose first Notice of her she stood indebted for being on the Stage at all, and whose dramatic Labours afterwards afforded her many happy Opportunities of recommending herself to the Public Favour on it.—And now, as I have mentioned this Lady, it may not be amiss to explain the Hint thrown out above, that it was wholly owing to Captain *Farqubar* that

she became an Actress, which was in Consequence of the following Incident.

That Gentleman dining one Day at her Aunt's, who kept the *Mitre* Tavern in St. *James's* Market, heard Miss *Narcy* reading a Play behind the Bar.——This drew his Attention to listen for a Time, when he was so pleased with the proper Emphasis and agreeable Turn she gave to each Character, that he swore the Girl was cut out for the Stage.—As she had always expressed an Inclination for that Way of Life, and a Desire of trying her Fortune in it, her Mother, on this Encouragement, the next Time she saw Captain *Vanbrugh* (afterwards Sir *John)* who had a great Respect for the Family, acquainted him with Captain *Farqubar's* Opinion; on which he desired to know whether her Bent was most to Tragedy or Comedy. — Miss being called in, informed him, that her principal Inclination was to the latter, having at that Time gone thro' all *Beaumont* and *Fletcher's* Comedies, and the Play she was reading when Captain *Farqubar* dined there having been the *Scornful Lady.*—Captain *Vanbrugh* shortly after recommended her to Mr. *Christopher Rich,* who took her into the House at the Allowance of fifteen Shillings *per* Week.—However, her agreeable Figure and Sweetness of Voice, soon gave her the Preference, in the Opinion of the whole Town, to all the young Actresses of that Time, and the Duke of *Bedford,* in particular, being pleased to speak to Mr. *Rich* in her Favour, he instantly raised her to twenty Shillings *per* Week. —After which her Fame and Salary gradually increased, till at

 length

length they both attained that Height which her Merit entitled her to.

Whether Mr. *Farquhar*'s Connections with this Lady extended beyond the Limits of mere Friendship, it is not my Intention here to enquire.—But of what Kind foever they were, it is evident they did not long interfere with any more regular Engagement; for in 1703 Capt. *Farquhar* was married, and according to general Report to a Lady of a very good Fortune; but in this Particular the Captain and the Public were both alike miftaken; for the real Fact was, that the Lady, who really had no Fortune at all, had fallen fo violently in Love with our Author, that, determined to have him at any Rate, and judging perhaps very juftly, that a Gentleman of his volatile and diffipated Humour would not eafily be drawn into the Matrimonial Cage, without the Bait of fome very confiderable Advantage to allure him to it, fhe contrived to have it given out that fhe was poffefs'd of a large Fortune; and finding Means afterwards to let Mr. *Farquhar* know her Attachment to him, the united Powers of Intereft and Vanity perfectly got the better of his Paffion for Liberty, and they were united in the hymeneal Bands.—But how great was his Difappointment, when he found all his Profpects overclouded fo early in Life (for he was then no more than four and twenty) by a Marriage from which he had Nothing to expect but an annual Increafe of Family, and an Enlargement of Expence in Confequence of it far beyond what his Income would fupport.—Yet to his immortal Honour be it recorded, tho' he found himfelf thus deceived in a moft effential

Particular, he never once was known to upbraid his Wife for it, but generoufly forgave an Impofition which Love for him alone had urg'd her to, and even behaved to her with all the Tendernefs and Delicacy of the moft indulgent Hufband.

Mis. *Farquhar*, however, did not very long enjoy the Happinefs fhe had purchafed by this Stratagem, for the Circumftances that attended this Union were in fome Refpect perhaps the Means of fhortening the Period of the Captain's Life, for finding himfelf confiderably involved in Debt in Confequence of their increafing Family, he was induced to make Application to a certain noble Courtier, who had frequently profeffed the greateft Friendfhip for him, and given him the ftrongeft Affurances of intended Services.—This pretended Patron repeated his former Declarations, but expreffing much Concern that he had nothing at prefent immediatcly in his Power, advifed him to convert his Commiffion into Money to anfwer his prefent Occafions, and affur'd him that in a very fhort Time he would procure another for him.—*Farquhar*, who could not bear the Thoughts of his Wife and Family being in Diftrefs, and was therefore ready to lay hold on any Expedient for their Relief, followed this Piece of Advice, and fold his Commiffion; but to his great Mortification and Difappointment found, on a Renewal of his Application to this inhuman Nobleman, that he had either entirely forgotten, or had never intended to perform, the Promife he had made him.—This diftracting Fruftration of all his Hopes fixed itfelf fo ftrongly on our Author's Mind, that it foon brought on him a fure,

tho'

tho' not a very fudden Declenfion of Nature, which at length carried him off the Stage of Life in the latter End of *April* 1707, before he could well be faid to have run half his Courfe, being not quite thirty Years of Age when he died.

Notwithftanding the feveral Difappointments and Vexations which this Gentleman met with during his fhort Stay in this tranfitory World, nothing feems to have been able to overcome the Readinefs of his Genius or the eafy Good-Nature of his Difpofition; for he began and finifhed his well-known Comedy of the *Beaux Stratagem* in about fix Weeks, during his laft Illnefs, notwithftanding that he, for great Part of the Time, was extremely fenfible of the Approaches of Death, and even foretold what actually happened, *viz.* that he fhould die before the Run of it was over.—Nay, in fo calm and manly a Manner did he treat the Expectation of that fatal Event, as even to be able to exercife his wonted Pleafantry on the very Subject.—For while his Play was in Rehearfal, his Friend Mr. *Wilks*, who frequently vifited him during his Illnefs, obferving to him that Mrs. *Oldfield* thought he had dealt too freely with the Character of Mrs. *Sullen*, in giving her to *Archer*, without fuch a proper Divorce as might be a Security for her Honour,—*Oh*, replied the Author, with his accuftom'd Vivacity, *I will, if fhe pleafes, falve that immediately, by getting a real Divorce, marrying her myfelf, and giving her my Bond that fhe fhall be a real Widow in lefs than a Fortnight.*——But nothing can give a more perfect Idea of that Difpofition I have hinted at in him, than the very

laconic but expreffive Billet which Mr. *Wilks* found after his Death among his Papers directed to himfelf, and which, as a Curiofity in its Kind, I cannot refrain from giving to my Readers; it was as follows,

Dear Bob,

" I have not any Thing to
" leave thee to perpetuate my
" Memory, but two helplefs
" Girls; look upon them fome-
" times, and think of him that
" was, to the laft Moment of
" his Life, thine,

George Farqubar."

nor would it be doing Juftice to Mr. *Wilks's* Memory not to obferve in this Place, that he paid the moft punctual Regard to the Requeft of his dying Friend, by fhewing them every Act of Regard, and when they became fit to be put out into the World, procured a Benefit for each of them for that Purpofe.

Mr. *Farqubar's* private Character may be fully gather'd from what has been already faid, yet it may not be improper to obferve, that from his Behaviour to his Wife, and his apparent Tendernefs towards his Children, he muft have been poffeffed of excellent moral Qualities, and deferved a much better Fate than what he met with.

As a Writer, the Opinions of Critics have been various; the general Character which has been given of his Comedies is, that the Succefs of moft of them far exceeded the Author's Expectations; that he was particularly happy in the Choice of his Subjects, which he always took Care to adorn with a great Variety of Characters and Incidents; that his Stile is pure and unaffected, his Wit natural and flowing, and his Plots generally well contrived.—

But

But then, on the contrary, it has been objected, that he was too hasty in his Productions; that his Works are loose, tho' indeed not so grosly Libertine as those of some other Wits of his Time; that his Imagination, tho' lively, was capable of no great Compass, and his Wit, tho' passable, not such as would gain Ground on Confideration.—In a Word, he seems to have been a Man of a Genius rather sprightly than great, rather flowing than solid; his Characters are natural, yet not ever strongly mark'd, nor peculiarly heightened; yet, as it is apparent he drew his Observations from those he conversed with, and formed all his Portraits from Nature, it is more than probable, that if he had lived to have gained a more general Knowledge of Life, or his Circumstances had not been so straitened as to prevent his mingling with Persons of Rank, we might have seen his Plays embellished with more finished Characters, and adorned with a more polished Dialogue.

On the whole, however, his Pieces are very entertaining, and almost all of them, after near three-score Years have passed over them, are still some of the greatest Favorites of the Public.—His *Twin Rivals* has been consider'd by the Critics as his most perfect, regular and finish'd Play, yet it is far from standing in the same Rank of Preference with the Audience; which is one Instance among many that serve to evince that the Art of Pleasing in dramatic Writings, and more especially in Comedy, frequently depends on a certain Happiness, which cannot be reduc'd within the Limits of any didactic Rules or critical Investigation.

FENTON, *Elijah*, Esq;—This Gentleman was the youngest of twelve Children, and was born at a Town call'd *Shelton*, near *Newcastle under Line*, in *Staffordshire*, in which County are several Families of the Name of *Fenton*, all of whom are Branches from the same original Stock, which was a very ancient and honourable one.—Nor had he less Right to boast of the Antiquity of his Family on the Female Side, his Mother being lineally descended from one *Mare*, who was an Officer in *William* the Conqueror's Army.—All the Writers of his Life are silent as to the Date of his Birth, but agree that he was intended for the Ministry, to prepare him for which he was sent to the University of *Cambridge*, and enter'd of *Jesus* College.—Here however he embrac'd Principles very opposite to the Government, whereby he became disqualified for the taking Orders.—Soon after his quitting the University, he was entertained by the Earl of *Orrery* as his Secretary; but how long he continued in that Office does not clearly appear.—He seems indeed to have pass'd the most of his Time in the Country, among his Friends and Relations.——But whether he had any Thing of an independent Fortune, or was assisted by his eldest Brother, who had an Estate of a Thousand Pounds *per Annum*, and to whom he constantly paid an annual Visit, I have not been able to determine.—Certain, however, it is, that he was a Man of great Humanity and Tenderness, and of a most affable and genteel Behaviour, which Qualities, joined to his great Good Sense and literary Abilities, highly endear'd him

him to all who knew him, and more especially to his Relations, by whom he was greatly caress'd.

His Life, not being intermingled with any Affairs of public Business, was like that of most studious Men, very barren of Incident.—It was, however, blest with an uninterrupted Calm, which he enjoy'd till the inevitable Stroke deprived the World of him and his Virtues, on the 13th of *July* 1730.——He died, and was buried at *East Hampstead* Park, near *Oakingham* in *Berkshire,* leaving behind him the same fair Reputation he had carried with him thro' Life.——In short, he was perhaps the very happiest Man among the whole extensive Number we shall have Occasion to mention in the Course of this Work.—He had that good Fortune which rarely befalls Authors, of having his Merits acknowledged and respected during his Life-Time, without having laid himself open to the Jealousy or Malevolence even of his Brother Writers.—And as, while living, he enjoy'd the Friendship of Mr. *Pope,* so after Death he received from that Poet the Tribute of a very elegant Epitaph, which is to be found in Mr. *Pope's* Works, and which more strongly characterizes the Goodness of the Person it was written upon, than all that I could add on this Occasion could possibly do.

Mr. *Fenton* wrote many Poems, but only one dramatic Piece, which is entitled,

MARIAMNE. T. This however met with perhaps as much Applause as any Play that had appeared for many Years both before and after it; and indeed much more than could be expected under the disadvantage-

ous Circumstances that attended on it's first Appearance.—For, in Consequence of the ill Behaviour of the Managers of *Drury Lane* Theatre, who, notwithstanding repeated Promises to the contrary, had delayed bringing it on for three or four Years together, he was induced, and indeed advised by his Friends, to carry it to the Theatre in *Lincoln's-Inn-Fields,* where he was assur'd that his Interest should be strongly supported; and indeed these Promises were amply performed; for altho' that Theatre was then so entirely out of Favour with the Town, which in general is guided by Caprice and Fashion alone, that for a long Time before the Managers had scarcely ever been able to defray their Charges, nay, frequently had acted to Audiences of five or six Pounds, the Merit of this Piece not only brought crowded Houses for several Nights together, but seem'd by so doing to have turn'd the Current of public Favour into a new Channel, from which, during the Existence of that Theatre, it never after so totally deviated, as it had done for a considerable while before.

FIELD, Mr. *Nathaniel.*—This Author lived in the Reigns of King *James* I. and King *Cha.* I. and was not only a Lover of the Muses, but belov'd by them, and the Poets his Cotemporaries.— He was also an Actor, and appears to have been held in considerable Estimation in that Light; for we find his Name joined with those of *Hemmings, Burbage, Condel,* &c. before the Folio Edition of *Shakespeare's* Works, and also in the *Dramatis Personæ* prefix'd to the *Cynthia's* Revels of *Ben Jonson.*—He was also a great Favorite with *Massinger* and *Chapman,*

man, the latter of whom adopted him for his Son.—He wrote two dramatic Pieces, whose Titles are as follow,

1. *Amends for Ladies.* C.
2. *Woman is a Weather-Cock.* Com.

Besides these, he was concerned with *Maffinger* in the writing of a very good Play, called,

The *Fatal Dowry*,

on which two Authors since have formed the Ground-work of their respective Tragedies, *viz.* Mr. *Rowe* that of his *Fair Penitent*, and *Aaron Hill* of one which he left behind him unfinished, by the Title of The *Infolvent*, or *Filial Piety*.

I have not been able to trace the just Period either of the Birth or Death of this Author.

FIELDING, *Henry*, Esq;—— This well-known and justly celebrated Writer of our own Time, was born at *Sharpham* Park in *Somersetshire*, *April* 22, 1707.— His Father *Edmund Fielding*, Esq; who was a younger Son of the Earl of *Denbigh*, was in the Army, and towards the Close of King *George* I's Reign or the Accession of *George* II. was promoted to the Rank of a Lieutenant-General. —— His Mother was Daughter to Judge *Gold*, and Aunt to the present Sir *Henry Gold*, one of the Barons of the Exchequer.—This Lady, besides our Author, who seems to have been her first born, had another Son and four Daughters, one of the latter being the celebrated Miss *Fielding* now living, and Author of *David Simple*, the Countess of *Delvin*, the *Cry*, and many other very ingenious Pieces. And, in Consequence of his Father's second Marriage, Mr. *Fielding* had six half Brothers, all of whom are dead, excepting the

present Sir *John Fielding*, now in the Commission of the Peace for the Counties of *Middlesex*, *Surry*, *Essex*, and the Liberties of *Westminster*.

Our Author received the first Rudiments of his Education at home, under the Care of the Rev. Mr. *Oliver*, for whom he seems to have had no very great Regard, as he is said to have designed a Portrait of his Character in the very humorous yet detestable one of Parson *Trulliber*, in his *Joseph Andrews*.— When taken from under this Gentleman's Charge, he was removed to *Eton* School, where he had an Opportunity of cultivating a very early Intimacy and Friendship with several, who afterwards became the first Persons in the Kingdom, such as Lord *Lyttleton*, Mr. *Fox*, Mr. *Pitt*, Sir *Charles Hanbury Williams*, &c. who ever thro' Life retained a warm Regard for him. —But these were not the only Advantages he reaped at that great Seminary of Education ; for by an assiduous Application to Study and the Possession of strong and peculiar Talents, he became, before he left that School, uncommonly versed in the *Greek* Authors, and a perfect Master of the *Latin* Classics.—Thus accomplished, at about eighteen Years of Age he left *Eton*, and went to *Leyden*, where he studied under the most celebrated Civilians for about two Years, at the Expiration of which Time, the Remittances from *England* not coming so regularly as at first, he was obliged to return to *London*.

In short, General *Fielding*'s Family being very greatly increased by his second Marriage, as may be seen from what we have said above, it became impossible for him to make such Appointments

for

for this his eldeſt Son, as he could have wiſhed; the utmoſt that he could afford to allow him being no more than two hundred Pounds a Year, with which ſlender Income, a ſtrong Conſtitution, a lively Imagination, and a Diſpoſition naturally but little formed for Oeconomy, he found himſelf his own Maſter, in a Place where the Temptations to every expenſive Pleaſure are ſo numerous, and the Means of gratifying them ſo eaſily attainable.——From this unfortunately pleaſing Situation ſprung the Source of every Misfortune or Uneaſineſs that Mr. *Fielding* afterwards felt thro' Life. ——He very ſoon found that his Finances were by no Means adequate to the frequent Draughts made on him from the Conſequences of the briſk Career of Diſſipation which he had launched into; yet, as diſagreeable Impreſſions never continued long upon his Mind, but only on the contrary rouzed him to ſtruggle thro' his Difficulties with the greater Spirit and Magnanimity, he flatter'd himſelf that he ſhould find his Reſources in his Wit and Invention, and accordingly commenced a Writer for the Stage in the Year 1727, at which Time he had not more than attained the Completion of his twentieth Year.

His firſt Attempt in the Drama was a Piece called *Love in ſeveral Maſques*, which, tho' it immediately ſucceeded the long and crowded Run of the *Provoked Huſband*, met with a favourable Reception, as did likewiſe his ſecond Play, which came out in the following Year, and was entitled, *The Temple Beau*.——He did not however meet with equal Succeſs in all his dramatic Works, for he has even printed in the

Title Page of one of his Farces, *as it was* damned *at the Theatre Royal in Drury Lane*; and he himſelf informs us, in the general Preface to his Miſcellanies, that for the *Wedding Day*, tho' acted ſix Nights, his Profits from the Houſe did not exceed Fifty Pounds.——Nor did a much better Fate attend on ſome of his earlier Productions, ſo that, tho' it was his Lot always to write from Neceſſity, he would probably, notwithſtanding his Writings, have laboured continually under that Neceſſity, had not the Severity of the Public and the Malice of his Enemies met with a noble Alleviation from the Patronage of ſeveral Perſons of diſtinguiſhed Rank and Character, particularly the late Dukes of *Richmond* and *Roxburgh*, *John* Duke of *Argyle*, the preſent Lord *Lyttleton*, &c. the laſt-named of which Noblemen not only by his Friendſhip ſoftened the Rigour of our Author's Misfortunes while he lived, but alſo by his generous Ardour has vindicated his Character and done Juſtice to his Memory after Death.

About ſix or ſeven Years, after Mr. *Fielding*'s commencing a Writer for the Stage, he fell in Love with and married one Miſs *Craddock*, a young Lady from *Saliſbury*, poſſeſſed of a very great Share of Beauty, and a Fortune of about fifteen hundred Pounds, and about the ſame Time his Mother dying, an Eſtate at *Stower* in *Dorſetſhire*, of ſomewhat better than two hundred Pounds *per Annum* came into his Poſſeſſion. ——With this Fortune, which, had it been conducted with Prudence and Oeconomy, might have ſecured to him a State of Independence for Life, and with the Helps it might have derived from

the

the Productions of a Genius un-
incumber'd with Anxieties and
Perplexity, might have even afforded him an affluent Income;
with this, I say, and a Wife
whom he was fond of to Distrac-
tion, and for whose Sake he had
taken up a Resolution of biding
Adieu to all the Follies and Intemperances to which he had addicted himself in that short but
very rapid Career of a Town Life
which he had run, he determined
to retire to his Country Seat, and
there reside entirely.

But here, in Spite of this prudent Resolution, one Folly only
took Place of another, and Family Pride now brought on him
all the Inconveniences in one
Place, that youthful Dissipation
and Libertinism had done in another.—The Income he possess'd,
tho' sufficient for Ease and even
some Degree of Elegance, yet was
in no Degree adequate to the
Support of either Luxury or
Splendour.—Yet, fond of Figure
and Magnificence, he incumber'd
himself with a large Retinue of
Servants, and his natural Turn
leading him to a Fondness for the
Delights of Society and Convivial
Mirth, he threw wide open the
Gates of Hospitality, and suffer'd
his whole Patrimony to be de-
vour'd up by Hounds, Horses and
Entertainments.—In short, in less
than three Years, from the mere
Passion of being esteem'd a Man
of great Fortune, he reduced himself to the displeasing Situation of
having no Fortune at all; and
thro' an Ambition of maintaining an open House for the Reception of *every one else*, he soon
found *himself* without a Habitation which he could call his own.
—In a Word, by a Desire, as
Shakespeare expresses it,

—— of shewing a more swelling
   Port
Than his faint Means would grant
   Continuance,

he was, in the Course of a very
short Period, brought back to the
same unfortunate Situation which
he had before experienced; but
with this Aggravation to it, that
he could now have none of those
Resources in future to look forward to, which he had thus indiscreetly lavished.—He had un-
dermined his own Supports, and
had now nothing but his own A-
bilities to depend on for the Recovery of what he had so wan-
tonly thrown from him, an easy
Competence. — Not discouraged,
however, he determined to exert
his best Abilities, betook himself
closely to the Study of the Law,
and after the customary Time of
Probation at the *Temple*, was called to the Bar, and made no inconsiderable Figure in *Westminster
Hall.*

To the Practice of the Law
Mr. *Fielding* now applied himself
with great Assiduity both in the
Courts here and on the Circuits,
so long as his Health permitted
him, and it is probable would have
risen to a considerable Degree of
Eminence in it, had not the Intemperances of his early Parts of
Life put a Check, by their Consequences, to the Progress of his
Success.——In short, tho' but a
young Man, he began now to be
molested with such violent Attacks from the Gout, as render'd
it impossible for him to be as
constant at the Bar as the Labo-
riousness of his Profession required, and would only permit
him to pursue the Law by
Snatches, at such Intervals as
were free from Indisposition.—
However,

However, under thefe united Severities of Pain and Want, he ftill found Refources in his Genius and Abilities.—He was concerned in a political Periodical Paper, called the *Champion*, which owed it's principal Support to his Pen; a Pen which feems never to have lain idle, fince it was perpetually producing, almoft as it were extempore, a Play, a Farce, a Pamphlet, or a News-paper, but whofe full Exertion of Power feem'd referved for a Kind of Writing different from, and indeed fuperior to, them all; nor will it perhaps be neceffary in Proof of this more than to mention his celebrated Novels of *Jofeph Andrews* and *Tom Jones*, which are too well known and too juftly admired to leave us any Room for expatiating on their Merits.—Precarious, however, as this Means of Subfiftence unavoidably muft be, it was fcarcely poffible he fhould be enabled by it to recover his fhattered Fortunes, and was therefore at length obliged to accept of the Office of an acting Magiftrate in the Commiffion of the Peace for the County of *Middlefex*, in which Station he continued till pretty near the Time of his Death;—an Office however which feldom fails of being hateful to the Populace, and of Courfe liable to many infamous and unjuft Imputations, particularly that of Venality; a Charge which the Illnatur'd World, not unacquainted with Mr. *Fielding*'s Want of Oeconomy and Paffion for Expence were but too ready to caft upon him.—Yet from this Charge Mr. *Murphy*, in the Life of this Author, prefixed to a late Edition of his Works, has taken great Pains to exculpate him, as has likewife Mr. *Fielding* himfelf, in his *Voyage*

to Lifbon, which was not only his laft Work, but may with fome Degree of Propriety be confider'd as the laft Words of a dying Man; that Voyage having been undertaken only as a *dernier Refort* in one laft defperate Effort for the Prefervation of Life, and the reftoring a Conftitution broken with Chagrin, Diftrefs, Vexation and public Bufinefs; for his Strength was at that Time entirely exhaufted, and in about two Months after his Arrival at *Lifbon*, he yielded his laft Breath, in the forty eighth Year of his Age, and of our Lord 1754.

Mr. *Fielding*'s Genius, as I have before obferved, was moft fuperior in thofe ftrong, lively and natural Paintings of the Characters of Mankind, and the Movements of the human Heart, which conftitute the Bafis of his Novels, yet, as Comedy bears the clofeft Affinity to this Kind of Writing, his dramatic Pieces, every one of which is comic, are far from being contemptible.— His Farces and Ballad Pieces, more efpecially, have a Sprightlinefs of Manner, and a Forciblenefs of Character, which it is impoffible to avoid the being agreeably entertained by, and in thofe among them which he has in any Degree borrowed from *Moliere* or any other Writer, he has done his Original great Honour and Juftice by the Manner in which he has handled the Subject.—The Number and Titles of his dramatic Works are as follows.

1. *Author's Farce.* C.
2. *Coffeehoufe Politician.* C.
3. *Covent Garden Tragedy.* F.
4. *Debauchees.* C.
5. *Don* QUIXOTE *in England.* Com.
6. EURIDICE. F.

     6 EURI-

7. EURIDICE *hiſs'd*. F.
8. *Grubſtreet Opera.*
9. *Hiſtorical Regiſter.* C.
10. *Interlude between* JUPITER, JUNO, *and* MERCURY.
11. *Intriguing Chambermaid.* B. Farce.
12. *Letter Writers.* C.
14. *Lottery.* Ballad Farce.
15. *Miſer.* C.
16. *Miſs* LUCY *in Town.* F.
17. *Mock Doſtor.* Ball. Farce.
18. *Modern Huſband.* C.
19. *Old Man taught Wiſdom.* Ball. Farce.
20. PASQUIN. C.
21. PLUTUS *the God of Riches.* Com. (Aſſiſted by Mr. *Young.*)
22. *Temple Beau.* C.
23. *Tragedy of Tragedies.*
24. *Tumble down Dick.* F.
25. *Wedding Day.* C.

As to Mr. *Fielding*'s Character, as a Man, it may in great Meaſure be deduced from the Incidents I have above related of his Life, but cannot perhaps be with more Candour ſet forth than by his Biographer Mr. *Murphy*, in the Work I before made Mention of, and with ſome of whoſe Words therefore I ſhall cloſe this Article.

" It will be, ſays that Gentle-
" man, an humane and generous
" Office to ſet down to the Ac-
" count of Slander and Defama-
" tion, a great Part of that A-
" buſe which was diſcharged a-
" gainſt him by his Enemies in
" his Life-Time ; deducing how-
" ever from the whole this uſe-
" ful Leſſon, *that quick and warm*
" *Paſſions ſhould be early controuled,*
" *and that Diſſipation and extra-*
" *vagant Pleaſures are the moſt*
" *dangerous Palliations that can be*
" *found for Diſappointments and*
" *Vexations in the firſt Stages of*

" *Life.*—We have ſeen, adds he,
" how Mr. *Fielding* very ſoon
" ſquander'd away his ſmall Pa-
" trimony, which, with Oeco-
" nomy, might have procur'd
" him Independence ;—we have
" ſeen how he ruined, into the
" Bargain, a Conſtitution, which
" in it's original Texture ſeem'd
" formed to laſt much longer.—
" When Illneſs and Indigence
" were once let in upon him, he
" no longer remained the Maſter
" of his own Actions ; and that
" nice Delicacy of Conduct which
" alone conſtitutes and preſerves
" a Character, was occaſionally
" obliged to give Way.—When
" he was not under the imme-
" diate Urgency of Want, thoſe
" who were intimate with him
" are ready to aver, that he had
" a Mind greatly ſuperior to any
" Thing mean or little ; when
" his Finances were exhauſted,
" he was not the moſt elegant in
" his Choice of the Means to
" redreſs himſelf, and he would
" inſtantly exhibit a Farce or a
" Puppet-Shew, in the *Haymar-*
" *ket* Theatre, which was wholly
" inconſiſtent with the Profeſſion
" he had embarked in.—But his
" Intimates are Witneſs how
" much his Pride ſuffer'd when
" he was forced into Meaſures of
" this Kind.—No Man having a
" juſter Senſe of Propriety, or
" more honourable Ideas of the
" Employment of an Author and
" a Scholar."

FILMER, Mr. *Edward.*——
This Gentleman was a Doctor of
Civil Law : He was ever a ſtrong
Advocate for dramatic Writings,
which, together with the Pro-
feſſors of dramatic Poetry, he has
warmly defended againſt their furious Enemy and Opponent *Je-*
remy Collier.—In the Decline of
his Life he produced a Play,
which,

which, tho' it bears ftrong Tefti-mony to the Underftanding and Abilities of the Author, yet fail-ed of Succefs on the Stage for the Want of that Force and Fire, which it is probable the Doctor, in a lefs advanced Time of Life, would have been able to have be-ftowed on it.—The Piece is en-titled,

The *Unnatural Brother.* T. What Time this Author was born or died I have not been able to trace ; yet, from what I have faid, it will appear that he muft have lived in the Reigns of *Charles* I. *Charles* II. and *James* the fecond, as the Date of his Play is in 1697, at which Time, as I before obferved, he was of an advanced Age.—It fhould feem, however, that he lived for fome Years afterwards, at leaft if the Edition which I have of his *Defence of Stage Plays* againft *Collier* is the firft, as that is dated in 1707.

FISHBOURNE, Mr.——This Gentleman belonged to the Inns of Court, and is only mentioned here by Way of perpetuating that Infamy which he has juftly in-curr'd, by being known to be the Author of a dramatic Piece, entitled,

SODOM. This Play is fo extremely ob-fcene, and beyond all Bounds in-decent and immoral, that even the Earl of *Rochefter*, whofe Li-bertinifm was fo profefs'd and open, and who fcarcely knew what the Senfe of Shame was, could not bear to undergo the Imputation of being the Author of this Piece (which, in Order to make it fell, was publifhed with initial Letters in the Title, intended to mifguide the Opinion of the Public, and induced them to fix it on that Nobleman) and

publifhed a Copy of Verfes to dif-claim his having had any Share in the Compofition.—Nor has it indeed any Spark of Refemblance to Lord *Rochefter's* Wit, could that even have attoned (which however it could by no Means have done) for the abominable Obfcenity.—To fuch Lengths did the Licence of that Court induce Perfons to imagine they might proceed in Vice with full Im-punity.

FLECKNOE, *Richard,* Efq;—This Writer lived in the Reign of King *Charles* II.—He is faid to have been originally a Jefuit, and, in Confequence of that Pro-feffion, to have had Connections with moft of the Perfons of Di-ftinction in *London,* who were of the *Roman* Catholic Perfuafion.—The Character that *Langbaine* gives of him is, that his Ac-quaintance with the Nobility was more than with the Mufes, and that he had a greater Propenfity to Rhyming than Genius for Poetry.

He wrote many Things both in Profe and Verfe, more efpecially the latter, and has left behind him five dramatic Pieces, only one of which he could ever ob-tain the Favour of having acted, and that met with but indiffer-ent Succefs.—Their Titles are;

1. *Damoifelles a-la-Mode.* C.
2. ERMINIA. T. C. *Vid.* Vol. I. APPENDIX.
3. *Love's Dominion.* Dramatic Paftoral.
4. *Love's Kingdom.* Paftoral Com.
5. *Marriage of* OCEANUS *and* BRITANNIA. Mafque.

The Author, however, wrapped up in his own Self-Opinion, has carried off this Difappointment in a Manner extremely cavalier and almoft peculiar to himfelf;

for,

for, in the Preface to his *Demoi-selles a-la-Mode*, which had been refused by the Players, he has these very remarkable Words. "For the acting this Comedy," says he, "those who have the "Government of the Stage have "their Humour, and would be "intreated; and I have mine, "and won't intreat them; and "were all dramatic Writers of "my Mind, they should wear "their old Plays Thread-bare, "e'er they should have any new, "till they better understood their "own Interest, and how to dif- "tinguish between Good and "Bad."——The Duke of *Buck-ingham*, in his *Rehearsal*, seems to have kept this Passage strongly in his Eye in the Anger he has put into *Bayes*'s Mouth when the Players were gone to Dinner.—However, notwithstanding all this important Bluster of Mr. *Fleck-noe*, and his having printed to his *Dramatis Personæ* the Names of the Actors he had intended the several Parts to be performed by, in order, as he says, "that the "Reader might have half the "Pleasure of seeing it acted," it is probable that he and his Works might have sunk together into ab-solute Oblivion, had not the Re-sentment of a much greater Poet against him, I mean Mr. *Dryden*, doom'd him to a different Kind of Immortality from that which he aim'd at, by giving his Name to one of the severest Satires he ever wrote, *viz.* his *Mac Fleck-noe*, which, tho' mostly pointed at *Shadwell*, has nevertheless some severe Strokes upon our Author, which, together with the Title of the Poem itself, will preserve his Memory, and, as he himself proposed by the Publication of his own Works, "continue his Name "to Posterity," so long as the

Writings of that admirable Poet continue to be read.

FLETCHER, Mr. *John*. Vid. BEAUMONT, *Francis*.

FLETCHER, Mr. *Phineas*.—This learned Writer was, ac-cording to *Winstanley*, Son to *Giles Fletcher*, Esq; Doctor of Civil Law and Ambassador from Queen *Eli-zabeth* to *Theodore Juanowick*, Duke of *Muscovy*.—He had two Brothers, viz. *George* and *Giles Fletcher*, who each of them wrote a Poem in a religious Strain, en-titled *Christ's Victory*.—Our Au-thor was a Fellow of *King*'s Col-lege, *Cambridge*, and exceeded both his Brothers in poetic Fame, which he acquired principally by a Poem, called the *Purple Island*, which however is now quite for-gotten.

Winstanley has attributed to him one dramatic Piece, entitled,

SICELIDES. Piscatory Drama. But as within a very few Pages he has ascribed a Piece of the very same Title, (with no other Dif-ference than the calling it a *Pas-toral)* to *Robert Chamberlaine*, and as the other Writers mention no more than one dramatic Work of that Title, and that without any Author's Name, it would be dif-ficult to know where to fix it, were it not for one Circumstance, which I think determines it to have been Mr. *Fletcher*'s, and that is, it's being declared in the Title Page to have been acted in *King*'s College, *Cambridge*, the very Spot where this Author was educated, whereas Mr. *Chamber-laine* was bred at *Exeter* College, *Oxford*.

By the Date of it's Publication, which is in 1631, the Author must have flourished in the Reign of *Charles* I. and been Cotempo-rary with Mr. *Chamberlaine*.

FOOTE,

FOOTE, *Samuel*, Efq; — This well-known living Author was born at *Truro* in *Cornwall*, but in what Year I know not.—His Father was Member of Parliament for *Tiverton* in *Devorſhire*, and enjoyed the Poſts of Commiſſioner of the Prize Office and Fine Contract. —— His Mother was Heireſs of the *Dinely* and *Goodere* Families, and to her, in Conſequence of an unhappy and fatal Quarrel between her two Brothers, Sir *John Dinely Goodere*, Bart. and Sir *Samuel Goodere*, Captain of his Majeſty's Ship the *Ruby*, which terminated in the Loſs of Life to both, the *Dinely* Eſtate, which was upwards of five Thouſand Pounds *per Annum*, deſcended.—He received his Education at *Worceſter* College, formerly *Glouceſter* Hall, *Oxon*, which ow'd its Foundation and Change of Name to Sir *Thomas Cooks Winford*, Bart. a ſecond Couſin of our Author's.—From the Univerſity he was removed to the *Temple*, being deſigned for the Study of the Law; in which it is moſt probable that his great Oratorical Talents and Powers of Mimickry and Humour, would have ſhewn themſelves in a very conſpicuous Light.—The Dryneſs and Gravity of this Study, however, not ſuiting the more volatile Vivacity of his Diſpoſition, he choſe rather to employ thoſe Talents in a Sphere of Action to which they ſeem'd better adapted, viz. on the Stage, in the Purſuit of which the repeated Proofs he has received of the Public Approbation, bear the ſtrongeſt Teſtimonials to his Merit.—His firſt Appearance was in the Part of *Othello*, but whether he early diſcovered that his *Forte* did not lye in Tragedy, or that his Genius could not bear the being only a Repeater of the

Works of others, he ſoon ſtruck out into a new and untrodden Path, in which he at once attained the two great Ends of affording Entertainment to the Public and Emolument to himſelf.——This was by taking on himſelf the double Character of Author and Performer, in which Light, in 1747, he opened the little Theatre in the *Haymarket*, with a dramatic Piece of his own writing, called the *Diverſions of the Morning*.—This Piece conſiſted of nothing more than the Introduction of ſeveral well-known Characters in real Life, whoſe Manner of Converſation and Expreſſion this Author had very happily hit in the Diction of his Drama, and ſtill more happily repreſented on the Stage by an exact and moſt amazing Imitation, not only of the Manner and Tone of Voice, but even of the very Perſons of thoſe whom he intended to *take off*.—Among theſe Characters there was in particular a certain Phyſician, who was much better known from the Oddity and Singularity of his Appearance and Converſation, than from his Eminence in the Practice of his Profeſſion.—The celebrated Chevalier *Taylor* the Oculiſt, who was at that Time in the Height of his Vogue and Popularity, was alſo another Object, and indeed a deſerved one, of Mr. *Foote's* Mimickry and Ridicule; and in the latter Part of his Piece, under the Character of a theatrical Director, this Gentleman took off with great Humour and Accuracy the ſeveral Stiles of acting of every principal Performer of the *Engliſh* Stage.

This Performance at firſt met with ſome little Oppoſition from the civil Magiſtrates of *Weſtminſter*, under the Sanction of the Act of

Parlia-

Parliament for limiting the Number of Play-houfes.—But the Author, being patronized by many of the principal Nobility and others, this Oppofition was over-ruled, and with an Alteration of the Title of his Piece to that of Mr. *Foote's giving Tea to his Friends*, he proceeded without farther Moleftation, and reprefented it thro' a Run of upwards of forty Mornings, to crowded and fplendid Audiences.

The enfuing Seafon he produced another Piece of the fame Kind, which he called *An Auction of Pictures.*——In this he introduced feveral new Characters, all however popular ones, and extremely well known, particularly Sir *Thomas De Veil*, then the acting Juftice of Peace for *Weftminfter*; Mr. *Cock*, the celebrated Auctioneer, and the equally famous Orator *Henley*.—This Piece had alfo a very great Run.

. Neither of the above-mentioned Pieces have yet appeared in Print, nor would they perhaps give any very great Pleafure in the Clofet; for, confifting principally of Characters whofe peculiar Singularities could never be perfectly reprefented in Black and White, they might probably appear flat and infipid, when divefted of that ftrong Colouring which Mr. *Foote* had given them in his perfonal Reprefentation; for it may not be improper to obferve in this Place, that he himfelf reprefented all the principal Characters in each Piece, which ftood in Need of his Mimick Powers to execute, fhifting from one to another with all the Dexterity of a *Proteus.*——He now, however, proceeded to Pieces of fomewhat more dramatic Regularity, his *Knights* being the Produce of an enfuing Seafon.—Yet

in this alfo, tho' his Plot and Characters feem'd lefs immediately perfonal, it was apparent that he kept fome particular real Perfonages ftrongly in his Eye in the Performance, and the Town took on themfelves to fix them where the Refemblance appear'd to be the moft ftriking.—It would be fuperfluous in this Place to enumerate the Courfe of this Gentleman's dramatic Progrefs as to all the refpective Pieces which he has fince written and performed, as a particular Account of each of them may be feen under it's proper Head, in the firft Volume of this Work.—Let it here fuffice therefore to obferve, that he has continued from Time to Time to entertain the Public, by felecting for their Ufe fuch Characters, as well general as individual, as feem'd moft likely to contribute to the exciting our innocent Laughter, and beft anfwer the principal End of dramatic Writings of the comic Kind, *viz.* the Relaxation of the Mind from the Fatigue of Bufinefs or Anxiety.—The Names of the feveral Pieces which he has hitherto publifhed, are as follows.

1. *Author.* C. of two Acts.
2. *Englifhman in Paris.* Com. of two Acts.
3. *Englifhman return'd from Paris.* C. of two Acts.
4. *Knights.* C. of two Acts. *Vid.* Vol. I. APPENDIX.
5. *Minor.* C. of two Acts.
6. ORATORS. C. of three Acts. *Vid.* Vol. I. APPENDIX.
7. *Tafte.* C. of two Acts.

Mr. *Foote's* dramatic Works are all to be ranked among the *Petite Pieces* of the Theatre, as he has not hitherto attempted any Thing which has reached to the Bulk of the more perfect Drama.

In

In the Execution of them they are sometimes loose, negligent and unfinished, seeming rather to be the hasty Productions of a Man of Genius, whose Pegasus, tho' indued with Fire, has no Inclination for Fatigue, than the labour'd Finishings of a profest Dramatist aiming at Immortality. —His Plots are somewhat irregular, and their Catastrophes not always conclusive or perfectly wound up.—Yet, with all these little Deficiencies, it must be confes'd that they contain more of one essential Property of Comedy, *viz.* strong Character, than the Writings of any other of our modern Authors, and altho' the Diction of his Dialogue may not, from the general Tenor of his Subjects, either require, or admit of, the Wit of a *Congreve* or the Elegance of an *Etherege*, yet it is constantly embellished with numberless Strokes of keen Satire, and Touches of Temporary Humour, such as only the clearest Judgment and deepest Discernment could dictate; and tho' the Language spoken by his Characters may at first Sight seem not the most accurate and correct, yet it will, on a closer Examination, be found entirely dramatical, as it contains Numbers of those natural Minutiæ of Expression, on which the very Basis of Character is frequently founded, and which render it the truest Mirrour of the Conversation of the Time he wrote in.

It has been objected against Mr. *Foote*, that the Introduction of real Characters on the Stage is not only ungenerous, but cruel and unjust; and that the rendering any Person the Object of public Ridicule and Laughter, is doing him the most essential Injury possible, as it is wounding the human Breast in the tenderest Point, *viz.* it's Pride and Self-Opinion.—Yet I cannot think this Charge so strong as the vehement Opponents of Mimickry would have it appear to be.—Mr. *Foote* himself, in his *Minor*, has very properly distinguished who are the proper Objects of Ridicule, and the legal Victims to the Lash of Satire; that is to say, those who appear what they are not, or would be what they cannot.—When Hypocrify and Dissimulation would lay Snares for the Fortunes, or contaminate the Principles of Mankind, it is surely but Justice to the World to withdraw the Mask, and shew their natural Faces with the Distortions and shocking Deformities they really are possessed of.— And when Affectation or Singularity overbear the more valuable Parts of any Person's Character, and render those disagreeable and wearisome Companions, who, divested of those characteristic Foibles, might be valuable, sensible and entertaining Members of Community, it is themselves surely who act the ridiculous Part on the more extensive Stage of the World; and it should rather be deemed an *Act* of Kindness both to the Persons themselves and their Acquaintance to set up such a Mirrour before them, as by pointing out to themselves their absurd Peculiarities, (and who is without some?) afford them an Opportunity, by Amendment, to destroy the Resemblance, and To avoid the Ridicule.—Such a Sort of Kindness as it would be to lead a Person to a Looking-Glass who had put on his Peruke the wrong Side foremost, instead of suffering him in that Condition to run the Gauntlet in the Mall or the Playhouse, where he muſt perceive the Titter of the whole Aſſembly raiſed againſt him, without knowing on what Account it is raiſed, or by what Means to put a Stop to it. —In a Word, if a Sir *Penurious Trifle*, a *Peter Paragraph*, or a *Cadwallader*, have ever had their Originals in ꞓeal Life, let thoſe Originals keep their own Counſel, remember the *qui capit, ille facit*, and reform their reſpective Follies.—Nor can I help being of Opinion, that an Author of this Kind in ſome Reſpects is more uſeful to the Age he lives in, than thoſe who only range abroad into the various Scenes of Life for general Character.—And altho' Mr. *Foote*'s dramatic Pieces may not perhaps have the good Fortune to attain Immortality, or be perfectly reliſhed by the Audiences of a *future* Age, yet I cannot deny him here the Juſtice of bearing ſtrong Teſtimony to his Merits, and ranking him among the firſt of the Dramatiſts of *this*.

Foꞃᴅ, Mr. *John*.—This Gentleman was a Member of the *Middle Temple*, and wrote in the Reign of *Charles* I.—He was not only himſelf a Well-wiſher and Devotee to the Muſes, but alſꝋ a Friend and Acquaintance of moſt of the Poets of his Time, particularly of *Rowley* and *Decker*, with whom he joined in the Compoſition of ſome of their Pieces.—He wrote however ſeven dramatic Pieces on his own Foundation entirely, all of which have conſiderable Merit, and met with good Succeſs.—Not only his Genius as a Writer, but his Diſpoſition as a Man, ſeems to have been more inclined to Tragedy than Comedy, at leaſt if we may be allowed to form our Judgment on

a Diſtich concerning him, written by a cotemporary Poet.

> *Deep in a Dump* John Ford *was alone got,*
> *With folded Arms, and melancholy Hat.*—

According to the Cuſtom of that Time his Name is not affixed to any of his Plays, but they may be known by an Anagram generally printed in the Title Page inſtead of a Name, *viz.*
    Fɪᴅᴇ Hᴏɴᴏʀ.
and the Titles of them are as in the following Liſt.
1. *Broken Heart.* T.
2. *Fancies chaſte and noble.* T.-Com.
3. *Ladies Tryal.* T. C.
4. *Lover's Melancholy.* T. C.
5. *Love's Sacrifice.* T.
6. Pᴇʀᴋɪɴ Wᴀʀʙᴇᴄᴋ. Hiſt. Play.
7. *Sun's Darling.* Maſque. (aſſiſted by *Decker*.)
8. *'Tis Pity ſhe's a Whore.* T.
The laſt of theſe is an admirable Play, and is to be found in *Dodſley*'s Collection, Vol. V.

He alſo aſſiſted *Decker* and *Rowley* in the writing of another Piece, entitled,
The *Witch of* Eᴅᴍᴏɴᴛᴏɴ. Com.

Winſtanley obſerves that this Author was very beneficial to the *Red Bull* and *Fortune* Play-houſes, as may appear by the Plays which he wrote.—But this is apparently a Miſtake, ſince in the ſeveral Title Pages to hiꞋ Plays they will be found to have been all acted either at the *Globe*, the *Phœnix*, or the *Cookpit*.

I know not when this Author was born, nor is there any particular Account of the Time of his Death, but as all his Plays
weꞃe

were publifhed between 1629 and 1639, it is fcarcely to be fuppofed fo rapid a Courfe of Genius could have been ftopped all at once, by any Thing but that great inevitable Stroke ;—I am therefore apt to believe he muft have died fhortly after the laft-mentioned Year.—For as to the *Sun's Darling*, written by him and *Decker*, tho' not publifhed till 1657, yet *Langbaine* has informed us with Refpect to it, that it did not make it's Appearance in Print till after the Death of both it's Authors.

Winftanley has alfo by Miftake attributed to this Author the Play of *Love's Labyrinth*, written by the Perfon I fhall next have occafion to mention.

FORD, Mr. *Thomas*.—Whether this Author was any Relation to the above-mentioned Gentleman or not, I have not been able to difcover.—All I can trace concerning him is, that he lived in the Reign of *Charles* I. and publifhed one dramatic Piece, entitled,

    Love's Labyrinth. Trag.-Com.

FOUNTAIN, Mr. *John.*—— This Gentleman lived in *Devonfhire*, and foon after the Reftoration publifhed a Play which he had written for the Amufement of fome leifure Hours and without any View to the Stage, entitled,

    The *Rewards of Virtue.* Com. About eight Years after it's firft Publication, however, the Author being dead, Mr. *Shadwell* took it in Hand, and making fome Alterations in it, brought it on the Stage, where it met with very good Succefs, under the Title of,

    The *Royal Shepherdefs.*

FRANCIS, Mr. *Philip.*——Of this Gentleman, though a living Writer, I know nothing more than that he is a Clergyman.— His poetical Abilities have been fufficiently evinced in a Tranflation of the works of *Horace,* which is very juftly efteemed the beft at prefent extant, but as a Dramatift he does not ftand in fo exalted a Light, having produced only two dramatic Pieces, neither of which met with any extraordinary Succefs.—Their Titles are,

    CONSTANTINE. T.

    EUGENIA. T.

FRAUNCE, Mr. *Abraham.*— This is an ancient Author, of fo diftant a Date as the Reig. of Queen *Elizabeth.*—He has written feveral Things in that awkwardeft of all Verfe, tho' at that Time greatly in Vogue, *Englifh Hexameter.*—Among other Things he has executed a Tranflation of *Taffo's Aminta,* which he has dedicated to the celebrated Countefs of *Pembroke,* under the Title of,

    AMYNTAS. Paft. It is however contained in the Body of another Piece, entitled,

    Countefs of PEMBROKE's *Ivy Church.* Play, in two Parts, or more properly fpeaking, a Paftoral and an Elegy, of which *Amyntas* is the former.

FREEMAN, Sir *Ralph.*—This Gentleman lived in the Time of King *Charles* I. and moft probably is the fame who was one of the Mafters of Requefts in the Reign of that Monarch.—During the inteftine Troubles he thought proper to bury himfelf in Retirement, during which he employed his Hours in the Purfuit of Poetry, and produced a Tragedy on which *Langbaine* and other Writers beftow a very high Character.—It is entitled,

    IMPERIALE. Trag.

FROWDE,

FROWDE, Mr. *Philip.*—This Gentleman's Father was Post-Master-General in the Reign of Q. *Anne.*—When or where our Author was born, or where he received his first Rudiments of Learning, I have not been able to ascertain.—It is sufficient, however, to observe, that he finished his Studies at the University of *Oxford,* where he had the Honour of being particularly distinguished by Mr. *Addison,* who was so extremely pleased with the Elegance and Purity of some of his poetical Performances, especially those in *Latin,* that he gave them a Place in his celebrated Collection, entitled the *Musæ Anglicanæ,* to whose Merit so strong a Testimonial was given as the Declaration of that great *French* Poet *M. Boileau Despreaux,* that from the Perusal of that Collection he first conceived an Idea of the Greatness of the *British* Genius.—In the dramatic Way Mr. *Frowde* produced two Pieces, both in the Tragic Walk, entitled,

1. *Fall of* SAGUNTUM. T.
2. PHILOTAS. T.

Neither of them however met with very great Success, tho' they had strong Interest to support them, and were allowed to have considerable Merit. — Especially the last, whose Fate the Author himself in his Dedication of it to the Earl of *Chesterfield* (who at the Time when it was acted was Ambassador to the States General, and consequently could not oblige the Piece by his Countenance at the Representation) describes by the Words of *Juvenal,* *Laudatur & alget.*——Thus far however the Judgment of the Public stands vindicated, that it must be confessed Mr. *Frowde's* Tragedies have more Poetry than Pathos, more Beauties of Language to please in the Closet, than Strokes of Incident and Action to strike and astonish in the Theatre, and consequently they might force a due Applause from the Reading, at the same Time that they might appear very heavy and even insipid in the Representation.

This elegant Writer died at his Lodgings in *Cecil* Street in the *Strand, Dec.* 19, 1738, equally lamented as he had been beloved, for tho' his Writings had recommended him to *public* Esteem, the Politeness of his Genius was the least amiable Part of his Character; for, besides the Possession of the great Talents of Wit and Learning, an agreeable Complacence of Behaviour, a chearful Benevolence of Mind, a punctual Sincerity in Friendship, and a strict Adherence to the Practice of Honour and Humanity, were what added the most brilliant Ornaments to that Character, and render'd him an Object of Esteem and Admiration to all who knew him.

FULWELL, Mr. *Ulpian.*—An ancient Writer, of whom *Wood* has recorded nothing farther than that he lived in the Reign of Queen *Elizabeth,* was a Native of *Somersetshire,* and descended from a good Family there, that he was born in 1556, and at the Age of thirty Years became a Commoner of St. *Mary's* Hall in *Oxford*; that it does not appear whether he took any Degree there or not: but that while he continued in that House he was esteemed a Person of Ingenuity by his Cotemporaries.—He wrote one moral dramatic Piece in Rhyme, *viz.*

Like will to like, quothe the Devil to Collier. Interl.

FYFE,

Fyfe, Mr.—All I know of this Gentleman is, that he lived in the Reign of *Charles* I. and immediately after the Reftoration prlifhed a Play founded on the Hiftory of that unhappy Monarch, entitled,

The *Royal Martyr*. Trag.

G.

G. J, *Vid.* Gough, J.

Gager, *Wm.* L.L.D. —This very learned and ancient Author I do not find mentioned in any of the Lifts of *Englifh* dramatic Writers, which he is undoubtedly entitled to be as a Native of this Kingdom, notwithftanding that his Pieces are written in the *Latin* Tongue.— In what Year he was born or died does not appear, but he received the Rudiments of his Education at *Weftminfter*, from which, being removed to the Univerfity of *Oxford*, he was enter'd a Student in *Chrift Church* College in 1574, where he took the Degrees in Arts, and afterwards, entering on the Law Line, took the Degrees in that Faculty alfo in 1589.—About which Time, being famed for his Excellencies therein, he became Chancellor of the Diocefe of *Ely*, being held in high Efteem by Dr. *Martin Heton*, the Bifhop of that See.—— The Commendation which *Anth. à Wood* gives of him as to his poetical Talents is fomewhat extraordinary.—He was (fays that Author) an excellent Poet, efpecially in the *Latin* Tongue, and reputed the beft *Comedian* (by which I fuppofe he means *dramatic Writer*) of his Time, whether, adds he, it was *Edward*

Earl of *Oxford*, *Will. Rowley*, the once Ornament for Wit and Ingenuity of *Pembroke* Hall in *Cambridge*, *Richard Edwards*, *John Lylie*, *Tho. Lodge*, *Geo. Gafcoigne*, *Will. Shakefpeare*, *Tho. Nafh*, or *John Heywood*.—A Combination of Names, by the bye, fo oddly jumbled together, as muft convince us that Mr. *Wood* was a much better Biographer than a Judge of dramatic Writings.—— He alfo tells us that Dr. *Gager* was a Man of great Gifts, a good Scholar, and an honeft Man, and that, in a Controverfy which he maintained in an Epiftolary Correfpondence with Dr. *John Rainolds*, concerning Stage Plays (which Controverfy was printed at *Oxford* in 4to. 1629) he had faid more for the Defence of Plays than can well be faid again by any Man that fhall fucceed or come after him.—He at length, however, gave up the Point, either convinced by Dr. *Rainold*'s Arguments, or perhaps afraid of incurring Cenfure, fhould he have purfued the Subject any farther. —*Wood* informs us that our Author wrote feveral Plays, of which however he gives us the Titles of no more than three, *viz.*

1. Meleager.
2. *Rivales.*
3. Ulysses *redux.*

which are all written in *Latin*, and, as we are informed by the above-cited Author, were acted with great Applaufe in the Refectory of *Chrift Church* College ; but only the firft of them does he affure us of having been printed, which it was at *Oxford*, in 4to. 1592, and occafioned the Letters between the Author and Dr. *Rainolds*, which I have before fpoken of.—Dr. *Gager* was living at, or near the City of *Ely*, in 1610.—— I cannot however omit one Circumftance cum.ftance of our Author, which I am afraid will be no very ftrong Recommendation of him to my fair Readers, *viz.* that in an Act at *Oxford* in 1608, he maintained a Thefis, *That it was lawful for Hufbands to beat their Wives.*—This Thefis was anfwer'd by Mr. *Heale,* of *Exeter* College, an avowed Champion for the Fair Sex.

GARDINER, Mr. *Matthew.*—This Author is mentioned no where but in the *Britifh Theatre,* the Writer of which informs us that he was a native of *Ireland,* and wrote two dramatic Pieces, moft probably performed in that Kingdom, whofe Titles were

1. *Parthian Hero.* Trag.
2. *Sharpers.* Ballad Opera.

GARRICK, *David,* Efq;—It would furely be needlefs here to mention, that the Gentleman juft nam'd is at this Time a living Writer, were it not for the Sake of future theatrical Chronology, which may at fome Period hereafter have Occafion for fuch Information.—He was born in the City of *Hereford,* in the Year 1717, his Father bearing a Captain's Commiffion in the Army, which Rank he maintained for feveral Years; and at the Time of his Death was poffefs'd of a Majority, which that Event however prevented him from ever enjoying.—Our Author received the firft Rudiments of his Education at the Free - School of *Litchfield,* which he afterwards compleated at *Rochefter,* under the celebrated Mr. *Colfon,* fince Mathematical Profeffor at *Cambridge.*—On the 9th of *March* 1736, he was enter'd of the honourable Society of *Lincoln's-Inn,* being intended for the Bar.—But whether he found the Study of the Law too heavy, faturnine, and

barren of Amufement for his more active and lively Difpofition, or that a Genius like his could not continue circumfcribed within the Limits of any Profeffion but that to which it was more peculiarly adapted, and like the magnetic Needle pointed directly to its proper Centre, or perhaps both, it is cer'ain that he did not long purfue the Municipal Law; for in the Year 1740-1, he quitted it entirely for the Stage, and made his firft Appearance at the Theatre in *Goodman's-Fields,* then under the Management of Mr. *Henry Giffard.*—The Character he firft reprefented was that of King *Richard* III. in which, like the Sun burfting from behind an obfcure Cloud, he difplayed, in the very earlieft Dawn, a fomewhat more than Meridian Brightnefs.—In fhort, his Excellence dazzled and aftonifhed every one, and the feeing a young Man, in no more than his twenty-fourth Year, and a Novice to the Stage, reaching at one fingle Step to that Height of Perfection which Maturity of Years and long practical Experience had not been able to beftow on the then capital Performers of the *Englifh* Stage, was a Phœnomenon which could not but become the Object of univerfal Speculation, and as univerfal Admiration.——The Rumour of this bright Star appearing in the Eaft flew with the Rapidity of Lightning through the Town, and drew all the theatrical *Magi* thither to pay their Devotions to this new-born Son of Genius; the Theatres towards the Court-End of the Town were deferted, Perfons of all Ranks flocking to *Goodman's - Fields,* where Mr. *Garrick* continued to act till the Clofe of the Seafon,

when

when, having very advantageous Terms offer'd him for the performing in *Dublin* during some Part of the Summer, he went over thither, where he found the same just Homage paid to his Merit, which he had received from his own Countrymen.——— To the Service of the latter, however, he esteemed himself more immediately bound; and therefore, in the ensuing Winter, engaged himself to Mr. *Fleetwood*, then Manager of *Drury Lane* Playhouse, in which Theatre he continued till the Year 1745, in the Winter of which he again went over to *Ireland*, and continued there through the whole of that Season, being joint Manager with Mr. *Sheridan* in the Direction and Profits of the Theatre Royal in *Smock-Alley*.— From thence he returned to *England*, and was engaged for the Season of 1746 with the late Mr. *Rich*, Patentee of *Covent Garden*. This, however, was his last Performance as an hired Actor, for in the Close of that Season, Mr. *Fleetwood*'s Patent for the Management of *Drury Lane* being expir'd, and that Gentleman having no Inclination farther to persue a Design by which, from his Want of Acquaintance with the proper Conduct of it, or some other Reasons, he had already considerably impair'd his Fortune, Mr. *Garrick*, in Conjunction with Mr. *Lacy*, purchased the Property of that Theatre, together with the Renovation of the Patent, and, in the Winter of 1747, opened it with the best Part of Mr. *Fleetwood*'s former Company, and the great additional Strength of Mr. *Barry*, Mrs. *Pritchard* and Mrs. *Cibber* from *Covent Garden*.

In this Station Mr. *Garrick* has continued ever since, and both by his Conduct as a Manager, and his unequal'd Merit as an Actor, has from Year to Year added to the Entertainment of the Public, which he has ever, with an indefatigable Assiduity, consulted.—Nor has the Public been by any Means ungrateful in its Returns for that Assiduity; but has, on the Contrary, by the warm and deserved Encouragement which it has given him, raised him to that State of Ease and Affluence, to which it must surely be the Wish of every honest Heart, to see superior Excellence of any Kind exalted.

To enter into a particular Detail of Mr. *Garrick*'s several Merits, or a Discussion of his peculiar Excellencies in the immense Variety of Characters he performs, would be a Task, not only too arduous for me to attempt, and too extensive for the Limits of the present Work, but also entirely impertinent and unnecessary, as very few Persons, for whose Entertainment or Information this Book is intended, can be supposed unacquainted with them.—However, as Readers in some more distant Periods, when, as Mr. *Cibber* expresses it, *the animated Graces of the Player will, at best, but faintly glimmer thro' the Memory, or imperfect Attestation, of a few surviving Spectators*; nay, when even these Testimonials shall be unattainable, will be desirous of forming to their Ideas a Portrait of the Person and Manner of this amazing Performer, I shall here bequeath my little Mite to future dramatic History, by offering such a rude Sketch of them, as when touched up hereafter by some other Pencil, may answer the intended Purpose, and prove a perfect Picture.

Mr. *Garrick* in his Perfon is low, yet well-fhap'd and neatly proportioned, and, having added the Qualifications of Dancing and Fencing to that natural Gentility of Manner, which no Art can beftow, but which our great Mother Nature endows many with, even from Infancy, his Deportment is conftantly eafy, natural and engaging.—His Complection is dark, and the Features of his Face, which are pleafingly regular, are animated by a full black Eye, brilliant and penetrating.—His Voice is clear, melodious and commanding, and, altho' it may not poffefs the ftrong overbearing Powers of Mr. *Moffop*'s, or the mufical Sweetnefs of Mr. *Barry*'s, yet it appears to have a much greater Compafs of Variety than either ; and, from Mr. *Garrick*'s judicious Manner of conducting it, enjoys that Articulation and piercing Diftinctnefs, which renders it equally intelligible, even to the moft diftant Parts of an Audience, in the gentle Whifpers of murmuring Love, the half-fmother'd Accents of infelt Paffion, or the profeffed and fometimes aukward Concealments of an Afide Speech in Comedy, as in the Rants of Rage, the Darings of Defpair, or all the open Violence of tragical Enthufiafm.

As to his particular *Forte* or fuperior Caft in acting, it would be perhaps as difficult to determine it, as it would be minutely to defcribe his feveral Excellencies in the very different Cafts in which he at different Times thinks proper to appear.—Particular Superiority is fwallowed up in his Univerfality, and fhould it even be contended, that there have been Performers equal to him in their own refpective *Fortes*

of Playing, yet even *their* Partifans muft acknowledge, there never exifted any one Performer that came near his Excellence in fo great a Variety of Parts.——Tragedy, Comedy and Farce, the Lover and the Hero, the jealous Hufband, who fufpects his Wife's Virtue without Caufe, and the thoughtlefs lively Rake, who attacks it without Defign, are all alike open to his Imitation, and all alike do Honour to his Execution.—Every Paffion of the human Breaft feems fubjected to his Powers of Expreffion, nay, even Time itfelf appears to ftand ftill or advance as he would have it.——Rage and Ridicule, Doubt and Defpair, Tranfport and Tendernefs, Compaffion and Contempt, Love, Jealoufy, Fear, Fury and Simplicity, all take in Turn Poffeffion of his Features, while each of them in Turn appears to be the fole Poffeffor of thofe Features.—One Night Old Age fits on his Countenance, as if the Wrinkles fhe had ftampt there were indelible ; the next the Gaiety and Bloom of Youth feems to o'erfpread his Face, and fmooth even thofe Marks which Time and mufcular Conformation may have really made there. —Of thefe Truths no one can be ignorant, who has ever feen him in the feveral Characters of *Lear* or *Hamlet*, *Richard*, *Dorilas*, *Romeo*, or *Lufignon* ; in his *Ranger*, *Bays*, *Drugger*, *Kitely*, *Brute*, or *Benedict*——In fhort, Nature, the Miftrefs from whom alone this great Performer has borrowed all his Leffons, being in herfelf inexhauftible, and her Variation not to be numbered, it is by no Means furprizing, that this, her darling Son, fhould find an unlimited Scope for Change and Diverfity in his Manner of copying

from

from her various Productions; and, as if she had from his Cradle marked him out for her truest Representative, she has bestowed on him such Powers of Expression in the Muscles of his Face, as no Performer ever yet possess'd; not only for the Display of a single Passion, but also for the Combination of those various Conflicts with which the human Breast at Times is fraught; so that in his Countenance, even when his Lips are silent, his Meaning stands portray'd in Characters too legible for any to mistake it.—In a Word, the Beholder feels himself affected he knows not how, and it may be truly said of him, by future Writers, what the Poet has said of *Shakespeare*, that in *his* acting, as in *the other*'s writing,

His powerful Strokes prevailing Truth impress'd,
And unresisted Passion storm'd the Breast.

During the Course of his Management, the Public has, undoubtedly, been much obliged to him for his indefatigable Labour in the Conduct of the Theatre, and in the Pains he has ever taken to discover and gratify its Taste; and, tho' the Situation of a Manager will perpetually be liable to Attacks from disappointed Authors and undeserving Performers; yet, it is apparent, from the Barrenness both of Plays and Players of Merit which has for some years past appear'd at the opposite Theatre, that this Gentleman cannot have refus'd Acceptance to many of either Kind, that was any Way deserving of the Town's Regard —In short, it does not appear that this is the Age of either dramatic or thea-

trical Genius; and yet it is very apparent, that the Pains Mr. *Garrick* has taken in rearing many tender Plants of the latter Kind, has added several valuable Performers to the *English* Stage, whose first Blossoms were far from promising so fair a Fruit as they have since produc'd:—and that, among the several dramatic Pieces which have within these fourteen Years made their first Appearance on the Theatre in *Drury Lane*, there are very few, whose Authors have not acknowledged themselves greatly indebted to this Gentleman for useful Hints or advantageous Alterations, to which their Success has in great Measure been owing.— Add to this Care, the Revival of many Pieces of the more early Writers: Pieces possess'd of great Merit, but which had, either thro' the Neglect or Ignorance of other Managers, lain for a long, Time unemployed and unregarded.——But there is one Part of theatrical Conduct which ought unquestionably to be recorded to Mr. *Garrick*'s Honour, since the Cause of Virtue and Morality, and the Formation of public Manners are very considerably dependant on it, and that is, the Zeal with which he has ever aimed to banish from the Stage all those Plays which carry with them an immoral Tendency, and to prune from those, which do not absolutely on the whole promote the Interests of Vice, such Scenes of Licentiousness and Liberty, as a Redundancy of Wit and too great Liveliness of Imagination has induced some of our comic Writers to indulge themselves in, and which the sympathetic Disposition of an Age of Gallantry and Intrigue had given a Sanction to.——The Purity of

the

the *English* Stage has certainly been much more fully established during the Administration of this theatrical Minister, than it had ever been during preceding Managements : For what the Public Taste had itself in some Measure began, he, by keeping that Taste within its proper Channel, and feeding it with a pure and untainted Stream, seems to have compleated; and to have endeavour'd as much as possible to keep up to the Promise made in the Prologue above quoted, and which was spoken at the first Opening of that Theatre under his Direction, viz.

Bade Scenic Virtue form the rising Age,
And Truth diffuse her Radiance from the Stage.

His Superiority to all others in one Branch of Excellence, however, must not make us overlook the Rank he is entitled to stand in as to another ; nor our Remembrance of his being the *first Actor* living, induce us to forget, that he is far from being the *last Writer.*——Notwithstanding the numberless and laborious Avocations attending on his Profession as an Actor, and his Station as a Manager, yet still his active Genius has been perpetually bursting forth in various little Productions both in the dramatic and poetical Way, whose Merit cannot but make us regret his Want of Time for the Pursuance of more extensive and important Works. Of these he has publicly avowed himself the Author of the following, some of which are Originals, and the rest Alterations from other Authors, with a Design to adapt them to the present Taste of the Public.

1. *Every Man in his Humour.* Com. (Alteration from *Ben Jonson*, with an additional Scene.)
2. *Farmer's Return.* Interlude.
3. *Guardian.* Com. of two Acts.
4. LETHE. Farce.
5. *Lying Valet.* Com. of two Acts.
6. *Miss in her Teens.* Farce.
7. ROMEO and JULIET. T. (Alter'd from *Shakespeare*, with an additional Scene.)
8. *Winter's Tale.* (Alter'd from *Shakespeare.*)

Besides these, Mr. *Garrick* has been reputed the Author of the following Pieces, *viz.*

1. CATHERINE and PETRUCHIO. Farce, in three Acts. (Alter'd from *Shakespeare.*)
2. CYMBELINE. T. (Alter'd from *Shakespears*, but by little more than a Transposition of several Scenes, for the Sake of adding Regularity to the Conduct of the Drama.)
3. *Enchanter.* Musical Entertainment.
4. *Gamesters.* C. (Alteration from *James Shirley.*)
5. HARLEQUIN's *Invasion.* A *Christmas* Gambol. (This is a Sort of speaking Pantomime, in which an admirable Scene of Lady *Doll Skip*, the Taylor's Daughter, was written by this Gentleman.)
6. ISABELLA. (Alteration from *Southerne's Fatal Marriage*)
7. LILLIPUT. An Entertainment, acted by Children.
8. *Male Coquette.* Com. in two Acts.

Besides

Befides thefe, Mr. *Garrick* has been fuppofed to be the Author of an Ode on the Death of Mr. *Pelham*, which, in lefs than fix Weeks, run thro' four Editions. The Prologues, Epilogues and Songs, which he has written, are almoft innumerable, and poffefs a Degree of Happinefs both in Conception and Execution, in which he ftands unequall'd.—It would, however, be in vain to attempt any Enumeration of them in this Place, and is indeed the lefs neceffary, as I have been informed there is Hope the Author himfelf will, e'er long, oblige the Public with a compleat Edition of all his Works.

GARTER, Mr. *Thomas.*——I meet with no mention of this Gentleman among any of the Writers, but only in *Coxeter*'s MS. Notes, where, without any farther Account, a very old Piece, publifhed about the Middle of Queen *Elizabeth*'s Reign, is afcribed to a Perfon of this Name. The Piece itfelf is entitled, *The Commody of,*

SUSANNA.

GASCOIGNE, *George*, Efq;——This Gentleman flourifhed in the Beginning of Queen *Elizabeth*'s Reign.——He was born at *Walthamftow in the Foreft*, in *Effex*, and had a Tafte of each of our famous Univerfities, before he was enter'd of *Gray's-Inn.*—For his volatile Temper made him foon leave one of thefe delightful Places for another, and all of them for the Army, where his Behaviour was fo fignally brave, as to entitle him very juftly to the Motto he took, of *Tam Marti quam Mercurio.*

In this Station he was for fome Time in various Cities of *Holland*, after which he went to *France*, in order to fee and ftudy the Manners of that Court, where he happen'd to meet with a *Scottifh* Lady, whom he fell in Love with and married.—At length, being tired of this rambling Way of Life, he came back to *England*, and returned to *Gray's-Inn*, where he compofed moft of his various Pieces; and afterwards to his native Place, where, fays *Coxeter*, he died, and was buried in his middle Age, *Anno* 1578.—*Coxeter*, however, tells us, that he has feen an old Piece in Verfe (in Black Letter and without Date, 4to. *London.*) entitled, *A Remembrance of the well imployed Life and godly End of* George Gafcoigne, *Efq; who deceafed at* Stalmford *in* Lincolnfhire, *the 7th of* October, 1577. *The Report of* Geor. Whetftones, *Gent. an Eye-Witnefs of his godly and charitable End in this World.*

The dramatic Pieces he has left behind him are four in Number, their Names as follow,

1. *Glafs of Government.* Tragi-Com.
2. JOCASTA. T. (Tranflation from *Euripides*, affifted by Mr. *Fra. Kynwellmerfh.*)
3. *Pleafures at* KENELWORTHE *Caftle.* Mafque.
4. *Suppofes.* Com. (Tranflation from *Ariofto.*)

Befides thefe Pieces, he wrote feveral other Things in Verfe and Profe, and at that early Time was efteemed not only a Perfon of Politenefs, Eloquence and Underftanding, but alfo the beft Love Poet extant, nor were his dramatic Works held in any trifling Eftimation.——Among the reft of his Pieces is a Satire, called *The Steel Glafs*, printed in 1576, to which is prefixed the Author's Picture in Armour, with a Ruff and a large Beard.—

                On

On his right Hand hangs a Muſquet and Bandileers, on his left ſtands an Ink-horn and ſome-Books, and underwritten is the Motto above-mentioned, *Tam Marti quam Mercurio.*—No very ſtriking Mark of the Author's Modeſty!

GAY, Mr. *John.*—This Gentleman was deſcended from an ancient Family in *Devonſhire,* was born at *Exeter,* and received his Education at the Free-School of *Barnſtaple,* in that County, under the Care of Mr. *William Rayner.*—He was bred a Mercer in the *Strand,* but having a ſmall Fortune, independent of Buſineſs, and conſidering the Attendance on a Shop as a Degradation of thoſe Talents which he found himſelf poſſeſſed of, he quitted that Occupation, and applied himſelf to other Views, and to the Indulgence of his Inclination for the Muſes.—In what Year Mr. *Gay* was born does not appear from the Accounts of any of his Hiſtoriographers, but in 1712 we find him Secretary, or rather Domeſtic Steward, to the Dutcheſs of *Monmouth,* in which Station he continued till the Beginning of the Year 1714, at which Time he accompanied the Earl of *Clarendon* to *Hanover,* whither that Nobleman was diſpatched by Qu. *Anne.*

In the latter End of the ſame Year, in Conſequence of the Queen's Death, he returned to *England,* where he lived in the higheſt Eſtimation and Intimacy of Friendſhip with many Perſons of the firſt Diſtinction both in Rank and Abilities.——He was even particularly taken Notice of by Queen *Caroline,* then Princeſs of *Wales,* to whom he had the Honour of reading in Manuſcript his Tragedy of the *Captives,* and

in 1726 dedicated his Fables, by Permiſſion, to the Duke of *Cumberland.*—From this Countenance ſhewn to him, and numberleſs Promiſes made him of Preferment, it was reaſonable to ſuppoſe, that he would have been genteelly provided for in ſome Office ſuitable to his Inclination and Abilities.—Inſtead of which, in 1727, he was offer'd the Place of Gentleman-Uſher to one of the youngeſt Princeſſes; an Office which, as he looked on it as rather an Indignity to a Man, whoſe Talents might have been ſo much better employed, he thought proper to refuſe, and ſome pretty warm Remonſtrances were made on the Occaſion by his ſincere Friends and zealous Patrons the Duke and Dutcheſs of *Queenſberry,* which terminated in thoſe two noble Perſonages withdrawing from Court in Diſguſt.

Mr. *Gay*'s Dependencies on the Promiſes of the Great, and the Diſappointments he met with, he has figuratively deſcribed in his Fable of the *Hare with many Friends.*—However, the very extraordinary Succeſs he met with from Public Encouragement made an ample Amends, both with Reſpect to Satisfaction and Emolument, for thoſe private Diſappointments.—For, in the Seaſon of 1727-8, appeared his *Beggar's Opera,* the vaſt Succeſs of which was not only unprecedented, but almoſt incredible.—It had an uninterrupted Run in *London* of ſixty-three Nights in the firſt Seaſon, and was renewed in the enſuing one with equal Approbation.—It ſpread into all the great Towns of *England;* was played in many Places to the thirtieth and fortieth Time, and at *Bath* and *Briſtol* fifty; made its Progreſs into

into *Wales*, *Scotland* and *Ireland*, in which laft Place it was acted for twenty-four fucceffive nights, and laft of all it was performed at *Minorca*.—Nor was the Fame of it confined to the Reading and Reprefentation alone, for the Card-Table and Drawing Room fhar'd with the Theatre and Clofet in this Refpect ; the Ladies carried about the favorite Songs of it engraven on their Fan Mounts, and Screens and other Pieces of Furniture, were decorated with the fame.— Mifs *Fenton*, who acted *Polly*, tho' till then perfectly obfcure, became all at once the Idol of the Town ; her Pictures were engraven and fold in great Numbers ; her Life written ; Books of Letters and Verfes to her publifhed ; and Pamphlets made of even her very Sayings and Jefts ; nay, fhe herfelf received to a Station, in Confequence of which fhe, before her Death, attained the higheft Rank a Female Subject can acquire.—In fhort, the Satire of this Piece was fo ftriking, fo apparent and fo perfectly adapted to the Tafte of all Degrees of People, that it even for that Seafon overthrew the *Italian* Opera, that *Dagon* of the Nobility and Gentry, which had fo long feduced them to Idolatry, and which *Dennis*, by the Labours and Outcries of a whole Life, and many other Writers, by the Force of Reafon and Reflection, had in vain endeavour'd to drive from the Throne of Public Tafte. —Yet the *Herculean* Exploit did this little Piece at once bring to its Completion, and for fome Time recalled the Devotion of the Town from an Adoration of mere Sound and Shew, to the Admiration of, and Relifh for, true Satire and found Underftanding.

The Profits of this Piece was fo very great, both to the Author and Mr. *Rich*, the Manager, that it gave Rife to a Quibble, which became frequent in the Mouths of many, viz. *That it had made* Rich gay, *and* Gay rich ; and I have heard it afferted, that the Author's own Advantages from it were not lefs than two thoufand Pounds.—In Confequence of this Succefs, Mr. *Gay* was induced to write a fecond Part to it, which he entitled *Polly*.—But the Difguft fubfifting between him and the Court, together with the Mifreprefentations made of him, as having been the Author of fome difaffected Libels and feditious Pamphlets, a Charge which, however, he warmly difavows in his Preface to this Opera, a Prohibition and Suppreffion of it was fent from the Lord Chamberlain, at the very Time when every Thing was in Readinefs for the Rehearfal of it.— This Difappointment, however, was far from being a Lofs to the Author, for, as it was afterwards confeffed, even by his very beft Friends, to be in every Refpect infinitely inferior to the firft Part, it is more than probable, that it might have failed of that great Succefs in the Reprefentation which Mr. *Gay* might promife himfelf from it, whereas, the Profits arifing from the Publication of it afterwards in Quarto, in Confequence of a very large Subfcription, which this Appearance of Perfecution, added to the Author's great perfonal Intereft procured for him, were at leaft adequate to what could have accrued to him from a moderate Run, had it been reprefented.——This was the laft dramatic Piece of Mr. *Gay*'s that made it's Appearance during his Life ; his Opera of *Achilles*, and

the

the Comedy of the *Diſtreſſ Wife*, being both brought on the Stage after his Death.——What other Works he executed in the dramatic Way will be ſeen in the enſuing Liſt, and their ſeveral Succeſſes in the reſpective Accounts of them in the firſt Volume of this Work.—Their Titles are as follow,

1. ACHILLES. Opera.
2. *Beggar's Opera.*
3. *Captives.* T.
4. DIONE. Paſt.
5. *Diſtreſſ Wife.* C.
6. *Mohocks.* F.
7. *No Fools like Wits.* C.
8. POLLY. Opera.
9. *Three Hours after Marriage.* Farce.
10. *What d'ye call it.* Tragi-Com.-Paſt.-Farce.
11. *Wife of* BATH. C.

Beſides theſe, Mr. *Gay* wrote many very valuable Pieces in Verſe, among which his *Trivia*, or the *Art of walking the Streets of London*, tho' I believe his firſt poetical Attempt, is far from being the leaſt conſiderable, and is what recommended him to the Eſteem and Friendſhip of Mr. *Pope*; but, as among his dramatic Works, his *Beggar's Opera* did at firſt, and perhaps ever will, ſtand as an unrivall'd Maſter-Piece, ſo, among his poetical Works, his *Fables* hold the ſame Rank of Eſtimation: the latter having been almoſt as univerſally read, as the former was repreſented, and both equally admired. It would therefore be ſuperfluous here to add any Thing farther to theſe ſelf-rear'd Monuments of his Fame as a Poet.—As a Man, he appears to have been morally amiable.——His Diſpoſition was ſweet and affable, his Temper generous, and his Converſation agreeable and entertaining.—He had indeed one Foible, too frequently incident to Men of great literary Abilities, and which ſubjected him at Times to Inconveniences, which otherwiſe he needed not to have experienced, *viz.* an Exceſs of Indolence, without any Knowledge of Oeconomy; ſo that, tho' his Emoluments were, at ſome Periods of his Life, very conſiderable, he was at others greatly ſtraitened in his Circumſtances; nor could he prevail on himſelf to follow the Advice of his Friend Dean *Swift*, whom we find in many of his Letters endeavouring to perſuade him to the Purchaſing of an Annuity, as a Reſerve for the Exigencies that might attend on Old Age.—Mr. *Gay* choſe rather to throw himſelf on Patronage, than ſecure to himſelf an independent Competency by the Means pointed out to him; ſo that, after having undergone many Viciſſitudes of Fortune, and being for ſome Time chiefly ſupported by the Liberality of the Duke and Dutcheſs of *Queenſberry*, he died at their Houſe in *Burlington* Gardens, on *December* 1732.——He was interred in *Weſtminſter-Abbey*, and a Monument erected to his Memory, at the Expence of his afore-mentioned noble Benefactors, with an Inſcription expreſſive of their Regards and his own Deſerts, and an Epitaph in Verſe by Mr. *Pope*; but, as both of them are ſtill in Exiſtence, and free of Acceſs to every one, it would be impertinent to repeat either of them in this Place.

GAY, *Joſeph.*——This Name is only a fictitious one, yet I could not avoid giving it a Place here, as otherwiſe ſome Readers might be miſled, by the finding it prefix'd to a dramatic Piece, entitled,

The *Confederates*. Farce.
For an Explanation of it, however, *Vid.* BREVAL, Capt. *John Durant*.

GENTLEMAN, Mr. *Francis*.—— Of this Gentleman I know nothing more than a Report of his having been formerly in the Army.———A ſtrong Inclination for theatrical Exhibitions engaged him to make an Attempt of that Kind himſelf at *Bath*, but not ſucceeding there, he went into ſome of the itinerant Companies of Players, which travel over the different Parts of this Kingdom, in one of which I believe he at preſent continues.—His Education appears to have been liberal, and he is far from being deficient of Genius, which has ſhewn itſelf in ſome dramatic Attempts he has made, which, tho' they have not had Intereſt, or perhaps Novelty ſufficient to entitle them to an Appearance on the Metropolitan Theatres, have ſome of them been preſented with Succeſs in the Country.—His Writings of that Kind, which have come to my Knowledge, are the following, *viz.*

   1. NARCISSUS and ELIZA. Dram. Tale.
   2. OSMAN. Tr. *Vid.* Vol. I. APPENDIX.
   3. SEJANUS. Trag.
If I miſtake not, I was ſhewn, when at *Bath*, by one of the principal Performers there, ſome Parts of an Alteration of *Banks's Albion Queens*, or *Mary Queen of Scots*, made by Mr. *Gentleman*, and either actually performed, or elſe intended ſo to be, at the Theatre there.

GILDON, Mr. *Charles*.—This Gentleman was born at *Gilling-*

ham, near *Shafteſbury*, in *Dorſetſhire*, in the Year 1665.—His Parents and Family were all of the *Romiſh* Perſuaſion, and conſequently endeavoured to inſtill the ſame Principles into our Author; but in vain, for no ſooner did he find himſelf capable of reaſoning, than he was alſo able to diſcover the Foppery, Errors and Abſurdity of that Church's Tenets.———His Father was a Member of the Society of *Gray's-Inn*, and had ſuffer'd conſiderably in the Royal Cauſe.—Mr. *Gildon* received the firſt Rudiments of his Education at the Place where he was born; but at no more than twelve Years of Age, his Parents ſent him over to *Doway* in *Hainault*, and enter'd him in the *Engliſh* College of Secular Prieſts there, with a View of bringing him up likewiſe to the Prieſthood; but all to no Purpoſe, for, during a Progreſs of five Years Study there, he only found his Inclinations more ſtrongly confirmed for a quite different Courſe of Life.

At nineteen Years of Age, his Parents probably being dead, he returned to *England*, and when he was of Age, and by the Entrance into his Paternal Fortune, which was not inconſiderable, render'd in every Reſpect capable of enjoying the Gaieties and Pleaſures of this polite Town, he came up to *London*, where, as Men of Genius and Vivacity are too often deficient in the Article of Oeconomy, he ſoon ſpent the beſt Part of what he had, and, that he might be ſure, as Lord *Townly* ſays, never to mend it, he crowned his other Imprudences by marrying a young Lady, without any Fortune, at about the Age of twenty-three, thereby adding to his other Incumbrances
that

that of a growing Family, without any Way improving his reduced Circumſtances thereby.

During the Reign of King *James* II. he dedicated a great Deal of Time to the Study of the religious Controverſies which then ſo ſtrongly prevailed; and he declares, in ſome of his Writings, that it coſt him above ſeven Years Study and Conteſt, and a very cloſe Application to Books, before he could entirely overcome the Prejudices of his Education.—For, tho' he never had given Credit to the abſurd Tenets of the Church of *Rome*, nor could ever be brought to embrace the ridiculous Doctrine of her Infallibility, yet, as he had been taught an early Reverence to the Prieſthood, and a ſubmiſſive Obedience to their Authority, it was a long Time before he aſſumed Courage to think freely for himſelf, or declare what he thought.

Having, as I have before obſerved, greatly injured his Fortune by Thoughtleſſneſs and Diſſipation, he was now obliged to conſider on ſome Method for the retrieving it, or indeed rather for the Means of Subſiſtence, and he himſelf candidly owns, in his Eſſays, that Neceſſity (the general Inducement) was his firſt Motive for venturing to be an Author; nor was it till he had arrived at his two and thirtieth Year, that he made any Attempt in the dramatic Way.

He died on *Sunday* the 12th of *Jan.* 1723-4, nor can I give a better Summary of his literary Character, than by mentioning what was at the Time ſaid of him in *Boyer's Political State*, Vol. XXVII. p. 102. where he is ſaid to have been " a Perſon of " great Literature, but a mean

" Genius; who, having attempt" ed ſeveral Kinds of writing, " never gained much Reputation " in any.—Among other Trea" tiſes he wrote the *Engliſh Art* " *of Poetry*, which he had prac" tiſed himſelf very unſucceſs" fully in his dramatic Perform" ances.—He alſo wrote an *Eng" liſh* Grammar; but what he " ſeemed to build his chief Hopes " of Fame upon was his late " Critical Commentary on the " Duke of *Buckingham*'s Eſſay on " Poetry, which laſt Piece was " peruſed, and highly approved " by his Grace."

His dramatic Pieces are as follow,

1. *Love's Victim.* Trag.
2. PHAETON. Trag.
3. ROMAN *Bride's Revenge.* Trag.

None of them met with any great Succeſs, and indeed, tho' they do not totally want Merit, yet, by too ſtrong an Emulation of the Stile of *Lee*, of whom he was a great Admirer, but without being poſſeſſed of that Brilliancy of poetical Imagination, which frequently atones for the mad Flights of that Poet, Mr. *Gildon*'s Verſe runs into a perpetual Train of Bombaſt and Rant.

Coxeter aſcribes to him a Piece publiſhed Anonymous, and which is only an Alteration from *Shakeſpeare*, entitled,

Meaſure for Meaſure, or *Beauty the beſt Advocate.*

He alſo, about two Years after Mrs. *Behn*'s Death, brought on the Stage, with ſome few Alterations of his own, a Comedy which that Lady had left behind her, entitled,

The *Younger Brother*, or the *Amorous Jilt.*

Tho' not a Man of capital Genius himſelf, yet he was a

pretty

pretty severe Critic on the Writings of others, and particularly the Freedom he took in remarking upon Mr. *Pope's Rape of the Lock*, excited the Resentment of that Gentleman, who was never remarkable for any great Readiness to forgive Injuries, to such a Height, that he has thought proper to immortalize his Name, together with that of the snarling *Dennis*, in his celebrated Poem the *Dunciad*.

GLAPTHORNE, Mr. *Henry*.—This Author lived in the Reign of *Charles* I. and *Winstanley* calls him one of the chiefest dramatic Poets of that Age.—Tho' that Commendation, however, is far beyond what his Merits can lay Claim to, yet we cannot but allow him to have been a good Writer, and tho' his Plays are now entirely laid aside, yet, at the Time they were written, they met with considerable Approbation and Success.—They are five in Number, and their Titles as follow,

1. ALBERTUS WALLEN-STEIN. T.
2. ARGALUS and PARTHE-NIA. Tragi-Com.
3. *Hollander.* C.
4. *Ladies Priviledge.* C.
5. *Wit in a Constable.* C.

GLOVER, *Richard*, Esq;——This very ingenious Author is still living.—He was brought up in the Mercantile Way, in which he made a conspicuous Figure, and by a remarkable Speech that he made in Behalf of the Merchants of *London*, at the Bar of the House of Commons, about the Year 1740, previous to the breaking out of the *Spanish* War, he acquir'd, and with great Justice, the Character of an able and steady Patriot; and indeed, on every Occasion, he has shewn

a most perfect Knowledge of, joined to the most ardent Zeal for, the commercial Interests of this Nation, and an inviolable Attachment to the Welfare of his Countrymen in general, and that of the City of *London* in particular. —— However, about 1751, having, in Consequence of unavoidable Losses in Trade, and perhaps, in some Measure, of his zealous Warmth for the public Interests, to the Neglect of his own private Emoluments, somewhat reduc'd his Fortunes, he condescended to stand Candidate for the Place of Chamberlain of the City of *London*, in Opposition to the present Sir *Thomas Harrison*, but lost his Election there by no very great Majority.

His public Abilities, however, are so well known, that I need no farther expatiate on them; in the *Belles Lettres*, however, he has also made no inconsiderable Figure, and in that View it is that we have Occasion to consider him in this Work.—Mr. *Glover* very early demonstrated a very strong Propensity to, and Genius for, Poetry; yet his Ardor for public, and the Hurry necessary attendant on his private, Affairs, so far interfer'd with that Inclination, that it was some Years before he had it in his Power to finish an Epic Poem, which he had begun when young, entitled LEONIDAS, the Subject of which was the gallant Actions of that great General, and his heroic Defence of, and Fall at, the Pass of, *Thermopylæ*.—This Piece, however, the Public were so long in Expectation of, and had encouraged such extravagant Ideas of, that altho' on it's Publication it was found to have very great Beauties, yet the Ardour of the Lovers of Poetry soon sunk into

a Kind

a Kind of cold Forgetfulnefs
with Regard to it, becaufe it did
not poffefs more than the narrow
Limits of the Defign itfelf would
admit of, or indeed than it was
in the Power of human Genius
to execute.—His poetical Abilities, therefore, lay for fome
Years dormant, till at length he
favoured the World with two
dramatic Pieces, the one of which
was acted, tho' with no very
great Succefs, the other not intended for the Stage, being written entirely on the Model of the
Greek Tragedy.—For a more particular Account of, and Obfervations on, them, fee under their
refpective Titles in the former
Part of this Work.—Their Titles are,

BOADICIA. Trag.
MEDEA. Trag. *Vid.* Vol. I.
APPENDIX.

GOFF, Rev. Mr. *Thomas.*—
This Gentleman flourifhed in the
Reign of *James* I.—He was born
in *Effex*, about the Year 1592,
and received his firft Introduction
to Learning at *Weftminfter* School,
from which Place, at the Age of
eighteen, he was removed to the
Univerfity of *Oxford*, and enter'd
as a Student of *Chrift Church* College.—Here he compleated his
Studies, and, by the Dint of
Application and Induftry, became
a very able Scholar, obtained the
Character of a good Poet, and,
being endowed with the Powers
of Oratory, was, after his taking
Orders, greatly efteemed as an
excellent Preacher.—He had the
Degree of Batchelor of Divinity
conferr'd on him before he quitted
the Univerfity, and, in the Year
1623, was preferr'd to the Living of *Eaft Clandon*, in *Surry*.—
Here, notwithftanding that he
had long been a profeffed Enemy
to the Female Sex, and even by

fome efteemed a Woman-Hater,
he unfortunately tied himfelf to
a Wife, the Widow of his Pre-
deceffor, who prov'd as great a
Plague to him as it was well poffible for a Shrew to be; and became a true *Xantippe* to our Ecclefiaftical *Socrates*, who, being
naturally of a mild and patient
Difpofition, which it feems fhe
gave him daily Opportunities for
the Exercife of, was unable to
cope with fo turbulent a Spirit,
back'd as fhe was by the Children fhe had had by her former
Hufband.—In a Word, it was believed by many, that the Uneafi-
nefs he met with in domeftic
Life from the provoking Temper
of this home-bred Scourge, fhort-
ened the Period of his Life,
which he refigned to him from
whom he had received it, in
July 1629, being then only thirty-five Years of Age, and was buried on the 27th of the fame
Month, at his own Parifh-
Church.

Mr. *Goff* wrote five dramatic
Pieces, which met with confiderable Applaufe, but were none
of them publifhed till after his
Death.—Their Names are as follow,

1. *Carelefs Shepherdefs.* Tragi-
Com.
2. *Couragious Turk.* Trag.
3. ORESTES. Trag.
4. *Raging Turk.* Trag.
5. SELIMUS, *Emperor of the
Turks.* Trag.

Towards the latter Part of his
Life he quitted dramatic Writing, and applied himfelf folely
to the Bufinefs of the Pulpit.—
Some of his Sermons appeared
in Print in 1627.

Philips and *Winftanley* have father'd a Comedy on this Author,
called,

Cupid's Whirligig.

than

than which nothing could be more oppofite to his Genius.——Befides, the true Author of that Piece has fo far declared himfelf, as to have affixed the Initial Letters *E. S.* to his Epiftle Dedicatory, which is moreover interlarded with fuch a Kind of ridiculous unmeaning Mirth, as could never have fallen from Mr. *Goff*, who was a Man of a grave, fedate Turn, and whofe Pen never produced any Thing but what was perfectly ferious, manly, and becoming of his Character as a Divine.

Wood, moreover, has attributed to him, but indeed with a Quære, a Tragedy, called,

The *Baftard.*

which, however, *Coxeter* has given to *Cofmo Manuche.*

GOLDSMITH, *Francis*, Efq;— This Gentleman lived in the Reign of King *Charles* I.——He was the Son of *Francis Goldfmith*, of St. *Giles's in the Fields*, Efq;— He received the earlier Parts of his Education at *Merchant Taylor's* School, under Dr. *Nicholas Guy*, from whence he was removed, in the Beginning of the Year 1629, to the Univerfity of *Oxford*, where he was entered a Gentleman-Commoner at *Pembroke* College, but foon after tranflated to St. *John's*, where, having taken a Degree in Arts, he returned to *London*, and for feveral Years ftudied the Common Law in *Gray's-Inn*, but probably, having an independent Fortune, and being more clofely attached to other Kinds of Learning, he indulged his Inclination, and favoured the World with a Tranflation from *Hugo Grotius*, of a Tragedy, or facred Drama, entitled,

Sophompaneas. Trag.

In what Year Mr. *Goldfmith* was born, is not recorded by any of the Writers, yet I fhould fuppofe it to have been about 1610 or 1612. He died at *Afhton* in *Northamptonfhire*, in *Sept.* 1655, and was buried there, leaving behind him one only Daughter named *Catharine*, who was afterwards married to Sir *Henry Dacres.*

GOMERSAL, The Rev. Mr. *Robert.*—This Gentleman, who was a Divine, flourifhed in the Reign of *Charles* I. and was born at *London* in 1600, from whence, at fourteen Years of Age, he was fent by his Father to *Chrift Church* College, in *Oxford*, where, foon after his being enter'd, he was elected a Student on the Royal Foundation.——At about feven Years ftanding, he here took his Degrees of Bachelor and Mafter of Arts, and before he left the Univerfity, which was in 1627, he had the Degree of Batchelor of Divinity conferr'd on him.—— Being now in Orders, he was preferr'd to the Living of *Flower* in *Northamptonfhire*, where it is probable that he refided till his Death, which was in 1646.—He was accounted a good Preacher, and publifhed fome Sermons, which were well eftcem'd.—As a Devotee to the Mufes, he publifhed feveral Poems, particularly one, called the *Levite's Revenge*, being Meditations, in Verfe, on the 19th and 20th Chapters of *Judges*, and one Play, which, whether it was ever performed or not, I cannot pretend to afcertain.—It's Title is

LODOWICK SFORZA, *Duke of* MILAN. Trag.

GORING, *Charles*, Efq;—Of this Gentleman I meet with nothing more than the bare Mention

tion

tion of his Name, and a Record of his having been Author of one dramatic Piece, which was acted at *Drury Lane* Theatre, entitled,

IRENE, or *the Fair Greek.* Trag.

Coxeter, however, in his MS. Notes, tells us, that there was a *Charles Goring,* Efq; of *Magdalen* College, *Oxford,* who took his Degree there as Mafter of Arts, *Apr.* 27. 1687. and annexes a Quære, with a Reference to our Author, the Date of whofe Play, tho' twenty Years later than that of the conferring this Degree, is far from totally difagreeing with the Probability of their being both the fame Perfon.

GOUGH, *J.* Gent. or *J. G.*— Who this Mr. *Gough* was I know not, only by the Date of the undermentioned Piece it is evident he muft have lived in the Reign of *Charles* I.——However, this Name, or the Initials annexed, ftand indifcriminately in the Title Page to different Copies of the only Edition of a dramatic Piece, entitled,

The *Strange Difcovery.* Tragi-Com.

GOULD, Mr.——I know nothing more of this Gentleman than of the preceding Writer, yet cannot omit his Name in this Place, as I find it in the Monthly Catalogues of Publications for the Year 1737, joined to that of a Play, which however was not acted, entitled,

Innocence diftreffed. Trag.

GOULD, Mr. *Robert.*——This Author was originally a Domeftic of the Earl of *Dorfet* and *Middlefex,* but afterwards, having had fome Education and Abilities, fet up a School in the Country.——He wrote one dramatic Piece, called,

The *Rival Sifters.* Trag.

GRANVILLE, *George.* Vid. LANSDOWNE, Lord.

GREBER, Sig. *Giacomo.*—Of this Gentleman I know nothing more than that, from his Name, he appears to have been a Foreigner (but whether *German* or *Italian* is not very evident) and that he was Author of one dramatic Piece, entitled,

The *Loves* of ERGASTO. Dram. Paft.

GREEN, Mr. *Alexander.*—— This Gentleman is mentioned by all the Writers, but with no farther Account of him, than that he lived in the Reign of *Cha.* II. and foon after the Reftoration prefented the World with one dramatic Piece, entitled,

The *Politician cheated.* Com. but whether it was ever acted or not I cannot trace.

GREEN, *George Smith.*—This Author is probably ftill living; he publifhed in 1761 a Tragedy, which was never acted, but which I find among the Catalogues of that Year, entitled,

OLIVER CROMWELL. Hift. Play.

GREEN, Mr. *Robert.*—This Author lived in the Reign of Q. *Elizabeth,* and had a liberal Education, having taken the Degree of Mafter of Arts at the Univerfity of *Cambridge,* and afterwards incorporated in that of *Oxford.*—— He was a Man of great Humour and Drollery, and by no Means deficient in Point of Wit, had he not too often proftituted that happy but dangerous Talent to the bafe Purpofes of Vice and Obfcenity.——In fhort, both in Theory and Practice, he feems to have been a moft perfect Libertine; for, altho' he appears to have been blefs'd with a beautiful, virtuous and very deferviug Lady to his Wife, yet we find that

that he bafely abandoned her and a Child which fhe had borne him to Penury and Diftrefs, lavifhing his Fortune and Subftance on Harlots and common Proftitutes. Unable, however, to maintain the Expences which the unlimited Extravagance of thofe Wretches neceffarily drew him into, he was obliged to have Refource to his Pen for a Maintenance, and indeed I think he is the firft *Englifh* Poet we have on Record as writing for Bread.—As he had a great Fund of that licentious Kind of Wit, which would moft ftrongly recommend his Works among the Rakes and Wou'd be-Bucks of that Age, his Writings fold well, and afforded him a confiderable Income.—Till at length, after a Courfe of Years fpent in Diffipation, Riot and Debauchery, whereby his Faculties, his Fortune and Conftitution had been deftroy'd, we find him fallen into a State of the moft wretched Penury, Difeafe and Self Condemnation. Nor can there be a ftronger Picture of the Repentance and miferable Condition of a Being thus pinch'd to Repentance by the griping Hand of Diftrefs, than a Letter which, in the Decline of Life, he wrote to his much-wronged Wife, and which, tho' too long to be here inferted, may be feen in *Theoph. Cibber's Lives of the Poets*, Vol. I. p. 89. by which it appears that he found himfelf deferted even by the very Companions of his Riots, deftitute of the common Neceffaries of Life, and in Confequence of a Courfe of repeated Falfhoods, Perjuries and Prophanenefs, became an Object of general Contempt and Deteftation.

His Letter is truly a penitential, and it is to be hop'd a fincere one; yet, from the Titles of fome of his latter Works, fuch as, GREEN's *Never too late*, in two Parts; GREEN's *Farewel to Folly*, GREEN's *Groatfworth of Wit*, &c. he feems to have chofe to affume the Habit of a Penitent, as if he was defirous of bringing himfelf back into the good Opinion of the World, by an Acknowledgment of thofe Faults which had been too openly committed for him to deny, and by the Appearance of an intended Reformation.—*Wood*, in his *Fafti*, Vol. I. p. 137. tells us, that our Author died in 1592, of a Surfeit gotten by eating too great a Quantity of Pickled Herrings and drinking Rhenifh Wine with them; a Death which feems in even poetical Juftice, to be the proper Conclufion for a Life fpent as his had been.—At this Feaft, his Friend *Thomas Nafh*, who had very humouroufly rallied him in a Poem called the Apology of *Pierce Pennilefs*, was likewife prefent.——His Works of different Kinds are very numerous, but as to his dramatic Ones, there are many Difficulties that ftand in the Way of coming, with any Degree of Certainty, at a Knowledge of them.—All the Writers, however agree in his having written one Play, called,

The *Hiftory of Fryar* Bacon *and Fryar* Bungay.

as alfo that he joined with Dr. *Lodge*, in his Comedy, entitled,

A Looking-Glafs for London *and* England.

But *Winftanley*, befides thefe, has attributed one entire Play to him, called,

Fair EMM.

which however is printed anonymous; and afferts that he was concerned with Dr. *Lodge* in the

Com...

Compofition of four other dramatic Pieces, called,

Lady Alimony. Com.
Laws of Nature. Com.
Liberality and Prodigality. C.
Luminalia. Mafque.

But for my Opinion in Regard to thefe, fee farther in my Account of Dr. *Lodge.*

Wood alfo mentions another Comedy, faid in the Title to have been written by *R. Green*, and which, from its Date, is probable to have been this Author.— It is entitled,

Planetomachia.

The fame Author alfo tells us, that Mr. *Green*, having written againft, or at leaft reflected upon, *Gabriel Harvey*, in feveral of his Writings, *Harvey*, not being able to bear his Abufes, did inhumanly trample upon him when he lay full low in his Grave, even as *Achilles* tortured the dead Body of *Hector.*

GREVILLE, Sir *Fulke.* Vid. BROOKE, Lord.

GRIFFIN, Mr. *Benjamin.*— This Gentleman was an Actor as well as an Author.—He was the Son of the Reverend Mr. *Benjamin Griffin*, Rector of *Buxton* and *Oxnead*, in the County of *Norfolk*, and Chaplain to the Earl of *Yarmouth.*—At the laft-mentioned of thefe two Places Mr. *Griffin* was born in 1689, and received his Education at the Free-School of *North Walfham* in the faid County, founded by the noble Family of the *Pafton*'s.——His Inclination leading him to the Stage preferably to any other Profeffion, he enter'd young into the Company of Comedians belonging to the City of *Norwich* and the Towns around it, from thence going into feveral Country Companies, where he acquired confiderable Improvement, till in the Year 1714, he made one at the Opening of the New Theatre in *Lincoln's-Inn-Fields.*—Here he gained great Applaufe, and eftablifhed a Character to himfelf in the Caft of Parts which he commonly performed; which were always in low Comedy, and moftly in the tefty old Men.—In fhort, he in a few Years became of fo much Confequence, that the Managers of *Drury Lane*, notwithftanding they had already *Norris* and *John-fon*, who were ftill more excellent in the fame Way of Playing, and therefore could make but little Ufe of Mr. *Griffin* at their own Houfe, found it, neverthelefs, worth their while to buy off his Weight againft them in the Rival Theatre, by engaging him at a larger Salary than he had hitherto had there; and, indeed, fo intrinfically great was our Author's Merit, that tho', in Confequence of the Circumftance above-mentioned, he made his Appearance but feldom, yet, whenever he did, it was conftantly with Applaufe, nor did the Excellence of the above-mention'd Actors by any Means eclipfe his, or feem to abate the favourable Opinion the Public had conceived of him, even when they at any Time appear'd on the Stage together with him.

Mr. *Chetwood*, in his *Britifh Theatre*, fays, that Mr. *Griffin* removed to *Drury Lane* Theatre in 1720; but this I think muft be a Miftake, as we find his Comedy of *Whig and Tory* brought on that Stage in 1721, which would hardly have been the Cafe, had the Author fo lately quitted that Theatre, and joined in an Oppofition at that Time of fo much Confequence againft them.

This Author died in 1739, being the 5oth Year of his Age,
and

and left behind him five dramatic Pieces, whose Titles are as follows, *viz.*

1. *Humours of Purgatory.* Far.
2. *Injur'd Virtue.* Trag.
3. *Love in a Sack.* Farce.
4. *Masquerade.* Farce.
5. *Whig and Tory.* Com.

GRIMALDI, Sign. *Nicolini.*—Of this Author I know nothing more than that he was an *Italian*, and probably one of the Directors of the King's Theatre in the *Haymarket*, for which he composed two *Italian* Operas, entitled,

1. HAMLET.
2. HYDASPES.

GRIMSTON, *James*, Lord Viscount.—This Nobleman, whose Title stands in the List of the *Irish* Peerage, was Father to the present Lord *Grimston*.—He was born about 1692, and in *April* 1719, was created Baron of *Dunboyne*, in the County of *Meath* in *Ireland*, and Viscount *Grimston*.—At the Age of thirteen Years, while at School, he wrote a Play, which was never acted, but printed in the Year 1705, entitled,

The *Lawyer's Fortune.* Com. It is true, this Piece, so far from having any dramatic Merit in it, is full of the grossest Absurdities; but when the Infantile Years of its Author come to be consider'd, and that it might probably be owing to the Partiality of Parents in the Gratification of a childish Vanity, that it was ever published:—If it is moreover known, that when, at a maturer Time of Life, the Author himself, on a Review of it, became sensible of its Faults, he took the utmost Pains to call in the Impression, and prevent, if possible, so indifferent a Performance to stand forth in Evidence against even his

Boyish Abilities, surely a first Fault, so amply repented, might easily be forgiven, and the Asperity with which the Author has been treated on the Account of it might well have been spar'd.

And indeed, the Public is scarcely to be blamed for the ill Usage he has received, as they would probably have suffer'd this Piece to have died in Obscurity, with many others of equal Merit, had it not been for the Malevolence of the late D—ch—fs of M—lb—gh, who, in the Course of an Opposition which she thought proper to make to this worthy Peer, in an Election for Members of Parliament, where his Lordship was a Candidate, caused a large Impression of this Play to be printed off, at her own sole Charge, and to be dispersed among the Electors, with a Frontispiece, conveying a most indecent and unmannerly Reflection on his Lordship's Understanding, under the allegorical Figure of an Elephant dancing on the Ropes.

Lord *Grimston*, however, carried his Election, in Spite of all those unfair Proceedings to prevent it, and by his Behaviour while he continued in Parliament; his Conduct in a rational and happy Retirement after his quitting Public Affairs, and his prudent Oeconomy thro' Life in the Management of an Estate, which, tho' a large one, was, at the Time it descended to him, loaded with the Incumbrance of numerous Fortunes and heavy Jointures saddled on it, gave ample Proof of the Injustice of the Insinuations, so artfully thrown out against him, and supported solely on this one trivial Error of his Childhood; and, it is but Justice to a valuable Character, thus attempted

tempted to be injur'd, to conclude our Account of him with the amiable Portrait drawn of him by the Author of the Lives annexed to *Whincop's Scanderbeg.*—— " This Nobleman," fays that Writer, " is a good Hufband to " one of the beft of Wives; an " indulgent Father to a hopeful " and numerous Offspring; a " kind Mafter to his Servants, a " generous Friend, and an affa- " ble and hofpitable Neighbour."

I cannot directly afcertain in what Year this Nobleman died, but find his Succeffor to have been Member in the laft Parliament for the ancient Town of *St. Alban's.*

H.

HABINGTON, *William*, Efq; —This Gentleman, who flourifhed in the Reign of King *Charles* I. was born on the 4th of *Nov.* 1605, at *Handlip* in *Worcefterfhire.*—Being of a *Roman* Catholic Family, he was fent to receive the early Parts of his Education at *Paris* and St. *Omers,* where he was very earneftly entreated to take on him the Habit of a Jefuit.—But an ecclefiaftical Life being by no Means agreeable to his Difpofition, he refifted all their Solicitations and returned to *England,* where, by his own Application and the Inftruction of his Father *Thomas Habington,* Efq; he made great Proficiency in the Study of Hiftory and other ufeful Branches of Literature, and became, according to the Account given of him by *Wood* in his *Athen. Oxon.* a very accomplifhed Gentleman.

His principal Bent was to Hiftory, as is apparent from his Writings, among which are fome *Obfervations on Hiftory,* in 1 Vol. 8vo. and a Hiftory of *Edw.* IV. written and publifhed at the Defire of King *Charles* I.—Yet, for the Amufement of fome leifure Hours, he wrote a Play, called,

    Queen of ARRAGON. Tragi-Com.

which he appears himfelf to have had a very diffident Opinion of; but having fhewed it to *Philip* Earl of *Pembroke,* that Nobleman was fo much pleafed with it, that he caufed it to be acted at Court, and afterwards to be publifhed, tho' contrary to the Author's Inclination.——*Wood* acquaints us, that, during the Civil War, Mr. *Habington* (probably for the Sake of preferving to himfelf that Calm, which is ever moft agreeable to a ftudious and fedentary Difpofition) temporized with thofe in Power, and was not unknown to *Oliver Cromwell.* Yet, it is probable, this temporizing was no more than a mere Non-Refiftance, as we have no Account of his having been raifed to any Kind of Preferment during the Protector's Government. —He died *November* 30, 1654, being juft entered into his 50th Year.

HAINES, Mr. *Jofeph,* (commonly called COUNT HAINES). —This Gentleman was a very eminent low Comedian and a Perfon of great Facetioufnefs of Temper and Readinefs of Wit. — When, or where, or of what Parents he was born, are Particulars which the Hiftorians of his Life are totally filent about.—It is certain, however, that the earlier Parts of his Education were communicated to him at the School of

St. Martin's in the Fields, where he made fo rapid a Progrefs as to become the Admiration of all who knew him.

From this Place he was fent by the voluntary Subfcription of a Number of Gentlemen, to whofe Notice his Quicknefs of Parts had ftrongly recommended him, to *Queen's* College, *Oxford*, where his Learning and great Fund of Humour gain'd him the Efteem and Regard of Sir *Jofeph Williamfon*, who was afterwards Secretary of State, and Minifter Plenipotentiary at the concluding the Peace of *Ryfwick*.——When Sir *Jofeph* was appointed to the firft of thofe high Offices, he took our Author as his *Latin* Secretary.——But Taciturnity not being one of thofe Qualities which *Haines* was eminent for, Sir *Jofeph* found that, thro' his Means, Affairs of great Importance frequently tranfpir'd even before they came to the Knowledge of thofe who were more immediately concerned in them.—He was, therefore, obliged to remove him from an Employment for which he feem'd fo ill calculated, but recommended him, however, to one of the Heads of the Univerfity of *Cambridge*, where he was very kindly received ; but a Company of Comedians coming to perform at *Stourbridge* Fair, Mr. *Haines* took fo fudden an Inclination for their Employment and Way of living, that he threw away his Cap and Band, and immediately joined their Company.

It was not long, however, before the Reputation of his theatrical Abilities procur'd him an Invitation to the Theatre Royal in *Drury Lane*, where his inimitable Performance on the Public Stage, together with his Vivacity and Pleafantry in private Conver-

fation, introduced him not only to the Acquaintance, but even the Familiarity of Perfons of the moft exalted Abilities, and of the firft Rank in the Kingdom.—— Infomuch, that a certain noble Duke, being appointed Ambaffador to the *French* Court, thought it no Difgrace to take *Joe Haines* with him as a Companion, who being, befides his Knowledge of the dead Languages, as perfect Mafter of the *French* and *Italian*, as if he had been a Native of the refpective Capitals of *Paris* and *Rome*, was greatly careffed by many of the *French* Nobility.

In his Return from *France*, where he had affumed the Title of Count, he again applied himfelf to the Stage, on which he continued till 1701, on the 4th of *April* in which Year he died of a Fever, after a very fhort Illnefs, at his Lodgings in *Hart-Street, Long-Acre*, and was buried in the Church-Yard of St. *Paul's, Covent-Garden*.

There is one dramatic Piece, faid to be his, entitled,

The *Fatal Miftake*. Com. But the Compofition of it is fo very miferable, and fo devoid of any Marks of that Humour and Sprightlinefs which ran thro' his whole Converfation, that fome of the Writers feem inclinable to acquit him of being the Author of it.—Yet I know not whether that is quite a fufficient Reafon for fo doing, as it is by no Means uncommon to find, among Men of profeffed Drollery, that the Manner is much more than the Matter; and the Table, as *Shakefpeare* has it, is often fet in a Roar, by Jokes, which, if repeated without the immediate Humour of the Speaker, to accompany them, would fcarcely excite a Smile, unlefs of Contempt.——

And.

And it is remarkable of the very Perſon we are now treating of, that ſome of his Prologues and Epilogues, which uſed to force Thunder Claps of Applauſe from the Audience when ſpoken by himſelf, and according to his own Conceptions in the writing of them, appear but flat and inſipid when we come to read them in the Cloſet.—I do not mean this, however, in any Degree to depreciate Mr. Haines's Merit.— That he poſſeſſed a great Share of genuine Wit, I do not in the leaſt queſtion; and altho' every Jeſt Book will furniſh Numbers of droll Turns of Humour, which are ſaid to have come from him, I think I cannot better cloſe this Account of him, than by the Repetition of one undoubtedly authentic *Bon Mot* of his, handed down to us by his Cotemporary *Colley Cibber*, who, in his Apology, relates this Story.—" *Joe* " *Haines*," ſays he, " being aſk-" ed what could tranſport *Collier* " into ſo blind a Zeal for the ge-" neral Suppreſſion of the Stage, " when only ſome particular Au-" thors had abuſed it, whereas " the Stage, he could not but " know, was generally allowed, " when rightly conducted, to be " a delightful Method of mend-" ing our Morals ?"—" *For that* " *very Reaſon*," replied *Haines*: " *Collier is by Profeſſion a Moral-* " *Mender bimſelf, and two of a* " *Trade, you know, can never* " *agree.*"

HAMILTON, Mr. *Newburgh.* —This Gentleman lived in the Family of Duke *Hamilton*, and was probably related to his Grace. He wrote two dramatic Pieces, entitl d,

1. *Doating Lovers.* Com.
2. *Petticoat Plotter.* Farce.

Neither of theſe Pieces met with Succeſs.——The firſt of them, however, was ſupported through three Performances, for the Sake of the Author's Benefit, whoſe Intereſt was ſo ſtrong, and his Acquaintance ſo extenſive, that he was enabled to lay the Pit and Boxes together, at the advanced Price of ſix Shillings for each Ticket.

HAMMOND, *William.* — This Writer is mentioned no where but in the *Britiſh Theatre*, where he is ſaid to have been a young Gentleman in the Army, and to have written a dramatic Piece of one Act, entitled,

Preceptor. Ball. Opera.

HARDHAM, Mr. *John.*—This Author is yet living, and extremely well known among Perſons of Genius and Taſte.—He was born at *Chicheſter*, and bred in the Lapidary or Diamond-cutting Buſineſs; but quitting that, and entering into the Snuff Trade, became, and ſtill continues to be, very eminent in that Buſineſs, being, perhaps, poſſeſſed of the largeſt Shop and the moſt extenſive Trade of that Kind in or about this Metropolis, *viz.* the *Black Lion*, near the *Fleet-Market*, in *Fleet-Street.*—Beſides this, he has for ſome Years been principal Numberer to the Theatre Royal in *Drury Lane.*—What Mr. *Hardbam's* Advantages from Education may have been, I never could learn, but, by the Dint of ſtrong natural Parts, he has render'd himſelf agreeable to Numbers of the moſt conſiderable Wits and Critics of the Age and has even himſelf made one Attempt in the dramatic Way, which, altho', I believe, it was not even intended for the Stage, is in Print, and is far from being devoid of Genius

nius or poetical Imagination.—It is entitled,

The *Fortune-Tellers*. Com.

HARRIS, Mr. *Joseph*.—This Person was a Comedian, but of no great Reputation in his Profession.—Yet, as *Jacob* informs us, by the Assistance of his Friends, he aimed at being an Author, and produced the four following dramatic Pieces, all of which seems to have miscarried in the Representation, *viz.*

1. The *City Bride*. Com.
2. *Love's a Lottery, and a Woman the Prize*. Com.
3. *Love and Riches reconciled*. Masque.
4. The *Miftakes*. Com.

HARRISON, Mr. *William*.—This Author was a Man of mean Employment, being by Trade no other than a Patten Maker.——Yet he was esteemed to be Master of excellent natural Parts.—He wrote one Play, which, tho' it was never acted, probably from Want of Intereft, is far from being devoid of Merit; it is entitled,

The *Pilgrims*. Paft. Trag.

HATCHET, Mr.——Of this Gentleman I know nothing more than his having been concerned, in Conjunction with Mrs. *Eliza Heywood*, in the converting Mr. *Fielding*'s Tragedy of *Tom Thumb*, into a Ballad Opera, which was set to Mufick, and performed under the Title of

The *Opera of Operas*,

and having brought one Play on the Stage, entitled,

The *Rival Father*. Trag.

HAVARD, Mr. *William*.—— This Gentleman is ftill living, and at prefent an Actor belonging to the Theatre Royal in *Drury Lane*.—He is the Son of a Vintner in *Dublin*, and ferved his Time as Apprentice to a Surgeon;

but, having an early Inclination for the Stage, he quitted the Profeffion he was intended for, and engaged himfelf firft at the Theatre in *Goodman's-Fields*, from whence he removed to the Theatres Royal, in both which he at different Times has been received.——As an Actor he ftands in very good Eftimation with the Public.—His Perfon is comely and genteel, his Voice clear and articulate, and his critical Judgment, and perfect Underftanding of the Meaning of his Author, fhine forth confpicuoufly in every Part he performs.—He does not want Feeling, but, from a Degree of Monotomy, which feems natural to his Voice, he fometimes falls fhort with Refpect to empaffioned Execution.—He is, however, always decent, fenfible and perfect, and has acquir'd an Eafe in his Manner and Deportment, which it is uncommon to meet with, and which renders him, if not a capital, at leaft a very ufeful Performer; and if, on any Occafion, Neceffity or Accident throws him into Parts which may appear above the Rank of Characters in which he ufually appears, he conftantly makes Way thro' them with lefs Difguft than fome Performers would do, who, with greater particular Beauties, intermingle an equal Number of glaring deformities.

As an Author, Mr. *Havard* ftands nearly in the fame Predicament that he does as an Actor, for, tho' much inferior to our firft Rate Dramatifts, he is at the fame Time as greatly fuperior to many; whofe Pieces have even met with Succefs.—Good-Senfe, Correctnefs and Senfibility run thro' his Writings, and tho' he does not aftonifh us with the fublime Flafhes of a *Shakefpeare*,

or

or touch our Hearts with the tender Senfations of an *Otway*, yet he neither ftarts out into the puerile Bombaft of a *Banks*, nor finks into the infenfible profaical Coldnefs of a *Trapp*.—In a Word, the fenfible Leffon of the *medio tutiſſimus ibis*, ſeems to be the Rule of Mr. *Havard*'s Conduct both on the Stage and in the Study, and, indeed, he feems to have fufficiently availed himfelf of an Adherence to the Maxim; the filent Attention conftantly paid to his Performance in the Theatre avouching the Truth of it on the one Hand, and the Succefs his dramatic Pieces, efpecially one of them, met with on their Reprefentation, evincing it on tne other.—The Names of his Plays, which are three in Number, are as follow,

1. *King* CHARLES I. Trag.
2. REGULUS. Trag.
3. SCANDERBEG. Trag.

Mr. *Havard* is, moreover, in his private Character, extremely amiable, being polite, humane and friendly.—In a Word, he is generally efteemed and beloved by all who know him, and whenever he fhall be obliged to quit the great Stage of Life, Society will lofe a valuable Member, and the Theatre a ferviceable and ornamental Pillar.

HAUSTED, the Rev. Mr. *Peter*.—This Gentleman was born at *Oundle* in *Northamptonfhire*, towards the Beginning of the Reign of King *James* the firft.—He received his Education in *Queen*'s College, *Cambridge*, where, after paffing thro' the proper Exercifes, he took his Degree as Mafter of Arts, and, after quitting the Univerfity, entering into holy Orders, he became, firft, Curate of *Uppingham* in *Rutlandfhire*, and ome Time afterwards Rector of

Hadham in *Hertfordfhire*.——In 1641, he had a Degree of Doctor of Divinity conferr'd on him.

On the breaking out of the Civil Wars, he was made Chaplain to *Spencer*, Earl of *Northampton*, to whom he adher'd in all his Engagements for the Royal Intereft, and was with him in the Caftle of *Banbury* in *Oxfordfhire* at the very Time it made fo vigorous a Defence againft the Parliament's Forces.——In that Caftle *Wood*, in his *Fafti*, informs us, that Mr. *Haufted* concluded his laft Moments in the Year 1645, and was buried wirhin the Precincts of it, or elfe in the Church belonging to *Banbury*.

Both *Langbaine* and *Wood* give this Author the Character of a very ingenious Man and a good Foet; all the Teftimonials we have extant of the latter Character, are a fmall Poem, called a *Lecture to the People*, and one dramatic Piece, which it is pretty apparent, from the very Title Page the Author has prefixed to it, met with but indifferent Succefs.—It is entitled,

The *Rival Friends*. Com.

HAWKINS, Mr. *William*.—This Gentleman is now living, and is a Fellow of *Pembroke* College, *Oxford*.——He has obliged the Public with but two dramatic Pieces, the firft only an Alteration of a Tragedy of the immortal *Shakefpeare*; in which indeed it were to be wifhed that he had either fix'd on the Story only, and made the Conduct and Language of it entirely his own, or elfe that he had taken fomewhat lefs Liberty with his Original, fince, as it now ftands, there appears too great a Diffimilarity between the different Parts of it, to render it perfectly pleafing, either as the Work of
Shakefpeare

Shakespeare or of Mr. *Hawkins.*—— The Play, thus alter'd, is

    CYMBELINE. T.

The other Piece, which may more properly be called his own, is far from wanting Merit, and is entitled,

    HENRY *and* ROSAMOND. Trag.

HAWKS, Mr.—Of this Gentleman I find no farther Mention made than bareley his Name, and that he was the Author of an unsuccefsful Piece, called,

    The *Country Wedding.* Tragi-Comi-Paftoral-Farcical-Opera.

HAWKSWORTH, *John,* L.L.D. —This Gentleman is ftill living, and has been more remarkable for his Effays in a periodical Paper, entitled the ADVENTURER, whofe Merit certainly ftands ftrongly in Competition even with the celebrated *Spectators* and *Ramblers,* than for his dramatic Pieces. However, what little he has done in the dramatic Way, is far from wantiug Merit, and may be feen in the following Lift.

    1. EDGAR *and* EMMELINE. Fairy Tale.

    2. OROONOKO. T, (alter'd from *Southerne.*)

    3. ZIMRI. Oratorio.

Befides thefe, he has, not long fince, favoured the World with a very ingenious Romance in the Eaftern Manner, entitled *Almoran* and *Hamet,* which, however, exclufive of it's being foreign to our prefent Purpofe, is too recent in every one's Acquaintance to need any farther Mention here.

HAYM, Mr. *Nicholas.*—What Country this Gentleman was of I know not, nor whether he was himfelf the Author of the Pieces to which his Name is prefixed : I am apt to believe, however, that he was a *German,* and preceded

Mr. *Heidegger* in the Management of the Opera Houfe in the *Haymarket,* and that therefore in that Light only he has figned his Name to the Dedication of the following dramatic Pieces performed at that Theatre, the Authors of which were probably obfcure Hirelings, employed by this Gentleman to write, or rather put together, a Set of Words, the only Merit requir'd in which was an Aptnefs to go well by Way of Accompanyment to, or Vehicle for, thofe *Italian* Airs and Voices, which were to charm away the Senfes and drain the Pockets of all the Perfons of either real or pretended Tafte in this poor infatuated Nation.—The Titles of the Pieces, which I thus find with his Name to them as Dedicator, are the fix following.

    1. ASTYANAX. Ital. Op.

    2. FLAVIUS, *King of* LOMBARDY. Ital. Op.

    3. PTOLEMY, *King of* EGYPT. Ital. Op.

    4. RODELINDA. *Queen of* LOMBARDY. Ital. Op.

    5. TAMERLANE. Ital. Op.

    6. VESPASIAN. Ital. Op.

HEAD, Mr. *Richard.*——This Author was the Son of a Minifter in *Ireland,* who, being murder'd, among many Thoufands more, in the dreadful Maffacre in that Kingdom in 1641, Mrs. *Head,* with this Son, then but young, came over to *England,* where, having been train'd up in Learning, he was fent, thro' the Friendfhip of fome Perfons who had had a Regard for his Father, to *Oxford,* and compleated his Studies in the very fame College that his Father had formerly belonged to.—His Circumftances, however, being mean, he was taken away from the Univerfity before he had got any Degree, and was bound

                  Apprentice

Apprentice to a Bookſeller, and when out of his Time married, and ſet up for himſelf; but, having a ſtrong Propenſity to two pernicious Paſſions, *viz.* Poetry and Gaming, the one of which is for the moſt Part unprofitable, and the other almoſt always deſtructive, he quickly ruined his Circumſtances, and was obliged to retire for a Time to *Ireland.*— Here he wrote his only dramatic Piece, which was entitled,

Hic & ubique. Com. By this Piece he acquired very great Reputation and ſome Money; on which he returned to *England,* reprinted his Comedy, and dedicated it to the Duke of *Monmouth*; but, meeting with no Encouragement, he once more had Recourſe to his Trade of Bookſelling.—But, no ſooner had he a little recover'd himſelf, than he again lent an Ear to the Syren Allurements of Pleaſure and Poetry, in the latter of which he ſeems never to have made any great Proficiency.—He failed a ſecond Time in the World; on which he had again Recourſe to his Pen for Support, and wrote ſeveral different Pieces, particularly the firſt Part of the *Engliſh Rogue,* in which, however, he had given Scope to ſo much Licentiouſneſs, that he could not get an *Imprimatur* granted to it, till he had expunged ſome of the moſt luſcious Deſcriptions out of it.—To this firſt Part three more were afterwards added by Mr. *Head,* in Conjunction with Mr. *Francis Kirkman,* who had alſo been his Partner in Trade.

The Buſineſs of an Author, however, and it's Emoluments being very precarious, it appears from *Winſtanley,* who was perſonally acquainted with him, that he afterwards met with a great many Croſſes and Afflictions, and was at laſt caſt away at Sea as he was going to the *Iſle of Wight,* in the Year 1678.

HEIDEGGER, *John James,* Eſq;—This Gentleman I imagine to have been by Birth a *Dutchman* or *Fleming.*——He was for many Years Manager of the King's Theatre, or Opera Houſe, in the *Haymarket*; by which he raiſed a very large Fortune,—Among the infinite Number of new Pieces, which are annually brought on at that Theatre, and are for the moſt Part as regularly forgotten by the following Seaſon, I find the following with Mr. *Heidegger*'s Name annexed to the Dedication, *viz.*

1. ALMAHIDE. Ital. Op.
2. AMADIS *of* GAUL. Ital. Opera.
3. ANTIOCHUS. Ital.. Op.
4. ARMINIUS. Ital. Opera.

Mr. *Heidegger* died about the Year 1750.

HEMINGS, Mr. *William.*—— This Gentleman was Son of *John Hemings,* the famous Player, who was Cotemporary with *Shakeſpeare,* and whoſe Name we find, together with thoſe of *Burbidge, Condel, Taylor,* &c. before the Folio Edition of that Author's Works.—He was born at *London,* about the Beginning of the Reign of *James* I. and received his Education at *Chriſt Church* College in *Oxford,* where he was enter'd as a Student in the Year 1621, and in 1628 took his Degree of Maſter of Arts.—During the Time of the Troubles he wrote ſome dramatic Pieces, which were at that Time very well eſteem'd, and after the Reſtoration were revived with great Succeſs.—— Their Titles are as follow,

1. The

1. The *Eunuch*. Trag. (N. B. This is only the Title by which the next-mentioned Play was revived, in the Year 1687.)
2. The *Fatal Contract*.   T.
3. The *Jew's Tragedy*.

HENDERSON, Mr. *A.*—This Author is, I think, a Clergyman, and still living.——In the Year 1752 he published one dramatic Piece, of very little Merit, entitled,

ARSINOE.   Trag.

HERBERT, *Mary*.   Vid. PEMBROKE, Countess of.

HEWIT, Mr. *John.*—Of this Gentleman I know nothing more than that he is Author of one dramatic Piece, borrowed almost entirely from the *French*, but which never was acted, entitled,

A *Tutor for the Beaus*.   Com.

HEYWOOD, Mrs. *Eliza.*—— This Lady was perhaps the most voluminous Female Writer this Kingdom ever produced. — Her Genius lay for the most Part in the Novel Kind of Writing.—In the early Part of her Life, her natural Vivacity, her Sex's constitutional Fondness for Gallantry, and the Passion which then prevailed in the public Taste for personal Scandal, and diving into the Intrigues of the Great, guided her Pen to Works, in which a Scope was given for great Licentiousness.——The celebrated *Atalantis* of Mrs. *Manley* served her for a Model, and the Court of *Carimania*, the *New Utopia*, and some other Pieces of a like Nature, were the Copies her Genius produced.——Whether the Looseness of the Pieces themselves, or some more private Reasons, provoked the Resentment of Mr. *Pope* against her, I cannot pretend to determine; but, certain it is, that that great Poet has

taken some Pains to perpetuate her Name to immortal Infamy; having, in his *Dunciad*, propos'd her as one of the Prizes to be run for, in the Games instituted in Honour of the Inauguration of the Monarch of *Dulness*.—This, however, I own I cannot readily subscribe to; for, altho' I should be far from vindicating the Libertinism of her Subjects, or the exposing with Aggravation to the Public the private Errors of Individuals, yet, I think, it cannot be denied, that there is great Spirit and Ingenuity in Mrs. *Heywood's* Mann.r of treating Subjects, which the Friends of Virtue may perhaps wish she had never enter'd on at all; and that in those of her Novels, where personal Character has not been admitted to take Place, and where the Stories have been of her own Creation, such as her *Love in Excess, Fruitless Enquiry*, &c. she has given Proofs of great inventive Powers, and a perfect Knowledge of the Affections of the human Heart.—And thus much must be granted in her Favour, that whatever Liberty she might at first give to her Pen, to the Offence either of Morality or Delicacy, she seem'd to be soon convinced of her Error, and determined not only to reform, but even attone for it; since, in the numerous Volumes which she gave to the World towards the latter Part of her Life, no Author has appear'd more the Votary of Virtue, nor are there any Novels in which a stricter Purity, or a greater Delicacy of Sentiment, has been preserv'd.—It may not, perhaps, be disagreeable in this Place to point out what these latter Works were, as they are very voluminous, and are not perfectly known to every one.—They may therefore, tho' somewhat foreign to the Purport of this Work, be found in the following Lift, *viz.*

The Female Spectator, 4 vol.
Epiftle for the Ladies, 2 vol.
Fortunase Foundling, 1 vol.
Adventures of Nature, 1 vol.
Hift. of Betfy Thoughtlefs, 4 vol.
Jenny and Jemmy Jeffamy, 3 v.
Invifible Spy, 2 vol.
Hufband and Wife, 2 vol.

and a Pamphlet, entitled,

A Prefent for a Servant Maid.

When young, fhe dabbled in dramatic Poetry, but with no great Succefs.—None of her Plays either meeting with much Approbation at the firft, nor having been admitted to Repetition fince.—Their Titles were as follow,

1. *Fair Captive.* T.
2. F R E D E R I C K *Duke of* B R U N S W I C K. T.
3. *Opera of Operas.* (joined with Mr. *Hatchet*.)
4. *Wife to be let.* Com.

She had alfo an Inclination for the Stage as a Performer, which appears from her having acted a principal Part in her own Comedy of the *Wife to be let*, and her Name ftanding in the Drama of a Tragedy, entitled, the *Rival Father*, written by Mr. *Hatchet*, a Gentleman with whom fhe appears to have had a clofe literary Intimacy.

As to the Circumftances of Mrs. *Heywood*'s Life, very little Light feems to appear; for, tho' the World feem'd inclinable, probably induced by the general Tenor of her earlier Writings, to affix on her the Character of a Lady of Gallantry, yet I have never heard of any particular Intrigues or Connections directly laid to her Charge; and have been credibly informed that, from a Suppofition of fome improper Liberties being taken with her

Character after Death, by the Intermixture of Truth and Falfhood with her Hiftory, fhe laid a folemn Injunction on a particular Perfon, who was well acquainted with all the Particulars of it, not to communicate to any one the leaft Circumftance relating to her; fo that probably, unlefs fome very ample Account fhould appear from that Quarter itfelf, whereby her Story may be placed in a true and favourable Light, the World will ftill be left in the dark with Regard to it.—All I have been able to learn is, that her Father was in the Mercantile Way, that fhe was born at *London*, and that, at the Time of her Death, which was, I think, in 1759, fhe was about fixty three Years of Age.

With Refpect to her Genius and Abilities, her Works, which are very numerous, muft ftand in Evidence; but I cannot help obferving, as to her perfonal Character, that I was told by one, who was well acquainted with her for many Years before her Clofe of Life, that fhe was goodnatured, affable, lively and entertaining; and that, whatever Errors fhe might in any Refpect have run into in her youthful Days, fhe was, during the whole Courfe of his Knowledge of her, remarkable for the moft rigid and fcrupulous Decorum, Delicacy and Prudence, both with Refpect to her Conduct and Converfation.

H E Y W O O D, *Jafper*, D. D.—This Writer, who flourifhed in the Reign of Queen *Elizabeth*, was Son of the famous Poet and Epigrammatift of that Name, whom we fhall immediately have Occafion to mention.——He was born in *London* in 1535, and in the twelfth Year of his Age was fent to the Univerfity of *Oxford*, and enter'd a Student in *Merton* College.

College.—Here he received those useful Parts of Education, Grammar and Logic; and in 1553 took his Degree as Master of Arts, and was admitted to a Probationary Fellowship in that College, where he gained a Superiority over all his Fellow Students in Disputations at the Public School, and was (as appears from an Oration written in his Praise by *David De la Hyde*, entitled *De Ligno & Fæno)* nominated there *Rex Regni Fabarum*, or a Kind of *Christmas* Lord.——*Langbaine* and *Jacob* both say that he quitted this College, at which he only passed his younger Days, for a Fellowship in *All-Souls* College in the same University.——But *Wood* informs us, that, having been guilty of several Misdemeanours, such as are peculiar to Youth, Wildness and Rakishness, which in those Days were punished with great Severity, and which probably he run into the more readily from being, in Consequence of his Father's quitting *England*, left very early to himself, he was obliged, in Order to prevent Expulsion, to resign his Fellowship, upon a third Admonition from the Warden and Society of *Merton* College, on the 4th of *April* 1558.

Soon after this he quitted *England*, and, going over to St. *Omer's*, enter'd himself into the Society of *Jesus* at that Place, from whence, after having spent two Years in the Study of Divinity among the Priests, he was sent to *Diling* in *Switzerland*, where he spent upwards of seventeen Years in discussing certain Points of Controversy among those whom he called Heretics; in which Time, on Account of his distinguished Learning, and his ardent Zeal for the holy Mother, he was promoted to the

Degree of Doctor of Divinity and of the four Vows.

In the Year 1581 Pope *Gregory* XIII. called him away from *Diling*, in order to plant him at the Head of the first Mission of *Jesuits* to *England*; in which Office, being settled in the Metropolis of his native Country, and esteemed as Provincial of the Order in that great Kingdom, he ran into great Luxury and Magnificence, affecting more the exterior Shew of a Grandee than the Humility of a Priest, and supporting as splendid an Equipage as Money could then furnish him with.

Dr. *Fuller*, in his *British Worthies*, *(London*, p. 222.) has run into an Error with Respect to our Author, telling us that he was executed in the Reign of Queen *Elizabeth*.—But *Anth. à Wood* *(Athen. Oxon.* Vol. I. Col. 252.) informs us, that he paid the great Debt to Nature at *Naples*, on the 9th of *Jan.* 1598, and Sir *Richard Baker* relates, that he was one of the Chief of the seventy Priests that were taken in 1585. and that, when some of them were condemned, and the rest in Danger of the Law, her Majesty caused them all to be shipped away, and sent out of *England:* From whence it seems probable, that he went immediately to *Rome*, and at length settled in the City of *Naples*, where he contracted an Intimacy with that zealous Catholic *John Pitseus*, by whom he is spoken of with great Respect and Honour.

This Account seems also confirmed by a Copy of Verses, preserved by Sir *John Harrington*, which were written by this Author on his being taken and carried to Prison, and the Readiness shewn by the Earl of *Warwick* to afford him Relief. — Which laſt Circumſtance he hints at, in the following Words,

> — *Thanks to that Lord that wills me good,*
> *For I want all Things, ſaving Hay and Wood.*

During the Courſe of his Studies at the Univerſity, he tranſlated three of thoſe Tragedies which are attributed to *Seneca*, viz.

1. HERCULES *furens.* T.
2. THYESTES. T.
3. TROAS. T.

He has choſen an uncouth Sort of Verſe for theſe Tranſlations, *viz.* that of fourteen Feet.—Yet he has been very correct in the Meaning of his Author, where he has ſtuck to the Original, and in ſome Alterations, which he has profeſſedly made in the Conduct of the Pieces, has ſhewn great Judgment and Ingenuity.

HEYWOOD, Mr. *John.*—This Poet is one of the very firſt dramatic Writers that this Iſland produced; he was born at *North Mims*, near St. *Albans* in *Hertfordſhire*, and received the firſt Rudiments of his Education at *Oxford*; but the Sprightlineſs of his Diſpoſition not being well adapted to the ſedentary Life of an Academician, he went back to his Native Place, which being in the Neighbourhood of the great Sir *Tho. Moore*, he preſently contracted an Intimacy with that Patron of Wit and Genius, who introduced him to the Knowledge and Patronage of the Princeſs *Mary.*—*Heywood*'s ready Wit and Aptneſs for Jeſt and Repartee, together with the Poſſeſſion of great Skill both in vocal and inſtrumental Muſic, render'd him a Favorite with *Henry* VIII. who frequently rewarded him very

highly.——On the Acceſſion of *Edward* VI. he ſtill continued in Favour, tho' the Author of the *Art of* Engliſh *Poetry* ſays, it was " for the Mirth and Quickneſs of " Conceit, more than any good " Learning that was in him."— When his old Patroneſs, Queen *Mary*, came to the Throne, he ſtood in higher Eſtimation than ever, being admitted into the moſt intimate Converſation with her, on Account of his happy Talent of telling diverting Stories, which he did to amuſe her painful Hours, even when ſhe was languiſhing on her Death-Bed.

At the Deceaſe of that Princeſs, however, being a bigotted *Roman* Catholic, perceiving that the Proteſtant Intereſt was likely to prevail under the Patronage of her Succeſſor Queen *Elizabeth*, and perhaps apprehenſive, that ſome of the Severities, which had been practiſed on the Proteſtants in the preceding Reign, might be retaliated on thoſe of a contrary Perſuaſion in the enſuing one, and more eſpecially on the peculiar Favorites of Qu. *Mary*, he thought it beſt, for the Security of his Perſon, and the Preſervation of his Religion to quit the Kingdom.—Thus, throwing himſelf into a voluntary Exile, he ſettled at *Mecklin* in *Brabant*, where he died in 1565, leaving ſeveral Children behind him, to all of whom he had given liberal Educations.—Among the reſt was *Jaſper*, ſome Account of whom we gave in the laſt Article.

From what has been ſaid above his Character in private Life may be gather'd to have been that of a ſprightly, humourous and entertaining Companion.—As a Poet he was held in no inconſiderable Eſteem by his Cotemporaries, tho' none of his Writings extended

tended to any great Length, but seem, like his Conversation, to have been the Result of little sudden Sallies of Mirth and Humour.—His longest Work is entitled *A Parable of the Spider and the Fly*, and forms a pretty thick Quarto in *Old English* Verse, and printed in the Black Letter.—By Way of Frontispiece to this Book is a wooden Print of the Author at full Length, and most probably in the Habit he usually wore; for he is drest in a Fur Gown, somewhat resembling that of a Master of Arts, excepting that the Bottom of the Sleeves reach no lower than his Knees.—He has a round Cap on his Head and a Dagger hanging to his Girdle, and his Chin and Lips are close shaven.

His other Works are, a Dialogue composed of all the Proverbs in the *English* Language, and three Quarto Volumes, containing five hundred Epigrams. —None of his dramatic Works, which are six in Number, have extended beyond the Limits of an Interlude.—The Titles of them are as follow,

1. *Four P's*. Interlude.
2. *Play between* JOHN *the Husband*, TIB *the Wife, and Sir* JOHN *the Priest*. Interlude.
3. *Play between the* PARDONER, *the* FRIAR, *the* CURATE, *and Neighbour* PRAT. Interlude.
4. *Play of Gentleness and Nobility*. Interlude.
5. *Play of Love*. Interlude.
6. *Play of the Weather*. Interlude.

Phillips and *Winstanley* have attributed two other Pieces to him, *viz.*

The *Pindar of* WAKEFIELD. *Philotas*, Scotch.

but *Langbaine* rejects their Authority, and I think with very good Reason, as both those Pieces are printed anonymous, and the one was not published till twenty, the other not till upwards of forty Years after this Author's Death.

I do not find any Writer who ascertains the exact Time of *John Heywood*'s Birth, or his Age at the Time of his Death, but he could not have died a young Man, as we find him to have survived the Birth of his Son *Jasper* by full thirty Years.

HEYWOOD, Mr. *Matthew*.— I do not find any such Person mentioned by any of the Writers but *Winstanley*, who, (*Lives of the Poets*, p. 97.) after mentioning *John*, *Thomas* and *Jasper Heywood*, adds, " and, as if the " Names of *Heywood* were desti- " nated to the Stage, in my Time " I knew one *Matthew Heywood*, " who wrote a Comedy, call'd, " The *Changling*, " that should have been acted at " *Audley-End* House, but, by I " know not what Accident, was " prevented."

It is difficult to controvert what our Author thus asserts on his Knowledge, but *Winstanley* was very liable to Mistakes, and, it is well known that there is a Comedy of that Name extant, which was written by *Middleton* and *Rowley* in Conjunction, and that no other stands in any of the Catalogues.

HEYWOOD, Mr. *Thomas*.— This Author was an Actor as well as a Writer, and flourished in the Reigns of Queen *Elizabeth*, King *James* I. and King *Charles* I. tho' what particular Year gave him to the World, or robb'd it of him, seems not easy to ascertain.—He appears to have been a

 Native

Native of *Lincolnſhire*, from a Copy of Verſes to his Friend *James Yorke*, on his Book of Heraldry, prefix'd to that Work.— He was certainly the moſt voluminous dramatic Writer that this Nation, or indeed any other, ever produced, excepting the celebrated *Spaniſh* Play-Wright, *Lopez de Vega*, for, in the Preface to one of his Plays, called the *Engliſh Travellers*, he tells us, that it was one preſerved amongſt two hundred and twenty, in which, ſays he, " I had either "an entire Hand, or at leaſt a " main Finger."—Of this prodigious Number, however, all the Writers agree in the Opinion, that there are only twenty-four remaining.——For this different Reaſons might perhaps be aſſigned.—Thoſe that *Winſtanley* has given us are romantic and extravagant to the greateſt Degree.— " It is ſaid (relates *Winſtanley*) " that he not only acted himſelf " every Day, but alſo wrote every " Day a Sheet; and, that he " might loſe no Time, many of " his Plays were compoſed in " the Tavern, on the Backſide " of Tavern-Bills, which may be " the Occaſion that ſo many of " them are loſt."—But this Account is inconſiſtent with all Belief, for, beſides, that it is not apparent that *Heywood's* Circumſtances were ever ſuch as ſhould compel him to make ſuch Shifts, or that a Man, who was a conſtant Frequenter of Taverns, ſhould at the ſame Time be ſo penurious, as to make Uſe of Bills to ſpare himſelf the Expence of a few Sheets of Paper; yet, had even this been the Caſe, it would not occaſion the Loſs of his Pieces, ſince, before they could poſſibly be performed, theſe Scraps muſt have been all collect-

ed together, and tranſcribed in Body, for the Uſe of the Performers and Prompter.—But, the Reaſons he himſelf has given us in the above-mentioned Preface, ſeem to be the moſt rational ones; for, tho' it is probable that ſo active a Genius as, it is evident, from the Bulk of his Works, Mr. *Heywood's* muſt have been, could never be idle, nor afford to loſe any Time, or even let a ſingle Thought paſs by him unemployed at the very Moment it occurr'd; and that, conſequently, he might have planned ſome of his Plays in Taverns, and even have ſecur'd ſome occaſional Hints, by penning them down on the Back of Tavern Bills, or any occaſional Scraps of Paper he might have about him; yet, it is extremely unlikely that he ſhould ſuffer thoſe Thoughts, he had been ſo careful to preſerve, to be afterwards loſt by an unaccountable Negligence. — But he gives us three very good Reaſons for no more of his Pieces having appear'd in Print; the firſt, " that many of them, by the " Shifting and Change of Com- " panies," (at a Time when there were ſo many Theatres in the Metropolis, and that the Performers, moreover, frequently travelled the Country) " had been " negligently loſt."—The ſecond, " that others of them were ſtill " retained in the Hands of ſome " Actors, who thought it againſt " their Profit to have them come " in Print."—And here it will be proper to obſerve, that at that Time the Profits of an Author were not determined by the Succeſs of his Works, no ſuch Thing as third Nights being known or thought of till after the Reſtoration, but that the Actors purchaſed to themſelves the ſole Pro-

peity

perty of the Copy, by which Means, as it could not be their Intereſt to publiſh any Piece, till the Public Curioſity in Regard to it was entirely ſated, it is probable many very good Plays may have been entirely loſt.——The third Reaſon he gives us is, "that it was never any great "Ambition in him to be volu- "minouſly read."

Thoſe of his Works, which are to be met with in Print, are as follows,

1. *Brazen Age.* Hiſt. Play.
2. *Challenge for Beauty.* Tr.-Com.
3. *Dutcheſs of* SUFFOLK. Hiſt. Play.
4. EDWARD IV. Hiſt. Play. two Parts.
5. ENGLISH *Traveller.* Tragi-Com.
6. *Fair Maid of the Exchange.* Com.
7. *Fair Maid of the Weſt.* C. two Parts.
8. *Fortune by Land and Sea.* Tragi-Com. (Aſſiſted by *William Rowley.*)
9. *Four 'Prentices of* LONDON. Hiſt. Play.
10. *Golden Age.* Hiſt. Play.
11. *If you know not me, you know Nobody.* Hiſt. Play.
12. *Iron Age.* Hiſt. Play, two Parts.
13. LANCASHIRE *Witches.* Com. (Aſſiſted by *Rich. Brome.*)
14. *Love's Miſtreſs.* Maſque.
15. *Maidenhead well loſt.* Com.
16. *Rape of* LUCRECE. Trag.
17. ROBERT *Earl of* HUNTINGDON's *Downfall.*
18. ROBERT *Earl of* HUNTINGDON's *Death.* Hiſt. Play.
19. *Royal King and Loyal Subject.* Tragi-Com.

20. *Silver Age.* Hiſt. Play.
21. *Wiſe Woman of* HOGSDON. Com.
22. *Woman kill'd with Kindneſs.* Trag.

Mr. *Heywood* appears to have been a very favourite Author with *Langbain*, who ranks him in the ſecond Claſs of Dramatic Writers, tho' his Cotemporaries would not allow his Performances to ſtand ſo high in Deſert, as may be gather'd from the following Lines, which *Langbaine* has quoted from one of the Poets of that Time, who, after mentioning ſome other Authors, thus proceeds,

————— *And* Heywood
    Sage,
Th' apologetic Atlas of the
    Stage ;
Well! of the Golden Age he could
    entreat,
But little of the Metal he could
    get ;
Threeſcore ſweet Babes be chriſ-
    ten'd at a Lump,
For he was chriſten'd in Parnaſ-
    ſus' Pump ;
The Muſes Goſſip to Aurora's
    Bed,
And, ever ſince that Time, his
    Face was red.

It muſt be allowed, however, that he was a good general Scholar, and a very tolerable Maſter of the Claſſical Languages, as appears from the great Uſe he made of the Ancients, and his various Quotations from them in his Works, eſpecially his *Actor's Vindication*, in which he has diſplay'd great Erudition.——What Rank he held as an Actor, I know not, but it is probable no very conſiderable one, as all his Biographers are ſilent on that

Head ;

Head; and, indeed, if we confider how much he wrote, it is fcarcely poffible to conceive he could have fo much Time to fpare for an Application to that Art, as 'was neceffaiy for the attaining any Perfection in it.

HIFFERMAN, Dr. *Paul.*—This Gentleman is an Author now living; he is a Native of *Ireland*, received Part of his Education in the Univerfity of *Dublin*, and I believe took the Degree of Doctor of Phyfic in fome of the foreign Univerfities; but, not having met with any great Succefs in the Profeffion he was bred to, he has been obliged to rely on his Pen for an additional Affiftance.—While in *Dublin* he was for fome Time concerned in a public Political Paper, written in Oppofition to the famous Dr. *Lucas*, and, fince his coming over to this Kingdom. has been employ'd by the Bookfellers in various Works of Tranflation, Compilement, *&c.*—A Circumftance which, in this Age, but too frequently happens to Men of liberal Educations, whofe Neceffities, obliging them thus to enlift under the Banner of Bookfellers, their Geniufes have fcarcely ever fair Play with the Public, but, compelled to pufh forward in anv Road prefcribed them indifcriminately, without either Time for Invention, or Leifure for Amendment, their Productions muft neceffarily be dull, cold and erroneous; and many a fertile Genius, which, under the aufpicious Sunfhine or happier Circumftances, might have grown up and yielded to the World the faireft Fruit, has thus been nipp'd in the very Bud, and never been able afterwards to rear its blighted Head.—But, to return, among the Doctor's other Wotks,

he has produced three dramatic Pieces, none of which, however, met with any Succefs, *viz.*

1. *Choice.* Farce.
2. *New* HIPPOCRATES. Far.
3. *Wifhes of a free People.* Dram. Entert.

HIGDEN, *Henry*, Efq;—This Gentleman was a Member of the Honourable Society of the *Middle Temple*, during the Reigns of *James* II. and King *William* III. He was a Gentleman of great Wit, an agreeable and facetious Companion, and well known to all the fprightly and converfible Part of the Town.—He was Author of one dramatic Piece, entitled,

The *Wary Widow.* Com. and, indeed, his Fondnefs for the convivial and focial Delights feem'd to fhew itfelf very apparent even in the Conduct of his Play, for he had introduced fo many drinking Scenes into it, that the Performers got drunk before the End of the third Act, and, being unable to proceed with the Reprefentation, were obliged to difmifs the Audience. The Behaviour of the Bear Garden Criticks (as the Author calls them) on this Occafion, he ftrongly complains of in his Preface.

HIGGONS, *Bevil*, Efq;—This Gentleman was Son of a Sir *Thomas Higgons*, but from what Part of the Kingdom his Family claim'd their Defcent I know not.—Our Author received his Education at *Trinity* College, *Cambridge*, of which he was a Fellow Commoner in 1688.——After the Revolution he followed the Fortunes of K. *James* II. into *France*, where he refided till his Death, and, it is faid, retained his Wit and Good Humour, of both which he had an

inex-

inexhauftible Fund, undepreffed by his Misfortunes.—The Time of his Birth or Death, however, do not appear from any Accounts that have reach'd me.—He wrote one dramatic Piece, entitled,

The *Generous Conqueror*. Trag.

HILL, *Aaron*, Efq; — This Gentleman, who was born in *Beaufort-Buildings* in the *Strand*, *Feb*. 10. 1684-5, was the eldeft Son of *Geo. Hill*, Efq; of *Malmf-bury-Abbey* in *Wiltfhire*; and, in Confequence of this Defcent, the legal Heir to an entailed Eftate of about 2000l. *per Annum*; but, the Indifcretions and Mifconducts of his Father having, by a Sale of the Eftate, which he had no Right to execute, render'd it hitherto of no Advantage to the Family it juftly belongs to, our Author was left, together with Mr. *Hill's* other Children, to the Care of, and a Dependance on, his Mother and Grand-Mother; the latter of whom (Mrs. *Anne Gregory*) was more particularly anxious for his Education and Improvement.—The firft Rudiments of Learning he received from Mr. *Reyner*, of *Barnftaple* in *Devonfhire*, to whom he was fent at nine Years old, and, on his Removal from thence, was placed at *Weftminfter* School, under the Care of the celebrated Dr. *Knipe*.—Here his Genius foon rendered itfelf confpicuous, and, by enabling him at Times to perform the Tafks of others as well as his own, frequently procur'd for him, from fome of his School-Fellows of more limited Abilities, an ample Amends for the very fcanty Allowance of Pocket-Money which the Circumftances of his Family laid him under the Neceffity of being contented with.

Our Author left *Weftminfter* School in the Year 1699, being then only fourteen Years of Age; and, having heard his Mother frequently made warm Mention of the Lord *Paget*, who was a pretty near Relation of her's, and was at that Time at *Conftantinople*, in the Rank of Ambaffador from the *Englifh* to the *Ottoman* Court, he conceived a very ftrong Inclination of paying a Vifit, and making himfelf known to that Nobleman.——This Defign he communicated to Mrs. *Gregory*, and, meeting with no Oppofition from her in it, he embarked on the 2d of *March* 1700, being then but juft fifteen, on board a Veffel that was going to *Conftantinople*, in which City he arrived after a fafe and profperous Voyage.

On his Arrival he was received with the utmoft Kindnefs and Cordiality by the Ambaffador, who was no lefs pleafed than furprized at that Ardour for Improvement, which could induce a Youth of his tender Years to adventure fuch a Voyage, on a Vifit to a Relation whom he knew by Character only. —He immediately provided him a Tutor in the Houfe with himfelf, under whofe Tuition he very foon fent him to travel, being defirous of indulging to the utmoft that laudable Curiofity and Thirft of Knowledge, which feem'd fo ftrongly impreffed on the amiable Mind of our young Adventurer.—With this Gentleman, who was a learned Ecclefiaftic, he travelled through *Egypt*, *Paleftine*, and the greateft Part of the *Eaft*; and, on Lord *Paget's* returning home, as that Nobleman chofe to take his Journey by Land, Mr. *Hill* had an Opportunity of feeing

great

great Part of *Europe*, at most of the Courts of which the Ambassador made some little Stay.

With Lord *Paget* our Author continued in great Estimation; and, it is not improbable, that his Lordship might have provided genteely for him at his Death, had not the Envy and Malevolence of a certain Female, who had great Influence with him, by Falshoods and Misrepresentations, in great Measure, prevented his good Intentions towards him.—Fortune, however, and his own Merits, made him Amends for the Loss of this Patronage; for his known Sobriety and good Understanding recommended him soon after to Sir *William Wentworth*, a worthy Baronet of *Yorkshire*, who, being inclinable to make the Tour of *Europe*, his Relations engaged Mr. *Hill* to accompany him as a Sort of Governor or travelling Tutor, which Office, tho' himself of an Age which might rather be expected to require the being put under Tuition itself, than to become the Guide and Director of others, he executed so well, as to bring home the young Gentleman, after a Course of two or three Years, very greatly improved, to the entire Satisfaction, not only of himself, but of all his Friends.

In the Year 1709 he commenced Author, by the Publication of an History of the *Ottoman* Empire, compiled from the Materials which he had collected in the Course of his different Travels, and during his Residence at the *Turkish* Court.—This Work, tho' it met with Success, Mr. *Hill* frequently afterwards repented the having printed, and would himself, at Times, very severely criticize on it; and indeed, to say

the Truth of it, there are in it a great Number of Puerilities, which render it far inferior to the Merit of his subsequent Writings; in which Correctness has ever been so strong a Characteristic, that his Critics have even attributed it to him as a Fault.—Whereas, in this Work, there at best appears the Labour of a juvenile Genius, rather chusing to give the full Rein to fiery Fancy, and indulge the Imagination of the Poet, than make Use of the Curb of cooler Judgment, or aim at the Plainness and Perspicuity of the Historian.—About the same Year he published his first poetical Piece, entitled *Camillus*, in Vindication and Honour of the Earl of *Peterborough*, who had been General in *Spain*.—This Poem was printed without any Author's Name; but Lord *Peterborough*, having made it his Business to find out to whom he was indebted for this Compliment, appointed Mr. *Hill* his Secretary; which Post, however, he quitted the Year following, on Occasion of his Marriage.

In 1709 he was also made Master of the Theatre Royal in *Drury Lane*, and, at the Desire of Mr. *Booth*, wrote his first Tragedy of *Elfrid*, or the *Fair Inconstant*.—This Play was written in little more than a Week, on which Account it is no Wonder that it should be, as he himself has described it, " An unprun'd " Wilderness of Fancy, with here " and there a Flower among the " Leaves; but without any Fruit " of Judgment." — This, however, he alter'd, and brought on the Stage again about twenty Years afterwards, under the Title of *Athelwold*.—Yet, even in its first Form, it met with sufficient Encouragement to induce
him

him to a fecond Attempt in the dramatic Way, tho' of another Kind, viz. the Opera of *Rinaldo*, the Mufic of which was the firft Piece of Compofition of that admirable Mafter Mr. *Handel*, after his Arrival in *England*.—This Piece, in the Year 1710, Mr. *Hill* brought on the Stage at the King's Theatre in the *Haymarket*, of which alfo he was at that Time Director, and where it met with very great and deferved Succefs.

It appears, from the above Account, that Mr. *Hill* was, at one and the fame Period, Manager of two Theatres, both of which he conducted entirely to the Satisfaction of the Public; and, indeed, no Man feem'd better qualified for fuch a Station, if we may be allowed to form our Opinion from that admirable Judgment in theatrical Affairs, and perfect Acquaintance, both with the Laws of the Drama, and the Rules of acting, which he gives Proofs of, not only in a Poem entitled, the *Art of Acting*, and in the Courfe of his periodical Effays, entitled the *Prompter*, which appear'd in his Life-Time, but alfo in many Parts of an Epiftolary Correfpondence which he maintained with various Perfons of Tafte and Genius, and which have fince been publifhed among his pofthumous Works, in four Volumes in Octavo.—This Poft, however, he relinquifhed in a few Months, from fome Mifunderftanding with the then Lord Chamberlain; and tho' he was not long after very earneftly folicited, and that too by a Perfon of the firft Diftinction and Confequence, to take the Charge on him again, yet he could not be prevailed on, by any Means, to re-accept it.

It is probable, however, that neither Pride, nor any harbour'd Refentment, were the Motives of this Refufal, but one much more amiable, *viz.* an ardent Zeal for general Improvement, and an Earneftnefs for the public Good, which ever attended him thro' Life, in which he was at all Times indefatigable, and to which he, on different Occafions, frequently facrificed, not only his Eafe and Satisfaction, but even large Sums of Money alfo; and, indeed, this valuable Property of Public Spirit feems to have been his Soul's Darling Paffion; for he himfelf, in one of his Prefaces, fpeaking of Poetry, tells us, "that he has no better Reafon "for wifhing it well than his "Love for a Miftrefs, whom he "fhould never be married to; for "that, whenever he grew ambi- "tious, he would wifh to build "higher, and owe his Memory "to fome Occafion of more Im- "portance than his Writings."— To this Motive, therefore, I fay, it is probable that we ought to attribute his declining the Theatrical Direction, for in the fame Year he married the only Daughter of *Edward Norris*, Efq; of *Stratford* in *Effex*, and, as the Fortune that Lady brought him was very confiderable, he was now better able to purfue fome of his more public Defigns than he had before been.

The firft Project which Mr. *Hill* fet on Foot, for which he obtained a Patent, and of which he was himfelf the fole Difcoverer, was the making an Oil, as fweet as that from Olives, from the Beech Nuts, which are a very plentiful Produce of fome Parts of thefe Kingdoms.—This was an Improvement apparently and acknowledgely of great Utility, and muſt have turned out to great Advantage, had the Conduct of it continued in the Hands of the original Inventor.— But, being an Undertaking of too great Extent for his own Fortune ſingly to purſue, he was obliged to call in the Aſſiſtance of others; and took a Subſcription of twenty-five thouſand Pounds on Shares and Annuities, in Security of which he aſſigned over his Patent in Truſt for the Proprietors, forming from amongſt themſelves a Body, who were to act in Concert with the Patentee, under the Denomination of the Beech Oil Company.—However, as Mankind are apt to be over ſanguine in their Expectations, and too impatient, under any the leaſt Diſappointment of thoſe Expectations, there ſoon aroſe Diſputes among them, which obliged Mr. Hill, in Vindication of ſome Miſrepreſentations concerning himſelf, to publiſh a fair State of the Caſe, by which it appear'd plainly that all the Money, that had hitherto been employed, had been fairly and candidly expended for the public Benefit, and that the Patentee had even waved all the Advantages, to which, by Agreement, he had been entitled to.— Theſe Diſputes, however, terminated in the over-throwing the whole Deſign, without any Emolument either to the Patentee or the Adventurers, at a Time when Profits were already ariſing from it, and, if purſued with Vigour, would, in all Probability, have continued increaſing and permanent.—Mr. Hill procured his Patent for this Invention in October 1713, and the Date of his public Appeal, in Regard to the Affair, is the 30th of Nov. 1716.—— Thus, excluſive of the Time employed in bringing the Invention

itſelf to Maturity, we ſee a full three Years Labour of a Gentleman of Abilities and Ingenuity entirely fruſtrated, thro' the Inequality of his own Fortune to carry his Plan into Execution ſingly, and the erroneous Warmth and Impatience of thoſe various Tempers with which he was, in Conſequence of that Inſufficiency, obliged to unite himſelf for the Perfection of it.

He was alſo concerned with Sir *Robert Montgomery*, in a Deſign for eſtabliſhing a Plantation of a vaſt Tract of Land in the South of *Carolina*, for which Purpoſe a Grant had been purchaſed from the Lords Proprietors of that Province; but here again the Want of a larger Fortune then he was Maſter of, ſtood as a Bar in his Way; for, tho' it has many Years ſince been largely cultivated under the Name of *Georgia*, yet it never proved of any Advantage to him.

Another very valuable Project he ſet on Foot in the Year 1728, which was the turning to a great Account many Woods of very large Extent in the North of *Scotland*, by applying the Timber, produced by them, to the Uſes of the Navy, for which it had been long erroneouſly imagined, they were totally unfit.—The Falſity of this Suppoſition, however, he clearly evinced; for one entire Veſſel was built of it, and, on Trial, was found to be of as good Timber as that brought from any Part of the World; and altho', indeed, there were not many Trees in theſe Woods large enough for Maſts to Ships of the largeſt Burthen, yet there were Millions fit for thoſe of all ſmaller Veſſels, and for every other Branch of Ship-Building.—In this Undertaking, however, he met with various

various Obſtacles, not only from the Ignorance of the Natives of that Country, but even from Nature herſelf; yet, Mr. *Hill*'s Aſſiduity and Perſeverance ſurmounted them all.—For when the Trees were by his Order chained together into Floats, the unexperienced Highlanders refuſed to venture themſelves on them down the River *Spey*; nor would have been prevailed on, had not he firſt gone himſelf to convince them that there was no Danger.——And now the great Number of Rocks, which choaked up different Parts of this River, and ſeemed to render it impoſſible, were another Impediment to his Expedition.—But, by ordering great Fires to be made upon them at the Time of low Tide, when they were moſt expoſed, and throwing Quantities of Water upon them, they were, by the Help of proper Tools, broke to Pieces and thrown down, and a free Paſſage opened for the Floats.

This Deſign was, for ſome Time, carried on with great Vigour, and turned out to very good Account; till ſome of the Perſons concerned in it thought proper to call off the Men and Horſes from the Woods of *Abernethy*, in order to employ them in their Lead Mines in the ſame Country, from whence they promiſed themſelves to reap a ſtill more conſiderable Advantage.—What private Emolument Mr. *Hill* received from this Affair, or whether any at all, I am uninformed of.—However, the Magiſtrates of *Inverneſs*, *Aberdeen*, &c. paid him the Compliment of the Freedom of their reſpective Towns, and entertained him with all imaginary Honours. — Yet, notwithſtanding theſe Honours,

which were publicly paid to our Author, and the diſtinguiſhed Civilities which he met with from the Duke and Dutcheſs of *Gordon*, and other Perſons of Rank to whom he became known during his Reſidence in the Highlands, this Northern Expedition was near proving of very unhappy Conſequences to his Fortune; for, in his Return, his Lady being at that Time in *Yorkſhire* for the Recovery of her Health, he made ſo long a Continuance with her in that County, as afforded an Opportunity to ſome Perſons, to whoſe Hands he had confided the Management of certain important Affairs, to be guilty of a Breach of Truſt, that aimed at the Deſtruction of the greateſt Part of what he was worth.—However, he happily returned Time enough to fruſtrate their villainous Intentions.

In the Year 1731 he met with a ſevere Shock by the Loſs of his Lady, with whom he had paſſed upwards of twenty happy Years, and to whom he had ever had the ſincereſt and tendereſt Attachment.—The Thought of the following Epitaph, which he wrote on her, is original and entirely poetical.

Enough, co'd Stone !—Suffice her
  long-lov'd Name :
Words are too weak to pay her
  Virtue's Claim.—
Temples, and Tombs, and Tongues
  ſhall waſte away ;
And Pow'r's vain Pomp, in
  mould'ring Duſt decay ;
But e'er Mankind a Wife more
  perfect ſee,
Eternity, O Time ! ſhall bury
  thee.

Mr. *Hill*, after this, continued in *London* and an Intercourſe with the

the Public, till about the Year 1738, when he, in a Manner, withdrew himfelf from the World, by retiring to *Plaiftow* in *Effex,* where he devoted himfelf entirely to Study, and the Cultivation of his Family and Garden. Yet the Concerns of the Public became by no Means a Matter of Indifference to him ; for, even in this Retirement, he clofely applied to the bringing to Perfection many profitable Improvements. — One more particularly he lived to compleat, tho' not to reap any Benefit from it himfelf, *viz.* the Art of making Pot-Afh equal to that brought from *Ruffia,* to which Place an immenfe Sum of Money ufed annually to be fent from thefe Kingdoms for that Article alone.—In his Solitude he wrote and publifhed feveral poetical Pieces, particularly an Heroic Poem, entitled the *Fanciad,* another of the fame Kind, called the *Impartial,* a *Poem upon Faith,* and three Books of an Epic Poem which he had many Years before begun, on the Story of *Gideon.*— He alfo tranflated and adapted to the *Englifh* Stage *Monf. de Voltaire's* Tragedy of *Merope,* which was the laft Work he lived to compleat ; for, from about the Time he was folliciting the bringing it on the Stage, an Illnefs feized him, from the tormenting Pains of which he had fcarce an Hour's Intermiffion; and, after trying, in vain, all the Aids that Medicine could afford him, he at laft returned to *London,* in Hopes that his native Air might have proved beneficial to him ; but, alas ! he was paft Recovery, being wafted almoft to a Skeleton, from fome internal Caufe, which had occafioned a general Decay, and was believed to be an Inflammation in the Kidneys, the Foundation of which

moft probably had been laid by his intenfe and indefatigable Application to his Studies.——He juft lived to fee his Tragedy introduced to the Public, but the Day before it was, by Command of *Frederic* Prince of *Wales,* to have been reprefented for his Benefit, he died. in the very Minute of the Earthquake, *Feb.* 8. 1749-50, of the Shock of which, tho' fpeechlefs. he appeared fenfible.——This Event happened within two Days of the full Completion of his fixty-fifth Year, the laft Twelvemonth of which he had paffed in the utmoft Torment of Body, but with a Calmnefs and Refignation that gave Teftimony of the moft unfhaken Fortitude of Soul.—He was interred near Lord *Godolphin's* Monument, in the great Cloifter of *Weftminfter-Abbey,* in the fame Grave with her, who had, while living, been the deareft to him.

With Regard to Mr. *Hill's* private Character, he was in every Refpect perfectly amiable.—His Perfon was, in his Youth, extremely fair and handfome,—He was tall, not too thin, yet genteeliy made.—His Eyes were a dark Blue, bright and penetrating ; his Hair brown, and his Face oval.—His Countenance was moft generally animated by a Smile, which was more particularly diftinguifhable whenever he entered into Converfation ; in the doing which his Addrefs was moft engagingly affable, yet mingled with a native unaffumed Dignity, which render'd him equally the Object of Admiration and Refpect, with thofe who had the Pleafure of his Acquaintance.— His Voice was fweet, and his Converfation elegant ; and fo extenfive was his Knowledge in all Subjects,

Subjects, that scarcely any could occur on which he did not acquit himself in a most masterly and entertaining Manner.—His Temper, tho' naturally warm when rouz'd by Injuries, was equally noble in a Readiness to forgive them; and so much inclinable was he to repay Evil with Good, that he frequently exercised that Christian Lesson, even to the Prejudice of his own Circumstances. —He was a generous Master, a sincere Friend, an affectionate Husband, and an indulgent and tender Parent; and indeed, so benevolent was his Disposition in general, even beyond the Power of the Fortune he was blessed with, that the Calamities of those he knew, and valued as deserving, affected him more deeply than his own.—In Consequence of this we find him bestowing the Profits of many of his Works for the Relief of his Friends, and particularly his dramatic ones, none of which he could ever be prevailed on to accept of a Benefit for till at the very Close of his Life, when, Oh Grief! his narrow Circumstances compelled him to sollicit the acting of his *Merope*, for the Relief of its Author from those Difficulties, out of which he had frequently been the generous Instrument of extricating others.—His Manner of living was temperate to the greatest Degree in every Respect but that of late Hours, which, as the Night is less liable to Interruptions than the Day, his indefatigable Love of Study frequently drew him into.—No Labour deterr'd him from the Prosecution of any Design which appeared to him to be praise-worthy and feasible; nor was it in the Power of the greatest Misfortunes (and, indeed, from his Birth, he seem-

ed destined to encounter many) to overcome, or even shake his Fortitude of Mind.

As a Writer, he must be allowed to stand in a very exalted Rank of Merit.——The greatest Elevation of Thought and Dignity of Sentiment; the strongest Powers of affecting the Mind and alarming the Passions; a Fancy, which took its Flight on the most unlimited Pinions; and an Originality of Expression, which true Genius alone could be capable of, are the striking Characteristics of Mr. *Hill*'s Writings.— And altho' it may be confessed that the rigid Correctness, with which he constantly reperused his Works for Alteration, the frequent Use of compound Epithets, and an *Ordo Verborum* in great Measure peculiar to himself, have justly laid him open to the Charge of being, in some Places, rather too turgid, and in others somewhat obscure; yet, the nervous Power we find in them, will surely attone for the former Fault, and, as to the latter, the intrinsic Sterling Sense we constantly find on a close Examination of every Passage of his Writings, ought to make us overlook our having been obliged to take some little Pains in digging thro' the Rock in which it was contained. —As I have, however, in this Place, nothing to do with any but his dramatic Writings, the Reader may see a compleat Catalogue of them in the following List, *viz.*

1. ALZIRA. Trag.
2. ATHELWOLD. Trag. (alter'd from *Elfrid.*)
3. ELFRID. Trag.
4. *Fatal Vision.* Trag.
5. HENRY V. Trag.
6. *Insolvent.* Trag.
7. MEROPE. Trag.

 8. *Muses*

8. *Muses in Mourning.* Opera.
9. RINALDO. Ital. Opera. (the Plan only laid by this Author.)
10. *Roman Revenge.* Trag.
11. SAUL. Trag.
12. *Snake in the Grass.* Dram. Entertainment.
13. *Trick upon Trick.* Com.
14. *Walking Statue.* Farce.
15. ZARA. Trag.

Our Author seems to have lived in perfect Harmony with all the Writers of his Time excepting Mr. *Pope,* with whom he had a short Paper War, occasioned by that Gentleman's introducing him in the *Dunciad,* as one of the Competitors for the Prize offer'd by the Goddess of Dulness, in the following Lines.

Then Hill *essay'd; scarce vanish'd out of Sight,*
He buoys up instant, and returns to Light;
He bears no Token of the sabler Streams,
And mounts, far off, among the Swans of Thames.

This, though far the gentlest Piece of Satire in the whole Poem, and conveying at the same Time an oblique Compliment, rous'd Mr. *Hill* to the taking some Notice of it, which he did by a Poem, written during his Peregrination in the North, entitled, The *Progress of Wit,* a *Caveat for the Use of an eminent Writer,* which he begins with the following eight Lines, in which Mr. *Pope's* too well-known Disposition is elegantly, yet very severely characterized.

Tuneful ALEXIS, *on the* Thames' *fair Side,*
The Ladies' Play-thing, and the Muse's Pride;

With Merit popular, with Wit polite,
Easy, tho' vain, and elegant, tho' light;
Desiring, and deserving *other's Praise,*
Poorly accepts *a Fame he ne'er* repays :
Unborn to cherish, SNEAKINGLY APPROVES,
And wants the Soul to spread *the Worth he* loves.

The " *sneakingly approves,*" in the last Couplet, Mr. *Pope* was much affected by ; and, indeed, thro' their whole Controversy afterwards, in which it was generally thought Mr. *Hill* had considerably the Advantage, Mr. *Pope* seems rather to express his Repentance by denying the Offence, than to vindicate himself, supposing it to have been given.

HILL, Dr. *John.*—This Gentleman, who may very justly be esteemed as a Phœnomenon in Literary History, is yet living, and perhaps one of the most voluminous Writers that this or any other Age has produced ; yet, on an Examination of his Works, it will, I am afraid, appear, that he has just inverted that Sentiment of *Horace,* which his Name-Sake last-mentioned chose for the Motto of his *Fatal Vision,* and that the Doctor's Maxim will appear the direct contrary to the

I not for vulgar Admiration write ;
To be well *read, not* much, *is my Delight.*

but of this more hereafter.—He is the second Son of one Mr. *Theophilus Hill,* a Clergyman, if I mistake not, of either *Peterborough* or *Spalding.*—The Year of
our

our Author's Birth I am not absolutely afcertained of, but fhould, from a Collection of Circumftances, be apt to conclude it about 1716 or 1717, as in the Year 1740 we find him engaged in a Controverfy with Mr. *Rich*, in Regard to a little Opera called *Orpheus and Euridice*, in which much perfonal Abufe appeared on both Sides.—He was originally bound Apprentice to an Apothecary, after ferving his Time to whom, he fet up in that Profeffion in a little Shop in *St. Martin's Lane*; but. having very early incumbered himfelf with the Cares of a Family, by an hafty Marriage with a young Woman of no Fortune, the Daughter of one Mr. *Tauver*, who was Houfbold Steward to the late Earl of *Burlington*, and whom he fell in Love with at a Dancing. he found the little Bufinefs he had in his Profeffion infufficient for the Support of it, and therefore was obliged to apply to other Refources to help out the poor Pittance he could obtain by his regular Avocation.—Having, during his Apprenticefhip, regularly attended on the Botanical Lectures which are periodically given under the Patronage of the Company of Apothecaries, and being poffeffed of quick natural Parts and ready Abilities, he had made himfelf a very compleat Mafter of the practical, and indeed the theoretical Part alfo, of Botany; and, having procured a Recommendation to the late Duke of *Richmond*, and the Lord *Petre*, two Noblemen, whofe Love of Science and conftant Encouragement of Genius, ever did Honour to their Country, he was by them employed in the Regulation of their refpective botanic Gardens, and the Arrangement of certain cu-

rious dried Plants, which they were in Poffeffion of.—Affifted by the Gratuities he received from thefe Noblemen, he was enabled to put a Scheme in Execution of travelling over feveral Parts of this Kingdom, to gather certain of the more rare and uncommon Plants; a felect Number of which, prepared in a peculiar Manner, he propofed to publifh, as it were, by Subfcription, at a certain Price.—The Labour and Expences attending on an Undertaking of this Kind, however, being very great, and the Number of even probable Purchafers very few, the Emoluments accruing to him from all his Induftry, which was indeed indefatigable, were by no Means adequate either to his Expectations or his Merits.—The Stage now prefented itfelf to him as a Soil in which Genius might ftand a Chance of flourifhing.—But this Plan proved likewife abortive, and, after two or three unfuccefsful Attempts at the Little Theatre in the *Haymarket*, and the Theatre Royal in *Covent Garden*, (particularly in the Character of the fecond Spirit of *Comus*, which he performed during the firft Run of that Mafque, as alter'd by Dr. *Dalton*, and in the *Dramatis Perfonæ* of which Mr. *Hill*'s Name may to this Day be feen) he was obliged to relinquifh his Pretenfions to the Sock and Bufkin, and apply again to his Botanical Advantages, and his Bufinefs as an Apothecary.

During the Courfe of thefe Occurrences, he was introduced to the Acquaintance of *Martin Folkes*, Efq; the late Prefident of the Royal Society, to Dr. *Alexander Stuart*, Mr. *Henry Baker*, F. R. S. and many other Gentlemen eminent in the literary

 and

and philosophical World, by all of whom he was received and entertained, on every Occasion, with the utmost Candour and Warmth of Friendship; being esteemed as a young Man of very considerable Abilities, struggling with the most laudable Assiduity against the Stream of Misfortune, yet, with a Degree of bashful Diffidence, which seemed an unsurmountable Bar to his ever being able to stem the Torrent, or make that Figure in Life which his Merit justly entitled him to. —In this Point of View Mr. *Hill* appeared for a considerable Time, admitted to every literary Assembly, esteem'd and caressed by all the Individuals which composed them, yet indigent and distress'd, and sometimes put to Difficulties for the obtaining even the common Necessaries of Life. At length, about the Year 1745 or 1746, at which Time he had a trifling Appointment of Apothecary to a Regiment or two in the *Savoy*, he translated from the *Greek* a small Tract, written by *Theophrastus*, on Stones and Gems, which, by the Addition of a great Number of very judicious and curious Notes, he enlarged into an Octavo Volume of three Shillings and Six-pence Price, which formed almost a compleat System of that Branch of Natural History. —This Work he published by Subscription, and, being extremely well executed, and as strongly recommended by all his literary Friends, it not only answered his Expectations from it with Respect to pecuniary Advantages, but also established a Reputation for him as a Writer, in Consequence of which he was immediately engaged in Works of more Extent, and of greater Importance.—The first Work he

undertook was a general Natural History, in three Volumes, Folio, the first of which, exclusive of other Writings, he compleated in less than a Twelve-Month.—He was also engaged, in Conjunction with *George Lewis Scott*, Esq; in a Supplement to *Chambers's Dictionary*.——He took on him the Management of a Monthly Publication, entitled the *British Magazine*, in which he wrote a great Variety of Essays on different Subjects; and was at the same Time concerned in many other Works. —In short, the Rapidity of his Pen was astonishing, nor will it perhaps readily gain Credit with Posterity, that while he was thus employed in several very voluminous Concerns at one Time, some of which were on Subjects which seemed to claim singly the whole of his Attention, and which he brought to Perfection with an Expedition that is scarcely to be conceived, he solely, and without any Assistance, carried on a *daily* periodical Essay, under the Title of the *Inspector*.—Nor was this the only extraordinary Circumstance attending on it; for, notwithstanding all this Employment, so much Leisure did he find Means ever to reserve to himself, that he was, at the same Time, a constant Frequenter of every Place of Public Amusement. — No Play, Opera, Ball or Assembly, but Mr. *Hill* was sure to be seen at, where he collected, by Wholesale, a great Variety of private Intrigue and personal Scandal, which he as freely retailed again to the Public, in his *Inspectors* and *Magazines*.

But now a Disposition began to shew itself in this Gentleman, which those, who had been the most intimate with him in his earlier

earlier Parts of Life, could never have suspected in him, *viz.* an unbounded Share of Vanity and Self-Sufficiency, which had for Years lain dormant behind the Mask of their direct opposite Qualities of Humility and Diffidence; a Pride, which was perpetually laying Claim to Homage by no Means his Due, and a Vindictiveness, which never could forgive the Refusal of it to him.——Hence it was that personal Abuse and the most licentious and uncandid Scurrility continually flowed from his Pen; every Affront, tho' ever so trivial, which his Pride met with, being assuredly revenged by a public Attack on the Morals, Understandings or Peculiarities of the Person from whom it had been received.—In Consequence of this Disposition we find him very frequently engaged in personal Disputes and Quarrels. — Particularly in one with an *Irish* Gentleman, of the Name of *Browne*, who, on finding himself universally considered as the Person intended by a very ridiculous Character drawn in one of the *Inspectors*, thought proper to bestow some Correction on him, not of the gentlest Kind, in the public Gardens of *Ranelagh*, which however Mr. *Hill* does not appear to have replied to with any other Weapon but his Pen.—He also engaged himself in a little Paper War with Mr. *Woodward*, the Comedian, in Consequence of an Insult that Gentleman received, in the Execution of his Profession, from a Gentleman in one of the Boxes——Mr. *Hill* was also extremel busy in the Opposition against the late Mr. *Henry Fielding*, in that intricate and inexplicable Affair of *Elizabeth Canning*.——But the most important Contest he was ever concerned in

was his Attack on the Royal Society of *London*, which, as his Writings on the Subject are of some Extent, and may be handed down to Posterity when the Cause of them is forgotten, it will not, perhaps, be disagreeable to my Readers, if I take up a small Portion of their Time in a Detail of the Origin and Progress of it.

When Mr. *Hill* had started all at once, as I have before related, from a State of Indigence and Distress, to taste the Comforts of very considerable Emoluments from his Labour, giddy with Success, and elated, beyond Bounds, with the warm Sunshine of Prosperity, he seemed to be seized with a Kind of Infatuation.—— Vanity took entire Possession of his Bosom, and banished from thence every Consideration but of Self.—His Conversation turn'd on little else, and even his very Writings were tainted with perpetual Details of every little Occurrence that happened to him.—A Passion for Dress, Shew and Parade, the natural Attendants on Self-Love, now broke forth; he set up his Chariot, and, professing to assume the Character of a meer Man of Pleasure, Gallantry and *Bon Ton*, affected to express, on every Occasion, the highest Contempt for Business and the drier Kinds of Study —His Raillery both in Company and in his Writings frequently turned on those who closely attached themselves to Philosophical Investigations, more especially in the Branches of Natural Philosophy.——The Common Place Wit of abusing the Medal-Scraper, the Butterfly-Hunter, the Cockle-Shell-Merchant, &c. now appeared in some of his *Magazines* and *Inspectors*, and in two or three Places he

even

even indulged some distant Glance of Satire at the Royal Society.——Notwithstanding which, however, when the Supplement to *Chambers's Dictionary* was nearly finished, the Proprietors of that Work, very sensible of the Weight which an F. R. S. annexed to the Author's Name, ever has in the Recommendation of a Work of that Nature, were very desirous that Mr. *Hill* (who had just before this purchased a Diploma for the Degree of Doctor of Physic from the *Scotch* University of *St. Andrews*) should also have this Addition as well as Mr. *Scott*, his Colleague in the Work.——In Consequence of this their Design, the new Dr. *Hill* procured Mr. *Scott* to propose him for Election into that honourable Body; but the Doctor's Conduct for some Time past having been such as had render'd him the Object of Contempt to some, of Disgust to others, and of Ridicule to almost all the rest of his former grave and philosophical Acquaintances, he now stood but a very indifferent Chance for carrying an Election, where an Opposition of one third was sufficient to reject the Candidate; and as the failing in that Attempt might have done our Author more essential Prejudice than the succeeding in it could even have brought him Advantage, the late ingenious and worthy President *Martin Folkes*, Esq; whose Remembrance must ever live in the highest Estimation with all who ever had the Honour of knowing him, notwithstanding that Dr. *Hill* had given him personal Occasion of Offence against him, yet, with the utmost Generosity and Candour, advised Mr. *Scott* to dissuade his Friend, for his own Sake, against a Design which

then appeared so little Probability of his succeeding in.——This Advice, however, Dr. *Hill*, instead of considering it in the generous Light it was meant, misinterpreted into a prejudiced Opposition against his Interest; and would have persisted in his Intention even in Despight of it, had not his being unable to obtain the Subscription of the requisite Number of Members to his Recommendation, obliged him to lay it aside, from a Conviction that he could not expect to carry an Election in a Body composed of three hundred Members, of which he could not prevail on three to set their Names to the barely recommending him as a Candidate.——Thus disappointed, his Vanity piqued, and his Pride lower'd, no Relief was left him but railing and Scurrility, for which Purpose, declaring open War with the Society in general, he first published a Pamphlet, entitled *A Dissertation on Royal Societies*, in a Letter from a *Sclavonian* Nobleman in *London* to his Friend in *Sclavonia* which, besides the most ill-manner'd and unjust Abuse on the whole learned Body, he had been just aiming, in vain, to become a Member of, is interlarded with the grossest personal Scurrility on the Characters of Mr. *Folkes* and Mr. *Henry Baker*, two Gentlemen to whom Dr. *Hill* had formerly been under the greatest Obligations, and whose respective Reputations in both the moral and literary World, had long been too firmly established for the weak Efforts of a disappointed Scribbler to shake or undermine.——Not contented with this, he proceeded to compile together a large Quarto Volume, entitled a *Review of the Works of the Royal Society*, in which,

which, by the moſt unfair Quotations, Mutilations and Miſreprefentations, Numbers of the Papers, read in that illuſtrious Aſſembly, and publiſhed under the Title of the *Philoſophical Tranſactions*, are endeavoured to be rendered ridiculous.—This Work is uſhered into the World with a moſt abuſive and infamous Dedication to *Martin Folkes*, Efq; againſt whom and the afore-mentioned Mr. *Henry Baker*, the Weight of this furious Attack was chiefly aimed, ſince of the few other Authors, who have been dragged in to ſuffer the Laſh of the Doctor's Abuſe, much the greateſt Part of them ſeem to have had no Claim to his Reſentment, but that of being Correſpondents of, or their Pieces being communicated by, one or the other of theſe Gentlemen.—But here again Dr. *Hill* met with a Diſappointment; for the Perſons, whom he had thus unjuſtly and ungratefully attacked, being greatly above the Reach of his Malice he found the ill Effects of it, like a recoiling Piece, revert on himſelf; the World, inſtead of laughing with him, deſpiſed him; thoſe, who would have otherwiſe been the principal Purchaſers of his Philoſophical Writings, were now too much exaſperated to afford him the leaſt Encouragement or Aſſiſtance.—By giving ſo ample a Scope to perſonal Slander and ſcurrilous Abuſe in ſome of his Works, and by his too great Hurry and the Impoſſibility of giving a proper Digeſtion to others, he made himſelf ſo many perſonal Enemies on the one Hand, and wrote himſelf ſo out of Repute, both with the Town and the Bookſellers, on the other, that at length, even when employed by the latter, he was ob-

liged, by Contract, to conceal from the former his being the Author, from the Conſideration that his very Name was ſufficient to damp the Sale of any Piece to which it might be affixed.—This, however, did not prevent his engaging in many Works, tho' not ſo voluminouſly as before, till at length he hit upon another Method for getting Money, which, as I am informed, ſtill continues to bring him a very conſiderable Income.—This is no other than the Preparation of certain ſimple Medicines, whoſe Effects are very ſerviceable in many Caſes, and, being moſtly of the vegetable Kind, are, I believe, very inoffenſive in all.—Theſe Medicines, in Conſequence of conſtant Advertiſements and Puffing, have had a very extenſive Sale and Conſumption, and are, I think, only of four Sorts, *viz.* The *Eſſence of Water-Dock*, *Tincture of Valerian*, *Pectoral Balſam of Honey*, and *Tincture of Bardana.*— Dr. *Hill* has, for ſome Time paſt, been warmly patronized by the Earl of *Bute*, thro' whoſe Intereſt, I have been informed, he was appointed, about two Years ago, to the Management of the Royal Gardens, but, by what Means I know not, the Grant was never confirmed.—Under that Nobleman's Patronage, and, I believe. at his Expence, the Doctor is alſo now publiſhing a very pompous and voluminous botanical Work, entitled, a *Syſtem of Botany*, of which five Volumes in Folio, with a great Number of very elegant and magnificent Copper-Plates, have already appeared.

And now, having related what peculiar Circumſtances I have been able to collect in Regard to his Life, it may be expected that

I ſhould

I fhould give fome Obfervations with Refpect to his Character; yet, thefe I fhall here confine only to his literary one, and the Rank of Merit which his Writings ought to ftand in.——Dr. *Hill*'s greateft Enemies cannot deny that he is Mafter of great Abilities, and an amazing Quicknefs of Parts.—The Rapidity of his Pen has been ever aftonifhing, and, I have even been credibly informed, that he has been known to receive, within one Year, no lefs than fifteen hundred Pounds, for the Works of his own fingle Pen, which, as he was never in fuch Eftimation as to be entitled to any extraordinary Price for his Copies, is, I believe, at leaft three Times as much as ever was made by any one Writer in the fame Period of Time.—But, had he wrote much lefs, he would probably have been much more read.—The vaft Variety of Subjects he has handled, certainly requir'd fuch a Fund of univerfal Knowledge, and fuch a boundlefs Genius as were never, perhaps, known to center in any one Man; and therefore it is not to be wondered at, if, in Regard to fome, he appears very inaccurate, in fome very fuperficial, and, in others, very inadequate to the Tafk he had undertaken. His Works, in the Philofophical Way, are what he feems moft likely to have purchafed future Fame by, had he allowed himfelf Time to have digefted the Knowledge he was poffeffed of, or adhered to that Precifion with Regard to Veracity, which the Relation of literary Facts fo rigidly demands.—His Novels, of which he has written many, fuch as the Hiftory of Mr. *Loveill* (in which he had endeavoured to perfuade the World he had given it the

Detail of his own Life) The Adventures of a *Creole*, The Life of Lady *Frail*, &c. have, in fome Parts of them, Incidents not difagreeably related, but the moft of them are no more than Narratives of private Intrigues, containing, throughout, the groffeft Calumnies, and aiming at the blackening and undermining the private Characters of many refpectable and amiable Perfonages.—In his Effays, which are by much the beft of his Writings, there is, in general, a Livelinefs of Imagination, and a Prettinefs in the Manner of extending perhaps fome very trivial Thought, which, at the firft *Coup D'Oeil*, is pleafing enough, and may, with many, be miftaken for Wit; but, on a nearer Examination, the imagined Sterling will be found to dwindle down into meer *French* Plate.—A continued Ufe of fmart fhort Periods, bold Affertions, and a Rotain of Egotiafms, for the moft Part give a glitter to them, which, however, prefently fallies to the Eye, and feldom tempts the Spectator to a fecond Glance.—In a Word, the utmoft that can be faid of Dr. *Hill* is, that he has Talents, but that he has, in the general, either greatly mifapplied them, or moft miferably/hackney'd them out.

As a dramatic Writer he ftands in no Eftimation, nor has been known in that View by any Thing but two very infignificant little Pieces, one of which I have mentioned above.—Their Titles are,

1. ORPHEUS and EURIDICE. Opera.

2. The *Rout*. Farce.

HOADLY, Dr. *Benjamin*.—— This Gentleman was a Doctor of Phyfic, and eminent in his Profeffion.—He was fecond Son of the

the great Dr. *Benjamin Hoadly*, late Lord Bishop of *Winchester.*— The Doctor was, in his private Character, an amiable humane Man, and an agreeable sprightly Companion.—In his Profession he was learned and judicious, and, as a Writer, there needs no farther Testimony to be borne to his Merit, than the very pleasing Comedy he has left behind him, and which, whenever represented, continually affords fresh Pleasure to the Audience.—We scarce have need to mention to any one, the least conversant with theatrical Affairs, that we mean

The *Suspicious Husband*. Com. Doctor *Hoadly* died about the Year 1760.

HOLYDAY, Dr. *Barten.*—— This Gentleman was Son of one *Thomas Holyday*, a Taylor, and was born in the Parish of *All-Saints*, in the City of *Oxford*, about the latter End of Queen *Elizabeth*'s Reign.——He was very early entered of *Christ Church* in the University of *Oxford*, during the Time of Dr. *Ravis*, who was not only his Patron, but a Relation also.——In this College he took his Degrees of Batchelor and Master of Arts, and, in 1615, enter'd into Holy Orders, in which his Abilities very soon made him taken Notice of, and render'd him a very popular Preacher.—He soon after obtained two good Livings, both of them in *Oxfordshire*, and, in the Year 1618, he went as Chaplain to Sir *Francis Stewart*, when he accompanied, to his own Country, the famous Count *Gundamore*, who had been many Years Ambassador from the Court of *Spain* to that of *England*.——In this Journey the Doctor's facetious and agreeable Manner greatly in-

gratiated him in the Favour of Count *Gundamore*.

Soon after his Return he was appointed, by King *Charles* I. as one of his Chaplains, and, before 1626, succeeded Dr. *Bridges*, as Archdeacon of *Oxford*.—In 1642 he was, by Virtue of the King's Letters, created, with several others, Doctor of Divinity.—And now, the Rebellion being broke out, he sheltered himself near *Oxford*; but very soon began to give Proofs of a Want of Stedfastness, which occasioned him the Blame and Censure of many of his ancient Friends among the Clergy; the most of whom chose rather to live in Poverty during the Usurpation, than by a mean Compliance with the Times to betray the Interests of the Church, and the Cause of their unhappy exil'd Sovereign.—For, when he saw the Royal Party so far declining, that their Cause began to appear desperate, he thought it the most for his own Interest to temporize, and appear to join in with the prevailing Power.—— Nay, on *Oliver Cromwell*'s being raised to the Protectorship, he even so far coincided with the Measures then pursued, as to submit to an Examination by the Friars, in order to his being inducted into the Rectory of *Shilton* in *Berkshire*, which had been vacated by the Ejectment of one *Thomas Lawrence*, on Account of his being *non Compos Mentis*.—He lived, however, to see the Restoration of King *Charles* II. in Consequence of which Event the Doctor threw up the Living he had held under the Protector, and returned to *Eisley* near *Oxford*, to live on his Archdeaconry, and, it is thought, that had he survived, his Poetry, and the Fame

of

of his Learning and Abilities, gave him so fair a Chance for Preferment, that, notwithstanding his having acted a temporizing Part, which had greatly injured him with the Royalists, it was probable he would soon have been raised to a Bishoprick, or at the least to a very rich Deanery.—But the irresistable Monarch summoned him away from the Village of *Eisley*, on the 2d Day of *Oct.* 1661.—Three Days after which he was interred at the Foot of Bishop *King*'s Monument, under the South Wall of the Isle, joining, on the South Side, to the Choir of *Christ Church* Cathedral, near the Remains of *William Cartwright* and *John Gregory*.

His Writings are very numerous both in the classical and theological Way, but he has only left one dramatic Piece behind him, which is entitled,

ΤΕΧΝΟΓΑΜΙΑ.

Wood relates an Anecdote in Relation to this Play, which has some Humour in it, and therefore may not prove unentertaining to our Readers.—He tells us that this Piece had been publickly acted in *Christ Church* Hall, in the Year 1617, but with no very great Applause.—But that the Wits of those Times, being willing to distinguish themselves before the King, were resolved, with Leave, to act the same Comedy at *Woodstock*.—Permission being obtained, it was accordingly acted, on *Sunday* Evening, *Aug.* 26, 1621.—But, whether it was too grave for his Majesty and too scholastic for the Audience, or whether, as some said, the Actors had taken too much Wine, before they began, in order to remove their Timidity, his Majesty grew so tir'd with the Per-

formance, that, after the first two Acts were over, he several Times made Efforts to be gone.—At length, however, being persuaded by those, who were about him, to have Patience till it was over, lest the young Men should be discouraged by so apparent a Slight shewn to them, he did sit it out, though much against his Will.—On which the following Smart and ingenious Epigram was made by a certain Scholar.

At Christ Church *Marriage, done*
   before the King,
Lest that their Mates should want
   an Offering,
The King himself did offer.—
   What, I pray?
He offer'd *twice or thrice*—to
   go away.

HOPER, Mrs ——This Lady was the Daughter of one Mr. *Harford*, a very eminent Upholsterer and Cabinet-Maker in the City, and married to a Person of the same Avocation in *Cornhill*, to whom she brought no inconsiderable Fortune.—But, tho' Mr. *Hoper*'s Circumstances were, at the first setting out in Life, fully adequate to that Fortune, and that, for some Time, he continued successful in Business, yet a vain Desire, which is no uncommon Frailty among Persons in Trade in this Metropolis, of supporting a Figure somewhat greater than his Rank in Life requir'd, together with a real Decline in the Business itself, in a few Years considerably impair'd his Circumstances.—Yet, even at his Death, they were found not so much shatter'd, but that a little Care and a Continuance of good Fortune might have fully retrieved them.—But, having left behind him only a Wife and one Son,

neither

neither of them experienced in Trade, and the latter even too young to conduct it, the Busincss was now obliged to be carried on by Journeymen only, who, probably taking Advantage of the Ignorance of their Miftrefs, or at leaft not acting with the fame Affiduity for another as they might have done for their own immediate Emolument, fhe foon found herfelf involved in too large a Concern for her to manage, and therefore prudently threw up Bufinefs before it had plunged her into Difficulties beyond her Power of extricating herfelf from.——Having fold off her Stock in Trade, and fettled her Affairs, fhe now confidered of fome Method, whereby fhe might find Means to increafe, rather than diminifh, the little Pittance fhe was at prefent poffeffed of. Being a Woman of a fprightly Imagination and active Mind, the Pen appeared to her no improbable Refource; and dramatic Writing was that to which her Genius found its ftrongeft Bent.——Here, however, fhe had, *Phaeton* like, undertaken too arduous a Tafk for her to perform.——For, though fhe wrote three or four Pieces, none of them were accepted by the Managers, and when, at her own Expence, fhe found Means to have two of them reprefented, one at the little Playhoufe in *Goodman's-Fields* and the other at the little Theatre in the *Haymarket*, the Succefs they met with was a fufficient Vindication of the Manager's Refufal of them.——Their Titles were,

1. EDWARD *the black Prince.* Trag.

2. *Queen Tragedy reflor'd.* Burlefque.

Mrs. *Hoper's* good Underftanding, however, at length, opening

her Eyes to the Difficulties that attended on the Performance of this Plan, fhe retired with her Son, now grown up, to *Enfield* in *Middlefex*, where the latter, who had a literal Education, fet up a School, in which he met with good Succefs; and which, fince his Death, which happened four or five Years ago, has been continued under the Care of our Authorefs.

HOPKINS, *Charles*, Efq;—— This Gentleman was Son of that Right Reverend and eminent Divine, Dr. *Ezekiel Hopkins*, Bifhop of *Londonderry* in *Ireland*, to which Kingdom our Author, who was born in *Devonfhire*, was carried over very young, and received the early Parts of his Education in *Trinity* College, *Dublin*. ——From thence he was fent over to *England*, and compleated his Studies in the Univerfity of *Cambridge*.——On the breaking out of the Wars in *Ireland*, he went thither, and, entering into the Service of King *William*, exerted his early Valour in the Caufe of his Country, its Religion and Liberties.——Thefe Wars being at an End, he returned again to his native Land, where he fell into the Acquaintance and Efteem of fuch Gentlemen, whofe Age and Genius were moft agreeable to his own.

Writers do not mention his having purfued any Profeffion, and, indeed, it is probable, he had an independent Fortune, his Father having attained fo high a Rank in the Church.——*Whincop*, and *Chetwood* after him, informs us, that he died young.——He had certainly a promifing Genius, and his poetical Writings bear ftrong Teftimony, both from the Eafe of the Thoughts, and the Harmony of the Numbers, that their

Author

Author muft have been born a Poet.—In his dramatic Writings his Genius led him to Tragedy; the Pieces he has left behind him being the three following,

1. BOADICEA, *Queen of* BRI-TAIN. Trag.
2. *Friendfhip improv'd.* Trag.
3. PYRRHUS, *King of* EPI-RUS. Trag.

HORDEN, Mr. *Hildebrand*, was the Son of Dr. *Horden*, Minifter of *Twickenham* in *Middlefex.*—He was an Actor as well as an Author.—He flourifhed in the Reign of *William* III. and, being poffeffed of almoft every requifite for Eminence in the dramatic Profeffion, was daily growing into Favour with the Public, when unfortunately, after having been about feven Years upon the Stage, he loft his Life in a frivolous, rafh, accidental Quarrel, which he fell into at the Bar of the *Rofe* Tavern, as he was paffing thro' that Houfe, in order to go to Rehearfal.—On Occafion of his Death one Colonel *Burgefs*, a Gentleman who was Refident at *Venice*, and fome other Perfons of Diftinction, were obliged to take their Trial, but were honourably acquitted, it appearing to have been a mere accidental *Rencontre.*

Among other Perfections, neceffary to his Profeffion, he poffeffed a Perfon fo remarkably handfome, that, after he was killed, feveral Ladies, very well dreffed, came in Mafks, which were then greatly worn, and fome even openly and in their own Coaches, to vifit him in his Shrowd.

The Authors of the dramatic Catalogues have afcribed to him one Play, entitled,

Neglected Virtue. Trag. But it appears, from the Preface,

&c. that it was only put into his Hands by a Friend.

Mr. *Horden* was buried in a Vault in the Parifh Church of St. *Clement's-Danes.*

HOWARD, The Hon. *Edward*, Efq; ——— This Gentleman was much more illuftrious from his Birth and Family, than from the Brilliance of his Genius, being Brother to the Earl of *Berkfhire* and to Sir *Robert Howard*, whom we fhall have Occafion hereafter to mention.—Poetry was his Paffion rather than his Talent, and, tho' he wrote no lefs than four Plays and an Epic Poem, he gained no Reputation by any of them; but, on the contrary, only furnifhed Food for the Wits of that Time, who have treated him very feverely; particularly the Earl of *Rochefter*, in an Invective againft his Comedy of the *Six Day's Adventure*; and the Earl of *Dorfet*, that *beft good Man with the worft-natur'd Mufe*, in a Copy of Verfes addreffed to him on his Poem of the *Britifh Princes.*

Mr. *Howard* lived in King *Charles* II's Reign, but the particular Dates either of his Birth or Death, do not ftand on Record. —The dramatic Pieces he has left behind him are the following:

1. *Man of New-Market.* C.
2. *Six Day's Adventure.* C.
3. *Ufurper.* Trag.
4. *Woman's Conqueft.* T. C.

HOWARD, The Hon. *James*, Efq;—This Gentleman was alfo of the *Berkfhire* Family, and was cotemporary with the laft-mentioned Author.—He wrote two Plays, which were reprefented with Succefs, and held in Efteem in their Time, and likewife altered another, which was frequently acted.—Their Titles are,

1. *All Miftaken.* C.

2. *The*

2. *The* ENGLISH *Monſieur.* C.
3. ROMEO *and* JULIET. T.-
Com. (not printed.)

In Regard to the laſt-mentioned Piece, a more particular Account of it may be ſeen in the firſt Volume of this Work, under it's own Title.

HOWARD, Hon. Sir *Robert,* Knight.—This Gentleman was Brother to the Earl of *Berkſhire,* and to Mr. *Edward Howard* before-mentioned.—His Mother was one of the Daughters and Coheireſſes of *William* Lord *Burghley.*—*Cibber* acquaints us, but on what Authority I know not, that he received his Education under Dr. *Edward Drope,* at *Magdalen* College, *Oxford,* but *Wood* has made no Mention at all of him. He was no leſs ſteadily attached, then the reſt of his Family, to the Intereſts of that unhappy Monarch King *Charles* I and, with the reſt of them, ſuffer'd conſiderably in the maintaining his Loyalty to that Cauſe.—He had, however, the Honour of Knighthood beſtowed on him for his gallant Behaviour in reſcuing the Lord *Wilmot,* Lieutenant-General of the King's Forces, who was wounded and taken Priſoner at *Cropley - Bridge* Fight, on the 29th of *June* 1644.—At the Reſtoration he was choſen one of the Burgeſſes for *Stockbridge* in *Hampſhire,* to ſerve in the Parliament which began at *Weſtminſter* on the 8th of *May* 1661. and, on the 19th of *June* 1678, was promoted to the Place of Auditor of the *Exchequer,* at that Time worth ſeveral Thouſand Pounds *per Ann.* But this Preferment was generally conſider'd as a Reward for the Services he had done the Crown in aſſiſting to cajole the Parliament out of Money.— In 1679 he was elected Member for *Caſtle-Riſing,* in *Norfolk,* for which Place, after the Reſtoration was effected, we find him ſitting as Repreſentative in the firſt Parliament under King *William* III. and, about the 16th of *Feb.* 1688, he was admitted to the Privy - Council, took the Oaths, and became a very rigid Proſecutor of the Nonjurors, diſclaiming all Kind of Converſation or Intercourſe with any of that Character.—The Incidents of his Life are not very numerous, or at leaſt not recorded ; nor can I trace, with any Degree of Preciſion, the Time of either his Birth or Death ; yet, it is pretty apparent, he lived to a very advanced Age, and, in the Year 1692, at which Time he can ſcarcely be ſuppoſed much leſs than ſeventy Years of Age, he married Mrs. *Dives,* who was one of the Maids of Honour to Queen *Mary.*

With Reſpect to Sir *Robert Howard's* Abilities, they appear to have occaſioned Debates among the Writers. —— *Langbaine, Jacob* and *Gildon* ſpeaking in very warm Terms in his Commendation, while *Cibber,* on the contrary, will allow him no higher Claim to Notice in the Republic of Letters, than that of being Brother-in-Law to *Dryden.* —It is true, indeed, that ſome of his Cotemporary Writers, and thoſe of Eminence too, among whom were Mr. *Dryden* himſelf, Mr. *Shadwell,* and the Duke of *Buckingham,* have pretty rigidly handled him and his Works ; but, as it is generally acknowledged that Sir *Robert* was a Man of a very obſtinate and poſitive Temper, ſupercilious, haughty, and over-bearing to the greateſt Degree in his Behaviour to others, and poſſeſſed of an inſufferable

Share

Share of Vanity and Self-Sufficiency in Regard to his own Abilities. It is not improbable that these Qualities might create him an Enmity among his Cotemporary Wits, who would perhaps have readily subscribed to the Merits he really possessed, had he not seemed to aim at a Superiority which he had no Claim to; in Consequence of which *Dryden* wrote a severe Criticism on his *Duke* of *Lerma, Shadwell* pointed him out under the Character of Sir *Positive Atall*, in his Comedy called the *Impertinents*, and the Duke of *Buckingham* intended, and had even made him, the Hero of his *Rehearsal*, under the Name of *Bilboa*, altho', after the Play had been stopped from Representation by the Plague in 1665, that Nobleman alter'd his Plan, and pointed the Artillery of his Satire against a much greater Name, in the Character of *Bayes*, retaining only some few Strokes against Sir *Robert*, in Parodies on certain Passages in his Plays.—Yet, notwithstanding all this Virulence against him, I cannot look on him as an Author devoid of Genius, since two of his Plays, *viz.* the *Indian Queen* and the *Committee*, continued for a long Time Favorites with the Public, and the latter, even to this Day, where even the Species of Character, against which the Satire of it is principally aimed, *viz.* the Roundheads and puritanical Zealots is totally abolished and forgotten among us, is still frequently performed, and never makes it's Appearance without giving Satisfaction to the Audience, and producing all the Effects which the true *Vis comica* ever has on the Mind.—A certain Sign that the Piece must possess some, if not a

capital Share of Merit. ——His List of dramatic Pieces is confined to six in Number, *viz.*

1. *Blind Lady.* C.
2. *Committee.* C.
3. *Great Favourite.* T. C.
4. Indian *Queen.* T.
5. *Surprizal.* T. C.
6. *Vestal Virgin.* T.

Howell, *James*, Esq;—This Gentleman was born about the latter End of *June* or Beginning of *July* 1594, at *Abermarlis* in *Caermarthenshire, South-Wales*; of which Place his Father, at that Time, was Minister.—He received the first Part of his Education and Grammar-Learning at the Free-School of *Hereford*, from whence, before he was quite sixteen Years of Age, he was sent to *Jesus* College in *Oxford.*—Here he finished his Academical Studies, and took the Degree of Master of Arts.—On his quitting the University, he acquired the Esteem and Friendship of Sir *Robert Mansel*, by whose Means, together with some small Assistances from his Father, he was enabled, in the Year 1618, to go abroad, where he continued three Years on his Travels thro' *France, Italy* and the *Low-Countries*, by which he made himself perfectly Master of the living Languages, and every other Branch of useful Knowledge; and, so great was the Reputation of his Abilities, that, soon after his Return, he was made Choice of by King *James* I. to be sent on a Negotiation to the Court of *Madrid*, for the Recovery of the *Spanish Monarch*, a very rich *English* Ship, which had been seized by the Vice-Roy of *Sardinia*, for his Master's Use, under Pretence of prohibited Goods having been found in it.

During

During his Abfence he was e-lected, in 1623, Fellow of *Jefus* College, and, being in Favour with *Emanuel*, Lord *Scroop*, Lord Prefident of the North, was by him appointed his Secretary, on his Return.—This Poft calling him to refide at *York*, he formed fuch an Intereft in that County, as to procure his being elected Burgefs for the Corporation of *Richmond*, by the Suffrages of the Mayor and Aldermen of that Corporation, to fit in the Parliament, which began at *Weftminfter* in 1627; and, in the Year 1631, was made Secretary to *Robert* Earl of *Leicefter*, who was appointed Ambaffador Extraordinary at the Court of *Copenhagen*, on a Commiffion of Condolement on the Death of King *Charles* I's Grandmother, *Sophia*, Queen-Dowager of *Denmark*; on which Occafion Mr. *Howell* very eminently diftinguifhed himfelf, by feveral Speeches delivered in *Latin* before the King of *Denmark*, fetting forth the Occafion of the Embaffy.

On his Return to *England*, he was put into many beneficial Employments, and, about the Beginning of the Civil War, was appointed, by King *Charles* I. one of the Clerks of the Privy Council.—But, altho' thefe Pofts were equally lucrative and honourable, he does not feem to have been Mafter of much Oeconomy, for when, in the Year 1643, he was feized by the Committee of Parliament, and fent to the *Fleet* Prifon, where, by the Courfe of his Letters, it is evident he continued till after the Death of the King, we find he was obliged to have Recourfe to his Pen for a Subfiftence, which at that Time, before the Trade of Authorfhip had been fo hackney'd,

as of late Years it has been, was no defpicable Employment; and *Wood* tells us that it brought him in a very comfortable Subfiftance.

This long and difagreeable Confinement, together with the Narrownefs of his Circumftances, and the laborious Manner in which he was compelled to provide for himfelf, feemed to have fhaken the Firmnefs of Mr. *Howell*'s political Attachments; for, during the Rebellion, we find him temporizing with the prevailing Party, and inclinable to enter into their Meafures; for which Reafon, tho' they feem not to have accepted of his Services, yet, at the Reftoration, he was not reinftated in his Place of Clerk of the Council, but only appointed the King's Hiftoriographer, being the firft in *England* who ever bore that Title.—But this being a Place of no great Emolument, he was obliged to continue his Trade of Writing, to the laft.—He lived to an advanced Age, and died in the Beginning of *November* 1666, being then in his 73d Year.

As he was almoft one of the firft among our *Englifh* Authors, who introduced Writing for a Livelihood, fo is he likewife one among the moft voluminous of thofe who have applied the Advantages of Literature to that Purpofe, having written and tranflated no lefs than forty-nine feveral Books, exclufive of one dramatic Piece, which he wrote while he was at *Paris*, and which was prefented there at Court no lefs than fix Times, by the King and Grandees in Perfon, entitled, *Nuptials of* PELEUS *and* THETIS. Com. and Mafque.

Mr. *Howell* was, undoubtedly, a Man of moft extenfive Know-

ledge,

ledge, a moft perfect Linguift, and very well verfed in Modern Hiftory, more efpecially thofe of the Countries through which he had travelled.——His Letters are extremely entertaining, and convey Anecdotes and Obfervations that might by no other Means have been handed down to us, and fpeak their Author to have been no bad Politician.—And as to Poetry, tho' he has been little more than a Dabbler in it, yet he has a confiderable Share of Fancy, and his Numbers are fmother and more harmonious than thofe of moft of the Writers of that Time.—He lies buried on the North-Side of the *Temple* Church, with the following Infcription over him, probably written by himfelf in his Life-Time.

Jacobus Howell. *Cambro-Britannus, Regius Hiftoriographus (in Anglia primus); qui, poft varias perigrinationes, tandem Naturæ Curfum peregit; fatur Annorum & Famæ, Domi, forifque huc ufque erraticus; hic fixus.* 1666.

HIPPESLEY, Mr. *John*, was much more noted as an Actor than as an Author.——In the former of thefe Characters his Genius was very great, and, without Affiftance, would have render'd him famous from his great Judgment and comic Execution.——But accidental Defects, in fome particular Circumftances, have been known to turn out to the Advantage of thofe who have met with them, and fo it peculiarly happened to Mr. *Hippefley*; for a Burn or Scald in his Face, which he by Chance had undergone the Pain of in his younger Days, had implanted fomewhat fo Caricature and truly rifible in his Countenance, that it was almoft impoffible to look

at him with any Steadinefs of Mufcles; and it had, moreover, fo far affected his Voice, as to render it peculiarly happy for the Caft of Parts he ufually performed, which, in the general, was that of the feeble Old Man in Comedy.——He, however, ftill lives fo perfectly in the Memory of moft of the Frequenters of the Theatres, that it is needlefs to fay any more of him in that Capacity, than barely to hint, to thofe who never did fee him, that the Idea neareft to Truth, that they can poffibly form to themfelves of his Performance, will be attained by an Attention to Mr. *Shuter* in his Juftice *Clack*, in the *Jovial Crew*, and other Parts of the fame Nature.

Mr. *Hippefley* died at *Briftol* in the Summer of 1748, to which Place it had been his Cuftom for feveral Years to go, every Summer, as Manager of a Company of Comedians, felected from the Theatres in *London*.—He wrote one dramatic Piece, entitled,

A Journey to BRISTOL. Farce. Mr. *Hippefley* left two Daughters behind him, one of whom is the prefent Mrs. *Green*, a comic Actrefs of confiderable Merit, belonging to the Theatre in *Covent-Garden*, and the other, ftill unmarried, is a Performer in *Drury Lane* Theatre.

HUGHES, Mr. *John*.—This amiable Man, and elegant Author, was the Son of a Citizen of *London*, and was born at *Marlborough* in *Wiltfhire*, on the 29th of *Jan.* 1677, but received the Rudiments of his Education in private Schools at *London*.—Even in the very earlieft Parts of Life his Genius feem'd to fhew itfelf equally inclined to each of the three Sifter Arts, Mufic, Poetry and Defign, in all which he made
a very

a very confiderable Progrefs. To his Excellence in thefe Qualifications his Cotemporary and Friend, Sir *Richard Steele*, bears the following extraordinary Teftimonial. "He may" (fays that Author) "be the Emulation of " more Perfons of different Ta- " lents than any one I have ever " known.—His Head, Hands, or " Heart were always employed in " fomething worthy Imitation. " His Pencil, his Bow, or his " Pen, each of which he ufed in " a Mafterly Manner, were al- " ways directed to raife and en- " tertain his own Mind, or that " of others, to a more chearful " Profecution of what is noble " and virtuous."——Such is the Evidence borne to his Talents by a Writer of the firft Rank; yet, he feems, for the moft Part, to have purfued thefe and other polite Studies, little farther than by the Way of agreeable Amufements, under frequent Confinement, occafioned by Indifpofition and a valetudinarian State of Health.

Mr. *Hughes* had, for fome Time, an Employment in the Office of Ordnance, and was Secretary to two or three Commiffioners under the Great-Seal for the Purchafe of Lands, in Order to the better ferving the Docks and Harbours at *Portfmouth*, *Chatham* and *Harwich*.

In the Year 1717 the Lord Chancellor *Cowper*, to whom our Author had not long been known, thought proper, without any previous Solicitation, to nominate him his Secretary for the Commiffions of the Peace, and to diftinguifh him with fingular Marks of his Favour and Affection; and, upon his Lordfhip's laying down the great Seal, he was, at the

particular Recommendation of this his Patron, and with the ready Concurrence of his Succeffor, the Earl of *Macclesfield*, continued in the fame Employment, which he held till the Time of his Deceafe, the 17th of *Feb.* 1719, being the very Night on which his celebrated Tragedy of the *Siege of Damafcus* made its firft Appearance on the Stage; when, after a Life moftly fpent in Pain and Sicknefs, he was carried off by a Confumption, having but barely compleated his 42d Year, and at a Period in which he had juft arrived at an agreeable Competence, and was advancing, with rapid Steps, towards the Pinnacle of Fame and Fortune.—He was privately buried in the Vault under the Chancel of St. *Andrew*'s Church in *Holbourn*.

As a Man, the worthy Mention made of him by Numbers of his Cotemporary Writers, are fufficient to give us the moft exalted Idea of his Virtues; and, as a Writer, no ftronger Proof can be offer'd of the Efteem he was held in by the trueft Judges of Poetry, than to mention that the great Mr. *Addifon*, after having fuffer'd the four firft Acts of his Tragedy to lie by him for feveral Years, without putting the finifhing Hand to the Piece, at length fix'd on Mr. *Hughes*, whom he earneftly perfuaded to undertake the Tafk, as the only Perfon capable of it, to add a fifth Act to it.—And though that Author afterwards thought proper to undertake it himfelf, yet it was by no Means from any Diffidence of this Gentleman's Abilities, but from the juft Reflection that no one could have fo perfect a Notion of his
Defign

Defign as himfelf, who had been fo long and fo carefully thinking of it.

Our Author's Poetical Works are numerous, but it is not our Bufinefs in this Place to take Notice of any but his dramatic Writings, which are as follows,

1. AMALASONT, *Queen of the* GOTHS. Trag.

2. APOLLO *and* DAPHNE. Mafque.

3. CALYPSO *and* TELEMACHUS. Opera.

4. CUPID *and* HYMEN. Mafque.

5. *Mifanthrope.* Com. from *Moliere.* (Printed with Ozell's Tranfiation of that Author.)

6. *Mifer.* Com. from *Moliere.* (1ft Act only.)

7. ORESTES. Trag. from *Euripides.* (Act I. Sce. II. only.)

8. *Siege of* DAMASCUS. Trag.

HUME, or HOME, The Rev. Mr. *John.*—This Gentleman is a Native of *Scotland*, and, I believe, related to *David Hume* the Hiftorian, whofe Worth, did the Nature of this Work admit us to introduce any Writers into it but thofe who have had fome Connection with the Theatre, it would be Injuftice not to enlarge upon.—Our Author was bred to the Miniftry in the Kirk of *Scotland.*—But, notwithftanding the Rigour of that Church, finding in his natural Genius a Bent to Poetry, and not conceiving that Tragedy, in which the Principles of Virtue, of Morality, of Filial Duty, of Patriotic Zeal, and of Reverence for an over-ruling Power, could be inconfiftent with the Profeffion of a Religion, in which all thefe are in the ftrongeft Manner inculcated and en-

joined, he formed a dramatic Piece, and prefenting it to the Managers of the Theatre at *Edinburgh*, at that Time in a more flourifhing Condition than it had been for many Years before, and vying, in every Refpect, as far as Circumftances would permit, with thofe of this Metropolis, they faw its Merit, readily accepted it, put it into a Rehearfal, and prepared for the Performance of it in fuch a Manner as might do Honour to the Author, and bring both Credit and Emolument to themfelves.——Thefe Tranfactions, however, coming to the Knowledge of the Elders of the Kirk, they, in their great Zeal, firft remonftrated with the Author on the *heinous Crime* he was committing; but he, not quite fo perfectly convinced as they would have had him, of the Iniquity of the Act itfelf, unconfcious of any ill Intention, and pretty thoroughly perfuaded that his Play would meet with a Succefs, from which he fhould reap both Fame and Profit, was not willing at once to defift, nor with his own Hands to pull down a Fabrick he had, at the Expence of much Time and Labour, been rearing.—They now endeavoured to terrify the Performers from reprefenting it, but with no better Succefs.—— Author and Actors were both equally incorrigible; the Piece was brought on, and met with that Encouragement which its Merit very juftly entitled it to.——What remained then for thefe incenfed Elders to do, but in a public Convocation to expel and for ever difqualify for the Miniftry, not only this difobedient Son, but even others, his Friends, who were wicked enough either to

keep

keep him Company, or go to fee his Piece performed, and by various Pamphlets, Advertisements, &c. to thunder their *Anathemas* against those Implements of *Satan* the Actors, who had thus led aside, or at least abetted in his wandering, this lost Sheep of the Flock.—However, as Persecution most commonly defeats its own Purposes, so did it happen in this Case, for the ill Treatment which Mr. *Hume* had met with in his own Country, procured him a most valuable Protection in an adjacent one.—Being known to the Earl of *Bute*. and that Nobleman representing the Circumstances of this unreasonable Oppression, exercised on a Man of Genius, to our present most gracious Sovereign, then Prince of *Wales*, his Royal Highness, who even at that Time gave the strongest Assurances of that Inclination to, and Zeal for, the Polite Arts, which have since shone so conspicuously a Part of his Character, stretch'd out his princely and protecting Hand to the Author of *Douglas*, and, by settling a very handsome Pension on him, and sheltering him under the Shade of his own Patronage, put it out of the Power of either the Thunderbolts of Bigotry or the Flashes of Envy or Malevolence to blast his Laurels.—Mr. *Hume* has since pursued his poetical Talents, and produced two more dramatic Pieces, both of which have been brought on the Stage in this City, but, whether thro' an Eagerness to prove still farther his Inclination to deserve the Favour he has met with, he has not allowed himself a sufficient Time for the planning, digesting, reconsidering and correct-

ing his Works, or that in his first Play the Diffidence of a young Author might make him more ready to ask and to pursue the Judgment of others, or from any other Cause I know not, but *Douglas* seems still to stand as Mr. *Hume*'s Master-Piece in dramatic Writing.—His three Plays, which are all Tragedies, are entitled as follows,

1. Douglas. Trag.
2. Agis. Trag.
3. *Siege of* Aquileia. Tr.

HUNT, Mr. *William*.—This Gentleman, *Whincop* tells us, was a Collector of Excise, and wrote one Play, which was never acted, but was printed at *York*, (tho' we are not told when) entitled,

The *Fall of* Tarquin. Tr. The same Author informs us that it is a most wretched Piece, and, as a Specimen of it's Merit, quotes us the following very extraordinary Line,

And the tall Trees stood Circling *in a* Row.

HUNTER, Governor.——Of this Gentleman we know nothing farther than his being mentioned by *Coxeter*, who says that, in a Copy which he had seen of the under-named Piece, there was a MS. which declared him to be the Author of it, *viz.*

Androboros. Farce.

HURST, Captain.—This Gentleman I know nothing of, only find his Name mentioned by the Compiler of *Whincop*'s List, and by *Chetwood* in his *British Theatre*, as the Author of one Play, which was acted with no very great Success, entitled,

The Roman *Maid*. Trag.

J. B.

J.

J. B.—By thefe Initials we find a Piece diftinguifhed, which bears the Title of

The *Bafhful Lovers*. T. C.

J. G. or JACOB, *Giles*. —— By thefe Initials Mr. *Jacob* has thought proper to diftinguifh himfelf in his *Poetical Regifter*, or *Lives and Charaɛters of the* Englifh *Dramatic Poets*, 8vo. 1719. p. 318. —And, as no Writer has given us any Account of him but himfelf, I cannot pretend to offer to my Readers any Thing fo fatisfaɛtory concerning him as the Repetition of his own Words.

He is, (fays he, fpeaking in the third Perfon) the Son of a confiderable Malfter of *Romfey*, in the County of *SoutLampton*, at which Place he was born Anno 1686.—His Mother is of the Family of the *Thornburgh*'s in *Wilts*, one of whom was Bifhop of *Worcefter*, in the Reign of K. *Cha.* I. and two of them attended the Royal Exile.—He was bred to the Law under a very eminent Attorney; and has fince been Steward and Secretary to the Honourable *William Blathwayt*, Efq; a celebrated Courtier in the Reign of King *William*, and who enjoyed great Preferments in the State in the late and prefent Reign.

He was Author of two dramatic Pieces, *viz.*

1. *Love in a Wood*. Farce.
2. *Soldier's laft Stake*. C.

For the fiift of thefe, which, however, was never aɛted, he apologized that it was written in three or four Days, and before the Author was any Ways acquainted with the Stage, or poetical Writings; and as to the latter, he only informs us that he had fuch a Piece prepared for the Stage.

Mr. *Jacob* followed the Profeffion of the Law, and wrote feveral Books in that Science, fome of which are ftill held in Efteem, particularly his *Law Diɛionary*, and indeed Works of Compilement feem to have fuited his Talent rather than thofe of Genius; for it muft be confeffed that his *Poetical Regifter*, notwithftanding fome few Errors in it, is by much the beft Book of the Kind hitherto extant; and yet fo little Merit had his own dramatic Pieces, that, according to *Whincop*, Dr. *Sewel*, who was by no Means remarkable for Ill-Nature, on reading his Farce called *Love in a Wood*, wrote the following very fevere Lines in the Title Page.

Parent of Darknefs ! genuine Son
 of Night ;
Total Eclipfe, without one Ray of
 Light :
Born when dull Midnight Bells
 for Funerals chime,
Juft at the clofing of the Bellman's
 Rhime.

At what Time Mr. *Jacob* quitted the Stage of Life, I have not been able to trace; but as by his own Account he was no more than thirty-three Years of Age at the Publication of his *Poetical Regifter* in 1719. it is probable he might furvive that Publication feveral Years.

JACOB, *Hildebrand*, Efq;—— This Author was a Gentleman of Family and Fortune, and gained confiderable Reputation by a poetical Tale, called the *Curious Maid*, and fome other humourous Poems.—He alfo wrote the following dramatic Pieces:

1. *Fatal*

1. *Fatal Conflancy.* T.
2. *Neft of Plays,* confifting of three fhort Comedies, entitled,

The *Prodigal Reform'd,*
The *Happy Conflancy,* and
The *Tryal of Conjugal Love.*

JEFFERIES, Mr.——Of this Gentleman I find no farther Mention made by any of the Writers than that he enjoyed fome Poft in the *Cuftom-Houfe,* and that he was Author of one dramatic Piece, which met with very little Succefs, entitled,

EDWIN. T.

JEVON, Mr. *Thomas.*—— This Author flourifhed in the Reigns of K. *Charles* II. and K. *James* II. —He was an Actor and a Dancing Mafter, and attained great Eminence in both thofe Profeffions, efpecially in the former, in which his general Caft was that of low Comedy.—He did not however, long enjoy that Sunfhine of popular Applaufe, which was darting in full Luftre upon him, for he was taken off in the very Prime of Life, *viz.* at the Age of 36 Years, on the 20th of *December* 1688, and was interred in *Hampftead* Church Yard.

He wrote one dramatic Piece, which even in its original Form met with Succefs, but has fince undergone almoft as many Tranf-formations as the *Banjans* of the *Eaft-Indies* fable their Deity *Wift-non* to have paffed thro'—It was originally entitled,

The *Devil of a Wife.* Farce.
Vid. APPENDIX.

INGELAND, Mr. *Thomas.* —— This Gentleman is one of our oldeft dramatic Writers, having been a Student in the Univerfity of *Cambridge* in the Reign of Queen *Elizabeth.*—He wrote one dramatic Piece, which he himfelf

ftiles a *prettie and merrie Interlude.*—It is entitled,

The *Difobedient Child.* Interl.

JOHNSON, Mr. *Charles,* was originally bred to the Law, but being a great Admirer of the Mufes, and finding in himfelf a ftrong Propenfity to dramatic Writing, he quitted the ftudious Labour of the one, for the more fpirited Amufements of the other ; and, by contracting an Intimacy with Mr. *Wilks,* found Means, thro' that Gentleman's Intereft, to get his Plays on the Stage without much Difficulty.—Some of them met with very good Succefs, and by being a conftant Frequenter of thofe grand Rendezvouz of the Wits of that Time, *Will's* and *Button's* Coffeehoufes, he, by a polite and inoffenfive Behaviour, formed fo extenfive an Acquaintance and Intimacy, as conftantly enfured him great Emoluments on his Benefit Night, by which Means, being a Man of Oeconomy, he was enabled to fubfift very genteely.— He at length married a young Widow, with a tolerable Fortune, on which he fet up a Tavern in *Bow - Street, Covent-Garden,* but quitted Bufinefs at his Wife's Death, and lived privately on an eafy Competence which he had faved.—What Time he was born I know not, but he flourifhed during the Reigns of Queen *Anne,* K. *George* I. and Part of *Geo.* II. His firft Play was acted in 1702, and his lateft is dated in 1732, but *Cibber* informs us that he did not die till about 1744.——As a dramatic Writer, he is far from deferving to be placed amongft the loweft Clafs ; for tho' his Plots are feldom original, yet he has given them fo many Additions of his own, and has cloathed the

Defigns

Defigns of others in fo pleafing
a Drefs, that a great Share of
the Merit they poffefs ought
to be attributed to him.——
The Language of his Comedies,
which are greatly fuperior to his
Trajedies, is eafy, and the Dialogue natural and fprightly; and
two of them, *viz.* the *Wife's Relief* and the *Country Laffes*, ftill
continue on the Lift of acting
Plays.

'Tho' I have obferved before,
that he was a Man of a very inoffenfive Behaviour, yet he could
not efcape the Satire of Mr. *Pope*,
who, too ready to refent even any
fuppos'd Offence, has, on fome
trivial Pique, immortalized him
in the *Dunciad*, and in one of the
Notes to that Poem has quoted
from another Piece, called *The
Characters of the Times*, the following Account of our Author.

" *Charles Johnfon*, famous for
" writing a Play every Year, and
" for being at *Button*'s every Day.
" He had probably thriven better
" in his Vocation had he been a
" fmall Matter leaner; he may
" be juftly called a Martyr to
" Obefity, and be faid to have
" fallen a Victim to the Rotun-
" dity of his Parts."

I do not repeat this Quotation
by any Means with a View to reflect on Mr. *Johnfon*, but think
on the contrary, that it fhould
rather turn to his Honour, fince
that Man's Character muft be extremely unexceptionable, on whom
his Enemies can fix no greater
Imputation than the Defects of
his Perfon; but rather to point
out how low Refentment may
fometimes plunge even the moft
brilliant Geniufes, when it can
lead them to encourage Scurrility
without Wit, and mere perfonal
Reflection without even the Sha-
dow of Humour.

The dramatic Pieces this Author produced, notwithftanding
that he appears to have quitted
writing for the Stage for fome
Years before his Death, are very
numerous, and will be feen in the
following Lift.

1. *Cobler of* PRESTON. Farce.
2. CELIA. Trag.
3. *Country Laffes.* Com.
4. EPHESIAN *Matron.* F.
5. *Force of Friendfhip.* Trag.
6. *Fortune in her Wits.* Com.
7. *Generous Hufband.* Com.
8. *Gentleman Cully.* Com. (afcribed to him by *Coxeter*
   only.)
9. *Love and Liberty.* Trag.
10. *Love in a Cheft.* Farce.
11. *Love in a Foreft.* Com.
12. *Mafquerade.* Com.
13. MEDEA. Trag.
14. *Succefsful Pirate.* Tr.-Com.
15. *Sultanefs.* Trag.
16. *Victim.* Trag.
17. *Village Opera.*
18. *Wife's Relief.* Com.

JOHNSON, Mr. *Samuel*, M. A.
—This excellent Writer, who
is no lefs the Glory of the prefent Age and Nation, than he
will be the Admiration of all
fucceeding ones, received his E-
ducation and took his Degrees at
the Univerfity of *Oxford*, after
quitting which Place I have been
informed he for fome Time was
Mafter of a private Academy at
Litchfield.——A Genius like his,
however, could not long content
itfelf with that moft difagreeable
of all Drudgery, the mere claffical
Inftruction of Youth, nor fuffer
its Brightnefs to be conceal'd in
the dull Obfcurity of a Country
Academy.—He came up therefore
to *London*, where he immediately
gave Proofs how high a Rank in
the World of Letters he deferved
to hold. —— Having conceived
the Defign of one of the nobleft

and moſt uſeful, tho' at the ſame Time the moſt laborious Works that could be poſſibly undertaken, *viz.* A compleat *Grammar* and *Dictionary* of our hitherto unſettled Language ; he drew up a Plan of the ſaid Deſign, in a Letter to the Right Honourable the Earl of *Cheſterfield,* which being publiſhed, gave the ſtrongeſt Proof, in its own Compoſition, how great a Degree of grammatical Perfection and claſſical Elegance the *Engliſh* Tongue was capable of being brought to.——The Execution of this Plan coſt him the Labour of many Years ; but the Manner in which it was at laſt executed made ample Amends for all the Expectations of the Public in Regard to it for ſo long a Time ; and the Honours paid him on the Occaſion of its Publication by ſeveral of the foreign Academies, particularly by the *Academia della Cruſca,* leave all Encomium on the Work in this Place entirely unneceſſary.——During ſome Intervals of Receſs neceſſary to the Fatigue of this ſtupendous Undertaking, Mr. *Johnſon* publiſhed many other Pieces which are moſt truly capital in their Kind ; among which the *Rambler,* a Series of periodical Eſſays which came out twice a Week for two Years ſucceſſively, ſtood in the foremoſt Rank.——In the Courſe of ſo great a Number of theſe Papers as this long Period demanded, the Number which the Undertaker of them was favoured with by others, was inconſiderable; and yet, on the whole, the Product of this ſingle Genius, thus perpetually employed, proved at leaſt equal, if not ſuperior, to that of the Club of firſt-rate Wits, who were concerned in thoſe celebrated Works the *Spectator* and *Tatler.* —— Mr.

Johnſon's Stile in Proſe is nervous and claſſically correct; in Verſe his Numbers are harmonious and muſical, yet bold and poignant, and on the whole approach nearer to Mr. *Pope's* Manner of Verſification than that of any other Writer ; and tho' he has favoured the World with but little in *abſolute Verſe* (for all his *Proſe* is *Poetry)* yet that little, like Diamonds of the firſt Water, will ever be held in the higheſt Eſtimation, whilſt Gems of larger Bulk, with leſs intrinſic Worth, are ſcarcely look'd upon.——In ſhort, while the Name of *Juvenal* ſhall be remember'd, this Gentleman's improved Imitations of him, in his two Poems, entitled *London,* and *The Vanity of Human Wiſhes,* muſt be read with Delight.——His Imagination is amazingly extenſive, and his Knowledge of Men and Manners unbounded, as may be plainly traced in his *Eaſtern* Stories in the *Rambler,* in which he has not only ſupported to the utmoſt the Sublimity of the *Eaſtern* Manner of Expreſſion, but even greatly excelled any of the Oriental Writers in the Fertility of his Invention, the Conduct of his Plots, and the Juſtice and Strength of his Sentiments. —— His capital Work of that Kind, however, is a Novel entitled *Raſſelas* Prince of *Abyſſinia,* too well known and univerſally read to need any Comment here, and in which, as he does at preſent, ſo he probably ever will, ſtand without an equal.

Our Author has wrote only one dramatic Piece, the Succeſs of which was not equal to its Merit, owing entirely to his having too ſtrictly adhered to the *Ariſtotelian* Rules of the Drama to render his Piece agreeable to the Taſte of our preſent theatrical Audiences,

who

who look for little more than Plot and Incident, without paying any great Regard either to Character, Language, or Sentiment; it was performed at *Drury-Lane* Theatre, and entitled,

IRENE. Trag.

It would, however, be the highest Injustice, after bestowing these undeniable Encomiums on his Genius, were I not to observe, that nothing *but* that Genius can possibly exceed the Extent of his Erudition, and it would be adding a greater Injury to his still more valuable Qualities, were we to stop here, since, together with the *ablest Head*, he seems possessed of the very *best Heart* at present existing.——Every Line, every Sentiment, that issues from his Pen, tends to the great Centre of all his Views, the Promotion of Virtue, Religion and Humanity; nor are his Actions less pointed towards the same great End.——Benevolence, Charity and Piety are the most striking Features in his Character, and while his Writings point out to us what a good Man *ought to be*, his own Conduct sets us an Example of what he *is*.

JOHNSON, Mr. *Samuel*.——This Gentleman, tho' Namesake to the last-mentioned Author, must not be confounded with him.——He is the Author of the three following dramatic Pieces, all of which, at the Time of their first Appearance, greatly attracted the Notice of the Public, *viz.*

1. *All alive and merry.*
2. *Cheshire Comics.*
3. *Hurlothrumbo.*

All these Pieces were represented at the Theatre in the *Haymarket*; but the last, in particular, took an amazing Run, owing to the whimsical Madness and Extravagance which ran thro' the whole Piece and its Author, who him-

self presented a principal Character in it called Lord *Flame*, into which he had thrown such a Mixture of fine Thoughts and unintelligible Fustian that no one could possibly understand what he was aiming at; and if at any Time this Unintelligibleness was objected to him as a Fault in his Piece, his constant Reply was, that the Fault did not lie in that, but in the Audience, who did not take the proper Method for attaining a Knowledge of his Meaning; that no one could possibly understand our Author perfectly unless they examined his Works in the same Situation and State of Mind, as they were written; and therefore, as he himself never sate down to write without a Fiddle in his Hand, it was impossible for any one to comprehend the Sense of what he wrote, without an Instrument of the very same Kind to quicken their Understandings. —But, in Order in some Measure to remedy this Deficiency in the Audience, he used to act his Part of Lord *Flame* in a Manner equally extravagant with the rest of the Affair, *viz.* with a Violin in his Hand, which he occasionally played upon, and sometimes walking in high Stilts.

Mr. *Johnson* is a Native of *Cheshire*, and was bred to and followed the Profession of a Dancing Master, yet, from what has been above related, it is apparent he must have been infected with a strong Tincture of Insanity, in Consequence of which, it is probable, that not many Persons would be willing to entrust their Children in his Hands; yet, as his Madness did not take any dangerous or mischievous Turn; and, as it was accompanied with Flights of Wit and Humour that render'd him, tho' an extraordinary, yet far from

a disa difagreeable Companion, his Acquaintance has been fought by moft of the Gentlemen of Fortune in that Country, at whofe Houfes he ufed to refide alternately for a confiderable Time, in fuch Manner as to render the Purfuit of Bufinefs unneceffary to him.—He is ftill living, and continues the fame Kind of Life and Humour, but has quitted writing for the Stage, as that original Oddity which, like *Triftram Shandy*, the World run mad in Admiration of, only becaufe they did not underftand it, at length grew tirefome, and like that became as univerfally decried, as at firft it had been univerfally followed. — The following humourous Anecdote, which was related to me by a Gentleman who left *Chefhire* not long fince, may ferve to give the Reader fome Idea of Mr. *Johnfon's* general Turn, and unconcerned Manner.—Some little Time ago our Author having been invited to pafs fome Months at the Country Houfe of a Gentleman who had a great Regard for him, but whom he had never vifited before ; he accepted the Invitation, and was for fome Time treated with the utmoft Hofpitality and Kindnefs. —But at length, having fhewn in fome of his Expreffions and Actions that wild and unaccountable Extravagance and Oddity which runs thro' his Compofition, the Lady of the Houfe, who happened to enjoy but a very indifferent State of Health, which rendered her hippifh and low-fpirited, and being moreover naturally of a timorous Difpofition, began to be extremely alarmed at his Behaviour, and apprehenfive that at fome Time or other he might do Mifchief either to himfelf or others.—On this fhe repeatedly remonftrated to her Hufband, in-

treating him to find fome Means of getting rid of Mr. *Johnfon.*— The Gentleman, however, who was better acquainted with *Johnfon's* Manner, and therefore under no fuch Apprehenfions, was unwilling to proceed to an Act of fo much feeming Inhofpitality, as the forbidding his Houfe to a Perfon whom he had himfelf invited to it, and therefore declined fo doing for fome Time ; till at length, on the continued Solicitations of his Lady, whom he found he could not make eafy on any other Terms, he commiffioned a mutual Friend to both, to break the Affair to Mr. *Johnfon.* —This being done with all the Tendernefs imaginable, and the true Reafon affign'd by Way of Vindication of the Gentleman himfelf, Mr. *Johnfon*, with great Coolnefs, and a Gaiety of Temper peculiar to himfelf, replied, *That he was moft perfectly perfuaded of Mr. ——'s Regard for him, and fhould ever retain the moft grateful Senfe of the Civilities he had received from him; that he alfo maintained the higheft Refpect for his Lady ; and thought it his Duty, by every Means in his Power, to contribute to the Reftoration of her Peace of Mind, which it appears that he had been the innocent Caufe of difturbing ; that he, therefore, might give her the ftrongeft Affurances from him, together with his Compliments, that he never would again trouble her Houfe whilft living, but, as a Teftimonial of his fincere Efteem, fhe might depend on it that, after his Death, he fhould confider her as the very firft Perfon to whom, on a Vifit back to this World, he fhould think himfelf under an Obligation to pay his Refpects.*—This Meffage being delivered to the Lady, who we have before obferved was of an *Hypochondriac* Complexion, threw her

her into still greater Apprehen-
sions than before; and, fearing
that he would be as good as his
Word, intreated the Gentleman
to go back to Mr. *Johnson*, and
beg from her that he would continue where he was, or at least favour them with his Company as
often as possible, for that, with
all his Wildness, *she had much rather see him* alive *than* dead.

Mr. *Johnson* as a Writer stands
in the same Predicament as in his
personal Character; his Writings
have Madness in them, but at the
same Time it is evidently the
Madness of a Man of great Abilities.—In his *Hurlothrumbo*, more
particularly, there are some Beauties, in the Midst of numberless
Absurdities, that would do Honour even to our first Rate Geniuses.—In Proof of which I shall
present my Readers with a few
Quotations from that Piece, which
may prove by no Means unentertaining, not only as Specimens of
his Manner of Writing, but as
they are in themselves truly worth
preserving; and that the Book itself being extremely scarce, and
moreover, from the general Idea
formed of it, hardly considered
as worth looking into.——The
greatest Part of them may possibly
be unacquainted with that Piece;
without Regard to Order, therefore, be pleased to accept the following Sentiments selected from
it.

" *Pride* is the Serpent's Egg,
" laid in the Hearts of all, but
" hatch'd by none but Fools."

" Conscience is an intellectual
" Caul that covers the Heart, up-
" on which all the Faculties sport
" in Terror, like Boys that dance
" upon the Ice."

" You are the most covetous
" Man in the Universe; you give
" what you have away to the
" Poor, that you may enjoy it all
" yourself; and when your Time
" is to die, you'll not leave a
" Farthing behind you to fling
" away."

" He that lives in Pleasure runs
" up a Score, and he that is af-
" flicted is paying Debts."

" A Coquet is a Whore in the
" Soul, a Harlot for the Devil."

" Oh! who shall deliver me
" from the Contagion of Mor-
" tals;—Of my Lambs, that in-
" nocently sport all round me, of
" them will I learn Humility,
" and despise your Arrogance:
" My Dog, that scouts upon the
" Plain, I'll compare him with
" you, and blush for you. He
" loves me and is constant, a fer-
" vent Friend, will fight till
" Death for his Master, rises not
" up against him when he smites
" him; he's grateful, he flatters
" not, and to your Shame has
" more Compassion; for with his
" Tongue he'll heal the Wound
" of the Oppressed.—Ye Ratio-
" nals, learn of Brutes, they teach
" me to abhor Mankind."

Sementory's Sentiments of Happiness in Love are ingenious.—
" Of all Happiness (says she) that
" is the most sweet, that is near-
" est to us; Riches lie in the
" Purse, Love in the Heart; ne-
" ver marry for Honour or Title;
" Fame is always at a Distance;
" the Man I love is near. What
" is Fame? A Word; that Word
" is Wind, the Humming of a
" Bee; but when I sleep by the
" Man I love, no Wind can come
" to me."

The Scene between *Urbandenny*
and *Puny* the Miser, contains the
following very just Remarks on
Avarice and upstart Gentility.—
The Miser is in Alarm on a Rebellion being raised in the City,
and exclaims to himself thus,
" Oh!

" Oh ! thefe Rogues are coming,
" they'll rob me, take my Plate
" and break my Windows; O!
" fweet Heaven, forgive me all
" my ill-dreamt vifionary Lewd-
" nefs.—If they come I fhall ne-
" ver purchafe *Kemp*'s Eftate, and
" buy a Coat of Arms and a Pa-
" tent for my Son.

Enter Urbandenny.

" *Urban.* So, old *Gaddecar*,
" you're at Prayers; cry aloud,
" thy Deity is deaf, with your
" fquinting Soul that ken both
" Earth and Heaven; fling your
" Bags into the Elements, then
" will you look ftraight up right.
" Begone, what haft thou to do
" in this World ? What doft thou
" mean ?

" *Puny.* I mean to be the Root
" of a Family.

" *Urban.* If the Root be Ava-
" rice, what will the Body,
" Branches, Leaves and Fruit be ?
" Twenty Generations muft pafs
" away before thy Seed can be
" refin'd fo far as to produce a
" Gentleman.

" *Puny.* Is not Gold a Gentle-
" man; a Perfon of Quality ?—
" What makes a Gentleman ?

" *Urban.* Education, Honour
" and Generofity; add to a fine
" Gentleman, Love, Refolution,
" Tafte : A Perfon of Quality
" has all thefe Perfections, and
" is difcerning; with a fublime
" Thirft in the Soul; a Longing
" to reward Merit; fervent to
" ferve the Meaneft, and punctual
" to his Word; his Blood is dou-
" ble and treble refin'd; he's full
" of Heaven; a Sun Fire; a
" Light that quenches all the
" Flame of Nature.

" *Puny.* Cannot a new-born
" Gentleman have all thefe Per-
" fections ?

" *Urban.* No, your Upftarts are

" huge and tall, converfe with a
" Prince of the Air, and their
" Noftrils are full of the Devil."

Dologodelmo's Curfe on *Hurlothrumbo* is perhaps equal to any
Thing of the Kind in our own or
any other Language.—It is as follows,

" May Heaven pour down up-
" on him the bitter Blefling, the
" Honey Curfe, the gilded Pill
" that fatisfies Defire and infects
" the Mind; give him Riches,
" and make him love them ; then
" will he be abhorr'd of Men, the
" Spirits, the Angels, and the
" Gods; may a proud Sign ap-
" pear in his Face, that he may
" be a Tavern for Devils to riot
" and banquet in; let him pam-
" per Nature, feed high to de-
" ftroy his Tafte, fo blind all the
" Beauties of his Mind; then
" will his hungry Pleafure de-
" vour up all the eternal Treafure
" of his Soul."

I fhall clofe this Set of Quotations with Part of a Speech of
Lord *Flame*'s, which being the
moft extravagant Character in the
whole Piece, will fhew how much
Originality and inventive Imagination this Writer poffeffes even
in his wildeft Flights.—It is Part
of a Defcription of the next
World, where, after he has given
fome general Account of the State
of Spirits there, he then proceeds,

" Queen *Elizabeth* is in her
" Hut felling of fry'd Fritters;
" *Pompey* and *Alexander* carry
" Charcoal to feed her Fires; the
" Great *Mogul*, the *Czar*, the
" grim *Bafhaw*, the *Emperor*, the
" Grand *Turk* and *Cæfar*, are
" fcrambling for the Drops of the
" Pan; and, as they are wont,
" are fcuffling for Trifles, till it
" raifes their inextinguifhable
" Rage to Loggerheads,"

[T 3]　　　　Jo&n-

JOHNSON, Mr.—Who or what this Gentleman was I know not, but find his Name prefixed to a Comedy, entitled,

The *Female Fortune-teller*. Com.

JONES, Mr. *Henry*.—This Author, who is still living, is a Native of *Ireland*, being born at *Drogheda*, in the County of *Meath* in that Kingdom.—He was bred a Bricklayer, but, having a natural Inclination for the Muses, he pursued his Devotions to them even during the Labours of his mere mechanical Avocations, and composing a Line of Brick and a Line of Verse alternately, his Walls and Poems rose in Growth together; but which of his Labours will be most durable Time alone must determine.—His Turn, as is most generally the Case with mean Poets, or Bards of humble Origin, was Panegyrick.—This procur'd him some Friends, and, in the Year 1745, when the Earl of *Chesterfield* went over to *Ireland* as Lord Lieutenant, Mr. *Jones* was recommended to the Notice of that Nobleman, who has not been more remarkable for his own shining Talents and Brilliancy of Parts, than for his zealous and generous Patronage of Genius in whatever Person or of whatever Rank he may chance to meet with it.—His Excellency, delighted with the Discovery of this mechanic Muse, not only favoured him with his own Notice and generous Munificence, thought proper to transplant this opening Flower into a warmer and more thriving Climate.——He brought him with him to *England*, recommended him to many of the Nobility there, and not only by his Influence and Interest procured him a large Subscription for the publishing a Collection of his Poems, but it is said even took on himself the Alteration and Correction of his Tragedy, and also the Care of prevailing on the Managers of *Covent-Garden* Theatre to bring it on the Stage.—This Nobleman also recommended him in the warmest Manner to the late Mr. *Colley Cibber*, whose friendly and humane Disposition induced him to shew him a thousand Acts of Friendship, and I have even been informed that he made strong Efforts by his Interest at Court to have secured to him the Succession of the Laurel after his Death.

The Appearance of Mr. *Jones's* Play is so recent, and its Representation so frequently repeated, that, excepting for the Sake of more distant Readers, it would scarcely be necessary to mention that the Title of it is

The *Earl of* ESSEX. Trag. My Opinion of Mr. *Jones's* Merit as a dramatic Writer may be seen in my Account of this Play in the first Part of the present Work.—His poetical Worth in his other Writings is certainly not in itself contemptible, yet is far from being of the first rate Kind. —In short, it is pretty nearly on a Par with that of another rustic bred Bard of this Century, whom the Royal Favour having given a Sanction to, it became a Fashion to admire his Writings, tho' the greatest Value that either that Gentleman's Poems or those of our Author possessed to call them into Notice above Hundreds of the humbler Inhabitants of *Parnassus*, was their being produced by Geniuses entirely uncultivated; so that, the Wonder was not how Men of a poetical Turn should produce such Verses as theirs, but how any Verses at all

should

should be the Produce of a Thatcher or a Bricklayer.

JONES, Mr. *John*.—Of this Author I find no farther Mention than that he lived in the Reign of *Charles* I. and wrote one very indifferent Play, intitled,

ADRASTA.

JONSON, *Ben*, one of the most considerable dramatic Poets of the last Age; whether we consider the Number or the Merit of his Productions.——He was born at *Westminster* in 1574, and was educated at the public School there, under the great *Camden*.—He was descended from a *Scots* Family; and his Father, who lost his Estate under Q. *Mary*, dying before our Poet was born, and his Mother marrying a Bricklayer for her second Husband, *Ben* was taken from School to work at his Father-in-Law's Trade.—Not being captivated with this Employment, he went into the Low Countries, and distinguished himself in a military Capacity.

On his Return to *England* he entered himself at St. *John's* College *Cambridge*, and having killed a Person in a Duel, was condemned, and narrowly escaped Execution.—After this he turned Actor, and *Shakespeare* is said to have first introduced him to the World, by recommending a Play of his to the Stage, aiter it had been rejected.——His *Alchymist* gained him such Reputation that in 1619 he was, at the Death of Mr. *Daniel*, made Poet Laureat to K. *James* I. and Master of Arts at *Oxford*.

As we do not find *Jonson's* œconomical Virtues any where recorded, it is the less to be wondered at, that after this we find him petitioning K. *Charles*, on his Accession, to enlarge his Father's Allowance of a hundred

Marks into Pounds; and quickly after we learn that he was very poor and sick, lodging in an obscure Alley: On which Occasion it was, that *Charles* being prevailed on in his Favour, sent him ten Guineas; which *Ben* receiving, said, " His Majesty has sent me ten " Guineas because I am poor, " and live in an Alley, go and " tell him that his Soul lives in " an Alley."

He died in *August* 1637, aged 63 Years, and was buried in *Westminster-Abbey*.

His dramatic Compositions are very numerous, and are as follows.

1. *Alchymist.* Com.
2. *Bartholomew-Fair.* Com.
3. *Cataline's Conspiracy.* Trag.
4. *Challenge at Tilt.* At a Marriage, printed in 1640.
5. *Christmas's Masque.*
6. *Cloridia.* A Masque.
7. *Cynthia's Revels.* Masque.
8. *The Devil is an Ass.* Com.
9. *Entertainment of King James,* in passing his Coronation.
10. *Entertainment in private* of the King and Queen, on *May* Day in the Morning. At Sir *Wm. Cornwallis's,* at *Highgate*.
11. *Ditto at Theobald's,* on the Delivery up of the House by the E. of *Salisbury*.
12. *Entertainment in particular* of the Queen and Prince, on their first coming into the Kingdom.
13. *Entertainment of the two Kings* of Great-Britain and Denmark, at *Theobald's*.
14. *Every Man in his Humour.* Com.
15. *Every Man out of his Humour.* Com.
16. *Fortunate Isles, and their Union celebrated.* Masque.
17. *Golden Age restored.* Masque.
18. *Hy-*

18. *Hymenæi*, &c. Mafque.
19. *Irifh Mafque*.
20. *King's Entertainment at Welbeck*, on his going to *Scotland*.
21. *Love freed from Ignorance and Folly*. Mafque.
22. *Love reftored*. Mafque.
23. *Love's Welcome*. Mafque, for the King and Queen at *Bolfover*.
24. *Magnetic Lady*. Com.
25. *Mafque*, on Lord *Hadington's* Marriage.
26. *Mafque of Augurs*.
27. *Mafque of Owls*.
28. *Mafque of Queens*.
29. *Mafque* for the *French Ambaffador*.
30. *Metamorphofed Gypfies*. M.
31. *Mercury vindicated from the Alchymifts*.
32. *Mortimer's Fall*. Fragment of a Trag.
33. *Neptune's Triumph*. Mafq;
34. *News from the new World in the Moon*.
35. *Oberon, the Fairy Prince*. Mafque.
36. *Paris Anniverfary*. Mafq;
37. *Pleafure reconciled to Virtue*. Mafque.
38. *Poetafter, or his Arraignment*.
39. *Queen's Mafques*.
40. *Sad Shepherd, or a Tale of Robin-Hood*. Paftoral.
41. *Sejanus's Fall*. Trag.
42. *Silent Woman*. Com.
43. *Staple of News*. Com.
44. *Tale of a Tub* Com.
45. *Time vindicated to himfelf, and to his Honour*.
46. *Volpone*. Com.
47. *Cafe is altered*. Com.
48. *Widow*. Com.
49. *New Inn, or the light Heart*. Com.

JORDON, Mr. *Thomas*, lived in the Reign of King *Charles* I.

and wrote the three following regular dramatic Pieces, *viz.*

1. *Fancy's Feftivals*. Mafque.
2. *Money's an Afs*. Com.
3. *Walks of* ISLINGTON *and* HOGSDON. Com.

I alfo imagine that he muft have fucceeded Mr. *Tatcham* in the diftinguifhed Honour of City Poet, as we find fome of his Pieces written for the Pageant Ceremonials of Lord Mayor's Day, in the fame Manner as thofe which are mentioned in our Account of that Author.—Thefe, of this Gentleman's which I have been able to trace, are no more than four, and thofe at broken Periods ; but it is moft probable that the City Poet was obliged to fupply one for every Year.—The Titles of the four I have hinted at are

1. *London's Refurrection*, 1671.
2. *London triumphant*, 1673.
3. *London's Glory*, 1680.
4. *London's Joy*, 1681.

Whether Mr. *Jordon* was an Actor by Profeffion I know not, but am rather apt to imagine the contrary.—*Langbaine* however takes Notice of his having acted the Part of *Lepida*, *Meffalina's* Mother, in a Tragedy written by Mr. *Richards*, called *Meffalina, Emprefs of Rome*.

JOYNER, Mr. *William*, was born in *Oxfordfhire* in the latter End of King *Charles* I's Reign, and was educated at *Magdalen* College, where he obtained a Fellowfhip, which he kept till he changed his Religion, on which he made a voluntary Refignation of it, and being fond of Retirement, took great Delight in the Favour and Good-Will of his private Friends, which a natural Sweetnefs of Difpofition that he poffeffed, and an inoffenfive Prudence

dence in his Behaviour, obtained for him in a very perfect Degree ; nor did he think proper to interfere either in the public Controverfies of Religion or the Affairs of State, till, on the new modelling of the Univerfity under the *Ecclefiaftical Commiffioners* in King *James* II's Reign, he was reinftated in his former Rank in the College, which however he did not very long enjoy, for fhortly af er, *viz.* at the Revolution, the College was reftored to its former Settlement, and he and the reft of the Fellows removed.——On which Occafion he again betook himfelf to Solitude, in an obfcure Village in *Buckinghamfhire,* where he lived for many Years in the moft retir'd Manner, not dying till the 14th of *Sept.* 1706.—— When he firft withdrew from *Oxford,* he wrote one dramatic Piece, entitled,

The *Roman Emprefs.* Trag. *Langbaine* informs us that the ancient Name belonging to Mr. *Joyner's* Family had been *Lyde,* and takes Notice of a little Book written by this Gentleman, entitled *Obfervations on the Life of Cardinal* Reginaldus Polus, in the Title Page of which the Author difguifes himfelf under the Initials *G. L.* which he interprets to ftand for *Gulielmus Lyde.*

K.

K F.——Thefe two Letters *Langbaine* interprets to mean *Francis Kirkman,* and ftand affixed to the Dedication of a Piece of dramatic Satire, entitled,

The *Prefbyterian Lafs.* Tragi-Com.

Kirkman was a very great Publifher of dramatic Works foon after the Reftoration, whether therefore he was the Author or only the Editor of this Piece, is not extremely apparent, even allowing Mr. *Langbaine's* Explication of the Initials, which moreover *Coxeter's MS.* has given us to be *K. E.*

This *Kirkman,* in whofe Name by the Way *Langbaine* makes fome Degree of Confufion, calling him at one Time *Francis,* and at others *John Kirkman,* was the Publifher of a Collection of dramatic Pieces, under the Title of

The W I T S, or *Sport upon Sport,*

confifting of the following Farces or Drolls, intended for Fairs.

1. *Bouncing Knight.*
2. *Bubble.*
3. *Clubmen.*
4. *Empirick.*
5. *Equal Match.*
6. *Falfe Heir.*
7. *Forc'd Valour.*
8. *French Dancing-Mafter.*
9. *Grave-makers.*
10. *Jenkins's Love Courfe.*
11. *Invifible Smirk.*
12. *Lame Commonwealth.*
13. *Landlady.*
14. *Mock Teftator.*
15. *Prince in Conceit.*
16. *Simpleton.*
17. *Stallion.*
18. *Surprize.*
19. *Tefty Lover.*
20. *Three merry Boys.*

As alfo a fecond Part of this Collection, for which *Vid.* C o x, *Robert.*

KELLY, *John,* Efq;——This Gentleman, who may be ftill living, was a Member of the Honourable Society of the *Middle Temple.*——He was concerned with others in the writing a daily periodical Paper, called the *Univerfal*

fal Spectator, and in some other literary Undertakings; and is Author of five dramatic Pieces, the Titles of which are as follow.

1. *Fall of* Bob. Farce.
2. *Levee.* Farce.
3. *Married Philosopher.* Com.
4. *Fill and Drop.* Farce.
5. Timon *in Love.* Com.

KILLIGREW, Dr. *Henry.*— This Gentleman, who was one of the most eminent Wits in *Charles* I's Reign, was educated at *Christ Church* College, *Oxford,* and there, according to *Coxeter,* he took the Degree of Doctor of Laws.— In what Year he was born is not apparent, as the Play, on which Account we have admitted him to a Place, seems not to have been acted till some Time after the Occasion was past, for which it was originally designed, *viz.* the Celebration of the Nuptials of Lord *Charles Herbert* with the Lady *Mary Villiers,* at which Time the Author was no more than seventeen Years of Age.—Which Circumstance we gather from an Anecdote concerning it, related by *Langbaine,* that reflects Honour on the Author.———For he tells us, that on its first Representation at *Black-Friars,* certain Critics cavilled at the Character of *Cleanthes* in it, objecting that it was *monstrous* and *impossible,* for a Person of only seventeen Years old, as that Character is supposed to be, to conceive and utter such Sentiments as he is made to speak, and which would better suit the Lips of one of thirty Years of Age; to which Objection the learned and ingenious Lord *Falkland* made this very judicious Reply in Vindication of the Author, viz. *that it was neither* monstrous *nor* impossible *for one of seventeen Years to speak at such a Rate; when He that made him speak in that Man-*

ner, and wrote the whole Play, was himself no older.—The Title of the Piece, which has also been highly commended by *Ben Jonson,* is

The *Conspiracy.* Trag.

Mr. *Killigrew* was in *Italy,* most probably upon his Travels, at the Time that this Play was first published, which was in 1638, by which Means it came out very imperfect and incorrect.—But after his Return, it is probable he might himself make some Alterations in it, and it was republished in 1653, with the altered Title of

PALLANTUS and EUDORA.

I find no Hints whereby to trace out the exact Time either of the Birth or Death of this Author.

KILLIGREW, *Thomas,* Esq;— This Gentleman most probably might be related to the last-mentioned Writer, at least it is apparent that they were Cotemporaries, for our present Author was first Page of Honour to K. *Cha.* I. and being afterwards appointed Groom of the Bed - Chamber to his Son *Charles* II, attended that Prince during his Exile.—While abroad he made the Tour of *France, Italy* and *Spain,* and in 1651 was honoured by his Majesty with the Employment of Resident at the Republic of *Venice.*

After the Restoration he continued in high Favour with the King, and had frequently Access to him when he was denied to the first Peers in the Realm; and being a Man of great Wit and Liveliness of Parts, and having from his long Intimacy with that Monarch, and being continually about his Person during his Troubles, acquired a Freedom and Familiarity with him, which even the Pomp of Majesty afterwards could not check in him, he sometimes,

by

by Way of Jeſt, which King *Charles* was ever fond of, if genuine, even tho' himſelf was the Object of the Satire, would adventure bold Truths which ſcarcely any one beſides would have dared even to hint at.——One Story in particular is related of him, which, if true, is a ſtrong Proof of the great Lengths he would ſometimes proceed in his Freedoms of this Kind, which is as follows ;——When the King's unbounded Paſſion for Women had given his Miſtreſs ſuch an Aſcendant over him, that, like the effeminate *Perſian* Monarch, he was much fitter to have handled a Diſtaff than to wield a Sceptre, and for the Converſation of his Concubines utterly neglected the moſt important Affairs of State, Mr. *Killigrew* went to pay his Majeſty a Viſit in his private Apartments, habited like a Pilgrim who was bent on a long Journey. ——The King, ſurprized at the Oddity of his Appearance, immediately aſked him what was the Meaning of it, and whither he was going ?——*To Hell*, bluntly replied the Wag.——*Prithee*, ſaid the King, *what can your Errand be to that Place ?——To fetch back* Oliver Cromwell, (rejoined he) *that he may take ſome Care of the Affairs of* England, *for his Succeſſor takes none at all.*

One more Story is related of him, which is not barren of Humour.——King *Charles*'s Fondneſs for Pleaſure, to which he almoſt always made Buſineſs give Way, uſed frequently to delay Affairs of Conſequence from his Majeſty's diſappointing the Council of his Preſence when met for the Diſpatch of Buſineſs, which Neglect gave great Diſguſt and Offence to many of thoſe who were treated with this ſeeming Diſreſpect.——

On one of theſe Occaſions the Duke of *Lauderdale*, who was naturally impetuous and turbulent, quitted the Council-Chamber in a violent Paſſion, and, meeting Mr. *Killigrew* preſently after, expreſſed himſelf on the Occaſion in very diſreſpectful Terms of his Majeſty.——*Killigrew* begg'd his Grace to moderate his Paſſion, and offer'd to lay him a Wager of an hundred Pounds that he himſelf would prevail on his Majeſty to come to Council in half an Hour. ——The Duke, ſurprized at the Boldneſs of the Aſſertion, and warmed by his Reſentment againſt the King, accepted the Wager, on which *Killigrew* immediately went to the King, and, without Ceremony, told him what had happen'd ; adding theſe Words, " I know that your Majeſty hates " *Lauderdale*, tho', the Neceſſity " of your Affairs compels you to " carry an outward Appearance " of Civility ; now, if you chuſe " to be rid of a Man who is thus " diſagreeable to you, you need " only go this once to Council ; " for I know his covetous Diſpo- " ſition ſo perfectly, that I am " well perſuaded, rather than pay " this hundred Pounds he wouid " hang himſelf out of the Way, " and never plague you more."—— The King was ſo pleaſed with the Archneſs of this Obſervation, that he immediately replied, *Well then*, Killigrew, *I poſitively* will *go*.—— And kept his Word accordingly.

During his Reſidence abroad he applied the greateſt Part of his leiſure Hours to the Study and Practice of Poetry, and particularly dramatic Writings, ſeveral of his Plays being compoſed in that Period of Time.——To this Sir *John Denham* humorouſly alludes, and alſo draws a Character of our Author extremely conſiſtent

with

with the Circumftances we have been relating of him, in his Copy of Verfes on Mr. Killigrew's Return from his Embaffy at Venice.

I.

Our Refident Tom,
From Venice is come,
And has left the Statefman behind
bim ;
Talks at the fame Pitch,
Is as wife, is as rich,
And juft where you left bim, you
find bim.

II.

But who fays be is not
A Man of much Plot,
May repent this falfe Accufation ;
Having plotted and penn'd
Six Plays to attend
The Farce of bis Negociation.

However, tho' Sir *John Denbam* here hints at only fix, Mr. *Killigrew* wrote nine Plays while abroad, and two after he came home ; the Names of them all are as follows,

1. BELLAMIRA, *her Dream,* two Parts. Tragi-Com.
2. CICILIA and CLORINDA, two Parts. Tragi-Com.
3. CLARAXILLA. Tr.-Com.
4. *Parfon's Wedding.* Com.
5. *Pilgrim.* Trag.
6. *Princefs.* Tragi-Com.
7. *Prifoners.* Com.
8. THORNASO, two Parts. C.

KILLIGREW, *Thomas,* Efq;— As if the Name of *Killigrew* was of itfelf a Warrant to the Title of Wit, this Century has, as well as the two preceding ones, produced an Author of that Name. —He was Gentleman of the Bed-Chamber to his late Majefty when Prince of *Wales,* and wrote one Play, entitled,

Cbit Cbat. Com.

KILLIGREW, Sir *William,* Knt.—This Gentleman's Father was Sir *Robert Killigrew,* Knight, Chamberlain to Queen *Elizabeth.* —He was born in *May* 1605, at the Manor of *Hamworth,* near *Hampton-Court,* and was enter'd a Gentleman Commoner in St. *John's* College, *Oxford,* in Midfummer Term of the Year 1622. —Here he continued for about three Years, at the Expiration of which he fet out on his Travels, and made the Tour of *Europe.*— What Time he fpent abroad does not exactly appear ; but we find him, after his Return, appointed Governor of *Pendennis* Caftle and *Falmouth* Haven, both in the County of *Cornwall,* and alfo put in the Command of the Militia of the Weftern Part of that County.

His next Promotion brought him to Court, as an immediate Attendant on the King's own Perfon, being made one of the Gentlemen Ufhers of the Privy Chamber, which Poft he kept till the breaking out of the Civil Wars, when he had the Command of the two great Troops of thofe that guarded the King's Perfon during the whole Courfe of the War between the King and Parliament beftowed on him.——He was in Attendance on the King at the Time that the Court refided at *Oxford* in the Year 1642, at which Time he alfo was admitted to the Degree of Doctor of Civil Law.— But, when the King's Affairs had fallen into fuch a Situation as to be apparently paft Recovery, he thought it the moft prudent Step, tho' he was under a Neceffity of fuffering by his Attachment to the Royal Caufe to enter into a Compofition for his Eftate

with

with the Committee of Sequestrations.

Tho' King *Charles* II. was not remarkable for his Returns of Gratitude to thofe who had been Sufferers in the Interefts of his Family, yet in this Inftance he contradicted his general Conduct, for this Gentleman was one of the firft among his Father's Servants that he took Notice of, firft reftoring him to the Poft of Gentleman Ufher of the Privy Chamber, which he had held under *Charles* I. and afterwards, on his own Marriage with *Donna Catbarine* of *Portugal*, creating him her Majefty's firft Vice-Chamberlain, which honourable Station he held for two and twenty Years, when, being greatly advanced in Life, retired from Court, and, from fome Books which he publifhed after that Time, feems to have devoted the Remainder of his Life to a due Preparation for his being called to another World, which Event happened to him in the Year 1693, at which Time he was eighty - eight Years of Age.

I do not find any Mention made by former Writers of what Eftimation he was held in by his Cotemporaries with Refpect to Genius.——And indeed, excepting his dramatic Pieces, I find nothing of his in Print till the Time when, in the entire Decline of Life, he publifhed a Collection of detached Thoughts and Reflections on the Inftability of human Happinefs, when fixed on any other Views than thofe which are to arife from the Enjoyments of another State.—His dramatic Works, however, received the Commendations of Mr. *Waller*, Sir *Robert Stapleton*, and others, and they are the following.

1. *Imperial Tragedy*. (attributed to him only.)
2. ORMASDES. Tragi-Com.
3. PANDORA. Tragi-Com.
4. SELINDRA. Tragi-Com.
5. *Siege of* URBIN. Tragi-Com.

KIRKE, Mr. *John*.—Of this Author I can trace nothing farther than that all Writers agree in placing him in the Reign of King *Charles* I. and naming him as the Author of one Piece, entitled,

Seven Champions of Chriftendom. Play.

KNEVET, Mr. *Ralph*, was a *Norfolk* Gentleman, and Cotemporary with Mr. *Kirke* abovementioned.—He wrote one little Piece, which was intended only for a private Reprefentation at the Florift's Feaft at *Norwich*, entitled,

RHODON *and* IRIS. Paftoral.

KNIFE, Mr. *Charles*.—Of this Gentleman I know little more than of the foregoing Author.— He was, however, one of the Genii of the Infancy of the prefent Century, and Author of one *Petite Piece* of the Theatre, which met with fome Applaufe at its firft Appearance, entitled,

A *City Ramble*. Farce of two Acts.

KYD, Mr. *Thomas*, lived in the Reign of Queen *Elizabeth*, and wrote, or rather tranflated, one dramatic Piece, entitled,

POMPEY *the Great*, *bis Fair* CORNELIA's *Tragedy*.

KYFFIN, Mr. *Maurice*. — Of this Gentleman I know nothing more than the finding his Name in *Coxeter's MS.* Notes, as one of the firft Tranflators into *Englifh* of one of the Comedies of *Terence*, viz.

ANDRIA. Com. *Vid.* APPENDIX.

He wrote in the Reign of Queen *Elizabeth*, and seems, from Circumstances relating to this Play, to have been Tutor to the Children of the celebrated Lord *Buckhurst*, a particular which of itself is sufficient to give us a very favourable Idea of his literary Abilities.

L.

LACY, Mr. *John*, flourished in the Reign of King *Charles* II.——He was born near *Doncaster* in *Yorkshire*, and was at first bred a Dancing-Master, but afterwards went into the Army, having a Lieutenant's Commission and Warrant as Quarter-Master under Colonel *Charles Gerrard*.—— The Charms of a military Life, however, he quitted to go upon the Stage, in which Profession, from the Advantages of a fine Person, being well shaped, of a good Stature, and well proportioned, added to a sound critical Judgment, and a large Share of comic Humour, he arrived at so great a Height of Excellence, as to be universally admired; and in particular was so high in the Esteem of King *Charles* II. that his Majesty had his Picture painted in three several Characters, viz. *Teague* in the *Committee*, *Scruple* in the *Cheats*, and *Galliard* in the *Variety*; which Picture is still preserved at *Windsor* Castle.—His Cast of acting was chiefly in Comedy, and his Writings are all of that Kind, he being the Author of the four following Plays,

1. *Dumb Lady.* Com.
2. *Old Troop.* Com.

3. *Sawney the Scot.* Com.
4. *Sir* Hercules Buffoon. Com.

The last of these was not brought on the Stage till three Years after the Author's Death, which happened on the 17th of *Sept.* 1681. Mr. *Durfey*, who wrote the Prologue to it, has, in the following Lines, paid a very great, but, as it appears, a very deserving Compliment to Mr. *Lacy*'s theatrical Abilities, in Reference to the Advantages the Piece might have received from the Author's own Performance in it, had he been living.

Know, that fam'd Lacy, *Ornament o'th' Stage,*
That Standard *of* true Comedy *in our Age,*
Wrote this new Play.——
And if it takes not, all that we can say on't,
Is, we've his Fiddle, *not his* Hands, *to play on't.*

LANGFORD, Mr.—This Gentleman is perhaps better known in the *polite* than in the *poetical* World, standing at this Time the foremost in Renown among a Set of Orators, whose Eloquence must be confessed of the most perfect and powerful Kind, since it has that amazing Prevalence of perfuading Mankind to part with even their Money.—In a Word, to leave Ambiguities, he is the most celebrated Auctioneer of this Age, and Successor in that Profession to the great Mr. *Cock*.—— His Success, or perhaps his Merit, has not been equally great in the Exercise of his Pen as in that of another more valuable Weapon; for the only dramatic Piece, I believe, which he has attempted, tho' it is in print, was never acted,

acted, nor indeed seems to lay any just Claim to that Honour.—It was entitled,

The *Mad Captain.* Com.

LANSDOWNE, Lord, was second Son of *Bernard Granville,* and Grand-Son of the famous Sir *Beville Granville,* who was killed at the Battle of *Lansdowne* in 1643.—This Nobleman received the first Principles of Education in *France,* under Sir *Wm. Ellis,* a Gentleman afterward distinguished in many public Employments. When the Nation was disturbed by the Commotions occasioned by the Endeavours of *James* II. to introduce the Popish Religion, Lord *Lansdowne,* who had early imbibed Principles of Loyalty, being of a Family which had suffered in the Cause of *Charles* I. solicited his Father's Permission to engage in the Party of this infatuated Prince : Whether he really did, or did not join him, is not known; but there was no Opportunity for him to signalize his Courage, as the Revolution was accomplished without any Loss of Blood.

In 1702 he translated the second *Olynthian* of *Demosthenes :* he was elected Member for the County of *Cornwall* in 1710; and soon after made Secretary at War. He was next made Comptroller of the Houshold, then Treasurer; and sworn of the Privy Council: and created Baron *Lansdowne* of *Bidd-ford* in *Devonshire.*—On the Accession of King *George* I. he was committed to the *Tower* on an Impeachment for High Treason; but was honourably discharged without Trial.—He died in 1735.

He wrote,

1. *She Gallants.* Com.
2. *Heroic Love.* Trag.

3. BRITISH *Enchanters.* Dram. Opera.
4. PELEUS and THETIS. M.

LEANARD, or LEANERD, Mr. *John.*—So *Coxeter* has corrected the Name of this Gentleman, who lived in the Reign of *Charles* II.— Mr. *Langbaine* has treated him with great Severity, and indeed a Degree of Scurrility, which had somewhat the Appearance of personal Pique and Resentment.—He has called him " a confident Plagiary, whom he " disdains to stile an Author; " one, who, tho' he wou'd be " esteem'd the Father, is at best " but the Midwife to the Labours " of others;" and that, " *Gipsy-* " *like,* he begs with stolen Chil- " dren, that he may raise the " more Compassion."—Yet, begging Mr. *Langbaine*'s Pardon, who by the bye on many Occasions shews himself to be far from an impartial Writer, tho' Plagiarism be a Fault, this Gentleman is not more guilty of it than many whom he has let pass without so severe a Censure.—And altho' he may have borrowed from others, yet he seems to have had at least some Merit of his own, since *Jacob* has attributed to him an original Play, from which one of our most entertaining Comic Writers, viz. *Colley Cibber,* has borrowed the greatest Part of a very entertaining Comedy, and which is frequently acted to this Day, viz. *She wou'd and she wou'd not.*—The Play of Mr. *Leanerd*'s is entitled

—.The *Counterfeits.* Com.

The two other dramatic Pieces, which our Author has published under his own Name, and for which Mr. *Langbaine* has attacked him with so much Warmth and Violence, are entitled,

 1. *Coun*

1. *Country Innocence.* Com.
2. *Rambling Justice.* Com.

LEE, *Nathaniel,* a very eminent dramatic Poet of the last Century, was the Son of a Clergyman, who gave him a liberal Education.—He received his first Rudiments of Learning at *Westminster* School, from whence he went to *Trinity* College, *Cambridge.*—Coming to *London,* however, his Inclination promoted him to appear on the Theatre; but he was not more successful in representing the Thoughts of other Men, than many a Genius besides, who have been equally unfortunate in treading the Stage, although they knew so well how to write for it. He produced eleven Tragedies, all of which contain a very great Portion of true Poetic Enthusiasm.—Now, if any ever felt the Passion of Love more truly; nor could any one describe it with more Tenderness.—*Addison* commends his Genius highly; observing that none of our *English* Poets had a happier Turn for Tragedy, although his natural Fire and unbridled Impetuosity hurried him beyond all Bounds of Probability, and sometimes were quite out of Nature.—The Truth is, this Poet's Imagination ran away with his Reason; so that at length he became quite crazy: and grew so bad, that his Friends were obliged to confine him in *Bedlam*; where he made that famous witty Reply to a Coxcomb Scribbler, who had the Cruelty to jeer him with his Misfortune, by observing that it was an easy Thing to write like a Madman:—*No,* said Lee, *it is* not *an easy Thing to write like a Madman; but it is very easy to write like a Fool.*

Lee had the good Fortune to recover the Use of his Reason so far as to be discharged from his melancholy Confinement; but he did not long survive his Enlargement: dying at the early Age of Thirty-four. *Cibber,* in his Lives of the Poets, says he perished unfortunately in a Night Ramble, in *London* Streets; and other Writers mention the same Thing: and probably this was the End of poor *Nat. Lee* !—His dramatic Pieces are,

1. NERO, *Emperor of* ROME.
2. SOPHONISBA, or HANNIBAL's *Overthrow.*
3. The *Rival Queens,* or ALEXANDER *the Great.*
4. MITHRIDATES, *King of* PONTUS.
5. THEODOSIUS, or *the Force of Love.*
6. CÆSAR BORGIA.
7. LUCIUS JUNIUS BRUTUS. (*Cibber* deems this the best of his Tragedies.)
8. CONSTANTINE *the Great.*
9. The *Princess of* CLEVE.
10. The *Massacre of* PARIS.
11. GLORIANA, or *the Court of* AUGUSTUS.

Besides the above Tragedies, *Lee* was concerned with *Dryden* in writing the *Duke of Guise,* and that other excellent Tragedy entitled *Oedipus.*—He also revived *Shakespear's King Lear,* in which he made some Alterations, and brought it on the Stage in 1681.—His *Theodosius* and *Alexander the Great* are Stock-Plays, and to this Day are often acted with great Applause.—Mr. *Barry* has been particularly fortunate in the Character of the *Macedonian* Hero.

LEGGE, *Thomas.*——Of this Writer I know nothing more than the Name, which *Langbaine* tells us is inserted in a Catalogue of Plays printed with *Massinger's Old Law,*

Law, and there said to be the Author of a Play, called

The *Destruction of* Jerusalem.

Leigh, Mr. *John*, was an Actor, but of no very great Eminence, and therefore should be distinguished from the great *Leigh*, who was Cotemporary with *Underkill*, *Betterton*, &c.—He was a Native of *Ireland*, and made his first theatrical Essay on the Stage in *Dublin*.—From thence he came over to *London*, where, from his having the Advantage of a good Figure, he was engaged by the late Mr. *Rich* in a Company with which, in the Year 1714, he opened the Theatre Royal at *Lincoln's-Inn-Fields*.—But, tho' he continued on the Stage for twelve Years after, he made no considerable Advances towards theatrical Excellence.—He died in 1726, in the 37th Year of his Age, and left behind him two dramatic Pieces, entitl'd,

1. *Hob's Wedding.* Farce.
2. *Kensington Gardens.* Com.

* Lennox, Mrs. *Arabella*—This Lady, who is now living, and an Authoress by Profession, has raised her Fame on the Foundation of Novel-Writing, of which she has produced several, *viz.* the *Female Quixote*, *Henrietta*, *Sophia*, &c. which are far from wanting Merit in their Way; yet she would have had no Right to any Mention in this Place but for one little Piece that she has published, which, tho' never act-

---

* *Her Maiden Name was* Ramsay. *She was the Daughter of a* North-American *Gentleman; and it should seem, from some of her Poems, that she is a Native of* New-York; *on which Place she has written a severe Satire.*

ed, has yet some Connection with the Drama; it is entitled,

Philander. Dram. Pastoral.

Lewis, Mr.—This Gentleman, according to *Whincop*, was living in the Year 1747, and probably may be so at this Time.—The same Writer also informs us, that he was favoured with the Esteem and Friendship of Mr. *Pope*, as likewise that he was Author of one Dramatic Piece, entitled,

Philip *of* Macedon. Trag.

Lillo, *George*, was by Profession a Jeweller, and was born in the Neighbourhood of *Moorgate* in *London*, on the 4th of *Feb.* 1693, in which Neighbourhood he pursued his Occupation for many Years with the fairest and most unblemished Character.—He was bred up in the Principles of the Protestant Dissenters; but let his Religious Tracts have been what they would, he would have been an Honour to any Sect he had adher'd to.—He was strongly attached to the Muses, yet seem'd to have laid it down as a Maxim, that the Devotion paid to them ought always to tend to the Promotion of Virtue, Morality and Religion.—In the Pursuance of this Aim Mr. *Lillo* was happy in the Choice of his Subjects, and shew'd great Power of affecting the Heart, by working up the Passions to such a Height, as to render the Distresses of common and domestic Life equally interesting to the Audiences as that of Kings and Heroes, and the Ruin brought on private Families by an Indulgence of Avarice, Lust, &c. as the Havock made in States and Empires, by Ambition, Cruelty or Tyranny.——His *George Barnwell*, *Fatal Curiosity*, and *Arden of Feversham*, are all planned on common and well known Stories; yet they have perhaps more frequently drawn Tears from an Audience, than the more pompous Tragedies of *Alexander the Great*, *All for Love*, &c. particularly the first of them, which, being founded on a well-known old Ballad, many of the Critics of that Time, who went to the first Representation of it, formed so contemptible an Idea of the Piece in their Expectations, that they purchased the Ballad, some Thousands of which were used in one Day on this Account, in order to draw Comparisons between that and the Play.——But the Merit of the Play soon got the better of this Contempt, and presented them with Scenes written so truly to the Heart, that they were compelled to subscribe to the Power, and drop their Ballads to take up their Handkerchiefs.

Mr. *Lillo*, as I before observed, has been happy in the Choice of his Subjects; his Conduct in the Management of them is no less meritorious, and his *Pathos* very great.——If there is any Fault to be objected to his Writings, it is that sometimes he affects an Elevation of Stile somewhat above the Simplicity of his Subject, and the supposed Rank of his Characters; but the Custom of Tragedy will stand in some Degree of Excuse for this, and a still better Argument perhaps may be admited in Vindication, not only of our present Author, but of other Writers in the like Predicament, which is, that even Nature itself will justify this Conduct, since we find even the most humble Characters in real Life, when under peculiar Circumstances of Distress, or actuated by the Influence of any violent Passions, will at Times be elevated to an Aptness of Expression and Power of Language, not only greatly superior to themselves, but even to the general Language of Conversation of Persons of much higher Rank in Life, and of Minds more perfectly cultivated.

This Author died *September* 3, 1739, in the 47th Year of his Age, leaving behind him the Character of a Man of strict Morals, great Good-Nature, and a sound Understanding; and, what added a double Lustre to all these Perfections, endued with an uncommon Share of Modesty.—— *Whincop* (or the Compiler of the List of Plays affixed to his *Scanderbeg*) has indeed spoke but slightingly of his Genius, on Account of some little Sort of Rivalship and Pique subsisting between that Gentleman and our Author, with Respect to a Tragedy of the latter's, entitled the *Christian Hero*, written on the same Story with the *Scanderbeg* of the former.——Notwithstanding which, under the Sanction not only of the Success of his Pieces, but also of the Commendations bestowed on them by Mr. *Pope*, and other indisputable Judges, I shall venture to affirm that Mr. *Lillo* is far from standing in the lowest Rank of Merit (however he may be ranged with Respect to Fame) among our dramatic Writers.

His dramatic Pieces are seven in Number, and their Titles as follow,

1. ARDEN *of* FEVERSHAM. Trag. *Vid.* ADDENDA to Vol. I.
2. *Christian Hero.* Trag.
3. *Elmerick.* Trag.
4. *Fatal Curiosity.* Trag.
5. LONDON *Merchant.* Trag. *Vid.* APPENDIX.
6. MARINA. Play, 3 Acts.
7. SYLVIA. Ballad Opera.

LLOYD,

LLOYD, Mr. *Robert*, was formerly one of the Ushers of *Westminster* School, but at present I believe employs his literary Talents mostly in the Service of the Press.——He was Author of a Poem called the *Actor*, which not only gave Proofs of great Judgment in the Subject he was treating of, but had also the Merit of smooth Versification and great Strength of Poetry.—Some little Poems, however, which he has published since, seem scarcely equal to the Specimen of Abilities set forth in that Piece.——In the Beginning of the *Poetical War*, which for some Time past raged among the living Wits of this Age, and to which the celebrated *Rosciad* founded the first Charge, Mr. *Lloyd* was suspected to be the Author of that Poem.——That Charge, however, he exculpated himself from, by an Advertisement in the public Papers, on which Occasion the real Author, Mr. *Churchill*, boldly step'd forth, and in the same public Manner declared himself; and drew on that Torrent of *Anti - Rosciads*, *Apologies*, *Murphiads*, *Churchiliads*, *Examiners*, &c. which for a long Time kept up the Attention and employed the Geniuses of the greatest Part of the critical World.

Mr. *Lloyd* is said to be Author of one little dramatic Piece of last Season's Growth, entitled,

ARCADIA. Dram. Pastoral. *Vid.* APPENDIX.

LOCKMAN, Mr. *John*, Secretary to the *British Herring Fishery*.—His poetical Talents seem not very extensive, as the greatest Part of what he has favoured the World with of that Sort, have been only a few Songs, Odes, &c. written on temporary Subjects, and intended to receive the Advantage of musical Composition

before they reached the Public.——I find, however, two Pieces of the dramatic Kind, both of them designed to be set to Music, but only the first of them, I believe, ever performed. They are entitled,

1. DAVID's *Lamentations*. Oratorio.

2. ROSALINDA. Dram. Piece.

Mr. *Lockman* has been concerned in several Translations and Compilements of very considerable Works; particularly the *General Dictionary* and *Blainvill's Travels*.

LODGE, *Thomas*, M. D.—The Family from which this Gentleman was descended had its Residence in *Lincolnshire*, but whether the Doctor himself was born there, seems not very easy to ascertain.—*Langbaine* and *Jacob*, and after them *Whincop* and *Chetwood*, who in the general are little more than Copiers, run into the Mistake of giving this Gentleman his Education at the University of *Cambridge*, whereas *Wood* informs us that it was at *Oxford* he was educated, where he made his first Appearance about 1573, and was afterwards a Scholar under the learned Dr. *Hobye* of *Trinity* College.—Here he made very considerable Advances in Learning, dedicated some Time to reading the Poets of Antiquity, and having himself a Turn to Poetry, more especially of the satirical Kind, his Genius soon render'd itself conspicuous in various Compositions of that Nature, and obtained him no inconsiderable Reputation as a Wit and Poet.——However, Mr. *Lodge* being very sensible of the Barrenness of the Soil throughout the whole Neighbourhood of *Parnassus*, and how seldom the Study of Poetry yields a competent Provision to its Professors, very prudently considered

it as only an Amufement for leifure Hours, a Relaxation from
more important Labours; and
therefore, after having taken one
Degree in Arts, applied himfelf
with great Affiduity, to the more
profitable Study of Phyfick, for
the Improvement of which he
went abroad, and after ftaying a
fufficient Time at *Avignon* to be
entitled to the Degree of Doctor
in that Univerfity, he returned,
and in the latter End of Queen
Elizabeth's Reign was incorporated in the Univerfity of *Cambridge*.
—He afterwards fettled in *London*,
where, by his Skill and Intereft
with the *Roman* Catholic Party, in
which Perfuafion it is faid he was
brought up, he met with good
Succefs, and came into great
Practice.

In what Year Dr. *Lodge* was
born does not evidently appear,
but he died in 1625, and had
Tributes paid to his Memory by
many of his Cotemporary Poets,
who have characterized him as a
Man of very confiderable Genius.

His dramatic Works are as follow,

   1. *Looking Glafs for* London
     and England. Tragi-Com.
     (affifted by *Robert Green*.)
   2. *Wounds of Civil War.* Tr.
Winftanley has named four more
dramatic Pieces, befides the firft
of the two above-named, which
he afferts to have been written in
Conjunction by this Author, affifted by *Robert Green,* viz.

   Lady ALIMONY. Com.
   Laws of Nature. Com.
   Liberalitie and Prodigalitie. C.
   LUMINALIA. Mafque.
But the three firft of thefe, tho'
they might be brought to agree in
Point of Time, yet are all printed
anonymous:—And, as to the laft,
it was written on a particular Oc-
cafion, and that not till two Years

after Dr. *Lodge*'s Death, and full
thirty-five after that of *Robert
Green*.

LOWER, Sir *William*, Knt. was
a noted Cavalier in the Reign of
King *Charles* I.—He was born at
a Place called *Tremare* in *Cornwall*.
—During the Heat of the Civil
Wars he took Refuge in *Holland*,
where, being ftrongly attached to
the Mufes, he had an Opportunity of enjoying their Society, and
purfuing his Studies in Peace and
Privacy.—He was a very great
Admirer of the *French* Poets, particularly *Corneille* and *Quinault*, on
whofe Works he has built the
Plans of four out of the fix Plays
which he wrote; the Titles of
all his dramatic Works in general are,

   1. *Amorous Phantafm.* T.-C.
   2. HORATIUS. Trag.
   3. *Inchanted Lovers.* Dram. Paft.
   4. *Martyr.* Trag.
   5. *Noble Ingratitude.* Paft.-
     Tragi-Comedy.
   6. PHÆNIX *in her Flames.* T.
Sir *William Lower* died in 1662.

LUPTON, Mr. *Thomas.* — Of
this Author *Langbaine* tells us he
was unable to recover any Particulars, either as to the Time of
his Birth, the Place where he
lived, or any Thing he wrote, excepting one Tragedy mentioned in
former Catalogues, entitled,

   All for Money.
As to all the former Particulars I
know as little as Mr. *Langbaine*,
but happening to have feen the
Play, which that Writer honeftly
confeffes he had not, am able to
afcertain the Author's Name,
which Mr. *Langbaine* has mif-
takenly called *Lupon*.—The Name
as I have given it is printed, together with that of the Publifher,
at the End of the Piece, which
is apparently very old, being written in Rhime, and printed in the
                old

old black Letter, without any numbering to the Pages.—The Manner of the Writing, moreover, is as old as that of the Printing.—The Characters being all figurative, *All for Money, Wit without Money, Money without Wit, Pleasure, &c.* being personalized and made Interlocutors in the Play or Interlude.—*Coxeter*, in his *Manuscript* Additions to *Jacob's Lives*, has peremptorily, and without assigning any Reason for so doing, affixed to it the Date of 1578.—But if, as is most probable, he has taken this Liberty from having seen some Edition of it so dated, it must have been an Impression subsequent to that which fell into my Hands, and which has no Date ; and therefore we may conclude the Play is in Reality still older than what even he has made it to be.

LYDE, *William.* Vid. JOYNER, *William.*

LYLLY, or LILLY, *John,* M. A. lived in the Reign of Q. *Elizabeth.*—He was a Native of *Kent,* and received his Education in St. *Mary Magdalen* College, *Oxford,* at which University he took his Degree of Master of Arts in the Year 1575.——He was a very assiduous Student, and warmly addicted, more especially to the Study of Poetry, in which he made so great a Proficiency, that he has bequeathed to the World no less than nine dramatic Pieces. —He was the first who attempted to reform and purify the *English* Language, by purging it of obsolete and uncouth Expressions : For this Purpose he wrote a Book entitled EUPHEUS *and his England,* which seems to have met with a Degree of Success unusual with the first Attempters of Reformation, the being almost immedi-

ately and universally followed.— At least, if we may give Credit to the Words of Mr. *Blount,* who published six of Mr. *Lilly's* Plays together, in one Volume in twelves, in a Preface to which he says of our Author, that " *Our Nation are in his Debt for a* " *new English, which he taught* " *them :* Eupheus *and his* England " *(says he) began first that Lan-* " *guage; all our Ladies were his* " *Scholars ; and that Beauty at* " *Court, which could not parley* " *Eupheisme, (that is to say)* " *who was unable to converse in* " *that pure and reformed* English, " *which he had formed his Work* " *to be the Standard of) was as* " *little regarded as she which now* " *there, speaks not* French."

According to this Mr. *Blount,* Mr. *Lilly* was deserving of the highest Encomiums.——He stiles him, in his Title Page, *the only rare Poet of that Time, the Witty, Comical, Facetiously-quick, and un-paralleled* John Lilly ; and in his Epistle Dedicatory says, " *that he* " *sate at* Apollo's *Table; that A-* " *pollo gave him a Wreath of his* " *own* Bayes *without snatching,* " *and that the* Lyre *he played on* " *had no borrowed Strings.*"—And indeed, if what has been above-hinted with Regard to the Reformation of the *English* Language be Fact, he certainly has a Claim to the highest Honours from his Countrymen, and even to have a Statue erected to his Memory, since, in the Foundation of what he thus begun, our Language seems all at once to have started out into a Degree of Perfection, which it has scarcely exceeded at any Period since.

His Plays, which were in that Age very well esteemed both by the Court and the University, are, as I said before, nine in Number, and their Titles as follow,

1. ALEXANDER *and* CAMPASPE. Tragi-Com.
2. ENDIMION. Com.
3. GALATEA. Com.
4. *Love his Metamorphosis.* Dram. Past.
5. *Maid her Metamorphosis.*
6. *Mother* BOMBIE. Com.
7. MYDAS. Com.
8. SAPPHO *and* PHAON. C.
9. *Woman in the Moon.* Com.

Winstanley has attributed another Piece to this Author, entitled,

A Warning for Fair Women,

but very erroneously, that having been written by an anonymous Author.

LYNCH, *Francis,* Esq;—Of this Gentleman I can trace nothing farther than that he was a Writer of the present Century (probably still living) and Author of two dramatic Pieces, *viz.*

The *Independant Patriot.* Com.
The *Man of Honour.* Com.

* * *

M.

M E.—These Initials stand to a dramatic Piece, published in the Reign of *Charles* II. entitled,

Saint CICILY. Trag.

But I cannot find out any known Author of that Time, with whose Name the Letters will correspond, or by whom therefore I can with any Appearance of Probability form a Conjecture of its having been written.

M. W.—These Letters stand in the Title Page of a dramatic Piece, called

The *Female Wits.* Com.

Coxeter, in his Remarks on *Jacob,* has altered with his Pen the Letters of W. N. which that Author had mentioned as belonging to a Piece, entitled,

HUNTINGTON's *Divertisement.* Interlude,

to those at the Head of this Article.—I therefore imagine these to be the Letters properly belonging to it, and *Jacob* to have been in a Mistake.—*Whincop,* however, has implicitly copied the W. N. from *Jacob.*

MACHIN, Mr. *Lewis.*—Concerning this Author I find nothing upon Record but that he lived in the Reign of K. *Char.* I. and wrote one Play, which we find reprinted in *Dodsley*'s Collection of old Plays, entitled,

The *Dumb Knight.* Com.

MACKLIN, Mr. *Charles.*——This Author is a Native of *Ireland,* born, as I have been informed, in the County of *West Meath,* and that the Name of his Family was M‘*Laughlin,* which seeming somewhat uncouth to the Pronunciation of an *English* Tongue, he, on his coming upon the Stage, *anglicized* it to that by which he has ever since been known.—His Merit as a Comedian in various Characters is too well known to need our taking up much Time in expatiating on it, particularly in Sir *Gilbert Wrangle* in the *Refusal,* Don *Manuel* in the *Kind Impostor,* Sir *Archibald* M‘*Sarcasm* in his own Farce of *Love a-la-Mode*; he has also been esteemed as very capital in the Character of *Shakespeare's Iago*; but the Part in which he has ever been allowed to shine without a Competitor, is that of *Shyleck* in the *Merchant of Venice,* which he performed in so natural a Manner, that a Gentleman in the

the Audience, on his firſt Appearance in it, by Way of Diſtinction
of his ſuperior Excellence, ſtarted
out into this accidental Extempore,

This is the Jew
That Shakeſpeare *drew.*

which Expreſſion being ready to
every one's Remembrance, eſtabliſhed Mr. *Macklin*'s very deſerved Reputation in the Character.
Mr. *Macklin* had the Misfortune
ſome Years ago, in Conſequence
of a ſudden Act of Paſſion, to occaſion the Death of a Brother Comedian (one Mr. *Hallam*) and
ſtood his Trial on Account of it,
but was honourably acquitted, it
appearing to be merely accidental, and without any Malice *pre-
penſe.*—However, he does not appear to be of the happieſt or moſt
complacent Diſpoſition, and that
Turbulence of Temper which has
at ſome Times induced him to
Steps whereby he has offended
the Audience, and at others involved in Diſputes with the Managers, has, at different Periods,
and that for a long while together,
deprived the Public of a very good
Performer, and himſelf of thoſe
Emoluments and Rewards that his
Merit had a perfect Right to, to
the great Loſs of both.—He is
now in the Decline of Life, a
Veteran of the Stage, and as he
has ſpent much the greateſt Part
of that Life in the Service of the
Public, it were much to be wiſhed, that the Remainder of it
might take a quiet Repoſe, free
from thoſe Storms and Hurricanes
which have but too frequently
diſturbed it.—He was formerly
conſidered as an excellent Tutor
in the Theatrical Arts, and indeed the Succeſs Miſs *Macklin* has
very juſtly met with, ſeems a
ſtrong Proof of the Truth of this
Aſſertion, as I have been informed ſhe ſtands almoſt entirely indebted to the Judgment and Inſtruction of her Father, in Oppoſition, if not to Genius, at
leaſt to Inclination, for that theatrical Execution which has gained her ſo much of the Favour of
the Town.

Mr. *Macklin*'s Merit as a Writer is more particularly enlarged
on in our reſpective Accounts of
his Works in the firſt Volume,
it will be therefore needleſs to recapitulate here what we have
there ſaid, and conſequently ſufficient to point them out to the
Reader's farther Obſervation, by
an Enumeration of their Titles in
the following Liſt, *viz.*

1. *Fortune Hunters.* Farce.
2. Henry VII. Trag.
3. *Love a la Mode.* Farce.
4. *Married Libertine.* Com.
5. *Suſpicious Huſband Criticiſed.*
Farce.
6. *Will or no Will.* Farce.

Maidwell, Mr. *John.*—The
Times of this Gentleman's Birth
and Death are not recorded by
any of the Writers.—It appears,
however, that he lived in the
Reign of *Charles* I. and kept a
private School in *London* for the
Education of young Gentlemen;
during the Receſſes from which
very fatiguing Employment it is
probable that, by Way of Amuſement, he wrote the Play publiſhed in his Name, *viz.*

The *Loving Enemies.* Com.
Coxeter (on what Authority I
know not) has ſtruck out the
Chriſtian Name of *John*, by which
both *Langbaine* and *Jacob* have
diſtinguiſhed this Author, and
put the Letter *L.* in its Room, as
the Initial of his Name.

Maine, or Mayne, *Jaſper*,
D. D.—This very learned and ingenious Gentleman was born in
1604,

1604, the second Year of King *James* I's Reign, at a little Market Town called *Hatherleigh* in *Devonſhire*.—He received his Education at *Weſtminſter* School, where he continued till the Age of nineteen, when he was removed to the Univerſity of *Oxford*, where he was admitted into *Chriſt-Church* College in the Rank of a *Servitor*; but in the enſuing Year, *viz.* 1624, he was choſen into the Number of Students on that noble Foundation.—Here he took his Degree of Batchelor and Maſter of Arts, after which he enter'd into Orders, and was prefer'd to two Livings in the Gift of the College, one of which was ſituated pretty near *Oxford*.—It does not, however, ſeem to have been ſo much the Doctor's own Inclination that led him to the Pulpit, as the Sollicitation of certain Perſons of Eminence, who, on Account of the Figure he made at the Univerſity in the Study of Arts and Sciences, and from an Eſteem for his Abilities, which they were deſirous of being enabled to reward, urged him to go into Orders.

On the breaking out of the Civil Wars, when King *Cha.* I. was obliged to fly for Shelter to *Oxford*, and keep his Court there, in order to avoid the Reſentment of the Populace in *London*, where continual Tumults were prevailing, Mr. *Maine* was made Choice of, among others, to preach before his Majeſty.—Soon after this, *viz.* in 1646, he was elected Doctor in Divinity, and reſided at *Oxford* till the Time of the Mock Viſitation of that Univerſity by *Oliver Cromwell*'s Creatures, when, with many others, equally diſtinguiſhed for their Zeal and Loyalty to the poor unhappy King, he was not only ejected

from the College, but alſo deprived of both his Livings.

During the Rage of the Civil War, he found an hoſpitable Refuge in the Family of the Earl of *Devonſhire*, where he continued till the Reſtoration, when he was not only reſtored to his former Benefices, but made one of the Canons of *Chriſt Church*, Chaplain in Ordinary to his Majeſty, and Archdeacon of *Chichbeſter*, all which Preferments he kept till his Death, which happened on the 6th of *Dec.* 1672.—He lies buried on the North Side of the Choir in the Cathedral of *Chriſt Church*.

Dr. *Maine* was held in very high Eſteem both for his natural Parts and his acquired Accompliſhments.—He was an orthodox Preacher, and a Man of ſevere Virtue and exemplary Behaviour, yet of a ready and facetious Wit, and a very ſingular Turn of Humour.—From ſome Stories that are related of him, he ſeems to have borne ſome Degree of Reſemblance in his Manner to the celebrated Dr. *Swift*; but, if he did not poſſeſs thoſe very brilliant Parts that diſtinguiſhed the Dean, he probably was leſs ſubject to that capricious and thoſe unaccountable Whimſies, which at Times ſo greatly eclipſed the Abilities of the latter.—Yet there is one Anecdote related of him, which, although I cannot be of Opinion that it reflects any great Honour to his Memory, as it ſeems to carry ſome Degree of Cruelty with it, yet is it a ſtrong Mark of his Reſemblance to the Dean, and a Proof that his Propenſity for Drollery and Joke did not quit him even in his lateſt Moments.—The Story is this; The Doctor had an old Servant, who had lived with him ſome
Years,

Years, to whom he bequeathed an old Trunk, in which he told him he would find *something that would make him drink after his Death.*—The Servant, full of Expectation that his Master, under this familiar Expression, had left him somewhat that would be a Reward for the Affiduity of his past Services, as soon as Decency would permit, flew to the Trunk, when behold, to his great Disappointment, the boasted Legacy proved to be—*a Red Herring.*

The Doctor, however, bequeathed many Legacies by Will to pious Uses, particularly fifty Pounds towards the Rebuilding of St. *Paul*'s Cathedral, and two Hundred Pounds to be distributed to the Poor of the Parishes of *Caffington*, and *Pyrton* near *Wattington*, of both which Places he had been Vicar.

In his younger Years he had an Attachment to Poetry, and wrote two Plays, the latter of which may be seen in the tenth Volume of *Dodfley's Collection*, viz.

1. *Amorous War.* Tragi-Com.
2. The *City Match.* Com.

MALLET, *David*, Efq; a North-Briton, was Tutor to the Duke of *Montrofe*, and to his Brother Lord *George Graham.*—He was Secretary to the late Prince of *Wales*.—He married a Lady of very confiderable Fortune; and has always lived, and been refpected as a Gentleman.—He is now Keeper of the Book of Entries for Ships in the Port of *London*.

He was the Editor of a new and compleat Edition of Lord *Bacon*'s Works, to which he prefixed a Life of that great Man; and publifhed the Philofophical Works of the late Lord *Bolingbroke*, agreeable to his Lordfhip's laft Will and Teftament.

His dramatic Pieces are,
1. EURYDICE. Trag.
2. MUSTAPHA. Trag.
3. ALFRED. Mafque, written in Conjunction with the late Mr. *James Thomfon*, Author of the *Seafons*.
4. BRITANNIA, a Mafque. 1755.
5. ELVIRA. Trag. altered from *La Motte*; who founded this Play on the famous Story of *Agnes de Caftro*, which *Camoëns* has fo beautifully introduced in his *Lufiad*. — Mr. *Mallet*'s Tragedy was acted with moderate Applaufe, at *Drury-Lane* Houfe, in *January* 1763.—The indifferent Succefs it met with may, in Part, be afcribed to the unlucky Juncture in which it appeared; at a Time when Party-Prejudice ran high againft the *Scottifh* Nation, on Account of the unpopular Adminiftration of the Earl of *Bute*, to whom *Elvira* was dedicated.

Mr. *Mallet*'s other Works are collected in three vol. 12mo. among which the moft confiderable are,
1. That fweet Ballad, entitled *William and Margaret.*
2. The *Excurfion*, a Poem, in two Cantos.
3. *Amyntor* and *Theodora*, or *the Hermit.*—This Piece was originally intended for the Stage; but the Author afterwards chofe to alter his Plan.

There was likewife an additional Collection of Poems by this Author, publifhed in 1762, in a thin Volume, Octavo; confifting of fmall Pieces on feveral Occafions.

MANNING, Mr *Francis*, was a Gentleman of eminent Learning, who flourifhed in the Reign of *William* III.—He has obliged the World with a Tranflation of

Dion

Dion Caſſius from the Original, and with two dramatic Pieces, entitled,

1. *All for the better.* Com.
2. *Generous Choice.* Com.

MANUCHE, Major *Coſmo.*—This Gentleman appears to have been an *Italian* by Birth, and *Phillips* has given us his Name *Manuci*, in which it is not improbable that he may for once have been in the Right.——He took up Arms for King *Charles*, and had a Major's Commiſſion, but whether of Horſe or Foot does not appear.—He wrote three Plays in the *Engliſh* Language, and, conſidering that he was a Foreigner, and that he only wrote for his Diverſion, and not by Way of a Profeſſion, and that at leaſt he has the Merit of their being original, wholly his own and unborrowed, they are very far from being contemptible.——Their Titles are,

1. The *Juſt General.* Trag.
2. The *Loyal Lovers.* T. C.
3. The *Baſtard.* Trag. (attributed to him by *Coxeter.*)

MARKHAM, *Gervaſe*, Eſq; was the Son of *Robert Markham*, of *Cotham* in *Nottinghamſhire*, Eſq; —He flouriſhed in the Reigns of Queen *Elizabeth*, King *James* I. and King *Charles* I. for the laſt of whom he took up Arms, and bore a Captain's Commiſſion.—He was a good Scholar, being perfect Maſter of the *French, Italian* and *Spaniſh* Languages.—He was extremely well verſed both in the Theory and Practice of military Diſcipline, and was a great Adept in Horſemanſhip, Farriery and Huſbandry; by which Means he was fully qualified for the Tranſlation and Compilement of numerous Volumes on all theſe Subjects, ma-

ny of which are even now held in very high Eſteem.—He alſo wrote ſome Books on rural Recreations; nor among his other Attentions were the Muſes neglected, for we find one Play extant in his Name, tho' he was indeed aſſiſted in it by Mr. *Sampſon*, of whom we ſhall hereafter have Occaſion to ſpeak, entitled,

HEROD *and* ANTIPATER. Trag.

Langbaine ſpeaks very highly in his Commendation, and very juſtly, as a great Benefactor to the Public, by his numerous and uſeful Publications, but ſays little of his Poetry; and indeed both him and *Jacob*, and ſince them *Cibber* in his *Lives of the Poets*, ſeem not to know of any other poetical Works that he was concerned in: But *Coxeter*, in his *MS.* Notes, has mentioned two Pieces of Poetry by this Author (both indeed Tranſlations) of conſiderable Conſequence, *viz.*

1. *Arioſto's Satires, in ſeven famous Diſcourſes*, 4to. 1608. and
2. *The Famous Whore, or Noble Courtezan: containing the lamentable Complaint of* Paulina, *the famous* Roman *Courtezan; ſometime Miſtreſs unto the great Cardinal* Hippolyto *of* Eſte, *tranſlated into Verſe from the* Italian, 8vo. 1609.

Beſides theſe *Coxeter* mentions the following Works in Proſe, not taken Notice of by the Writers of his Life, which he attributes to him, *viz.*

1. DEVEREUX. *Vertue's Tears for the Loſs of the moſt Chriſtian King* Henry, *third of that Name, King of* France, *and the untimely Death of the moſt noble and heroical* Walter Devereux, *who was ſlain before* Roan *in* Fraunce. *Firſt written in* French, *by that moſt excellent and learned Gentlewoman* Madame

Madame Gennoiſne Pelan Mau-
lette, *and paraphraſtically tranſlated into* Engliſh *by* Jarvis Markham, 4to. 1597.

2. *The Art of Archerie,* 8vo.
1634.

3. *The Soldier's Exerciſe,* &c. in
three Books, of which there was
a 3d Edition, 4to. 1643.

At what Time Mr. *Markham*
was born, or when he died, I
have not been able to trace ; but,
if all the Dates of his Publications
are rightly ſet down, he muſt
have lived to a very great Age,
ſince the *Devereux,* according to
Coxeter, was publiſhed in 1597,
and his *Perfect Horſemanſhip,* according to *Langbaine,* not till
1671, a Space, of itſelf, of 74
Years, which is ſcarcely credible.
I cannot help, therefore, ſuppoſing either that *Langbaine* muſt
have been miſtaken, and not
mentioned the firſt Editions of
ſome of his Works, or that the
Devereux at leaſt, and perhaps
ſome other of the Pieces attributed to him, might have been
by ſome other Perſon of the ſame
Family, and, which is not uncommon, of the ſame Chriſtian
Name.

MARLOE, Mr. *Chriſtopher,*
lived in the Reign of Queen *Elizabeth,* and was not only an Author but an Actor alſo, being very conſiderable in both.——There
is no Account extant of his Family, but it is well known that
he was entered as a Student in the
Univerſity of *Cambridge* ; but that
he early quitted the Academic
Life, and went on the Stage,
where he was Cotemporary with
the immortal *Shakeſpeare* and with
Thomas Heywood, whom we have
mentioned before ; the latter of
whom ſtiles him the *beſt of Poets* ;
nay, even *Ben Jonſon,* who was
never apt to be over laviſh of

Commendation, has beſtowed a
high Panegyrick on him, in a
Copy of Verſes called the *Cenſure
of the Poets,* in which he ſpeaks
of him in the following Manner ;

Next Marloe, *bathed in* Theſ-
pian *Springs,*
*Had in him thoſe brave ſublunary
Things,*
*That your firſt Poets had ; his
Raptures were*
*All Air and Fire, which made
his Verſes clear ;*
*For that fine Madneſs ſtill he did
retain,*
*Which rightly ſhould poſſeſs a
Poet's Brain.*

Mr. *Marloe* came to an untimely End, falling a Victim to
the moſt torturing Paſſion of the
human Breaſt, Jealouſy.——For,
being deeply in Love with a Girl
of a low Station, he found himſelf rivalled by a Fellow in Li
very, who, as *Wood* informs us,
had more the Appearance of a
Pimp than a Man formed for the
tender and generous Paſſion of
Love.——*Marloe* finding the Fellow
with his Miſtreſs, and having
ſome Reaſons to ſuſpect that ſhe
granted him Favours, drew his
Dagger, a Weapon at that Time
moſt univerſally worn, and ruſh-
ed on him to ſtab him, but the
Footman being nimble, warded
off the impending Stroke, and,
ſeizing hold of *Marloe's* Wriſt,
turned the fatal Point, and plunged the Poignard into its Maſter's
Head, of which Wound, notwithſtanding all poſſible Care being
taken of him, he died ſoon after,
in the Year 1593.

Wood conſiders this Cataſtrophe
as an immediate Judgment on the
unhappy Sufferer for his Blaſphe-
mies and Impiety ; for he tells
us that *Marloe,* preſuming upon

 his

his own little Wit, thought proper to practife the moft Epicurean Indulgence, and openly profeffed Atheifm; that he denied God our Saviour; blafphemed the adorable Trinity; and, as it was reported, wrote feveral Difcourfes againft it; affirming our Saviour to be a Deceiver, the facred Scriptures to entertain nothing but idle Stories, and all Religion to be a Device of Policy and Prieftcraft.

This Character, if juft, is fuch a one, as fhould induce us to look back with Contempt and Pity, on the Memory of the Perfon who poffeffed it, and recal to our Mind that inimitable Sentiment of the great and good Dr. *Young*, in his Complaint,

> *When I behold a Genius bright and bafe,*
> *Of tow'ring Talents, but terreftrial Aims,*
> *Methinks I fee, as fallen from it's high Sphere,*
> *The glorious Image of a Soul immortal;*
> *With   mix'd, and grov'ling in the Duft.*

I would, however, rather wifh to take this Character with fome Degree of Abatement, and, allowing that Mr. *Marloe* might be inclinable to Free-thinking, yet that he could not run to the unhappy Lengths he is reported to have done, especially as the Time he lived in was a Period of Bigotry; and that even, in thefe calmer Times of Controverfy, we find a great Aptnefs in Perfons, who differ in Opinion with Regard to the fpeculative Points of Religion, either wilfully or from the miftaking of Terms, to tax each other with Deifm, Herefy, and even Atheifm, on even the moft trivial Tenets, which have

the leaft Appearance of being unorthodox.

But, to quit his Character in a religious View, let us now confider him as a Poet, and in this Light he muft be allowed to have had great Merit.—His Turn was entirely to Tragedy, in which Kind of Writing he has left the fix following Teftimonials of Abilities.

1. Dr. FAUSTUS's *Tragical. Hiftory.*
2. EDWARD II.   Trag.
3. *Jew of Malta.*   T. C.
4. *Luft's Dominion.*   Trag.
5. *Maffacre of Paris.*   Trag.
6. TAMBERLAINE *the Great.*   Trag. in two Parts.

He alfo joined with *Nafh*, in the writing a Play called

DIDO, *Queen of* CARTHAGE, and had begun a very fine Poem, called *Hero and Leander*, which was afterwards finifhed by *Chapman*, tho' not with the fame Spirit and Invention that its Author had begun it with.

MARMION, or MARMYON, *Shakerley*, M. A.—This Writer, who flourifhed in the Reign of *Charles* I. was born in the Hereditary Manfion-Houfe of his Family at *Ainoe* in *Northamptonfhire*, about the Beginning of *January* 1602.—When a Boy he was put to School at *Thame* in *Oxfordfhire*, from whence, at about the Age of Sixteen, he was removed to *Wadham* College *Oxford*, where he was enter'd firft as a Gentleman-Commoner, and afterwards, in 1624, took his Degree of Mafter of Arts.

Mr. *Marmion* is not a voluminous Writer, Death having moft probably ftopped the Career of his Genius; yet I cannot help confidering him as one of the beft among the dramatic Authors of that Time.—His Plots are ingenious,

nious, his Characters well drawn, and his Language not only easy and dramatic, but full of lively Wit, and solid Understanding.—He died in a middle Age of Life, some Time between 1641 and 1650, tho' I have not been able to trace the particular Year, and has left only three Plays behind him, one of which, *viz.* The *Antiquary*, is to be seen among *Dodsley's Old Plays*, Vol. V.——The Titles of his Pieces are

1. *Antiquary.* Com.
2. *Fine Companion.* Com.
3. *Holland's Leaguer.* Com.

Phillips and *Winstanley*, according to their usual Custom of fathering anonymous Plays on any Authors that they think proper to find out for them, have attributed to Mr. *Marmion* a Play which is not his, nor bears any Resemblance to his Manner of writing, entitled,

The *Faithful Shepherd.*

MARSH, Mr. *Charles*, a Bookseller and a Dealer also in Poetry, but not very extensively; being Author only of one Play, *viz.*

AMASIS *King of* EGYPT. Trag. printed, but never acted.

He has also republished *Shakespeare's Cymbeline*, with some Alterations, but it has not yet been acted.

MARSTON, Mr. *John.*—Of this eminent Poet, who flourished in the Reigns of Queen *Elizabeth* and King *James* I. but few Circumstances remain on Record. *Wood* only informs us that he was a Student in *Corpus Christi* College *Oxford*, but has neither fixed the Place of his Birth, nor the Family from which he was descended ; and *Langbaine* tells us, that he was able to recover no farther Information of him than what he had learned from the Testimony of his Bookseller,

and, as that relates only to the Merit of his Writings, it is little more than what might have been gathered from the Perusal of his Works, *viz.* that he was a chaste and pure Writer, avoiding all that Obscenity, Ribaldry, and Scurrility, which too many of the Play-wrights of that Time, and indeed much more so in some Periods since, have made the Basis of their Wit, to the great Disgrace and Scandal of the Stage.—That he abhorred such Writers and their Works, and pursued so opposite a Practice in his own Performances, that " whatsoever " even in the Spring of his Years " he presented upon the private " and public Theatre, in his Au- " tumn and declining Age he " needed not to be ashamed of."

His Plays are eight in Number, and their Titles as follow, *viz.*

1. ANTONIO *and* MELIDA. Hist. Play.
2. ANTONIO's *Revenge.* Trag.
3. *Dutch Courtezan.* Com.
4. *Insatiate Countess.* Trag.
5. *Malecontent.* Tragi-Com.
6. *Parasitaster.* Com.
7. SOPHONISBA. Trag.
8. *What you will.* Com.

It is evident that *Marston* must have lived in Friendship with *Ben Jonson* at the Time of his writing the *Malecontent*, which Play he has warmly dedicated to him, yet it is probable that *Ben's* Self-Sufficiency and natural Arrogance might in Time lessen that Friendship, as we afterwards find our Author, in his Epistle to the Reader prefixed to his *Sophonisba*, casting some very severe Glances at the Pedantry and Plagiarism of that Poet, in borrowing Orations from *Sallust* and other of the classical Writers, and making Use of them in his Tragedies of *Sejanus* and *Cataline*.

The

The exact Period of Mr. *Marston*'s Death is not known; but, as *Cibber* tells us that his Works were publifhed after his Death by *Shakefpeare*, who himfelf died in 1616, it is evident that it muft have been fome Time before that Year.—As a Specimen of his Poetry, Mr. *Dodfley* has republifhed his *Malecontent* in his *Collection*, Vol. IV.

MARTYN, *Benjamin*, Efq;—Who or what this Gentleman was, or whether ftill living, I know not.—He, however, lays Claim to a Place in this Work, as being Author of one Play, which was acted with fome Succefs, and is entitled,

TIMOLEON. Trag.

MASON, *John*, M. A. lived in the Time of King *James* I. and about the Middle of that Reign publifhed one dramatic Piece, which he has entitled

MULCASSES *the Turk*. A worthy Tragedy.

Whether it merits the Title of *worthy* I cannot pretend to determine, as it has not happened to fall in my Way, but it is evident that the Author had himfelf a very high Opinion of its Worth, from the following Motto which he has prefixed to it, quoted from *Horace*, viz.

Sume Superbiam quæfitam meritis.

MASSINGER, Mr. *Philip*.—This excellent Poet was Son to Mr. *Philip Maffinger*, a Gentleman who had fome Employment under the Earl of *Montgomery*, in whofe Service he died, after having fpent feveral happy Years in his Family.——Our Author was born at *Salifbury* in Queen *Elizabeth*'s Reign, Anno 1584, and at the Age of eighteen was entered a Fellow-Commoner of St.

Alban's Hall in *Oxford*, in which Station he remained three or four Years, in Order to compleat his Education.—Yet, tho' he was encouraged in the Purfuit of his Studies by his Father's Patron, the Earl of *Pembroke*, yet the natural Bent of his Genius leading him much more to Poetry and polite Literature, than to dryer and more abftrufe Studies of Logic and Philofophy; and, being impatient for an Opportunity of moving in a more public Sphere of Action, and improving his Poetical Fancy and his Knowledge of the *Belles Lettres*, by Converfation with the World, and an Intercourfe with Men of Wit and Genius, he quitted the Univerfity without taking any Degree, and came up to *London*, where, applying himfelf to writing for the Stage, he prefently rofe into high Reputation, his Plays meeting with the univerfal Approbation of the Public, both for the Purity of their Stile, and the Ingenuity and Oeconomy of their Plots.—Tho' his Pieces befpeak him a Man of the Firft-Rate Abilities, and well qualified both as to Learning and a moft perfect Acquaintance with the Methods of dramatic Writings, yet he was at the fame Time a Perfon of the moft confummate Modefty, which render'd him extremely beloved by all his Cotemporary Poets, few of whom but what efteemed it as an Honour to join with him in the Compofition of their Works.— The Pieces he has left behind him are as follow,

1. *Bafhful Lover*. Tragi-Com.
2. *Believe as you lift*. Com.
3. *Bondman*. Trag.
4. *City Madam*. Com.
5. *Duke of* MILAN. Trag.
6. *Emperor of the Eaft*. T. C.
7. *Fatal Dowry*. Trag.

8. *Great*

8. *Great Duke of* FLORENCE. Com.
9. *Guardian.* Com. Hift.
10. *Maid of Honour.* T. C.
11. *New Way to pay old Debts.* Com.
12. *Old Law.* Com. (affifted by *Rowley* and *Middleton.*)
13. *Picture.* Tragi-Com.
14. *Powerful Favourite.* Hift. Play.
15. *Renegado.* Tragi-Com.
16. *Roman Actor.* Trag.
17. *Very Woman.* Tragi-Com.
18. *Virgin Martyr.* Trag. (affifted by *Decker.*)
19. *Unnatural Combat.* Trag.

Almoft all the Writers agree very nearly in their Accounts of the Time of his Birth, but *Coxeter's MS.* points out a Miftake in the Æra of his Death, which he makes to have happened in *March* 1639, in which he is fupported by the Authority of *Wood's Athen. Oxon.* whereas *Langbaine* and *Jacob,* and after them *Whincop* and *Cibber* have placed in it 1669.—*Coxeter,* however, feems to have the greater apparent Probability on his Side, both with a Confideration of the very great Age, (*viz.* 85 Years) that he muft have lived to, according to the latter Suppofition, and moreover from the Epitaph written on him by Sir *Afton Cockain,* in which he is faid to be buried in the very fame Grave with *Fletcher,* who died in 1625; and which, had there been a Diftance of forty-four Years between their refpective Departures, it is probable would have been a Circumftance fcarcely known, and much lefs worth recording.

There is one Thing, however, fomewhat unaccountable, which is, that *Chetwood,* who, in his double Capacity of Bookfeller and Prompter had great Opportuni-

ties, and indeed wanted not Curiofity, to enquire into thofe Affairs, has, in his *Britifh Theatre,* varied from all the other Writers in both the Beginning and End of his Mortal Exiftence; and, without affigning any Authority but his own *ipfe dixit,* has pofitively afferted, that *he was born in* 1578, *and died in* 1659, *in the* 81ft *Year of his Age.*

It is, however, univerfally agreed, that his Body was buried in the Church Yard of St. *Saviour's, Southwark,* and that he was attended to the Grave by all the Comedians then in Town.——His Death was fudden, and the Place of it his own Houfe, near to the Play-Houfe, on the *Bank* Side, *Southwark,* where he went to Bed in good Health, and was found dead the next Morning.

In the above Lift of his Works, that numbered 2, is mentioned by no one but *Chetwood,* who tells us that he had feen it in MS. and is affured by the proper Quotations, (i. e. The Markings of the Prompter for his own Ufe and that of the Performers) that it was acted.——The Title, he fays, runs thus,

Believe as you Lift, written by
Mr. *Maffinger,*

and that it had the following Licence, figned by Lord *Herbert,* who, I imagine, was Mafter of the Revels in King *Charles* I's Reign, *viz.*

THIS Play, called *Believe as you Lift,* may be acted this 6th of *May* 1631. HENRY HERBERT.

And now, it is but a Piece of Juftice due to the Memory of this very great Man, to make fome little farther Mention of his Merit, which feems in good Meafure to have been buried in Obfcurity, and forgotten amongft the extenfive Number of Writers of the

the same Period, whose Ashes it was not worth awakening or calling forth from the Caverns of Oblivion.—But when we consider how long many of those Pieces, even of the immortal *Shakespeare* himself, which are now the greatest Ornaments of the present Stage, lay by neglected, although they wanted no more than a judicious Pruning of some few Luxuriances, some little straggling Branches, which over-hung the fairer Flowers, and hid some of the choicest Fruits, it is the less to be wonder'd that this Author, who, tho' second, stands no more *than* second to him, should share for a while the same Destiny.

Those who are unacquainted with *Massinger*'s Writings will, perhaps, be surprized to find one placing him in an equal Rank with *Beaumont* and *Fletcher*, and the immortal *Ben*; but I flatter myself that, if they will but give themselves the Trouble of perusing his Plays, their Astonishment will cease, that they will acquiesce with me in my Opinion, and think themselves obliged to me for pointing out to them so vast a Treasury of Entertainment and Delight.

Massinger has certainly equal Invention, equal Ingenuity in the Conduct of his Plots, and an equal Knowledge of Character and Nature with *Beaumont* and *Fletcher*; and if it should be objected that he has less of the *Vis comica*, it will surely be allowed that that Deficiency is amply made Amends for by that Purity and Decorum which he has preserved, and a Rejection of that Looseness and Obscenity which runs through most of their Comedies.—As to *Ben Jonson*, I shall readily allow that he excels this Author with Respect to the studied Accuracy

and Classical Correctness of his Stile; yet Mr. *Massinger* has so greatly the Superiority of him in Fire, *Pathos,* and the Fancy and Management of his Plots, that I cannot help thinking the Ballance stands pretty even between them.

However, to the Credit of the present Age, this Author seems to be rising out of Obscurity, as by a late Republication of his Works, compleat in four Volumes, 8vo. to which I refer my Readers, every one has an Opportunity of conversing with him in the Study; and as Mr. *Garrick*, to whom the Town has been obliged for many valuable Revivals, has already brought one of his Pieces on the Stage (viz. *The New Way to pay Old Debts*) and may probably bestow the same Honour on others of them, should some able Hand take on itself the Task of adapting them ever so little more than they are to the Taste of the present Time.

MAY, *Thomas,* Esq; was both a Poet and an Historian, and flourished in the Reigns of *James* I. and *Cha.* I.—He was born in the Year 1595, and was the Son of Sir *Thomas May*, of an ancient, but somewhat declining Family, in the County of *Sussex.*—He received his Education in the University of *Cambridge*, where he was enter'd a Fellow-Commoner of *Sidney* College; during his Residence at which Place, he applied very close to his Studies, and acquired that Fund of Learning of which his various Works give such apparent Testimony. —— From thence he removed to *London,* and frequently made his Appearance at Court, where he contracted the Friendship, and obtained the Esteem of several Persons of Fashion and Distinction, more especially with the accomplished

Endymion

Endymion Porter, Efq; one of the Gentlemen of the Bed-Chamber to the King; a Perfon fo dearly valued by Sir *William D'Avenant*, that he has ftiled him *Lord of his Mufe and Heart*.

On the Death of *Ben Jonfon* in 1637, Mr. *May* ftood Candidate for the vacant Laurel, in Competition with Sir *William D'Avenant*, but the latter carrying the Day, our Author was fo extremely exafperated at his Difappointment, that, notwithftanding he had hitherto been a zealous Courtier, yet, through Refentment to the Queen, to whofe Intereft he imagined Sir *William* was indebted for his Succefs, he commenced a violent and inveterate Enemy to the King's Party, and became not only an Advocate, but Hiftorian for the Parliament.—In that Hiftory, however, he has fhewn entirely the Spleen of a Malecontent, and indeed it is fcarcely poffible it fhould happen otherwife, fince it is apparent that he efpoufed the Party merely thro' Pique and Refentment, and not from any public-fpirited Principles ; and confequently that, had he happened to have obtained the Bayes, it is reafonable to fuppofe he would, with equal Warmth, have efpoufed and fupported the Royal Caufe, as under his prefent Circumftances he did the Republican.

He died fuddenly, in the Year 1650, and the 55th of his Age ; for, going well to Bed, he was there found next Morning dead, occafioned, as fome fay, by tying his Night-Cap too clofe under his fat Chin and Cheeks, which choaked him when he turned on the other Side ; and, as Dr. *Fuller* expreffes it, " if he " were himfelf a *byaffed* and *par-* " *tial* Writer, yet he lieth buried

" near a good and true Hiftorian " indeed, *viz.* the great Mr. *John* " *Cambden*, in the Weft Side of " the South Ifle of *Weftminfter-* " *Abbey.*"——He had a Monument, with a *Latin* Infcription, raifed over him by Order of the Parliament, who had made him their Hiftoriographer. —— But, before his Body had refted there eleven Years, it was taken up (with other Bodies that had been unwarrantably buried there from 1641 till the Reftauration) and buried in a large Pit in the Church Yard belonging to St. *Margaret's, Weftminfter.*—At the fame Time his Monument alfo was taken down and thrown afide, and in the Place of it was fet up that of Dr. *Thomas Triplet*, Anno 1670.

Tho' the Circumftance abovementioned in Regard to King *Charles* feems to fpeak him fomewhat opinionated, and jealous of the Refpect due to his own Merits, yet we muft allow fomewhat for the Frailty of human Nature, and even his Enemies cannot furely deny him to have been a very good Poet.

His Works are numerous, but thofe of the greateft Note are, A Tranflation of *Lucan's Pharfalia*, together with a Continuation of it, in feven Books, both in *Latin* and *English* Verfe.——He wrote likewife an *Hiftory of Henry* II. and the above-mentioned *Hiftory of the Parliament*, in Profe.—He alfo wrote the five following Plays, *viz.*

1. Agrippina, *Emprefs of Rome.* Trag.
2. Antigone. Trag.
3. Cleopatra, *Queen of Egypt.* Trag.
4. The *Heir.* Com.
5. *Old Couple.* Com.

The two laft of thefe are reprinted

ed by *Dodſley*, in the VIIth Volume of his Collection, to which
is prefixed ſome ſhort Account of
the Author, and a very ſevere
Epitaph written on him in *Latin*,
by one of the Cavalier Party,
which he had ſo much abuſed.

Phillips and *Winſtanley* have attributed two other Plays to this
Author, but without any Regard
to Chronology, the one of them
having been printed when Mr.
May could not have been above
three Years old, and the other a
Year before he was born. — The
Pieces are,

   1. The *Old Wiſe's Tale*. Com.
   2. ORLANDO FURIOSO. C.

MEAD, *Robert*, M. D. was
born in *Fleetſtreet London*, in the
Year 1616.—He received the firſt
Parts of Education at *Weſtminſter*
School, from whence, in his
eighteenth Year, he removed to
Oxford, and was elected a Student
of *Chriſt Church* College in that
Univerſity.—As ſoon as he had
taken the Degree of Maſter of
Arts, he quitted his Academical
Studies, and took up Arms for
King *Charles* I. who gave him a
Captain's Commiſſion in the Garriſon at *Oxford*.—In *May* 1646,
he was appointed, by the Governor thereof, one of the Commiſſioners to treat with thoſe of the
Parliament concerning a Surrender, and in the next Month was
actually created a Doctor of Phyſic.

He followed King *Charles* II.
into *France*, and was ſent by
him as an Agent into *Sweden*.
—Soon after this he returned to
the Place of his Nativity, died in
the very ſame Houſe in which he
had been born, on the 12th of
Feb. 1652, Æt. 30, and lies buried in the Church of St. *Dun-
ſtan's in the Weſt*.

While he was an Under Gra-
duate in the Univerſity, he wrote
one Play, which however was never publiſhed till after his Deceaſe.—It is entitled,
   The *Combat of Love and Friendſhip*. Com.

Phillips has alſo, but without
Foundation, attributed to this
Author an anonymous Piece, en-
titled,
   The *Coſtly Whore*. A Comical
Hiſtory.

MEDBOURN, Mr. *Matth.w*,
an Actor of conſiderable Eminence, belonging to the Duke of
York's Theatre, in the Reign of
King *Charles* II. but being a *Roman* Catholic, and inflamed with
a too forward and indiſcreet Zeal
for the Religion he had been
brought up in, he became engaged in *Titus Oates's* Plot, on
which Account he was committed
to *Newgate*, in which Place he
died, altho', as *Langbaine* obſerves, he merited a much better
Fate.—He wrote, or rather made
a Tranſlation at Large from *Moliere*, of a Comedy, entitled,
   TARTUFFE.

This Gentleman alſo publiſhed
another dramatic Piece, which
he dedicated to the Queen, of
which *Gildon* ſays, notwithſtanding the Letters E. M. in the Title Page, he was ſuppoſed to have
been the Author; it is entitled,
   Saint CECILY. Trag.

Tho' all the Writers mention his
having died in Priſon, yet none
of them have informed us in
what Year that Cataſtrophe happened.

MENDEZ, *Moſes*, Eſq;—This
Gentleman, who has been but a
very few Years dead, was a Jew,
and, if I do not miſtake, either
a Stock-Broker or a Notary Public.—He was a Perſon of conſi-
de   rable

derable Genius, of an agreeable Behaviour and entertaining in Converfation, and had a very pretty Turn for Poetry.—He was Author of two little dramatic Pieces, both of which met with good Succefs, and fome of the Songs in both ftill juftly continue Favorites with Perfons of poetical and mufical Tafte.

1. *Chaplet.* Mufical Entertainment.

2. *Shepherd's Lottery.* Ditto.

MERITON, Mr. *Thomas*, lived in the Reign of King *Charles* II. *Langbaine* has been extremely fevere upon him, telling us that he was certainly the meaneft dramatic Writer that ever *England* produced; and, applying to his Stupidity a Parody on the Expreffion of *Menedemus* the Philofopher, relating to the Wickednefs of *Perfeus*, fays, that *He is indeed a Poet, but of all Men that are, were, or ever fhall be, the dulleft :* that never Man's Stile was more Bom--baft, and that, as he himfelf did not pretend to fuch a Quicknefs of Apprehenfion as to underftand either of his Plays, he can only inform us that they are two in Number, and that their Titles are,

1. *Love and War.* Trag.

2. *Wandering Lovers.* T. C.

He alfo informs us, from Mr. *Meriton's* own Authority, that he had written another Play, called,

The *Several Wits.* Com. which, however, he made only his Pocket Companions, fhewing them only to a few feleét and private Friends, on which, moreover, he remarks, that thofe were certainly happieft who were not reckoned in the Number of this Author's Friends, and confequently compelled to liften to fuch Fuftian, which, like an empty

Cafk, makes a great Sound, but yields at beft nothing but Lees.

In Proof of thefe Affertions Mr. *Langbaine* has given his Readers a Copy of Part of the Epiftle Dedicatory to the *Wandering Lover,* which is indeed a Curiofity in its Way, and to which I refer thofe who are fond of grafping a Cloud, or regaling their Appetites with Whipp'd Syllabub.

METASTASIO, Abbè.—This Gentleman, as a Foreigner, has little Right to a Place here; yet, as fome of his Pieces have been reprefented on our *Italian* Theatre in the *Haymarket,* that Kind of Naturalization gives me an Opportunity of doing fome little Juftice to the Merit of a Poet of the very firft Rate, who feems to be little thought of, only becaufe his Works, being written in a Language not much in Vogue in this Nation, are but little known.— Whereas, were they but once introduced to the Acquaintance of our Countrymen, they would certainly be as univerfally admired as thofe of *Racine, Corneille,* &c. among the *French*, to which, in Refpeét of Plot, Language, Charaéter and Sentiment, they are by no Means inferior; and, which is ftill a ftronger Proof of the poetical Powers of their Author, he has found Means of fupporting the Dignity of Tragedy, and all the more nervous Beauties of Tragic Poetry, amidft the Jingle of Rhime and the Effeminacy of Sing-Song, to which, in Compliance with the depraved Tafte of his Countrymen, he has been compelled to fubmit.—He is, I believe, ftill living, and hold the Station of Poet-Laureat to the Emperor.—He has written a great Number of dramatic Pieces, of which it were to be wifhed we
had

had a Tranflation by fome capital Hand.—Of thefe, as I before obferved, feveral have made their Appearance at the King's Theatre in the *Haymarket*, where, notwithftanding their capital Degree of Merit, they have paffed with juft the fame Sort of Approbation that has been beftowed on the contemptible Pieces which are frequently reprefented there, and in which the Words have been intended for nothing but a mere Vehicle to the Sound of mufical Notes ; that is to fay, the Audience have been enraptured with Mufic that they did not underftand, and never concerned themfelves about underftanding the Piece itfelf, which would have done Honour to their Judgments.

I fhall, however, only mention three, and in my Choice of them fhall be directed by the Confideration of their having been all introduced into our own Language, either in Imitation, Tranflation or Paraphrafe, *viz.*

1. ARTASERSE. Ital. Opera.
2. *Clemenza di* TITO. Ital. Opera.
3. *L'Ifola defabitata.* Italian Opera.

The firft of thefe has been tranflated, greatly mangled, yet moft nobly fet to Mufic by Dr. *Arne,* under the Title of the *Englifh* Opera of *Artaxerxes.*—Mr. *Cleland* has made the fecond the Model of his Tragedy called *Titus Vefpafian* ; and the *Defert Ifland* of Mr. *Murphy* is only a very greatly extended Paraphrafe of the laft.

MIDDLETON, Mr. *Thomas,* was a very voluminous Writer, and lived fo late as the Time of *Charles* I. yet I can meet with very few Particulars relating to him ; for, notwithftanding that he has certainly fhewn confidera-

ble Genius in thofe Plays, which are unqueftionably all his own, and which are very numerous, yet he feems in his Life-Time to have owed the greateft Part of the Reputation he acquired, to his Connection with *Jonfon, Fletcher, Maffinger* and *Rowley,* with whom he was concerned in the writing of feveral dramatic Pieces, but to have been confider'd in himfelf as a Genius of a very inferior Clafs, and concerning whom the World was not greatly interefted in the purfuing any Memoirs.— Yet, furely it is a Proof of Merit fufficient to eftablifh him in a Rank far from the moft contemptible among our dramatic Writers, that a Set of Men of fuch acknowledged Abilities confider'd him as deferving to be admitted a joint Labourer with them in the Fields of poetical Fame ; and more efpecially by *Fletcher* and *Jonfon,* the firft of whom, like a Widow'd Mufe, could not be fuppofed readily to admit another Partner after the Lofs of his long and well-beloved Mate *Beaumont* ; and the latter, who entertained fo high an Opinion of his own Talents as fcarcely to admit any Brother near the Throne, and would hardly have permitted the clear Waters of his own *Heliconian* Springs to have been muddied by the Mixture of any Streams, that did not apparently flow from the fame Source, and, however narrow their Currents, were not the genuine Produce of *Parnaffus.*

The Pieces which *Middleton* wrote entirely, and thofe in which he only fhared the Honour with others, are diftinguifhed in the following Lift.

1. *Any Thing for a quiet Life.* Com.
2. BLUST *Mr. Conftable.* Com.
3. *Change-*

3. *Changeling.* Trag. (The Author affifted by *Rowley*.)
4. *Chafte Maid in Cheapfide.* Com.
5. *CORONA MINERVÆ.* Mafque.
6. *Fair Quarrel.* Com. (In this Play *Rowley* alfo joined with our Author.)
7. *Family of Love.* Com.
8. *Fine Gallants.* Com. *Vid.* APPENDIX.
9. *Game at Cheffe.*
10. *Inner Temple Mafque.*
11. *Mad World my Mafters.* Com.
12. *Mayor of* QUEENBOROUGH. Com.
13. *Michaelmas Term.* Com.
14. *More Diffemblers befides Women.* Com.
15. *No Wit, no Help like a Woman's.* Com.
16. *Old Law.* Com. (This Author and *Rowley* affifted *Maffinger* in writing this Comedy.)
17. PHÆNIX. Tragi-Com.
18. *Roaring Girl.* Com.
19. *Spanifh Gypfie.* Com. (The Author affifted by *Rowley*.)
20. *Sun in Aries.* Entertain.
21. *Trick to catch the old One.* Com.
22. *Triumphs of Love and Antiquity.* Mafque.
23. *Triumphs of Truth.*
24. *Widow.* Com. (In this *Middleton* only joined with *Fletcher* and *Jonfon*.)
25. *World tofs'd at Tennis.* M.
26. *Women beware Women.* T.

MILLER, the Rev. Mr. *James*, was the Son of a Clergyman, who poffeffed two Livings of confiderable Value in *Dorfetfhire*.— He was born in the Year 1703, and received his Education at *Wadham* College in *Oxford*.—His natural Genius and Turn for Satire, however, led him, by Way of Relaxation from his more ferious Studies, to apply fome Portion of his Time to the Mufes; and, during his Refidence at the Univerfity, he compofed great Part of a Comedy called the *Humours of Oxford*, fome of the Characters in which being either really defigned for, or at leaft pointed out, as bearing a ftrong Refemblance to fome of the Students, and indeed Heads, of that Univerfity, gave confiderable Umbrage, created the Author many Enemies, and probably laid the Foundation of the greateft Part of his Misfortunes thro' Life.

On his quitting the Univerfity he entered into holy Orders, and got immediately preferred to the Lecturefhip of *Trinity* College in *Conduit* Street, and to be Preacher of *Roehampton* in *Surry*.

The Emoluments of thefe Livings, however, being not very confiderable, he having married an amiable young lady with a very genteel Fortune, finding the Expences of a Family growing upon him, and having perhaps, from the Vivacity of his Difpofition, a Defire, as *Shakefpeare* expreffes it,

*Of fhewing fomewhat a more
 fwelling Port
Than his faint Means could grant
 Continuance,*

he was encouraged, by the Succefs of his firft Play, which had been brought on the Stage at the particular Recommendation of Mrs. *Oldfield*, to have Recourfe to dramatic Writing, as a Means of enlarging his Finances.—But this Kind of Compofition being confider'd, in this fqueamifh Age, as fomewhat foreign to, and inconfiftent with, a clerical Profeffion, a certain Right Reverend Prelate, from whom Mr. *Miller* had perhaps fome Expectations of Preferment, made fome very harfh Remonftrances with him on the Subject, and, on not perceiving him perfectly inclinable at once to quit the Advantages he received from the Theatre, without the Affurance of fomewhat adequate to it from the Church, thought proper to withdraw his Patronage.— On which, in a fatyrical Poem which our Author publifhed foon after, there appeared a Character, which being univerfally fixed on as intended for the Bifhop, occafioned an irreconcileable Breach between his Lordfhip and the Author, and was for many Years afterwards thought to have retarded his Advancement in the Church.

Mr. *Miller* proceeded with his dramatic Productions, and met with fo good Succefs that, from the Reprefentation of three or four other Pieces, he reaped very confiderable Emoluments, and very probably might have continued fo to do, had not his Wit and Propenfity to Satire involved him in a *Brulée* with the Body of Critics, the Supporters or Deftroyers of this Kind of Writing, for having, in a Comedy called the *Coffeehoufe*, drawn certain Characters, which were imagined to be defigned for Mrs. *Yarrow* and her Daughter, who kept *Dick's* Coffeehoufe between the *Temple* Gates, and for fome of the Perfons who frequented that Houfe, the *Templars*, who confider'd this Step as touching their own Copyhold, went in a Body to the Play-houfe, with a Refolution, very far from uncommon at that Time, of damning the Piece right or wrong.

The Author, however, denying the Charge laid againft him, the Inns of Court Wits might perhaps have been reconciled to him, had not the Engraver, who was employed to draw a Frontifpiece for the Play, unfortunately taken the Sketch of his Defign from the very Coffeehoufe in Queftion.—This Circumftance, rendering them entirely implacable, all Attempts that he made afterwards proved entirely unfuccefsful, it being of itfelf a fufficient Reafon, with thofe Gentlemen, to damn any Piece if it was known, or but fufpected to be his. —Thus was Mr. *Miller's* great Refource ftop'd at once, and he again reduced to a Dependance on his little Pittance in the Church, with fcarcely a Profpect of any Advancement; for, befides the Enmities he had created by the feveral Circumftances above-mentioned, he was in his Principles a fteady High Church Man, which was a Circumftance at that Time no Way favourable to his Promotion.

His Integrity, however, in thefe Principles was fo firm, that he had Refolution enough to withftand the Temptation of a very large Offer made him by the Agents of the Miniftry in the Time of general Oppofition, notwithftanding that his Circumftances were at that Period very far from being eafy.—He has, indeed, frequently acknowledged that this was the fevereft Trial his Conftancy ever endur'd, and that his Tendernefs for the moft amiable of Wives, whofe Dependence had been fwallowed up in his Misfortunes, had even ftagger'd his Firmnefs, and induced him to found her Difpofition, by hinting to her on which Terms Preferment might be purchafed; but
fhe,

she, with an Intrepidity and Indignation which almost made him blush at the Thought of having hesitated for a single Moment, rejected all Proposals of so servile a Nature, and silenced every Scruple that could on her Account have suggested itself to him.—— However, thus far he was willing to have temporized, that tho' he would not eat the Bread purchased by writing in the Vindication of Principles he disapproved, yet he would have stipulated with the Ministry on the same Terms never to have drawn his Pen against them.—But this Proposal was rejected on the other Side, and so terminated their Negociations.

Thus did Mr. *Miller*'s Wit and Honesty stand for many Years the most powerful Bars to his Fortune; and, as if some over-ruling Planet hung over his Destiny, and determined to banish Success entirely from him, the Stroke of Death hurried him away, just as his Prospects appeared to be clearing up in more Respects than one.—For, by the Gift of Mr. *Carey* of *Dorsetshire*, he was at length presented to the very profitable Living of *Upsun*, which his Father had before possessed; besides which, having translated the *Mahomet* of Monsieur *de Voltaire*, and adapted it to the *English* Stage, it made its Appearance at *Drury Lane* Theatre, and, as all his former Attempts having been in Comedy, by which Means the Author of this Tragedy was not suspected, it passed with very considerable Approbation, and a Probability of a reasonable Success, when behold, on the very Night that should have been that of his first Benefit, and before he had received a Twelve-Month's Revenue from his own Benefice, he

died at his Lodgings in *Cheyne Walk*, *Chelsea*; without ever having it in his Power to make that Provision for his Family which he had so long solicited.

As a Man, his Character may partly be deduced from the foregoing Relation of his Life.—He was firm and stedfast in his Principles, ardent in his Friendships, and somewhat precipitate in his Resentments.—In his Conversation he was sprightly, chearful, and a great Master of ready Repartee, till towards the latter Part of his Life, when a Depression of Circumstances threw a Gloom and Hypochondria over his Temper, which got the better of his natural Gaiety and Disposition.

As a Writer, he certainly has a Right to stand in a very estimable Light.——His *Humours of Oxford* is perfectly his own, and is much the best of his dramatic Pieces; for it is probable, that when he applied to that Kind of Writing by Way of Support, he had both less Leisure and less Spirits for the retouching and finishing them, than when he wrote merely for Amusement.—Besides, the most of his other Plays are more or less built on the Foundation of other Writers, altho' the ornamental Parts of the Structure have been added to them by their present Fabricator.—The Names of them are,

1. *Art and Nature.* Com.
2. *Coffeehouse.* Com.
3. *Hospital for Fools.* Farce.
4. *Humours of* OXFORD. C.
5. JOSEPH *and his Brethren.* Oratorio.
6. MAHOMET *the Impostor.* Trag.
7. *Man of Taste.* Com.
8. *Mother in Law.* Com. (Assisted by Mr. *Henry Baker.*)

[Y 2]   9. *Pic-*

9. *Picture.* Ballad Opera.
10. *Savage.* (Attributed to this Author.)
11. *Universal Passion.* Com.

Besides thefe dramatic Pieces, he wrote feveral political Pamphlets, particularly one called *Are thefe Things fo?* which was taken very great Notice of; he was Author of a Poem called *Harlequin Horace*, a Satire, occafioned by fome ill Treatment he had received from Mr. *Rich*, the Manager of *Covent Garden* Theatre; and was likewife concerned, together with Mr. *Henry Baker*, F. R. S. now living, in a compleat Tranflation of the Comedies of *Moliere*, printed together with the original *French*, and publifhed by Mr. *Watts*.

Mr. *Miller* died in 1743, leaving behind him a Wife and two Children, a Son and Daughter, the latter of whom is fince dead, but the other two are ftill living; and, altho' it may feem fomewhat foreign to our prefent Purpofe, yet it would be unjuft to the Character of that Lady, whofe heroical and noble Behaviour we have already recorded one Inftance of above, not here to convey to Pofterity the Record of that ftill continued Attachment to the Honour and Reputation of her Hufband even after Death, which induced her to devote the whole Profits both of a Benefit Play, which Mr. *Fleetwood* gave her a little Time after Mr. *Miller*'s Deceafe, and alfo of a large Subfcription to a Volume of admirable Sermons of that Gentleman's, which fhe publifhed, to the Satisfaction of his Creditors, and the Payment of thofe Debts which his limited Circumftances had unavoidably engaged him in, even tho' by the fo doing fhe left herfelf and Family almoft deftitute of the common Neceffaries of Life.

Mr. *Miller*'s Son was bred a Surgeon, and was fome Time in that Station in the Navy; but has fince applied to literary Avocations for his Livelihood.—Among other Works he has been concerned in, he has publifhed a Volume of original Poems, and a Tranflation of the Abbè *Batteaux*'s *Cours des Belles Lettres*.

MILTON, *John*, the moft illuftrious of the *English* Poets, was defcended of a genteel Family, feated at a Place of their own Name, viz. *Milton*, in *Oxfordfhire*.—He was born *Dec.* 9, 1608, and received his firft Rudiments of Education under the Care of his Parents, affifted by a private Tutor. He afterwards paffed fome Time at St. *Paul*'s School, *London*; in which City his Father had fettled, being engaged in the Bufinefs of a Scrivener.—At the Age of feventeen, he was fent to *Chrift*'s College, *Cambridge*; where he made a great Progrefs in all Parts of academical Learning; but his chief Delight was in Poetry.—In 1698 he proceeded Batchelor of Arts, having performed his Exercife for it with great Applaufe. His Father defigned him for the Church; but the young Gentleman's Attachments to the Mufes was fo ftrong, it became impoffible to engage him in any other Purfuits.—In 1632, he took the Degree of Mafter of Arts; and, having now fpent as much Time in the Univerfity as became a Perfon who determined not to engage in any of the three Profeffions, he left the College, greatly regretted by his Acquaintance, but highly difpleafed with the ufual Method of training up Youth there, for the Study of Divinity; and being much out of Humour

Humour with the public Administration of Ecclefiaftical Affairs, he grew diffatisfied with the eftablifhed Form of Church Government, and difliked the whole Plan of Education practifed in the Univerfity.——His Parents, who now dwelt at *Horton*, near *Colnbrook*, in *Buckinghamfhire*, received him with unabated Affection, notwithftanding he had thwarted their Views of providing for him in the Church, and they amply indulged him in his Love of Retirement; wherein he enriched his Mind with the choiceft Stories of *Grecian* and *Roman* Literature: and his Poems of *Comus*, *L'Allegro*, *Il Penferofo* and *Lycidas*, all wrote at this Time, would have been fufficient, had he never produced any Thing more confiderable, to have tranfmitted his Fame to lateft Pofterity.——However, he was not fo abforbed in his Studies, as not to make frequent Excurfions to *London*; neither did fo much Excellence pafs unnoticed among his Neighbours in the Country, with the moft diftinguifhed of whom he fometimes chofe to relax his Mind, and improve his Acquaintance with the World, as well as with Books.

After five Years fpent in this Manner, he obtained his Father's Permiffion to travel, for farther Improvement.——In the Spring of the Year 1638, he fet out for *Paris*, where he was introduced to the celebrated *Grotius*; from thence he departed for *Genoa*, and from *Genoa* he went to *Florence*; where he fpent two Months with great Satisfaction, in the Company of Perfons the moft eminent for Rank, Parts, or Learning.—— Hence he went to *Rome*, where he paffed the fame Time in the fame Manner.——His next Re-

move was to *Naples*; whence his Defign was to proceed into *Sicily* and *Greece*; but, hearing of the Commotions then beginning to ftir in *England*, he refolved to fhorten his Tour, in Order to return to his native Country: being of too public-fpirited a Difpofition to remain an unconcerned Spectator of the great Struggle for Liberty which he faw approaching.——Returning therefore to *Rome*, and from thence to *Florence*, he croffed the *Appenine*, and paffed by the Way of *Bologna* and *Ferrara* to *Venice*, where he fhiped off the Books he had collected in his Travels.——After a Month's Stay at *Venice*, he went through *Verona*, *Milan* and along the *Alps*, down *Leman* Lake to *Geneva*, where he fpent fome Time, and then fet out on his Return thro' *France*, whence he arrived in *England*, towards the Clofe of the Year 1639.

The Times, however, not being yet ripe for his Defign of attacking the Epifcopal Order, he determined to lie *perdue* for the prefent; but, that he might not be idle, he fet up a genteel Academy in *Alderfgate-ftreet*.——In 1641, he began to draw his Pen in Defence of the Prefbyterian Party; and the next Year he married the Daughter of *Richard Powell*, Efq; of *Foreft-Hill* in *Oxfordfhire*.——This Lady, however, whether from a Difference on Account of Party, her Father being a zealous Royalift, or fome other Caufe, foon thought proper to return to her Relations; which fo incenfed her Hufband, that he refolved never to take her again, and wrote and publifhed feveral Tracts in Defence of the Doctrine and Difcipline of *Divorce*.——He even made his Addreffes to another Lady; but this Incident

proved

proved the Means of a Reconciliation with Mrs. *Milton*.

In 1644 he wrote his Tract upon Education ; and the Reſtraint on the Liberty of the Preſs being continued by Act of Parliament, he wrote boldly and nobly againſt that Reſtraint : For which ſeaſonable Effort eternal Honour and Glory be to the Memory of the admirable Author ! That infamous Scheme of *licencing* continued, however, to the Year 1649 ; when Mr. *Mabbot*, who held the Office of Licenſer, was ſo much aſhamed of it, and ſo diſguſted with the Practice, that he threw up the Employment ; and the Council of State totally annulled the Office : For which be due Reverence paid to their Memory alſo !

In 1645, he publiſhed his *Juvenile* Poems ; and about two Years after, on the Death of his Father, he took a ſmaller Houſe in *High Holborn*, the Back of which opened into *Lincoln's-Inn-Fields* ; and here he kept cloſe to his Studies, pleaſed to obſerve the public Affairs daily tending toward the great End of his Wiſhes, 'till it was compleated in the Deſtruction of Monarchy, by the fatal Cataſtrophe and Death of *Charles* the Firſt.

But after this dreadful Blow was ſtruck, the Preſbyterians made ſo much Out-cry againſt it, that *Milton* grew apprehenſive leſt the Deſign of ſettling a Commonwealth ſhould miſcarry ; for which Reaſon he publiſhed his *Tenure of Kings and Magiſtrates. Proving that it is lawful for any to have the Power, to call to Account a Tyrant or wicked King, and, after due Conviction, to depoſe and put him to Death.*—Soon after this, he entered upon his *Hiſtory of England,*

a Work planned in the ſame Republican Spirit, being undertaken with a View of preſerving the Country from ſubmitting to monarchical Government, in any future Time, by Example from the paſt : But, before he had made any great Progreſs in this Work, the Common-wealth was formed, the Council of State erected, and he was pitched upon for their *Latin* Secretary.—The famous εικων Βασιλικη coming out about the ſame Time, our Author, by Command, wrote and publiſhed his *Iconoclaſtes* the ſame Year. It was alſo by Order of his Maſters, backed by the Reward of one thouſand Pounds, that, in 1651. he publiſhed his celebrated Piece, entitled *Pro Populo Anglicano Defenſio,* a Defence of the People of *England*, in Anſwer to *Salmaſius's Defence of the King* ; which Performance ſpread his Fame over all *Europe.*—He now dwelt in a pleaſant Houſe, with a Garden, in *Petty France, Weſtminſter*, opening into St. *James's Park.* In 1652 he buried his Wife, who died not long after the Delivery of her 4th Child ; and about the ſame Time he alſo loſt his Eye-Sight, by a *Gutta Serena,* which had been growing upon him many Years.

Cromwell took the Reins of Government into his own Hands in the Year 1653 ; but *Milton* ſtill held his Office.—His leiſure Hours he employed in proſecuting his Studies, wherein he was ſo far from being diſcouraged by the Loſs of his Sight, that he even conceived Hopes this Misfortune would add new Vigour to his Genius ; which, in Fact, ſeems to have been the Caſe.—Thus animated, he again ventured upon Matrimony : His ſecond Lady

was

was the Daughter of Captain *Woodcock* of *Hackney:* She died in Childbed, about a Year after.

On the Depofition of the Protector, *Richard Cromwell,* and on the Return of the Long Parliament, *Milton* being ftill continued Secretary, he appeared again in Print; pleading for a farther Reformation of the Laws relating to Religion; and, during the Anarchy that enfued, he drew up feveral Schemes for re-eftablifhing the Common-wealth, exerting all his Faculties to prevent the Return of *Charles* II. — *England*'s Deftiny, however, and *Charles*'s good Fortune prevailing, our Author chofe to confult his Safety, and retired to a Friend's Houfe in *Bartholomew Clofe.*—A particular Profecution was intended againft him; but the juft efteem to which his admirable Genius and extraordinary Accomplifhments entitled him, had raifed him fo many Friends, even among thofe of the oppofite Party, that he was included in the general Amnefty.

This Storm over, he married a third Wife: *Elizabeth* Daughter of Mr. *Minfhall,* a *Chefhire* Gentleman; and not long after he took a Houfe in the *Artillery Walk,* leading to *Bunhill-Fields.*— This was his laft Stage; here he fat down for a longer Continuance than he had before been able to do any where; and though he had loft his Fortune (for every Thing belonging to him went to wreck at the Reftoration) he did not lofe his Tafte for Literature, but continued his Studies with almoft as much Ardor as ever; and applied himfelf particularly to the finifhing his grand Work, the PARADISE LOST; one of the nobleft Poems that ever was produced by human Genius!—We

could enlarge with Pleafure on the numberlefs exquifite Beauties of this *Englifh* Epic; but this has been fo copioufly done by Mr. *Addifon* and many others, that any Attempt of that Kind *here* would be altogether fuperfluous. —It was publifhed in 1667, and his *Paradife Regained* came out in 1670.——This latter Work fell fhort of the Excellence of the former Production; altho', were it not for the tranfcendent Merit of the *Paradife Loft,* the fecond Compofition would doubtlefs have ftood foremoft in the Rank of *Englifh* Epic Poems:—But, perhaps, the Ground-work was unfavorable to the Poet, many being of Opinion that the Mifteries of the *Chriftian* Scheme are improper Subjects for the Mufe.—After this he publifhed many Pieces in Profe; for which we refer our Readers to the Edition of his *Hiftorical, Poetical* and *Mifcellaneous Works,* printed by *Millar,* in 2 vol. 4to. in 1753.

In 1674, this great and worthy Man paid the laft Debt to Nature, at his Houfe in *Bunhill-Fields,* in the 66th Year of his Age; and was interred on the 12th of *Nov.* in the Chancel of St. *Giles's Cripplegate.*—A decent Monument was erected to his Memory, in 1737, in *Weftminfter-Abbey,* by Mr. *Benfon,* one of the Auditors of the impreft.—As to his Perfon, it was remarkably handfome, but his Conftitution was tender, and by no Means equal to his inceffant Application to his Studies.—Tho' greatly reduced in his Circumftances, yet he died worth 1500 l. in Money, befide his Houfhold Goods.—He had no Son, but left behind him three Daughters, whom he had by his firft Wife.

His

His dramatic Works are
1. COMUS. Mafque.
2. SAMSON AGONISTES. T.
The former of thefe Pieces hath long been, and ftill continues to be, a favorite Entertainment on the *Britifh* Theatre; but it was firft performed at *Ludlow* Caftle, by Perfons of Diftinction.—The fecond, tho' an admirable Performance on the Plan of the Ancients, is not adapted to the modern Stage.

MITCHELL, Mr. *Jofeph*, was the Son of a Stone-Cutter in *North Britain*, and was born about the Year 1684.—Mr. *Cibber* tells us that he received an Univerfity Education while he remained in that Kingdom, but does not fpecify to which of the Seminaries of Academical Literature he ftood indebted for that Advantage.—He quitted his own Country, however, and repaired to the Metropolis of its Neighbour Nation, with a View of improving his Fortune.—Here he got into Favour with the Earl of *Stair* and Sir *Robert Walpole*; on the latter of whom he was for great Part of his Life almoft entirely dependant.—In fhort, he received fo many Obligations from that openhanded Statefman, and from a Senfe of Gratitude which feems to have been ftrongly Mr. *Mitchell*'s Characteriftic, was fo zealous in his Intereft, that he was even diftinguifhed by the Title of Sir *Robert Walpole*'s Poet.—Notwithftanding this valuable Patronage, however, his natural Diffipation of Temper, his Fondnefs of Pleafure, and Eagernefs in the Gratification of every irregular Appetite, threw him into perpetual Diftreffes, and all thofe uneafy Situations, which are the natural Confequences of Extravagance.—Nor does it appear that,

after having experienced more than once the fatal Effects of thofe dangerous Follies, he thought of correcting his Conduct at a Time when Fortune put it in his Power fo to do.—For when, by the Death of his Wife's Uncle, feveral thoufand Pounds devolved to him, he feems not to have been relieved, by that Acquifition, from the Incumbrances which he laboured under; but, on the contrary, inftead of difcharging thofe Debts which he had already contracted, he lavifhed away, in the Repetition of his former Follies, thofe Sums, which would not only have cleared his Reputation in the Eye of the World, but alfo, with Prudence and Oeconomy, might have render'd him eafy for the Remainder of his Life.

As to the Particulars of his Hiftory, there are not many on Record, for his Eminence in public Character not rifing to fuch an Height as to make the Tranfactions of his Life important to Strangers, and the Follies of his private Behaviour inducing thofe, who were more intimate with him, rather to conceal than publifh his Actions, there is a Cloud of Obfcurity hanging over them, which is neither eafy, nor indeed much worth while attempting, to withdraw from them.——His Genius was of the third or fourth Rate, yet he lived in good Correfpondence with moft of the eminent Wits of his Time; particularly with *Aaron Hill*, Efq; whofe eftimable Character render'd it an Honour, and almoft a Stamp of Merit, to be noticed by him.—That Gentleman, on a particular Occafion, in which Mr. *Mitchell* had laid open the diftreffed Situation of his Circumftances to him, finding himfelf unable,

unable, confiftently with Prudence, to relieve him by an immediately pecuniary Affiftance (as he had indeed but too greatly injured his own Fortune by Acts of almoft unbounded Generofity) yet found Means of affifting him effentially by another Method, which was by prefenting him with the Profits and Reputation alfo of a very beautiful dramatic Piece in one Act, entitled the *Fatal Extravagance*, a Piece which feemed in its very Title to convey a gentle Reproof to Mr. *Mitchell* on the Occafion of his own Diftreffes. — It was acted and printed in Mr. *Mitchell*'s Name, and the Emoluments arifing from it amounted to a very confiderable Sum.—Mr. *Mitchell* was ingenuous enough, however, to undeceive the World with Regard to its true Author, and on every Occafion acknowledged the Obligations he lay under to Mr. *Hill*.—The dramatic Pieces however, which appear under this Gentleman's Name, are,

1. *Fatal Extravagance*. Trag.
2. The *Highland Fair*. Ballad Opera.

The latter of thefe, however, is really Mr. *Mitchell*'s, and does not want Merit in its Way.

This Author died in 1738, and Mr. *Cibber* gives the following Character of him, with which I fhall clofe this Account.

" He feems (fays that Writer) " to have been a Poet of the " third Rate; he has feldom " reached the Sublime; his Hu- " mour, in which he more fuc- " ceeded, is not ftrong enough to " laft; his Verfification holds a " State of Mediocrity; he pof- " feffed but little Invention; and, " if he was not a bad Rhimefter, " he cannot be denominated a

" fine Poet, for there are but few " Marks of Genius in his Wri- " tings."

His Poems were printed in two Volumes, 8vo. 1729.

MONCRIEF, Mr.—This Gentleman is a *Scotfman*.—He is Author of one dramatic Piece, acted feven Years ago at the Theatre Royal in *Covent - Garden*, with middling Succefs, and entitled,

APPIUS. Trag. *Vid.* APPENDIX.

MONTAGUE, The Hon. *Walter*, Efq;—This Gentleman was a younger Son of *Henry* the firft Earl of *Manchefter* of that Name, and from whom the prefent Dukes of *Manchefter* are lineally defcended.—He was born in the Parifh of St. *Botolph*, without *Alderfgate*, about the Clofe of Queen *Elizabeth*'s, or the Beginning of King *James* the firft's Reign, but the particular Year is not fpecified by any of the Biographers.— He received fome Years Education at *Sidney* College *Cambridge*, and afterwards met with Preferment in the Government under King *Charles* I. being frequently fent into *France* upon public Bufinefs.—At length, he bid an entire Farewell, not only to the Religion in which he had been born and baptized, but alfo to his Native Country and all his Friends and Relations, and paffed fome Time in a Monaftery, determining to fettle for the Remainder of his Life in *France*; his Reafons for which Step he affigned in a Letter to his Father, *in Vindication of his Change*, together with an Anfwer to the fame, written by *Lucius* Lord *Falkland*, in 4to. 1641.

While he was abroad he ingratiated himfelf fo well with the Queen Mother of *France*, that fhe made him her Almoner and one
of

of her Cabinet Council.—She also procured him the Dignity, firſt of Abbot of *Nantueil* of the *Benedictine* Order in the Dioceſe of *Metz*, and afterwards of Abbot of the *Benedictines* of St. *Martin's* near *Pontoiſe*, a pleaſant Abbey in the Dioceſe of *Roan*, in the Room of the Abbot *John Francis de Goudy*, deceaſed.——He was alſo, thro' his Intereſt with that Princeſs, a great Friend to *Mazarine*, and a principal Inſtrument in eſtabliſhing him in her Favour; for which, however, the Cardinal afterwards ſhewed, on many Occaſions, but a very ungrateful Return.

This Gentleman, who was uſually called the *Abbé Montague*, and ſometimes Lord *Abbot* of *Pontoiſe*, did not long ſurvive the Queen Mother of *England*, *Henrietta Maria*, that Princeſs dying on the laſt Day of *Auguſt* 1669, and Mr. *Montague* before the End of the ſame Year.—He was buried in the Church or Chapel belonging to the Hoſpital of *Incurables* at *Paris*.

Before his quitting his Country, and Deſertion from the Proteſtant Religion, he wrote one dramatic Piece, entitled,

The *Shepherd's Paradiſe*. Paſt.

MOLLOY, *Charles*, Eſq;—This Gentleman is deſcended from a very good Family in the Kingdom of *Ireland*, and was himſelf born in the City of *Dublin*, altho' he received the greateſt Part of his Education abroad.—At his firſt coming to *England* he enter'd himſelf of the *Middle Temple*, and was ſuppoſed to have had a very conſiderable Hand in the writing of a periodical Paper, called *Fog's Journal*, as alſo ſince that Time to have been almoſt the ſole Author of another well-known Paper, entitled *Common Senſe*.—All theſe Papers give Teſtimony of ſtrong Abilities, great Depth of Underſtanding, and Clearneſs of Reaſoning.—He has alſo written three dramatic Pieces, entitled,

1. The *Coquet*. Com.
2. *Half-pay Officers*. Farce.
3. *Perplexed Couple*. Com.

None of theſe Pieces met with any very extraordinary Succeſs, but the Author of *Whincop's* Catalogue relates an Anecdote relating to one of them, *viz.* the *Half-pay Officers*, which, beſides its having ſome Humour in itſelf, has ſo much Concern with theatrical Hiſtory, that I cannot deny it a Place here.

There was, ſays that Writer, one Thing very remarkable at the Repreſentation of this Farce; the Part of an Old Grandmother was performed by Mrs. *Fryer*, who was then 85 Years of Age, and had quitted the Stage ever ſince the Reign of King *Charles* II.—It was put in the Bills, *The Part of Lady* Richlove *to be performed by* Peg Fryer, *who has not appeared upon the Stage theſe* fifty *Years*; which drew together a great Houſe.—The Character in the Farce was ſuppoſed to be a very old Woman, and *Peg* went thro' it very well, as if ſhe had exerted her utmoſt Abilities.—But the Farce being ended, ſhe was brought again upon the Stage to dance a Jigg, which had been promiſed in the Bills.—She came tottering in, as if ready to fall, and made two or three pretended Offers to go out again; but all on a ſudden, the Muſic ſtriking up the *Iriſh Trot*, ſhe danced and footed it almoſt as nimbly as any Wench of five and twenty could have done. —This Woman afterwards ſet up a Public Houſe at *Tottenham Court*,

and

and great Numbers frequently went to fatisfy their Curiofity in feeing fo extraordinary a Perfon.

This Story recalls to Mind a very extraordinary Particular fomewhat of the like Kind, in the Life of the celebrated M. *Baron*, the *Garrick* or the *Betterton* of the *French* Nation.——That great Actor having, on fome Occafion, taken Difguft at the Reception he had met with in the Purfuance of his Profeffion, quitted the Stage, after having been on it for feveral Years, 'altho' at that Time in the very Height of his Reputation. He continued in a private and retired Manner for many Years, after which, at a Time of Life when moft Men would have confidered themfelves as Veterans, would have found their Faculties abating, and been defirous of retiring, if poffible, from the Hurry of public Bufinefs, he returned again to the Stage with renewed Vigour and improved Abilities; rofe to a higher Rank of Fame than even that which he had before obtained; playing the youngeft and moft fpirited Characters with unabated Vivacity; and continuing fo to do for many Years afterwards, till Death fnatched him away in a very advanced Age.

MOORE, Mr. *Edward*, was bred a Linnen Draper, but having probably a ftronger Attachment to the Study than the Counter, and a more ardent Zeal in the Purfuit of Fame than in the Search after Fortune, he quitted Bufinefs, and applied to the Mufes for a Support.——In Verfe he had certainly a very happy and pleafing Manner; in his Trial of *Sclim* the *Perfian*, which is a Compliment to the ingenious Lord *Lyttleton*, he has fhewn himfelf a perfect Mafter of the moft elegant Kind of Panegyrick, *viz.* that which is couched under the Appearance of Accufation; and his *Fables for the Female Sex* feem, not only in the Freedom and Eafe of the Verfification, but alfo in the Forciblenefs of the Moral and Poignancy of the Satire, to approach nearer to the Manner of Mr. *Gay*, than any of the numerous Imitations of that Author, which have been attempted fince the Publication of his Fables.——As a dramatic Writer Mr. *Moore* has, I think, by no Means met with the Succefs his Works have merited, fince, out of three Plays which he wrote, one of them has been condemned for its fuppofed Refemblance to a very celebrated Comedy, (The *Confcious Lovers*) but to which I cannot avoid giving it greatly the Preference; and another, *viz.* The *Gamefter*, met with a cold Reception, for no other apparent Reafon, but becaufe it too nearly touched a favourite and fafhionable Vice.——Yet on the whole his Plots are interefting, his Characters well drawn, his Sentiments delicate, and his Language poetical and pleafing; and, what crowns the whole of his Recommendation, the greateft Purity runs thro' all his Writings, and the apparent Tendency of every Piece is towards the Promotion of Morality and Virtue.——The two Plays I have mentioned, and one more, make the whole of his dramatic Works, as follows,

1. *Foundling.* Com.
2. *Gamefter.* Trag.
3. GIL BLAS. Com.

Mr. *Moore* married a Lady of the Name of *Hamilton*, Daughter to Mr. *H.* Table - Decker to the Princeffes; who had herfelf a very poetical Turn, and has been faid to have affifted him in the Writing of his Tragedy.——One

Specimen

Specimen of her Poetry, however, was handed about before their Marriage, and has since appeared in Print in different Collections of Songs, particularly in one called the *Gold-Finch*.—It was addressed to a Daughter of the famous *Stephen Duck*; and begins with the following Stanza,

> *Would you think it, my Duck, for*
> *the Fault I must own,*
> *Your Jenny, at last, is quite co-*
> *vetous grown;*
> *Tho' Millions if Fortune should*
> *lavishly pour,*
> *I still shou'd be wretched, if I*
> *had not* MORE.

And after half a Dozen Stanzas more, in which, with great Ingenuity and Delicacy, and yet in a Manner that expresses a sincere Affection, she has quibbled on our Author's Name, she concludes with the following Lines,

> *You will wonder, my Girl, who*
> *this dear one can be,*
> *Whose Merit can boast such a*
> *Conquest as me;*
> *But you shan't know his Name,*
> *tho' I told you before,*
> *It begins with an M, but I dare*
> *not say* MORE.

Mr. *Moore* died soon after his celebrated Papers, entitled *The World*, were collected into Volumes.

MOORE, Sir *Thomas*.——This Gentleman lived in the Reign of King *George* I. which Monarch bestowed on him the Honour of Knighthood.—On what Occasion is not recorded; but, as some Writers have observed, it was scarcely on Account of his Poetry.—He only wrote one Play, which is remarkable only for its Absurdities.—It is entitled,

MANGORA, *King of the* TIMBUSIANS. Trag.
This Play, partly thro' the Necessity of the Actors of *Lincoln's-Inn-Fields* Theatre, who were then only a young Company, and had met with but small Encouragement from the Public, and were glad of making Trial of any Thing that had but the Nature of Novelty to recommend it, and partly thro' the Influence of many good Dinners and Suppers which Sir *Thomas* gave them while it was in Rehearsal, at length made its Way to the Stage; but we need do no more, to give our Readers an Idea of the Merit of the Piece and the Genius of its Author, than the quoting a few Lines from it, which Mr. *Victor* has given us in his *History of the Stage*.—In one Part of the Play the King makes use of the following very extraordinary Exclamation,

> *By all the ancient Gods of* Rome
> *and* Greece,
> *I love my Daughter better than*
> *my Niece;*
> *If any one should ask the Reason*
> *why;—*
> *I'd tell 'em—Nature makes the*
> *strongest Tie.*

And, in another Place, having conceived a Suspicion of some Design being formed against his Life, he thus emphatically calls for and commands Assistance,

> *Call up my Guards! call 'em up*
> *ev'ry one!*
> *If you don't call all—you'd as*
> *good call none.*

MORGAN, M'*Namara*, Esq; a Native of *Ireland*; was, if I am not mistaken, a Member of the Honourable

Honourable Society of *Lincoln's-Inn*, and has since been called to the Bar, and practised as a Counsellor in the Courts of Justice in *Dublin*.—He contracted a close Friendship with Mr. *Barry* the celebrated Actor, thro' whose Influence a Tragedy of his, founded on Part of Sir *Philip Sidney's Arcadia*, was brought on the Stage in 1754.—It met with some Success from the strong Manner in which it was supported in the Performance, and from the potent Interest of the *Irish* Gentlemen in *London*, excited in Favour of their Countryman's Work.—A Kind of national Zeal, which is highly Praise-worthy, and which indeed we meet with in the People of every Country but our own, the Natives of which, when they chance to meet abroad, seem to pay no more peculiar Regard for each other, than for the Natives of *North-America*, or the Coast of *Coromandel*.——Mr. *M'Namara's* Tragedy, however, certainly found as favourable a Reception as it could lay any Claim to, as it was in many Respects very far from being limited within the strict Rules of the Drama, and of a Species of Writing much too romantic for the present Taste.—It is entitled,

PHILOCLEA. Trag.

A particular and very diverting Account of this Piece may be found in the tenth Volume of the *Monthly Review*, p. 157, *seq.*

Mr. *Morgan* died in the Year 1762.

Moss, Mr. *Theophilus*, is Author of one most contemptible Piece, which was never acted, but which the Vanity of seeing his Name in Print has seduced him to the Publication of, entitled,

The *General Lover*. C. 1748. We have been informed, however, that the real Name of this Writer is not *Moss*, but *Marriot*.

MOTTEUX, Mr. *Peter Anthony*.—This Gentleman was a Native of *France*, being born in 1660, at *Rohan* in *Normandy*, where also he received his Education.—Being bred to Trade, in which he made a considerable Figure, he came over to *England*, and resided for many Years in this Kingdom, where he acquir'd so perfect a Mastery of the *English* Language, that he not only was qualified to oblige the World with a very good Translation of Don *Quixote*, but also wrote several Songs, Prologues, Epilogues, *&c.* and, what was still more extraordinary, became a very eminent dramatic Writer in a Language to which he was not native.—The respective Titles of his numerous Pieces of that Kind are as follow,

1. ACIS *and* GALATEA. Masque.
2. ARSINOE, *Queen of* CYPRUS. Opera.
3. *Amorous Miser.* Com.
4. *Beauty in Distress.* Trag.
5. BRITAIN's *Happiness.* Musical Interlude.
6. EUROPE's *Revels.* Musical Interlude.
7. *Four Seasons.* Musical Interlude. *Vid.* Vol. I. APPENDIX.
8. *Island Princess.* Dramatic Opera. *Vid.* Vol. I. APPENDIX.
9. *Love dragoon'd.* Farce.
10. *Love's a Jest.* Com.
11. *Loves of* MARS *and* VENUS. Play, set to Music.
12. *Novelty.*
13. *Temple of Love.* Pastoral Opera. *Vid.* Vol. I. APPENDIX.
14. THOMYRIS, *Queen of* SCYTHIA. Opera.

 This

This Gentleman, who feems to have led a very comfortable Life, his Circumftances having been perfectly eafy, was yet unfortunate in his Death; for he was found dead in a diforderly Houfe in the Parifh of St. *Clement Danes*, not without Sufpicion of having been murdered, tho' other Accounts fay, that he met with his Fate in trying a very odd Experiment.—This Accident happened to him on the 19th of *Feb.* 1717-18, which, being his Birth-Day, exactly compleated his 58th Year. His Body was interr'd in his own Parifh Church, which was that of St. *Mary Axe*, in the City of *London*.

MOTTLEY, *John*, Efq; is the Son of Colonel *Mottley*, who was a great Favorite with King *James* the Second, and followed the Fortunes of that Prince into *France*. *James*, not being able himfelf to provide for him fo well as he defired, procured for him, by his Intereft, the Command of a Regiment in the Service of *Louis* XIV. at the Head of which he loft his Life, in the Battle of *Turin*, in the Year 1706.——The Colonel married a Daughter of *John Guife*, Efq; of *Abledfcurt* in *Gloucefterfhire*, with whom, by the Death of a Brother who left her his whole Eftate, he had a very confiderable Fortune.—The Family of the *Guifes*, however, being of Principles diametrically oppofite to thofe of the Colonel, and zealous Friends to the Revolution, Mrs. *Mottley*, notwithftanding the tendereft Affection for her Hufband, and repeated Invitations from the King and Queen then at St. *Germains*, could not be prevailed on to follow him, but rather chofe to live on the Remains of what he had left her behind. The Colonel being fent over to

England, three or four Years after the Revolution, on a fecret Commiffion from King *James*, and cohabiting with his Wife during his fhort Stay there, occafioned the Birth of our Author in the Year 1692.

Mr. *Mottley* received the firft Rudiments of his Education at St. *Mark*'s Library School, founded by Archbifhop *Tennifon*, but was foon called forth into Bufinefs, being placed in the *Excife Office* at fixteen Years of Age under the Comptroller, Lord Vifcount *Howe*, whofe Brother and Sifter were both related by Marriage to his Mother.—This Place he kept till the Year 1720, when, in Confequence of an unhappy Contract that he had made, probably in Purfuit of fome of the Bubbles of that infatuated Year, he was obliged to refign it.

Soon after the Acceffion of King *George* I. Mr. *Mottley* had been promifed by the Lord *Hallifax*, at that Time firft Lord of the Treafury, the Place of one of the Commiffioners of the *Wine Licence Office*; but when the Day came that his Name fhould have been inferted in the Patent, a more powerful Intereft, to his great Surprize, had ftep'd in between him and the Preferment of which he had fo pofitive a Promife. —This, however, was not the only Difappointment of that Kind which this Gentleman met with, for, at the Period above-mentioned, when he parted with his Place in the *Excife*, he had one in the *Exchequer* abfolutely given to him by Sir *Robert Walpole*, to whom he lay under many other Obligations.—But in this Cafe, as well as the preceding one, at the very Time that he imagined himfelf the fureft, he was doomed to find his Hopes fruftrated; for
that

that Minister, no longer than three Days afterwards, recollecting that he had made a prior Promise of it to another, Mr. *Mottley* was obliged to relinquish his Claim to him who had, in Honour, an earlier Right to it.

Mr. *Guise*, our Author's Grandfather by the Mother's Side, had settled an Estate on him after the Death of his Mother, she being to receive the Income of it during her Life-Time; but that Lady, whose Inclination for Expence, or what the World commonly calls Spirit, was greatly above her Circumstances, thus diminished as they were in Consequence of her Husband's Party Principles, being considerably involved in Debt, Mr. *Mottley*, in Order to free her from those Incumbrances, consented to the Sale of the Estate, altho' she was no more than Tenant for Life.—This Step was taken at the very Time that he lost his Place in the *Excise*, which might perhaps be one Motive for his joining in the Sale, and when he was almost twenty-eight Years of Age.

In the same Year, finding his Fortunes in some Measure impaired, and his Prospects overclouded, he applied to his Pen, which had hitherto been only his Amusement, for the Means of immediate Support, and wrote his first Play, which met with tolerable Success.—From that Time he depended chiefly on his literary Abilities for the Amendment of his Fortune, and wrote the following dramatic Pieces; some of which met with tolerable Success,

  1. Antiochus. Trag.
  2. *Craftsman.* Farce.
  3. *Imperial Captives.* Trag.
  4. Penelope. Mock Ball. Op.
  5. *Widow bewitch'd.* Com.

He had also a Hand in the Composition of that many-father'd Piece, the *Devil to pay*; as well as in that of the Farce of *Penelope*; as may be seen in our Account of those Pieces in the first Vol. of this Work.—He published a Life of the great Czar *Peter*, by Subscription, in which he met with the Sanction of some of the Royal Family and great Numbers of the Nobility and Gentry; and, on Occasion of one of his Benefits, which happened on the 3d of *November*, her late Majesty Queen *Caroline*, on the 30th of the preceding Month) being the Prince of *Wales*'s Birth - Day) did the Author the singular Honour of disposing of a great Number of his Tickets, with her own Hand, in the Drawing-Room, most of which were paid for in Gold, into the Hands of Colonel *Schutz*, his Royal Highness's Privy-Purse, from whom Mr. *Mottley* received it, with the Addition of a very liberal Present from the Prince himself.

Chetwood, in his *British Theatre*, has hinted a Surmise, and I think with some Appearance of Reason, that Mr. *Mottley* was the Compiler of the Lives of the dramatic Writers, published at the End of *Whincop's Scanderbeg*.—It is certain, that the Life of Mr. *Mottley*, in that Work, is rendered one of the most important in it, and is particularized by such a Number of various Incidents, as it seems improbable should be known by any but either himself or some one nearly related to him. Among others he relates the following Anecdote, with which, as it contains some Humour, I shall close this Article.

When Colonel *Mottley*, our Author's Father, came over, as has been before related, on a secret

Commiſſion from the abdicated Monarch, the Government, who had by ſome Means Intelligence of it, were very diligent in the Endeavours to have him ſeized. The Colonel, however, was happy enough to elude their Search, but ſeveral other Perſons were, at different Times, ſeized thro' Miſtake for him.—Among the reſt, it being well known that he frequently ſupped at the *Blue Poſts* Tavern in the *Haymarket*, with one Mr. *Tredenham*, a *Corniſh* Gentleman, particular Directions were given for ſearching that Houſe.—Colonel *Mottley*, however, happening not to be there, the Meſſengers found Mr. *Tredenham* alone, and with a Heap of Papers before him, which, being a ſuſpicious Circumſtance, they immediately ſeized, and carried him before the Earl of *Nottingham*, then Secretary of State.

His Lordſhip, who, however, could not avoid knowing him, as he was a Member of the Houſe of Commons, and Nephew to the famous Sir *Edward Seymour*, aſked him what all thoſe Papers contained.——Mr. *Tredenham* made Anſwer, that they were only the ſeveral Scenes of a Play, which he had been ſcribbling for the Amuſemnt of a few leiſure Hours. Lord *Nottingham* then only deſired Leave juſt to look over them, which having done for ſome little Time, he returned them again to the Author, aſſuring him that he was perfectly ſatisfied; for, *Upon my Word*, ſaid he, *I can find no Plot in them.*

MOUNTFORT, Mr. *William.*—This Gentleman, who is far from a contemptible Writer, tho' in much greater Eminence as an Actor, was born in the Year 1659, but of what Family no Particulars are extant, farther than that they were of *Staffordſhire.*—It is probable that he went early upon the Stage, as it is certain that he died young, and *Jacob* informs us that, after his attaining that Degree of Excellence which ſhewed itſelf in his Performance of the Character of *Tallboy* and Sir *Courtly Nice*, he was entertained for ſome Time in the Family of the Lord Chancellor *Jefferies*; after which he again returned to the Stage, in which Profeſſion he continued till his Death, which happened in 1692.

Mr. *Colley Cibber*, who has, in his Apology, ſhewn great Candour and Warmth in his beſtowing all due Commendations on his Cotemporaries, has drawn one of the moſt amiable Portraits of Mr. *Mountfort* as an Actor.—He tells us that he was tall, well made, fair, and of an agreeable Aſpect. His Voice clear, full and melodious; a moſt affecting Lover in Tragedy, and in Comedy gave the trueſt Life to the real Character of a fine Gentleman.—In Scenes of Gaiety he never broke into that Reſpect that was due to the Preſence of equal or ſuperior Characters, though inferior Actors played them, nor ſought to acquire any Advantage over other Performers by *Fineſſe*, or Stage-Tricks, but only by ſurpaſſing them in true and maſterly Touches of Nature.—He had in himſelf a ſufficient Share of Wit, and a Pleaſantry of Humour that gave new Life to the more ſprightly Characters which he appeared in; and ſo much Decency did he preſerve even in the more diſſolute Parts in Comedy, that Queen *Mary* II. who was remarkable for her Solicitude in the Cauſe of Virtue, and Diſcouragement of even the Appearance of Vice, did, on ſeeing Mrs. *Behn*'s Comedy

medy of the *Rover* performed, at the same Time that she expressed her Disapprobation of the Piece itself, make a very just Distinction between the Author and Actor, and allowed a due Praise to the admirable Performance of Mr. *Mountfort* in the Character. —He had, besides this, such an amazing Variety in his Manner, as very few Actors have been able to attain; and was so excellent in the Cast of Fops and *Petit Maitres*, that Mr. *Cibber*, who was himself in high Esteem in that Manner of playing, not only acknowledges that he was greatly indebted to his Observation of this Gentleman for his own Success afterwards, but even confesses a great Inferiority to him, more especially in personal Advantage; and says moreover, that had Mr. *Mountfort* been remember'd when he first attempted them, his Defects would have been more easily discovered, and consequently his favourable Reception in them very much and very justly abated.

Such were the Excellencies of this great Performer, who did not, however, in all Probability, reach that Summit of Perfection which he might have arrived at, had he not been untimely cut off by the Hands of a base Assassin, in the 33d Year of his Age.—As the Affair was in itself of an extraordinary Nature, and so essential a Circumstance in Mr. *Mountfort*'s History, I need make no Apology for giving a short Detail of it in this Place, collected from the Circumstances which appeared on the Trial of the Murderer's Accomplice.

Lord *Mohun*, who was a Man of loose Morals, and of a turbulent and rancourous Spirit, had, from a Kind of Sympathy of Disposition, contracted the closest In-

timacy with one Captain *Hill*, whom Nature, by with-holding from him every valuable Quality, seem'd to have intended for a Cut-Throat.—*Hill* had long entertained a Passion for that celebrated Actress Mrs. *Bracegirdle*, which that Lady had rejected, with that contemptuous Disdain which his Character justly deserved.—Fir'd with Resentment for this Treatment, *Hill*'s Vanity would not suffer him to attribute it to any other Cause than a Pre-Engagement of her Affections in favour of some other Lover.—*Mountfort*'s agreeable Person, his frequently performing the Counterparts in Love-Scenes with Mrs. *Bracegirdle*, and the Respect which he used always to pay her, induced Captain *Hill* to fix on him, tho' a married Man, as the supposed Bar to his own Success.—Grown desperate then of succeeding by fair Means, he determined to attempt Force; and, communicating his Design to Lord *Mohun*, whose Attachment to him was so great, as to render him the Accomplice in all his Schemes, and the Promoter of even his most criminal Pleasures, they determined on a Plan for carrying her away from the Play-House; but, not finding her there, they got Intelligence where she was to sup, and, having hired a Number of Soldiers and a Coach for the Purpose, waited near the Door for her coming out, and, on her so doing, the Ruffians actually seized her, and were going to force her into the Coach; but her Mother, and the Gentleman whose House she came out of, interposing till farther Assistance could come up, she was rescued from them, and safely escorted to her own House.——Lord *Mohun* and Captain *Hill*, however, enraged at their Difappointment in this Attempt, immediately re-refolved on one of another Kind, and with violent Imprecations openly vowed Revenge on Mr. *Mountfort*.

Mrs. *Bracegirdle*'s Mother, and a Gentleman who were Ear-Witneffes to their Threats, immediately fent to inform Mrs. *Mountfort* of her Hufband's Danger, with their Opinion that fhe fhould warn him of it, and advife him not to come home that Night; but unfortunately, no Meffenger Mrs. *Mountfort* fent was able to find him.—In the mean Time his Lordfhip and the Captain paraded the Streets with their Swords drawn, till about Midnight, when Mr. *Mountfort*, on his Return home, was met and faluted in a friendly Manner by Lord *Mohun*; but, while that Scandal to the Rank and Title which he bore was treacheroufly holding him in a Converfation which he could form no Sufpicion from, the Affaffin *Hill*, being at his Back, firft gave him a defperate Blow on the Head with his left Hand, and immediately afterwards, before Mr. *Mountfort* had Time to draw and ftand on his Defence, he, with the Sword he held ready in his right, run him through the Body.—This laft Circumftance Mr. *Mountfort* declar'd, as a dying Man, to Mr. *Bancroft*, the Surgeon who attended him. —*Hill* immediately made his Efcape, but Lord *Mohun* was feized, and ftood his Trial; but, as it did not appear that he immediately affifted *Hill* in perpetrating this Affaffination, and that, altho' Lord *Mohun* had joined with the Captain in his Threats of Revenge, yet the actual Mention of Murther could not be proved, his Lordfhip was acquitted by his

Peers.—He afterwards, however, himfelf loft his Life in a Duel with the Duke of *Hamilton*, in which it has been hinted that fome of the fame Kind of Treachery, which he had been an Abettor of in the above-mentioned Affair, was put in Practice againft himfelf.—Mr. *Mountfort*'s Death happened in *Norfolk-Street* in the *Strand*, in the Winter of 1692. —His Body was interred in the Church Yard of St. *Clements Danes*.

He left behind him the five following dramatic Pieces, which he brought on the Stage.—The firft of them, however, is nominated as his by no Writer but *Chetwood*; and *Coxeter* tells us it was written by *John Bancroft*, and given by him to Mr. *Mountfort*.

1. EDWARD III. Trag.
2. GREENWICH *Park*. Com.
3. *Injur'd Lovers*. Trag.
4. *Life and Death of Dr.* FAUSTUS. Farce.
5. *Succefsful Strangers*. Com.

Coxeter, in his *MS.* Notes, has unaccountably altered the Date of his Death, having altered 1692 to 1696, and added *Ætat.* 35, whereas all the other Writers agree in his having been killed in his 33d Year.—The Date of Lord *Mohun*'s Trial, however, which is by no Means difficult to have Accefs to, determines that Point beyond all Difpute.

MOZEEN, Mr. *William*.—This Gentleman, who is an Actor on the Theatre Royal in *Drury Lane*, was, as I have been informed, originally bred to the Law; but, probably finding the Laborioufnefs or Gravity of that Profeffion unfuitable to his natural Difpofition, he quitted it for the Stage, on which, however, he makes no very confpicuous Figure.—Yet he has given fome Proofs of Genius and Humour in the Writing Way,

being

being reputed the Author of a very humorous Account of the Adventures of a Summer Company of Comedians, detached from the Metropolitan Theatres, commencing capital Heroes within the Limits of a Barn, and to the Audience of a Country Town.——The Book is entitled *Young Scarron*, and gives evident Proofs of the Author's having a perfect Knowledge of the Scenes and Characters he attempts to describe, and no very unskilful Pencil for the pourtraying them with their most striking Features, and in the liveliest Colours.—He has also written some little Poems, for the Publication of which, by Subscription, Proposals have been delivered; and also a Farce, entitled,

The ANTIGALLICAN. *Vid.* APPENDIX.

N.

N M.—These Letters stand as the Initials of a young Lady's Name, who introduced on the Stage an Alteration of *Beaumont* and *Fletcher's Loyal Subject*, under the Title of,

The *Faithful General*. Trag.

NABBES, Mr. *Thomas*, wrote in the Reign of *Charles* I.—*Langbaine* ranks him as a third Rate Poet, but *Cibber* will not admit to above a fifth Rate Degree of Merit. Yet he appears to have been well esteemed by his Cotemporaries, *Richard Erome* and *Rob. Chamberlaine* having publickly professed themselves his Friends, and Sir *John Suckling* having warmly patronized him.——One Degree of Merit at least he has a Claim to, and that is, that his Plays are

truly and entirely his own, not having had Recourse to any preceding Writer for Assistance; on which Account his Deficiencies are certainly more pardonable, and the Applause due to his Beauties more truly his own, than those of many other Bards. ——This *Langbaine*, whose great Reading enabled him very accurately to trace the Plagiaries of Authors, seems to confirm, at the same Time that he quotes the Author's own Assertion of it in his Prologue to the Comedy of *Covent Garden*, in these Words,

> He justifies that 'tis no borrow'd
>   Strain
> From the Invention of another's
>   Brain;
> Nor did he steal the Fancy, &c.

The dramatic Pieces extant by this Author are the following,

1. *Bride*. Com.
2. *Covent Garden*. Com.
3. *Entertainment on the Prince's Birth-Day*. Masque.
4. HANNIBAL and SCIPIO. Hist. Trag.
5. *Microcosmus*. Masque.
6. *Spring's Glory*. Masque.
7. *Tottenham Court*. Com.
8. *Unfortunate Mother*. Trag.

Phillips and *Winstanley*, according to their usual Custom, have ascribed two other anonymous Plays to him, which however *Langbaine* has proved not to be his.—— They are entitled,

CHARLES I. Trag.

Woman Hater arraigned. Com.

Wood informs us, that Mr. *Nabbes* made a Continuation of *Knolles's History of the Turks*, from the Year 1628 to the End of 1637, collected from the Dispatches of Sir *Peter Wycke*, Knt. Ambassador at *Constantinople*, and others.

Coxeter seems to be of Opinion, that

that this is the *Thomas Nabbes*, who lies buried in the *Temple* Church, under the Organ on the Inner Side.

NASH, Mr. *Thomas*, was Cotemporary with the foregoing Writer.—He was born at the Sea-port Town of *Leoftoff* in *Suffolk*, and was defcended from a Family whofe Refidence was in *Hertford-fhire.*—He received his Education in the Univerfity of *Cambridge*, and was defigned for Holy Orders, but it does not appear that he either met with any Patronage, or obtained any Preferment in the Church.—On the contrary, if we may judge from his Poem entitled *Pierce Pennilefs*, which, tho' writ-ten with a confiderable Spirit of Poetry, feems to breathe the Sentiments of a Man in the Height of Defpair and Rage againft the World, it appears probable that he had met with many Difappointments and much Diftrefs.—And indeed, it feems not improbable, from the Raillery which he vents at *Robert Green* in his *Pierce Pennilefs*, and from his hav-ing been with that Writer at the Feaft in which he took the Surfeit that carried him off the Stage of Life, that he had been, and even continued to the laft to be, a Companion and Intimate to that loofe and riotous Genius, whofe Hiftory I have before related.—And, as Diffipation moft gene-rally feeks out Companions of its own Kind to confort and affociate with, it will not, perhaps, ap-pear an improbable Suggeftion, that fome of *Green*'s Comrades might run into the fame Extra-vagances, and meet with the fame Diftreffes in Confequence of them, that he himfelf had done, and that *Nafh*'s Poem above-mention-ed might be no lefs a Picture of the Situation of his Mind, than

the Recantation Pieces which I have taken Notice of in the Life of *Green*.

Nafh's Talent was Satire, in which he muft have had great Excellence, if we may give Cre-dit to the Authority of an old Copy of Verfes which *Langbaine* has quoted concerning him, in which it is faid of him,

Sharply fatyric was he; and that Way
He went, that fince his Being, to this Day,
Few have attempted; and I furely think
Thofe Words fhall hardly be fet down in Ink
Shall fcorch and blaft, fo as his could, when he
Would inflict Vengeance.

Particularly, he was engaged in a moft virulent Paper-War with the fame Dr. *Gabriel Harvey*, whom his Friend *Rob. Green* had fatirized in fome of his Writings and whofe rancorous Revenge led him even to treat his Body ill af-ter Death, as I have before given an Account of under GREEN.

His dramatic Works are only two in Number, *viz.*

1. DIDO, *Queen of* CAR-THAGE. Trag.
2. *Summer's laft Will and Tef-tament.* Com.

Befides thefe, *Phillips* and *Win-ftanley* have very unjuftly afcribed to this Author Mr. *Dewbridge-Court Reichier*'s Comedy of *Hans Beer Pot*, (which I have reftored to the right Owner) and at the fame Time omitted the Mention of the Tragedy of *Dido*, which was unqueftionably his; or at leaft he had a confiderable Hand in it in Conjunction with *Mar-los*.

NEVIL,

NEVIL, Mr. *Robert*, lived in the Reign of King *Charles* I.—There are no Particulars relating to him extant, farther than that he received his Education at *King's* College, in the Univerſity of *Cambridge*, where he obtained a Fellowſhip; and that he wrote one Play, which is far from deficient in Point of Merit, entitled,

The *Poor Scholar*. Com.

NEVILL, Mr. *Alexander*. — This Author was a Native of *Kent*, lived in the Reign of Queen *Elizabeth*, and was Brother to Dr. *Thomas Nevill*, who ſucceeded to the Deanery of *Canterbury* on the Deceaſe of Biſhop *Rogers*.—He made a very early Progreſs in Learning, particularly in the Study of Poetry, for, at ſixteen Years of Age, he was fixed on by the celebrated *Jaſper Heywood*, as one of thoſe whom he thought capable of joining with himſelf in a Tranſlation of the Tragedies of *Seneca*.—That which this Youth undertook was the fifth, entitled

OEDIPUS. Trag.

This Piece was executed in the Year 1560, tho' not publiſhed till the reſt, by *Heywood, Newton, Nuce* and *Stadley*, in 1581; beſides which, *Wood* acquaints us of another Work of this Author, entitled, *Kettus, ſive de Fumoribus Norfolcienſium*, &c. 1582.—Mr. *Nevill* was born in 1544.—It is not apparent when he died, but he was buried in the Chapel belonging to the Cathedral Church of *Canterbury*, in a Monument erected for that Purpoſe by his Brother the Dean, ſome Years before the Deceaſe of either of them.—The Dean died in 1615, and, according to *Wood*, ſeems to have ſurvived our Author.

NEWCASTLE, *William Cavendiſh*, Duke of.—This noble Author, who was juſtly eſteemed one of the moſt finiſhed Gentlemen, as well as the moſt diſtinguiſhed General and Stateſman of the Age he lived in, was the Son of Sir *Charles Cavendiſh*, whoſe Father was Sir *William Cavendiſh*, and his elder Brother the firſt Earl of *Devonſhire* of that Family. His Mother was *Catharine*, Daughter of *Cuthbert*, Lord *Ogle*.—He was born in 1592, and his Father, who diſcovered in him, even from Infancy, a great Quickneſs of Genius, and a ſtrong Propenſity to Literature, took Care to improve thoſe Advantages, by procuring for him the beſt Maſters in every Science.

His Courſe of Education being early compleated, he appeared at Court with ſo high a Reputation for Abilities, as drew on him the peculiar Attention and Regard of King *James* I. who, at the Creation of *Henry* Prince of *Wales* in 1610, made him a Knight of the *Bath*, and, in 1620, his Father having been dead three Years, by whoſe Deceaſe he became poſſeſſed of a large Eſtate, he was created a Peer by the Title of Baron *Ogle* and Viſcount *Mansfield*, which Titles were afterwards farther ennobled in the third Year of King *Charles* I's Reign, by the Addition of that of Lord *Cavendiſh* of *Balſover*, and the ſtill higher one of Earl of *Newcaſtle* upon *Tyne*.

The high Favour, however, in which his Lordſhip ſtood at Court, excited the Jealouſy of the Miniſters, and more particularly of the Favorite Duke of *Buckingham*, notwithſtanding which, his Lordſhip preſerved the King's Affection towards him in ſo perfect a Degree, that, in 1638, his Majeſty gave the ſtrongeſt Teſtimony of his Confidence, both in his Abilities and Honour, by aſſigning figning him the very important Office of Governor to the Prince of *Wales.*—In 1639, when the Troubles broke out in *Scotland,* the King being obliged, not only to affemble an Army in the North, but alfo to put himfelf at the Head of it, which was an Expedition that could not but require immenfe Sums, and that at a Time when the Royal Finances were extremely low, his Lordfhip, in Demonftration of his Zeal and Loyalty, not only contributed ten Thoufand Pounds to the Treafury, but alfo raifed a Troop of Horfe, confifting of about two Hundred Knights and Gentlemen, who ferved at their own Charge, and were incorporated under the Title of the Prince's Troop; on which Occafion a very remarkable Inftance was given of how far his Loyalty, however it might eftablifh him in the King's Efteem, continued to give Umbrage to thofe who were defirous of a fuperior Influence at Court.—And, as his Lordfhip's Behaviour on the Occafion was fuch, as exalted his Reputation, at the fame Time that it confiderably leffened that of a Rival, I fhall take the Liberty of relating the Story in this Place.

In the Number of thofe who looked with an envious Eye on the particular Diftinctions fhewn to our Author by the King, was the Earl of *Holland,* at that Time General in Chief of the Horfe. He was a Man remarkably felfifh in his Temper, and of a Difpofition, altho' his Courage had never before been fufpected, rather cunning and penetrating, than brave or open.—The Troop which the Earl of *Newcaftle* had raifed, was, as I have before obferved, called the *Prince's;* but was commanded by the Earl himfelf, in

Perfon, as its Captain.—When the Army drew near *Berwick,* the Earl fent Sir *William Carnaby,* his Aid de Camp, to Lord *Holland,* to know where his Troop fhould march; whofe Anfwer was, *Next after the Troops of the general Officers.*—The Earl on this fent again to reprefent, *That having the Honour to march under the* Prince's *Colours, he thought it not becoming for him to give Place to any of the Officers of the Field.*—The General, however, repeated his Orders with great Peremptorinefs, which the Earl of *Newcaftle,* therefore, obeyed, taking no farther Notice of it at that Time, than by ordering the Prince's Colours to be taken off the Staff, and marching without any.—But, as foon as ever the Service was over, he fent the Earl of *Holland* a Challenge, which his Lordfhip accepted, and agreed to the Time and Place of meeting; to which, however, when our Author came, he found not his Antagonift, but his Second.—The Affair had been difclofed to the King, by whofe Authority, according to Lord *Clarendon,* the Matter was compofed; but not without leaving an Imputation, in the Minds of many, of fome Want of perfonal Bravery in Lord *Holland.*

But, though in this Conteft he had apparently the Advantage, yet, as it convinc'd him, in Concurrence with other Circumftances, how hard the Minifterial Faction was inclinable to bear upon him, and being unwilling to give his Majefty any Trouble about himfelf, he voluntarily refigned the Place of Governor to the Prince, and retired into the Country, where he remained quiet till he received the King's Orders to revifit *Hull,* which important Fortrefs, and all the Magazines

that

that were in it, he offered to his Majesty to have secured for him; but when, instead of receiving Directions for that Purpose, he found his Instructions were to obey the Orders of the Parliament, he drop'd his Design, and once more retired into the Country.

Here he remained totally inactive, till the Flame of Civil War being kindled to such a Blaze, that it would have appeared Cowardice to continue longer so, he engaged in the Royal Cause, and accepted of a Commission for the raising Men to take Care of the Town of *Newcastle*, and the four adjacent Counties, in which he was so expeditious and successful, that his Majesty constituted him General and Commander in Chief of all the Forces raised North of *Trent*, and also of those that might be levied in many of the Southern Counties, with a most extraordinary plenipotentiary Power of conferring the Honour of Knighthood, coining Money, and printing and setting forth all such Declarations as should to him appear expedient.—Of all these extensive Powers, however, his Lordship made a very sparing Use, excepting that of raising Men, which he pursued with such Diligence, that in three Months he had levied an Army of eight Thousand Horse, Foot and Dragoons, with which he marched directly into *Yorkshire*, and, after defeating the Enemy at *Peirce* Bridge, advanced to *York*, the Governor of which City surrendered up the Keys to him.

During the Course of the Civil War, the Earl of *Newcastle* was very successful, having more than once defeated General *Fairfax*, and even gained several important Forts and Battles.—For which Service

King *Charles*, in the Year 1643, advanced him to the Dignity of Marquis of *Newcastle*, but when, in 1644, thro' the Precipitancy of Prince *Rupert*, his Majesty's Forces received a total Defeat at *Marston Moor*, in which the Marquis's Infantry was cut to Pieces, this Nobleman, finding the King's Affairs in that Part of the Kingdom irretrievably ruined, he made the best of his Way to *Scarborough*, and from thence, with a few of the principal Officers of his Army, embarked for *Hamburgh*.—After staying for about six Months at that Place, he went by Sea to *Amsterdam*, and from thence took a Journey to *Paris*, where he married and resided some Time.—He afterwards removed to *Antwerp*, where he passed the Remainder of his Exile, during which he underwent a Variety of Misfortunes and Distress, his Circumstances being at some Times so bad, that the Dutchess herself, in the Life she has written of her Husband, confesses they were both reduced to the Necessity of pawning their Cloaths for Subsistence.—For, altho' his Estates in *England* were valued at upwards of twenty Thousand Pounds *per Annum*, yet they were left entirely at the Mercy of the Parliament, who levied immense Sums on them.

Yet, notwithstanding all these Severities of Fortune, during the Course of a sixteen Years Banishment, he never lost his Spirit, but retained his Vigour to the last, recruiting his natural Vivacity by the sprightly Conversation of his Lady, the frequent Company of the young King, who made him Knight of the Garter, and a full Prepossession that the Clouds, which then over-hung his own Fortunes and those of

his

his Country, would at length be difperfed by the King's Reftoration.—In this his Lordfhip proved a true Prophet, for the gloomy Period at length came to an End, and the Marquis returned to his own Country with his Sovereign; where, after being, by Letters Patent, dated *March* 16, 1664, created Earl of *Ogle* and Duke of *Newcaftle*, his Grace withdrew to a happy Country Retirement, where he fpent the Evening of his Days in calm Repofe, and in the Indulgence of thofe Studies, with which he was the moft affected.

At length, after a Life of great Action and great Variety, having attained to the higheft Honours, and defervedly purchas'd the faireft Reputation, this truly noble Lord took his Flight to a better World, on the 25th of *Dec.* 1676. *Ætatis* 84. and lies interred in *Weftminfter - Abbey*, againft the Screen of the Chapel of St. *Michael*, under a moft fpacious and noble Tomb, which a little before his Death he had caufed to be erected to the Memory of his Dutchefs.—The Monument is all of white Marble, but adorned with two Pillars of black Marble, with Entablatures of the *Corinthian* Order, embellifhed with Arms, as in the Pedeftal, with various Trophy Works, whereon are two Images of white Marble, excellently well carved, and in full Proportion, in a cumbent Pofture, reprefenting the Duke and Dutchefs.

With Refpect to this Nobleman's public Character, it will be needlefs to add any Thing to what has been already faid, in Regard to his private one.—Some of his Hiftorians have feemed to condemn him for a Profufenefs and Paffion for Magnificence, which fometimes had too great a Ten-

dency to the Encouragement of Luxury and Diffipation, of which they produce as Inftances the two fumptuous Entertainments which he gave to King *Charles* I. at his Seat at *Welbech*, the Expences of which, according to the Dutchefs's own Computations, muft have amounted to upwards of ten Thoufand Pounds.—And others, of the graver Kind, have cenfured him for too ftrong an Attachment to Poetry and the polite Arts, in which, however, they have done no Honour to the Delicacy of their own Tafte.—It is certain, indeed, that this noble Perfonage was, from his earlieft Youth, celebrated for his Love of the Mufes, that he had a true Tafte for the liberal Arts, was ever delighted with having Men of Genius about him, and took a fingular Pleafure in refcuing neceffitous Merit from Obfcurity.—In a Word, that he was truly the *Mecenas* of King *Charles* I's Reign: But it does not appear that, in the bufy Scenes of Life, his Lordfhip fuffered his Thoughts to ftray fo far from his Employment as to turn Author.

In his Exile, indeed, being extremely fond of the breaking and managing Horfes, than which there cannot be a more manly Exercife, tho' in our delicate Age almoft entirely left to Grooms and Jockeys, he thought fit to publifh his Sentiments on thofe Subjects, in that very pompous Work printed in his Name, and which is ftill held in high Efteem.—He alfo, for the Amufement of fome leifure Hours, applied himfelf to dramatic Poetry, the Produce of which cannot but give us a ftrong Idea of his Fortitude and Chearfulnefs of Temper, even under the greateft Difficulties, fince, tho' written during his Banifhment, and in the Midft of De-

preffion

preſſion and Poverty, all the Pieces he has left us in that Way of Writing, are of the comic Kind. Their Titles are,

1. The *Country Captain*. Com.
2. *Exile*. Com.
3. *Humorous Lovers*. Com.
4. *Triumphant Widow*. Com.
5. *Variety*. Com.

His Grace had been twice married, but had Iſſue only by his firſt Lady.—His Titles deſcended to his Son *Henry* Earl of *Ogle*, who was the laſt Heir Male of his Family, and who, dying without Iſſue in 1691, the Title of *Newcaſtle*, in the Line of *Cavendiſh*, became extinct.

NEWCASTLE, *Margaret*, Ducheſs of, Conſort of the above-mentioned noble Duke, was remarkable for her *many* Writings; but ſhe was a mere Pedant in Pettycoats.—She wrote 28 theatrical Pieces, many of which, indeed, are only ſhort unfiniſhed Scenes;—and, on the whole, it is not worth while to preſerve the Memory of their numerous Titles, which would take up a great Deal of Room to very little Purpoſe.

NEWMAN, *Thomas*.—All that we know of this Gentleman is, that he lived in the Beginning of the 17th Century, and that he tranſlated two of *Terence*'s Comedies, for School-Exhibitions, *viz.*

1. ANDRIA. *Vid.* APPENDIX.
2. EUNUCH. *Vid.* APPENDIX.

NEWTON, *Thomas*. —— This learned Writer was the eldeſt Son of *Edward Newton*, of *Butley*, in the Pariſh of *Preſtbury* in *Cheſhire*, by *Alice* his Wife.—He was born in that Country, and received his firſt Rudiments of grammatical Erudition under the celebrated *John Brownſword*, for whom he

appears ever to have retained the moſt ardent and almoſt filial Affection ; for, in his Encomium on ſeveral illuſtrious Men of *England*, he has this very remarkable Diſtich on his

Rhetora, Grammaticum, Polyhiſtora Teque Poetam
Quis negat ?—is Lippus, luſcus, obeſus, iners.

Nay, ſo great was his Reſpect for the Memory of this Gentleman, that he afterwards erected a Monument for him, on the South Wall of the Chancel of the Church of *Macclesfield* in *Cheſhire*, with a *Latin* Inſcription, highly in his Commendation.—But, to return to our Author.—He was ſent very young to *Oxford*; but, whether thro' any Diſguſt, or from what other Cauſe I know not, he made no long Stay there, but removed to *Cambridge*, where he ſettled in *Queen*'s College, and became ſo eminent for his *Latin* Poetry, as to be eſteemed by his Cotemporaries as deſerving to rank with the moſt celebrated Poets who have written in that Language.

After this he retired to his own Country, making ſome Reſidence at *Oxford*, which he took in his Way; and, having obtained the warm Patronage of *Robert* Earl of *Eſſex*, he taught School and practiſed Phyſick with Succeſs at *Macclesfield*. It appears, however, that he was in holy Orders alſo, for *Wood* ſays, that at length, being *beneficed* at *Little Ilford* in *Eſſex*, he taught School there, and continued at that Place till the Time of his Death, which, after his having acquired a conſiderable Eſtate, happened in the Month of *May* 1607. —— He was buried in the Church belonging to that Village, and for

the

the Decoration of which he left a confiderable Legacy.—He wrote and tranflated many Books, and, among the latter, the third Tragedy of *Seneca*, entitled,

    Thebais.

Yet, tho' he tranflated only this one Play, he took on himfelf the Publication of all the reft, as tranflated by *Heywood*, *Nevill*, *Nuci*, &c.

Phillips has wrongfully attributed to this Author the Compofition of *Marloe*'s Tragedy of TAMBERLAIN *the Great*, or *The* Scythian *Shepherd*.

Le NOBLE, Monfieur, a *French* Writer, produced one *petite Piece*, which was acted here by a Set of Strollers, of his own Country, on the Theatre in *Lincoln's-Inn-Fields.*—It met with but little Succefs, and was entitled,

    The *Two Harlequins*. Farce,
        of three Acts.

NORRIS, Mr. *Henry*, was Son to Mr. *Henry Norris* the Comedian, who, from his admirable Performance in *Farquhar*'s Comedy of the *Trip to the Jubilee*, acquir'd the Nick-Name of *Jubilee Dicky*.—This Gentleman alfo trod in his Father's Steps as an Actor, though not with equal Succefs, nor perhaps equal Merit ; yet, notwithftanding the flighting Manner in which *Chetwood*, both in his *Hiftory of the Stage*, and in his *Britifh Theatre*, fpeaks of him, Mr. *Norris* had certainly great Merit, and in many Parts equalled, if not excelled, the beft Actors who have attempted them fince.——He performed for many Years in the Theatres of *London* and *Dublin*, but, in the Decline of his Life, retired to *York*, where he joined the eftablifhed Company of Comedians belonging to that City, among whom he died a few Years

ago.—He publifhed a Collection of Poems, and two dramatic Pieces, entitled,

  1. The *Deceit*. Farce.
  2. *Royal Merchant*. Com. (fuppos'd to be this Author's, from the Initial Letters annexed *H. N.*) This is only an Alteration of the *Beggar's Bufh* of *Beaumont* and *Fletcher*.

NORTON, *Thomas*, Efq;—All that can be traced concerning this Gentleman is, that he was an Inhabitant, if not a Native, of *Sharpenhaule*, or *Sharpenhoe*, in *Bedfordfhire*, that he was a Barrifter at Law, and a zealous Calvinift in the Beginning of Queen *Elizabeth*'s Reign, as appears by feveral Tracts, printed together in 8vo. 1569.—He was Cotemporary with *Sternhold* and *Hopkins*, and Affiftant to them in their noted Verfion of the Pfalms, twenty feven of which he turned into *Englifh* Metre, to which, in all the Editions of them, the Initials of his Name are prefix'd. —He alfo tranflated into *Englifh* feveral fmall *Latin* Pieces, and, being a clofe Intimate and Fellow-Student with *Thomas Sackville*, Efq; afterwards Earl of *Dorfet*, he joined with him in the compofing one dramatic Piece, of which Mr. *Norton* wrote the three firft Acts, entitled,

    FERREX *and* PORREX, afterwards reprinted with confiderable Alterations under the Title of GORBODUC.

NUCI, Mr. *Thomas*, was a Cotemporary with Mr. *Thomas Newton* before-mentioned, and concerned with him in the Tranflation of *Seneca*'s Tragedies, of which one only fell to his Share, *viz.* the eleventh, which is entitled,

    OCTAVIA. Trag.

Some

Some Authors, *Delrio* in particular, have denied this Play's having been written by *Seneca*, and indeed, the Story of it being founded on History so near the Time of the supposed Author, and the Consideration of the tyrannical Period in which *Seneca* lived, seem to furnish a reasonable Ground of Suspicion on this Head.—But this, being a Particular, the Discussion of which is somewhat foreign to our present Purpose, any farther Enquiry on it in this Place will be needless.

O.

ODELL, *Thomas*, Esq; was born in *Buckinghamshire*, towards the Conclusion of the last or the Beginning of this Century; in which County he had a very handsome paternal Estate, the greatest Part of which he expended in the Service of the Court Interest; but, on the Death of Lord *Wharton*, who had been his Patron, and who, with other Friends of the same Principles, had procured him a Pension from the Government, Mr. *Odell*, finding both his Fortunes and Interest impaired, erected a Theatre in *Goodman's-Fields*, which he opened in *October* 1729.—For the first Season it met with all the Success that could be wished for, and fully answered his Expectations; and indeed, it is probable, that it would still have gone on with like Success, had not a Connection, which it was said the Son of a respectable and honourable Magistrate of the City of *London* had with the said Theatre, given Umbrage to the Lord Mayor and

Court of Aldermen, who, under the Appearance of an Apprehension that the Apprentices and Journeymen of the trading Part of the City would be led too readily in Dissipation, by having a Theatre brought so near home to them, made an Application to Court for the Suppression of it.— In Consequence of this, an Order came down for the shutting it up; in Complaisance to which, (for at that Time there was no Act of Parliament for limiting the Number of the Theatres) Mr. *Odell* put a Stop to his Performances, and, in the End, found himself under a Necessity of disposing of his Theatre to Mr. *Henry Giffard*, who, not meeting with the same Opposition as our Author, raised a Subscription for the building of a more ample Play-house on the same Spot, to which, assembling a very tolerable Company of Performers, he went on successfully, till the passing of the said Act; for the immediate Occasion of which, *Vid.* Vol. I. APPENDIX, under GOLDEN RUMP.—I cannot, however, help observing in this Place one Particular, for which that Theatre, which is even now standing, and which has been at different Periods since opened for some Time by Permission, has been remarkable, and that is, for the first Appearance, in, or about, the Year 1740, of our *English Roscius*, Mr. *Garrick*.——In that Eastern Hemisphere it was that first this brilliant Star arose, and shone with that dazzling Brightness which surprized all who viewed it, and which since, proceeding Westward, has blazed with that Meridian Lustre which has illuminated the whole theatrical World.—But, to return to our Author.

Mr.

Mr. *Odell* was, for some Years, and even so late as 1752, Deputy Master of the Revels, under his Grace the late Duke of *Grafton*, when Lord Chamberlain, and Mr. *Chetwynd*, the Licenser of the Stage.—This Place he held till his Death, which happened a few Years ago.—He has brought four dramatic Pieces on the Stage, all of which met with some Share of Success.—Their Titles are as follows,

1. *Chimera.* Farce.
2. *Patron.* Opera.
3. *Prodigal.* Com.
4. *Smugglers.* Farce.

ODINGSELS, Mr. *Gabriel.*— Of this Gentleman's Life I can find nothing farther on Record, than that he was born in *London*, that he was matriculated of *Pembroke* College, *Oxford*, 23d of *April* 1707. and that, becoming lunatic, he put an End to his own Life, by the Assistance of a Cord, on the 10th of *Feb.* 1734, at his House in *Thatch'd-Court*, *Westminster.*—He wrote three dramatic Pieces, the Titles of which are as follow,

1. The *Bath unmask'd.* Com.
2. BAYES's *Opera.* Com.
3. The *Capricious Lovers.* C.

OLDMIXON, Mr. *John.*—This Gentleman was descended from an ancient Family of the Name, originally seated at *Oldmixon*, near *Bridgwater*, in *Somersetshire.*—He was a violent Party Writer, and a very severe and malevolent Critic; in the former Light he was a strong Opponent of the *Stuart* Family, whom he has, on every Occasion, as much as possible endeavoured to blacken and calumniate, without any Regard to that Impartiality which ought ever to be the most essential Characteristic of an Historian.—In the other Character he was perpetually attacking, with the most apparent Tokens of Envy and Ill-Nature, his several Cotemporaries. Particularly Messrs. *Addison, Eusden* and *Pope.*—The last of these, however, whom he had attacked in different Letters which he wrote in the *Flying Post*, and repeatedly reflected on in his Prose Essays on Criticism, and in his Art of Logic and Rhetoric, written in Imitation of *Bouhours*, has condemn'd him to an Immortality of Infamy, by introducing him into his *Dunciad*, with some very distinguishing Marks of Eminence among the Devotees of Dulness. For, in the second Book of that severe Poem, where he introduces the Dunces contending for the Prize of Dulness, by diving in the Mud of *Fleet-Ditch*, he represents our Author as mounting the Sides of a Lighter, in order to enable him to take a more efficacious Plunge.—His Words are as follows,

> In naked *Majesty* Oldmixon
> *stands*,
> *And*, Milo *like, surveys his Arms*
> *and Hands*;
> *Then, sighing, thus:* "*And am*
> "*I now threescore?*
> "*Ah, why, ye Gods! should two*
> "*and two make four?*"
> *He said, and climb'd a stranded*
> *lighter's Height,*
> *Shot to the black Abyss, and*
> *plung'd downright.—*
> *The Senior's Judgment all the*
> *Crowd admire,*
> *Who, but to sink the deeper, rose*
> *the higher.*

Mr. *Oldmixon*, tho' rigid with Regard to others, is far from unblameable himself, in the very Particulars concerning which he is so free in his Accusations, and that sometimes even without a strict

ſtrict Adherence to Truth, one remarkable Inſtance of this Kind it is but Juſtice to take Notice of, and that his having advanced a particular Fact to charge three eminent Perſons with Interpolation in Lord *Clarendon*'s Hiſtory, which Fact was diſproved by Dr. *Atterbury*, the only Survivor of them; and the pretended Interpolation, after a Space of almoſt ninety Years, produced in his Lordſhip's own Hand-Writing; and yet this very Author himſelf, when employ'd by Biſhop *Kennet* in publiſhing the Hiſtorians in his Collection, has made no Scruple of perverting *Daniel*'s Chronicle in numberleſs Places.

What Year Mr. *Oldmixon* was born in, is not mentioned by any of the Writers, nor where he received his Education.—He was, however, undoubtedly a Man of Learning and Abilities; and, excluſive of his ſtrong-biaſs'd Prejudice, and natural Moroſeneſs and Petulance, far from a bad Writer.—He has left behind him three dramatic Pieces, the Titles of which are,

1. AMYNTAS. Paſt.
2. *Governor of* CYPRUS. T.
3. *Grove.* Opera.

He alſo wrote a Paſtoral, called *Thyrſis*, which forms one Act of Mr. *Motteux*'s *Novelty*, or *Every Act a Play*.—As he was always a violent Party Writer, on the Whig Side, he was at length rewarded with a ſmall Poſt in the Revenue at *Liverpoole*, at which Place he died in a very advanced Age, in the Year 1745.

ORRERY, *Roger Boyle*, Earl of, was the younger Brother of *Richard*, Earl of *Burlington* and *Cork*, and fifth Son of *Richard*, ſtyled the Great Earl of *Cork*.—He was born *April* 25, 1621, and was raiſed to the Dignity of Baron *Broghill* in *Ireland*, when only

ſeven Years old.—His Education was in the College of *Dublin*; where he applied himſelf with ſuch Diligence to his Books, and ſo happily digeſted what he gathered from them, that he was very ſoon diſtinguiſhed as an early and promiſing Genius.—In 1636, his Father ſent him to make the Tour of *France* and *Italy*, in Company with Lord *Kynalmeaky*, his elder Brother.—After his Return from his Travels, this gallant young Nobleman found all Things in great Confuſion in *England*, and a War on the Point of breaking out with *Scotland*; in which he was invited to ſerve, with Marks of peculiar Diſtinction; but his Thoughts were turned another Way.—As the old Earl of *Cork* loved to ſettle his Children very early in the World, a Marriage was at this Time propoſed for Lord *Broghill*, with the Lady *Margaret Howard*, Daughter to the Earl of *Suffolk*, and it was quickly concluded: Immediately after which his Lordſhip, with his new-married Lady, ſet out for *Ireland*, where they landed *Oct.* 23, 1641, the very Day on which the Rebellion broke out in that Kingdom.

The Family of Lord *Cork* were inſtantly obliged to take Arms, in Order to their own Security, as well as that of the Public; and the Poſt aſſigned to Lord *Broghill*, was the Defence of his Father's Caſtle of *Liſmore*; in which he behaved with all the Spirit of a young Officer, and all the Diſcretion of an old one.— He afterwards diſtinguiſhed himſelf on many ſignal Occaſions; in the Courſe of which he equally manifeſted his Abilities for the Field and the Cabinet.—At the Death of *Charles* I. however, he was induced to quit both his Eſtate

 and

and his Country, as ruined paſt all Hopes.—For ſome Time he remained in cloſe Retirement; but at length *Cromwell*, to whom the Merit of Lord *Broghill* was well known, found Means to gain him over to that Party, which he had hitherto ſo rigorouſly oppoſed; but they were ſuch Means as reflect no Diſhonour to his Memory.—The Story is told at length in the *Biographia Britannica*, under the Article BOYLE; to which we refer, being too circumſtantial for ſo brief a Compilation as the preſent.—By his own Intereſt he now raiſed a gallant Troop of Horſe, conſiſting chiefly of Gentlemen attached to him by perſonal Friendſhip; which Corps was ſoon increaſed to a compleat Regiment of 1500 Men.—Theſe he led into the Field againſt the *Iriſh* Rebels; and was ſpeedily joined by *Cromwell*, who placed the higheſt Confidence in his new Ally; and found him of the greateſt Conſequence to the Intereſt of the Commonwealth.—Among other conſiderable Exploits performed by Lord *Broghill*, his Victory at *Maccroom* deſerves to be particularly mentioned; where, with 2000 Horſe and Dragoons, he briſkly attacked above 5000 of the Rebels, and totally defeated them.——He afterwards relieved *Cromwell* himſelf, at *Clonmell*, where that great Commander happened to be ſo dangerouſly ſituated, that he confeſſed nothing but the ſeaſonable Relief afforded him by Lord *Broghill*, could have ſaved him from Deſtruction.—He likewiſe worſted Lord *Muſkerry*, who came againſt him with an Army raiſed by the Pope's Nuncio, and which conſiſted of three Times the Number of Lord *Broghill*'s forces; beſides the Advant-

age of being well officer'd by Veteran Commanders from *Spain*.

When *Cromwell* became Protector, he ſent for Lord *Broghill*, merely to take his Advice, occaſionally.—And we are told, that not long after his coming to *England*, he formed a Project for engaging *Cromwell* to reſtore the old Conſtitution.—The Baſis of the Scheme was to be a Match between the King (*Charles* II.) and the Protector's Daughter.——As his Lordſhip maintained a ſecret Correſpondence with the exiled Monarch and his Friends, it is imagined he was, before-hand, pretty ſure that *Charles* was not averſe to the Scheme, or he would not have ventured to propoſe it ſeriouſly to *Cromwell*:—who, at firſt, ſeemed to think it not unfeaſible.—He ſoon changed his Mind, however, and told *Broghill* that he thought the Project impracticable; for, ſaid he, " *Charles* can never forgive me the " Death of his Father."—In fine, this Buſineſs came to nothing, although his Lordſhip had engaged *Cromwell*'s Wife and Daughter in the Scheme; but he never durſt let the Protector know that he had previouſly treated with *Charles* about it.

On the Death of the Protector, Lord *Broghill* continued firmly attached to his Son *Richard*, 'till he ſaw that the Honeſty and Good-Nature of that worthy Man would infallibly render him a Prey to his many Enemies, he did not think it adviſable to ſink with a Man he could not ſave.— The dark Clouds of Anarchy ſeemed now to be hovering over the *Britiſh* Iſland.—Lord *Broghill* ſaw the Storm gathering, and he deemed it prudent to retire to his Command in *Ireland*, where he ſhortly

shortly after had the Satisfaction of seeing Things take a Turn extremely favorable to the Design he had long been well-wisher to—that of the King's Restoration. In this great Event, Lord *Brog-hill* was not a little instrumental; 'and, in Consideration of his eminent Services, in this Respect, *Charles* created him Earl of *Orrery*, by Letters-Patent, bearing Date *Sept.* 5, 1660.—He was soon after made one of the Lords Justices of *Ireland*; and his Conduct, while at the Head of Affairs in that Kingdom, was such, as greatly added to the general Esteem in which his Character was before held.

His Lordship's active and free Course of Life, at length, brought upon him some Diseases and Infirmities, which gave him much Pain and Uneasiness; and a Fever, which fell into his Feet, joined to the Gout, with which he was often afflicted, abated much of that Vigour which he had shewn in the early Part of his Life; but his Industry and Application were still the same, and bent to the same Purposes; as appears from his *Letters*, which shew at once a Capacity and an Attention to Business, which do Honour to that Age, and may serve as an Example to this.

Notwithstanding his Infirmities, on the King's desiring to see his Lordship in *England*, he went over in 1665.——He found the Court in some Disorder; where his Majesty was on the Point of removing the Great Earl of *Clarendon*, Lord High Chancellor; and there was also a great Misunderstanding between the Royal Brothers.—Lord *Orrery* undertook to reconcile the King with the Duke of York; which he effected by prevailing on the latter to

ask his Majesty's Pardon for some Steps he had taken in Support of the Chancellor.

On his Return to *Ireland*, he found himself called to a new Scene of Action.——The *Dutch* war was then in its Height; and the *French*, in Confederacy with the *Hollanders*, were endeavouring to stir up the Ashes of Rebellion in *Ireland*.—The Duke *de Beaufort*, Admiral of *France*, had formed a Scheme for a Descent upon that Island; but this was rendered abortive by the extraordinary Diligence, military Skill, and prudent Measures of Lord *Orrery*.

But, in the Midst of all his Labours, a Dispute arose, founded on a mutual Jealousy of each other's Greatness, betwixt him and his old Friend the Duke of *Ormond*, then Lord Lieutenant; the bad Effects of which were soon felt by both the Disputants; who resorted to *England*, to defend their respective Interests and Pretensions; both having been attacked by secret Enemies, who suggested many Things to their Prejudice. — This Quarrel, tho' of a private Beginning, became at last of a Public Nature; and, producing first an Attempt to frame an Impeachment against the Duke of *Ormond*, occasioned in the End, by Way of Revenge, an actual Impeachment of the Earl of *Orrery*.——He defended himself so well, however, against a Charge of high Crimes, and even of Treason itself, that the Prosecution came to nothing.—He, nevertheless, lost his public Employments; but not the King's Favour; he still came frequently to Court, and sometimes to Council.—After this Revolution in his Affairs, he made several Voyages to and from *Ireland*; was

often

often confulted by his Majefty on Affairs of the utmoft Confequence ; and, on all Occafions, gave his Opinion and Advice with the Freedom of an honeft plain dealing Man, and a fincere Friend ; —which the King always found him, and refpe&ed him accordingly.

In 1678, being attacked more cruelly than ever by his old Enemy the Gout, he made his laft Voyage to *England*, for Advice in the Medical Way.—But his Diforder was beyond the Power of Medicine ; and having, in his laft Illnefs, given the ftrongeft Proofs of Chriftian Patience, manly Courage, and rational Fortitude, he breathed his laft, on the 16th of *October*, 1679 ; in the 59th Year of his Age.

As to the literary Character of this amiable and worthy Nobleman, it may be given in few Words.——His Wit was manly, pregnant and folid ; the early Bloffoms of it were fair, but not fairer than the Fruit.—He wrote feveral political Tracts and fome ingenious Poems ; but the Pieces which particularly entitled him to a Place in this Collection, were the following Plays, *viz.*

  1. Henry V. Trag. acted with the peculiar Favor of the Royal Family.

  2. Mustapha. Trag. well received.—This is written in Rhyme, which was the Mode at that Time.

  3. *Black Prince.* Trag. acted at the Duke of *York's* Theatre.

  4. Tryphon. Trag. from a Story in *Josephus.*

OSSORY, *John Bale*, Bifhop of.——This learned Prelate was born at *Covie* in *Suffolk*, in 1495, and, for his early and extenfive Learning, made one of the Car-

melites at *Norwich*, and from thence was enter'd a Student of St. *John's* College, *Cambridge.*

He was one of the firft that embraced the Proteftant Religion before the Time of the Reformation's taking Place in thefe Kingdoms, on which Account he found himfelf under a Neceffity of flying to avoid the Perfecution of *Lee* Bifhop of *York*, and *Stukeley* Bifhop of *London.*—He was, however, recalled by King *Edw.* VI. and made Bifhop of *Offory* in *Ireland* in 1552 ; but, about fix Months after this Promotion, Qu. *Mary* afcending the Throne, he retired again from the Dread of Perfecution, and, in his Voyage to *Brabant*, where he intended to have fought for Refuge, he was taken by Pyrates ; but, finding Means not long after to procure his Ranfom, he found an Afylum at *Bafil*, till Queen *Elizabeth* came to the Crown, when, being once more recalled, he rather chofe to accept of a Prebendary of *Canterbury*, than to fue for his former See of *Offory.*

Bifhop *Bale* died in *November* 1563, being the 68th Year of his Age.——He was fo fevere a Writer againft the Church of *Rome*, that his Books are particularly prohibited in the expurgatory Index, publifhed at *Madrid*, in Fol.o, in the Year 1667 ; and *Wood* accufes him of great Scurrility and Abufe againft various Perfons, in his Book entitled *De Scriptoribus majoribus Britannicæ.* He is the earlieft dramatic Writer in the *Englifh* Language, or at leaft Author of the firft Pieces of that Kind that we find in Print, and his Writings in that Way, that we have been able to trace, are very numerous, as will be feen in the fubfequent Catalogue of them, *viz.*

  1. *A-

1. *Againſt Momus's and Zoi-lus's.* A dramatic Piece.
2. *Againſt thoſe who adulterate the Word of God.* Ditto.
3. *Of Baptiſm and Temptation.* Two Comedies.
4. *Of Chriſt when he was twelve Years old.* Com.
5. *Corruption of the Divine Laws.* Dramatic Piece.
6. *Of the Counſels of Biſhops.* Com.
7. *God's Promiſes.* Interlude.
8. *Image of Love.* Dramatic Piece.
9. *Impoſtures of* THOMAS BECKET. Dram. Piece.
10. St. JOHN BAPTIST *Preaching in the Wilderneſs.* Interlude.
11. St. JOHN *the Baptiſt's Life.* Interlude.
12. *Of* JOHN *King of* ENG-LAND.
13. *Concerning the Laws of Na-ture corrupted.* Com.
14. *Of* LAZARUS *rais'd from the Dead.* Com.
15. *Of the Lord's Supper and waſhing of Feet.* Com.
16. *On both Marriages of the King.* Com.
17. *Of the Paſſion of* CHRIST. Two Comedies.
18. *Of the Sepulture and Reſur-rection.* Two Comedies.
19. *Of* SIMON *the Leper.* Com.
20. *Of the Temptation of* CHRIST. Dram. Piece.
21. *Treacheries of the Papiſts.* Dram. Piece.

Of theſe only thoſe number'd 7, 10 and 13 have been ſeen in Print; the firſt of which has been reprinted by *Dodſley* in the firſt Volume of his Collection of old Plays, and the only Copy I be-lieve extant of the laſt is preſerv-ed in St. *Sepulchre*'s Library in *Dublin.*—As to the reſt they are

mentioned by himſelf, as his own, in his Account of the Writers of *Britain* before-mentioned.——He alſo tranſlated the Tragedies of *Pammachius.*

OTWAY, *Thomas,* was not more remarkable, ſays *Cibber,* in his *Lives of the Poets,* for moving the tender Paſſions, than for the Variety of Fortune to which he himſelf was ſubjected.—He was the Son of the Rev. Mr. *Hum-phry Otway,* Rector of *Wolbeding* in *Suſſex,* and was born in the Year 1651.—He received his E-ducation at *Wickham* School near *Wincheſter,* and became a Com-moner of *Chriſt* Church, in *Ox-ford,* in 1669.—But, on his quit-ting the Univerſity, and coming to *London,* he turned Player.— His Succeſs as an Actor was but indifferent; he was more valued for the Sprightlineſs of his Con-verſation and the Acuteneſs of his Wit; which gained him the Friendſhip of the Earl of *Ply-mouth,* who procured him a Cor-net's Commiſſion in the Troops which then ſerved in *Flanders.*

Poor *Tom Otway,* like the reſt of the Wits and Bloods of every Age, was but a bad Oeconomiſt; and therefore it is no Wonder that we generally find him in very neceſſitous Circumſtances.—This was particularly the Caſe with him at his Return from *Flanders.* —He was, moreover, averſe to the Military Profeſſion, and it is therefore not extraordinary, all Things conſidered, that *Tom* and his Commiſſion ſoon quarrel'd, and parted, never to meet again.

After this, he had Recourſe to writing for the Stage; and now it was that he found out the only Employment that Nature ſeems to have fitted him for.—In Comedy he has been deemed too licentious; which, however, was no great

Objection

Objection to them in the profligate Days of *Charles* II.—But in Tragedy few of our *English* Poets ever equalled him ; and perhaps none ever excelled him, in touching the Paſſions, particularly the tender Paſſion.—There is generally ſomething familiar and domeſtic in the Fable of his Tragedy, and there is amazing Energy in his Expreſſion.—The Heart that does not melt at the Diſtreſſes of his *Orphan*, muſt be hard indeed !

But, tho' *Otway* poſſeſſed, in ſo eminent a Degree, the rare Talent of writing to the Heart, yet he was not very favorably regarded by ſome of his cotemporary Poets ; nor was he always ſuccefsful in his dramatic Compoſitions.—After experiencing many Reverſes of Fortune, in Regard to his Circumſtances, but generally changing for the worſe, he had at laſt died wretchedly in a Public-Houſe on *Tower-Hill*, whither it is ſuppoſed he had retired to avoid the Preſſure of his Creditors.—Some have ſaid that downright Hunger, compelling him to fall too eagerly upon a Piece of Bread, of which he had been ſome Time in Want, the firſt Mouthful choaked him, and inſtantly put a Period to his Days.

His dramatic Writings are,

1. ALCIBIADES. Trag.
2. TITUS and BERENICE. Trag.
3. *Don* CARLOS *Prince of* SPAIN. Trag.
4. *The Orphan.* Trag.
5. CAIUS MARIUS. Trag.
6. VENICE *Preſerved.* Trag.
7. The *Soldier's Fortune.* Com.
8. The *Atheiſt,* or the ſecond Part of the *Soldier's Fortune.* Com.
9. *Friendſhip in Faſhion.* Com.

Beſide theſe Plays, Mr. *Otway* made ſome Tranſlations, and wrote ſeveral Miſcellaneous Poems.—His whole Works are printed in two Pocket Volumes.

D'OUVILLE, *Geo. Gerbier,* Eſq;—Of this Gentleman I know nothing more than that, from his Name, he appears to have been a *Frenchman,* and that *Coxeter* has poſitively ſet him down as the Author of one dramatic Piece never acted, but which, by the Date, muſt have been written, or at leaſt publiſhed, during the Time of the *Inter-regnum.*—It is entitled,

The *Falſe Favorite diſgrac'd.* Tragi-Com.

All the other Writers have inſerted this Play in their Catalogues as anonymous, excepting *Langbaine,* who only tells us that it was aſcribed to the above-mentioned Gentleman.

OWEN, *Robert,* Eſq;—Of this Gentleman I can find no farther Account, than that he lived in the Reign of Q. *Anne,* and that he received the earlier Parts of his Education at *Eton* School, from whence he removed, for the finiſhing of his Studies, to *King's* College in *Cambridge.*—He wrote one dramatic Piece, founded on the *Grecian* Hiſtory, and entitled,

HYPERMNESTRA. Trag.

OZELL, Mr. *John.*—This Writer, to whoſe Induſtry, if not to his Genius, the World lies under very conſiderable Obligations, received the firſt Rudiments of his Education from Mr. *Shaw,* an excellent Grammarian, and Maſter of the Free-School at *Aſhby de la Zouch* in *Leiceſterſhire.* — He afterwards compleated his grammatical Studies under the Reverend Mr. *Mountford,* of *Chriſt's* Hoſpital, where, having attained a great Degree of Perfection

fection in the dead Languages, *viz.* the *Latin, Greek* and *Hebrew*, it was next the Intention of his Friends to have sent him to the University of *Cambridge*, there to finish his Studies, with a View to his being admitted into Holy Orders.—But Mr. *Ozell*, averse to the Confinement of a College Life, and perhaps disinclined to the clerical Profession, and desirous of being sooner brought out into, and settled in the World, than the regular Course of Academical Gradations would permit, sollicited and obtained an Employment in a Public Office of Accompts, with a View to which he had taken previous Care to qualify himself by a most perfect Knowledge of Arithmetic in all its Branches, and a great Degree of Excellence in writing all the necessary Hands.

Notwithstanding, however, this grave Attention to Business, he still retained an Inclination for, and an Attention to, even polite Literature, that could scarcely have been expected; and, by entering into much Conversation with Foreigners abroad, and a close Application to reading at Home, he made himself Master of most of the living Languages, more especially the *French, Italian* and *Spanish*, from all which, as well as from the *Latin* and *Greek*, he has favoured the World with many valuable Translations. —But, as it is in the Light of a dramatic Writer only that he has any Claim to a Place in this Work, I shall not enter into a Recapitulation of any of his Pieces but those which have some Connection with the Theatre.—These, however, tho' all Translations, are very numerous, there being included in them an *English* Ver-

sion of all the dramatic Pieces of that justly celebrated *French* Writer, Monf. *Moliere*, besides some others from *Corneille, Racine,* &c. the Titles of which are all to be found in the following List.

1. *Affected Ladies.* Com.
2. ALEXANDER. Trag.
3. *Amorous Quarrel.* Com.
4. AMPHYTRION. Com.
5. BRITANNICUS. Trag.
6. CATO *of* UTICA. Trag.
7. *Cheats of* SCAPIN. Farce.
8. *Cid.* Trag.
9. *Countess of* ESCARBORGNAS. Com.
10. *Don* GARCIAN *of* NAVARRE. Com.
11. *Fair of Saint* GERMAINS. Farce.
12. *Forc'd Marriage.* Com.
13. *Forc'd Physician.* Com.
14. *Gentleman Cit.* Com.
15. GEORGE DANDIN. Com.
16. *Hypochondriack.* Com.
17. *Imaginary Cuckold.* Com.
18. *Impertinents.* Com.
19. *Impromptu of* VERSAILLES. Com.
20. *Learned Ladies.* Com.
21. *Libertine.* Trag.
22. *Litigants.* Com.
23. *Love the best Physician.* C.
24. *Magnificent Lovers.* Com.
25. *Manhater.* Com.
26. MANLIUS CAPITOLINUS. Trag.
27. MELICERTA. Heroic Pastoral.
28. *Miser.* Com.
29. *Monsieur De* POURCEAUGNEC. Com.
30. *Princess of* ELIS. Dram. Piece, in three Parts.
31. PSYCHE. Opera.
32. *School for Husbands.* Com.
33. *School for Women.* Com.
34. *School for Women criticis'd.* Farce.
35. *Sicilian.* Com.

36. *Sir* MARTIN MARR-
ALL. Com.

37. TARTUFFE. Com.

Mr. *Ozell* had the good Fortune to efcape all thofe Viciffitudes and Anxieties in Regard to pecuniary Circumftances, which too frequently attend on Men of literary Abilities; for, befides that he was, from his earlieft fetting out in Life, conftantly in the Poffeffion of very good Places, having been for fome Years Auditor-General of the City and Bridge Accounts; and, to the Time of his Deceafe, Auditor of the Accounts of St. *Paul*'s Cathedral and St. *Thomas*'s Hofpital, all of them Pofts of confiderable Emolument, a Gentleman, who was a Native of the fame Country with him, who had known him from a School-Boy, and it is faid lay under particular Obligations to his Family, dying when Mr. *Ozell* was in the very Prime of Life, left him fuch a Fortune as would have been a competent Support for him, if he fhould, at any Time, have chofe to retire from Bufinefs entirely, which however it does not appear he ever did.—Our Author died about the Middle of *October* 1743, and was buried in a Vault of a Church belonging to the Parifh of St. *Mary Aldermanbury*; but what Year he was born in, and confequently his Age at the Time of his Death, are Particulars that I do not find on Record.

That Mr. *Ozell* was rather a Man of Application than Genius, is apparent from many Circumftances; nor is any Thing, perhaps, a ftronger Proof of it, than the very Employment he made Choice of, fince it has been much oftener feen, that Men of brilliant Talents have quitted the more fedentary Avocations they have fortuitoufly been bred to, than that they have fix'd on any fuch by their own Election; and perhaps our Author is the only Inftance of a Perfon, even of a Turn to the heavier and more abftrufe Branches of Literature, who ever chofe to bury the greateft Part of his Hours behind the Defk of a Compting-Houfe.

Notwithftanding this Obfervation, however, Mr. *Ozell*'s Abilities, if lefs entertaining, were not perhaps lefs ufeful to the World, than thofe of fome other Writers; for, tho' he produced nothing originally his own, yet he has cloathed in an *Englifh* Habit feveral very valuable Pieces, and, tho' his Tranflations may not, perhaps, have all that Elegance and Spirit which the Originals poffefs'd, yet, in the general, it muft be confeffed that they are very juft, and convey, if not the poetical, at leaft the literary Meaning of their refpective Authors: And indeed, it were rather to be wifhed, that this Writer had confined himfelf to the Tranflation of Works of a more ferious Nature, than have engaged in thofe of Humour and Genius, which were Qualities he feemed not to poffefs himfelf, and therefore could not do Juftice to in others.—*Moliere*, more particularly, is an Author of that fuperior Genius, that it would require Abilities almoft equal to his own, to tranflate him in fuch a Manner, as to give him, in the Cloathing of our own Language, the perfect Air and Manner of a Native.—There is a peculiar Spirit, a peculiar Manner, adapted to the Dialogue and Language of the Stage, more particularly in Comedy, which is only attainable by Obfervation and Practice, and renders a Writer of dramatic Genius

nius alone properly qualified for the Tranflation of dramatic Pieces. And this is apparently the Reafon that, notwithftanding we have many very good Comedies in our own Language, founded almoft entirely on thofe of Foreign Authors, yet very few of the Pieces themfelves, from which they have been borrowed, have afforded much Pleafure to the Reader, in the Tranflations that have appeared of them. —— Celebrated as the Name of *Moliere* has been for above a Century paft, notwithftanding that there have been more than one perfect Tranflation of his Works publifhed in *Englifh*, yet I will venture to affirm, that his Pieces are very little known, excepting to thofe who, from their Acquaintance with the *French* Language, are enabled to read them in the Original; nor can I help hinting my Wifh, that fome Writer of Eminence would undertake the Tafk, which would beftow fo valuable an Addition to the Libraries of the *Belles Lettres*, introduce M. *de Moliere* among the Set of our intimate Acquaintances, as perfectly as *Cervantes* or *Le Sage*, and enable us to converfe as familiarly with the *Mifer* and *Hypecbondriac* of the one, as with the *Don Quixote* and *Gil Blas* of the others.—But this is a Digreffion for which I beg Pardon, and will therefore proceed.

Mr. *Ozell* feems to have had a more exalted Idea of his own Abilities than the World feemed willing to allow them, for, on his being introduced by Mr. *Pope* into the *Dunciad*, (for what Caufe however does not appear) he publifhed a very extraordinary Advertifement, figned with his Name, in a Paper called the *Weekly Medley*, *Sept.* 1729, in which he ex-

preffes his Refentment, and at the fame Time draws a Comparifon, in his own Favour, between Mr. *Pope* and himfelf, both with Refpect to Learning and poetical Genius.—The Advertifement at length may be feen in the Notes to the *Dunciad*.—But, tho' I confefs I cannot readily fubfcribe to this felf-affum'd Preference, yet, as Mr. *Coxeter* informs us, that his Converfation was furprizingly agreeable, and his Knowledge of Men and Things confiderable; and, as it is probable that, with an Underftanding fomewhat above the Common Rank, he poffeffed a confiderable Share of Good-Nature, I will readily allow, that a Perfon of this Character might be much more amiable than one of a greater Brilliance of Parts, if deficient in thefe good Qualities.

P.

P P. *Monfieur.*—In this Manner, but without giving us any Explanations of thefe Initials, has *Langbaine* diftinguifhed the Author of a mufical dramatic Piece, performed in *K. Cha.* II's Reign, entitled,

Ariadne. Opera.

P. R.—*Coxeter*, in his Notes, has given us the full Title of a very old Play, with thefe Letters in the Title-Page, called,

Appius *and* Virginia. Tragi-Com.

Neither *Langbaine*, *Jacob*, nor *Whincop*'s Editor, have taken any Notice of this Play; but *Chetwood* (*Britifh Theatre*, p. 21.) mentions the Piece, with its very early Date of 1575, but has not hinted at any Author's Name or Initials.

P. S.—Thefe Letters are prefixed to a Tranflation of one of *Seneca*'s Tragedies, to which are added Poems on feveral Occafions, all which *Langbaine* imagines ought to be afcribed to *Samuel Pordage*, Efq; of whom hereafter.—The Title of the Play is

Troades.

P. T. —Thefe Initial Letters are printed to two Plays, both publifhed in *Charles* II's Reign. Tho' at fifteen Years Diftance from each other, yet it is not improbable they might both be the Work of the fame Author.—In looking back to the Writers of that Time, I can find only one dramatic Author whofe Name will correfpond with thefe Letters, and that is *Thomas Porter*, Efq; of whom I fhall have Occafion to make farther Mention.——It is indeed only Conjecture; yet, as the Walk of Writing in both thefe Pieces is the fame with thofe which are declaredly that Gentleman's, as the Dates of all come within a reafonable Compafs as to Time, as it was no uncommon Practife at that Period for known Authors to fubfcribe only Initials to their Works, and as, laftly, Mr. *Langbaine* feems to hint at Mr. *Porter*'s having written more than had come to his Knowledge, I hope I fhall be pardoned, on all thefe Circumftances of Probability, If I prefume to attribute thefe two Pieces to him.—Their refpective Titles are,

1. *French Conjuror.* Com.

2. *Witty Combat.* Tragi-Com.

PALSGRAVE, Rev. Mr. *John.* —This learned and ancient Writer flourifhed in the Reigns of *Henry* VII. and *Henry* VIII.

—He received his Grammatical Learning at *London*, in which City he was born.—He ftudied Logic and Philofophy at *Cambridge*, at which Univerfity he refided till he had attained the Degree of Batchelor of Arts, after which he went to *Paris*, where he fpent feveral Years in the Study of Philofophical and other Learning, took the Degree of Mafter of Arts, and acquired fuch Excellence in the *French* Tongue, that, in 1514, when a Treaty of Marriage was negociated between *Louis* XII. King of *France*, and the Princefs *Mary*, Sifter of King *Henry* VIII. of *England*, Mr. *Palfgrave* was chofen to be her Tutor in that Language.—But *Louis* XII. dying almoft immediately after his Marriage, *Palfgrave* attended his fair Pupil back to *England*, where he taught the *French* Language to many of the young Nobility, obtained good Church Preferment, and was appointed by the King one of his Chaplains in Ordinary.

In the Year 1631, he fettled at *Oxford* for fome Time, and the next Year was incorporated Mafter of Arts in that Univerfity, as he had before been in that of *Paris*, and a few Days after was admitted to the Degree of Batchelor of Divinity.

At this Time he was highly efteemed for his Learning; and, what is very remarkable, tho' an *Englifhman*, he was the firft Author who reduced the *French* Tongue under grammatical Rules, or that had attempted to fix it to any Kind of Standard, which he undertook, and that with great Ingenuity and Succefs, in a large Work which he publifhed in that Language at *London*, entitled, *L'Ecclairciffement de la Language Francois*, containing three Books, in a thick Folio, 1530, to which he has prefixed a large Introduction in *English*.——So that the *French* Nation seems to stand indebted to our Country originally, for that Univerſality which their Language at preſent poſſeſſes, and on which they ſo greatly pride themſelves.——Theſe Works, however, would not have entitled him to a Place in this Regiſter of Authors, had he not tranſlated into the *English* a *Latin* Play, written by one *Will. Fullonius* (an Author then living at *Hagen* in *Holland*) entitled

ACCOLASTUS. Com.

When Mr. *Palſgrave* was born, or to what Age he lived, are Particulars which I have not been able to trace ; yet, from the Concurrence of various Facts, I cannot ſuppoſe him to have been much leſs than ſixty Years of Age at the Time of his publiſhing the above-mentioned Tranſlation, which was in the Year 1540.

PATRICK, The Rev. Dr. *S.* Of this Gentleman, who I imagine is ſtill living, I know nothing farther to entitle him to a Place in this Work, than his having favoured the World with a very careful and accurate Edition, with a very perfect Tranſlation, Page againſt Page, of the Works of the *Latin* Comic Poet, *Terence*, in three Vol. 12mo. 1745.

PATTISON, Mr.——This Gentleman wrote one dramatic Piece, which was never acted, having been refuſed a Licence from the Lord Chamberlain's Office.——It did not, however, want Merit, and is in Print by the Title of

ARMINIUS. Trag.

PEAPS, Mr. *William.*——*Langbaine*, who lived the neareſt to the Time of Publication of the dramatic Piece I am on the Point of mentioning, has inſerted it in his Catalogue of Plays by unknown Authors, and only tells us, that it was ſuppoſed by *Kirkman*, but on what Ground he knows not, to have been written by one *Peaps*, from which it is apparent it had been only publiſhed anonymous.——*Jacob*, *Gildon* and *Whincop*, however, have, on this Authority, poſitively affixed the Right of it to that Name.——But *Chetwood*, in his *British Theatre*, has gone ſtill farther, and annexed the Chriſtian Name I have made Uſe of at the Head of this Article.——How far he is right in this Particular, or on what Foundation he has ſo done, I know not.——It is, however, agreed by all the Writers, that the Author lived in the Reign of *Charles* I. and was a Student at *Eton*, as alſo that the Piece was compoſed when he was but ſeventeen Years of Age, which Information I ſuppoſe they derive from the Date, Title - Page and Preface to the Piece itſelf.——It is entitled,

Love in its Extaſy. Paſt. *Coxeter*, in his MS. Notes, has made a Quære with Regard to the Spelling of the Author's Name, ſuppoſing that it might have been one *Pepys* of *Cottenham* in *Cambridgeſhire*, of which Family was Secretary *Pepys*.

PEELE, *George*, M. A.——This Poet, who flouriſhed in the Reign of Queen *Elizabeth*, was a Native of *Devonſhire*, from whence, being ſent to *Broadgate*'s Hall, he was, ſome Time afterwards, made a Student of *Chriſt Church* College, *Oxford*, about the Year 1573, where, after going thro' all the ſeveral Forms of Logic and Philoſophy, and taking all the neceſſary Steps, he was admitted to his Maſter of Arts Degree in

1579.

1579.—After this it appears that he removed to *London*, where he maintained the Estimation in his Poetical Capacity which he had acquired at the University, and which seems to have been of no inconsiderable Rank.—He was a good pastoral Poet, and *Wood* informs us, that his Plays were not only often acted with great Applause in his Life-Time, but did also endure reading, with due Commendation, many Years after his Death.—He speaks of him, however, as a more voluminous Writer in that Way than he appears to have been, mentioning his dramatic Pieces by the Distinction of Tragedies and Comedies, and has given us a List of those which he says he had seen, but in this he must have made some Mistake, as he has divided the several Incidents in one of them, *viz.* his *Edwa,d* I. in such Manner as to make the *Life of Llewellin*, and the *Sinking of Queen Elinor*, two detached and separate Pieces of themselves; the Error of which will be seen in the Perusal of the whole Title of this Play {*Vid.* Vol. I. EDWARD I.) — He, moreover, tells us, that the last-mentioned Piece, together with a Ballad on the same Subject, was, in his Time, usually sold by the common Ballad Mongers.—The real Titles of the Plays written by this Author, and which are but two in Number, are,

   1. DAVID *and* BATHSHEBA. Trag.

   2. EDWARD *the First*. Hist. Play.

Wood and *Winstanley*, misguided by former Catalogues, have also attributed to him another Tragedy, entitled,

   ALPHONSUS, *Emperor of* GERMANY.

But this *Langbaine* assures us was written by *Chapman*, he himself having the Play in his Possession, with that Author's Name to it.

In the latter End of Queen *Elizabeth*'s Reign, that is to say in 1699, *Wood* tells us Mr. *Peele* was living, and in his Middle Age, but is not able to inform us when or where he died ; on which Account he closes with an Observation which I am sorry History does not enable me to contradict, *viz.* " that so it is, and always " hath been, that most Poets die " poor, and consequently ob- " scurely, and a hard Matter it is " to trace them to their Graves."

PEMBROKE , *Mary Herbert*, Countess of.—This Noble Female Author was Wife of *Henry* Earl of *Pembroke*, and lived in the Reigns of Queen *Elizabeth* and King *James* I.—She was also the Sister of the famous Sir *Philip Sidney*, to whom that great Genius dedicated his incomparable Romance called the *Arcadia*, and from whom it has been almost constantly named the Countess of *Pembroke's Arcadia.* — This Circumstance was of itself sufficient to have entailed Immortality on her Memory ; but her Merits stood in Need of no derived Honour, being in themselves entitled to the highest Praise and Commendation.—She was not only a Lover of the Muses, but also a great Encourager of polite Literature ; a Quality not very frequently met with among the Fair. And, not contented with affording her Sanction to those Talents in others, she was careful to cultivate them, and set Example of the Use of them in her own Person.—In the dramatic Way, on which Account she is entitled to a Place here, she translated one Piece from the *French*, call'd,

AN-

ANTONIUS. _Trag._
Coxeter says that, with the Affist-
ance of her Lord's Chaplain, Dr.
Gervase Babington, afterwards Bishop of _Exeter_, she made an exact
Translation of the _Psalms_ of _Da-
vid_ into _English_ Metre.——He,
however, makes a Quere as to
their being ever printed; but
Wood (Athen. Oxon. Vol. I. p.
184.) ascribes such a Translation
to her Brother Sir _Philip Sidney_,
and informs us that it is in MS.
in the Library of the Earl of _Pem-
broke_ at _Wilton_, curiously bound
in a Crimson Velvet Cover, left
thereto by this Lady

In what Year she was born,
I have not been able to trace;
but it is apparent that she was
not married in 1597, from the
Dedication (of that Date) to
Fenton's Tragical Discourses, in
which she is addressed by the Ti-
tle of the Right Hon. the Lady
Mary Sidney.——She died at her
House in _Aldersgate street, London,
Sept._ 25, 1621, and lies in the
Cathedral Church of _Salisbury_,
among the Graves of the _Pem-
brokian_ Family.

I cannot close my Account of
this most excellent Lady, better
than by transcribing for my Readers the Character given of her
by _Francis Osborn_, in his _Memoirs
of the Reign of King_ James, Paragraph 24.

" She was (says he) that Sif-
" ter of Sir _Philip Sidney_, to whom
" she addressed his _Arcadia_, and
" of whom he had no other Ad-
" vantage than what he received
" from the partial Benevolence
" of Fortune in making him a
" Man; which yet she did, in
" some Judgments, recompense
" in Beauty, her Pen being no-
" thing short of his, as I am rea-
" dy to attest, so far as so infe-
" rior a Reason may be taken,

" having seen incomparable Let-
" ters of hers.—But, lest I should
" seem to trespass upon Truth,
" which few do unsuborned (as I
" protest I am, unless by her
" Rhetoric) I shall leave the
" World her Epitaph, in which
" the Author doth manifest him-
" self a Poet in all Things but
" Untruth."

_Underneath this sable Hearse
Lies the Subject of all Verse;_
Sydney's _Sister,_ Pembroke's
_Mother,
Death! e'er thou kill'st such an-
other;
Fair and good, and learn'd as she,
Time shall throw a Dart at thee.
Marble Piles let no Man raise
To her Fame,—for after Days
Some kind Woman, born as she,
Reading this, like_ Niobe,
_Shall turn Statue, and become
Both her Mourner, and her Tomb._

PHILLIPS, Mr. _Ambrose_, was
descended from a very ancient and
considerable Family of that Name
in _Leicestershire._—He was born, as
I should imagine, not much later
than 1680, and received his Education at St. _John's_ College, _Cam-
bridge_; during his Stay at which
University he wrote his Pastorals,
which acquir'd him at the Time
so high a Reputation, and concerning the Merits of which the
Critical World has since been so
much divided; and also a Life of
John Williams, Lord Keeper of
the Great Seal, Bishop of _Lincoln_,
and Archbishop of _York_, in the
Reigns of King _James_ and _Cha._ I.
in which are related some remarkable Occurrences in those
Times, both in Church and State;
with an Appendix, giving an Account of his Benefactions to St.
John's College.—This Work _Cib-
ber_ seems to imagine Mr. _Phillips_

 made

made Ufe of the better to make known his own political Princi-ples, which, in the Courfe of it, he had a free Opportunity of do-ing, as the Archbifhop, who is the Hero of his Work, was a ftrong Opponent to the High Church Meafures.

When he quitted the Univer-fity, and came to *London*, he be-came a conftant Attendant at, and one of the Wits of, *Button's* Cof-fee-Houfe, where he obtained the Friendfhip and Intimacy of many of the celebrated Geniufes of that Age, more particularly of Sir *Richard Steele*, who, in the firft Volume of his *Tatler*, has in-ferted a little Poem of Mr. *Phil-lips's*, which he calls a *Winter Piece*, dated from *Copenhagen*, and addreffed to the Earl of *Dorfet*, on which he beftows the higheft En-comiums; and, indeed, fo much Juftice is there in thefe his Com-mendations, that even Mr. *Pope* himfelf, who, for Reafons that I fhall prefently mention, had a fixed Averfion for the Author, while he affected to defpife his o-ther Works, ufed always to ex-cept this from the Number.

The firft Diflike Mr. *Pope* con-ceived againft Mr. *Phillips*, pro-ceeded from that Jealoufy of Fame which was fo confpicuous in the Character of that great Poet, for Sir *Richard Steele*, who, as I have before obferved, was an Ad-mirer of *Phillips*, had taken fo ftrong a Liking to the Paftorals of the latter, as to have formed a Defign for a critical Comparifon of them with thofe of *Pope*, in the Conclufion of which the Pre-ference was to have been given to *Phillips*.—This Defign, however, coming to Mr. *Pope's* Knowledge, that Gentleman, who could not bear a Rival near the Throne, determined to ward off this Stroke,

by a Stratagem of the moft artfu Kind, which was no other than taking the fame Tafk on himfelf, and, in a Paper in the Guardian, by drawing the like Comparifon, and giving a like Preference, but on Principles of Criticifm appa-rently fallacious, to point out the Abfurdity of fuch a Judgment.— However, notwithftanding the Ridicule that was drawn on him in Confequence of his ftanding as it were in Competition with fo powerful an Antagonift, I cannot help giving it as my Opinion that there are, in fome Parts of *Phillips's* Paftorals, certain Strokes of Nature, and a Degree of Sim-plicity, that are much better fuit-ed to the Purpofes of Paftoral, than the more correctly turned Periods of Mr. *Pope's* Verfifica-tion.—But, as I am on the Sub-ject of Paftoral Writing, I cannot omit obferving that we have an Author at prefent living, who feems, tho' lefs noticed than ei-ther of thefe Gentlemen, not only to excell them both, but even every other Writer of this or any other Period; nor do I doubt that many of my Readers will join with me in Opinion, if they either have read, or will give themfelves the Pleafure of perufing, Mr. *Shenftone's* little Pieces, publifhed in the IVth Volume of *Dodfley's Collection of Poems*, particularly one Poem, en-titled a Paftoral Ballad, in four Parts, confifting of *Abfence, Sol-licitude, Hope* and *Difappointment*. But to proceed.—Mr. *Phillips* and Mr. *Pope* being of different Poli-tical Principles, was another Caufe of Enmity between them, which arofe at length to fo great a Height, that the former, finding his Antagonift too hard for him at the Weapon of Wit, had even determined on making Ufe of a

rougher

rougher Kind of Argument, for which Purpose he even went fo far as to hang up a Rod at *Button*'s for the Chaftifement of his Adverfary whenever he fhould come thither, which, however, Mr. *Pope* declining to do, avoided the *Argumentum baculinum*, in which he would, no doubt, have found himfelf on the weakeft Side of the Queftion.

Befides Mr. *Pope*, there were fome other Writers who have written in Burlefque of Mr. *Phillips*'s Poetry, which was fingular in its Manner, and not difficult to imitate, particularly Mr. *Henry Carey*, who, by fome Lines in *Phillips*'s Stile, and which were for fometime thought to be Dean *Swift*'s, fixed on that Author the Name of *Namby-Pamby*; and *Hawkins Browne*, Efq; in his Foem called a *Pipe of Tobacco*, which, however, is written with great good Humour, and, tho' intended to *burlefque*, is by no Means defigned to ridicule Mr. *Phillips*, he having taken the very fame Liberty with *Swift*, *Pope*, *Thomfon*, *Young* and *Cibber*.

As a dramatic Writer, our Author has certainly confiderable Merit.—All his Pieces of that Kind met with Succefs, and one of them is at this Time a Standard of Entertainment at both Theatres, being generally repeated feveral Times in every Seafon. The Titles of them all, being three in Number, are,

1. The *Briton*. Trag.
2. *Diftreft Mother*. Trag.
3. Humphry *Duke of* Gloucester. Trag.

Mr. *Phillips*'s Circumftances were in general, through his Life, not only eafy, but rather affluent, in Confequence of his being connected, by his political Principles, with Perfons of great Rank and

Confequence.—He was concerned with Dr. *Hugh Boulter*, afterwards Archbifhop of *Armagh*, the Right Hon. *Richard Weft*, Efq; Lord Chancellor of *Ireland*, the Rev. Mr. *Gilbert Burnet*, and the Rev. Mr. *Henry Stevens*, in writing a Series of Papers called the *Free Thinker*, which were all publifhed together by Mr. *Phillips*, in three vol. in 12mo. —— In the latter Part of Queen *Anne*'s Reign, he was Secretary to the *Hanover* Club, who were a Set of Noblemen and Gentlemen who had formed an Affociation in Honour of that Succeffion, and for the Support of its Interefts, and who ufed particularly to diftinguifh in their Toafts fuch of the Fair Sex as were moft zealoufly attached to the illuftrious Houfe of *Brunfwick*.—In Honour of which Ladies our Bard wrote the following Lines,

While thefe, the chofen Beauties of our Ifle,
Propitious on the Caufe of Freedom fmile;
The rafh Pretender's Hopes we may defpife,
And truft Britannia's *Safety to their Eyes.*

Mr. *Phillips*'s Station in this Club, together with the Zeal fhewn in his Writings, recommending him to the Notice and Favour of the new Government, he was, foon after the Acceffion of King *George* I. put into the Commiffion of the Peace, and appointed one of the Commiffioners of the Lottery.—And, on his Friend Dr. *Boulton*'s being made Primate of *Ireland*, he accompanied that Prelate acrofs St. *George*'s Channel, where he had confiderable Preferments beftowed on him, and was elected a Member

of

of the Houfe of Commons there, as Reprefentative for the County of *Armagh*.

At length, having purchafed an Annuity for Life of four hundred Pounds *per Annum*, he came over to *England* fome Time in the Year 1748, but, having a very bad State of Health, and being moreover of an advanced Age, he died foon after, at his Lodgings near *Vauxhall*, in *Surry*.

PHILLIPS, Mr. *Edward*.—Of this Gentleman I can trace nothing farther than his Name, that he was a Writer of the laft Reign, and produced four little dramatic Pieces, entitled,

 1. *Britons ftrike Home.* Farce.
 2. *Chambermaid.* Ball. Opera.
 3. *Livery Rake and Country Lafs.* Opera.
 4. *Mock Lawyer.* Farce.

PHILLIPS, Mr. *John*.—This Name is put to the three following Pieces, none of which, I believe were ever acted; the firft and laft of them, however, being written entirely on Party Subjects, and at a Time that every Act of Zeal fhewn for the Intereft of the Houfe of *Hanover*, which was as yet not fo firmly eftablifhed in the Hearts of the People, as it has fince moft happily and moft defervedly render'd itfelf, met with a generous and kind Return, Mr. *Chetwood* has informed us, that the Author received a handfome Prefent from the Government, in Confideration of them.—The Compiler of *Whincop*'s Catalogue feems to furmife, that this Name of *Phillips* was not a real, but only an affumed one, but on what Grounds he builds his Suppofition I know not, as I can fee no Reafon why an Author, who only wrote in Contempt of an unjuftifiable Rebellion, and in Ridicule of the pro-

feffed or detected Enemies of a juft and an amiable Monarch, fhould either be afraid or afhamed of as openly declaring his Name as his Opinions.—Be this as it will, the Titles of the Pieces publifhed under this Name, (the fecond of which, however, I find mentioned by nobody but *Coxeter*) are as follow,

 1. *Earl of* MAR *marr'd.* Farce.
 2. *Inquifition.* Farce.
 3. *Pretender's Flight.* Farce.

PHILLIPS, Mr. *R*.——This Writer's Name is mentioned by *Coxeter*, as Author of a Series of poetical Stories, printed in 4to. 1683, under the Title of *The Victory of Cupid over the Gods and Goddeffes*, and of one dramatic Piece, dated 1701, entitled,

 Fatal Inconftancy. Trag. *Vid.* APPENDIX.

PHILLIPS, *William*, Efq;—Whether this Gentleman was a Native of *Ireland* or not, *Jacob* has informed us that he was educated in that Kingdom, and that he wrote a Tragedy, entitled

 The *Revengeful Queen*.

In this the Compiler of *Whincop*'s Catalogue agrees with him, but afterwards gives us the Name of another Gentleman, whom he ftiles

PHILLIPS, Capt. *William*, which Gentleman he informs us was the Author of another Tragedy, entitled,

 HIBERNIA *Freed*.

This Play, however, *Coxeter*, in his MS. Notes on *Jacob*, has inferted as the Work of the foregoing Gentleman, and *Chetwood*, in his *Britifh Theatre*, has gone ftill farther, making Mention of another Piece alfo by the Title of

 St. STEPHEN's *Green.* Com.

afcribing all the three Plays indifcriminately to a *William Phillips*, Efq;——And indeed, as we have

have Reason to believe the Author of the first Piece to have been an *Irishman*, and that the two others have an apparent Reference to that Country, I cannot help joining in Opinion, that these Authors must have been one and the same Person.—The only Objection to that Opinion is, the Distance of Time between 1698 the Date of the first Play, and 1721, which is that affix'd to the earliest of the other two.—But, as we find a Difference only in the Title of the Gentleman at the several Periods, it is not at all improbable that the *Revengeful Queen* might have been written before the Author had taken on himself the military Profession, the Employment of which might afterwards put a Stop to that Attachment to the *Muses*, which afterwards, in Times of Peace and Recess from martial Business, he could not avoid indulging himself by returning to.

PILKINGTON, Mrs. *Lætitia*, a Native of *Dublin*, was born in 1712.—Her Father was Dr. *Van-lewin*, an eminent Physician of that City.—Our Authoress was married, very young, to the Rev. Mr. *Matthew Pilkington*; who was also a Poet of no inconsiderable Merit.—This Pair of Wits, as is but too often the Case, lived very unhappily together; and at length were totally separated, in Consequence of an accidental Discovery which Mr. *Pilkington* made of a Gentleman in his Wife's Bed-Chamber. — Of this Affair, however, Mrs. *Pilkington*, in her celebrated Memoirs of her own Life, gives such an Account, as would persuade her Readers to believe that, in Reality, nothing criminal passed between her and the Gentleman; but, *Credat Judæus apella*.

After this unlucky Affair, Mrs. *Pilkington* had Recourse to her Pen for a Support, and raised a very considerable Subscription for her Memoirs, which are extremely entertaining, particularly on Account of the many lively Anecdotes she has given of Dean *Swift*, with whom she had the Honour of being very intimate.

This unhappy but ingenious Woman died, in great Penury, in the Year 1750; having had Recourse to the Bottle, in Order to drown her Sorrows; by which it is thought she shortened her Days.—She departed at the Age of 39, leaving several Children to take their Chance in the wide World; for her Husband renounced them at the same Time that he renounced her.—*John*, her eldest Son, turned out also something of a Poet; and has likewise published *his* Memoirs. He is still living, and therefore we shall say no more of him.

Mrs. *Pilkington*, besides her other Poems and her Memoirs, was Author of one burlesque dramatic Piece, entitled,

> The TURKISH *Court*, or the *London Prentice*; acted in *Dublin*.

PIX, Mrs. *Mary*. — Of this Lady, tho' a Woman of considerable Genius and Abilities, I can trace nothing farther than that she was born at *Nettlebed* in *Oxfordshire*, and that her Maiden Name was *Griffith*, being the Daughter of one Mr. *Griffith* a Clergyman, and that, by the Mother's Side, she was descended from a very considerable Family, *viz.* that of the *Wallis*'s.—By the Date of her Writings she must have flourished in K. *William* III's Reign, but in what Year she was born, to whom married, or when she died, are Particulars which seem feem buried in Obfcurity and Oblivion.——She was Cotemporary with Mrs. *Manley* and Mrs. *Trotter*, afterwards Mrs. *Cockburn*, one of the moft learned Ladies that ever lived in this or any other Country; and is ridiculed in Company with thefe Ladies in a little dramatic Piece called the *Female Wits (Vid.* Vol. I.) but, however near fhe may ftand on a Par with the latter, in Refpect to her poetical Talents, I can by no Means think her equal to the former. —— Her Works, however, will beft fpeak in her Commendation; they are feven in Number, and their Titles as follow,

1. *Czar of* MUSCOVY. Trag.
2. *Deceiver deceived.* Com.
3. *Double Diftrefs.* Trag.
4. IBRAHIM XII. Trag.
5. *Innocent Miftrefs.* Com.
6. *Queen* CATHARINE. T.
7. SPANISH *Wives.* Farce.

POPPLE, *William*, Efq;——This Gentleman, who is ftill living, is Governor of *Bermudas*, and is Author of a dramatic Piece, which met with fome Succefs, entitled,

The *Double Deceit.* Com. There are alfo feveral Pieces in Verfe, written by this Gentleman, to be found in a Collection of Mifcellaneous Poems, publifhed by *Richard Savage*, in 8vo. 1736.—He was alfo concerned in fome Periodical Papers; particularly *The Prompter;* in which he was jointly connected with the celebrated *Aaron Hill*, Efq;—Mr. *Popple* has likewife publifhed a Tranflation of *Horace's Art of Poetry;* See *Monthly Review*, for *Oct.* 1753.

PORDAGE, *Samuel*, Efq;—A Writer in the Reign of King *Charles* II.—He was Son of the Rev. Mr. *John Pordage*, Rector of *Bradfield* in *Berkfhire*, and formerly Head Steward of the Lands to *Philip* the fecond Earl of *Pembroke*.—He was probably born at *Bradfield*; where he received his Education I am unable to trace, but find him mentioned by *Wood*, as a Member of the Hon. Society of *Lincoln's-Inn*. Befides an Edition with Cuts (publifhed after the Author's Death) of *Reinalds's God's Revenge againft Murder and Adultery*, he has favoured the World, of his own Products, with a Romance entitled *Eliana*, two Plays of original Compofition, and a Tranflation of the third.—The Titles of the faid dramatic Pieces are,

1. HEROD *and* MARIAMNE. Trag.
2. *Siege of* BABYLON. Tragi-Com.
3. TROADES. Trag. (fuppos'd by *Langbaine*, from the Initial Letters S. P. annex'd, to have been tranflated by this Author.)

PORTAL, Mr. *Abraham*, is a Goldfmith and Jeweller on *Ludgate-Hill, London*.—He has publifhed one dramatic Piece which was never acted, founded on *Taffo*, and entitled,

OLINDA *and* SOPHRONIA. Trag.

He is likewife Author of fome other Poetical Pieces, not contemptible.—Mr. *Portal* is the Perfon upon whom an extraordinary and moft daring Attempt was made, in *February* 1763, by a young Man, named *John Freake*, in Order to obtain from him an hundred Guineas: The Affair made a great Noife in the Papers, and is, doubtlefs, frefh in the Memory of moft Readers, fo that we need not repeat it here. *Freake*, who was tried for this Offence, being a Perfon of a good

Family in the Kingdom of *Ireland*, had so much Favour shewn him, that his Life was saved.

PORTER, Mr. *Henry*, Author of a dramatic Piece, which made its Appearance in the latter Part of Queen *Elizabeth*'s Reign, entitled,

The *Two angry Women of A-BINGTON.* Com.

Wood (Atken. Oxon. Vol. I. p. 781.) mentions a Mr. *Henry Porter*, of *Christ Church* College, in the University of *Oxford*, and Batchelor of Music, who, he tells us, was Father to Mr. *Walter Porter*, some Time Gentleman of the Royal Chapel, and Master of the Choristers at *Westminster*, in the Reign of King *Charles* I.—And, altho' *Wood* does not mention that Gentleman as a Writer, yet, as the Date of his Degree, which was in *July* 16co, is but one Year subsequent to that of the above-mentioned Play, I think it is no very far-fetch'd Conjecture that he might be the Author of it.

PORTER, *Thomas*, Esq; a Major in the Army, in the Reigns of King *Charles* I. and II.—He is the avowed Author of two dramatic Pieces, entitled,

1. *Carnival.* Com.
2. *Villain.* Tragi-Com.

With Respect to a Conjecture of his having written more in the dramatic Way, see above, under the Initials P. T.

POWELL, Mr. *George*, was an Actor as well as an Author, and in neither Light deficient of Merit.—In the former Character he attained to great Eminence, and, tho' Cotemporary with *Betterton*, *Booth*, *Wilks*, *Cibber*, &c. maintained a very considerable Rank among others ; and, amidst the Brightness of such a dazzling Constellation as then illuminated the

theatrical World, shone no inglorious Star.—His Excellencies, however, suffered Abatements, from some very considerable Blemishes in his Manner of acting ; yet, on the whole, the Good outweigh'd the Bad, and his Beauties more than made Amends for his Deformities.—Whoever is desirous of a more particular Idea of him, need only look into *Colley Cibber*'s Apology, which is the most compleat History of Theatrical Affairs extant, for the Period of Time it includes.—Mr. *Powell*, however, in the latter Part of his Life, being somewhat too strongly attach'd to the Allurements of the Bottle, declined in great Measure from the Reputation he had acquir'd.

Mr. *Powell* died in the Year 1714, and was interred in the Vault of the Parish Church of St. *Clement's Danes*, leaving behind him the five following dramatic Pieces, all which he had brought on the Stage with Success.

1. ALPHONSO, *King of* NAPLES. Trag.
2. BONDUCA. Trag. (only an Alteration from *Beaumont* and *Fletcher*.)
3. BRUTUS *of* ALBA. Trag.
4. *Treacherous Brother.* Trag.
5. *Very good Wife.* Com.

Gildon informs us that Mr. *Powell*'s Father had also been a Player, and was but lately dead at the Time he wrote, which was in 1698.

PRESTON, *Thomas*, L. L. D. flourished in the earlier Part of Queen *Elizabeth*'s Reign, was first Master of Arts and Fellow of *King*'s College, *Cambridge*, and afterwards created a Doctor of Civil Law, and Master of *Trinity Hall* in the same University.—In the Year 1564, when Queen *Elizabeth* was entertained at *Cambridge*,

bridge, this Gentleman acted so admirably well in the Tragedy of *Dido*, written by *Tho. Nash*, and did moreover so genteely and gracefully dispute before her Majesty, that, as a Testimonial of her Approbation, she bestowed a Pension of twenty Pounds *per Annum* upon him.——On the 6th of *Sept.* 1566, when the *Oxonian* Muses, in their Turn, were honoured with a Visit from their Royal Mistress, our Author, with eight more *Cantabrigians*, were incorporated Masters of Arts in the University of *Oxford*.

Mr. *Preston* wrote one dramatic Piece, in the old Metre, entitled,

Lyfe of CAMBYSES. Trag. For a more particular Account of which, see Vol. I. CAMBYSES. This Play *Langbaine* imagines *Shakespeare* meant to ridicule, when, in his Play of *Henry* IV. Part I. Act II. he makes *Falstaff* talk of *speaking in King Cambyses* Vein.——In Proof of which Conjecture he has given his Readers a Quotation from the Beginng of the Play, being a Speech of King *Cambyses* himself, which, on the same Account that he quoted it, and also as being a good Specimen of the Manner of Writing of many Authors at that Period of Time, I shall take the Liberty of transcribing.————The Words are as follow,

My Counsile grave and sapient,
  With Lords of legal Train ;
Attentive Eares towards us bend,
  And mark what shall be sain.

So you, likewise, my valiant Knight,
  Whose manly Acts doth fly ;
Bye Brute of Fame the sounding
    Trump
Doth perse the azure Sky.

My sapient Words, I say, prepare,
  And so your Skill delate:
You know that Moss *vanquished*
    hath
  Cyrus, *that King of State :*

And I, by due Inheritance,
  Possess that princely Crown;
Ruling, by Sword of mighty Force,
  In Place of great Renown.

PRESTWICH, PRESTWITH, or PRESTWICK, Mr. *Edmund.*—— In all these several Manners have different Authors spelled the Name of a Writer of King *Charles* I's Reign, who, according to *Phillips* and *Winstanley*, (and indeed most of the Biographers have followed their Opinion) was Author of two dramatic Pieces, entitled,

  1. The *Hectors.* Trag. *Vid.* APPENDIX.
  2. HIPPOLITUS. Trag.

Q.

QUARLES, *Francis*, Esq; was Son of *James Quarles*, Esq; Clerk of the Board of *Green Cloth*, and Purvevor to Queen *Elizabeth*. He was born in 1592, at *Stewards*, an ancient Seat of the Family, near *Rumford* in *Essex* ; from whence he was first sent to *Peter House*, and afterwards to *Christ Church* College, *Cambridge*, for the compleating of his Studies ; and, on his Return to *London*, became a Member of *Lincoln's Inn.*——He was some Time Cup-bearer to the Queen of *Bohemia*, and Chronologer to the City of *London* ; and went over to *Ireland* as Secretary to that
      truly

truly great Prelate *James Uſher*, Archbiſhop of *Armagh*.—But the Troubles in that Kingdom forcing him from thence, he returned to his Native Country, where he died, on the 8th Day of *Sept.* 1644, *Ætat.* 52. and was buried in the Pariſh Church of St. *Vedaſt*, *Foſter-Lane*.—His Works, both in Verſe and Proſe, are numerous and well known, particularly his *Divine Emblems*, which has been a good Copy to the Bookſellers, and is to this Day in great Requeſt with one Sort of pious Readers; tho', on Account of the obſolete Quaintneſs of Stile, which many of the Writers of that Age made Uſe of, his Works, with thoſe of many of his Cotemporaries once in high Repute, are now totally neglected, or at leaſt held in but ſlight Eſtimation.—Among his other Works was a Piece entitled the *Loyal Convert*, for the writing of which he underwent a very ſevere Proſecution, from the uſurped Authority then in being.

Langbaine, a great Admirer of his Works, gives him this amiable Character.—"He was (ſays " he) a Poet that mixed Religion " and Fancy together; and was " very careful in all his Writings " not to intrench upon Good-" Manners, by any Scurrility in " his Works; or any Ways of-" fending againſt his Duty to " God, his Neighbour, or him-" ſelf."

In dramatic Writing he only produced one Piece, to which even his zealous Advocate *Langbaine* gives no higher Commendation to, than ſtyling it *an innocent, inoffenſive Play.*—It is entitled,

The *Virgin Widow.* Com. Mr. *Quarles* had, by one Wife, no leſs than eighteen Children; one of whom, *John*, inheriting both his Father's Genius and his Loyalty, received his Education at *Exeter* College, *Oxford*; and, in 1642, being then but eighteen Years of Age, bore Arms within the Garriſon of *Oxon*, for King *Charles* I. in whoſe Army, it is ſaid, he afterwards had a Captain's Commiſſion.—But, on the Declenſion of his Majeſty's Cauſe, he retired to *London*, where, in Conſequence of his Attachment to the Royal Party, he was reduced to write for a bare Subſiſtence, and there continued in a poor and mean Condition, till the great Plague, which, raging in and about *London*, ſwept him away, with many Thouſands more, in the fatal Year 1665.

R.

R J. *Vid.* SHEPHERD'S HOLIDAY. Vol. I. APPENDIX.

R. T.—Theſe Initial Letters ſtand in the Title of one dramatic Piece, entitled,

The *Extravagant Shepherd.* Paſt. Com.

There is no Author who wrote about that Time whoſe Name would ſuit with theſe Initials, excepting *Thomas Rawlins*, of whom hereafter: Yet, without ſome farther concominant Circumſtances, I cannot think myſelf authorized to father this Play upon him.

R. W.——Theſe two Letters ſtand before a Kind of Droll or Farce, play'd at *Bartholomew* and *Southwark* Fairs, and publiſhed in K. *Charles* II's Time, entitled,

The *Coronation of Queen* ELIZABETH.

[C c]   Theſe

These Letters are also affixed to a Piece, entitled,

The *Three Lords and Ladies of* LONDON. *Vid.* Vol. I. THREE LADIES OF LON-DON.

RALPH, *James*, Esq; one of the greatest political, tho' not one of the greatest poetical Writers of the present Age.—Of his Family we can trace no particulars; but it is said his Descent was but mean, and that he solely raised himself from Obscurity by his Merit; a Circumstance which redounds more to his Honour than would a long Bead-roll of great Ancestors, " stuck o'er with Ti-" tles and hung round with " strings."

Mr. *Ralph*'s first Appearance in the World, before he became distinguished for his Writings, was, as we are informed, in the Character of a School-Master, at *Philadelphia*, in *North-America*; which remote Situation not suiting his active Mind, he came to *England*, about the Beginning of the Reign of *George* I. We have not learnt what was then the immediate Object of his Pursuit, but it was probably something in the public Offices dependant on the Court; for he soon became a Frequenter of the *Levees*, and attach'd to some great Men, to whom his Abilities recommended him,—He did not, however, at first make any Figure in the political World, but rather applied himself to writing for the Stage, in which he was not very successful.—He also produced some Pieces of Poetry, particularly *Night*, a Poem, of which Mr. *Pope* thus takes Notice in his *Dunciad:*

Silence ye Wolves! while Ralph *to* Cynthia *howls,*

And makes Night hideous—answer him ye Owls!

This Passage Mr. *Pope* has illustrated by a very abusive Note, in which Mr. *Ralph*'s Character is most unmercifully torn to Pieces; which Severity, it seems, was occasioned by a Piece attributed to our Author, entitled *Sawney*, a Poem, in which the sacred triumvirate, Dean *Swift*, Mr. *Pope* and Mr. *Gay* were attacked.——This was high Treason itself.—Mr. *Ralph*, was very falsely and injuriously represented in the *Dunciad*.—Mr. *Pope* says, he was so illiterate, that he did not even understand *French* : Whereas, it is very certain, that he was Master of the *French* and *Latin* Languages; and not altogether ignorant of the *Italian*; and was, in Truth, a very ingenious Prose-Writer, although he did not succeed as a Poet.—His *History of England*, commencing with the Reign of the *Stuarts*, is much esteemed, as were his Political Pamphlets; some of which were looked upon as Master-Pieces.—He was likewise concerned in writing the Essays in several Periodical Papers; in which he became so formidable to the Ministry towards the End of Sir *Robert Walpole*'s Time, that it was deemed expedient to take him off by a Pension.—He had great Expectations from the late Prince of *Wales*, who frequently made use of Mr. *Ralph*'s Pen, in the Controversies in which it is well known that Prince was engaged : But, by the Death of his Royal Highness, all our Author's Views of Preferment were entirely cut off.—At the Accession of *Geo.* III. however, Mr. *Ralph*, tho' considerably advanced in Years, began to be again taken Notice of, and his Hopes were revived; but, alas! the great Circumventor of all human Expectations, Death, put a final Period to all his Schemes,

in

in the Beginning of the Year 1762, at his House in *Chifwick*; after fuffering a long and fevere Affliction from the Gout, of which Diforder alfo his only Daughter, about eighteen, died in a few Weeks after him.

His dramatic Writings are,

1. *Fafhionable Lady*, or *Harlequin's Opera*.
2. *Fall of the Earl of* ESSEX. Trag.
3. *Lawyer's Feaft*. Farce.
4. *Aftrologer*. Com.

One of Mr. *Ralph*'s laft Performances had alfo fome Relation to the Stage; and was efteemed a very excellent and very entertaining Performance.—It was entitled, *The Cafe of Authors*.

RAMSAY, *Allan*, is faid to have been a Barber in *Edinburgh*. His Tafte in Poetry, however, has juftly raifed him to a Degree of Fame that may in fome Meafure be confider'd as a Recompence for the Frowns of Fortune.—His Songs are in univerfal Efteem; as is alfo the only dramatic Performance attributed to him, *viz*.

ROGER and PATTIE, or *the Gentle Shepherd*. A Scots Paftoral.

This Piece is frequently acted at the Little Theatre in the *Haymarket*, for the Benefit of one *Lauder*, a Singer; who himfelf ufually performs a principal Part in it.

Our Northern Bard was Father to the ingenious Mr. *Ramfay*, a celebrated Painter of the prefent Age, and who has likewife diftinguifhed himfelf by fome wellwritten Tracts on various Branches of Polite Literature, particularly *the Inveftigator*.

RANDOLPHE, Mr. *Thomas*.—This valuable Poet was a Son of *William Randolphe*, of *Hamfey*, near *Lewes* in *Suffex*, Efq; Steward to *Edward* Lord *Zouch*, by *Elizabeth* his Wife, Daughter of *Thomas Smith*, Efq; of *Newnham*, near *Daintree* in *Northamptonfhire*, at which Place our Author was born, on the 15th of *June* 1605. —He received the early Parts of his Education at *Weftminfter School*, from whence, being one of the King's Scholars, he removed to *Trinity* College in *Cambridge*, at the Age of eighteen; in which College he obtained a Fellowfhip, and afterwards commenced Mafter of Arts, in which Degree he was incorporated at *Oxford*.—Very early in Life he gave Proofs of an amazing Quicknefs of Parts, and he was not only efteem'd and admir'd by Perfons of Genius at the Univerfity, but likewife highly valued and beloved by the beft Poets of that Age in the Metropolis.—His extenfive Learning, Gaiety of Humour, and Readinefs of Repartee, gain'd him Admirers throughout all Ranks of Mankind, and more efpecially recommended him to the Intimacy and Friendfhip of *Ben Jonfon*, who admitted him as one of his adopted Sons in the Mufes, and held him in equal Efteem with the ingenious Mr. *Cartwright*, of whom I have before made Mention.

Randolphe's Turn, in his dramatic Works, is entirely to Comedy; his Language is elegant, and his Sentiments are juft and forcible.—His Characters are, for the moft Part, ftrongly drawn, and his Satire well chofen and poignant.—In fhort, it were to be wifhed, that fome Writer of Merit would endeavour at the raifing him out of the Obfcurity in which his Writings at prefent feem buried, by altering his Pieces, fo as to render them fit for the prefent

 Stage,

Stage, or at the leaft giving the World a correct and critical Edition of them.

The dramatic Pieces he has left behind him, which were puhlifhed after his Death by his Brother Mr. *Thomas Randolphe*, of *Chrift-Church* College, *Oxford*, are the fix following, *viz.*

1. AMYNTAS. Paft.
2. ARISTIPPUS. Com.
3. *Conceited Pedlar*. Farce.
4. *Hey for Honefty, Down with Knavery*. Com.
5. *Jealous Lovers*. Com.
6. *Mufis Looking-Glafs*. Com.

The laft of thefe has, within a few Years paft, been revived at *Covent-Garden* Theatre, and is, moreover, reprinted in *Dodfley's* Collection of old Plays.——It is probable that, had a Length of Days been permitted to this Author, he would have produced many more valuable Pieces, fome. of which might have become brilliant Ornaments to the *Englifh* Stage ; but, alas ! at the very Time when he was attaining the Prime of Life, at the very Time when Genius was beginning to be temper'd by Judgment, and Fancy to be moderated by Experience, at the very Time, in a Word, when the moft fanguine Expectations were raifed of a future Harveft, of luxuriant Fruit, this flourifhing Bloffom was crop'd by the envious Hand of Death.—— In fhort, according to *Wood*, being too like the Generality of Men of Abilities, fomewhat addicted to libertine Indulgences, and, in Confequence of keeping too much Company, and running into fafhionable Exceffes with greater Freedom than his Conftitution could bear, he affifted in fhortening his own Days, and died before he had compleated the Age

of twenty-nine Years, at the Houfe of *William Stafford*, Efq; of *Blatherwyke* in *Northamptonfhire*, and was buried, with the Anceftors of the Family of *Stafford*, in an Ifle adjoining to the Church of that Place, on the 17th of *March* 1634, foon after which a Monument of white Marble was erected over his Grave, at the Charge of Sir *Chriftopher* (afterwards Lord) *Hatton*, of *Kirby*, with an Infcription upon it, in *Latin* and *Englifh* Verfe, written by our Author's intimate Friend *Peter Haufted*, of whom I have before had Occafion to make Mention, and give fome Account of in his proper Place.

RAVENSCROFT, Mr. *Edward*. This Writer, or rather Compiler of Plays, lived in the Reigns of *Charles* II. and *James* II.—He was fometime a Member of the *Middle Temple*, but, looking on the dry Study of the Law as greatly beneath the Attention of a Man of Genius, quitted it, for the Pleafure of ranging in the more flowery Fields of Poetry : But here again he feem'd averfe to Labour, rather chufing to pluck and form Nofegays of thofe Flowers which had been planted by others, than by the cultivating of any untill'd Spot, to obtain a genuine Right of Inheritance in the Product of his own Induftry.—In a Word, he was an errant Plagiary ; and altho', by boldly daring to enter the Lifts, in a vigorous Oppofition to Mr. *Dryden*, the Power of his Antagonift ftamp'd a Degree of Diftinction on him, which he would never otherwife have obtained ; yet it is, perhaps, the only Claim he can properly lay to public Notice : And Mr. *Dryden* might, with great Propriety, have retorted on him in the

R E

the Words of *Ajax*.

IPSE *tulit Pretium jam nunc Cer-
taminis hujus,
Qui, cum victus erit, MECUM
certasse feretur.*

Mr. *Ravenscroft's* dramatic Pieces
are twelve in Number, and are as
follow,
  1. *Anatomist.* Com.
  2. CANTERBURY *Guests.* C.
  3. *Careless Lovers.* Com.
  4. *Dame* DOBSON. Com.
  5. EDGAR *and* ALFREDA.
      Trag.
  6. ENGLISH *Lawyer.* Com.
  7. ITALIAN *Husband.* Trag.
  8. LONDON *Cuckolds.* Com.
  9. MAMAMOUCHI. Com.
  10. SCARAMOUCH, *a Philoso-
      pher,* &c. Com.
  11. TITUS ANDRONICUS. T.
  12. *Wrangling Lovers.* Com.

RAWLINS, *Thomas,* Esq; was
principal Engraver of the Mint,
in the Reigns both of King *Charles*
the First and Second, and died in
that Employment in 1670.—He
was intimately acquainted with
most of the Wits and Poets of his
Time, and wrote for Amusement
only, not for Profit; for, in the
Preface to his first Play, he thus
addresses the Reader.—" Take no
" Notice of my Name (says he)
" for a second Work of this Na-
" ture shall hardly bear it.—I
" have no Desire to be known by
" a Thread-bare Coat, having a
" Calling that will maintain it
" woolly."—The Pieces which
pass under his Name, are the
following,
  1. *Rebellion.* Trag.
  2. TOM ESSENCE. Com.
  3. TUNBRIDGE *Wells.* Com.
      (ascribed to this Author.)

REVET, Mr. *Edward.* — Of
this Author I can trace nothing
farther than that he must have

R I

lived in the Reign of K. *Cha.* II.
and that he wrote one dramatic
Piece, which was a very hasty,
and therefore probably not a very
extraordinary Performance, having been begun and finished in a
Fortnight, entitled,
  The *Town Shifts.* Com.

RHODES, *Richard,* M. D —
This Author was of a good Extraction, being the Son of a Gentleman of *London,* and probably
born in that Metropolis, tho' in
what Year is not apparent.—He
received the Rudiments of his
Education in *Westminster* School,
from whence, being at that Time
well grounded in Grammar, and
in the practical Part of Music, he
was transplanted to *Oxford,* where
he became a Student in *Christ
Church* College, but took only
one Degree in Arts, at which
Time he made certain Compositions in Music.—From thence he
went to *France,* and took the Degree of Doctor in Physic at *Mont-
pellier,* but, being of an unsetled
Disposition, or perhaps fond of
Travel, he from thence took a
Journey to *Spain,* where at *Madrid* he died, and was buried in
the Year 1668.—While he was
at the University of *Oxford,* he
wrote one Play, entitled,
  FLORA's *Vagaries.* Com.

RICHARD, Mr. *Nathaniel.*—
Of this Author I find nothing
farther on Record than that he
lived in the Reign of K. *Charles* I.
and, about the Beginning of the
Civil War, published one dramatic Piece, entitled,
  MESSALINA *the Roman Em-
      press.* Trag.

RIDER, *William,* M. A.—All
I can learn with Relation to this
Author is, that he was a Student
in *Merton* College, *Oxford,* where
he took his Degree of Master of
Arts, some Time in the Reign

 of

of *Charles* II. that he married a near Kinfwoman to Dr. *Armway*, Archdeacon of *Litchfield* and *Coventry*, and that he wrote one dramatic Piece, entitled,

The *Twins*. Com.

RIVERS, Mr.—This Author was a Jefuit, who lived, I believe, in the Reign of *James* I. and wrote one Play, entitled,

The *Traytor*. Trag.
which, I imagine, was never acted in its original Form; but, falling into the Hands of Mr. *James Shirley*, he, with very confiderable Alterations and Improvements of his own, brought it on the Stage, and publifhed it among his own Works.——Mr. *Rivers* compofed this Piece while he was in Confinement in *Newgate*, on Account of fome political and religious Concerns, in which Prifon he died.— It was afterwards, *viz.* in 1692, revived with Succefs, under the Title of *Amidea*; and after that again, with fome Alterations, but by its old Title, by Mr. *Chriftopher Bullock*, the Comedian.

ROCHESTER, *John Wilmot*, Earl of, was Son to the famous *Henry* Lord *Wilmot*, (afterwards Earl of *Rochefter*) who was fo very inftrumental in the Prefervation of *Charles* II. in his Flight from *Worcefter*, where he was defeated by *Cromwell*.—The memorable Wit, who is the Subject of this Article, was born in 1648, and was educated firft at *Burford* Free-School; from whence, in 1659, he was admitted a Nobleman of *Wadham* College in *Oxford*.—He afterwards travelled into *France* and *Italy*; and, at his Return, he frequented the debauched Court of *Cha.* II. where his natural Propenfities to Vice were not likely to be curbed or cured: Here he was firft made

one of the Gentlemen of his Majefty's Bed-Chamber, and then Comptroller of *Woodftock* Park.

In the Winter of 1665 he went to Sea, under the Earl of *Sandwich*, who commanded a Fleet employed in the War with the *Dutch*.—*Wilmot* behaved very well in the Attack made on the Enemy in the Port of *Bergen* in *Norway*, and gained a high Reputation for Courage; which he afterwards loft in an Adventure with the Earl of *Mulgrave*, who called him to an Account, for fome Words which he was reported to have too freely fpoken of the Earl.—*Wilmot* accepted the Challenge; but when he came to the Place appointed, he declined coming to Action; urging that he was fo weak with a certain Diftemper, that he found himfelf unfit to fight.—This unlucky Affair entirely ruined his Reputation for Courage, and fubjected him to farther Infults; which will ever be the Cafe, when once People know a Man's Weaknefs in this Refpect.—His Reputation for *Wit*, however, ftill kept him from totally finking in the Opinion of the World; but, on the other Hand, his exceffive Debaucheries were every Day more and more completing the Ruin of his Conftitution; and the natural Vivacity of his Imagination being ftill more inflamed with Wine, made his Company fo eagerly coveted by his gay Affociates, that they were ever contriving to engage him deeper and deeper in Extravagance and Intemperance, in order that they might be the more diverted by his Humour.—All this fo entirely fubdued him, that, as he afterwards acknowledged, he was for five Years together continually drunk; not, indeed, all the while under the

vifible

visible Effect of Liquor, but so inflamed in his Blood, that he was never cool enough to be Master of himself.—There were two Principles in the natural Temper of this lively and witty Nobleman, which hurried him into great Excesses; a violent Love of sensual Pleasure, and a Disposition to extravagant Mirth.—The one involved him in the grossest Debaucheries, and the other led him to many odd Adventures and Frolicks; some of which are related in the several Accounts that have been published of his Life, but we have not Room to repeat them here.

As to his Genius, his principal Turn seems to have been towards Satire; but, being in this Respect as licentious as in every Thing else, his Satires usually degenerated into mere Libels; in all which, he had so peculiar a Talent of mixing his Wit with his Malice, that all his Compositions were easily known.—In Regard to his other Poems, which have been so usually admired for their Wit, as well as for their Obscenity, they are too indelicate to deserve any particular Notice.—It is a Compliment justly due to the more refined Taste of the present Age, to say, that such gross Productions no longer please, or can be even endured.—They are indeed, as a more moral Bard justly expresses it, more apt to *put out* than to *kindle* the Fire.—His Tragedy of *Valentinian*, however, and some other Pieces published by *Tonson*, shew that he was not incapable of more serious and more innocent Productions.

By constant Indulgence in Sensuality, he entirely wore out an excellent Constitution, before he was 30 Years of Age.—In *October* 1679, when he was slowly re-

covering from a Disease which had proved sufficiently powerful to make a serious Impression on him, he was visited by Bishop *Burnet*, on an Intimation that such a Visit would not be disagreeable.—It is natural to suppose that the good Bishop has made the most of this Affair.—We have only his Account of the Matter; and, as far as that Account may be relied upon, he made a perfect Convert of this illustrious Profligate: So that he, who lived the Life of a Libertine and an Atheist, died the Death of a good Christian and a sincere Penitent.—How far, however, that Penitence which is extorted by Affliction, and the Horrors of an approaching Dissolution, can be esteemed *genuine*, or *effectual*, is a Question which it would not be very proper to discuss in this Place.

Lord *Rochester* died in *July* 1680, of mere old Age, before he had compleated his 33d Year; quite worn down, so that Nature had not Strength even for a dying Groan.—He left behind him a Son named *Charles*, and three Daughters; the Son died the Year after his Father, so the Male Line ceasing, the Title of Earl of *Rochester* was transferred, by the King, to the Family of *Hyde*, in the Person of *Laurence*, a younger Son of *Edward* Earl of *Clarendon*.

Lord *Rochester*'s dramatic Works consisted only of one Play, *viz.*

VALENTINIAN. Trag. (alter'd from *Beaumont* and *Fletcher*.)

ROLLI, Sign. *Paolo Antonio.*— This Gentleman, who I believe is yet living, is by Birth a *Florentine*, has an Estate in the *Campania* of *Rome*, and stiles himself a *Roman* Senator, —— He resided several

several Years in this Kingdom, during which Time he had some Concern in the Management of the King's Theatre in the *Haymarket*, and wrote the greatest Part of the Operas which were represented there in that Period; and indeed, to do him Justice, they were in general much superior to those which have been since introduced to the Publick thro' the Channel of that Theatre. At length, however, after having, I believe, considerably better'd his Fortune by his Residence in *England*, and the Encouragement he met with from the Nobility and Gentry, he chose to retire to his own patrimonial Estate, and spend the Remainder of his Days in Ease and Indulgence; for which Purpose he quitted *England* about the Year 1744.—The Pieces that he wrote are very numerous; and, as the Publication of these Operas, which is intended principally for the Use of the Audience within the Theatre, by Way of Direction to the Ear during the Time of Representation, by no Means give a Chance for Immortality, since the Number of them which are destroyed greatly exceeds those which are preserved, I am aware that the following List is very imperfect; but as, in a Course of Time, the Remainder may fall into my Hands, that Deficiency, and such others in this Work, as even the utmost Assiduity and most diligent Search has not been able to avoid during the Time allotted to a *first* Compilement, the Reader may depend on finding supplied, if it should have the good Fortune to reach to a *second* Edition. — Those Pieces, however, which have come to my Hands of this Author's, are entitled as follow,

1. ARSACE. Ital. Opera.
2. ASTARTUS. Ital. Opera.
3. CRISPUS. Ital. Op.
4. FLORIDANTE. Ital. Op.
5. GRISELDA. Ital. Op.
6. IPHIGENIA IN AULIS. Ital. Opera.
7. MUTIUS SCÆVOLA. Ital. Opera.
8. NARCISSUS. Ital. Op.
9. NUMITOR. Ital. Opera.

Signior *Rolli* has also obliged the World with a good Translation of *Milton's Paradise Lost*, in *Italian*; a Work which does him great Honour.

ROOME, Mr.—This Gentleman was bred to the Law, and altered a Comedy of *Richard Broome's* into a Ballad Opera.—He has, however, been honest enough to make an Acknowledgment to the Founder of his Feast, by suffering the Piece to retain its original Title of

The *Jovial Crew*. Ball. Op. and, under the Form in which Mr. *Roome* left it, or at least with some very trivial Alterations, it has within these three Years been revived, and played with amazing Success at *Covent-Garden* Theatre.

* ROSSI, Sign. *Giacomo*, an *Italian*, who, on a Plan laid down for him by *Aaron Hill*, Esq; wrote the Words of one dramatic Piece, which, being set to Music by Mr. *Handel*, was performed with Success at the Opera House in the *Haymarket*.—It was entitled,

RINALDO. Ital. Opera.

ROWE, *Nicholas*, Esq; Son to *John Rowe*, Esq; Serjeant at Law, was born at *Little Berkford*, in *Bedfordshire*, Anno 1673. — His Education was begun at a private School in *Highgate*, from whence he was removed to *Westminster* School, where he was perfected in Classical Literature, under the famous severe Doctor *Busby*. — His

Father

Father defigning him for his own Profeffion, enter'd him, at 16 Years of Age, a Student of the *Middle Temple.*—He foon made a great Progrefs in the Law, and might have made a great Figure in that Profeffion, if the Love of Poetry and the *Belles Lettres* had not too much attracted his Attention.—At the Age of 25 he wrote his firft Tragedy, the *Ambitious Step-Mother*; the great Succefs of which made him entirely lay afide all Thoughts of the Law.—His Talent was altogether for Tragedy; all his Pieces of that Kind being juftly efteemed for the Poetry and Sentiments, although they are by many deemed faulty in Refpect to the Plots, which, in general, are too thin and fimple.—Being a great Admirer of *Shakefpeare*, he gave the Public an Edition of his Plays; to which he prefixed an Account of that great Man's Life.—But the moft confiderable of Mr. *Rowe*'s Performances, was a Tranflation of *Lucan's Pharfalia*, which he juft lived to finifh, but not to publifh; for it did not appear in Print till ten Years after his Death.

His Attachment to the Mufes, however, did not entirely unfit him for Bufinefs; and when the Duke of *Queenfbury* was Secretary of State, he made Mr. *Rowe* his Under-Secretary for Public Affairs: But, after the Duke's Death, the Avenues to his Preferment being ftopped, he paffed his Time in Retirement during the reft of Queen *Anne*'s Reign. On the Acceffion of *Geo.* I. he was made Poet Laureat, and one of the Land Surveyors of the Cuftoms in the Port of *London.*—He was alfo Clerk of the Council to the Prince of *Wales*, and the Lord Chancellor *Parker* made him his Secretary for the Prefen-

tations; but he did not long enjoy thefe Promotions, for he died in 1718, in the 45th Year of his Age.—His dramatic Pieces are,

1. The *Ambitious Step-Mother.* Trag.
2. TAMERLANE. Trag.
3. *Royal Convert.* Trag.
4. *Fair Penitent.* Trag.
5. JANE SHORE. Trag.
6. *Lady* JANE GREY. Trag.
7. ULYSSES. Trag.
8. The *Biter.* Com.

The laft Piece did not meet with the fame Succefs that he had with his Tragedies; for his Genius by no Means fuited the Comic Mufe.

Mr. *Rowe* was twice married; had a Son by his firft Wife, and a Daughter by the fecond.

He was a handfome, genteel Man; and his Mind was as amiable as his Perfon.—He lived beloved, and at his Death, had the Honour to be lamented by Mr. *Pope*, in an Epitaph which is printed in *Pope*'s Works, although it was not affixed on Mr. *Rowe*'s Monument, in *Weftminfter-Abbey*, where he was interred in the Poet's Corner, oppofite to *Chaucer.*

ROWLEY, Mr. *Samuel.*—This Gentleman lived in the Reign of *Charles* I. and confequently was Cotemporary with another Writer of his Name, of whom I fhall give fome Account in the next Article; but, whether he was any Way related to him, is not apparent.—He ftiles himfelf Servant to the Prince of *Wales*, but it does not appear what Place he enjoyed under his Royal Highnefs.—There are two Plays in Print under his Name, the Titles of which are,

1. *Noble Spanifh Soldier.* Trag.
2. *When You fee me You know me.* Hift. Play.

ROWLEY, Mr. *William*, who ftands in the third Clafs of dramatic

matic Writers, lived in the Reign of King *Charles* I. and received his Education at the Univerſity of *Cambridge*, but whether he took any Degree there is not evident, there being few Particulars preſerved in Regard to him, more than his cloſe Intimacy and Connection with all the principal Wits and poetical Geniuſes of that Age, by whom he was well beloved, and with ſome of whom he joined in their Writings.—*Wood* ſtiles him, " the " Ornament for Wit and Inge- " nuity of *Pembroke-Hall* in *Cam-* " *bridge*."—In a Word, he was a very great Benefactor to the *Engliſh* Stage, having, excluſive of his Aid lent to *Middleton, Day, Heywood, Webſter,* &c. left us five Plays of his own compoſing, and one in which even the immortal *Shakeſpeare* afforded him ſome Aſſiſtance.—Their Titles in alphabetical Order are as follow,

1. *All's loſt by Luſt.* Trag.
2. *Birth of* MERLIN. Tragi-Com. (aſſiſted by *Shakeſpeare.*)
3. *Match at Midnight.* Com.
4. *New Wonder, a Woman never vext.* Com.
5. *Shoemaker is a Gentleman.* Com.
6. *Witch of* EDMONTON. Tragi Com.

The Plays in which he was concerned with others, but, not having the principal Hand, are not aſcribed to him, are the following, to which I have ſubjoined the Author's Name who joined with him.

1. *Changling.* Trag. *Tho. Middleton.*
2. *Cure for a Cuckold.* Com. *John Webſter.*
3. *Fair Quarrel.* Com. *Tho. Middleton.*

4. *Fortune by Land and Sea.* C. *Tho. Heywood.*
5. *Old Law.* Tragi-Com. *Philip Maſſinger* and *Tho. Middleton.*
6. *Parliament of Bees.* Maſque. *John Day* and *Geo. Wilkins.*
7. *Spaniſh Gipſey.* Com. *Tho. Middleton.*
8. *Thracian Wonder.* Comic Hiſtory. *John Webſter,* (on the Authority of *Winſtanley* only.)
9. *Travels of the three* Engliſh *Brothers. John Day* and *Geo. Wilkins.*

RUGGLES, *Ralph,* A. M.— All I can diſcover concerning this Writer is, he belonged to *Clare-Hall, Cambridge,* and was Author of a very celebrated and very humorous *Latin* Play, which was acted at that Univerſity before King *James* I. on the 8th of *March* 1614, entitled,

IGNORAMUS. Com.

RUTTER, Mr. *Joſeph.*—This Author lived in the Reign of King *Charles* I. and was a Dependant on the Family of *Edward* Earl of *Dorſet,* Lord Chamberlain to the Queen, being Tutor to his Son.—At the Command of his Patron, he undertook a Tranſlation of the firſt Part of the *Cid,* from the *French* of *Corneille,* which, when executed, was ſo well approved of by the King, to whom it was ſhewn, that, at his Majeſty's own Deſire, the ſecond Part of the ſame Piece was put into Mr. *Rutter*'s Hands, with an Injunction to tranſlate it, which he immediately obey'd.—He beſides wrote one original dramatic Piece of his own, ſo that the Works of this Kind, which he has left behind him, are,

1. *Cid.*

1. *Cid.* Tragi-Com. in two Parts.
2. *Shepherd's Holiday.* Trag. Com. Pastoral.

RYAN, Mr. *Lacy.*—This Gentleman, tho' generally, I believe, esteemed a Native of *Ireland*, was born in *England*, in the Year 1694.—What Profession he was originally intended for I have never heard; but a strong theatrical Passion led him to that of the Stage, on which he made a very early Appearance, and was even taken considerable Notice of in the Part of *Marcus* in 'Cato, during the first Run of that Play in the Year 1712, tho' then but eighteen Years of Age.—He from that Time increased in Favour, arose to a very conspicuous Rank in his Profession, and constantly maintained a very useful and even important Cast of Parts, both in Tragedy and Comedy. — In his Person he was genteel and well made; his Judgment was critical and correct; his Understanding of an Author's Sense most accurately just, and his Emphasis, or Manner of pointing out that Sense to the Audience, ever constantly true, even to a musical Exactness; his Feelings were strong, and nothing could give more honourable Evidence of his Powers as an Actor, than the Sympathy to those Sensations, which was ever apparent in the Audience when he thought proper to make them feel with him.

Yet, so many are the Requisites that should go to the forming a capital Actor, somewhat so very near absolute Perfection is expected in those who are to convey to us the Idea, at Times, of even more than Mortality, that, with all the above-mentioned great Qualities, this Actor was still excluded from the List of first Rate Performers, by a Deficiency in only one Article, *viz.* that of Voice.

It is probable that Mr. *Ryan's* Voice might not naturally have been a very good one, as the Cadence of it seem'd always inclinable to a sharp shrill Treble; but an unlucky Fray with some Watermen, at the very earliest Part of his theatrical Life, in which he received a Blow on the Nose, which turned that Feature a little out of its Place, tho' not so much as to occasion any Deformity, made an Alteration in his Voice also, by no Means to its Advantage; yet still it continued not disgustful, till, several Years afterwards, being attacked in the Street by some Ruffians, who, as it appear'd afterwards, mistook him for some other Person, he received a Brace of Pistol Bullets in his Mouth, which broke some Part of his Jaw, and prevented his being able to perform at all for a long Time afterwards; and tho' he did at length recover from the Hurt, yet his Voice ever after retained a *Tremulum* or Quaver, when drawn out to any Length, which render'd his Manner very particular, and, by being extremely easy to imitate, laid him much more open to the Powers of Mimickry and Ridicule, than he would otherwise have been. Notwithstanding this, however, by being always extremely perfect in the Words of his Author, and just in the speaking of them, added to the Sensibility I before-mentioned, an exact Propriety in Dress, and an Ease and Gentility of Deportment on the Stage, he remained even to the last a very deserved Favorite with many; which, moreover, his amiable Character in private Life did not a little contribute to.—And a very striking

Instance

Inſtance of the perſonal Eſteem he was held in by the Public, ſhewed itſelf on the Occaſion of the Accident I related above, at which Time his late Royal Highneſs, *Frederick* Prince of *Wales*, contributed a very handſome Preſent to make him ſome Amends for the Injury he muſt receive from the being out of Employment, and ſeveral of the Nobility and Gentry followed the laudable Example ſet them by his Highneſs.

The Friendſhip ſubſiſting between him and his great theatrical Cotemporary Mr. *Quin*, is well known to have been inviolable, and reflects Honour to them both.—That valuable and juſtly-admir'd Veteran of the *Engliſh* Stage, even after he had quitted it as to general Performance, did, for ſome Years afterwards, make an annual Appearance in his favorite Character of Sir *John Falſtaff*, for the Benefit of his Friend Mr. *Ryan*; and when, at laſt, he prudently declined hazarding any longer that Reputation, which he had in ſo many hardy Campaigns nobly purchaſed, by adventuring into the Field under the Diſadvantages of Age and Infirmity; yet, even then, in the Service of that Friend, he continued to exert himſelf; and, where his Perſon could no longer avail him, he, to ſpeak in *Falſtaff's* Language, *us'd his Credit; Yea, and to us'd it,*—that he has been known, by his Intereſt with the Nobility and Gentry, to have diſpoſed, in the Rooms of *Bath*, among Perſons who could very few of them be preſent at the Play, as many Tickets for Mr. *Ryan's* Benefit as have amounted to an hundred Guineas.

At length this Gentleman, in the 68th Year of a Life, fifty Years of which he had ſpent in the Service and Entertainment of the Public, paid the great Debt to Nature at *Bath*, to which Place he had retired for his Health, in the Year 1760.

What entitles him to a Place in this Work is, his having given to the Stage a little dramatic Piece of one Act, entitled,

The *Cobler's Opera.*

RYMER, *Thomas*, Eſq; was born in the North of *England*, and educaced at the Univerſity of *Cambridge*, but in what College I know not.——On his ſettling in *London*, he became a Member of the Society of *Gray's-Inn*, and, in 1692, ſucceeded Mr. *Shadwell* as Hiſtoriographer to King *William* III.—He was a Man of great Learning and a Lover of Poetry; but, when he ſets up for a Critic, ſeems to prove that he has very few of the Requiſites for that Character; and was indeed almoſt totally diſqualified for it, by his Want of Candour.—The Severity which he has exerted, in his View of the Tragedies of the laſt Age, againſt the inimitable *Shakeſpeare*, are ſcarcely to be forgiven, and muſt ſurely be conſidered as a Kind of Sacrilege committed on the *Sanctum Sanctorum* of the Muſes. And, that his own Talents for dramatic Poetry were extremely inferior to thoſe of the Perſons whoſe Writing he has with ſo much Rigour attacked, will be apparent to any one who will give himſelf the Trouble of peruſing one Play, which he has given to the World, entitled,

EDGAR. Trag.

But, altho' I cannot ſubſcribe either to his Fame or his Judgment as a Poet or Critic, yet it cannot be denied that he was a very excellent Antiquarian and Hiſtorian.—Some of his Pieces relating

ing to our Conftitution are extremely good, and his well-known, valuable, and moft ufeful Work, entitled the FÆDERA, printed in feventeen Volumes in Folio, will ftand an everlafting Monument of his Worth, his indefatigable Affiduity, and, Clearnefs of Judgment as an hiftorical Compiler.—He died on the 14th Day of *Dec.* 1713, and was buried in the Parifh Church of St. *Clement's-Danes.*

S.

S' Mr. was Author of one of the very oldeft regular Comedies ever written in our Language.—The Piece itfelf is reprinted in Mr. *Dodfley*'s Collection of old Plays, Vol. I. and is entitled,

Gammer Gurton's Needle. Com.

S. E.—Thefe Initial Letters are prefixed to a Piece which appears to have been enter'd at Stationer's-Hall as *Shakefpeare*'s, tho' at the Time confider'd as an Impofition, contriv'd with a View to promote the Sale of the Book. Yet there appears a Degree of Inconfiftency in the Story, as in the firft Place the Public can know nothing of the Entries made in the Books of private Corporations; and fecondly, as *Shakefpeare*'s Chriftian Name was too univerfally known to admit of any Impofition under falfe Initials, or for any one to miftake E. S. for *William Shakefpeare.*—The Title of the Piece is,

Cupid's Whirligig. Com.
Phillips and *Winftanley* have committed a Miftake in Regard to

this Play, by attributing it to Mr. *Thomas Goff,* whofe Genius and Manner of Writing were as oppofite to Comedy as Light to Darknefs, and ftill more fo, if poffible, to that ludicrous Turn which runs thro' great Part of this Piece, and is particularly confpicuous in the Epiftle Dedicatory.

S. J.—We find no lefs than five feveral dramatic Pieces with thefe Initials in the Title Page.—One of them, *viz.* the *Mafquerade du Ciel,* moft Authors have attributed to *James Shirley,* and as the Dates of all the reft, excepting the *Athenian Comedy,* come within the Period of Mr. *Shirley*'s Writing, I cannot think it ftretching Conjecture beyond the Limits of Probability, to afcribe them all, or at leaft the beft Part of them, to him.—Yet I muft not omit obferving that *Coxeter,* in Confequence of fome Lines written by Mr. *Stanley,* feems of Opinion that the *Phillis of Scyros* was tranflated by Sir. *Edward Sherbourne,* yet, as the Initials affixed to that Piece do not agree with that Gentleman's Name, and correfpond perfectly with that of the Author I have mentioned, I think a diftant Hint of that Nature is fcarcely fufficient to fully invalidate the Surmife I have ventured to throw out.—The dramatic Works are,

1. ANDROMANA. Trag.
2. *Mafquerade du Ciel.* Com.
3. *New Athenian Comedy.*
4. PHILLIS *of* SCYROS. Paft.
5. *Prince of Prig's Revels.* C.

S. S.—Thefe Initials only ftand in the Title Page of one Play, written, or at leaft printed, in the Reign of King *James* I. nor do I find any known Authors of that Period with whofe Name these Letters can be brought to correspond.—The Play is entitled,

The *Honest Lawyer*. Com.

SACKVILLE, *Thomas*. Vid. DORSET, Earl of.

SADLER, *Anthony*, D. D.—This Gentleman was Son of *Thomas Sadler*, of *Chilton* in *Wiltshire*, Esq; at which Place he was born towards the Beginning of the Reign of *James* I.—At seventeen Years of Age, *viz.* in the *Lent* Term of the Year 1627, he was enter'd Butler of St. *Edmund's-Hall* in *Oxford*, and, in 1631, was admitted to the Degree of Bachelor of Arts, and received into Holy Orders, soon after which he became Chaplain to a Gentleman in *Hertfordshire*, his Name-Sake, and most probably a Relation.—Towards the Beginning of the Civil War he was Curate of *Bishopstoke* in *Hampshire*, was afterwards Chaplain to *Letitia*, Dowager Lady *Paget*, till at length, in the Year 1654, being presented to the Living of *Compton Hanway* in *Dorsetshire*, he was refused to pass by the *Triers*, which was the Occasion of a troublesome Contest between him and those Gentlemen.—Soon after this he was made Vicar of *Mitcham* in *Surry*.—But, indeed, he seems to have been a Man of a turbulent Disposition, for we find him, in the Year 1564, engaged in a violent Quarrel with one *Robert Cramer*, a Merchant of *London*, but an Inhabitant of *Mitcham*, of whose Behaviour he complains, in a little Pamphlet of one Sheet in Quarto, entitled, *Strange News indeed from Mitcham in Surry.*—After this, however, he took the Degree of Doctor of Divinity, and was appointed one of his Majesty's Chaplains extraordinary, in which Rank I imagine he continued till his Death, which hap-

pened about the Year 1680, and the 70th of his Age.—He was no very voluminous Writer, but has left one small dramatic Piece behind him, written on a loyal Occasion, but which I imagine, from a Circumstance in the Title Page, was never represented.—It is entitled,

The *Subject's Joy for the King's Restoration*. Masque.

ST. SERFE, Sir *Thomas*.——This Title *Jacob* has given to a Gentleman whom neither *Langbaine* nor *Gildon* have dignified with any Thing but his plain Name.——He was a Native of *North Briton*, and it appears, by the Dedication of a Play which he wrote, and will be presently mentioned, that he was in the King's Service in the North of *Scotland*, in the Times of the Troubles; tho' in what Post is not mentioned; yet, it is evident, that he ventured his Person on a Service of considerable Danger, no less than that of a Spy, from the following four Lines which *Coxeter* has quoted concerning him from the *Covent Garden Drollery*, 8vo. 1672. p. 84. *viz.*

Once like a Pedlar *they* * *have heard thee brag,*
How thou didst cheat their Sight, and save thy Craig;
When to the great Montrofs, *under Pretence*
Of godly Bukes, *thou broughtst* Intelligence.
* *The Covenanters.*

The Title of the above-mentioned Play, the Ground-Work of which, however, is borrowed from the *Spanish*, is,

TARUGO's *Wiles*. Com. *Langbaine* gives it a good Character, and, in *Dryden's* Miscellanies, Part V. (8vo. 1704.) p. 272.

272. may be seen a very elegant Copy of Verses by the Earl of *Dorset*, in Compliment to the Author, on its Publication.

SAMPSON, Mr. *William*.—All I can trace relating to this Author is, that he lived in the Reign of King *Charles* I. and was for some Time retain'd in, and a Dependant on, the Family of Sir *Henry Willoughby*, of *Richley* in *Derbyshire*.—He was the sole Author of one Play, entitled,

The *Vow Breaker*. Trag.
He was also Assistant to Mr. *Markham*, in the Composition of his Tragedy of

HEROD *and* ANTIPATER.

SANDYS, *George*, Esq;—This very accomplished Gentleman was a younger Son of *Edwin* Archbishop of *York*, and was born at *Bishops Thorp*, in that County, in 1577.—At eleven Years of Age he was sent to the University of *Oxford*, where he was matriculated of Saint *Mary's-Hall*.—In the Year 1610, remarkable for the Murder of that great and good Prince, *Henry* IV. of *France*, Mr. *Sandys* set out on his Travels, and, in the Course of two Years, made a very extensive Tour, having not only travelled thro' several Parts of *Europe*, but also visited many Cities and Countries of the East under the *Turkish* Empire, as *Constantinople*, *Greece*, *Egypt*, and the *Holy Land*, after which, taking a View of the remote Parts of *Italy* and the Islands adjoining, he went to *Rome*, where he met with one *Nicholas Fitzherbert*, his Countryman, and formerly his Fellow-Student, by whom he was shewn all the Antiquities of that once renowned City. —— From thence he went to *Venice*, and being by this Time very greatly improved, and become not only a

perfect Scholar but a compleat Gentleman, he returned to his Native Country, where, after properly digesting the Observations he had made, he published an Account of his Travels in Folio, which is held in very considerable Estimation.—He had also an Inclination for Poetry, his Exercises in which, however, seem to have been mostly on religious Subjects, except his Translation of *Ovid's Metamorphoses*.—He also paraphrased the Psalms, and has left behind him a Translation, with Notes, of one sacred Drama, written originally by *Grotius*, under the Title of *Christus Patiens*, and which is the Piece that *W. Lauder*, some few Years ago, thought proper to fix on, as the Foundation of his vile Charge of Plagiarism against our immortal *Milton*. —— Mr. *Sandys*, in his Translation, has entitled it,

Christ's Passion.
There are but few Incidents known concerning our Author, but all the Writers who have mentioned him, agree in bestowing on him the Character, not only of a Man of Genius, but of singular Worth and Piety.—For the most Part of his latter Days he lived with Sir *Francis Wenman*, of *Caswell* near *Whitney* in *Oxfordshire*, to whom his Sister was married; probably chusing that Situation in some Measure on Account of its Proximity to *Burford*, the Retirement of his intimate Acquaintance and valuable Friend *Lucius*, Lord Viscount *Falkland*. —He died, however, at the House of his Nephew, Sir *Francis Wyat*, at *Bexley* in *Kent*, in 1643; and was interred in the Chancel of that Parish Church.

He had no Monument erected

to his Memory, but various Writers have handed down the following Inscription, as one that was due to his Merit.

Georgius Sandys, *Poetarum Anglorum sui saeculi* Princeps.

And the high Commendations given of him by the above-mentioned ingenious Nobleman, in a Copy of Verses address'd to *Grotius* on his *Christus Patiens*, are a most honourable Tribute to, and an immortal Record of, our Author's great Worth and Abilities.

SAVAGE, *Richard*, one of the most remarkable Characters that we have met with, in all the Records of Biography.—He was the unfortunate Son of the most unnatural of Mothers, *Ann*, Countess of *Macclesfield*; who confessed that her Husband, the Earl of *Macclesfield*, was not the Father of the Child, but that he was adulterously begotten by the Earl of *Rivers*, whose Name was *Savage*.—This Declaration she voluntarily made, Anno 1697, (in which Year our Author was born) in order to procure a Separation from her Husband, with whom she had lived, for some Time, on very uneasy Terms.—As to the Truth of the Fact, there was no Doubt made of it; for Lord *Rivers* acquiesced in her Declaration, and appeared, by the Measures he took to provide for him, to consider the Child as his own. —But his Mother, who was certainly his Mother, whoever was the Father, had other, and less natural Sentiments, with Respect to the Duty which all Parents owe to their Offspring.— Strange as it may appear, the Countess looked upon her Son, from the Moment of his Birth, with a Kind of Resentment and

Abhorrence.——She resolved to disown him, and therefore committed him to the Care of a poor Woman, whom she directed to educate him as her own, enjoining her never to inform him who were his real Parents.

The hapless Infant, however, was not wholly abandoned.—The Lady *Mason*, Mother to the Countess, took some Charge of his Education, and placed him at a Grammar School near St. *Albans*, where he went by the Name of his Nurse.

While he was at this School, his Father, the Earl *Rivers*, was seized with a Distemper which threatened his Life; and, as he lay on his Death-Bed, he was desirous of providing for *this*, among *others* of his natural Children.—Accordingly he sent to the Countess, to enquire after her Son; and she had the monstrous Cruelty to *declare him dead!*—— The Earl, not suspecting that there could exist in Nature, a Mother who could thus causelessly ruin her Child, without procuring any Advantage to herself by so doing, believed her wicked Report; and thereupon bestowed upon another the Sum of six Thousand Pounds, which he had before bequeathed to his Son by Lady *Macclesfield*.

This unnatural Woman did not stop here, in her Enmity to, and even Persecution of, her Son.— She formed a Scheme, on his quitting the above-mentioned School, to have him kid-napped away to the Plantations; but this Contrivance was, by some Accident, defeated.—She then hatched another Device, with the View of burying him in Poverty and Obscurity, for the Remainder of his Days; and had him placed with a Shoemaker

ker in *Holborn.*—In this Station, however, he did not long continue; for his Nurse dying, he went to take Care of the Effects of his supposed Mother, and found in her Boxes some of Lady *Mason*'s Letters to the good Woman, which informed young *Savage* of his Birth, and the Cause of its Concealment.

From the Moment of this Discovery, it was natural for him to grow dissatisfied with his Station and Employment in *Holborn.*—He now conceived he had a Right to share in the Affluence of his real Mother, and therefore he directly, and perhaps indiscreetly, applied to her, and made use of every Art to awake her Tenderness and attract her Regard.—But in vain did he solicit this unfeeling Parent; she avoided him with the utmost Precaution, and took Measures to prevent his ever entering her House, on any Pretence whatever.

Savage was at this Time so touched with the Discovery of his Birth, that he frequently made it his Practice to walk in the Evening before his Mother's Door, in the Hope of seeing her by Accident; and often did he warmly solicit her to admit him to see her; but all to no Effect,—he could neither soften her Heart, nor open her Hand.

Mean time, while he was assiduously endeavouring to rouse the Affections of a Mother, in whom all natural Affection was extinct, he was destitute of the Means of Support, and reduced to the Miseries of Want.—We are not told by what Means he got rid of his Obligation to the Shoe-maker, or whether he ever was actually bound to him; but we now find him very differently employed, in order to procure a Subsistence.

In short, the Youth had Parts, and a strong Inclination toward literary Pursuits, especially Poetry. — Necessity, however, first made him an Author; and he was very oddly initiated into the Mysteries of the Press, by a little Poem on a very singular Subject, for such a Person as our young Author to meddle with: *viz.* the famous *Bangorian* Controversy, then warmly agitated by the polemical Writers of that Time.

This was, however, but a crude Effort of uncultivated Genius, of which the Author was afterward much ashamed.——He then attempted another Kind of Writing; and, at only eighteen Years of Age, offered a Comedy to the Stage, entitled *Woman's a Riddle,* which was refused by the Players; for, in Fact, the Piece was not *Savage*'s Property, it not being his own Performance, but the Work of a Lady who had translated it from the *Spanish,* and given *Savage* a Copy of it: The Story is circumstantially related in our first Volume, under the above-mentioned Title of this Play.—Two Years after this, he wrote *Love in a Veil,* borrowed likewise from the *Spanish,* but with little better Success than before; for it was acted so late in the Year, that the Author received scarce any other Advantage from it than the Acquaintance of Sir *Richard Steele,* and Mr. *Wilkes,* the celebrated Comedian, by whom he was pitied, countenanced, and relieved.—The former espoused his Interest with the most benevolent Zeal, declaring that the Inhumanity of his Mother had given him a right to find every good Man his Father. *Steele* proposed to have established him in a settled Scheme of Life,

 and

and to have married him to a natural Daughter of his, on whom he intended to bestow a thousand Pounds; but Sir *Richard* conducted his own Affairs so badly, that he found too much Difficulty in raising so considerable a Sum; on which Account the Marriage was delayed.—In the mean Time some officious Person informed the good-natured Knight, that his intended Son-in-Law had ridiculed him; which, whether true or not, so provoked Sir *Richard*, that he withdrew his Friendship from *Savage*, and never afterwards admitted him into his House.

Mr. *Wilkes*, however, still remained in his Interest; and even found Means to soften the Heart of *Savage*'s Mother, so far as to obtain from her the Sum of fifty Pounds, with a Promise of farther Relief for this her out-cast Offspring; but we do not find that this Promise was performed.

Being thus obliged to depend on Mr. *Wilkes*, he became an assiduous Frequenter of the Theatres, and thence the Amusements of the Stage took such Possession of his Mind, that he was never absent from a Play in several Years.

In 1723 he brought on the Stage his Tragedy of *Sir Thomas Overbury*; in which he himself performed the principal Character, but with so little Reputation, that he used to blot his Name out of the *Dramatis Personæ*, whenever any of the printed Copies of the Play fell into his Hands.—The whole Profits of this Performance, from the acting, printing, and the Dedication, amounted to about £ 200. The celebrated *Aaron Hill*, Esq; was of great Service to him in correcting and fitting this Piece

for the Stage and the Press; and extended his Patronage and good Offices still farther.—*Savage* was, like many other Wits, a bad Manager, and was ever in Distress. As fast as his Friends raised him out of one Difficulty, he sunk into another; and when he found himself greatly involved, he would ramble about like a Vagabond, with scarce a Shirt on his Back. He was in one of these Situations all the Time wherein he wrote his Tragedy above-mentioned; without a Lodging, and often without a Dinner: So that he used to scribble on Scraps of Paper picked up by Accident, or begged in the Shops which he occasionally stepped into, as Thoughts occurred to him, craving the Favour of the Pen and Ink, as it were just to take a Memorandum.

Mr. *Hill* also earnestly promoted a Subscription to a Volume of Miscellanies, by *Savage*; and likewise furnished Part of the Poems of which the Volume was composed. — To this Miscellany *Savage* wrote a Preface, in which he gives an Account of his Mother's Cruelty, in a very uncommon Strain of Humour.

The Profits of his Tragedy and his Miscellanies together had now, for a Time, somewhat raised poor *Savage*, both in Circumstances and Credit; so that the World just began to behold him with a more favourable Eye than formerly, when a Misfortune befel him, by which not only his Reputation but his *Life* was endangered.

On the 20th of *Nov.* 1727, Mr. *Savage* came from *Richmond*, whither he had for some Time retired, in Order to pursue his Studies without Interruption; and accidentally meeting with two Acquaintances, whose Names were *Merchant* and *Gregory*, he went

in

in with them to a Coffee-houfe, where they fat drinking till it was late.—He would willingly have gone to Bed in the fame Houfe, but there was not Room for the whole Company, and therefore they agreed to ramble about the Streets, and divert themfelves with fuch Incidents as fhould occur till Morning.—Happening to difcover a Light in a Coffee-houfe near *Charing Crofs*, they went in and demanded a Room.—They were told the next Parlour would be empty prefently; as a Company were then paying their reckoning, in order to leave it.——*Marchant*, not fatisfied with this Anfwer, abruptly rufhed into the Room, and behaved very rudely. This produced a Quarrel; Swords were drawn, and, in the Confufion, one Mr. *James Sinclair* was killed.—A Woman Servant, likewife, was accidently wounded by *Savage*, as fhe was endeavouring to hold him.

Savage and his Companions, being taken into Cuftody, were tried for this Offence, and both he and *Gregory* were capitally convicted of Murder.—*Savage* pleaded his own Caufe, and behaved with great Refolution; but it was too plainly proved that he gave *Sinclair* his Death's Wound, while *Gregory* commanded the Sword of the Deceafed.

The Convicts being reconducted to Prifon, were heavily ironed, and remained with no Hopes of Life, but from the Royal Mercy: But, can it be believed! *this* his own Mother (yes, it may be believed of *her*) endeavoured to intercept.—She was now in Hopes of entirely getting rid of him for ever; and that the laft Chance for his Life might be totally turned againft him, fhe had the horrible Inhumanity to Prejudice the Queen againft him, at this critical Juncture, by telling her Majefty the moft malicious Stories, and even downright Falfhoods, of her unhappy Son; which fo far anfwered her diabolical Purpofe, that for a long while the Queen totally rejected all Petitions that were offer'd to her, in Favour of this unhappy Man.

At length, however, Compaffion raifed him a Friend, whofe Rank and Character were too eminent to fail of Succefs: This was the amiable Countefs of *Hertford*, who laid before the Queen a true Account of the extraordinary Story and Sufferings of poor *Savage*; and, in Confequence of fuch feafonable and powerful Interpofition in his Favour, he was foon after admitted to Bail, and, in *March* 1728, he pleaded the Royal Pardon: To which alfo the Petition deliver'd to his Majefty by the Lord *Tyrconnel*, and the Sollicitations in his Behalf made to Sir *R. Walpole* by Mrs. *Oldfield*, were not a little conducive.

Tho' Misfortune made an Impreffion on the Mind of the indifcreet *Savage*, it had not fufficient Weight with him to produce a thorough Change in his Life and Manners.——He feems fated to be wretched, throughout the whole Courfe of his Life.—He had now recovered his Liberty, but he had no Means of Subfiftence. — The lucky Thought now ftruck him (lucky indeed, had he known how to have improved it to the moft Advantage) that he might *compel* his Mother to do fomething for him, and extort from her, by a Lampoon, what fhe refufed to natural Affection.—He threatned, that he would feverely expofe her, and the Expedient proved fuccefsful.

Whether

Whether Shame prevailed with her, or whether her Relations had more Delicacy than herself, is not very clear, but the Event might have made *Savage* happy for the Remainder of his Days, had he poſſeſſed but common Prudence.—— In ſhort, Lord *Tyrconnel* received him into his Family, treated him upon an equal Footing, and allowed him 200 l. a Year.

Savage was now, for once, on the Top of Fortune's Wheel; but, alaſs! his Head ſoon grew giddy, his Brain turned, and down he came Head-long, with ſuch a Fall as he never could recover.—— For ſome Time he lived with his noble Friend, in the utmoſt Eaſe and Affluence; and the World ſeemed to ſmile upon him, as tho' he had never experienced the ſlighteſt of its Frowns.——This Interval of Proſperity furniſhed him with Opportunities of enlarging his Knowledge of Human Nature, by contemplating Life from its higheſt Gradation to its loweſt; and in this gay Period of his Days, he publiſhed the *Wanderer*, a Moral Poem, which was approved by Mr. *Pope*, and which the Author himſelf conſidered as his Maſter-Piece.——It was addreſſed to the Earl of *Tyrconnel*, with the higheſt Strains of Panegyric.——Theſe Praiſes, however, in a ſhort Time, he found himſelf inclined to retract, being diſcarded by the Nobleman on whom he had beſtowed them.

The Cauſe aſſigned by his Lordſhip, for withdrawing his Protection from this ill-fated Man, was, that *Savage* was guilty of the moſt licentious Behaviour, introducing Company into his Houſe, with whom he practiſed the moſt licentious Frolics, and committed all the Outrages of Drunkenneſs: Moreover, that he pawned or ſold

the Books of which his Lordſhip had made him a Preſent, ſo that he had often the Mortification to ſee them expoſed to Sale upon Stalls.——On the other Hand, *Savage* alledged, that Lord *Tyrconnel* quarrel'd with him, becauſe he would not ſubſtract from his own Luxury, what he had promiſed to allow him; but this is by no Means probable.——Our Author's known Character pleads too ſtrongly againſt him; for his Conduct was ever ſuch as made all his Friends, ſooner or later, grow weary of him; and, even forced moſt of them to become his Enemies.

Being thus once more turned adriſt upon the World, *Savage*, whoſe Paſſions were very ſtrong, and whoſe Gratitude was very ſmall, became extremely diligent in expoſing the Faults of Lord *Tyrconnel*; and he, moreover, now thought himſelf again at Liberty to take his Revenge upon his Mother.————Accordingly, he wrote *The Baſtard*, a Poem, remarkable for the Vivacity in the Beginning, (where he finely enumerates the imaginary Advantages of baſe Birth) and for the pathetic Concluſion, wherein he recounts the real Calamities which he ſuffered by the Crime of his Parents.——The Reader will not be diſpleaſed with a Tranſcript of ſome of the Lines, in the Opening of the Poem, as a Specimen of this Writer's Spirit and Manner of Verſification.

Bleſt be the Baſtard's Birth!
  thro' wond'rous Ways,
He ſhines excentric like a Comet's
  Blaze.
No ſickly Fruit of faint Compliance he;
He! ſtamp'd in Nature's Mint
  with Extaſy!

He

He lives to build, not boaſt a
  gen'rous Race;
No tenth Tranſmitter of a fooliſh
  Face.—
He, kindling from within requires
  no Flame,
He glories in a Baſtard's glowing
  Name.
—Nature's unbounded Son, he
  ſtands alone,
His Heart unbias'd, and his Mind
  his own.
—O Mother! yet no Mother!—
  'tis to you
My Thanks for ſuch diſtinguiſh'd
  Claims are due.

This Poem had an extraordinary Sale; and its Appearance happening at the Time when his Mother was at *Bath*, many Perſons there took frequent Opportunities of repeating Paſſages from *the Baſtard* in her hearing; ſo that ſhe was obliged to fly the Place, and take Shelter in *London*.

Some Time after this, *Savage* formed the Reſolution of applying to the Queen; who, having once given him Life, he hoped ſhe might farther extend her Goodneſs to him, by enabling him to ſupport it.—With this View he publiſhed a Poem on her Birth-Day, which he entitled *The Volunteer-Laureat.*—He had not, at that Time, one Friend to preſent his Verſes to her Majeſty; who, nevertheleſs, ſent him fifty Pounds, with an Intimation that he might annually expeſt the ſame Bounty.——According he continued to pay her Majeſty this Compliment on every enſuing Birth-Day, and had the Honour of preſenting his Compoſitions, and of kiſſing her Majeſty's Hand.

But Satire was rather his Turn than Panegyrick; and, among other Exerciſes of his Propenſity this Way, was a Lampoon upon the Clergy, with a View to expoſe the Biſhop of *London*, who was then engaged in a Diſpute with the Lord Chancellor, which, being the Subjeſt of general Converſation, furniſhed *Savage* with a popular Topic.—The Piece was entitled *the Progreſs of a Divine*, in which he painted the Charaſter of a profligate Prieſt in ſuch odious Colours, as drew upon him the utmoſt Reſentment of the Eccleſiaſtics; who endeavoured to take their Revenge on him by a Proſecution in the *King's-Bench* for Obſcenity, in Regard to ſome Paſſages in this Performance.—In Anſwer to this Charge *Savage* juſtly pleaded that he had only introduced obſcene Ideas with the View of expoſing them to Deteſtation, and of diſcouraging Vice by ſhewing its Deformity.—As the Reſtitude of this Plea was obvious, it was readily admitted by Sir *Philip Yorke*, afterwards Lord Chancellor, who then preſided in that Court; and who accordingly diſmiſſed the Information.

But, tho' *Savage* found ſo many Friends, and had ſo many Reſources and Supplies, he was ever in Diſtreſs.—The Queen's annual Allowance was nothing to a Man of his ſtrange and ſingular Extravagance.—His uſual Cuſtom was, as ſoon as he had received his Penſion, to diſappear with it, and ſecrete himſelf from his moſt intimate Friends, till every Shilling of the fifty Pounds was ſpent; which done, he again appeared, pennyleſs as before: But he would never inform any Perſon where he had been, nor in what Manner his Money had been diſſipated.—From the Reports, however, of ſome who found Means to penetrate his Haunts, it would
ſeem

seem that he expended both his Time and his Cash in the most sordid and despicable Sensuality; particularly in eating and drinking, in which he would indulge in the most unsocial Manner, sitting whole Days and Nights by himself, in obscure Houses of Entertainment, over his Bottle and Trencher, immersed in Filth and Sloth, with scarce decent Apparel; generally wrapped up in a Horseman's great Coat; and, on the whole, with his very homely Countenance, and altogether, exhibiting an Object the most disgusting to the Sight, if not to some other of the Senses.

His Wit and Parts, however, still raised him new Friends, as fast as his Misbehaviour lost him his old ones; and Sir *R. Walpole*, the Prime Minister, was warmly sollicited in his Favour.——But, tho' Promises were made, nothing more than Promises were obtained, from that celebrated Statesman: Whether it was that some Enemy to *Savage* hinted to Sir *Robert*, that any Thing done for that unhappy Man, would be a mere Waste of Benevolence, and Charity utterly thrown away; or, to whatever Cause it was owing, certain it is, that our Author's Disappointment, with Respect to his Expectations from this Minister, could not proceed from any Want of Generosity in Sir *Robert*, who was confessedly a most munificent Patron, and bounteous Rewarder of literary Merit; especially where Men of Letters employed their Talents in his Service.

His Poverty still increasing, he was even reduced so low, as to be destitute of a Lodging; insomuch that he often passed his Nights in those mean Houses which are set open for casual Wanderers; some-times in Cellars, amidst the Riot and Filth of the most profligate of the Rabble; and not seldom would he walk the Streets 'till he was weary, and then lie down (in Summer) on a Bulk, or (in Winter) with his Associates, among the Ashes of a Glass House.

Yet, amidst all this Penury and Wretchedness, had this Man so much Pride, so high an Opinion of his own Merit, that he ever kept up his Spirits, and was always ready to repress, with Scorn and Contempt, the least Appearance of any Slight or Indignity towards himself, in the Behaviour of his Acquaintance; among whom he looked upon none as his Superiour: He *would* be treated as an equal, even by Persons of the highest Rank! We have an Instance of this preposterous and inconsistent Pride, in his refusing to wait upon a Gentleman who was desirous of relieving him when at the lowest Ebb of Distress, only because the Message signified the Gentleman's Desire to see him at nine o'Clock in the Morning: *Savage* could not bear that any one should presume to prescribe the Hour of his Attendance; and therefore he absolutely rejected the proffer'd Kindness.

This Life, unhappy as it may be already imagined, was yet rendered more unhappy, by the Death of the Queen, in 1738; which Stroke deprived him of all Hopes from the Court. — His Pension was discontinued, and the insolent Manner in which he *demanded* of Sir *Robert Walpole*, to have it restored, for ever cut off this considerable Supply; which possibly had been only delayed, and might have been recovered by proper Application.

His Distress now became so
great,

great, and so notorious, that a Scheme was at length concerted for procuring him a permanent Relief.—It was proposed that he should retire into *Wales*, with an Allowance of 50 l. *per Ann.* on which he was to live privately, in a cheap Place, for ever quiting his Town-Haunts and resigning all farther Pretensions to Fame. This Offer he seemed gladly to accept, but his Intentions were only to deceive his Friends, by retiring for a while, to write another Tragedy, and then to return with it to *London*, in order to bring it upon the Stage.

In 1739, he set out for *Swansey* in the *Bristol* Stage-Coach, and was furnished with 15 Guineas to bear the Expence of his Journey.—But, on the 14th Day after his Departure, his Friends and Benefactors, the principal of whom was no other than the great Mr. *Pope*, who expected to hear of his Arrival in *Wales*, were surprized with a Letter from *Savage*, informing them that he was yet upon the Road, and could not proceed for Want of Money.— There was no other Remedy than a Remittance; which was sent him, and by the Help of which he was enabled to reach *Bristol*; from whence he was to proceed to *Swansey* by Water.—At *Bristol*, however, he found an Embargo laid upon the Shipping; so that he could not immediately obtain a Passage.—Here, therefore, being obliged to stay for some Time, he, with his usual Facility, so ingratiated himself with the principal Inhabitants, that he was frequently invited to their Houses, distinguished at their public Entertainments, and treated with a Regard that highly gratified his Vanity, and there-

fore easily engaged his Affections. —At length, with great Reluctance, he proceeded to *Swansey*, where he lived about a Year, very much dissatisfied with the Diminution of his Salary; for he had, in his Letters, treated his Contributors so insolently, that most of them withdrew their Subscriptions.—Here he finished his Tragedy, and resolved to return with it to *London*; which was strenuously opposed by his great and constant Friend Mr. *Pope*; who proposed that *Savage* should put this Play into the Hands of Mr. *Thomson* and Mr. *Mallet*, in order that they might fit it for the Stage, that his Friends should receive the Profits it might bring in, and that the Author should receive the Produce by Way of Annuity.—This kind and prudent Scheme was rejected by *Savage*, with the utmost Contempt.—— He declared he would not submit his Works to any one's Correction; and that he would no longer be kept in leading Strings. Accordingly he soon returned to *Bristol*, in his Way to *London*; but at *Bristol*, meeting with a Repetition of the same kind Treatment he had before found there, he was tempted to make a second Stay in that opulent City, for some Time.—Here he was again not only caressed and treated, but the Sum of thirty Pounds was raised for him, with which it had been happy if he had immediately departed for *London*: But he never considered that a frequent Repetition of such Kindness was not to be expected, and that it was possible to tire out the Generosity of his *Bristol* Friends, as he had before tired his Friends every where else.—In short, he remained here, till his Company was no longer welcome. — His

Visits

Vifits in every Family were too often repeated ; his Wit had loft its Novelty, and his irregular Behaviour grew troublefome.—Neceffity came upon him before he was aware ; his Money was fpent, his Cloaths worn out, his Appearance was fhabby, and his Prefence was difguftful at every Table.—He now began to find every Man from Home, at whofe Houfe he called, and he found it difficult to obtain a Dinner.—Thus reduced, it would have been prudent in him to have withdrawn from the Place ; but Prudence and *Savage* were never acquainted.—He ftaid, in the Midft of Poverty, Hunger and Contempt, till the Miftrefs of a Coffee-Houfe, to whom he owed about eight Pounds, arrefted him for the Debt. He remained for fome Time, at a great Expence, in the Houfe of the Sheriff's Officer, in Hopes of procuring Bail ; which Expence he was enabled to defray, by a Prefent of five Guineas, from Mr. *Nafh* at *Bath*.——No Bail, however, was to be found ; fo that poor *Savage* was at laft lodged in *Newgate*, a Prifon fo named in *Briftol*.

But it was the Fortune of this extraordinary Mortal, always to find more Friends than he deferved. The Keeper of the Prifon took Compaffion on him, and greatly foftened the Rigours of his Confinement, by every Kind of Indulgence ; he fupported him at his own Table, gave him a commodious Room to himfelf, allowed him to ftand at the Door of the Goal, and even frequently took him into the Fields, for the Benefit of the Air and Exercife : So that, in Reality, *Savage* endured fewer Hardfhips in this Place, than he had ufually fuffer'd, during the greateft Part of his Life.

While he remained in this not intolerable Prifon, his Ingratitude again broke out, in a bitter Satire on the City of *Briftol*, to which he certainly owed great Obligations, notwithftanding the Circumftances of his Arreft, which was but the Act of an individual, and that attended with no Circumftances of Injuftice or Cruelty.—This Satire he entitled *London and Briftol Compared* ; and in it he abufed the Inhabitants of the latter, with fuch a Spirit of Refentment, that the Reader would imagine he had never received any other than the moft injurious Treatment in that City.—But this is ever the Behaviour of ungrateful People.—If a thoufand Favours are beftowed on them, and afterwards but the fmalleft Offence is given, all the previous Obligations are immediately cancel'd, and the fingle Offence, perhaps too an imaginary one, is returned with as much Rancour and Refentment, as if no Act of Friendfhip or Kindnefs had ever exifted, or had the leaft Right to be brought into the Account : — As tho' Injuries only, whether real or fuppofed, ought to be remember'd, and Favours to be as readily forgot, as they were liberally confer'd !

When *Savage* had remained about fix Months in this hofpitable Prifon, he received a Letter from Mr. *Pope*, (who ftill continued to allow him 20l. a Year) containing a Charge of very attrocious Ingratitude.—What were the Particulars of this Charge, we are not informed ; but, from the notorious Character of the Man, there is Reafon to fear that *Savage* was but too juftly accufed.

He,

He, however, folemnly protefted his innocence; but he was very unufually affected on this Occafion.—In a few Days after, he was feized with a Diforder, which at firft was not fufpected to be dangerous; but, growing daily more languid and dejected, at laft a Fever feized him, and he expired on the firft of *Auguft*, 1743, in the 46th Year of his Age.

Thus lived, and thus died, *Richard Savage*, Efq; leaving behind him a Character ftrangely chequer'd with Vices and good Qualities.—Of the former we have feen a Variety of Inftances in this Abftract of his Life; of the latter, his peculiar Situation in the World, gave him but few Opportunities of making any confiderable Difplay.—He was, however, undoubtedly a Man of excellent Parts; and, had he received the full benefits of a liberal Education, and had his natural Talents been cultivated to the beft Advantage, he might have made a refpectable Figure in Life.—He was happy in an agreeable Temper, and a lively Flow of Wit, which made his Company much coveted; nor was his Judgment, both of Writings and of Men, inferior to his Wit, but he was too much a Slave to his Paffions, and his Paffions were too eafily excited.—He was warm in his Friendfhips, but implacable in his Enmity; and his greateft Fault, which is indeed the greateft of all Faults, was Ingratitude.——He feemed to think every Thing due to his Merit, and that he was little obliged to any one for thofe Favours which he thought it their Duty to confer on him: It is therefore the lefs to be wonder'd at, that he never rightly

eftimated the Kindnefs of his many Friends and Benefactors, or preferved a grateful and due Senfe of their Generofity towards him.

The dramatic Works of this unhappy Bard, which are only two in Number, have been already mentioned; but we muft, in Conformity to our Method, here recapitulate them:

1. *Love in a Veil.* Com. from the *Spanifh*.
2. *Sir* THOMAS OVERBURY. Trag.

To which may be added the Tragedy which he finifhed during his Refidence in *Wales*, and which was a kind of Supplement to his firft Tragedy; being alfo founded on the Story of *Overbury*.—It is not certain what became of this Piece, nor into whofe Hands it fell at the Author's Death.

SAUNDERS, Mr. *Charles*.—A young Gentleman, who lived in the Reign of King *Charles* II. whofe Wit, *Langbaine* informs us, began to bud as early as that of the incomparable *Cowley*; and was like him a King's Scholar at *Weftminfter* School, at the Time that he wrote a Play, *viz.*

Tamerlane the Great. Trag. Mr. *Banks* has complimented our young Author in a Copy of Verfes prefixed to this Play, and Mr. *Dryden* did him the Honour of writing the Prologue to it.—Whether the Stroke of Fate deprived the World foon of this promifing Genius we know not, but there are no later Fruits of it on Record in the dramatic Lifts.

SCOTT, Mr. *Thomas*, was educated at *Weftminfter* School, from whence he was removed to the Univerfity of *Cambridge*, in the Reign of King *William* III. and, during the latter Part of Queen *Anne's* Reign, he was Secretary to the Earl of *Roxburgh.*—He was Author of the following dramatic Pieces,

  1. *Mock Marriage.* Com.
  2. *Unhappy Marriage.* Trag.
  3. *Unhappy Kindness.* Trag.

The two laſt, however, are no more than the ſame Play, under two different Titles, whence different Writers have riftakenly mentioned it in their Catalogues.—The latter of them is its real Title.

SEDLEY, Sir *Charles,* Bart. one of the gay Wits that enlivened the pleaſurable Court of King *Charles* the Second, was Grandſon of Sir *William Sedley,* Bart. the munificent Founder of the *Sedleian* Lecture of Natural Philoſophy at *Oxford,* and Son of Sir *John Sedley,* of *Aylesford* in *Kent,* Bart. by his Wife *Elizabeth,* Daughter and Heir of Sir *Henry Saville,* Knt. the learned Warden of *Merton* College in *Oxford,* and Provoſt of *Eton.*—Sir *Charles* was born about the Year 1639; and, after a proper Foundation of Grammar Learning, was ſent to *Oxford,* where he was admitted a Fellow-Commoner of *Wadham* College, in *Lent* Term, 1655-6.—But he left the Univerſity without taking any Degree, and, retiring into his own Country, lived privately there, out of Humour, as it ſhould ſeem, with the governing Powers, till the Reſtoration of *Cha.* II. when he came to *London,* in Order to join in the general Jubilee, the Gaiety of which was both agreeable to his Years, and exactly ſuitable to his Taſte and Temper.—He was ſoon introduced to the King, and it was not long before they, who recommended him to his Majeſty, found they had thereby, in ſome Meaſure, ſupplanted themſelves.——Sir

Charles had ſuch a diſtinguiſhingly polite Eaſineſs in his Manner and Converſation, as ſet him higher in the Royal Notice and Favour, than any of the Courtiers his Rivals, notwithſtanding they all aimed at the ſame Turn, and ſome of them even excelled in it. In the View of heightening their Pleaſures, our Author, among the reſt, did not neglect to exert his Talents in Writing.—The Productions of his Pen were ſome Plays, and ſeveral delicately tender amorous Poems. in which the Softneſs of the Verſes was ſo exquiſite, as to be called, by the Duke of *Buckingham,* *Sedley's Witchcraft.*——" There were no " Marks of Genius or true Po-" etry to be deſcried (ſay the Au-" thors of the *Biographia Britan-* " *nica)* the Art wholly conſiſted " in raiſing looſe Thoughts and " lewd Deſires, without giving " any Alarm, and ſo the Poiſon " worked gently and irreſiſtibly. " Our Author, we may be ſure, " did not eſcape the Infection of " his own Art, or rather was firſt " tainted himſelf, before he " ſpread the Infection to others."

A very ingenious Writer of the preſent Day, however, ſpeaks much more favorably of Sir *Charles Sedley's* Writings. " He " ſtudied human Nature, and was " diſtinguiſhed for the Art of " making *himſelf* agreeable, par-" ticularly to the Ladies; for the " Verſes of Lord *Rocheſter,* be-" ginning with, *Sedley has that* " *prevailing gentle Art,* &c. ſo of-" ten quoted, allude not to his " *Writings,* but to his *perſonal* " *Addreſs.*" LANGHORNE's *Effuſions,* &c.

Diſſoluteneſs and Debauchery were the ſcandalous Characteriſtics of the Times, and it was Sir *Charles's* Ambition to diſtinguiſh himſelf himfelf among the Foremoſt in the Faſhion.—In *June* 1663, our Author, Lord *Buckhurſt*, and Sir *Thomas Ogle*, were convened at a Public Houſe in *Bow-Street, Covent-Garden*, and, being enflamed with ſtrong Liquors, they went up to the Balcony belonging to that Houſe, and there ſhewed indecent Poſtures, and gave great Offence to the Paſſengers in the Street, by very unmannerly Diſcharges upon them; which done, *Sedley* ſtripped himſelf naked, and preached to the People in a groſs and ſcandalous manner: Whereupon a Riot being raiſed, the Mob became clamorous, and would have forced the Door next to the Street; but being oppoſed, the Preacher and his Company were driven from the Balcony, and the Windows of a Room into which they retired were broken by the Mob.—The Frolic being foon reported abroad, and as Perſons of Faſhion were concerned in it, it was ſo much the more aggravated. The Company were ſummoned to appear before a Court of Juſtice in *Weſtminſter-Hall*, where, being indicted for a Riot, they were all fined, and our Author was ſentenced to pay 500 l.

After this Affair Sir *Charles* took a more ſerious Turn, applied himſelf to Buſineſs, and became a Member of Parliament, in which he was a frequent Speaker.—We find him alſo in the Houſe of Commons in the Reign of *James* II. whoſe Attempts upon the Conſtitution he vigorouſly withſtood.—When the Defeat of the Rebels under the Duke of *Monmouth*, made it neceſſary, in the Language of the Court, to have a ſtanding Army, it was oppoſed ſtrongly by the Gentlemen of the Country Party, among whom were the Earl of *Dorſet*,

and Sir *Charles Sedley*, one of which bore a great Sway in the Houſe of Peers, and the other in that of the Commons.—Their Intereſt was ſo conſiderable in both, eſpecially Sir *Charles Sedley's*, that the King, foreſeeing it would be a Work of the greateſt Difficulty, to gain their Conſent for the Payment of more Troops than what were upon the Eſtabliſhment of the laſt Reign, contented himſelf with dropping the Purſuit of it, by a Diſſolution of the Parliament.—In the ſame Spirit, our Patriot was very active in bringing on the Revolution.—This was thought more extraordinary, as he had received Favours from *James:* But that Prince had taken a Fancy to Sir *Charles's* Daughter, (tho' it ſeems ſhe was not very handſome) and, in Conſequence of his Intrigues with her, he created Miſs *Sedley* Counteſs of *Dorcheſter.*—This Honour, ſo far from pleaſing, greatly ſhocked Sir *Charles.*—However Libertine himſelf had been, yet he could not bear the Thoughts of his Daughter's Diſhonour; and, with Regard to this her Exaltation, he only conſidered it as rendering her more conſpicuouſly infamous.——He therefore conceived a Hatred for the King, and from this, as well as other Motives, readily joined to diſpoſſeſs him of the Throne.

A witty Saying of *Sedley's*, on this Occaſion, is recorded. " I " hate Ingratitude, ſaid Sir " *Charles*; and therefore, as the " King has made my Daughter a " Counteſs, I will endeavour to " make his Daughter a Queen;" meaning the Princeſs *Mary*, married to the Prince of *Orange*, who diſpoſſeſſed *James* of the Throne, at the ever-glorious Revolution.

Sir *Charles* lived many Years

 after

after the Revolution, in full Poffeffion of his Wit and Humour,
and was, to the laft, an agreeable
Companion.—He died at a good
old Age, about the Year 1722,
when his Works were publifhed,
in two Volumes, 8vo.

His dramatic Writings are,

1. The *Mulberry Garden.* C.

2. ANTHONY *and* CLEOPA-
TRA. Trag.

3. BELLAMIRA, or *the Miftrefs.* Com.

4. *Beauty the Conqueror,* or *the
Death of Mark Antbony.*
Trag.

5. The *Grumbler.* Com. three
Acts.

6. The *Tyrant King of* CRETE.
Trag.

SETTLE, *Elkanah,* Son of
Jofeph Settle of *Dunftable* in *Bedfordfhire,* was born in 1648; and
in the 18th Year of his Age was
entered Commoner of *Trin.* Coll.
Oxon; but he quitted the Univerfity without taking any Degree,
and came to *London,* where he
applied himfelf to the Study of
Poetry; in which he lived to
make no inconfiderable Figure.
Finding the Nation divided between the Opinions of Whig and
Tory, he thought proper, on firft
fetting out in Life, to join the
Whigs, who were then, though
the Minor, yet a powerful Party,
and in Support of which he employed his Talents as a Writer.
Afterwards, if we may credit the
Oxford Antiquary, *Settle* changed
Sides, turned Tory, and wrote
for that Party with as much Zeal
as he had formerly fhewn for the
Intereft of the Whigs; by which
we fee that Politicians, as well
as Patriots, were made of the
fame Sort of Stuff in thofe Times,
as in the prefent.—He alfo wrote
an Heroic Poem on the Coronation of the high and mighty Mo-

narch *James* II. 1685. commenced a Journalift for the Court,
and publifhed Weekly an Effay
in Behalf of the Adminiftration.
If *Settle* was capable of thus
meanly writing for, or againft a
Party, as he was hired, he muft
have been totally devoid of all
Principles of Honour; but, as
there is no other Authority for
it than *Wood's,* the Reader may
give what Credit he pleafes to the
Report.

Mr. *Settle's* dramatic Works
are,

1. The *Emprefs of* MOROCCO.
Trag. This Play was acted
at Court, as appears by the
two Prologues, which were
both fpoken by the Lady
Elizabeth Howard; the firft
was written by the Earl of
Mulgrave, the other by Lord
Rochefter: When it was performed at Court, the Lords
and Ladies of the Bed-Chamber played in it.—*Dryden,
Shadwell* and *Crowne,* however, wrote againft it, which
began a famous Controverfy
among the Wits of the
Town.

2. *Love and Revenge.* Trag.
Printed in 4to. 1675.

3. CAMBYSES, *King of* PER-
SIA. Trag. Written in
Heroic Verfe.

4. *The Conqueft of* CHINA *by
the* TARTARS. Trag. 4to.
1676. written alfo in Heroic
Verfe.

5. IBRAHIM, *the Illuftrious
Baffa.* Trag. in Heroic
Verfe. 1677.

6. *Paftor Fido,* or *the Faithful
Shepherd.* Paftoral. This
is Sir *Richard Fanfhaw's*
Tranflation from the *Italian*
of *Guarini* improved.—This,
and the four preceding
Pieces, were all acted at the
Duke

Duke of *York's* Theatre.——
The Firſt was likewiſe acted
at the ſame Theatre, as well
as at Court.

7. *Fatal Love,* or *the Forced In-
conſtancy.* Trag. 1680.

8. The *Female Prelate,* being the
Hiſtory of the Life and Death
of Pope *Joan.* Trag. 1680.

9. The *Heir of* Morocco. T.
1682.

10. *Diſtreſſed Innocence,* or *the
Princeſs of* Persia. Trag.
This Play was acted with
Applauſe; the Author ack-
nowledges his Obligations to
Betterton, for ſome valuable
Hints in this Play, and that
Mr. *Mountford* wrote the laſt
Scene of it.

11. The *Ambitious Slave,* or *A
generous Revenge.* Trag.
acted with Succeſs at the
Theatre-Royal, 4to. 1694.
No. 7, 8, 9 and 10 were
likewiſe acted at the ſame
Theatre.

12. The *World in the Moon.* A
Dramatic Comic Opera, per-
formed at the Theatre in
Dorſet-Garden, 1698.

13. *City Rambler,* or *the Playhouſe Wedding.* Com. acted
at the Theatre-Royal.

14. The *Virgin Propheteſs,* or *the
Fate of* Troy. An Opera,
performed 1701.

15. The *Ladies Triumph.* A Co-
mic Opera, preſented at the
Theatre in *Lincoln's-Inn-
Fields,* by Subſcription, 1710.

This Author had a Penſion
from the City, for an annual Panegyric to celebrate the Feſtival
of the Lord Mayor; in Conſequence of which he wrote various
Poems, called *Triumphs for the
Inauguration of the Lord Mayor.*——
Beſides his dramatic Pieces, he
publiſhed many occaſional Poems,
addreſſed to his Patrons. —— He

died in the *Charter-Houſe,* 1724;
ſome Months before his Deceaſe,
he offered a Play to the Managers
of the Theatre-Royal in *Drury-
Lane,* but he lived not to bring
it on the Stage: It was called,
*The Expulſion of the Danes from
Britain.*

Sewell, Dr. *George.*——This
Author was born, in what Year
we know not, at the College
of *Windſor,* of which Place his
Father, Mr. *John Sewell,* was
Treaſurer and Chapter Clerk.——
He received his early Education
at *Eton* School, but was afterwards ſent to the Univerſity of
Cambridge, where he was entered
of *Peter-Houſe* College, and there
took the Degree of Batchelor of
Phyſic.——From thence he went
over to *Leyden,* where he ſtudied
under the famous Dr. *Boerhaave,*
and, on his Return to *London,*
practiſed Phyſick in that Metropolis for ſeveral Years with very
good Succeſs.——At length, towards the latter Part of his Life,
he retired to *Hampſtead,* where
he continued the Practice of his
Profeſſion till the Year 1726, on
the 8th of *Feb.* in which he departed this Life, and was buried
at *Hampſtead.*

He was a Man of an amiable
Diſpoſition, and greatly eſteemed
among his Acquaintance.——In his
Political Principles he was inclined to the Tory Party, which
might in ſome Meaſure be the
Reaſon of his being ſo warm an
Antagoniſt to the Biſhop of *Saliſbury,* whoſe Zeal had ſo eminently exerted itſelf in the Cauſe
of the Whigs.——As an Author,
he was undoubtedly poſſeſſed of a
conſiderable Share of Genius, and
wrote in Concert with ſeveral of
his Cotemporary Geniuſes, particularly in the *Spectators* and *Tatlers,* in the fifth Volume of the

 latter,

latter, and the ninth of the former of which he was principally concerned, as also in the Translation of the *Metamorphoses* of *Ovid*, with Dr. *Garth* and others.—He has left only one dramatic Piece behind him, which met with good Success at first, but has not been acted for several Years past, entitled,

Sir WALTER RALEIGH. Trag.

SHADWELL, Mr. *Charles.*—This Gentleman, *Jacob* tells us, was Nephew to the Poet-Laureat, whose Life we shall record in the next Article.—But *Chetwood*, in his *British Theatre*, makes him more nearly related, being, as he says, his younger Son.—He enjoyed a Post in the Revenue in *Dublin*, in which City he died on the 12th of *August* 1726.—He wrote seven dramatic Pieces, the Titles of which are,

1. *Fair Quaker of* DEAL. C.
2. *Hasty Wedding.* Com.
3. *Humours of the Army.* C.
4. IRISH *Hospitality.* Com.
5. *Plotting Lovers.* Farce.
6. ROTHERIC O'CONNOR. Trag.
7. *Sham Prince.* Com.

All these, excepting the *Fair Quaker of Deal*, and the *Humours of the Army*, made their Appearance on the *Irish* Stage only, and are printed together in one Vol. small Octavo.

SHADWELL, *Thomas*, Poet-Laureat to King *William* III. was descended from an ancient Family in *Staffordshire*, and was born about the Year 1640, at *Lauton Hall* in *Norfolk*, a Seat belonging to his Father, who was bred to the Law; but, having an ample Fortune, did not trouble himself with the Practice, chusing rather to serve his Country as a Justice of Peace.—He was in that Com-

mission for three Counties, *Middlesex*, *Norfolk* and *Suffolk*, and discharged the Office with distinguished Ability and exact Integrity.—In the Civil Wars he was a great Sufferer for the Royal Cause; so that, having a numerous Family, he was reduced to the Necessity of selling and spending a considerable Part of his Estate, to support it.—In these Circumstances he resolved to breed his Son to his own Profession; but the young Gentleman, having as little Disposition to plod in the Drudgery of the Law, as his Father had, quitted the *Temple*, and resolved to travel.—He had a Taste, and some Genius, for polite Literature; and, upon his Return home, falling into Acquaintance with the most celebrated Wits of the Age, he applied himself wholly to cultivate those elegant Studies, which were the fashionable Amusements of the Times; and it was not long before he became eminent in dramatic Poetry, a Specimen of which appeared in a Comedy called the *Sullen Lovers*, or *the Impertinents*, which was acted at the Duke's Theatre.——As the Play was well received, he wrote a great many more Comedies, which met with good Success.

In the mean while, as it was impossible in these Times to shine among the great ones, which is the Poet's Ambition, without siding with one of the Parties, Whig or Tory.—Mr. *Shadwell*'s Lot fell among the Whigs; and, in Consequence thereof, he was set up as a Rival to *Dryden*.—— Hence there grew a mutual Dislike between them; and, upon the Appearance of *Dryden*'s Tragedy, called *the Duke of Guise*, in 1683, our Author was charged with having the principal Hand

in

in writing a Piece, intitled, *Some Reflections on the pretended Parallel, in the Play-called the* Duke of Guise, *in a Letter to a Friend*; which was printed the fame Year, in four Sheets, 4to.—Mr. *Dryden* wrote a Vindication of the Parallel; and fuch a Storm was raifed, both againft *Shadwell*, and his Friend *Hunt*, who affifted him in it, that this latter was forced to fly into *Holland*, and we find our Author complaining, that in thefe, which he calls the worft of Times, his Ruin was defigned, and his Life fought; and that, for near ten Years, he was kept from the Exercife of that Profeffion, which had afforded him a competent Subfiftence.——However, he at laft faw himfelf crowned with the Laurel, which was ftripped from the Brows of his Antagonift; who thereupon, by Way of Revenge, wrote the bittereft Satire againft him that ever was penned; this was the celebrated *Mac-Flecnoe*.

Our new Laureat had the Misfortune to enjoy his Honour but a very few Years, for he died fuddenly in 1692, in the fifty-fecond Year of his Age, at *Chelfea*, and was interred in the Church there. His Friend, Dr. *Nicholas Brady*, preached his Funeral Sermon; wherein he affures us, that our Author was " a Man of great " Honefty and Integrity, and had " a real Love of Truth and Sin-" cerity, an inviolable Fidelity " and Strictnefs to his Word, an " unalterable Friendfhip where-" ever he profeffed it, and a " much deeper Senfe of Religion, " than many others have, who " pretend to it more openly. His " natural and acquired Abilities, " (continues the Dr.) made him " fufficiently remarkable to all " that he converfed with, very

" few being equal to him, in all " the becoming Qualities and Ac-" complifhments of a compleat " Gentleman."—After his Death came out *The Volunteers*, or *the Stock-Jobbers*, a Comedy, acted by their Majefties Servants, with a Dedication to the Queen by Mrs. *Shadwell*, our Author's Widow; and an Epilogue, wherein his Character as a Poet is fet in the beft and moft advantageous Light; which, perhaps, was judged neceffary to ballance the very different Drawing, and even abufive Reprefentation of it, by *Dryden*, who is generally condemned for treating our Author too unmercifully; his Refentment carrying him beyond the Bounds of Truth, for that, though it muft be owned he fell vaftly fhort of *Ben Jonfon*, whom he fet to himfelf as a Model of Excellence; yet it is certain there are high Authorities in favour of many of his Comedies, and the beft Judges of that Age gave their Teftimony for them.—They have in them fine Strokes of Humour; the Characters are often originals, ftrongly marked, and well fuftained.—Add to this, that he had the greateft Expedition imaginable in writing, and fometimes produced a Play in lefs than a Month.—Befides feventeen Plays, he wrote feveral other Pieces of Poetry, fome of which have been commended.—An Edition of his Works, with fome Account of his Life and Writings prefixed, was publifhed in 1720, in four Volumes, 8vo.—His dramatic Works are,

1. The *Sullen Lovers*, or *the Impertinents*. Com.
2. The *Humorift*. Com.
3. The *Royal Shepherdefs*. Tr.-Com. acted by the Duke of *York*'s Servants, 1669.

This

This Play was originally written by Mr. *Fountain* of *Devonshire*, but altered throughout by *Shadwell*.

4. The *Virtuoso*. Com. 1676.
5. PSYCHE. Trag. 1675.
6. The *Libertine*. Trag. 1676. The Story from which he took the Hint of this Play, is famous all over *Spain*, *Italy* and *France* ——It was firſt uſed in a *Spaniſh* Play, the *Spaniards* having a Tradition of ſuch a vicious *Spaniard*, as is repreſented in this Piece; from them the *Italian* Comedians took it; the *French* borrowed it from the *Italians*, and four ſeveral Plays have been founded on the ſame Story.
7. EPSOM *Wells*. Com. 1676. Mr. *Langbaine* ſays, this is ſo diverting and ſo true a Comedy, that even Foreigners, who are not in general kind to the Wit of our Nation, have extremely commended it.
8. The *Hiſtory of* TIMON *of* ATHENS, *the Manhater*. 1678.——In the Dedication to *George* Duke of *Buckingham* he obſerves, that this Play was originally *Shakeſpeare's*, who never made, ſays he, more maſterly Strokes than in this; yet I can truly ſay, I have made it into a Play.
9. The *Miſer*. Com. from *Moliere's L'Avare*.
10. *A true Widow*. Com. 1679. The Prologue was written by Mr. *Dryden*; for at this Time they lived in Friendſhip.
11. The LANCASHIRE *Witches*, *and* TEAGUE O'DIVELLY, *the* IRISH *Prieſt*. C. 1682;
12. The *Woman Captain*. Com.

13. The *Squire of* ALSATIA. Com. 1688.
14. BURY *Fair*. Com. 1689.
15. *Amorous Bigot*, with the ſecond Part ef TEAGUE O'DIVELLY. 1690.
16. The *Scowerers*. Com. 1690.
17. The *Volunteers*, or *the Stock-Jobbers*. A poſthumous Comedy, already mentioned.

SHAKESPEARE, *William*, the great Poet of Nature, and the Glory of the *Britiſh* Nation, was deſcended of a reputable Family, at *Stratford* upon *Avon*.——His Father was in the Wool-trade, and dealt conſiderably that Way.—— He had ten Children, of whom our immortal Poet was the eldeſt, and was born in *April* 1564. At a proper Age he was put to the Free-School in *Stratford*, where he acquired the Rudiments of Grammar-Learning. ——Whether he diſcovered at this Time any extraordinary Genius or Inclination for Literature is uncertain.——His Father had no Deſign to make a Scholar of him; on the contrary, he took him early from School, and employed him in his own Buſineſs, but he did not continue long in it, under the Controul of his Father; for at ſeventeen Years of Age he married, commenced Maſter of a Family, and became the Father of Children, before he was out of his Minority.——He now ſettled in Buſineſs for himſelf, and had no other Thoughts than of purſuing the Wool-trade, when, happening to fall into Acquaintance with ſome Perſons who followed the Practice of Deer-ſtealing, he was prevailed upon to engage with them in robbing Sir *Thomas Lucy's* Park, near *Stratford*.——The Injury being repeated more than once, that Gentleman

was

was provoked to enter a Profecution againft the Delinquents, and
Shakefpeare, in Revenge, made
him the Subject of a Ballad,
which Tradition fays (for the
Piece is loft) was pointed with fo
much Bitternefs, that it became
unfafe for the Author to ftay any
longer in the Country.—To efcape the Law, he fled o *London*,
where, as might be expected from
a Man of Wit and Humour in
his Circumftances, he threw him
felf among the Players —Thus
was this grand Luminary driven,
by a very untoward Accident, into his genuine and proper Sphere.

His firft Admiffion into the
Play-houfe was fuitable to his
Appearance ; a Stranger, and ignorant of the Art, he was glad
to be taken into the Company in
a very mean Rank ; nor did his
Performance recommend him to
any diftinguifhed Notice.—The
Part of an under Actor neither
engaged nor deferved his Attention.—It was far from filling,
or being adequate to, the Powers of his Mind : and therefore
he turned the Advantage which
that Situation afforded him, to a
higher and nobler Ufe.—Having,
by Practice and Obfervation, acquainted himfelf with the mechanical Oeconomy of the Theatre,
his Native Genius fupplied the
reft : But the whole View of his
firft attempts in Stage-Poetry being to procure a Subfiftence, he
directed his Endeavours folely to
hit the Tafte and Humour that
then prevailed amongft the mean-
er Sort of People, of whom the
Audience was generally compofed ; and therefore his Images
of Life were drawn from thofe of
that Rank. —Thus did *Shakefpeare* fet out, without the Advantage of Education, the Advice or Affiftance of the Learned,

the Patronage of the better Sort,
or any Acquaintance amongthem.
But when his Performances had
merited the Protection of his
Prince, and the Encouragement
of the Court had fucceeded to
that of the Town, the Works of
his riper Years were manifeftly
raifed above the Level of his former Productions.

In this Way of Writing he
was an abfolute Original, and of
fuch a peculiar Caft, as hath perpetually raifed and confounded
the Emulation of his Succeffors ;
a Compound of fuch very fingular
Blemifhes, as well as Beauties,
that thefe latter have not more
mocked the Toil of every af-
piring Undertaker to emulate
them , than the former , as
flaws intimately united to Diamonds, have baffled every Attempt of the ableft Artifts to
take them out, without fpoiling
the whole.——Queen *Elizabeth*,
who fhewed *Shakefpeare* many
Marks of her Favour, was fo
much pleafed with the delightful
Character of Sir *John Falftaff*, in
the two Parts of *Henry the Fourth*,
that fhe commanded the Author
to continue it for one Play more,
and to fhew the Knight in Love ;
which he executed inimitably, in
the *Merry Wives of Windfor*.

Among his other Patrons, the
Earl of *Southampton* is particularly
honoured by him, in the Dedication of two Poems, *Venus and
Adonis*, and *Lucrece* ; in the latter
efpecially he expreffes himfelf in
fuch Terms, as gives Countenance
to what is related of that Patron's diftinguifhed Generofity to
him.—In the Beginning of King
James the Firft's Reign (if not
fooner) he was one of the principal Managers of the Play-houfe,
and continued in it feveral Years
afterwards ; till, having acquired
fuch

such a Fortune as satisfied his moderate Wishes and Views in Life, he quitted the Stage, and all other Business, and passed the Remainder of his Time in an honourable Ease, at his native Town of *Stratford*, where he lived in a handsome House of his own purchasing, to which he gave the Name of *New-Place*; and he had the good Fortune to save it from the Flames, in the dreadful Fire that consumed the greatest Part of the Town, in 1614.

In the Beginning of the Year 1616, he made his Will, wherein he testified his Respect to his quondam Partners in the Theatre; he appointed his youngest Daughter, jointly with her Husband, his Executors, and bequeathed to them the best Part of his Estate, which they came into the Possession of, not long after. He died on the 23d of *April* following, being the fifty-third Year of his Age, and was interred among his Ancestors, on the North Side of the Chancel, in the great Church of *Stratford*, where there is a handsome Monument erected for him, inscribed with the following elegiac Distich in *Latin*.

*Judicio Pylium, Genio Socratem,
Arte Maronem,
Terra tegit, Populus mæret, O-
lympus habet.*

In the Year 1740, another very noble one was raised to his Memory, at the public Expence, in *Westminster - Abbey*; an ample Contribution for this Purpose being made, upon exhibiting his Tragedy of *Julius Cæsar*, at the Theatre Royal in *Drury-Lane*, *April* the 28th, 1738.—Seven Years after his Death, his Plays were collected and published in 1623, in Folio, by two of his principal Friends in the Company of Comedians, *Heninge* and *Condale*; who likewise corrected a second Edition in Folio, in 1632.—Though both these Editions were extremely faulty, yet no other was attempted till 1714, when a third was published in 8vo. by Mr. *Nicholas Rowe*, but with few if any Corrections, only he prefixed some Account of the Author's Life and Writings.— But the Plays being in the same mangled Condition as at first, Mr. *Pope* was prevailed upon to undertake the Task of clearing away the Rubbish, and reducing them to a better Order; and accordingly he printed a new Edition of them in 1721, in 4to.— Hereupon Mr. *Lewis Theobald*, after many Years spent in the same Task, published a Piece, called *Shakespeare restored*, 8vo. 1726, which was followed by a new Edition of *Shakespeare*'s Works, in 1733, by the same Author.———In 1744, Sir *Thomas Hanmer* published at *Oxford* a pompous Edition, with Emendations, in six Volumes, 4to.—To these Mr. *Warburton*, now Bishop of *Gloucester*, added another new Edition, with a great Number of Corrections, in 1747. And Mr. *Theobald*'s Edition was reprinted, with several Alterations, in 1757.—In 1760, appeared an historical Play, entitled, *The Raigne of Edward the Third*, &c. which is ascribed to *Shakespeare*, upon these three concurring Circumstances, the Date, the Style, and the Plan, which is taken, as several of *Shakespeare*'s are, from *Holingshead*, and a Book of Novels, called the *Palace of Pleasure*.—Thus new Monuments are continually rising to honour *Shakespeare*'s Genius in the

the learned World; and we muſt not conclude, without adding another Teſtimony of the Veneration paid to his Manes by the Public in General, which is, that a Mulberry-Tree, planted upon his Eſtate by the Hands of this revered Bard, was cut down not many Years ago, and the Wood, being converted to ſeveral domeſtic Uſes, was all eagerly bought at a high Price, and each ſingle Piece treaſured up by its Purchaſer, as a precious Memorial of the Planter.

The Plays of this great Author, which are forty-three in Number, are as follow,

1. The *Tempeſt*. Com. firſt acted in *Black-Fryars*.
2. The *Two Gentlemen of* VERONA. Com. writ at the Command of Q. *Eliz.*
3. The firſt and ſecond Parts of *King* HENRY IV.— The Character of *Falſtaff* in theſe Plays is juſtly eſteemed a Maſter-Piece.
4. The *Merry Wives of* WINDSOR. Com. written at the Command of Queen *Elizabeth.*
5. *Meaſure for Meaſure.* Com. Plot taken from *Cynthio Ciralni.*
6. The *Comedy of Errors*, founded upon *Plautus Mænechmi.*
7. *Much ado about Nothing.* C. Plot taken from *Arioſto's Orlando Furioſo.*
8. *Love's Labour loſt.* Com.
9. *Midſummer Night's Dream.* Com.
10. The *Merchant of* VENICE, Tragi-Com.
11. *As you like it.* Com.
12. The *Taming of a Shrew.* Com.
13. *All's well that ends well.* Com.

14. The *Twelfth-Night, or What you will.* Com.—In this Play there is ſomething ſingularly ridiculous in the fantaſtical Steward *Malvolio.*—Part of the Plot taken from *Plautus's Mænechmi.*
15. The *Winter's Tale.* Tragi-Com. Plot taken from *Doraſtus* and *Faunia.*
16. The *Life and Death of King* JOHN. An Hiſt. Play.
17. The *Life and Death of King* RICHARD II. Trag.
18. The *Life of King* HENRY V. Hiſt. Play.
19. The firſt Part of *King* HENRY VI. Hiſt. Play.
20. The ſecond Part of *King* HENRY VI. *with the Death of the good Duke* HUMPHREY.
21. The third Part of *King* HEN. VI. *with the Death of the Duke of* YORK.— Theſe Plays contain the whole Reign of this Monarch.
22. The *Life and Death of King* RICHARD III.
23. The *famous Hiſtory of the Life of K.* HENRY VIII.
24. TROILUS *and* CRESSIDA. Trag. Plot from *Chaucer.*
25. CORIOLANUS. Trag.
26. TITUS ANDRONICUS. T.
27. ROMEO *and* JULIET. T. Plot from *Bandello's* Novels—This is perhaps one of the moſt affecting of *Shakeſpeare's* Plays; it was not long ſince acted fourteen Nights together at both Houſes, at the ſame Time, and it was a few Years before revived and acted twelve Nights with Applauſe, at the Little Theatre in the *Haymarket.*

28. Th

28. TIMON of ATHENS. Tr. The Plot from *Lucian*'s Dialogues.

29. JULIUS CÆSAR. Trag.

30. The *Tragedy of* MACBETH. Plot from *Buchanan*, and other *Scotch* Writers.

31. HAMLET *Prince of* DENMARK. Trag.

32. *King* LEAR. Trag. Plot, see *Leland*, *Monmouth*.

33. OTHELLO, *the Moor of* VENICE. Trag. Plot from *Cynthio*'s Novels.

34. ANTHONY *and* CLEOPATRA. Story from *Plutarch*.

35. CYMBELINE. Trag. Plot from *Boccace*'s Novels.

36. PERICLES *Prince of* TYRE. An Hiftorical Play.

37. The LONDON *Prodigal*. C.

38. The *Life and Death of* THOMAS *Lord* CROMWELL, *the Favourite of King* HENRY VIII.

39. The *Hiftory of Sir* JOHN OLDCASTLE, *the good Lord* COBHAM. Trag.— See *Fox*'s Book of Martyrs.

40. The *Puritan*, or *the Widow of Watling-ftreet*. Com.

41. *A* YORKSHIRE *Tragedy*. This is rather an Interlude than a Tragedy, being very fhort, and not divided into Acts.

42. The *Tragedy of* LOCRINE, *the eldeft Son of King* BRUTUS. Story from *Milton*'s Hiftory of *England*.

SHARP, Mr. *Lewis*.— This Gentleman lived in the Reign of *Charles* I. and wrote one Play, entitled,

The *Noble Stranger*. Com.

SHARPMAN, Mr. *Edward*, was a Member of the *Middle Temple* in the Reign of *James* I. and wrote a Play much refem-

bling, if not borrowed from, *Marfton*'s Comedy of the *Parafitafter*.—It is entitled,

The *Fleire*. Com.

SHAW, *Samuel*, was of *Afhby de la Zouch* in *Leicefterfhire*, and wrote one Interlude, which was only reprefented at a Country School.—It was entitled,

ΠΟΙΚΙΛΟΦΡΟΝΕΣΙΣ. Interl.

SHEPPARD, Mr. *S.* lived in the Reign of King *Charles* I. and, during the Prohibition of the Stage, wrote and publifhed two fmall dramatic Pieces on Party Subjects, which, however, bear much ftronger Teftimony to his Loyalty than to his poetical Abilities; for, befides the Shortnefs of each of them, being not longer than a fingle Act of a moderate Play, they are almoft entirely ftolen from other Authors.—The Titles of them both are the fame, the fecond being only a Continuation of the fame Subject with the firft.—They are entitled,

The *Committee Man curried*. Com. in two Parts.

SHERBURNE, Sir *Edward*, Knight.——This Author, or at leaft learned Tranflator, was born in *Goldfmith's Rents*, in the Parifh of St. *Giles's*, *Cripplegate*, *London*, in 1616, and was of the fame ancient Family with Sir *Nicholas Sherburne*, Bart. of *Stonyhurft* in *Lancafhire*.—He was Commiffary General of King *Charles* I's Artillery, was conftant in his Attachment to the Royal Caufe, and, in Confideration of many faithful Services and Sufferings, was knighted by *Charles* II. at *Whitehall*, in 1682.—*Wood* mentions him by the Title of late Clerk of his Majefty's Ordnance and Armories within the Kingdom of *England*, which Poft he muft have held under K. *Cha.* II.

He

He was a Perfon of great Learning, and tranflated four of the Tragedies of *Seneca*, viz.

1. HERCULES. *Vid.* APPENDIX. Vol. I.
2. MEDEA.
3. THEBAIS.
4. TROADES.

Coxeter alfo tells us, that he had been informed that the *Clouds* in *Stanley*'s Life of *Ariftophanes* was written by this Gentleman.—He alfo conjectures him to be the Tranflator of the

PHILLIS *of* SCYROS.

But with Regard to that Conjecture, fee before under the Initial Letters S. J.

SHERIDAN, *Thomas*, M. A.—This Gentleman, who is now living, and has lately made himfelf well known by his feveral Endeavours for the Promotion and Improvement of the Art of Oratory in thefe Kingdoms, is the fecond Son of Dr. *Thomas Sheridan*, whom a clofe Intimacy and continual Correfpondence with that Mafter of true Wit and original Humour, the Dean of St. *Patricks*, introduced more extenfively to the Notice of the World than any very extraordinary Abilities of his own.—The Object of our prefent Enquiries was, I believe, born at *Quilca*, a little Eftate in the County of *Cavan* in *Ireland*, which came into the Family in Right of his Mother, the Daughter of one Mr. *M'Pherfon*, a *Scots* Gentleman, who became poffeffed of it during the Troubles in *Ireland*.

The early Parts of his Education, no Doubt, he received under his Father, who was fo far from being a mere Country Pedagogue, that he was deemed as good a Schoolmafter as any in *Europe*, and one of the beft *Latinifts* and *Grecians* of the Age he lived in.

When grounded in thefe Languages, he removed to *Trinity* College, *Dublin*, where he went thro' his Academical Studies, and, I believe, took his Degree of Mafter of Arts.—This Courfe of Education finifhed, it was Time for Mr. *Sheridan* to fet forwards in Life; but his Father having no kind of Intereft to procure him Preferment had he thought of going into Orders, nor any Fortune to give him as a Means of providing for him in any of the other liberal Profeffions, till fuch Time as his own Talents might have infured his Succefs, what Step was to be taken became a Point of fome Confideration.—The young Gentleman's Inclinations, added to the Applaufe that he had frequently met with from thofe who had been prefent at the Delivery of fome of his academical Exercifes, in which, tho' very young, he had acquir'd great Reputation as a juft and critical Orator, pointed his Thoughts towards the Theatre.—That of *Dublin* was indeed, at that Time, at a very low Ebb, not only with Refpect to the Emoluments arifing from it, but alfo as to the theatrical Merit of the Performers, and ftill much more fo as to the internal Oeconomy and Conduct of it, and the private Characters of the greateft Part of its Members; and confequently not much frequented, excepting by the younger and more licentious Members of the Community, who went there more for the Sake of indulging an Inclination of Riot and Intrigue, than from any other Motive.—Notwithftanding thefe Difadvantages, however, Mr. *Sheridan*'s Merit, and the ftrong Support his Intereft met with from his Fellow Collegians, who, in that

 City,

City, bear great Sway in all the Affairs of public Entertainment, forc'd him into Notice and Approbation.—And, as if one Period had been fixed on by Fate for awakening the almoſt expiring Taſte of both Kingdoms, it was nearly at the ſame Time that our great brilliant Star appear'd at once with dazzling Luſtre in the Eaſt, and this other new Phænomenon ſhone forth with almoſt equal Luſtre from the Weſt of the Theatric Hemiſphere.—But there was a Piece of Service ſtill remaining to be done to the *Iriſh* Theatre, even of more Importance than the Acquiſition of capital Performers, and which was reſerved for Mr. *Sheridan* to accompliſh.——This was the curbing the Licentiouſneſs which had long reign'd with an unlimited Empire behind the Scenes, and the putting a Stop to the Liberties daily taken by the young and unruly among the Male Part of the Audience, who, by the Preſcription of Cuſtom almoſt immemorial, had conſtantly claimed a Right of coming into the Green-Room, attending Rehearſals, and carrying on Gallantries in the moſt open and offenſive Manner, with ſuch of the Actreſſes as would admit of them, while thoſe who would not, were perpetually expoſed to Inſult and Ill-Treatment.——Theſe Grievances Mr. *Sheridan,* as ſoon as he became Manager of the Theatre, which was not long after his firſt coming on the Stage, determined by Degrees to remove; which he at laſt happily effected, tho' not till after his having been involved in Conteſts with perhaps the moſt tumultuous Audiences in the World, not only at the Hazard of loſing his Means of Subſiſtence, but even at the Riſque

of his Life, from the Reſentment of a Set of lawleſs Rioters; who were, however, thro' a noble Exertion of Juſtice in the Magiſtracy of *Dublin,* in the Support of ſo good a Cauſe, at length convinced of their Error, or at leaſt of the Impracticability of purſuing it any farther with Impunity.—And thus to Mr. *Sheridan's* Care, Judgment, Aſſiduity and Spirit, the Theatre of *Dublin* ſtands indebted for the Regularity, Decorum and Propriety which it has ſince been conducted with, and the Reputation it has acquir'd; it having been brought to that Strictneſs of Conduct, that neither the Powers of Intereſt or of Violence could procure an Admittance for any one behind the Scenes during the Time either of Performance or Rehearſal.—Nor has the Public been under leſs conſiderable Obligations to this Gentleman, not only for the Eaſe and quiet Enjoyment of their moſt rational Amuſement, but alſo for the very Merit of the Performances, in Conſequence of his introducing ſuch a Degree of Regularity into them, as became a Temptation for other Perſons, as well as himſelf (poſſeſs'd of amiable Characters, deſcended from good Families, whoſe Educations had been liberal, and who were endowed with thoſe Virtues and Accompliſhments, without which theatrical Excellence can never be attained) to offer their Services to the Public, in a Profeſſion, which, for a long Time, with Reſpect to that Kingdom, none but Perſons, indifferent to that moſt valuable of all earthly Poſſeſſions, the good Opinion of the World, would venture to appear in.

During the Space of about eight
Years,

Years, Mr. *Sheridan* poſſeſſed this important Office of Manager of the Theatre Royal of *Dublin*, with all the Succeſs both with Reſpect to Fame and Fortune that could well be expected.— Till at length, an unfortunate Occurrence overthrew at once the ſeemingly ſtable Fabric he had ſo long and with ſo much Pains been rearing, prov'd the Shipwreck of his private Fortune, and indeed hitherto the Deſtruction of all thoſe flouriſhing Proſpects the *Iriſh* Stage ſeem'd then to have of an eſtabliſhed Succeſs.

In the Summer of the Year 1754, in which the Rancour of political Party aroſe to the greateſt Height that it had almoſt ever been known to do in *Dublin*, Mr. *Sheridan* unfortunately revived a Tragedy, *viz. Miller's Mahomet.* In this Play were many Paſſages, which, though no more than general Sentiments of Liberty, and the Deteſtation of Bribery and Corruption, in thoſe who have the Conduct of public Affairs, yet being fixed on by the Anti-Courtiers as expreſſive of their own Opinions in Regard to certain Perſons at that Time in Power, thoſe Paſſages were inſiſted on by them to be repeated; a Demand which, on the firſt Night of its Repreſentation, was complied with by Mr. *Digges*, by whom the Part of *Alcanor*, in which moſt of them occurr'd, was then perform'd.—On the ſucceeding Night, however, in Conſequence of ſome Remonſtrances which had been made by the Manager, on the Impropriety and Inconveniences attending on ſuch a Practice, the ſame Speeches, when again called for by the Audience, were refuſed by the Actor, and, on ſome Hints which

he could not avoid giving of his Inducement for that Refuſal, the Manager became the Object of their Reſentment. —— On his not appearing to appeaſe their Rage by ſome Kind of Apology, they flew out into the moſt outrageous Violence, cut the Scenery to Pieces with their Swords, tore up the Benches and Boxes, and, in a Word, totally deſpoiled the Theatre; concluding with a Reſolution never more to permit Mr. *Sheridan* to appear on that Stage.

In Conſequence of this Tumult he was obliged to place the Management of his ravaged Playhouſe in other Hands for the enſuing Seaſon, and come himſelf to *England*, where he continued till the Opening of the Winter of the Year 1756, when the Spirit of Party being in ſome Degree ſubſided, and Mr. *Sheridan's* perſonal Opponents ſomewhat convinced of the impetuous Raſhneſs of their Proceedings, he returned to his native Country, and having preceded his firſt Appearance in Character by a public Apology for ſuch Parts of his Conduct as might have been conſider'd as exceptionable, he was again received with the higheſt Favour by the Audience.——But now, though once more ſeated on the Throne of theatrical Sovereignty, his Reign, which had been thus diſturbed by an Inſurrection at home, was yet to undergo a ſecond Shock from an Affair ſtill, if poſſible, more fatal, being no leſs than an Invaſion from abroad. —Two mighty Potentates from *England*, viz. Mr. *Barry* and Mr. *Woodward*, having found Means to ſound the Diſpoſition of the People of *Dublin*, with whom the former, excluſive of his allowed theatrical Merit, had

 great

great Interest by being their Countryman, and finding it the Opinion of many, that a second Theatre in that City would be likely to meet with Encouragement, if supported by good Performers, immediately raised a large Subscription among the Nobility and Gentry, set Artificers to Work, erected a new Playhouse in *Crow-street* during the Summer Season, and, having engaged a Company selected from the two Theatres of *London*, were ready for opening by the Beginning of the ensuing Winter.—And now, at a Time when he needed the greatest Increase of theatrical Strength, he found himself deserted by some of his principal Performers, who had engaged themselves at the new House; and, as if Fate was determined to combat against him, some valuable Auxiliaries, which he had engaged from *England*, among whom were Mr. *Theophilus Cibber*, and Mr. *Maddox* the Wire-Dancer, lost their Lives in the Attempt to come to *Ireland*, being driven by a Storm, and cast away on the Coast of *Scotland*.

This was the finishing Stroke to that Ruin which had begun to take Place, and had been so long impending over his Head.—He was now compelled entirely to throw up his whole Concern with that Theatre, and to seek out for some other Means of providing for himself and Family.

In the Year 1757, Mr. *Sheridan* had published a Plan, whereby he proposed to the Natives of *Ireland* the Establishment of an Academy for the Accomplishment of Youth in every Qualification necessary for a Gentleman.—In the Formation of this Design he consider'd the Art of Oratory as one of the principal Essentials, and, in order to give a stronger Idea of the Utility of that Art, by Example as well as Theory, he opened his Plan to the Public in two or three Orations, which were so well written, and so admirably delivered, as to give the highest Proofs of the Abilities of the Proposer, and his Fitness for the Office of Superintendant of such an Academy; for which Post he offer'd his Service to the Public.—Yet how it happen'd I know not; but, tho' the Plan itself was in some Degree carried into Execution, Mr. *Sheridan* was unfortunately excluded from any Share in the Conduct of it.

He then came over once more to *England*, where he composed a Course of excellent Lectures on *Elocution* and *Oratory*, which he publicly read in the Theatre of the University of *Oxford*, to numerous and elegant Audiences, very considerably to his Emolument, and still more so to his Reputation; and, as a farther Testimony borne to his Abilities, was honoured by the University with a Master of Arts Degree.—From thence he again came to *London*, where, for these three Years past, his Time seems to have been divided between the Avocations of his former Profession (having performed frequently in some of his most favorite Characters in the Theatre Royal in *Drury-Lane*) and that of the reading Lectures.—Some Part of last Winter, also, he published Proposals for establishing an Academy for introducing the *English* Language in its Purity, both of Grammar and Pronunciation, into the Kingdom of *Scotland*, where moreover he had met

with

with Succefs in his Lectures ; but this Defign feems, for the prefent at leaft, to be laid afide.

I have been the fuller in my Account of this Gentleman, as his clofe Connection with, and his real Confequence in theatrical Hiftory, feem naturally to render the Events of his Life of fome Importance to the Devotees of the dramatic Mufes, and to entitle them to an ample mention in a Work of this nature.—What Plan he propofes to purfue hereafter I am not informed of, but, be it what it will, his Merits of various Kinds certainly entitle him to the Encouragement of the Public, in whofe Service he has ever been faithfully affiduous, although in many Inftances unfuccefsfully fo. As an Actor, the capital Station he fo long maintained in the good Opinion of an Audience who value themfelves fo highly on being critical Judges of the Performances, is furely fufficient to authorize our allowing him, if not a Place in the firft Rank of Actors, at leaft deferving of one fuperior to thofe in the fecond.— Nature has indeed been rather niggard of her Favour to him with Refpect to Voice and Perfon, but the Judgment in oratorical Execution, and the critical Underftanding of his Author, which are fo effentially his Characteriftics, muft ever afford Delight to the judicious and difcerning.— As a Scholar, all who know him muft acknowledge his Excellencies ; and as a Writer, his Effay on *Britifh Education,* and his Courfe of *Oratorical Lectures* lately publifhed, as well as the many little Pieces which, in his own Defence, he has at Times been obliged to fend forth into the World, fhew a Depth of Rea-

foning, a Fulnefs of Imagination, and a Command of Language, which fpeak his Praifes in nobler Terms than it is in the Power of my Pen to difplay them with.— In the dramatic Way he has only produced one original Piece, and prepared three more for the Stage from the Works of other Authors, *viz.*

1. *Captain* O'BLUNDER. Far.
2. CORIOLANUS. Trag. *Vid.* Vol. I. APPENDIX.
3. *Loyal Subject.* Tragi-Com. alter'd from *Beaumont* and *Fletcher.*
4. ROMEO *and* JULIET. T. alter'd from *Shakefpeare.*

SHERIDAN, Mrs. Wife to the above-mentioned Gentleman.— This very ingenious Lady has written fome Things in the Novel-Way, which have been well-received ; particularly the Hiftory of Mifs *Sidney Biddulph.*—She is likewife Author of a Comedy, acted laft Winter, with good Succefs, at the Theatre in *Drury-Lane,* entitled,

The Difcovery.

Her Hufband played a principal Part in it ; as did alfo Mr. *Garrick,* Mr. *Obrien,* Mr. *Holland,* Mrs. *Pritchard,* &c. — *Garrick's* Part, being that of a formal old Batchelor, (Sir *Anthony Branville*) kept the Houfe in a continual Roar of Laughter ; and feveral lively Scenes between Sir *Harry Flutter* (Mr. *Obrien*) and his Lady, (Mifs *Pope*) created much Mirth, and were greatly applauded.—As to the Character of the Play in general, the ingenious Authors of the *Monthly Review* obferve, that it is " fenti- " mental and moral in the Con- " duct, eafy and correct in the " Language, various and enter- " taining in the Characters ;"

to which they add, " the greateſt " Fault we find throughout the " whole, is the Length and Lan- " guor of ſome of the Scenes, " which almoſt deviate into " Preaching." —— This Fault, however, was judiciouſly rectified in the Performance, after the firſt Night.

This Lady is alſo ſaid to be the Tranſlator of the Memoirs and Letters of the celebrated *Niron de L'Enclos*, publiſhed in 1761, in two Pocket Volumes.—We mention this Circumſtance to diſtinguiſh her Edition from a prior Tranſlation in one Vol. which is deemed much inferior to Mrs. *Sheridan's* Performance.

SHIPMAN, *Thomas*, Eſq;—Of this Gentleman we have no farther Information, than that he was deſcended of a very good Family, and had, by Dint of an excellent Education, acquired all thoſe Accompliſhments which were neceſſary to fit him for Converſation, and render his Company deſirable by the beſt Wits of the Age.—We find only one dramatic Piece of his extant, whoſe Title is

HENRY III. *of France.* Trag. Yet it appears, from a Collection of his Poems, entitled *Carolina*, that he was held in high Eſteem by Mr. *Cowley*, and had written other Tragedies. — But what they were entitled, or whether ever publiſhed, it is not eaſy to trace.—He lived in the Reign of *Charles* II. and is ſuppoſed to have died in the Year 1691.

SHIRLEY, Mr.—A Gentleman of this Name I find to have been, about thirty Years ago, Author of one dramatic Piece; but whether he is yet living, has render'd himſelf any other Ways

known by literary Productions, or any other Particulars relating to him, I am totally ignorant of. The Title of his Play is,

The *Parricide.* Trag.

SHIRLEY, Mr. *Henry.* — Of this Gentleman I can trace no farther Particulars, than that he lived in the Reign of K. *Charles* I. and wrote one Play, entitled,

The *Martyr'd Soldier.* Trag. *Wood* imagines him to be Brother, or ſome near Relation of *James Shirley*, whom I now ſhall proceed to give ſome Account of.

SHIRLEY, *James*, was of an ancient Family, and born about the Year 1594, in *London*.—He was educated at *Merchant-Taylor's* School, and from thence removed to St. *John's* College in *Oxford*; where Dr. *Laud*, then Preſident of that College, conceived a great Affection for him, on Account of his excellent Parts, yet would often tell him, that " he was an unfit Perſon to take " the ſacred Function upon him, " and ſhould never have his Conſent ;" becauſe Mr. *Shirley* had a large Mole upon his left Cheek, which *Laud* eſteemed a Deformity. Afterwards, leaving *Oxford*, he went to *Cambridge*, and ſoon after, entering into Orders, he took a Cure at or near St. *Albans*.— In the mean Time, growing unſettled in his Principles, he changed his Religion for that of *Rome*, left his Living, and taught a Grammar-School in St. *Albans* ; but this Employment being uneaſy to him, he retired to *London*, lived in *Gray's-Inn*, and became a Writer of Plays.—By this he gained, not only a Livelihood, but alſo great Reſpect and Encouragement from Perſons of Quality, eſpecially from the Queen, Wife to King *Charles* I.

the

who made him her Servant.—
When the Rebellion broke out,
he was obliged to leave *London*
and his Family; for he had a
Wife and Children: And being
invited by his Patron *William*,
Earl, afterwards Duke, of *Newcastle*, to follow his Fortune
in the Civil Wars, he attend-
ed his Lordship.—On the Decline of the King's Cause, he
retired to *London*; where, among
other of his Friends, he found
Mr. *Stanley*, Author of the *Lives
of the Philosophers*, who supported him for the present.—The
acting of Plays being prohibited,
he then returned to his old Occupation of teaching School,
which he did in *White-Fryars*;
and, at the Restoration, several
of his Plays were brought upon
the Theatre again.—In 1666,
happen'd the great Fire of *London*, by which he was burnt out
of his House near *Fleet-street*;
from whence he removed into
the Parish of St. *Giles*'s in the
Fields; where, being extremely
affected with the Loss and Terror occasioned by that dreadful
Conflagration.—They both died
within the Space of twenty-four
Hours, and were interred in the
same Grave.

Besides thirty-nine Plays, Tragedies and Comedies, printed at
different Times, he published an
Octavo Volume of Poems in
1646, with three Tracts relating
to Grammar.—He assisted his
Patron, the Duke of *Newcastle*,
in composing several Plays, which
the Duke published; as likewise
Mr. *John Ogilby*, in his Translation of *Homer* and *Virgil*, with
writing Notes on them.—He was
by many consider'd as one of the
most noted dramatic Poets of
his Time; and some thought

him even equal to *Fletcher* himself.

Our Author's dramatic Pieces
are,

1. The *Changes*, or *Love in a
Maze*. Com. 1632.
2. *Contention for Honour and
Riches*. Masque, 1633.
3. HONORIA *and* MAMMON.
Com.
4. The *Witty Fair-One*. Com.
1633.
5. The *Triumphs of Peace*.
Masque, 1633.
6. The *Traytor*. Trag. 1635.
7. The *Young Admiral*. Tragi-Com. 1637.
8. The *Example*. Tragi-Com.
1637.
9. HYDE *Park*. Com. 1637.
10. The *Gamester*. Com. 1637.
11. The *Royal Master*. Tragi-Com. 1638.
12. The *Duke's Mistress*. Tragi-Com. 1638.
13. The *Lady of Pleasure*. Com.
1638.
14. The *Maid's Revenge*. Trag.
1638.
15. CHABOT *Admiral of France*.
Trag. 1639.
16. The *Ball*. Com. 1639.
17. ARCADIA. Dramatic Pastoral. 1640.
18. The *Humorous Courtier*. C.
1640.
19. St. PATRICK *for Ireland*.
Historical Play. 1640.
20. *Love's Cruelty*. Trag. 1640.
21. The *Triumph of Beauty*.
Masque, 1646.
22. The *Sisters*. Com. 1652.
23. The *Brothers*. Com. 1652.
24. The *Doubtful Heir*. Tragi-Com. 1652.
25. The *Court Secret*. Tragi-Com. 1653.
26. The *Impostor*. Tragi-Com.
1653.
27. The *Politician*. Trag. 1655.
28. The

28. The *Grateful Servant*. Tr.-Com. 1655.

29. The *Gentleman of* VENICE. Tragi-Com. 1655.

30. The *Contention of* AJAX *and* ULYSSES *for* A-CHILLES's *Armour*. M. 1658.

31. CUPID *and Death*. Mafq; 1658.

32. *Love-Tricks*, or *the School of Compliments*. C. 1658.

33. The *Conftant Maid*, or *Love will find out the Way*. C.

34. The *Opportunity*. Com.

35. The *Wedding*. Com.

36. *A Bird in a Cage*. Com.

37. The *Coronation*. Com.

38. The *Cardinal*. Trag.

39. ANDROMANA, or *the Merchant's Wife*. Trag. 1660.

SHIRLEY, *William*, Efq;—This Gentleman is ftill living, and was for fome Years Refident in *Portugal*, in the Character, if I miftake not, of a Conful or public Agent for Mercantile Affairs from this Kingdom.—On fome Difguft, however, or Difpute which he had involved himfelf in there, he returned to *England* about the Year 1749.—He has ever been efteemed a Perfon of deep Penetration, and well verfed in Affairs of Trade and the Commercial Interefts and Connections of different Kingdoms, more efpecially thofe of *Great Britain* and *Portugal*.——He has alfo been generally confider'd as the Author of feveral Letters on thofe Subjects publifhed in the *Daily Gazetteer*, and figned *Lufitanicus*.—In his poetical Capacity, however, Mr. *Shirley* does not ftand in fo confiderable a Light, there having only one dramatic Piece of his Writing as yet appear'd on the

Stage, and that, though ftrongly fupported with Refpect to the Performance, met with but very indifferent Succefs.—It was entitled,

EDWARD *the Black Prince*. Trag.

We are informed that this Gentleman has written another Tragedy, and that every Thing was ready for acting it, in the prefent Year 1763, at the Theatre in *Covent-Garden*; when it was prohibited by Authority: The Town were the more furprized at this, the Play being entirely built on an old Story ufed by the *Greek* Poets 3000 Years ago, and bearing no Affinity to the prefent Times.—This is one ill Confequence of invefting a Courtier with the Power of licenfing the Stage, which certainly ought to be as free as the Prefs; the Exertion of fuch a Power being, as we conceive, the higheft Infult on the Dignity of the Public.

SMITH, *Edmund*, a Poet of confiderable Reputation, was the only Son of Mr. *Neale*, an eminent Merchant, and was born in the Year 1668.—Some Misfortunes of his Father, which were foon after followed by his Death, occafioned the Son's being left very young in the Hands of Mr. *Smith*, who had married his Father's Sifter.—This Gentleman treated him as if he had been his own Child, and placed him at *Weftminfter* School, under Dr. *Bufby*.—After the Death of his generous Guardian, whofe Name in Gratitude he thought proper to affume, he was removed to *Chrift-Church* in *Oxford*, and was there, by his Aunt, handfomely maintained till her Death.——Some Time before his leaving
Chrift-

Chrift-Church, he was fent for by his Mother to *Worcefter*, and acknowledged by her as a legitimate Son; which his Friend Mr. *Oldifworth* mentions, to wipe off the Afperfions that fome had ignorantly caft on his Birth.—He paffed through the Exercifes of the College and Univerfity with unufual Applaufe, and acquired a great Reputation in the Schools both for Knowledge and Skill in Difputation.—Mr. *Smith*'s Works are not many.—His celebrated Tragedy, *Phædra and Hippolitus*, was acted at the Theatre-Royal in 1707; and was introduced upon the Stage, at a Time when the *Italian* Operas fo much engroffed the polite World, that Senfe was altogether facrificed to Sound: And this occafioned Mr. *Addifon*, who did our Poet the Honour to write the Prologue, to rally therein the vitiated Tafte of the Public, in preferring the un-ideal Entertainment of an Opera to the genuine Senfe of a *Britifh* Poet. — This Tragedy, with a Poem to the Memory of Mr. *John Phillips*, his moft intimate Friend, three or four Odes, and a *Latin* Oration, fpoken publickly at *Oxford*, in *Laudem Thomæ Bodleii*, were publifhed in the Year 1719, under the Name of his *Works*, by Mr. *Oldifworth*; who prefixed a Character of the Author, from whence this Account is taken.—Mr. *Smith* died in the Year 1710, in the 42d Year of his Age, at the Seat of *George Ducket*, Efq; called *Hartham* in *Wiltfhire*, and was buried in the Parifh Church there.— Mr. *Oldifworth* has reprefented Mr. *Smith*, as a Man abounding with Qualities equally good and great; and we have no Reafon to impute this Panegyric to the Par-

tiality of Friendfhip.—Mr. *Smith* had, neverthelefs, fome flight Defects in his Conduct; one was an extreme Careleffnefs in Drefs, which Singularity procured him the Name of Captain *Ragg*.— His Perfon was yet fo well form-ed, that no Neglect of this Kind could render it difagreeable; infomuch that the Fair Sex, who obferved and admired him, ufed at once to commend and reprove him, by the Name of the handfome Sloven.—It is acknowledged alfo, that he was much inclined to Intemperance; which funk him into that Sloth and Indolence, which has been the Bane of many a bright Genius. Upon the whole, he was a good-natured Man, a finifhed Scholar, a fine Poet, and a difcerning Critic.

SMITH, Mr. *Henry*, wrote in the Reign of *William* III.—He belonged to *Clifford's - Inn*, and was Author of one Play, entitled,

The *Princefs* of PARMA. T.

SMITH, Mr. *John*, was born at *York*, received his Education at *Oxford*, and was, for many Years, Under-Mafter of *Magdalen* School in that City.—He is faid to have lived afterwards in *Yorkfhire*; and to have wrote one dramatic Piece, refufed by the Players, but printed about the Year 1691, under the Title of,

CYTHEREA. Com.

SMITH, Mr. *William*.—This Gentleman wrote, in the Reign of King *James* I. two dramatic Pieces, whofe Titles are,

1. *Freeman's Honour*. Play. *Vid.* Vol. I. APPENDIX.

2. *Hector of Germany*. Hift. Play.

The firft of them, I believe, never

ver

ver appeared in Print, being only mentioned in the Epiſtle Dedicatory of the other.

Coxeter quæries, whether this Author is not the *William Smith, Rouge Dragon* Purſuivant at Arms, ſpoken of in the *Engliſh Topographer,* pag. 2.

SMOLLET, *Tobias,* M. D.—A well-known Writer of the preſent Age, is a Native of *North Briton,* and was bred a Sea Surgeon.—He ſerved in the War which was terminated by the Peace of *Aix la Chapelle,* in 1748. Having then no farther Employment at Sea, he betook himſelf to his Pen ; and, being happy in a lively Genius, he ſoon produced his celebrated Novel, entitled *Roderick Random ;* which met with great Succeſs.—This encouraged him to purſue the ſame Path, and he afterwards gave the Town another Novel, entitled *Peregrine Pickle ;* in which he luckily introduced the Hiſtory of the celebrated Lady *Vane.—* This Epiſode gave the Book a great Run ; but it had likewiſe no inconſiderable Merit, independent of that Lady's entertaining Story ; the Materials of which, it is ſaid, ſhe herſelf furniſhed.—He likewiſe wrote a third Novel, entitled *Ferdinand Count Fathom,* which was judged greatly inferior to the two former ; and to this Gentleman alſo the Public is obliged for a new Tranſlation of *Gil Blas,* which was well received.—He alſo made a new Tranſlation of *Don Quixote,* from the *Spaniſh :*—And, in 1752, he ſtruck into a different Branch of Literature, and publiſhed a Tract on Bathing and *Bath* Waters.—About this Time he obtained a Degree as Doctor of Phyſic.—He reſided at *Chelſea,* and had ſome Practice ; but writing was his chief Purſuit.—His *Hiſtory of England* met with amazing Succeſs ; but this was chiefly attributed to the uncommon Arts of Publication made uſe of by his Bookſeller ; nevertheleſs, there is conſiderable Merit in the Doctor's Hiſtory ; which, in Point of Style, is inferior to none.—He alſo unfortunately engaged in a periodical Work, entitled *The Critical Review ;* in which the Acrimony of his Strictures expoſed him to great Inconveniences, particularly a Proſecution from Admiral *Knowles ;* in Conſequence of which he underwent a heavy Fine and Impriſonment in the *King's Bench.*—This ſeems to have given him a Diſguſt towards Criticiſm ; and probably againſt Authorſhip in general.— Nevertheleſs, it is ſaid, he engaged (in the Year 1762) in the Political Controverſy relating to Lord *Bute,* and the Oppoſition formed againſt that Miniſter ; and that he wrote the periodical Paper, entitled *The Briton.*—However, his Health being ſomewhat impaired, he dropt that Paper, and retired into *France,* in Hopes of receiving Benefit from that milder Climate.

The Doctor had a very agreeable Vein of Poetry ; as appeared by ſome little occaſional Pieces, particularly *The Tears of Scotland,* printed in a Collection of ingenious Poems, entitled *The Union.* He is Author of two dramatic Pieces, *viz.*

1. The *Regicide.* Trag. printed in 1749, refuſed by Mr. *Garrick,* and never acted.

2. The *Repriſal,* or *the Tars of Old England.* Farce, acted, with no great Succeſs, at the Theatre in *Drury Lane,* 1757.

SMYTH,

SMYTH, *James More*, Efq; was the Son of *Arthur More*, Efq; one of the Lords Commiffioners of Trade in the Reign of Queen *Anne*; and his Mother was the Daughter of Mr. *Smyth*, who left this his Grandfon an handfome Eftate, upon which Account he obtained an Act of Parliament to change his Name from *More* to *Smyth*; and, befides this Eftate at the Death of his Grandfather, he had his Place of Pay-Mafter to the Band of Gentlemen Penfioners, jointly with his younger Brother, *Arthur More*, Efq;—He was bred at *Oxford*, and wrote one Comedy, called,

The *Rival Modes*, 1726.
He wrote feveral humorous Songs and Poems, and, in Conjunction with the late Duke of *Wharton*, began a weekly Paper, called *The Inquifitor*, which favoured fo much of Jacobitifm, that the Publifher thought it too dangerous to print, and it dropt of Courfe. He died in the Year 1734.—This Gentleman having the Misfortune to rank with the Enemies of Mr. *Pope*, was *honoured* with a Place in that immortal Satire, *The Dunciad*; in which he is damn'd to everlafting Fame.—He is particularly pointed at there, as a notorious Plagiary, inftanced in a remarkable Story, for which the Reader is referred to the Notes to the fecond Book of the *Dunciad*; in that Part which celebrates the Foot-Race of the Bookfellers.

SOMMER, Mr.—Of this Gentleman I know nothing farther than the finding his Name on the Lift of Authors of the Year 1740, for one dramatic Piece, entitled,

ORPHEUS *and* EURIDICE. Englifh Opera.

SOUTHERN, *Thomas.* — This eminent Poet was born in *Dublin*, in the Year 1660, and received his Education at the Univerfity there.—In the 18th Year of his Age he quitted *Ireland*, and, as his Intention was to purfue a lucrative Profeffion, he entered himfelf in the *Middle Temple*; but the natural Vivacity of his Mind overcoming all Confiderations of Advantage, he quitted that State of Life, and entered into the more agreeable Service of the Mufes.—The firft dramatic Performance of Mr. *Southern*, was his *Perfian Prince*, or *Loyal Brother*, acted in the Year 1682. This Play was introduced at a Time when the Tory Intereft was triumphant in *England*, and the Character of the *Loyal Brother* was intended to compliment *James* Duke of *York*, who afterwards rewarded the Poet.—His next Play was a Comedy, called *the Difappointment*, or *the Mother in Fafhion*, performed in the Year 1684.

After the Acceffion of King *James* II. to the Throne, when the Duke of *Monmouth* made an unfortunate Attempt upon his Uncle's Crown, Mr. *Southern* went into the Army, in the Regiment of Foot raifed by the Lord *Ferrers*, afterwards commanded by the Duke of *Berwick*; and he had three Commiffions, *viz.* Enfign, Lieutenant and Captain, under King *James*, in that Regiment.—During the Reign of this Prince, in the Year before the Revolution, he wrote a Tragedy, called the *Spartan Dame.*—This Play was inimitably acted. Mr. *Booth*, Mr. *Wilkes*, Mr. *Cibber*, Mr. *Mills*, fen. Mrs. *Oldfield*, and Mrs. *Porter*, all performed in it, in their Height of Reputation, and the full Vigour

of

of their Powers.—Mr. *Southern* acknowledged, that he received from the Book-feller, as a Price for this Play, 150l. which at that Time was very extraordinary.—He was the firft who raifed the Advantage of Play-writing to a fecond and third Night.—*Southern* was induftrious to draw all imaginable Profits from his poetical Labours.—*Dryden* once took Occafion to afk him, how much he got by one of his Plays? to which he anfwered, that he was really afhamed to inform him.—But Mr. *Dryden* being a little importunate to know, he plainly told him, that by his laft Play he cleared feven hundred Pounds; which appeared aftonifhing to *Dryden*, as he himfelf had never been able to acquire more than one hundred by his moft fuccefsful Pieces.—The Secret is, *Southern* was not beneath the Drudgery of Sollicitation, and often fold his Tickets at a very high Price, by making Applications to Perfons of Diftinction; which, perhaps, *Dryden* thought was much beneath the Dignity of a Poet.—Our Author continued, from Time to Time, to entertain the Public with his dramatic Pieces, the greateft Part of which met with the Succefs they deferved.

Of our Author's Comedies, none are in Poffeffion of the Stage, nor perhaps deferve to be fo; for in that Province he is lefs excellent than in Tragedy.—The moft finifhed, and the moft pathetic of his Plays, in the Opinion of the Critics, is his *Oroonoko*.——His *Fatal Marriage*, or *Innocent Adultery*, met with deferved Succefs; the affecting Incidents, and interefting Tale in the Tragic Part, fufficiently compenfate for the low, trifling, Co-

mic Part.—Mr. *Southern* died in the Year 1746, in the 86th Year of his Age; the latter Part of which he fpent in a peaceful Serenity, having, by his Commiffion as a Soldier, and the Profits of his dramatic Works, acquired a handfome Fortune; and, being an exact Occonomift, he improved what Fortune he gained, to the beft Advantage: He enjoyed the longeft Life of all our Poets, and died the richeft of them, a very few excepted.

His dramatic Pieces are,

1. The *Loyal Brother*. Trag. 1682.
2. The *Difappointment*. Com. 1684.
3. Sir ANTHONY LOVE, or *the Rambling Lady*. Com. 1690.
4. The *Wives Excufe*, or *Cuckolds make themfelves*. Com. 1692.
5. The *Maid's laft Prayer*, or *Any Thing rather than fail*. Com. 1693.
6. The *Fatal Marriage*, or *the Innocent Adultery*. Trag. 1694.
7. OROONOKO. Trag. 1696.
8. The *Fate of* CAPUA. Tr. 1700.
9. The SPARTAN *Dame*. T. 1722.
10. *Money's the Miftrefs*. Com. 1725.

STAPLETON, Sir *Robert*, was the third Son of *Richard Stapleton*, Efq; of *Carleton* in *Yorkfhire*, and was educated a *Roman* Catholic, in the College of the *Englifh* Benedictines, at *Doway*; but, being born with a poetical Turn, and too volatile to be confined within the Walls of a Cloifter, he threw off the Reftraint of his Education, quitted a reclufe Life, came over to *England*, and turned Proteftant.—Sir *Robert* having

good

good Intereft, the Change of his Religion, having prepared the Way to Preferment; he was made Gentleman-Ufher of the Privy-Chamber to the Prince of *Wales*, afterwards *Charles* II.—We find him afterwards adhering to the Intereft of his Royal Maf-ter; for when his Majefty was driven out of *London*, by the Threatnings and Tumults of the difcontented, he followed him, and, in 1642, he received the Honour of Knighthood.—After the Battle of *Edgebill*, when his Majefty was obliged to retire to *Oxford*, our Author then attend-ed him, and was created Doctor of the Civil Laws.—When the Royal Caufe declined, *Stapleton* thought proper to retire and ap-ply himfelf to Study; and, as he was not amongft the moft con-fpicuous of the Royalifts, he was fuffered to enjoy his Solitude un-molefted.—At the Reftoration he was again promoted in the Ser-vice of *Charles* II. and held a Place in that Monarch's Efteem 'till his Death.—*Langbaine* fays, that his Writings have made him not only known, but admired, throughout all *England*, and while *Mufæus* and *Juvenal* are in Efteem with the Learned, Sir *Robert*'s Fame will ftill furvive; the Tranflation of thefe two Au-thors having placed his Name in the Temple of Immortality.—As to *Mufæus*, he had fo great a Va-lue for him, that, after he had tranflated him, he reduced the Story into a dramatic Poem, called,

HERO *and* LEANDER. Trag. printed in 4to. 1669.

Whether this Play was ever act-ed is uncertain, though the Pro-logue and Epilogue feem to im-ply that it appeared on the Stage.

Befides thefe Tranflations and this Tragedy, our Author wrote

The *Slighted Maid*. Com. act-ed at the Theatre in *Lin-coln's-Inn-Fields*, by the Duke of *York*'s Servants, 1663.

STEELE, Sir *Richard*, was born about the Year 1676, in *Ireland*, in which Kingdom one Branch of the Family was pof-feffed of a confiderable Eftate in the County of *Wexford*.—His Fa-ther, a Counfellor at Law in *Dublin*, was private Secretary to *James* Duke of *Ormond*, but he was of *Englifh* Extraction, and his Son, while very young, be-ing carried to *London*, he put him to School at the *Charter-houfe*, whence he was removed to *Mer-ton* College in *Oxford*, where he was admitted a Poft-Mafter, in 1692.—His Inclination and Ge-nius being turned to polite Lite-rature, he commenced Author during his Refidence in the Uni-verfity, and actually finifhed a Comedy; which, however, he thought fit to fupprefs, as un-worthy of his Genius.—Mr. *Steele* was well beloved and refpected by the whole Society, and had a good Intereft with them after he left the Univerfity, which he did without taking any Degree, in the full Refolution to enter into the Army.—This Step was high-ly difpleafing to his Friends; but the Ardor of his Paffion for a military Life, rendered him deaf to any other Propofal.—Not be-ing able to procure a better Sta-tion, he entered as a private Gen-tleman in the Horfe-Guards, not-withftanding he thereby loft the Succeffion to his *Irifh* Eftate.—However, as he had a Flow of Good-Nature, a generous Open-nefs and Franknefs of Spirit, and

 a fparka fparkling Vivacity of Wit,—thefe Qualities rendered him the Delight of the Soldiery, and procured him an Enfign's Commiffion in the Guards.—In the mean Time, as he had made Choice of a Profeffion, which fet him free from all the ordinary Reftraints in Youth, he fpared not to indulge his Inclinations in the wildeft Exceffes.—Yet his Gaieties and Revels did not pafs without fome cool Hours of Reflection, and in thefe it was that he drew up his little Treatife, entitled *The Chriftian Hero*, with a Defign, if we may believe himfelf, to be a Check upon his Paffions.—For this Ufe and Purpofe it had lain fome Time by him, when he printed it in 1701, with a Dedication to Lord *Cutts*, who had not only appointed him his private Secretary, but procured for him a Company in Lord *Lucas*'s Regiment of Fufiliers.—The whole Plan and Tenour of our Author's Book was fuch a flat Contradiction to the general Courfe of his Life, that it became a Subject of much Mirth and Raillery: But thefe Shafts had no Effect; he perfevered invariably in the fame Contradiction, and, though he had no Power to change his Heart, yet his Pen was never proftituted to his Follies.—Under the Influence of that good Senfe, he wrote his Comedy, called,

The *Funeral*.

This Play procured him the Regard of King *William*, who refolved to give him fome effential Marks of his Favour; and tho', upon that Prince's Death, his Hopes were difappointed, yet, in the Beginning of Queen *Anne*'s Reign, he was appointed to the profitable Place of *Gazetteer*.—He owed this Poft to the Friend-

fhip of Lord *Halifax* and the Earl of *Sunderland*, to whom he had been recommended by his School-Fellow Mr. *Addifon*.—That Gentleman alfo lent him an helping Hand in promoting the Comedy, called *The Tender Hufband*, which was acted in 1704, with great Succefs.—But his next Play, *The Lying Lover*, found a very different Fate.—Upon this Rebuff from the Stage, he turned the fame humorous Current into another Channel; and, early in the Year 1709, he began to publifh *The Tatler*; which admirable Paper was undertaken in Concert with Dr. *Swift*.—His Reputation was perfectly eftablifhed by this Work; and, during the Courfe of it, he was made a Commiffioner of the Stamp-Duties, in 1710.—Upon the Change of the Miniftry the fame Year, he fided with the Duke of *Marlborough*, who had feveral Years entertained a Friendfhip for him; and, upon his Grace's Difmiffion from all Employments, in 1711, Mr. *Steele* addreffed a Letter of Thanks to him for the Services done to his Country.—However, as our Author ftill continued to hold his Place in the Stamp-Office under the new Adminiftration, he forbore entering with his Pen upon political Subjects.— But, adhering more clofely to Mr. *Addifon*, he dropt *the Tatler*; and afterwards, by the Affiftance chiefly of that fteady Friend, he carried on the fame Plan, under the Title of *The Spectator*.—The Succefs of this Paper was equal to that of the former, which encouraged him, before the Clofe of it, to proceed upon the fame Defign in the Character of *the Guardian*.—This was opened in the Beginning of the Year 1713, and was laid down in *October* the

fam e

ſame Year.—But, in the Courſe of it, his Thoughts took a ſtronger Turn to Politics; he engaged with great Warmth againſt the Miniſtry, and, being determined to proſecute his Views that Way, by procuring a Seat in the Houſe of Commons, he immediately removed all Obſtacles thereto.—For that Purpoſe, he took Care to prevent a forcible Diſmiſſion from his Poſt in the Stamp-Office, by a timely Reſignation of it to the Earl of *Oxford*; and, at the ſame Time, gave up a Penſion, which had been, till this Time, paid him by the Queen, as a Servant to the late Prince *George* of *Denmark*.—This done, he wrote the famous *Guardian* upon the Demolition of *Dunkirk*, which was publiſhed *Aug.* 7, 1713; and the Parliament being diſſolved the next Day, the *Guardian* was ſoon followed by ſeveral other warm political Tracts againſt the Adminiſtration.—Upon the Meeting of the new Parliament, Mr. *Steele* having been returned a Member for the Borough of *Stockbridge* in *Dorſetſhire*, took his Seat accordingly in the Houſe of Commons, but was expelled thence in a few Days after, for writing ſeveral ſeditious and ſcandalous Libels, as he had been indeed forewarned by the Author of a periodical Paper, called *The Examiner*.—Preſently after his Expulſion, he publiſhed Propoſals for writing the Hiſtory of the Duke of *Marlborough*.—At the ſame Time he alſo wrote *The Spinſter*; and, in Oppoſition to *The Examiner*, he ſet up a Paper called *The Reader*, and continued publiſhing ſeveral other Things in the ſame Spirit, 'till the Death of the Queen. Immediately after which, as a Reward for theſe Services, he was taken into Favour by her Suc

ceſſor to the Throne; King *George* I. and appointed Surveyor to the Royal Stables of *Hampton-Court*, and put into the Commiſſion of the Peace in the County of *Middleſex*; and, having procured a Licence for chief Manager of the Royal Company of Comedians, he eaſily obtained it to be changed the ſame Year, 1714, into a Patent from his Majeſty, appointing him Governor of the ſaid Company during his Life; and to his Executors, Adminiſtrators, or Aſſigns, for the Space of three Years afterwards.—He was alſo choſen one of the Repreſentatives for *Boroughbridge* in *Yorkſhire*, in the firſt Parliament of that King, who conferred the Honour of Knighthood upon him, *April* 28, 1715, and, in *Auguſt* following, he received five hundred Pounds from Sir *Robert Walpole*, for ſpecial Services.—Thus highly encouraged, he triumphed over his Opponents in ſeveral Pamphlets wrote in this and the following Year.—In 1717, he was appointed one of the Commiſſioners for enquiring into the Eſtates forfeited by the late Rebellian in *Scotland*.—This carried him into that Part of the united Kingdom, where, how unwelcome a Gueſt ſoever he might be to the Generality, yet he received from ſeveral of the Nobility and Gentry, the moſt diſtinguiſhing Marks of Reſpect.—In 1718, he buried his ſecond Wife, who had brought him a handſome Fortune, and a good Eſtate in *Wales*; but neither that, nor the ample Additions lately made to his Income, were ſufficient to anſwer his Demands. ——The thoughtleſs Vivacity of his Spirit often reduced him to little Shifts of Wit for its Support; and the Project of the *Fiſh-pool* this Year,

 owed

owed its Birth chiefly to the Projector's Necessities.——The following Year he opposed the remarkable Peerage Bill in the House of Commons, and, during the Course of this Opposition to the Court, his Licence for acting Plays was revoked, and his Patent rendered ineffectual, at the Instance of the Lord Chamberlain.——He did his utmost to prevent so great a Loss, and, finding every direct Avenue of Approach to his Royal Master effectually barred against him by his powerful Adversary, he had Recourse to the Method of applying to the Public, in Hopes that his Complaints would reach the Ear of his Sovereign, though in an indirect Course, by that Canal.——In this Spirit he formed the Plan of a periodical Paper, to be published twice a Week, under the Title of *the Theatre*; the first Number of which came out on the 2d of *January* 1719-20.——In the mean Time, the Misfortune of being out of Favour at Court, like other Misfortunes, drew after it a Train of more.——During the Course of this Paper, in which he had assumed the feigned Name of *Sir John Edgar*, he was outrageously attacked by Mr. *Dennis*, the noted Critic, in a very abusive Pamphlet, entitled *The Character and Conduct of Sir John Edgar*.——To this Insult our Author made a proper Reply in *The Theatre*.

While he was struggling, with all his Might, to save himself from Ruin, he found Time to turn his Pen against the mischievous *South - Sea* Scheme, which had nearly brought the Nation to Ruin, in 1720.——And the next Year he was restored to his Office and Authority in the Play-house in *Drury-Lane*.——Of

this it was not long before he made an additional Advantage, by bringing his celebrated Comedy, called *the Conscious Lovers*, upon that Stage, where it was acted with prodigious Success; so that the Receipt there must have been very considerable, besides the Profits accruing by the Sale of the Copy, and a Purse of five hundred Pounds given to him by the King, to whom he dedicated it.——Yet, notwithstanding these ample Recruits, about the Year following, being reduced to the utmost Extremity, he sold his Share in the Play-House, and soon after commenced a Law-Suit with the Managers, which in 1726, was determined to his Disadvantage.——Having now again, for the last Time, brought his Fortune, by the most heedless Profusion, into a desperate Condition, he was rendered altogether incapable of retrieving the Loss, by being seized with a paralytic Disorder, which greatly impaired his Understanding.——In these unhappy Circumstances, he retired to his Seat at *Languanor* near *Caermarthen* in *Wales*; where he paid the last Debt to Nature, on the 21st of *September*, 1729, and was privately interr'd, according to his own Desire, in the Church of *Caermarthen*.——Among his Papers were found the Manuscripts of two Plays; one called *the Gentleman*, founded upon *the Eunuch of Terence*; and the other entitled *the School of Action*, both nearly finished.

Of three Children which Sir *Richard* had by his second Wife, *Elizabeth*, being the only one then living, was married young, in 1731, to the honourable *John Trevor*, then one of the *Welch* Judges, and now Baron *Trevor* of *Bromham*.—— Sir *Richard* was a

Man

Man of undiſſembled and extenſive Benevolence, a Friend to the
Friendleſs, and, as far as his Circumſtances would permit, the
Father of every Orphan.—His
Works are chaſte and manly.—
He was a Stranger to the moſt
diſtant Appearance of Envy or
Malevolence, never jealous of any
Man's growing Reputation, and
ſo far from arrogating any Praiſe
to himſelf from his Conjunction
with Mr. *Addiſon*, that he was
the firſt who deſired him to diftinguiſh his Papers.—His greateſt
Error was Want of Oeconomy.
However, he was certainly the
moſt agreeable, and (if we may
be allowed the Expreſſion) the
moſt innocent Rake, that ever
trod the Rounds of Indulgence.

Stephens, Mr. *John*, lived
in the Reign of *James* II. was a
Member of the Honourable Society of *Lincoln's-Inn*, and Author
of one dramatic Piece, entitled,

Cynthia's *Revenge*. Trag.

Stephens, Capt. *John*.—To
this Gentleman, who was alſo
Author of a Dictionary of the
Spaniſh and *Engliſh* Languages,
publiſhed in the Reign of King
George I. *Coxeter* has aſcribed one
dramatic Piece, either tranſlated
or borrowed from the *Spaniſh*,
but which I do not find taken Notice of any where elſe.—The Title of which is,

An Evening's Intrigue.

Whether this Piece was ever acted, or when it was publiſhed, are
Circumſtances we are not acquainted with.—The Author died
in *Nov.* 1726.

Sterling, Rev. Mr.—This
Gentleman was a Native of *Ireland*,
and, indulging his Paſſion for the
Tragic Muſe, has obliged the
World with two Plays, entitled,

1. *Parricide.* Trag.
2. *Rival Generals.* Trag.

Stevens, Mr. *George Alexander.*—This Gentleman, who is
ſtill living, and is well known
both as an Actor and Author,
but ſtill more ſo as a Boon Companion, was born in *Ireland.*—
Inclination or Neceſſity, and probably both, led him early to the
Stage, in which Profeſſion he
paſſed ſome Years in itinerant
Companies, particularly in that
whoſe principal Station is at *Lincoln*, till at length he ſeems to
have fixed his Reſidence in *London*, where he is eſtabliſhed by an
Engagement at the Theatre Royal
in *Drury-Lane.*—As a Companion, he is chearful, humorous
and entertaining; particularly after the Manner of his Predeceſſor
Tom D'Urfey, by his Singing,
with much Drollery and Spirit,
a Variety of Songs of his own
Writing, many of which are not
only poſſeſſed of great Humour,
but true Wit, a happy Manner of
Expreſſion, and an Originality
of Fancy, not often exceeded by Authors in that Walk
of Poetry. —— He has, indeed,
been ſometimes condemned,
and that not entirely without
Cauſe, for having run into too
great a Degree of Libertiniſm in
his little Sallies of this Kind.—
Mr. *Stevens* is alſo Author of
a Novel in two Volumes, entitled
the Adventures of Tom Fool, and
has alſo of late been concerned in
ſeveral literary Productions of the
periodical Kind, *viz.* Eſſays in
the *Public Ledger*, *Beauties of the
Magazines*, &c. in which he gives
Proof of a conſiderable Share both
of Humour and Genius.—His
Claim to a Place in this Work is
his having been Author of one
Piece, never acted, nor I believe
intended for the Stage, but written after the Manner, and with
the ſame Deſign, of *Tom Thumb*,

Chronon

Chrononbotonthologos, &c. — It is entitled,

Diſtreſs upon Diſtreſs. Burleſque Trag. printed about the Year 1749, at *Dublin*, and reprinted by the Book-ſellers in *London.*

STEVENS, *John.*—This Perſon was by Profeſſion a Book-ſeller, but, failing in Buſineſs, applied for Subſiſtence to the col-lecting together any Materials he could meet with of the poetical Productions of his Acquaintance, and printing them for his own Advantage, ſometimes at his own, and ſometimes without any Men-tion of the Authors, but more frequently making Uſe of their Names for a Sanction to Pieces which he put forth without their Conſent, and, indeed, to their Prejudice, being generally print-ed from ſpurious and incorrect Copies, which he had by ſome clandeſtine Means or other pro-cur'd.—Among other of his Pub-lications is one dramatic Piece, for which he took Subſcription in his own Name; but, indif-ferent as it is, I am much in Doubt as to its being his own.— It is entitled,

The *Modern Wife.* Com. 1745.

STIRLING, *William Alexan-der,* Earl of.—The Family of this North *Britiſh* Bard was ori-ginally a Branch of the *Macdo-nalds.* —— *Alexander Macdonald,* their Anceſtor, obtained from the Family of *Argyle* a Grant of the Lands of *Menſtry,* in *Clacmanan-ſhire,* where they fixed their Re-ſidence, and took their Sirnames from the Chriſtian Name of their Predeceſſor. — Our Author was born in the Reign of Queen *Eli-zabeth,* and, during the Minority of *James* VI. of *Scotland,* he gave early Specimens of a riſing Ge-nius, and much improved the fine

Parts he had from Nature, by a very polite and extenſive Educa-tion.—He firſt travelled abroad as Tutor to the Earl of *Argyle,* and, after his Return, being hap-py in ſo great a Patron as the Earl, he was careſſed by Perſons of the firſt Faſhion, while he yet moved in the Sphere of a private Gentleman. — Mr. *Alexander,* having a ſtrong Propenſity to Po-etry, declined entering upon any public Employment for ſome Years, and dedicated all his Time to the Study of the ancient Poets, upon whom he formed his Taſte. Although King *James* had but few regal Qualities, yet he cer-tainly was an Encourager of learn-ed Men.—Accordingly, he ſoon took Mr. *Alexander* into his Fa-vour, and accepted the Poems, our Author preſented him, with the moſt condeſcending Marks of Eſteem.—In the Year 1614, he created him a Knight, and gave him the Place of Maſter of the Requeſts.—*Charles* I. alſo beſtow-ed on him great Marks of the Royal Favour, and made him Se-cretary of State for the *Scotch* Affairs, in Place of the Earl of *Haddington,* and a Peer, by the Title of Viſcount *Stirling;* ſoon after which he raiſed him to the Dignity of an Earl, by Let-ters Patent, dated *June* 14, 1633, upon the Solemnity of his Ma-jeſty's Coronation, at the Palace of *Holy-Rood-Houſe* in *Edinburgh.* His Lordſhip enjoyed the Place of Secretary with the moſt unble-miſhed Reputation, for the Space of fifteen Years, even to his Death, which happened on the 12th of *February,* 1640.

His Lordſhip's dramatic Pieces are,

1. The ALEXANDRIAN *Tra-gedie.*

2. CRÆSUS. Trag.

3. DA-

3. DARIUS. Trag.

4. JULIUS CÆSAR. Trag. These Plays are printed in Fol. 1599, 1629. — They are rather Historical Dialogues than dramatic Performances, and are written in alternate Verse.

STRODE, The Rev. Dr. *William*.—This Gentleman was only Son of *Philip Strode*, Esq; sometime living near *Plimpton*, and Grandson to Sir *Richard Strode*, of *Newinham* in *Devonshire*, in which County he was born towards the End of Queen *Elizabeth*'s Reign, and, at nineteen Years of Age, was admitted to his Degree of Arts in *Christ Church* College, *Oxford*, into which he had been received a Student from *Westminster* School.—He took holy Orders, and became a florid and celebrated Preacher in the University. — In 1620, he was chosen public Orator of the University, being then one of the Proctors of it; and two Years after was admitted to the Reading of the Sentences.—In 1638, he was installed Canon of *Christ Church*, and in the same Month created Doctor in Divinity.

Dr. *Strode* died of a middle Age, having only attained his 45th Year, on the 10th of *March* 1644, and was buried in the Divinity Chapel belonging to the Cathedral Church of *Christ Church*, *Oxon*.—He was a good Preacher, an exquisite Orator, an eminent Poet, and indeed, in the general, a Person of great Parts, tho', as *Wood* observes, not equal to those of *William Cartwright*, of whom see an Account before.—He published many Sermons, Speeches, Orations, Epistles and Poems, but has left behind him no more than one Attempt in the dramatic Way, which is entitled,

The *Floating Island*. Tr.-Com.

Wood has given us the Title of it as follows,

· *Passions calmed, or the settling of the Floating Island.*

STUDLY, Mr. *John*.—Of this Gentleman I can find no farther Mention made by any of the Writers, than that he stood in high Estimation as a Poet in the Reign of Queen *Elizabeth*, and that he received his Education at *Trinity* College, *Cambridge*.—All the Connection he has with dramatic History, is his having translated the fourth, seventh, eighth and tenth Tragedies of *Seneca*, viz.

1. AGAMEMNON.

2. HERCULÉS ORTUS.

3. HIPPOLITUS.

4. MEDEA.

STURMY, Mr. wrote three Plays, all of which seem to have met with Success.—Their respective Titles are,

1. The *Compromise*. Com.

2. *Love and Duty*. Trag.

3. SESOSTIS. Trag. *Vid.* Vol. I. APPENDIX.

SUCKLING, Sir *John*, was Son of Sir *John Suckling*, Comptroller of the Houshold to King *Charles* I. and was born in the Year 1613.—He cultivated Music and Poetry, and excelled in both; for, though he had a Vivacity and Sprightliness in his Nature, which would not suffer his Attention to be long confin'd to any Thing, yet he was made ample Amends for this by Strength of Genius and Quickness of Apprehension.—In his Youth he travelled into foreign Countries, and became a most accomplished Gentleman. — He was allowed to have the peculiar Happiness of making every Thing he did become him.—Yet he was not so devoted to Wit, Gallantry, and the Muses, as to be wholly

wholly a Stranger to the Camp. In his Travels he made a Campaign under the great *Guſtavus Adolphus*, where he was preſent at three Battles, five Sieges, and ſeveral Skirmiſhes; and, if his Valour was not ſo remarkable, ſays Mr. *Langbaine*, in the Beginning of our Civil Wars, yet his Loyalty was exceedingly ſo; for, after his Return to his Country, he raiſed a Troop of Horſe, for the King's Service entirely at his own Charge, and ſo richly and compleatly mounted, that it is ſaid to have coſt him 12000 l. But theſe Troops and their Leader diſtinguiſhed themſelves only by their Finery, for they did nothing for the King's Service, which Sir *John* laid very much to Heart.—He died of a Fever, at twenty-eight Years of Age.—The Advantages of Birth, Perſon, Education, Parts and Fortune, with which this Gentleman ſet out in the World, had raiſed the Expectations of Mankind to a prodigious Height; and, perhaps, his dying ſo young was better for his Fame, than if he had lived longer. — He was a ſprightly Wit and a courtly Writer, as *Dryden* ſomewhere calls him; but certainly not a great Genius, as ſome have affected to repreſent him; a polite and eaſy Verſifier, but not a Poet.—His Works conſiſt of a few Poems, Letters, &c. and four Plays.—Theſe laſt are,

1. AGLAURA. Tragi-Com.
2. The *Goblins*. Tragi-Com.
3. BRENNORALT, or *the Diſcontented Colonel*. Trag.
4. The *ſad One*. Trag. left unfiniſhed.

His Poems, Plays, Speeches, Tracts and Letters, are all collected into one Volume, in 8vo. 1709.

SWINEY, *Owen*, a Gentleman

born in *Ireland*, and formerly a Manager of *Drury-Lane* Theatre, and afterwards of the Queen's Theatre in the *Haymarket*.——After leaving that Office he reſided in *Italy* ſeveral Years, and, at his Return, procured a Place in the *Cuſtom - Houſe*. —He wrote, or rather tranſlated from *Moliere*, one Play, called

    The *Quacks*, or *Love's the Phyſician*. Com. 1710.

SWINHOE, *Gilbert*, Eſq; a Native of *Northumberland*, lived in the Reigns of King *Charles* I. and King *Charles* II. and, during the Uſurpation, publiſhed one Play, entitled,

    The *Unhappy Fair* IRENE. Trag.

SYDNEY, Sir *Philip*, the *Marcellus* of the *Engliſh* Nation, was born at *Penſhurſt* in *Kent* in 1554. His Father was Sir *Henry Sydney*, Bart and his Mother was *Mary*, Daughter to *John Dudley*, Duke of *Northumberland*. He was educated at *Oxford*, where he continued till ſeventeen Years of Age, when he ſet out on the Tour of *Europe*, and at *Paris* narrowly eſcaped the horrid Maſſacre in 1572, by taking Shelter in the Houſe of the *Engliſh* Ambaſſador. Queen *Elizabeth* ſo highly prized his Merit and Abilities, that ſhe ſent him Ambaſſador to *Vienna*, and to ſeveral other Courts in *Germany*; and, when the Fame of his Valour became ſo extenſive, that he was put in Election for the Crown of *Poland*, ſhe refuſed to further his Advancement; leſt ſhe ſhould loſe the brighteſt Jewel of her Crown.—The Brevity we are confined to in this Work, will not permit us to enlarge on the Tranſactions of his Life.—We ſhall therefore only add, that he was killed at the Battle of *Zutphen*, in 1586, while he was mounting
the

the third Horſe, having before had two killed under him.—Beſide his other Works, he wrote one dramatic Piece, which is printed with his Poems, and called,

The *Lady of May.* Maſque, preſented to Queen *Elizabeth,* in the Gardens of *Wanſtead* in *Eſſex.*

T.

TATE, *Nahum,* was born in *Ireland,* and there educated. He was, as Mr. *Pope* obſerves in the Notes to his *Dunciad,* a cold Writer, of no Invention, but tranſlated tolerably, when befriended by *Dryden,* with whom he ſometimes wrote in Conjunction.——He ſucceeded *Dryden* as Poet - Laureat, and was concerned with *Brady* in a new Verſion of the Pſalms.—He died in 1716, and was interred in St. *George*'s Church, *Southwark.*—His dramatic Pieces are,

1. BRUTUS *of* ALBA. Opera, 1678.
2. The *Loyal General.* Trag. 1680.
3. RICHARD III. or *the Sicilian Uſurper.* Hiſt. Play, 1681.
4. The *Ingratitude of a Commonwealth,* or *the Fall of* CORIOLANUS. 1682.
5. *Cuckold's Haven,* or *an Alderman no Conjuror.* Farce, 1685.
6. *A Duke and no Duke.* Farce, 1685. taken from *Cockain's Trappolin.*
7. The *Iſland Princeſs.* TragiCom. 1687.
8. *King* LEAR, altered from *Shakeſpeare.*
9. *Injured Love,* or *the Cruel Huſband.* Trag.

TATEHAM, *John,* City-Poet in the Reign of *Charles* I. wrote four Plays, *viz.*

1. The *Diſtracted State.* Trag. 1651.
2. SCOTS *Vagaries,* or *a Knot of Knaves.* Com. 1652.
3. *Love crowns the End.* Tr.-Com. 1657.
4. The *Rump,* or *the Mirror of the late Times.* Com. 1661.

TAVERNER, *William,* the Son of Mr. *Jeremiah Taverner,* a Portrait - Painter, was bred to the Civil-Law, which he practiſed in *Doctor's Commons.*—Having a Turn for dramatic Poetry, he wrote,

1. The *Faithful Bride of* GRANADA. Com. 1711.
2. The *Maid the Miſtreſs.* C. 1713.
3. The *Female Advocates,* or *the Stock-Jobbers.* Com. 1714.
4. The *Artful Huſband.* Com. 1716.
5. The *Artful Wife.* Com. 1717.
6. *'Tis well if it takes.* Com. 1720.

TAYLOR, *Robert,* wrote one Play, called,

The *Hog has loſt his Pearl.* Com. 1611.—See the Account of this Play in our firſt Volume.

THEOBALD, Mr. *Lewis.*—This Author, who was born at *Sittingborne* in *Kent,* was the Son of Mr. *Theobald,* an Attorney of that Town, and was bred to his Father's Buſineſs.—He was concerned in a Paper, called *The Cenſor,* and publiſhed an Edition of all *Shakeſpeare*'s Plays, which is ſtill in great Eſteem ; being in general prefered to thoſe Editions publiſhed by *Pope,* *Warburton,* and *Hanmer.*—His own dramatic Pieces are,

1. The

1. The PERSIAN *Princeſs*, or *the Royal Villain*. Trag. 1707.

2. ELECTRA. Trag. tranſlated from the *Greek* of *Sophocles*, with Notes, 1714.

3. OEDIPUS, *King of Thebes*. Trag. tranſlated from *Sophocles*, with Notes, 1715.

4. PLUTUS, or *the World's Idol*. Com. tranſlated from the *Greek* of *Ariſtophanes*, with Notes, 1715.

5. The *Clouds*, Com. tranſlated from *Ariſtophanes*, with Notes, 1715.

6. The *Perfidious Brother*. T. 1716.

7. PAN *and* SYRINX. Opera, 1717.

8. The *Tragedy of King* RICHARD II. altered from *Shakeſpeare*, 1719.

9. *Double Falſhood*. T. 1729.

THOMPSON, Mr. *Thomas.*—All we can ſay of this Author is, that he publiſhed the two following Plays,

1. The ENGLISH *Rogue*. C. 1668.

2. *Mother* SHIPTON. Com. 1671.

THOMSON, Mr. *James*, was born in 1700, at *Ednam*, in the Shire of *Roxburgh*, in *Scotland*. His Father was Miniſter of *Ednam*, and was highly reſpected for his Piety and Diligence in the paſtoral Duty.—At this Time the Study of Poetry was become general in *Scotland*, the beſt *Engliſh* Authors being univerſally read, and Imitations of them attempted.—*Thomſon*'s Genius led him this Way, and he ſoon relinquiſhed his Views of engaging in the ſacred Function; nor had he any Proſpect of being otherwiſe provided for in *Scotland*, where the firſt Fruits of his Ge-

nius were not ſo favourably received as they deſerved to be.—Hereupon he repaired to *London*, where Works of Genius ſeldom fail of meeting with a candid Reception and due Encouragement.—Nor were the Hopes which Mr. *Thomſon* had conceived, from his Journey to the Capital, in the leaſt diſappointed.—The Reception he met with, wherever he was introduced, emboldened him to riſque the Publication of his excellent Poem on *Winter*.—This Piece was publiſhed in 1726; and, from the univerſal Applauſe it met with, Mr. *Thomſon*'s Acquaintance was courted by People of the firſt Taſte and Faſhion.—But the chief Advantage which it procured him, was the Acquaintance of Dr. *Rundle*, afterward Biſhop of *Derry*, who introduced him to the late Lord Chancellor *Talbot*; and ſome Years after, when the eldeſt Son of that Nobleman was to make his Tour of Travelling, Mr. *Thomſon* was choſen as a proper Companion for him.—The Expectations which his *Winter* had raiſed, were fully ſatisfied by the ſucceſſive Publications of the other Seaſons: Of *Summer*, in the Year 1727; of *Spring*, in the following Year; and o. *Autumn*; in a Quarto Edition of his Works, in 1730.—Beſide the *Seaſons*, and his Tragedy of *Sophoniſba*, written and acted with Applauſe in the Year 1729, he had, in 1727. publiſhed his Poem to the Memory of Sir *Iſaac Newton*, with an Account of his chief Diſcoveries; in which he was aſſiſted by his Friend Mr. *Gray*, a Gentleman well verſed in the *Newtonian* Philoſophy.—That ſame Year the Reſentment of our Merchants, for the Interruption of their Trade by the

Spaniards

Spaniards in *America*, running very high, Mr. *Thomſon* zealouſly took part in it, and wrote his ſpirited and public-ſpirited *Britannia*, to rouſe the Nation to Revenge.

With the Hon. Mr. *Charles Talbot*, our Author viſited moſt of the Courts in *Europe*, and returned with his Views greatly enlarged; not of exterior Nature only, and the Works of Art, but of human Life and Manners, and of the Conſtitution and Policy of the ſeveral States, their Connections, and their religious Inſtitutions.—How particular and judicious his Obſervations were, we ſee in his Poem on LIBERTY, begun ſoon after his Return to *England*.—We ſee, at the ſame Time, to what a high Pitch his Care of his Country was raiſed, by the Compariſons he had all along been making of our happy Government with thoſe of other Nations.—*To* inſpire his Fellow Subjects with the like Sentiments, and ſhew them by what Means the precious Freedom we enjoy may be preſerved, and how it may be abuſed or loſt, he employed two Years in compoſing that noble Work; upon which he valued himſelf more than upon all his other Writings.—On his Return to *England* with Mr. *Talbot* (who ſoon after died) the Chancellor made him his Secretary of Briefs; a Place of little Attendance, ſuiting his retired indolent Way of Life, and equal to all his Wants.—This Place fell when Death, not long after, deprived him of his noble Patron, and he then found himſelf reduced to a State of precarious Dependance, in which he paſſed the Remainder of his Life; excepting only the two laſt Years of it, during which he enjoyed the

Place of Surveyor-General of the Leeward-Iſlands, procured for him by Lord *Lyttleton*.—His Genius, however, could not be ſuppreſſed by any Reverſe of Fortune.—He reſumed his uſual Chearfulneſs, and never abated one Article in his Way of living; which, tho' ſimple, was genial and elegant. The Profits ariſing from his Works were not inconſiderable; his Tragedy of *Agamemnon*, acted in 1738, yielded a good Sum.— But his chief Dependance was upon the late Prince of *Wales*, who ſettled on him a handſome Allowance, and honoured him with many Marks of particular Favour. — Notwithſtanding this, however, he was refuſed a Licence for his Tragedy of *Edward and Eleanora*, which he had prepared for the Stage in the Year 1739.

Mr. *Thomſon*'s next Performance was the Maſque of *Alfred*, written jointly with Mr. *Mallet*, by the Command of the Prince of *Wales*, for the Entertainment of his Royal Highneſs's Court, at *Clifden*, his Summer Reſidence, in the Year 1740.—Mr. *Thomſon*'s Poem, entitled the *Caſtle of Indolence*, was his laſt Work publiſhed by himſelf; his Tragedy of *Coriolanus* being only prepared for the Theatre, when a fatal Accident robbed the World of one of the beſt of Men and beſt of Poets. He would commonly walk the Diſtance between *London* and *Richmond*, (where he lived) with any Acquaintance that offered, with whom he might chat, and reſt himſelf, or perhaps dine by the Way.—One Summer Evening, being alone, in his Walk from Town to *Hammerſmith*, he had over-heated himſelf, and, in that Condition, imprudently took a Boat to carry him to *Kew*; apprehending no bad Conſequence from

from the chill Air on the River, which his Walk to his Houſe, towards the upper End of *Kew-Lane*, had always hitherto prevented.—But now, the Cold had ſo ſeized him, that the next Day he found himſelf in a high Fever.—This, however, by the Uſe of proper Medicines, was removed, ſo that he was thought to be out of Danger; till the fine Weather having tempted him to expoſe himſelf once more to the Evening Dews, his Fever returned with Violence, and with ſuch Symptoms, as left no Hopes of a Cure.—His lamented Death happened on the 27th of *Auguſt*, 1748.—His teſtamentary Executors were the Lord *Lyttleton*, whoſe Care of our Poet's Fortune and Fame ceaſed not with his Life; and Mr. *Mitchell*, a Gentleman equally noted for the Truth and Conſtancy of his private Friendſhip, and for his Addreſs and Spirit as a public Miniſter.—By their united Intereſt, the Orphan Play of *Coriolanus* was brought on the Stage, to the beſt Advantage; from the Profits of which, and the Sale of Manuſcripts and other Effects, a handſome Sum was remitted to his Siſters.—His Remains were depoſited in the Church of *Richmond*, under a plain Stone, without any Inſcription. A handſome Monument was erected to him in *Weſtminſter Abbey*, in the Year 1762, the Charge of which was defrayed by the Profits ariſing from a ſplendid Edition of all his Works in Quarto; Mr. *Millar*, the Bookſeller, who had purchaſed all Mr. *Thomſon's* Copies, generouſly giving up his Property, on this grateful Occaſion.—His dramatic Works are,

1. SOPHONISBA. T. 1730.
2. AGAMEMNON. T. 1734
3. EDWARD *and* ELLEONORA. Trag. 1736.
4. TANCRED *and* SIGISMUND. Trag. 1744.
5. CORIOLANUS.' T. 1748.
6. ALFRED. Maſque, written in Conjunction with Mr. *Mallet.*

TOLSON, Mr. was the Author of one Play, called

The *Earl of* WARWICK. Tr. 1721.

TRACY, *John*, a Gentleman of *Glouceſterſhire*, was Author of

PERIANDER, *King of* CORINTH. Trag. 1731.

TRAPP, Dr. *Joſeph*, a celebrated Divine and Poet, was the Son of Mr. *Joſeph Trapp*, Rector of *Cherington* in *Glouceſterſhire*, where he was born, in 1679.—He was educated at *Wadham* College, *Oxford*, where he took the uſual Degrees, and was choſen Fellow.—He was afterwards choſen to the Profeſſorſhip of Poetry, founded by Dr. *Birkhead*, formerly Fellow of *All-Souls* College.—He was the firſt Profeſſor; and publiſhed his Lectures under the Title of *Prælectiones Poeticæ*. He has ſhewn there, in very elegant *Latin*, how perfectly he underſtood every Species of Poetry, and how critically and juſtly he could give Directions towards the forming a Poem, on the moſt juſt and moſt eſtabliſhed Rules.—He ſhewed afterwards, by his Tranſlation of *Virgil*, that a Man may be able to direct, who cannot execute; that is, may have the Critic's Judgment, without the Poet's Fire.—Dr. *Trapp* was Rector of *Harlington* in *Middleſex*, of *Chriſt - Church* in *Newgate-Street*, and St. *Leonard's* in *Foſter-Lane*, *London*; alſo Lecturer of St. *Lawrence-Jury* and St. *Martin's in the Fields*: His very high Church

Church-principles, were probably the Reason why he did not rise higher.—He died in *November* 1747, and left behind him the Character of a pathetic and instructive Preacher, an excellent Scholar, a discerning Critic, and a very exemplary Liver.—He is Author of a Tragedy, called

> ABRAMULE, or *Love and Empire*, acted in the Year 1704.

Several occasional Poems were written by him in *English*; and there is one *Latin* Poem of his in the *Musæ Anglicanæ*.—He also translated *Milton's Paradise Lost* into *Latin* Verse, but with little Success.

TROTTER, Mrs. *Catharine*, was the Daughter of Captain *David Trotter*, a *Scots* Gentleman.—He was a Commander in the Royal Navy, in the Reign of *Charles* II. and at his Death, left two Daughters, the youngest of whom, *Catharine*, our celebrated Author, was born in *London*, *August* 16, 1679.—She gave early Marks of her Genius, and learned to write, and also made herself Mistress of the *French* Language, by her own Application and Diligence, without any Instructor; but she had some Assistance in the Study of the *Latin* Grammar and Logic, of which latter she drew up an Abstract for her own Use.—The most serious and important Subjects, and especially Religion, soon engaged her Attention. — But, notwithstanding her Education, her Intimacy with several Families of Distinction, of the *Romish* Persuasion exposed her, while very young, to Impressions in Favour of that Church, which, not being removed by her Conferences with some eminent and learned Members of the Church of *Eng-*

land, she embraced the *Romish* Communion, in which she continued till the Year 1707.—In 1695, she produced a Tragedy, called *Agnes de Castro*, which was acted at the Theatre-Royal, when she was only in her seventeenth Year.—The Reputation of this Performance, and the Verses which she addressed to Mr. *Congreve* upon his *Mourning Bride*, in 1697, were probably the Foundation of her Acquaintance with that celebrated Writer.—Her second Tragedy, *Fatal Friendship*, was acted in 1698, at the new Theatre in *Lincoln's-Inn-Fields.*— This Tragedy met with great Applause, and is still thought the most perfect of her dramatic Performances. — Her dramatic Talents not being confined to Tragedy, she brought upon the Stage, in 1701, a Comedy, called *Love at a Loss, or Most Votes carry it.*— In the same Year she gave the Public her third Tragedy, entitled, *the Unhappy Penitent*, acted at the Theatre-Royal in *Drury-Lane.*—But Poetry and dramatic Writing did not so far engross the Thoughts of our Author, but that she sometimes turned them to Subjects of a very different Nature —Though engaged in the Profession of a Religion not very favourable to so rational a Philosophy as that of Mr. *Locke*; yet she had read his incomparable *Essay on Human Understanding*, with so clear a Comprehension, and so biassed a Judgment, that her own Conviction of the Truth and Importance of the Notions contained in it, led her to endeavour that of others, by removing some of the Objections urged against them.—She drew up, therefore, a Defence of the Essay, against some Remarks which had been published against it in 1667; and farther diftinguifhed herfelf in an extraordinary Manner, in Defence of Mr. *Locke*'s Writings, a Female Metaphyfician being a remarkable Phænomenon in the Republic of Letters.

She returned to the Exercife of her dramatic Genius, in 1703, and fixed upon the Revolution of *Sweden*, under *Guftavus Erickfon*, for the Subject of a Tragedy.— This Tragedy was acted in 1706, at the Queen's Theatre in the *Haymarket*. In 1707, her Doubts concerning the *Romifh* Religion, which fhe had fo many Years profeffed, having led her to a thorough Examination of the Grounds of it, by confulting the beft Books on both Sides of the Queftion, and advifing with Men of the beft Judgment; the Refult was a Conviction of the Falfenefs of the Pretenfions of that Church, and a Return to that of *England*, to which fhe adhered during the Remainder of her Life.—In 1708, fhe was married to the Reverend Mr. *Cockburn*, then Curate of St. *Dunftan's* in *Fleet-ftreet*, but he afterwards obtained the Living of *Long-Horfely*, near *Morpeth* in *Northumberland.*—He was a Man of confiderable Abilities; and, among feveral other Things, wrote an Account of the *Mofaic* Deluge, which was much approved by the Learned.

Mrs. *Cockburn*'s Remarks upon fome Writers in the Controverfy concerning the Foundation of Moral Duty and Moral Obligation, were introduced to the World in *Auguft* 1743, in the Literary Journal, entitled, *The Hiftory of the Works of the Learned.* The Strength, Clearnefs and Vivacity fhewn in her Remarks upon the moft abftract and perplexed Queftions, immediately raifed the Curiofity of all good Judges about the concealed Writer; and their Admiration was greatly increafed when her Sex and advanced Age were known.—Dr. *Rutherforth*'s *Effay on the Nature and Obligations of Virtue*, publifhed in *May* 1744, foon engaged her Thoughts; and, notwithftanding the afthmatic Diforder, which had feized her many Years before, and now left her fmall Intervals of Eafe, fhe applied herfelf to the Confutation of that elaborate Difcourfe; and, having finifhed it with a Spirit, Elegance, and Perfpicuity equal, if not fuperior, to all her former Writings, tranfmitted her Manufcript to Mr. *Warburton*, now Bifhop of *Glocefter*; who publifhed it, with a Preface of his own, in *April* 1747, under the Title of, *Remarks upon the Principles and Reafonings of Dr. Rutherforth's Effay on the Nature and Obligations of Virtue, in Vindication of the contrary Principles and Reafons inforced in the Writings of the late Dr.* Samuel Clark.

The Lofs of her Hufband, on the 4th of *January* 1748, in the 71ft Year of his Age, was a fevere Shock to her; and fhe did not long furvive him, dying on the 11th of *May* 1749, in her 71ft Year, after having long fupported a painful Diforder, with a Refignation to the Divine Will, which had been the governing Principle of her whole Life, and her Support under the various Trials of it.—She was interred near her Hufband, at *Long-Horfley*.

Mrs. *Cockburn* was no lefs celebrated for her Beauty, in her younger Days, than for her Genius and Accomplifhments.—She was indeed fmall of Stature, but had a remarkable Livelinefs in her Eye, and a Delicacy of Complection, plextion, which continued to her Death. — Her private Character rendered her extremely amiable to thofe who intimately knew her.—Her Converfation was always innocent, ufeful and agreeable, without the leaft Affectation of being thought a Wit, and attended with a remarkable Modefty and Diffidence of herfelf, and a conftant Endeavour to adapt her Difcourfe to her Company.—Her Difpofition was generous and benevolent ; and ready upon all Occafions to forgive Injuries, and bear them, as well as Misfortunes, without interrupting her own Eafe, or that of others, with Complaints or Reproaches. — The Preffures of a very contracted Fortune were fupported by her with Calmnefs and in Silence ; nor did fhe ever attempt to improve it among thofe great Perfonages to whom fhe was known, by Importunities ; to which the beft Minds are moft averfe, and which her approved Merit and eftablifhed Reputation fhould have rendered unneceffary. But her Abilities as a Writer, and the Merit of her Works, will not have full Juftice done, without a due Attention to the peculiar Circumftances, in which they were produced : Her early Youth, when fhe wrote ; her advanced Age, and ill State of Health, when fhe drew up others ; the uneafy Situation of her Fortune, during the whole Courfe of her Life ; and an Interval of near twenty Years in the Vigour of it, fpent in the Cares of a Family, without the leaft Leifure for Reading or Contemplation : After which, with a Mind fo long diverted and incumbered, refuming her Studies, fhe inftantly recovered its intire Powers, and, in the Hours of Relaxation from

her domeftic Employments, purfued, to their utmoft Limits, fome of the deepeft Enquiries of which the human Mind is capable ! Her Works are collected into two large Volumes, 8vo. by Dr. *Birch* ; who has prefixed to them an Account of her Life and Writings, from which we have extracted the imperfect Narrative here given.—Her dramatic Pieces, having been all of them already mentioned in the Courfe of this Article, need not be here repeated.

Tuchin, *John*, was Author of a weekly Paper, called *The Obfervator* ; for which he was fentenced to be whipped thro' feveral Market-Towns in the Weft of *England* ; to avoid this, he petitioned K. *James* II. to change his Sentence to *hanging*. — He lived, however, to take his Revenge, by writing an Invective againft the Memory of that unfortunate Prince ; and died in the Reign of Queen *Anne*.—He wrote one dramatic Piece, called

 The *Unfortunate Shepherd*, a
  Paftoral, printed with a
  Collection of Poems, in
  1685.

Tuke, *Richard*, was Author of one religious Play, called,

 The *Divine Comedian*, or *the*
  Right Ufe of Plays, a Sacred Tragi-Com. 1672.

Tuke, Sir *Samuel*, was of the County of *Effex*, and a Colonel in the Army. — He wrote one Play, taken from the *Spanifh* of Don *Pedro Calderon*, called,

 The *Adventures of five Hours*.
  Tragi-Com. 1662.

Turner, Mr. *Cyril*, wrote two Plays :

 1. The *Atheift*, his *Tragedie*,
  1617.

 2. The *Revenger*, his *Tragedie*,
  1619.

V.

VANBRUGH, Sir *John*, was descended from an antient Family in *Cheshire*, which came originally from *France*; though, by his Name, he should appear to be of *Dutch* Extraction.—He was born about the middle of the Reign of *Charles* II. and became eminent for Poetry and Skill in Architecture; to both which he discovered an early Propension.— He had a most ready Wit, and was particularly turned for dramatic Productions.—His first Comedy, called *The Relapse, or Virtue in Danger*, was acted with great Applause in the Year 1697, which encouraged him to proceed in the same Track.—The Reputation which he gained by his Comedies, was rewarded with greater Advantages, than usually arise from the Profits of writing for the Stage.—He was appointed *Clarencieux* King at Arms; a Place, which he sometime held, and at last disposed of.—In *August* 1716, he was appointed Surveyor of the Works at *Greenwich* Hospital: He was likewise made Comptroller-General of his Majesty's Works, and Surveyor of the Gardens and Waters.—But we are rather to ascribe these Preferments to his Skill in Architecture, than to his dramatic Writings.—Several noble Structures were raised under his Direction, as *Blenheim* in *Oxfordshire*, *Claremont* in *Surry*, and the Opera-House in the *Haymarket*. — In some Part of Sir *John*'s Life, for we cannot ascertain the Time, he went over to *France*; where, his Taste for Architecture exciting him to view the Fortifica-

tions of the Country, he was one Day observed by an Engineer, whose Information caused him to be secured by Authority, and sent to the *Bastile*; but was soon set at Liberty.—He died of a Quinsey, at his House in *Whitehall*, in 1726.—He was the Contemporary and Friend of Mr. *Congreve*.—These two Comic Writers gave new Life to the *English* Stage, and restored it to Reputation, when it had, in reality, been sinking for some Time.—It would, however, have been more to their Credit, if, while they exerted their Wit upon this Occasion, they had preserved it pure and unmixed with that Obscenity and Licentiousness; which, while it pleased, tended to corrupt the Audience.—When Mr. *Collier* attacked the Immorality and Profaneness of the Stage, in the Year 1698, these two Writers were his principal Objects.

Sir *John*'s dramatic Pieces are,

1. The *Relapse, or Virtue in Danger*. This Comedy is a Sequel to *Cibber's Love's last Shift*, most of the Characters being the same.
2. ÆSOP. Com. in two Parts.
3. The *Provoked Wife*. Com.
4. The *False Friend*. Com.
5. The *Country-House*. Farce.
6. The *Confederacy*. Com.
7. The *Cuckold in Conceit*. C.
8. 'Squire TRELOOBY. Com.
9. The *Mistake*. Com.
10. *A Journey to* LONDON. C. left unfinished.

VEGERIUS, *Paul*, translated from the *German*, a Play, called, The *Royal Cuckold, or Great Bastard*. Tragi Com.

VICTOR, *Benjamin*, Esq; was first bred to Trade; but, having a Turn to Poetry and Theatrical Affairs, he became connected
with

with the *English* and *Irish* Theatres; of both which he has written an entertaining History, as a Supplement to the celebrated Account written by Mr. *Colley Cibber.*—Mr. *Victor* is now Poet-Laureat to the Lord-Lieutenant of *Ireland.*—He is reported to be the Author of several little Theatrical Pieces, and to have altered some others, from former Writers; particularly *Shakespeare's Two Gentlemen of Verona*; but his Name not being affixed we only speak of them thus briefly, as not having Authority to be more particular.—He is likewise Author of several Pieces of Poetry, which have been printed with his Name; besides his Birth-day Odes, &c. written by him as Poet-Laureat of *Ireland.*

VILLIERS, *George,* Duke of *Buckingham.* See BUCKINGHAM.

W.

WAGER, *Lewis,* wrote one Interlude, called

MARY MAGDALENE, *her Lyfe and Repentaunce,* 1567.

WALKER, *Thomas,* was both Author and Actor.—He was the original *Macheath* in the *Beggar's Opera*; but his Success in that Part made him so vain and careless, that he was at length dismissed the Theatre: He afterwards went over to *Ireland,* where he died in 1745.

He brought two dramatic Pieces on the Stage, *viz.*

1. The *Quaker's Opera,* 1729.
2. The *Fate of Villainy.* Trag. 1730.

WALKER, *William,* was born in the Island of *Barbadoes,* where his Father was a considerable Planter, who sent him over to *England* for Education at *Eton* College.—He wrote

1. *Victorious Love.* T. 1698.
2. *Marry, or do worse.* Com. 1707.

WALLER, *Edmund,* Esq; was the Son of *Robert Waller,* Esq; of *Agmondesham* in *Buckinghamshire,* by *Anne,* the Sister of the great *Hamden,* who distinguished himself so much in the Beginning of the Civil Wars.—He was born in 1605; and, his Father dying when he was very young, the Care of his Education fell to his Mother, who sent him to *Eton* School.—He was afterwards sent to *King's* College in *Cambridge,* where he could not continue long; for at sixteen or seventeen Years of Age, he was chosen into the last Parliament of King *James* I. and served as Burgess for *Agmondesham.*—He began to exercise his poetical Talent so early as the Year 1623, as appears from his Verses " Upon the Danger his Majesty (being Prince) " escaped in the Road of St. " Andero;" for there Prince *Charles,* returning from *Spain* that Year, had like to have been cast away.—It was not, however, Mr. *Waller's* Wit, his fine Parts, or his Poetry, that so much occasioned him to be first publicly known, as his carrying off the Daughter and sole Heiress of a rich Citizen, against a Rival, whose Interest was espoused by the Court.—It is not known at what Time he married his first Lady; but he was a Widower, before he was five and twenty, when he began to have a Passion for *Sacharissa,* which was a fictitious Name for the Lady *Dorothy Sidney*

Sidney, Daughter to the Earl of *Leicester*, and afterwards Wife to the Earl of *Sunderland*.—He was now known at Court, careffed by all who had any Relifh for Wit and polite Literature; and was one of the famous Club, of which the Lord *Falkland*, Mr. *Chillingworth*, and other eminent Men were Members.—He was returned Burgefs for *Agmondefham* in the Parliament, which met in *April* 1640.—An Intermiffion of Parliaments having difgufted the Nation, and raifed Jealoufies againft the Defigns of the Court, which would be fure to difcover themfelves, whenever the King came to afk for a Supply; Mr. *Waller* was one of the firft who condemned the preceding Meafures. He fhewed himfelf in Oppofition to the Court, and made a Speech in the Houfe on this Occafion; from which we may gather fome Notion of his general Principles in Government; wherein, however, he afterwards proved very variable and inconftant.—He oppofed the Court alfo in the Long Parliament, which met in *November* following, and was chofen to impeach Judge *Crawley*, which he did in a warm and eloquent Speech, *July* the 6th, 1641.— This Speech was fo highly applauded, that twenty thoufand of them were fold in one Day.—In 1642, he was one of the Commiffioners appointed by the Parliament, to prefent their Propofitions of Peace to the King at *Oxford*.—In 1643, he was deeply engaged in a Defign to reduce the City of *London* and the *Tower*, to the Service of the King, for which he was tried and condemned, together with Mr. *Tomkyns* his Brother-in-Law, and Mr. *Challoner*: The two latter fuffered Death, but Mr. *Waller*

obtained a Reprieve; he was, however, fentenced to fuffer a Year's Imprifonment, and to pay a Fine of ten thoufand Pounds. After this, he became particularly attached to *Oliver Cromwell*, upon whom he wrote a very handfome Panegyric.—He alfo wrote a noble Poem on the Death of that great Man.

At the Reftoration he was treated with great Civility by *Charles* II. who always made him one of the Party in his Diverfions at the Duke of *Buckingham*'s and other Places.—He fat in feveral Parliaments after the Reftoration. He continued in the full Vigour of his Genius to the End of his Life; and his natural Vivacity made his Company agreeable to the laft.—He died of a Dropfy, *October* the 1ft, 1687, and was interred in the Church-Yard of *Beconsfield*, where a Monument is erected to his Memory.—He is looked upon as the moft elegant and harmonious Verfifier of his Time, and a great Refiner of the *Englifh* Language.—His dramatic Pieces are,

1. POMPEY *the Great.* Trag. 1664.
2. The *Maid's Tragedy*; alter'd from *Fletcher.*

WAPUL, *George*, wrote one Play, called

Tide tarrieth for no Man. Com. 1611.

WARD, *Edward*, was a Man of low Extraction, and almoft deftitute of Education.—He was an Imitator of the famous *Butler*, and wrote *The Reformation*, a Burlefque Poem, in which he aimed at the fame Kind of Humour which has fo remarkably diftinguifhed *Hudibras.*—Of late Years, fays Mr. *Jacob*, he has kept a public Houfe in the City, but in a genteel Way.—*Ward* was,

was, in his own droll Manner, a violent Antagonist to the Whigs, and, in Consequence of this, drew to his House such People as had a Mind to indulge their Spleen against the Government. — He was thought to be a Man of strong natural Parts, and possessed a very agreeable Pleasantry of Temper.—*Ward* was much affronted when he read Mr. *Jacob*'s Account, in which he mentions his keeping a public House in the City ; and, in a Book called *Apollo's Maggot*, declared this Account to be a great Falsity, protesting that his public House was not in the City, but in *Moorfields*.—*Ward* is most distinguished by his well-known *London Spy.* — He wrote one dramatic Piece, called,

> The *Humours of a Coffee-House.* Com. as it is daily acted at most of the Coffee-Houses in *London.*

WARD, *Henry*, a Comedian, published three dramatic Pieces in 1747.

  1. The *Happy Lovers*, or *the Beau metamorphosed.* C.
  2. The *Petticoat Plotter*, or *More Ways than one for a Wife.* C.
  3. The *Widow's Wish*, or *An Equipage of Lovers.* C.

WAVER, Mr. *Robert*, the Author of one dramatic Piece, called

> *Lusty* JUVENTUS. Interlude, 1561.

WAYER, Mr. *William*, Author of one Play, called

> *The longer thou livest, the more Foole thou arte.* C. 1570.

WEAVER, Mr. *John.*—This Person is a celebrated *Dancing-Master*, who makes his chief Residence at *Shrewsbury.*—He differs from most of his Profession, not altogether depending upon his *Heels.*—He wrote, or invented, several Pieces, called dramatic Pantomimes.

  1. The *Loves of* MARS *and* VENUS. 1716.
  2. ORPHEUS *and* EURIDICE. 1717.
  3. The *Judgment of* PARIS. 1732.

He was wrote several judicious Books, that shew a *Head* is not wanting to his Heels, *viz.*

> *A History of the Mimes and Pantomimes of the Ancients.*
> *The Art of Dancing, with a Treatise on Action and Gesture.*

He was the first Restorer of Pantomimes after the ancient Manner, without speaking.

WEBSTER, *John*, was accounted a tolerable Poet, and was well esteemed by his Contemporary Authors, particularly *Decker*, *Marston* and *Rowley*, with whom he wrote in Conjunction. His Plays are,

  1. The *White Devil*, or *Tragedie of* P. Gordiano Ursini, *Duke of* Brachiano, *wythe the Lyfe and Deathe of* Vittoria Corombona, *the famous* Venetian *Courtezan.* 1612.
  2. The *Devil's Law-Case*, or *When Women go to Law, the Deville is fulle of Business.* Tragi-Com. 1623.
  3. The *Dutchess of* MALFRY. Trag. 1623. revived with some Alterations, 1709.
  4. APPIUS *and* VIRGINIA. Trag. 1659.
  5. The THRACIAN *Wonder.* Comic-Historical Play.
  6. *A Cure for a Cuckold.* Com.

WELSTED, *Leonard*, Esq; This Gentleman was descended from a very good Family in *Leicestershire*, and received the Rudiments of his Education in *Westminster* School.—In a Piece, said to have been written by Mr. *Welsted*, called the *Characters of the Times*, printed in 8vo, 1728, he says of himself, that " he had, " in his Youth, raised so great " Expectations of his future Ge- " nius, that there was a Kind of " Struggle between the two Uni- " versities, which should have the " Honour of his Education; to " compound this, he civilly be- " came a Member of both, and, " after having passed some Time " at the one, he removed to the " other. — From thence he re- " turned to Town, where he be- " came the darling Expectation " of all the polite Writers, whose " Encouragement he acknow- " ledged in his occasional Poems, " in a Manner that will make " no small Part of the Fame of " his Protectors. — It also ap- " pears from his Works, that he " was happy in the Patronage of " the most illustrious Characters " of the present Age.—Encou- " raged by such a Combination in " his Favour, he published a " Book of Poems, some in the " *Ovidian*, some in the *Horatian* " Manner, in both which the " most exquisite Judges pro- " nounced he even rivalled his " Masters. — His Love Verses " have rescued that Way of Wri- " ting from Contempt.—In the " Translations he has given us " the very Soul and Spirit of his " Author.—His Odes, his Epis- " tles, his Verses, his Love- " Tales, all are the most perfect " Things in all Poetry."—If this pleasant Representation of our Author's Abilities were just, it would seem no Wonder, if the two Universities should strive with each other for the Honour of his Education; but it is certain the World hath not coincided with this Opinion of Mr. *Welsted*;

who, by the Way, can hardly be thought to have been serious in such an extravagant Self-Appro-bation, which we can only look upon as a Piece of Merriment.—Our Author, however, does not appear to have been a mean Poet; he had certainly, from Nature, a good Genius, but, after he came to Town, he became a votary to Pleasure; and the Applauses of his Friends, which taught him to overvalue his Talents, perhaps slackened his Diligence, and, by making him trust solely to Na-ture, slight the Assistance of Art.

In the Year 1718, he wrote the *Triumvirate*, or a Letter in Verse from *Palemon* to *Celia* from *Bath*, which was meant as a Sa-tire against Mr. *Pope*.—He wrote several other occasional Pieces a-gainst this Gentleman, who, in Recompence of his Enmity, has mentioned him in his *Dunciad*; and also in his Parodie upon *Den-ham's Cooper's Hill*, as follows;

" Flow *Welsted*, flow; like thine
 " Inspirer, Beer,
" Tho' stale, not ripe; tho' thin,
 " yet never clear;
" So sweetly mawkish, and so
 " smoothly dull;
" Heady, not strong; and foam-
 " ing, tho' not full."

How far Mr. *Pope*'s Insinua-tion is true, that Mr. *Welsted* owed his Inspiration to Beer, they who read his Works may determine for themselves.—His only dramatic Piece is,

The *Dissembled Wanton*, or *My Son get Money*. Com. 1726.

WESTON, *John*, Esq; wrote a Play, called

The AMAZONIAN *Queen*, or *the Amours of* Thalestris *and* Alexander. Tr.-Com. 1667.

WE-

WETHERBY, *James*, belonged to the Revenue at *Briſtol*, and wrote

PAUL *the Spaniſh Sharper.* Farce, 1730.

WHINCOP, *Thomas*, Eſq;— This Gentleman wrote

SCANDERBEG, or *Love and Liberty.* Trag. not acted, but publiſhed with the Life of *Scanderbeg*, 1747.

WHITAKER, *William*, publiſhed a Play, called

The *Conſpiracy*, or *Change of Government.* Trag. 1680.

WHITEHEAD, *William*, Eſq; Poet-Laureat to their Majeſties King *George* II. and III. ſucceeded to the Laurel on the Death of Mr. *Colley Cibber*.—He is greatly eſteemed as a polite and elegant Writer, to which his Travels abroad, and particularly into *Italy*, the native Soil of the Muſes, have perhaps not a little contributed.

On his Return to *England*, about the Year 1749, he gave the Town a new Tragedy, intitled the *Roman Father*, founded on the celebrated Story of the *Horatii* and *Curiatii*; it was acted with tolerable Succeſs at the Theatre-Royal in *Drury-Lane*, 1750.—In 1754, he brought upon the ſame Stage another Tragedy, entitled, *Creuſa, Queen of Athens*; which had a tolerable Run, notwithſtanding it came out too late in the Year to bring crowded Audiences; however, the Appearance the Boxes made, was ſufficient to keep both the Poet and Players in Countenance. — In 1762, he likewiſe brought upon the ſame Theatre, a Comedy, entitled, *The School for Lovers*, formed on a Plan laid down by M. *De Fontenelle*; and, like moſt of the *French* Productions of this Kind, is rather a Converſation-

Piece than a Comedy.—The Converſation is, however, natural, decent and moral; and, if the Work does not abound with all that Variety of Buſineſs, Plot, Scenery, Character and Humour, which are requiſite to gratify the Taſte of an *Engliſh* Audience, it is, neverthelefs, not an uninteresting Performance, and may certainly rank among thoſe which are diſtinguiſhed by the Appellation of *Genteel Comedy*. — Mr. *Whitehead* has alſo publiſhed ſeveral detached Poems, which have been well received, beſides his Anniverſary Odes, &c. written, *ex Officio*, as Poet-Laureat.

WILD, *Robert*, a diſſenting Miniſter, was Author of *Iter Boreale*, and ſome other Poems: and alſo of

The *Benefice*. Com. 1689.

WILDER, Mr. was both Actor and Poet.—He wrote

The *Gentleman Gardener*. Far. 1749.

WILKINS, Mr. *George*.—This Author wrote a Play, called

The *Miſeries of enforced Marriage.* Tragi-Com. 1637.

WILKINSON, Mr. *William*, the Author of one Play, called

Vice Reclaimed, or *the Paſſionate Miſtreſs.* Com. 1699.

WILLAN, Mr. *Leonard*. — This Author wrote a Paſtoral, called

ASTREA, or *True Love's Mirrour*, 1651.

WILMOT, Mr. *Robert*. — A Gentleman of the *Temple*, who publiſhed a dramatic Piece, called

TANCRED *and* GISMUND, 1592. — This Play was not originally wrote by *Wilmot*, but many Years before the Publication, by a Set of *Templers*.

WILSON, Mr. *John.* — This Gentleman, who lived in *Ireland,* in the Reign of King *Charles* II. and was Recorder of *Londonderry,* was the Author of four Plays.

1. ANDRONICUS COMMENIUS. Trag. 1663.
2. The *Projectors.* C. 1665.
3. The *Cheats.* Com. 1671.
4. BELPHEGOR, or *the Marriage of the Devil.* Com. 1690.

WILSON, Mr. *Robert,* wrote one Play, called

The *Cobler by Prophecie.* Com. 1565.

WINCHELSEA, *Anne,* Countess of, was the Daughter of Sir *William Kingsmill,* of *Sidmonton,* in the County of *Southampton.* — She was Maid of Honour to the second Dutchess of the Duke of *York,* afterwards K. *James* II. She married *Heneage,* second Son of the Earl of *Winchelsea;* who afterwards succeeded to the Title of that Earldom.

One of the most considerable of this Lady's Poems was that *Upon the Spleen,* printed in a new Miscellany of original Poems on several Occasions, published by *Gildon,* in 1701. — A Collection of her Poems was printed in 1713, 8vo. containing likewise a Tragedy, called *Aristomenes,* never acted; and a great Number of her Pieces still continue unpublished. — She died *August* the 5th, 1720, without Issue: as did the Earl her Husband, *September* the 30th, 1726.

WISEMAN, Mrs. — This Gentlewoman wrote a Play, called

ANTIOCHUS *the Great,* or *the Fatal Relapse.* T. 1706.

WOOD, The Rev. Mr. *Nathaniel,* was a Clergyman of the City of *Norwich;* he wrote a dramatic Piece, called

The *Conflycte of Conscience,* a Pastoral, 1581.

WORSDALE, Mr. *James.* — This Author is both a Poet and a Painter; he has published several small Pieces, Songs, &c. beside the following dramatic Performances;

1. *A Cure for a Scold.* Ballad Farce, taken from *Shakespeare's Taming of the Shrew.*
2. The *Assembly.* Farce, in which Mr. *Worsdale* himself acted the Part of Old Lady *Scandal.*
3. The *Queen of* SPAIN.
4. The *Extravagant Justice.* Farce.

Of this Gentleman Mrs. *Pilkington* has related several pleasant Anecdotes, in her well-known *Memoirs.* — He is now possessed of a considerable Place under the Government, in his Capacity of Painter.

WRIGHT, *John.* — This Gentleman, who was of the *Middle-Temple,* wrote two dramatic Pieces.

1. THYESTES. Tr. 1674.
2. *Mock* THYESTES. Farce, in Burlesque Verse, 1674.

WRIGHT, *Thomas,* was Machinist to the Theatre, and wrote

The *Female Virtuosos.* Com. 1693.

WYCHERLY, *William.* — This eminent Comic Poet, who was born about the Year 1640, was the eldest Son of *Daniel Wycherly,* of *Cleve* in *Shropshire,* Esq; —— When he was about fifteen Years of Age, he was sent to *France,* where he became a *Roman* Catholick; but, on his Return to *England,* and becoming a Gentleman - Commoner of *Queen's* College in *Oxford,* he was reconciled to the Protestant Religion.

He

He afterwards entered himſelf in the *Middle Temple*; but, making his firſt Appearance in Town in the looſe Reign of *Cha.* II. when Wit and Gaiety were the favourite Diſtinctions, he ſoon quitted the dry Study of the Law, and purſued Things more agreeable to his own Genius, as well as to the Taſte of the Age.—As nothing was likely to take better than dramatic Performances, eſpecially Comedies, he applied himſelf to this Species of Writing.—On the Appearance of his firſt Play, he became acquainted with ſeveral of the firſt-rate Wits, and likewiſe with the Dutcheſs of *Cleuland*, with whom, according to the ſecret Hiſtory of thoſe Times, he was admitted to the laſt Degree of Intimacy.—*Villiers*, Duke of *Buckingham*, had alſo the higheſt Eſteem for him; and, as Maſter of the Horſe to the King, made him one of his Equerries; as Colonel of a Regiment, Captain-Lieutenant of his own Company, reſigning to him at the ſame Time his own Pay as Captain, with many other Advantages.—King *Charles* likewiſe ſhewed him ſignal Marks of Favour; and once gave him a Proof of his Eſteem, which perhaps never any Sovereign Prince before had given to a private Gentleman.—Mr. *Wycherly* being ill of a Fever, at his Lodgings in *Bow-ſtreet*, the King did him the Honour of a Viſit.—Finding him extreamly weakened, and his Spirits miſerably ſhattered, he commanded him to take a Journey to the South of *France*, believing that the Air of *Montpelier* would contribute to reſtore him, and aſſured him, at the ſame Time, that he would order him 500l. to defray the Charges of the Journey.—Mr. *Wycherly* accordingly

went into *France*, and, having ſpent the Winter there, returned to *England*, entirely reſtored to his former Vigour.—The King, ſhortly after his Arrival, told him, that he had a Son, who he was reſolved ſhould be educated like the Son of a King, and that he could not chuſe a more proper Man for his Governor than Mr. *Wycherly*; for which Service 1500 l. *per Annum* ſhould be ſettled upon him.

Mr. *Wycherly*, however, ſuch is the uncertain State of all human Affairs, loſt the Favour of the King, by the following Means:—Immediately after he had received the gracious Offer above-mentioned, he went down to *Tunbridge*, where, walking one Day upon the Wells-Walk, with his Friend Mr. *Fairbeard*, of *Gray's-Inn*, juſt as he came up to the Bookſeller's Shop, the Counteſs of *Drogheda*, a young Widow, rich, noble and beautiful, came there to enquire for *The Plain Dealer*; " Madam," ſays Mr. *Fairbeard*, " ſince you " are for the *Flain Dealer*, there " he is for you;" puſhing Mr. *Wycherly* towards her. " Yes," ſays Mr. *Wycherly*, " this Lady " can bear plain Dealing; for " ſhe appears to be ſo accompliſh- " ed, that what would be a Compliment to others, would be " plain Dealing to her."—" No, " truly, Sir," ſaid the Counteſs, " I am not without my Faults, " any more than the reſt of my " Sex; and yet, notwithſtand- " ing, I love plain Dealing, and " am never more fond of it, than " when it tells me of them."— " Then, Madam," ſays Mr. *Fairbeard*, " you and *The Plain* " *Dealer*, ſeem deſigned by Heaven for each other."—In ſhort, Mr. *Wycherly* walked a Turn or two with the Countess, waited upon her home, visited her daily at her Lodgings while she staid at *Tunbridge*, and at her Lodgings in *Hatton-Gardon*, after she went to *London*; where in a little Time he married her, without acquainting the King.—But this Match, so promising, in Appearance, to his Fortunes and Happiness, was the actual Ruin of both.—As soon as the News of it came to Court, it was looked upon as a Contempt of his Majesty's Orders; and Mr. *Wycherly*'s Conduct after his Marriage occasioned this to be resented still more heinously; for he seldom or never went near the Court, which made him thought downright ungrateful.—The true Cause of his Absence, however, was not known. In short, the Lady was jealous of him to that Degree, that she could not endure him to be one Moment out of her Sight.—Their Lodgings were in *Bow-street, Covent - Garden*, over against the *Cock*; whither, if he at any Time went with his Friends, he was obliged to leave the Windows open, that his Lady might see there was no Woman in Company.—Nevertheless, she made him some Amends, by dying in a reasonable Time.—She settled her Fortune on him: But his Title being disputed after her Death, the Expences of the Law and other Incumbrances so far reduced him, that, not being able to satisfy the Importunity of his Creditors, he was flung into Prison, where he languished several Years; nor was he released, till King *James* II. going to see his *Plain-Dealer*, was so charmed with the Entertainment, that he gave immediate Orders for the Payment of his Debts; adding withal a

Pension of 200 l. *per Annum*, while he continued in *England*. But the bountiful Intentions of that Prince had not all the designed Effect, for *Wycherly* was ashamed to give the Earl of *Mulgrave*, whom the King had sent to demand it, a full Account of his Debts.—He laboured under these Difficulties, till his Father died; and then too the Estate, that descended to him, was left under very uneasy Limitations, since, being only a Tenant for Life, he could not raise Money for the Payment of his Debts.—However, he took a Method of doing it, which few suspected to be his Choice; and this was making a Jointure.—He had often declared, that he was resolved to *die* married, though he could not bear the Thoughts of *living* in that State again: Accordingly, just at the Eve of his Death, he married a young Gentlewoman with 1500 l. Fortune, Part of which he applied to the Uses he wanted it for.—Eleven Days after the Celebration of these Nuptials, in *December* 1715, he died; and was interred in the Vault of *Covent-Garden* Church. He published a Volume of Poems in 1704, Folio; and, in 1728, his posthumous Works, in Prose and Verse, were published by Mr. *Lewis Theobald*, in 8vo.— His dramatic Pieces are,

1. *Love in a Wood*, or *St. James's Park*. C. 1672.
2. The *Gentleman Dancing - Master*. Com. 1673.
3. The *Plain - Dealer*. Com. 1678.
4. The *Country Wife*. Com. 1683.

Mr. *Pope*, when very young, made his Court to Mr. *Wycherly*, when very old; and the latter was fo well pleafed with the for-mer, and had fuch an Opinion of his rifing Genius, that he en-tered into an intimate Corref-pondence with him. See the Letters between *Pope* and *Wy-cherly*, printed in *Pope*'s Works.

Y.

YARRINGTON, Mr. *Robert*, wrote a Play, called *Two Tragedies in one*, printed not till many Years after it was wrote, 1592.

YOUNG, The Rev. Dr. *Ed-ward*.—This great Genius was bred at *Oxford*, being a Fellow of *All-Souls* College in that Univer-fity. — He took his Degree of Doctor of the Civil Law; and afterwards, going into Holy Or-ders, was made one of his Ma-jefty's Chaplains, and obtained the Living of *Welwyn* in *Hert-fordfhire*.—He married the Lady *Elizabeth Lee*, Daughter of the late Earl of *Litchfield*. — He is Author of thofe fine moral Sa-tires, called *The Univerfal Paffion*; but his greateft Reputation arifes from his celebrated *Complaint*, or *Night Thoughts*; which Work has fucceeded more than any other moral Poem, of fuch confiderable Bulk, fince *Milton's Paradife Loft*. His dramatic Pieces are,

1. *Bufiris*. Trag. 1719.
2. The *Revenge*. Trag. 1721.
3. The *Brothers*. Trag. 1753.

Dr. *Young*'s Works are collected into four Pocket Volumes. 1757.

MA

BICKERSTAFF, Mr. *Isaac*, a Native of the Kingdom of *Ireland*, is a Lieutenant of Marines, and Author of

1. THOMAS *and* SALLY, a Dramatic Entertainment.
2. *Love in a Village*, an English Opera.

This laft had a Run almoft equal to that of the famous *Beggar's Opera.*—Both thefe Pieces were acted at the Theatre Royal in *Covent Garden*; the firft in the Year 1760, and the fecond in 1762.

COCKBURN, Mrs. *Catherine.*— See this Life under the Lady's Maiden Name; *viz.* TROTTER.

MANLEY, Mrs. was the Daughter of Sir *Roger Manley*, who is faid to have been the Author of the firft Volume of that famous Work, the *Turkifh Spy*. Mrs. *Manley* received an Education fuitable to her Birth; and gave early Difcoveries of a Genius, much fuperior to what is ufually found among her Sex.— In her Infancy fhe loft her Mother; a Lofs which was attended by many other Misfortunes; for when fhe grew up, fhe was cheated into a falfe Marriage by a near Relation of the fame Name, to

MA

whom her Father had bequeathed the Care of her. We call it a falfe Marriage, becaufe the Gentleman had a former Wife then living; and pretended to marry her, only to gratify a criminal Paffion.——She was afterwards brought to *London*, where fhe was foon deferted by him; and thus, in the very Morning of her Life, when all Things fhould have been gay and promifing, fhe wore away three wretched Years in Solitude. When fhe appeared in the World again, fhe fell, by mere Accident, under the Patronage of the Dutchefs of *Cleveland*, a Miftrefs of *Charles* II. — She was introduced by an Acquaintance of her Grace's, to whom fhe was paying a Vifit; but the Dutchefs, being a Woman of a very fickle Temper, grew tired of Mrs. *Manley* in fix Months Time, and difcharged her upon a Pretence, whether groundlefs or not is uncertain, that fhe intrigued with her Son.—When our Authorefs was difmiffed by the Dutchefs, fhe was folicited by General *Tidcombe*, to pafs fome Time with him at his Country-Seat; but fhe excufed herfelf by faying, " That her Love of Solitude was " improved by a Difguft of the " World;

" World ; and since it was im-
" possible for her to be in Public
" with Reputation, she was re-
" solved to remain concealed."—
In this Solitude she wrote her
first Tragedy, called the *Royal
Mischief*, which was acted at the
Theatre in *Lincoln's-Inn-Fields*,
in the Year 1696.—As this Play
succeeded, she received such unbounded Incense from Admirers,
that her Apartment was crowded
with Men of Wit and Gaiety.—
This proved, in the End, very
fatal to her Virtue ; and she afterwards engaged in Intrigues,
and was taken into keeping —In
her retired Hours, she wrote her
four Volumes of the *Memoirs of
the New Atalantis*, in which she
was not only very free with her
own Sex, in her wanton Description of Love Adventures, but also
with the Characters of many
high and distinguished Personages.
Her Father had always been attached to the Cause of *Cha.* I.
and she herself had a confirmed
Aversion to the Whig Ministry ;
so that the Representations of
many Characters in her *Atalantis*,
are nothing else but Satires upon
those, who had brought about the
Revolution.—Upon this a Warrant was granted, from the Secretary of State's Office, to seize the
Printer and Publisher of those
Volumes.—Mrs. *Manley* had too
much Generosity, to let innocent
Persons suffer on her Account ;
and therefore voluntarily presented herself before the Court of
King's-Bench, as the Author of
the *Atalantis*. — When she was
examined before Lord *Sunderland*,
who was then Secretary, he was
curious to know, from whom she
got Information of some Particulars, which they imagined to
be above her own Intelligence.—

She replied, with great Humility, that she had no Design in
writing, farther than her own
Amusement and Diversion in the
Country, without intending particular Reflections and Characters ; and did assure them, that
nobody was concerned with her.
When this was not believed, and
the contrary urged against her by
several Circumstances, she said,
" then it must be by Inspiration,
" because, knowing her own In-
" nocence, she could account for
" it no other Way."—The Secretary replied, that " Inspira-
" tion used to be upon a good
" Account ; but that her Writ-
" ings were stark nought."—She
acknowledged, " that his Lord-
" ship's Observation might be
" true ; but, as there were evil
" Angels as well as good, that
" what she had wrote might still
" be by Inspiration."—The Consequence of this Examination was,
that Mrs. *Manley* was close shut
up in a Messenger's House, without being allowed Pen, Ink and
Paper. — However, her Council
sued out her *Habeas Corpus*, and
she was admitted to Bail.—Whether those in Power were ashamed
to bring a Woman to a Trial for
writing a few amorous Trifles, or
whether the Laws could not reach
her, because she had disguised her
Satire under romantic Names,
and a feigned Scene of Action,
she was discharged, after several
Times exposing herself in Person,
to cross the Court before the
Bench of Judges, with her three
Attendants, the Printer and two
Publishers.—Not long after, a
total Change of the Ministry ensued, when she lived in high Reputation and Gaiety, and amused
herself in writing Poems and
Letters, and conversing with
Wits.

Wits.—A second Edition of a Volume of her Letters was published in the Year 1713.—*Lucius, the first Christian King of Britain*, a Tragedy, was written by her, and acted in *Drury-Lane*, in the Year 1717.—She dedicated it to Sir *Richard Steele*, whom she had abused in her *New Atalantis*; but was now upon such friendly Terms with him, that he wrote the Prologue to this Play, as Mr. *Prior* did the Epilogue.—This, with the Tragedy before mentioned, and a Comedy called *the Lost Lover*, or *the Jealous Husband*, acted in the Year 1696, make up her dramatic Works.— She died *July* the 11th, 1724.

MURPHY, *Arthur*, Esq; is a Native of *Ireland*, was bred to Business, and was some Time employed in a Compting-House in the City of *London*; but, having a greater Love for the Muses than for Tare and Tret, he soon removed to the other Side of *Temple-Bar*, and commenced an early Acquaintance with the Theatres.

After writing some small Pieces of Poetry and Dramatic Essays, he at length resolved to try his Talent as an Actor.—Having the Advantage of a very good Figure, and being allowed an excellent Judge of the Performances of others, in that Profession, the Managers of *Drury-Lane* readily engaged him, at a genteel Salary. But, on the Expiration of the first Season, not having met with all the Success he possibly expected, in some of the principal Characters, he thought proper to quit the Stage; and then, applying himself to the Study of the Law, he became a Member of the Society of *Lincoln's-Inn*; and will

probably one Day make a considerable Figure in that liberal Profession.—He remained, however, constant in his Affection for the Muses, and has hitherto chosen to fill up those Intervals of Time, in which he was not employed in his necessary Attendance upon *Coke* and *Littleton*, and continued to entertain the Public with his dramatic Writings; which are as under:

1. The *Apprentice*. Farce, of two Acts; performed, with great Applause, at the Theatre in *Drury-Lane*, 1756.
2. The *Upholsterer*, or *What News?* Farce, of two Acts; performed, with very great Success, at the same Theatre, 1758.
3. The *Orphan of* CHINA. Trag. founded on *Voltaire*'s Trag. on the same Subject; acted with Success at the Theatre in *Drury-Lane*, 1759.
4. The *Desert Island*, a Dramatic Poem, in 3 Acts, performed at the same Theatre, with inferior Success, 1760.
5. The *Way to keep him*. Com. of three Acts, performed jointly with the foregoing Piece, but with greater Approbation; which the Author perceiving, enlarged the *Way to keep him*, and extended it to a Com. of five Acts, which he brought upon the same Stage, in 1761, with very good Success.
6. *All in the Wrong*. Com. acted at the same Theatre, with great Success, 1761.

7. The

7. The *Old Maid.* Com. in two Acts, performed likewise at the same Houſe, in the ſame Seaſon; and with no inconſiderable Applauſe.

8. The *Citizen.* Farce, acted with tolerable Succeſs, at the Theatre Royal in *Covent-Garden,* 1762.

Since our firſt Volume was printed off, we have been alſo informed, that Mr. *Murphy* was Author of the *Spouter,* or *Tripple Revenge,* a Comic Farce of two Acts, never brought on the Stage, and probably intended only for the Cloſet. — The *Monthly Reviewers,* in their Account of it, obſerve, that the Author has diſplayed a good Deal of Wit and Humour; and that his Satire is chiefly level'd at certain Theatrical Gentlemen, who are pleaſantly mimicked and ridiculed.— We are therefore convinced, that this Piece could not be intended to ridicule his own Farce of the *Apprentice;* whatever might be the Deſign of another Piece, bearing a ſimilar Title, but greatly inferior to Mr. *Murphy's* Performance.

This ingenious Gentleman is likewiſe Author of thoſe ſprightly and entertaining Papers, entitled *The Craftſman,* or *Gray's-Inn Journal;* which came out weekly; and were reprinted in two Pocket Volumes.—He has alſo been concerned in ſome Political Controverſies; and is ſuppoſed to have had a principal Hand in the famous *Teſt,* a periodical Paper, which came out in Oppoſition to Mr. *Pitt's* firſt Adminiſtration.—And the *Auditor,* in Defence of Lord *Bute,* was the Product of Mr. *Murphy's* Pen.— He has, moreover, given the Public a handſome Edition of Mr. *Henry Fielding's* Works, in 4to. to which he has prefixed an ingenious and copious Diſſertation on the Life and Writings of that witty and humorous Author.

PHILIPS, Mrs. *Catherine,* was the Daughter of Mr. *Fowler,* a Merchant of *London;* and was born in 1631.—She was educated at a Boarding-School in *Hackney;* where ſhe very early diſtinguiſhed herſelf for her Skill in Poetry. She was married to *James Philips,* of *Cardigan,* Eſq; and afterwards went with the Viſcounteſs of *Duncannon* into *Ireland.* — She tranſlated *Corneille's* Tragedy of *Pompey;* which was ſeveral Times acted in 1663 and 1664, in which laſt Year it was publiſhed. She tranſlated alſo the four firſt Acts of *Horace,* another Tragedy of *Corneille;* the fifth being done by Sir *John Denham.*—This amiable Lady died of the Small-Pox in *London, June* 22, 1664, to the Regret of all who knew her; and, among many others, the great *Cowley,* who expreſſed his Reſpect for her Memory, by an elegant Ode upon her Death.— Her Works were printed in Folio, under the Title of, " Poems " by the moſt deſervedly-admired " Mrs. *Catherine Philips,* the " matchleſs *Orinda,*" 1667. — There was likewiſe another Folio Edition, in 1678; and, in 1705, a ſmall Volume of her Letters to Sir *Charles Cotterel* were printed, under the Title of " Letters from *Orinda* to *Poliarchus;*" the Editor of which tells us, that " they were the Effect of an " happy Intimacy between her- " ſelf and the late famous *Poli-* " *archus;* and are an admirable " Pattern for the pleaſing Correſ- " pondence of a virtuous Friend- " ſhip.

" ſhip. — They will ſufficiently
" inſtruct us, how an Intercourſe
" of writing between Perſons of
" different Sexes ought to be ma-
" naged with Delight and Inno-
" cence; and teach the World
" not to load ſuch a Commerce
" with Cenſure and Detraction,
" when it is removed at ſuch a
" Diſtance from even the Ap-
" pearance of Guilt."

THOMPSON, Rev. Mr. *Wil-
liam*, an eſteemed Poet of the
preſent Age, was bred at the U-
niverſity of *Oxford*; where he became Fellow of *Queen*'s College.
The moſt conſiderable of his Performances, is his Poem, entitled
Sickneſs; in five Books, written
in blank Verſe. — The ingenious
Author firſt publiſhed this Poem
in Quarto, about the Year 1740;
and, in 1758, he republiſhed it,
together with ſeveral other Pieces,
in an 8vo. Volume; in which
was included the only dramatic
Piece he wrote, *viz.*

GONDIBERT *and* BIRTHA.
Trag. taken from *Dave-
nant*'s Poem of *Gondibert*;
never acted.

We are not ſure whether this
Gentleman be yet living or not.

F I N I S.